THE LEGEND LIVES

They awarded him a medal, which he has never collected.

His fellow survivors have never seen him in the decades since.

Yet still they talk about him—his wild adventures, his affair with the beautiful partisan fighter Yanka, his legendary escape.

He is called Paulo. This is his story. . . .

THE TUNNEL AT LOIBL PASS

"Written in the tough, jaunty language of *Papillon* but rigorously authentic in factual detail, this moving documentary novel about a little-known episode of World War II is yet another testament to the brutality and degeneracy of Nazism. Still more, however, it's a testament to the almost incredible heroism and endurance of which human beings are capable, and that's the factor that keeps the reader constantly engrossed."

—*Publishers Weekly*

THE TUNNEL AT LOIBL PASS

André Lacaze

Translated by
Barrett W. Dower, Julian Evans
and Anne Gray

BANTAM BOOKS
TORONTO · NEW YORK · LONDON · SYDNEY

This low-priced Bantam Book has been completely reset in a type face designed for easy reading, and was printed from new plates. It contains the complete text of the original hard-cover edition.
NOT ONE WORD AS BEEN OMITTED.

THE TUNNEL AT LOIBL PASS

A Bantam Book / published by arrangement with Doubleday & Company, Inc.

PRINTING HISTORY

This book, Le Tunnel, *was originally published in France by Julliard.* © *1978 by Julliard.*

Doubleday edition published March 1981
Bantam edition / September 1982

ISBN 0-553-22584-7

Published simultaneously in the United States and Canada

Bantam Books are published by Bantam Books, Inc. Its trademark, consisting of the words "Bantam Books" and the portrayal of a rooster, is Registered in U.S. Patent and Trademark Office and in other countries, Marca Registrada. Bantam Books, Inc., 666 Fifth Avenue, New York, New York 10103.

PRINTED IN THE UNITED STATES OF AMERICA

O 0 9 8 7 6 5 4 3 2 1

To the memory of André Ménard, a student from Rennes, who died at the age of twenty-three in his Mauthausen convict's uniform, but with a gun in his hand.

I

Paulo had instantly grasped the importance of the occasion. Flexing his muscles like a contender for the Mr. Universe title, rigid from head to toe, he struck the pose just as the judges passed in front of him. Funny kind of judges: SS officers in boots, riding crops in hand. Three of them began to poke him: arms, thighs, calves. As for the mouth, Paulo had anticipated the tap of the riding crop, and spontaneously opened his mouth wide and smiled, baring the teeth of a starving young wolf—white, magnificent, not one missing.

"*Gut,*" exclaimed one of the SS pokers, turning toward the head of the panel.

"*Rechts,*" replied the monocled Colonel Standartenführer, chief of the Mauthausen concentration camp.

Rechts, to the right. It didn't mean very much yet, on that spring morning of 1943, but *links,* to the left, meant the crematorium. Without appeal.

Unfortunately, the twenty-five hundred Frenchmen, heads shaven and standing at attention in their long underpants since four in the morning, had not all understood as Paulo had the reason for this slave market. They were already surprised enough to find themselves assembled in such large numbers, gotten up like this and complete strangers to one another. They were a wholly mixed bag: innocent men, who had done nothing either good or bad, rounded up simply because a Kraut had been shot in their neighborhood or because some poison pen in their village, just for kicks, had written to the *Kommandantur;* guinea pigs of the early Resistance networks; communists imprisoned since Deladier; petty criminals, pimps, police impersonators, black marketeers, all evicted from jail to make room.

Paulo Chastagnier belonged to this last group, but it was

one of the flukes of the war. Given his youth and his disregard for politics, he might just as easily have been one of the innocent men rounded up. Or even one of the Resistance fighters, since he preferred to choose his victims from among the collaborators.

He had vacillated at the beginning of his career, looking for his own specialty, sampling all the avenues. Nothing—theft, fraud, women—had really gotten him going, and it was only with the defeat of France that he discovered his vocation: the black market. The ideal territory for his imagination, as he called it. But his imagination had run into a bad patch and he kept quiet about the reason for his arrest: a dismal story involving tungsten which had ended in the jail of the rue Cherche-Midi.

The tungsten was bogus and so was the buyer, a Belgian who turned out to be a Nazi. Such a badly bungled affair would certainly not impress the battalion of delinquents who had landed up in Mauthausen. If Paulo was nonetheless considered a big shot by the hoods gathered in this rogues' gallery, it was only because some of them had had the misfortune to tangle with him in the course of some shady deals. They had had to admit, backing down, that Paulo was a "real man." And the word quickly got around. At the age of twenty-three, such an honor is rare in the underworld. On his arrival at the camp, Paulo seemed delighted with his reputation as a tough. His career had been so rapid and easy that he was quite convinced a little nerve was sufficient to succeed in life. Even in a camp. Furthermore, since he was strong, in good health, and knew himself to be smart, he had not fully understood on the first day that this captivity was the price of defeat for several million young French people. He was convinced he would soon be out of this mess, and crossing the threshold of the camp, he displayed a morale which was a pleasure to see.

This optimism lasted only a day. By the following day, Paulo looked much less like a big shot. He had shrunken in the crowd at Mauthausen. His thoughts had become brooding and sinister.

"This is crazy," he had proclaimed. "We're in a nuthouse, but it's the nurses who are nuts."

Nonetheless, upon his arrival Paulo, always one to appreciate a trick, couldn't help smiling: "What a two-timing bunch, these Krauts! They ask us to write to our women so that they stuff our suitcases with food and warm clothes. And then? Everybody strip, down to your shorts!"

The suitcases? They were all stacked up haphazardly in the courtyard, no labels, no names. Forget the little delicacies to ease the separation. Forget the overcoats stuffed with dollars, *louis d'or*, wristwatches, wedding rings and signet rings. Forget the sparklers in their flies to buy over the Kraut peasants with whom they, the Relief Troops, were going to work, before beating it into Switzerland as in *La Grande Illusion*. Even the sentimental ones no longer sniveled over their lovingly packed bags and their stolen treasures. They had been tricked. Some, like Paulo, had a good laugh and the hilarity overcame almost the whole shower room. Of course, these new boys didn't know that at Mauthausen the showers and the gas chamber were one and the same, an invention of an enterprising SS to send all corpses ready naked to the crematorium. Before we turn on the gas, please fold your clothes so they can be used by the new arrivals. The same outfit for ten people, according to the figures. But that day, there were no deliveries of Jews or Russkies to Mauthausen. The showers were really for washing. Even more than that. The hilarity that had overtaken the French was caused by their attending their first great crab hunt. The first of a long series. *Eine Laus . . . dein Tod*—One louse . . . your death—read the sign. Not one louse, not one crab, was to penetrate the sanctuary, and since for the Nazis the French were by definition filthy and pox-ridden, the crab hunt was particularly thorough that evening.

Everything—and woe to those with beards—fell to the clippers: scalps, pubic hair, buttocks, chest, armpits, mustaches—even eyebrows, a well-known crab reserve. Impossible to recognize your best friend in this sea of skin. Only the bald hadn't changed. It would have made anyone laugh, in spite of the stinging crab powder which was slapped onto the bald areas with rough brush strokes.

Paulo laughed heartily, and for the first time no longer cursed himself for having been pinched like a novice by the false Belgian. It was worth it to see this. A show like the one he was watching just couldn't be invented, and with his colorful spiel he'd have his friends roaring with laughter when he got back to Paris. The long striped underpants, the wooden clogs, the paving stones in the yard perversely arranged to break all their necks, but especially the extraordinary Popeye punching sessions, blows and kicks landing from all sides at once accompanied by the welcoming insult *Schweine Franzosen*—it was really an astonishing reception in this surrealist floodlit theater.

At night things went way beyond the lunatic asylum. Sleeping arrangements were five hundred per block, ranged like sardines on the floor. The calculations must have been made with the oldest and skinniest deportees in mind. With the newly arrived French, fat on black market brioches or just well-fed peasants, it wouldn't work. They all fitted in nevertheless, but it was quite a session. The helpless Kapos had called in the SS, who had taken the buckle end of their straps to the sleepers and stamped them down with their cleated boots. Nighty-night everybody, five to a square yard, a camp record. You had to cling on so as not to be ejected from the human mattress. No question of getting back in again, or only at the price of such a beating for oneself and one's neighbors that restlessness was very rare that first night.

Next morning, Paulo had found Mauthausen less amusing. He had slept badly, with two feet for a pillow and another guy for a blanket. His big smile had left him that day, and the one he sported three months later, when the SS animal dealers were feeling him up on the parade ground, was more like the smile of a whore at choosing time. But Paulo had no shame. His instinct told him that the selection was the chance of his life, and to seize it; this was no time to play the big shot. He would do anything to get out of this madhouse. An assembly as big as this, with all the officers of the fortress, had to mean a work force. Perhaps even on the outside.

Paulo had noticed that the young and the brawny were being assembled on the right; on the left, the skinny ones, the old ones, the dying, and the others—with heads swollen like balloons by erysipelas or necks deformed by enormous goiters. Of course, the Germans were perverse enough to send prisoners in the best of health to the crematorium without hesitation. *Im gleichen Schritt Marsch*, destination the showers... It was as simple as that, and not unusual at Mauthausen for whole convoys to have gone up in smoke before the *Schreiber* had had time to register them. Spaniards, Czechs, Hungarians, Ukrainians, young, old, women, children, entire trainloads. But it was now 1943, and the German youth was disposed in tight ranks on the fatal front line against the Soviets. The Reich needed manpower.

This was political science that Paulo could grasp. The gangland contingent and a few of the brighter ones had come to the same conclusion. Their biceps were bulging in the ranks. The rest of the flock—the majority—had understood nothing. The simple-soldier frame of mind got the better of certain unfortunates, who hollowed in their chests and coughed, hoping to arouse the adjutant's pity with their best malingering act.

Links.

With blows from the rubber clubs, they found themselves on the left-hand side of the yard. For them, ailing or not, their chance had passed. Paulo and the others—just under three hundred—were also beaten, but they were beaten into line, into a square formation: short men in front, tall behind, and no mistake. Each had to quickly learn his size to be seen by the Kommandant, who was himself going to explain the selection. It was just as Paulo had foreseen: the formation of bald heads was going to leave Mauthausen.

A *Dolmetscher* had translated: "You have been chosen to work for the glory of the great Reich. Mauthausen is a sanatorium compared to the camp you're going to. If one of you tries to escape, ten others will be shot immediately. From now on you belong to Kommando X." Perhaps this was delivered somewhat brutally, but the *Dolmetscher*'s last words were greeted by the prisoners with an enormous sigh.

The shaven heads looked at each other, eyes lit up, and imaginations went swiftly to work.

For Paulo it was about time. His nerves of steel were beginning to crack. "We'll end up dead here" had been on his lips for the last three months. Because the day after his arrival—after the brief hilarity of the shower session and his amused surprise at the sardine-can snooze—he had found the explanation for the smell. An unknown smell, a smell which infested the nostrils, throat, clothes and skin, and wouldn't leave. A smell which Paulo had detected on the road up to the camp, more than a mile away, but which he had not at the time been able to identify.

It was the smell of his fellows burning, one after the other, in their hundreds. It came from the crematorium whose chimney, as big as that of a suburban factory, billowed a dense black smoke by day and a frightening red flame at night. Smoke whose density varied according to the supply of human fuel, and enormous soaring flames when the chimney was drawing well.

"The fire hasn't gone out since nineteen forty-one, when we enlarged the camp with the Spaniards," the chief of Block 17 had explained, by way of improving the newcomers' morale.

Paulo thought he was joking, and it was only after seeing the cart that he understood the block chief's wit. Standing watch next to the window, he was trying to soak up a little timid March sun when he saw the cart coming from the direction of the kitchens.

"There'll be some meat in the soup today," he remarked to no one in particular.

Suddenly he fell silent, his eyes staring. The mountain of meat—pulled by five prisoners and trampled on by another man in a Kapo cap—was men, naked, dead, pallid, trickling with blood, men who were going to be burned. It was the morning roast. The first roast of the day.

Paulo turned green, and for the first time in his life he shook with fear.

The smell, the smoke, the flames, the ghostly cart, there was no longer any question of startling his pals back home with this *danse macabre*. Because in this atmosphere, he could no longer even imagine going back. Besides, his Montmartre friends would never believe such bullshit anyway. No more so than Paulo in the early days would have believed the tales going around the blocks: lampshades made of human skin, tattooed for preference; syphilis injections; and the quarry opposite where, from the top of 186 steps, the SS organized push parties among the prisoners. The strongest were supposed to push the weak ones, who would fall screaming to their death on the rocks below. If by chance one of the good-for-nothings, by a desperate reflex, made a strong and useful one fall, on his return he was hanged, as a matter of course. Sabotage. A refinement on the game was a push party between father and son. Jews if possible. Paulo believed the stories now. With his own eyes he had seen an SS shoot a

Polack too small to carry a cauldron which one of his fellow prisoners, an enormous skeleton, was lifting too high. The soup was spilling over. Sabotage. One shot from a revolver in the back of the neck at noon, in front of a thousand witnesses speechless with fear.

Every morning for three months Paulo had counted the dead from the night before. They were extracted from the sardine camping arrangement, stripped before they got too stiff, and left neatly lined up in front of the block until muster. It left a little more room, but it was bad for morale. Even for the morale of a professional tough, an ex-tough like Paulo. He had also witnessed about forty hangings. Assembly, fanfare, "Lili Marlene" and curtains. The reason? Stealing soup, a crab impervious to the powder, a face that didn't fit, a cap not removed quickly enough as an SS walked past. He had seen no more than a yard away fatal beatings and pursuits with club blows toward the electrified barbed-wire fence. He had spent icy nights standing at attention, stark naked, with a pail of cold water on the back from time to time, an efficient means of making the feverish ones croak more quickly. He had seen his friends become bloated, done for and sent to the *Revier,* the sick bay, last stop before the crematorium. But what had struck him most was the special treatment reserved for a few of the priests, ten or so, who had entered the camp in their cassocks. Some young SS, fresh out of Nazi school, had immediately taken them in hand for lack of Jews, who were being sent to camps with higher rates of consumption. Day and night they spent on their knees, those curates, with their prayer books in hand and a blow from the Kapo each time a prayer book fell.

These persecutions out of another age had convinced Paulo beyond doubt that he had fallen among madmen, ranting madmen whose orders were to do everyone in. So that no one could talk.

That is why—in spite of three months without sleep, without food, shivering and seventy pounds lighter—Paulo, now that he was on the right side of things, felt in surprisingly good shape. He belonged to Kommando X. He, the crook, might one day be history's witness. In the meantime he had to hang on. It was easy because the Krauts, anxious to preserve their livestock, had immediately separated the draftees from the sick and the mangy huddled in the quarantine blocks. For the hardy, it was muster every fifteen minutes. Paulo had very quickly learned how to yell his serial number in German. He wasn't exactly gifted at speaking Kraut, but he was so afraid of being forgotten that he made spectacular progress.

"Acht und zwanzig tausend zwei hundert vierzehn."

It was a long way of saying 28,214, but to mispronounce it would have brought a swinging right to the jaw, at attention. Very bad, consequently, for the pronunciation.

Muster, remuster, Kommando X could barely catch its breath. Showers and delousings; clippers and razors. The Spanish barbers, old hands at the camp, threw themselves into it with gusto, brandishing their battery of shaving brushes, unable to keep up with the pace. Three hundred shaves an hour, running on the treacherous cobblestones, razors flying. Ten Spanish shaving brushes hoping for extra soup, to do one barber's work. Paulo couldn't get over it. The torero would lift up his nose with a thumb, and each time in not more than four strokes, he found himself more close shaven than when in civilian life he set off for Auteuil to pick up Breton housemaids, tomorrow's hookers.

And every morning it was wash, cut, delouse and shave for the privileged Kommando. Wherever it was going, the Kommando was to be a credit to Mauthausen.

Worn shirts and torn underwear had been left to those who stayed behind. Brand-new clothing had replaced them. Of course it was also vertically striped, gray and blue, but hard-wearing and stitched with the insignia KLM, *Konzentrationslager Mauthausen*. After the underwear, the Kommando was issued its going-away outfit, the uniform of a successful jailbird: striped jacket and trousers of heavy cloth like those of the Kapos, but without the docker's cap. A beret instead, with horizontal stripes for harmony.

Finally, a long coat of the same material with the same stripes completed the ensemble. And, sure sign of an imminent departure, new real-leather shoes and a Wehrmacht-model mess bowl. One might almost have thought that the SS intended to have this impeccable Kommando parachuted somewhere. For propaganda.

Paulo couldn't keep still. It was his first uniform and he was taking good care of it. Like a real recruit. With spotless boots, creaseless uniform and gleaming mess tin, he ran to each assembly, taking his place in the last row among the tallest. Attention! Atten-shun! The *Dolmetscher* didn't seem to know how to translate "At ease," but the troops' morale was high and in the yard outside the quarantine blocks, the looks of those left to their fate changed from envy to admiration.

Half naked and shaking with cold and hunger, the failures and the inept clung together in the center of the yard to form a huddle. It was a patented invention of the Polish, past masters of suffering: a sort of human cluster, as many as possible squeezed against each other to get warm without movement or exertion.

These huddles were the only means of finding warmth, theoretically 98.6 degrees, the temperature of the human body. But with the dying trapped in the middle of the cluster, the temperature often rose to nearly 104, and a few of the selfish ones managed to find their way to the center. The temporary well-being they felt was well worth the inevitable blow of the club. When the Kapos arrived to break up the overgrown huddles, breeding grounds for an epidemic, they found a pitiful group who did not react, asleep standing up. Even the dead, who had sought a little warmth before finally turning the lights out, were open to a few blows of the club.

And without letup, watched by the huddles, the Kommando's training continued. Each drill was repeated for hours on end. First of all, *Mützen ab*, caps off, the most important exercise, executed all over occupied Europe a hundred times a day by millions of shaven heads when a Kapo spoke or an SS passed by. One had to see the executioner without looking at him. It was forbidden to focus one's eyes on an SS. This was the first camp commandment, and at Mauthausen forbidden meant under penalty of death.

The second drill, eyes left, eyes right, had been more swiftly assimilated by Kommando X. For the most part these recruits, from all ages and walks of life, had recently done time in the military, the majority thanks to General Gamelin, the others in youth work camps. And with block chiefs as adjutants, they had quickly remembered how to march. First of all on the spot for hours on end, *links, zwo, drei, vier,* without moving; then maneuvers in the maliciously paved courtyard. The leather shoes were steadier than the wooden clogs, but the treacherous paving stones caused a balancing act never before seen in a parade of troops. They looked like an army of cripples on the march. Only the about-turn, German style, interrupted the seasickness. The Germans had won the war, their way was the right way, and to do an about-turn French style was a pretext for a beating. One more pretext.

Paulo maneuvered like a professional sergeant. Forward march, eyes left, eyes front, company halt, *Mützen ab*. Those who didn't know him would have thought that with this display of zeal he was hoping to be promoted Kapo. He might even be drafted into the Luftwaffe. Why not? But his delinquent neighbors heard him mutter between two calls to attention: "What are these fuckers waiting for? Let's get started."

His impersonation of a volunteer looking for stripes concealed a deepening anguish. The fear of staying. And by staying, the certainty of dying, roasted like a live chicken. He was afraid of being exchanged at the last minute for a fatter newcomer, for every day he lost a kilo with the fucking exercise in his wood-fiber coat. They had even issued each man a navy-blue sweater. With the coat, the jacket, the sweater and the heavy shirt, the quart of so-called soup—the only meal of the day—was sweated out before there was even time to piss it. With no reserve of fat, it was Paulo's muscles which were shrinking with the sweat, and soon the superworker wasn't going to be much good for anything. He could feel it, he clenched his teeth, but fear seized him nonetheless. He feared catching fever and not being able to bound out of bed when the Kommando was called, twenty times a day, ten times a night. Already nearly a dozen worn-out men had been thrown out, sent to the *Revier* to wait for the roasting, and they were immediately replaced by young fools who moaned, the idiots, about being separated from their buddies. Buddies who were already as good as dead.

And then, one sunny morning at the end of May, after several false alarms and much false excitement, the *eins, zwei, drei, vier* had caused the doors of the quarantine barracks to open. Slave-market square was crossed in an impressive silence and order. The Kommandant was on the battlements above, and the departure of three hundred of his best prisoners certainly didn't seem to be breaking his heart. His camp would be filled up again during the day. With some extras probably. Extras who would go up in smoke that same night if the stationmasters had miscalculated the arrivals.

Abteilung halt, Mützen ab, bare heads. It was normal to stop and reflect at such a moment, when the doors of hell were about to open. One could hear the breathing in the ranks of the prisoners. Above, scoffing, the SS of the camp, all of them, perched on the granite walls, balancing on the narrow walkway, astride the huge cast-iron gate, in the watchtowers, everywhere. They found it amusing to see these pretentious *Franzosen* leaving disguised, ridiculous, shaven, striped like zebras, German mess tins in hand. Three months earlier, they had entered at this same gate with their long hair slicked down, wearing felt hats and warm overcoats, each one carrying a suitcase full of wonderful things from Paris. Three months earlier, the troop of prisoners had been greeted by yells, insults, beatings and spittle. Even the hideous *Fräulein* and the tattooed hookers from the bordello had joined in the reception.

Today, just laughter. The laughter of pleasure seekers proud of a job well done for the Führer.

The gate finally opened for the men of Kommando X. *Im gleich Schritt Marsch, Mützen auf*, caps on, forward march. The hideous bronze eagle holding the swastika in its claws was now behind them. "All hope abandon, ye who enter here," Dante's phrase, which might have been engraved over the gate, had been disproved. They were coming out alive. Anxious still, for they knew quite well they had not been freed from the asylum to be returned to their families.

The lustful looks of the Kapos and the guards surrounding them gave the men the feeling that Kommando X would be no piece of cake.

II

Guns had expedited the climb up to Mauthausen; the new arrivals had been encouraged by pistol-whipping and random shots. The descent was faster still. Kommando X found wings.

The slope which led toward a pine wood put a lively spring in the steps of the escaped deportees. With the sun firing their imaginations, some wishful thinkers saw themselves as soldiers off on leave for a picnic, a loaf of bread under their arms and a mess tin at their belts.

Paulo however wasn't dreaming about lunch in the country. The huge gulps of fresh air that he breathed in were not stimulating his appetite. They were the gulps of the shipwrecked sailor who has spotted land. And that land, spread out at his feet, was magnificent. It was almost indecent, only a few yards away from hell. Bizarre sense of irony, to set up a psychiatric fortress against the backdrop of a Viennese operetta. Paulo was regretting having been deprived for three months of this wonderful scenery. It would have helped him. But up in the camp, it had been strongly suggested that the newcomers should not approach the electrified barbed-wire fence. So he knew nothing of the area except for the sky, a sky which was always gray, always dirty. Today, all at once, he could see everything. In the far distance, barring the horizon, rose the snowy peaks of the Tyrolean Alps. Below, there were pine woods everywhere, green hills and, right in the middle of this picture postcard, the long silver ribbon of the Danube. The beautiful blue Danube, favorite waltz of the sentimental citadel butchers. Paulo shivered at the memory, but nonetheless he glanced back. Mauthausen would disappear after the next turn in the wood and he wanted to preserve an image of it from the outside. Seen from below, there was no doubt that Mauthausen was impressive. It was a fortified castle, with its towers, its battlements, its coat of arms above the gate, and its turret watchtowers. Even the subsidiary buildings, the blocks, the gas showers, the kitchens and the whorehouse, which were gaily and artistically covered with Virginia creeper and clumps of nasturtium, gave the impression of a nobleman's residence. Paulo wondered if there was a photo of it. He would need one to explain what went on inside, and already he saw himself impressing an audience:

"You see this castle? Well, that's Mauthausen, *Morderhausen* they called it, the house of murder, the house of a hundred thousand corpses. I was there."

He had hardly been out for ten minutes and already he was thinking about going back to Paris. The tin-plate bracelet which rattled on his skinny wrist was enough to remind him that he was not yet out of the death house. He was still registered there, 28,214, a lottery number. Maybe it was a lucky number, he thought, looking around him at the 26-, 27- and 28-thousand registrations scrawled in crude digits on the striped coats of his companions right next to the little red triangle marked with the letter *F* for *Frankreich*. At any rate, his picnic companions were in good form; they were almost running as the happy group crossed the wood to arrive at the first houses of Mauthausen village.

"*Zu fünf*," yelled the Kapos.

Always in fives; it made it easier for these thinkers to count. *Eins, zwei*, in measured step—they had to show the townspeople that up in the castle they knew how to whip anarchists into line. The Austrians liked this method of re-education. Like the SS on the way out of the fortress, they had gathered alongside the path of the column, on the pavements or at the windows of their white-and-pink houses, the better to enjoy the spectacle. Three months earlier, little albino-looking brats in *Lederhosen* had pitched stones and spat upon the prisoners on their way up to the castle, still in civilian clothing. These same little monsters, with a hard on at the sight of a uniform, even a convict's outfit, followed the column, keeping in step. *Eins, zwei*.

"Little shit," hissed Paulo to a redheaded kid who happened to be level with him.

Ruhe, silence, *schnell*.

The SS led their flock of zebras silently and quickly to the station, where the signboard "*Mauthausen fertig*" was still displayed at the end of the railway track. *Fertig*, the end of the line, terminus, came home to those men who had done time up there. Three months ago, nine tenths of the passengers on the train from Compiègne had not realized that this sign was their epitaph. For them life had stopped at the terminus of the small line from Linz, Hitler's birthplace. It was a crowded line, with twice, three times, a hundred times as many trains as in the past.

These reflections didn't trouble the mechanical minds of the SS escort. *Schnell, los*, they seemed to be in a great hurry to board the train, and from their excitement, one could deduce that Kommando X was not being sent to consolidate the Russian front. Good thing, thought Paulo, who analyzed everything. He was just contemplating this conclusion when a well-aimed boot helped him to hoist himself into a truck. It was obviously a livestock car. Eight horses, forty men, or a hundred deportees, according to the *Todt* transport regulations. However, the door had been closed by the SS who had kicked him, and although Paulo counted over and again, there were only forty deportees in the car, forty, eight rows of five plus a Kapo.

"That's a good sign," Paulo said to himself. "They still consider us human beings."

And he began to look at these "human beings" who surrounded him. A stranger would not have been able to tell one from the other. They all looked the same with their grotesque striped outfits, their shaven heads, their grayish skin and their dazed expressions. More difficult to identify than Chinamen. Paulo knew almost all of them, but for the last three months he had lived among them without really seeing them. Up in the asylum, one couldn't focus on an image. It all went too quickly, like a silent film before the war, the First World War. All that remained was a blurred impression. Besides, at that time Paulo had had only one idea in his head: not to roast. His fellows, the French, had ceased to exist for those three months. He was alone, there was no one. Every man for himself, since there was no God in that apocalyptic circus, had been his philosophy. He had almost come to blows with some commies begging for bread crumbs to help a dying comrade, for whom this charitable gesture was not enough to prevent his dying two days later. Suddenly these striped phantoms, whom Paulo had seen running in all directions to avoid the clubs, without feeling the slightest emotion, came into focus. Men's faces, at last. They belonged to the same race as himself, from his country, and they too must have trembled at the thought of the oven or at the sight of the cart. But for three months each one had kept his fear to himself. Today, for the first time, tongues were loosened by the unhoped-for joy of having escaped the massacre. Everyone in the car began to confide in the others.

Insensitive Paulo listened to them talk, the men he had regarded for so long as ghosts. But this public wailing, these maudlin exchanges ended up getting on his nerves. The man opposite him, who couldn't be taken for anything but a peasant, was moaning incessantly: "Seems this camp we're going to'll be a lot worse, disciplinary and that. We don't stand an earthly."

Paulo cut him short, almost shouting.

"Shut your face, peasant, and keep your crap to yourself."

This unusual display of dominance impressed both the yokel and his neighbors; silence reigned in the car. Besides, the train began to move, reviving memories of another trip: the trip to Mauthausen, a hundred to each locked car, in the course of which a certain number of courageous and inspired men had succeeded in jumping onto the track. Paulo was the first to break the lock on the door of his car, child's play, and was about to jump just before Saarbrücken when machine-gun fire broke out. After that it was too risky and Paulo, always calculating, had figured that because they were in Germany it would be better to quietly organize escape from the place they were being taken to. With a compass and maps of the area. No such luck. The place was Mauthausen, and Paulo had not foreseen that in his plans. He cursed himself over and over for not having jumped, in spite of the machine-gun fire.

The memory of that lost opportunity did not even bring to mind the thought that he might on this present journey find a similar opportunity. Head shaven, in convict's uniform with his Mauthausen registration, it would be madness to make a break for it in a country whose natives seemed more than usually fanatical. Paulo had let his mind wander for five minutes, but suddenly he came back to reality. He turned his attention back to the freight car, and to pass the time he began to examine his traveling companions one by one.

In deference to rank, the Kapo first of all. To find a more revolting specimen would be impossible. Under that cap he had it all: thug, traitor, thief, murderer, coward, queer—he could have filled a prison on his own. Instead of a head, an enormous meatball—red, lipless, cauliflower-eared with blackened lead-filled teeth. And one eye. This cyclops of indeterminate age, whom the French had immediately dubbed Bullseye, was no better endowed vocally. He did not speak, he barked. What a monster. Inevitably with all these trump cards, this frightful bulldog inspired fear, and in the half-light of the car the impression of terror was reinforced.

Sitting on the straw in orderly rows with their mess tins lined up, the forty numbers had fallen silent. Bullseye had bellowed three times "*Ruhe*." That was enough, because the normal Mauthausen tradition was for the beating to arrive before the order. All the men in the car began to think that in spite of his horrendous mask maybe their overseer was really a good guy. That said, no one dared risk talking. Paulo, who by now knew enough about the guard, took advantage of the silence to study the other travelers more closely. Looking over the group, he guessed that about one in four was a crook. About ten altogether. He knew them all: small-time thugs who had made overtures to him at Compiègne, where his cell had quickly become the reserve of the camp black market; and some proper criminals, real professionals, who did not take kindly to their prisoner's outfit.

First of all, there were the Campana brothers, obviously Corsican. Twelve cases dismissed, seven acquittals from murder charges between them, and if Paulo's memory was correct, Mauthausen must have been the first taste of prison for these two lambs.

On their right was Riton of Montparnasse, a pimp from the rue de la Gaîté, and another fellow from the Left Bank, Pierrot Martin, officially a professional boxer.

Finally, behind Riton, completing the bunch of sharks, was Berck of Strasbourg. Insignificant, but dangerous because he talked Kraut.

"Better be careful of that shit," Paulo said to himself, and he continued his observation.

He didn't see any other pimps. Three wasn't bad for one car. The other representatives of the criminal world were divided into two groups, thieves and gunmen. The latter group was made up almost entirely of young men. Completely lacking the business sense that was vital to survive in troubled times, they had opted for the pistol to bring in the bread. Their careers had been brief. They had been introduced to Paulo upon arrival at Compiègne, and he still remembered the calling cards of three of these customers opposite him: three natives of Lyons, Marco, Gégène and Roland, sole survivors of the attack on the Boulogne Savings Bank. The rest of the gang had been barbecued within a few days at Mauthausen. As Paulo continued he recognized one by one some of the small fry who at Compiègne had absolutely insisted upon telling him, the up-and-coming gang leader, of their small-time exploits: Aimé Vicaire, a swindler and a self-styled POW escapee; and a little fellow from Cannes, Angel Belloni, twenty years old and an apprentice criminal. However, from what Paulo understood, he showed promise, and Paulo knew about vice. This bright boy had also had the sense to flex his little biceps on the day of the slave market. Angel Belloni didn't look at all like a hard laborer, but the SS were pleased that he was such an energetic fellow, and despite his pocket size they had stuck him in Kommando X.

In spite of the rhythmic sound of the train as it gathered speed, the silence was beginning to weigh heavily inside the freight car. Then the Kapo barked again. The forty shaven heads looked at him apprehensively, but relieved that he had interrupted their pessimistic reflections. His barks were not addressed to them. Bullseye had found a friend in the man opposite, Pozzi, the only crook who had escaped Paulo's examination. His phoniness had instantly attracted the Kapo, and the unwholesome pair were jabbering in pidgin German, which Pozzi must have learned from the Gestapo of the rue Lauriston, where he served as caretaker. Paulo had spotted him there as he came out of an interrogation.

Pozzi was trying to suck up to the Kapo, explaining that he had nothing against the Germans. On the contrary. "It was all a mistake," Pozzi was saying, but the other didn't give a damn about judicial errors. He shoved the green triangle sewn onto his jacket under Pozzi's nose. This badge was the pride of the German common criminal.

"*Nicht politik, ich bin ein Berufsverbrecher.* Zwanzig jahre prison. Politiker alle ins Krematorium*." The temperature was rising and the cyclops was screaming louder and louder. "*Krematorium, Krematorium, Scheisse politiker.*"

The ten criminals in the car felt like yelling back at him: "We're one and the same, crooks, not politicos," but they decided it was better to shut up. Besides, Bullseye had punctuated his last sentence with the inevitable "*Ruhe*," and once more the car lapsed prudently into silent contemplation.

Politicos or not, criminals, honest citizens, you really had to be on the inside like Paulo to distinguish one from the other in this mixed bag. Even he was unsure of some types.

---

*Professional criminal.

The young Breton with the square head, for example, didn't look like a quitter and he seemed to know why he was there. He was bound to be a member of the Resistance, like his neighbor, who looked just as determined and was old enough to be his father. These two guys were so relaxed they were really setting Paulo's nerves on edge. He had already noticed them at Compiègne, then again at Mauthausen. Like the Campana brothers they always stuck to one another, at muster and at whipping sessions. The pair had managed to get aboard the same car and they seemed oblivious to the riffraff around them. On the contrary, this mystery trip seemed to be to their liking. They were smiling at each other.

"And yet they don't look like queers," Paulo said to himself. And he moved on to the next one, the ignorant peasant whose demoralizing remarks he had cut short. If this fellow had managed to make it through Mauthausen, it was thanks to his reserves of butter and tripe. He was still living off them, but the puffy mug of this alcoholic, scarlet when he arrived, was now merely rosy. It could have been taken as a sign of good health next to the greenish tinge of the others. This hick would already have been dead if the SS had not rinsed his cider-soaked liver with the soup water for three months. In fact he had a hell of a lot to thank them for, but the ungrateful oaf was always the first to moan and groan. Like his fellow countryman, another much younger peasant who had wasted away to nothing in Block 18. There was nothing but shoulders left.

The peasants were well represented in the car—five or six according to Paulo's calculations, who wondered by what stroke of misfortune these rustics had ended up in such a slave ship. Doubtless by tradition, which dictates that country people should pay more heavily than others for war.

"Crazy war," thought Paulo, continuing his inspection. "There are all kinds of people involved: thieves, peasants, queers." But there were fifteen or so whom he couldn't quite place. Two or three students certainly—*lycée* students perhaps—in any case, less than twenty years old. And then there were the bourgeois, in their forties or fifties, well preserved, at least what was left of them. And one or two professional officers whose air of authority had disappeared with the first blows.

Members of the Resistance, bums, riffraff? Paulo gave

up. He was sick of it and felt terribly alone in the midst of all this company. No friend possible. The criminals he scorned; the straights he had no desire to know. Clearly the cure at the citadel had had its effect. Paulo, such a live wire when it came to survival, so cocky on his arrival, found when he came out that for the first time he felt completely empty and depressed. And yet, over the period of time, there had been changes, some hope especially. It didn't seem possible that they would dress these men so warmly merely to send them to the slaughterhouse. Paulo didn't understand anymore. Like the others he was waiting for information. The Kapo ought to know, but that dullard had obviously celebrated his nomination as escort by drinking schnaps. He was slumped forward, eye staring into space, mouth open, snoring.

The train had been on the move for almost four hours. There seemed no end to the silence, when suddenly a rough switch onto another track woke up Bullseye. His giant meatball of a head had banged violently against the partition.

"*Scheissdreck, merde, merde,*" thundered the one-eyed guard in German and in French, and his eye swept over the whole car in a single glance to see if by chance anybody had dared to find his painful awakening funny.

Fortunately, Pozzi took advantage of the moment to continue his earlier policy of ass-licking.

"D'you hurt yourself, chief?"

"If I'm a Kapo, it's because I have an iron head," answered Bullseye, delighted to explain that he had received thousands of blows on his skull since the Nazis had taken him out of jail in '34 to send him to Buchenwald. And he embarked on an account of his life to Pozzi. At each anecdote Pozzi opened his shifty eyes wide, full of admiration. His neighbors plucked up their courage and risked a few admiring interjections. Soon the whole car was buzzing. From neighbor to neighbor everybody commented on the exploits of their chief.

"He's been lucky," Aimé Vicaire said to Paulo. "Without Hitler, he'd still be moldering away in Düsseldorf jail. He's a lifer, he says."

"With a kisser like that, it's not surprising he got himself noticed," retorted Paulo.

"It's still unbelievable that the Germans would have enough confidence in thieves and murderers to put them in charge of camp discipline," one of the bourgeois muttered very low, prudently. "It's against all the rules of war."

"You haven't got it, have you?" Riton cut in. "Christ, you must have learned politics at St.-Cyr.* You aren't with it at all. Believe me, they haven't finished with your education. It's because of silly fools like you that we're here in the first place."

"Not so loud, boys, there's no point in quarreling," interrupted a tall, thin, distinguished-looking fellow seated among the savings bank gunmen. "We're all in this together. Do better trying to work out where they're taking us. I've an idea our convoy's heading north, probably toward Poland to reinforce the antitank defenses. That's why the warm clothes were handed out to us. What do you think, old fellow?"

The old fellow in question was the inseparable companion of the stubborn-looking Breton. He was still smiling.

"I don't think so," he answered. "Our Kommando is attached to Mauthausen and it wouldn't be logical to send part of its SS contingent so far from the garrison. In my opinion the trip will be short and it's likely our camp will be in Austria, or very close to the border."

The conversation was taking a lofty turn.

"My God, they're incurable," Paulo said to himself. "Anyone would think they were colonels changing duty stations. The older they get, the more ridiculous they become."

But suddenly the high-level exchanges came to a halt.

"*Essen*," the Kapo had yelled.

There was a general rush, no holds barred, on the loaves of bread. The gentlemen officers were transformed in a second into ill-bred old convicts. They tore at their dry bread like animals. As for the Kapo, he had taken out a long switchblade to fix himself some thin slices of bread on which he piled enormous chunks of sausage. His leaden jaws crushed the sandwich as the envious Pozzi looked on.

The loaves of bread had been heavily attacked when Bullseye, with his mouth full, asked Pozzi to translate. "I warn you, you bunch of guzzlers, that loaf of bread is your ration for three days."

The picnic stopped dead. Everyone put what remained in the bottom of his coat and the conversation began again.

---

*The French military academy.

"You slipped up," said the little Breton to his friend. "Three days has got to be outside Austria."

"I still think we're not being sent far," answered the other. "Three days at the speed we're making is not many miles."

"I'd just as soon we made tracks. The farther we get away from that nuthouse the better I'll feel," threw in Paulo, who was fed up with keeping to himself. "You from Paname?"* he asked the Breton's companion.

"No, I'm a Basque."

"What was your line of business?"

"I'm a history teacher."

"And your friend, is he a Basque too?" continued Paulo, well aware that the kid was a Breton, but wanted to find out what these two smiling faces were up to.

"No, he's a Breton, from St.-Malo."

"Is he a teacher too?"

"Yeah, does that surprise you?" the little guy broke in. "Don't worry, I'm no intellectual. I'm a gym teacher."

His reply was a little aggressive. Paulo noticed, but he let it pass.

"Not ideal for landing a soft job in prison," he commented after a moment.

"Oh, it might be useful."

They were certainly not keen to talk about themselves, those two. Paulo was not making much progress. But he persisted:

"Why did you get picked up? Resistance?"

"We weren't together," answered the elder one. "I was denounced and arrested. No reason."

"For me," added the other, "it was the same thing."

"A long time ago?"

"Eighteen months."

"Eighteen months? How have you stuck it out for so long? Where were you before Compiègne?" questioned Paulo, beginning to understand that the two comrades were suspicious of him.

"In solitary, at Fresnes."**

Paulo exploded. "And you don't know why you were

**Paname:* slang word for Paris.

**A prison in the suburbs of Paris.

hauled in? What kind of a cunt do you two take me for? Some kind of squealer? My God! I don't give a shit about your stories. Let me tell you something: I'm a crook and you can go to hell for all I care. Why don't you all go fuck yourselves, Resistance, commies, Yanks, Krauts, all of you? A great state you're in now, you heroes. Just look at you, and when I think it's because of types like you—"

"That's enough, big shot, nobody asked your opinion—"

It was the little gym teacher, who had stood up with his fists clenched and his blue eyes flashing.

Paulo saw it coming. "Listen, pint-size, you're not big enough. But if you want your head beaten in, you'll get it. Just wait till we arrive. You'll have your day."

The atmosphere was getting heated, and a few hungry men, sickened at the sight of Bullseye stuffing himself, thought they would add their bit.

"Beat him up," shouted one of the crooks at Paulo.

"Between Frenchmen? Have you no shame?" interjected the tall, distinguished skeleton.

"For Christ's sake shut up, or we'll all get in trouble."

For once the peasant had gotten it right. Bullseye had just put down his third sandwich, and came running with his club in hand, bruising shins and scattering blows on the skulls all around. He stopped in front of the Breton.

"Get up, *schnell*, *Scheisskubel*, bucket of shit. *Was willst du?* Boxing? *Gut, mein Herr.*"

And with all his might he punched him viciously on the jaw. Unbelievably, the small gym teacher didn't flinch. Even Bullseye, who had given it all he had, couldn't get over it. His punch was famous in the concentration camps and whoever was on the receiving end was invariably laid out. All the more easily since he had to stand at attention and it was out of the question to duck. That was going to cost the Breton dearly. Blind with rage, Bullseye took his club and deliberately set about the Breton's face. He hit him at least ten times, but as the blood began to spurt, he began to calm down.

"Who did you want to fight with, *Dreck Franzose*? Come on, *los*, out wth it or I'll start all over again."

"With no one, chief."

"No one, *mein lieber Mann*, no one?" The monster looked around, his club at the ready. He repeated, "No one, no one," and each time he lashed out again. Paulo, like his companions, got one behind the ears, but he did not feel all that proud of having provoked the Breton.

Back in his place, the chief felt obliged to give an explanation. "You're still at Mauthausen, you syphilitic bastards, and at Mauthausen it is forbidden to fight. Under penalty of death."

He sat down, pleased with himself, and attacked what was left of the sandwich, which he had left on his cap to be freer to beat the man. But the glutton wasn't hungry anymore, and in a gesture of magnanimity he turned toward Pozzi and handed him his crust. "*Du, Mensch, essen.*"

It was hard to turn it down. Pozzi grabbed the sandwich, but he actually looked embarrassed at being obliged, in front of everyone, to bite into the sausage which bore the fresh marks of the chief's lead-filled fangs.

"He doesn't even seem disgusted, the shit," muttered Paulo, secretly wondering what he would have done in the place of the Gestapo's caretaker. The same thing no doubt, but what a disgrace for a criminal! He was feeling more and more sickened when Bullseye barked his next order.

"*Alle schlafen, schnell.*"

No one had to be asked twice, Within a second, the forty *Politiker* had disappeared under their coats. Fifteen minutes later they were all snoring. For the first time in three months the reddish glow of the flames from the crematorium didn't invade their nightmares.

The sun was filtering through the wooden slats of the car when they awoke. During their sleep the train had carried them a little farther away from the death house. They were now several hundred miles distant, and this was their first thought as they began to stretch. It must also have occurred to Bullseye, for in the half-light he appeared suddenly less ugly and less evil. His eye was smiling.

"It smells of shit in here," he yelled as he got up. "*Schnell, zwei Mann.* Empty crapper." And he approached the door to draw back the bolt. The door slid back and the car was flooded with sunlight. The prisoners were blinded, then stupefied to see open country rolling by no more than two yards away—friendly countryside, no barbed wire and no watchtowers, countryside which invited escape. Freedom was waiting, one step away. All they had to do was jump. The same thought struck all forty prisoners at once, the cowards as well as the others. It was more than tempting.

"How about it, big shot, too chicken to jump? This is your big moment."

The jibe was addressed at Paulo by the little Breton. Blows he could take, but not insults.

"Leave me alone," Paulo answered gloomily.

The striped jacket had taken its toll on this scrapper, who had never been shaken by looking down the barrel of a gun. And all the brave men in the car—gunmen, members of the Resistance, officers, terrorists—were in the same bad way. Each found an excuse to hesitate. What country were they in? How fast were they going? A blue-striped zebra in this green countryside would be too easy to shoot, and so on. The real reason was that all these heroes had turned milky. But the idea of bungling it—the tragic irony of wearing with pride the Mauthausen brand over their hearts, the return to fanfares and a public hanging or a snack for the mastiffs—all this excused their hesitation.

They all knew that to be caught meant inevitable death, and not a quiet and easy death by firing squad. What the SS wanted for the escapees was a spectacle, a Roman circus, in public, to the strains of an orchestra. With all the population assembled and whipped into watching the agony from beginning to end. Before leaving, the men of Kommando X had been invited to two or three such sessions, and the memory of the torture cooled the escape candidates more effectively than the knowledge that ten of their fellows would be shot, as they had been warned upon their departure.

That is why nothing happened as the green fields continued to roll past the wide-open door. The train slowed down and even stopped, and the convicts remained very well behaved. Bullseye rejoiced. He watched his prisoners as they got up one after the other to go to the buckets near the door. He was sure of himself. In ten years he had never seen an escape from any establishment directed by the SS, those experts in residential institutions.

The crapper was filling up in spite of the meager reserves in the men's stomachs, and Angel Belloni, who had been detailed the duty of emptying, looked as if he didn't much care for his role of lavatory lady. Handling the piss and shit of his fellow criminals and especially of the "straights" was not much of a way for an ambitious boy to make an impression. In addition Bullseye seemed to be down on him. Between two of these excrement duties, he had yelled at him in an incomprehensible slang, and three times since waking he had viciously slapped him without apparent reason. Angel Belloni trembled with shame and rage, but no one pitied him.

It was now more than twenty-four hours since the convoy had left Mauthausen.

"According to the sun, we're heading south," announced the history teacher, pursuing his original idea.

"It's all the same," answered the whining peasant. "No point trying to understand."

The beauty of the countryside didn't improve the group's morale and the conversations Bullseye allowed were of a wretched banality for men experiencing such an adventure into the unknown. Difficult to deny that it was humiliating for these hard-bitten men to tremble when they were forty against one. This realization of their impotence mortified even the strongest, and as the countryside and freedom slipped by, they felt less and less proud of themselves. Once again it was Bullseye, always down-to-earth, who came to the aid of their failing spirits.

"*Essen*," he yelled. One had to eat on command. The chunks of bread reappeared. But not all of them; there had been a theft during the night. A sleepwalker had made off with the history teacher's loaf. Paulo thought the old man was ready to weep when he discovered the theft, but he held back his tears and instead of causing a fuss, he whispered quietly in his Breton friend's ear.

"My bread's been stolen, while I was asleep. It doesn't matter, I'm not hungry. Anyway, it won't be long now before we arrive."

Without a word his small square-headed friend broke his own bread in half and gave him the bigger piece. His open expression and his cheerful smile indicated there was to be no argument, and the old teacher, very moved but very hungry too, began to gnaw on the bread, oblivious of table manners.

The scene had only one witness, Paulo. Reluctantly he had to admit that he was impressed by the purity of this testimony of friendship. If it had been his crust, Paulo would have killed to get it back. He certainly thought so, but in any case he would easily have been capable of beating all his neighbors to make the thief vomit up the bread, even at the risk of a beating all around. The behavior of these two smiling men no longer annoyed him, it astonished him. They showed themselves to be bigger men than all ten criminals put together. The more so since the chances were that the bread thief was one of the pimps of the gang. Riton, for example, the old man's closest neighbor, who was munching away with an exaggerated air of innocence.

The famished prisoners were trying to make their final mouthfuls of bread last when the train began to slow down, labor as if it were climbing and finally stop. They were in the middle of a forest. The temptation to get out and walk around had become sorely trying, but for a good while now the thought of jumping had left even the most enterprising souls. Besides, an SS had just appeared, spoiling the scenery, his submachine gun pointing at the bucket of excrement.

"*Schweine Franzosen*," he articulated clearly, and he spat on the deportee nearest to him.

Each scene was more unpleasant than the last. Paulo was getting more and more disgusted with everything. But especially with himself, with his cowardice and with that of his companions. He repeated to himself: "We're just shits; all just shits." And the rhythm of the train, which had moved off again and was gathering some speed, accompanied his words: "We're just shits, all just shits."

Once again the change of scenery intervened to dispel black thoughts. The train was laboring as the locomotive steamed noisily. Now they were climbing, and soon meadows and woods gave way to miles of steep black rock right next to the train. They were penetrating the mountains. Bullseye was the only one who didn't look surprised. The bastard must have known what country this famous mystery camp was in. Pozzi must have caught on because he started to pump him, partly for his own information but especially to redeem himself in the eyes of his peers, the gang. He had lacked nerve in front of too many witnesses.

"Are we still in Austria, chief?"

"Austria doesn't exist anymore, *Dummkopf*. There's only the Reich, the great Reich. The whole of Europe is the Reich with *Konzentrationslager* everywhere. I know them all."

"And where we're going, do you know that too, chief?"

"No, shitface, it doesn't exist yet."

"You think the discipline will be rougher than at Mauthausen?"

"You don't get discipline in camps that are being built, you get killed. Like the Spaniards at Mauthausen. *Alle kaputt.*"

And he almost choked at his wonderful wit. The whole car had anxiously followed the dialogue with Pozzi. Their faces had become longer, if that was possible. Paulo, who had taken hold of himself again, wanted to make some sort of an effort in the face of this general depression.

"That queer's talking bullshit, he doesn't know any more than we do. It can't be any worse than where we've just come from. It'll stink, but it can't be worse."

"I agree," said the history teacher, who had understood Paulo's intentions, "and now I'm positive we're not in Austria anymore. We can only be in Hungary or Yugoslavia. Even the Germans will think twice about mass murder in a foreign country."

These words of hope were spread from ear to ear, from one end of the car to the other. Resignation had given way to excitement, and everyone was bending forward to scan the mountainside only inches away, as the train clattered by with an ear-splitting roar. But an icy cold quickly engulfed the car and Bullseye, full of loving attention, got up to close the door. In their little box night fell and conversation ceased.

III

Bullseye had lied. He knew very well that the journey would not last three days, and if he had bothered to get up and close the door of the car himself, it was not to prevent his chicks from catching pneumonia. The SS had told him that the train journey would be over by the end of that day and, as the history teacher had foreseen, the terminus was indeed in a foreign country. Given these circumstances, an escape could no longer be considered an act of madness. The SS had warned their assistants: a single escape, and the Kapo would find himself having to explain things, at the end of a rope, like the comrades in stripes. The thought of it was giving Bullseye the shakes. He opened his good eye—obviously. With his back to the door, he once again called for silence in order to detect any movement in the darkness as the train slowed down and then stopped.

"*Ruhe*," he yelled. Pointlessly, since one could have heard a pin drop, but he added immediately, "Nobody move," and the forty prisoners realized this was an important moment. The noise of a cavalcade of boots put an end to the suspense.

"*Alle raus*."

No need for an interpreter, even for the thickest peasant. *Alle raus*, everybody out, the key phrase of the Nazi camps. It cleared out barracks at any time of day or night, and throughout the whole of Europe it greeted the arrival of passengers on the death trains.

In a second, the convicts had stood up like robots, mess tins in hand. And when Bullseye slid back the door, there was a great rush for the exit. Each one had learned by experience that the club was reserved for the stragglers. But this time they miscalculated, because the reception had been arranged for everyone. Blows from the butts of the escort's guns rained on those who were first out, the quick ones and the eager beavers, as they jumped down onto the platform. Extra painful blows, on their backs, in their ribs and on their necks. Curiously, the flurry of the wooden butts was not accompanied by the usual yells. The *schnell*, *los*, *geh mal*, of the SS were uttered in low voices, almost whispered.

The teacher was right, the SS did not feel at home. The mysterious town, Hungarian or Yugoslavian, could not have been very far from the station, which appeared to be at the end of the track. In fifteen seconds, the company of workers had been ejected and Bullseye, helpfully cooperating with his club, could breathe again. His responsibility was over, he would not be hanged tonight. Forty, full strength. "*Zu fünf*," he yelled, by fives; and just to be sure, he recounted.

Paulo, as usual in the last row because of his height, glanced to the right and left like a hunting dog. He sniffed the night air, trying to find his bearings in the darkness.

A gun butt on a shoulder blade interrupted his efforts to

ascertain his whereabouts. The order to advance had been passed in low voices from group to group, and in a trice Kommando X found itself re-established. *Eins, zwei, links, rechts*, in impeccable order the column advanced toward the lights of the station buildings. But no one was there to see this proud march-past. The station was empty; there was not even a stationmaster. And the troops continued their silent march beyond the station buildings toward an illuminated strip of land. The light came from the headlights of vehicles or, more precisely, from old gas-burning flatloaders, about fifteen of them, motors already ticking over.

A few yards from the trucks about fifty SS, elbow to elbow, were having difficulty holding back a hundred or so civilians, men, women and children. Even from a distance, it was evident from the behavior of these civilians and the way in which they were dressed that they were not German. What were they then? Hungarian? Yugoslavian?

"*Halt*," an officer yelled at the head of the column, and the order reverberated back down the ranks.

"Attention, dressing by fives." Always the same old tune: count, recount. The officer responsible for the journey wanted to be certain no one had managed to escape in the three hundred yards they had just covered, between a double row of submachine guns held barrel to barrel.

"*Drei hundert Stücken, Kommandoführer*," cried a young NCO with an exaggerated click of his heels.

Stücken, pieces, they were exactly that. It was the only possible label for these strange creatures in striped pajamas, on a mountain road at this late hour.

At any rate, that's what the civilians must have thought. They had managed to come closer and they stared incredulously at the spectacle. Convicts in their quiet village? What had these bandits done to deserve being dressed like this, with heads like billiard balls? The only thing missing from the outfit of these dangerous men was a ball and chain on their ankles. And they must have been dangerous to need such a heavy escort, armed to the teeth. There were almost as many guards as prisoners. Not quite, but at least one SS for every three men, and it began to worry Paulo seriously.

The flaxen-haired escort, who had just wielded their butts with such dexterity, also looked worried. They had not been warned there would be so many spectators to witness their heroic mission, and they were anxious to get the trucks rolling to be rid of the source of their embarrassment.

Too late. The civilians had managed to get close to the trucks, and the column would have to march past only a few yards away. It was no longer possible to speed up the loading of the trucks with gun butts, because these civilians, lit up in the glare of the headlights, looked very attentive and not by any means hostile. The hangdog expression of the prisoners did not frighten them in the least. On the contrary, hands waved as the group moved toward the first trucks. Friendly hands, not holding rocks, unlike those little Tyrolean tossers of Mauthausen-on-the-Danube. There was no doubt that Kommando X had left the Reich. When Bullseye's group passed in front of the sympathetic inhabitants, a single voice was heard in the ranks.

"What country?"

"Trzic, Yugoslavia," the crowd replied in unison. "You French, too?"

"Yes, all French."

"Vive les Français, vive la France!"

This last cry, repeated every few yards by these unknown friends, electrified them. A shock wave of emotion swept through the wretched prisoners. *Vive la France!* Spines straightened, eyes filled with tears and among the delinquents, as among officers, students, bourgeois and peasants, hearts swelled. A current of patriotic fervor ran through the striped column. Even Paulo felt an involuntary thrill, like a hero acclaimed by the crowd.

"If they only knew what sort of a mob they're cheering," he murmured to himself, a little ashamed in spite of it all. His realistic reflections might have spoiled the moving illusion shared by the convicts and their admirers. He kept them to himself and joined the others, yelling at random to the groups of sympathetic bystanders:

"Thanks, thank you all, we'll have 'em!"

But his heart was no longer in it. He had realized that the warm welcome extended to him and his companions was the result of an error on the part of the guards. The bastards must have planned to whisk them off to the mysterious camp under cover of darkness, without witnesses. Their plans had failed; but wherever the men were being taken, there would certainly be no civilians to blow them kisses from the other side of the fence. They had to take advantage of it now. Paulo drew himself up again and, since he was a head taller than the rest, the smiles and little gestures and even the kisses of the Yugoslavians seemed to be addressed to him personally. A little kid in rags looked up at him with wide-open eyes, and when Paulo passed in front of him, the child surreptitiously threw him a loaf of newly baked bread. Too newly baked, for as it caught the light of the headlamps an SS spotted it. Furiously he stamped on it and, still marching, managed to grind it into crumbs with his heel, under the despairing eyes of the starving men. Paulo, with great dignity, did not even turn his head. His anxious gaze was focused on the boards of the truck assigned to his group. Contact with civilization had come to an end. SS and Kapos would be able to continue their education in private.

The élite Mauthausen troops were clearly annoyed at having to cross this courageous village. So anxious were the SS to take off into the night and settle their accounts that the prisoners had to jump into the trucks almost without breaking step. At the first bend in the road, the pistol-whipping took up where it had left off.

"Everybody sit, eyes on the floor or else," was the order, which would not be repeated twice. A ridiculous measure, since this was hardly a *route touristique*. On the right was the mountain, on the left a ravine, and it was pitch-dark. No houses, no signposts, not the slightest sign of life. This nighttime trip was taking a sinister turn, and all around Paulo patriotic sentiments had given way to fear and anguish.

This dejected state lasted a good quarter of an hour and only came to an end independently of their numbed spirits. The road was now no more than a series of zigzags, and the hairpin bends taken by a bad driver on a worse road had created havoc on the bed of the truck. The deportees were falling and rolling on each other, landing on their skinny backsides and painfully bumping their heads and shoulders on the metal panels. Paulo had linked arms with his neighbors to stop this St. Vitus's dance, and everyone followed suit. Immediately the excursion became less dramatic. The SS guards had noticed the stratagem, but did not react. Their worries seemed to be elsewhere, toward the mountain at which their submachine guns had been pointed for a while.

This detail had not escaped Paulo's notice, and with the relief of no longer having a gun trained on him, he found his voice again. He whispered in his neighbor's ear:

"This road isn't safe. Someone must have told these little cunts there were highwaymen in this desert, and they seem to believe it."

"Perhaps you're not far off the mark, except that the highwaymen might be partisans," answered the neighbor, who was in fact the old history teacher.

"Tell that to the Marines," retorted Paulo. But seeing the thoroughness with which the guards were studying the roadside verges, he kept quiet.

The thought that a skirmish might occur in the darkness gave Paulo a sudden shock. He could already see himself dodging machine-gun fire down the sloping side of the ravine. He unlinked his arms to be ready to jump at the first shot.

Suddenly he was in his element again, tougher than ever, ready to kill and be killed. He turned right around to study the disposition of the enemy. There were two SS on his side and another two at the back of the truck. He was in all their lines of fire, preventing a jump even if partisans were in the vicinity. Not a chance in a thousand of getting through. He just had to sit back and wait for the attack. But the farther they went, the more this attack seemed doubtful. Paulo's imagination had run away with him. Mechanically he took the teacher's arm. It was over, he had come back into the flock. His questions continued nonetheless, though more wearily now.

"What makes you say there are partisans in the area?"

"It's logical," answered the teacher. "Since we're in a very mountainous region, Resistance forces must be based here as in the rest of the country from Macedonia to Dalmatia. The proof is in our escort's change of attitude as we climb higher. For the moment our guards are no longer interested in us, and if our convoy has been marked, they would have good reason to fear a partisan attack. When we're in a camp, behind barbed wire, a surprise attack would be more difficult."

"Why do you think the partisans would take any notice of poor slobs like us?" asked Paulo, taking heart again.

"Didn't you see the welcome of the inhabitants at Trzic? They're Slavs and they love France. Napoleon came this way before us. As a matter of fact, I think we're now on the same road. The road to Vienna."

"In other words, they're bringing us back to Austria?"

"That would be surprising, and in that case I don't see why they would have brought us to Yugoslavia. Our guardian angels didn't seem too proud of showing us to the locals. More a case of hustling us away. I have a feeling we'll stop before the peak, but I really don't know where. My knowledge of the Karawanken is limited—that's the chain of mountains we're climbing now—and I have no memory of a village or an important town between Trzic and the frontier. It's all rather strange."

"Bullseye told you, didn't he? We're going to build a new camp," ended Paulo, who had been distracted for a few moments by the history lesson. But as the time passed, he felt the chances diminishing for the only thing that really interested him: the interception of the convoy by local members of the Resistance. The road wound more and more, the engines were laboring like locomotives on the steep slope and the air was getting a sharp edge. They were approaching the summit. Paulo realized the pitched battle was not for tonight. Discouraged, he whispered in the teacher's ear:

"Not much traffic on your historic road."

The teacher didn't reply. He too had hoped that the partisans would try something, and Paulo, stealing a glance at him, had the impression that if the ambush had taken place, the old man would have risen to the occasion. His dejected look suggested they would have to wait a long time for another opportunity. In a few hours, brand-new barbed wire would stand between them and freedom. That was the fate they could expect, these prisoners. After all, wearing clothes like this they could hardly expect to be sent on nature rambles.

The other prisoners, arm in arm on the floor of the truck, didn't seem to have shared the same dreams as Paulo and the teacher. Very few had made the connection between Napoleon, the Slavic patriots and the direction in which the submachine guns were pointing. "No point trying to understand," they would say. The only thing they had noticed was that the pistol-whipping had stopped. End of observations.

The mountain ride seemed endless, and the lack of

orders began to create a climate of panic. It was a terrible realization, but the poor devils, survivors of hell itself, were beginning to miss all the insults and blows, their daily bread. Left alone to think, they just couldn't cope. Where would they sleep tonight? Would they be given any soup? Or bread? What sort of work was waiting for them? Were they being escorted to the deserted mountain simply to be discreetly killed? Too many problems at once for their diminished faculties. They were anxious to get there, to be taken in hand.

Their wish was soon granted. The trucks at the head of the convoy had stopped and already the usual shouts, echoing around the mountain, let everybody know that the unloading of the trucks was taking place in the right tradition, under a hail of blows. There was no doubt—Kommando X had arrived at its destination. The mysterious camp appeared to consist of three or four wooden barracks, barely visible in the dark, and the running shadows were fellow prisoners from the first trucks being hustled toward the barracks by the SS gun butts. Searchlights had just been switched on, illuminating the whole scene. As on the evening of their arrival at Mauthausen, the lights were concentrated on a few yards inside and outside the gate. The beams were enormously powerful and direct; without diffusion or shadow. The concentration camp SS had an indisputable talent for dramatic lighting.

For the moment, the task of the SS was to empty the trucks in the minimum of time and to force the three hundred convicts even more quickly into the camp. They carried it out to perfection. A rifle butt for each man, on his head, on his hands, it didn't matter where. *Alle raus, schnell*, ten seconds per truck and the obligatory sprint across the illuminated strip. They were counted as they ran past a group of soldiers, probably the vanguard, who yelled in chorus: *eins, zwei, zehn, hundert*. The count would obviously be right, and they were wasting their time worrying, for under the avalanche of blows the deportees became more and more submissive. Paulo, like the others, ran his absurd little race. He ran into the prison on the double, his elbows tucked into his sides, and arrived among the last in front of the barracks. In the semidarkness he could make out an assembly taking place. Bullseye was already there, standing on the steps with half a dozen of his colleagues in their docker's caps. The stragglers knew the clubs were flying. They couldn't see them, but they could hear them whistling through the air, and they would have given a lot to know how to avoid a thrashing. But the answer was simple: move quickly, the quicker the better, get into the barracks, grab a straw mattress and come back out again, running the gauntlet by the same door. On the way in everybody got it, but on the way out the wily ones contrived to carry their straw mattresses on their heads to soften the blows from above. Paulo had managed all right, and it was really only the dawdlers who were coming off badly and beginning to find the welcome in this new camp a little excessive.

In spite of the bottleneck at the door, the mattress operation had been quick. Within five minutes the three hundred deportees were standing at attention, each with a mattress under his arm, more or less lined up on an uneven path illuminated by the searchlights. The formation didn't last long. Kapos and SS were in a hurry to tuck their charges up in bed, and with the usual clubbing they recounted their flock, and then divided it into three groups which they drove running and yelling toward the barracks.

Paulo and most of the men who had been in Bullseye's car found themselves completely breathless in front of a block bearing the number 3. But the one-eyed guard was not there to greet them. He had been assigned to Block 2. In his place a giant in a docker's cap was doing the honors. He seemed particularly expert at wielding the rubber hose, which landed with great precision on their heads, and equally good at distributing well-placed and vicious kicks.

"Another jailbird," mused Paulo to himself, landing with a thud in the block. When everyone was inside, the giant bawled in a rasping vulgar voice, "*Schnell, alle schlafen, Schweinerei.*"

He must have been at the same school as Bullseye. He spoke the same polished language, but his voice was even more commanding than his school friend's and it brought about a rush toward the *Schlafstube*. With his piece of hose filled with sand, the chief indicated the direction of the sleeping quarters to the first in line. Each one on entering got a taste of the rubber hose, more or less viciously, but it was a small price to pay to find, incredibly, that there were beds in the dormitory, real beds. The convicts thought they were dreaming. But they really were beds, and at first glance there had to be one each. Three months at Mauthausen had convinced them that the Nazis had abolished this bourgeois custom forever in the camps. And so their surprise was total, and morale took a distinct turn for the better.

With these bunk beds, which reminded them of a barracks, they would soon have re-created the cozy atmosphere of communal quarters had it not been for the enormous brute of a Kapo who carried on systematically thumping all those who were blocking the entrance in their astonishment. But the giant had specified *Ruhe*, and everyone slipped his mattress silently onto a bedstead. Paulo had chosen one of the beds at the back, near a window. He placed his mess tin carefully on the top bunk and began to undress. In the dark, using the pullover, the *Mütze* and the striped uniform, he quickly made himself a well-stuffed pillow. Thirty seconds later, after stretching his arms, he lay on his back with his long thin frame under the overcoat and began to ponder. His train of thought for the first time in a long while was optimistic. A bed! For three months he had wanted a bed even more than a fried chicken, in spite of his gnawing hunger. Sleeping in the sardine-can atmosphere of the quarantine had been his nightmare, more exhausting than standing at attention in the pouring rain for five hours on end, or sleeping naked in five degrees below zero. He had panicked at the promiscuity of tubercular prisoners who handed you their germs in the night so indiscriminately, mouth to mouth; at the dying who died in your arms without warning; and at the squirterers who let go in their sleep.

It was during those nights in their kennel, back in Block 17 at Mauthausen, that he had first been really afraid of dying. It was more than a fear; it would have been a certainty had the selection on the *Appelplatz* taken place a few weeks later. That night in his bed he finally admitted to himself his enormous fears, unworthy of a tough, and he congratulated himself on his intuition. Kommando X was a good spot, and it was tough luck for those poor slobs who had lacked initiative and hesitated to join up. Now he was certain it was a good assignment: the SS don't give beds to those they're going to grill. A real bed makes a deportee last longer, too long.

"This number's all right," Paulo concluded. And he fell asleep.

IV

A violent blow on the head wrenched him out of his dreams. The blow was the more vicious because the dreams had been very pleasant. The softness of the bed and the illusion of comfort had carried him far away. As he jumped to his feet, he tried to recall where his dreams had taken him. To Paris, obviously, and to freedom. He vaguely remembered girls around him, admiring friends and a table groaning with food. He was swanning about in a perfectly tailored tweed suit and his shirt, curiously, was striped. It reflected nothing more than his everyday life, but he didn't usually dream about it.

"*Aufstehen*, on your feet," yelled the Kapo, hitting him again. Nothing like a smack in the mouth to drive away rubbishy dreams. Paulo's head cleared as he ran with the others toward the exit. At the door of the *Schlafstube*, he collided with a bunch of men in shorts who were blocking the passage. Paulo's dream had lasted only an instant. It wasn't yet eleven o'clock, and they had been ordered to get up in the middle of the night for a general inspection for lice and crabs. The doyen of the camp Kapos—Superkapo—was anxious to assure himself personally that the vermin had remained at Mauthausen. He was seated on a stool in the main room of the block with two inspectors in caps on his right, who wore a green triangle, as he did. One of them also sported a black band on his left arm on which the word *Schreiber* was painted in crude letters. This "secretary" was writing, and under the circumstances one might have thought he was applying himself to statistics on crabs. As Paulo approached, however, he realized that he was merely asking each deportee for his name, age and profession. The official opening of the crab hunt would only take place when these formalities had been completed.

When the *Schreiber*, in excellent French without a trace of an accent, asked him his profession, Paulo hesitated. It was the first time in three months that any interest had been shown in anything but his registration number, and he was not prepared. It was essential to come up with a good answer. He knew that certain smart guys at Mauthausen had landed soft jobs by giving occupations such as hairdresser, cook, electrician or nurse. He also knew that other bullshitters had paid very heavily for their apprenticeship. Paulo was good for nothing except playing cards, screwing girls and conning straights. All the same, he was not going to announce that he was a crook, although that might have intrigued these fairies in caps who were interrogating him. He was going to say salesman, but that old trick only impressed the junior plain-clothesmen of the *Police Judiciaire*. With the Fritzes, he would have to come up with something else.

"Driver," he blurted out, for lack of time to come up with anything better. And he thought to himself: "You never know, there might be wood to fetch in the forest or food to collect from those sympathizers down in Trzic.." But he didn't really delude himself. The *Schreiber* wrote it down anyway in a separate column. Smiling and pleased with himself, Paulo returned to the mass of prisoners in their underclothes.

"Everybody strip, vests and shorts on the left arm, and one at a time in front of the vermin committee!"

It was the *Lagerschreiber* who had just translated these orders from the *Lageraltester*. The committee had set itself up a very powerful lamp. Bullseye was among them, along with two or three other thugs in the same mold, who must have been in charge of the other blocks. There was obviously going to be some sport for all these men to have stirred themselves in the middle of the night.

In the last row, Paulo conducted a frantic but surreptitious inspection of his clothes. He had just discovered a nice fat louse in the folds of a shirt-sleeve. He crushed it fiercely with his fingernail, and continued his inspection with his finger-tips while observing what was going on in the room.

It struck him, as it must have the Kapos and the *Schreiber*, that these eighty shaven fellows whom they were trying to humiliate yet again by making them parade around naked, did not in any way have the expected air of wretchedness, nor the look of conscripts anxiously seeking exemption. From all sorts of backgrounds, of every age and size, they had one common denominator: in spite of their horrible skinniness, their undernourished look and the ribs which showed through their distended skin, they were all well built. The ghastly regime at Mauthausen had not succeeded in wearing away all their muscles, which still clung almost transparently to their arms, thighs and shoulders. And, in spite of the new trial they were being made to undergo, the slaves were rather proud of showing all their persecutors here that the French were not always a bunch of weaklings.

One thing they had learned at Mauthausen was that the Germans, because of their queer tendencies, could be relied upon to go easy with the young and muscular at the expense of the old and weak, whom they flogged pitilessly. And so, as they went before the crab tribunal, the small Frenchmen drew themselves up, making the best of their matchstick appearance and smiling to look younger. One might have thought they were in a whorehouse, but that their clients were never satisfied. These degenerates were far more interested in playing the Marquis de Sade. The flagellation began with the third in line, a little old man, the average Frenchman. Neither villain nor peasant. One of the Kapo inspectors had just noticed a louse hidden in the folds of his shorts.

"*Knie nieder,* on your knees, you bucket of shit, you filthy animal. You ought to be hanged for having brought lice into my camp," screamed the doyen, and turning to the chief of Block 3 he said in a low voice: "*Fünf und zwanzig, Karl!*"

Fünf und zwanzig, twenty-five, that meant twenty-five strokes of the rubber hose on his naked buttocks. But not just ordinary lashes. The *fünf und zwanzig* were to be accompanied by a ceremony. Karl got up and calmly placed a stool in the middle of the room.

To give his full attention to this premiere, the doyen suspended the parasite inspection; Bullseye seized the old man by the ear and placed him none too gently on the stool. Not seated, but on all fours, his stomach against the seat, his hands and feet on the floor. The one-eyed Kapo clamped the lice-ridden head between his knees and held the old man's arms in a viselike grip. His buttocks properly exposed, they could now begin. In order to work unencumbered Karl stripped to the waist; but the striptease must have been part of the act, for the ugly bastard was tattooed from his belly button to his Adam's apple. There wasn't one inch of white skin on his torso, back or arms. A gaudy Spanish galley sailed in full rig across his entire chest. On his back, all over, were naked girls with enormous breasts and complicated suspender belts. It was a masterpiece of bad taste, evidence of a past crammed with seamy exploits. A real sailor.

The first stroke resounded in an anguished silence. The Frenchman hadn't flinched. On the fourth stroke he let out a whimper which was nearly lost in the lumberjack's grunt let out by Karl as he took his backswing. The block chiefs counted in chorus: "*Vier, fünf, sechs, sieben.*"

It was dragging on, the tattooed sailor was running out of breath. One of his Kapo friends came to give him a hand to maintain the rhythm. As one rubber hose left the skin of the tortured man the next one landed, more violent and hysterical than before. Enormous red-and-blue welts appeared on the back and buttocks of the victim. His skin split open and the blood flowed. Bullseye let go his grip and announced *fünf und zwanzig*, but the miserable creature did not get up. He had fainted.

He couldn't get away with that. The one-eyed Kapo brought him around with three vicious slaps, and with a brutal kick in the small of his bleeding back, he sent him sprawling into the midst of his horrified comrades.

The sadistic show had so shocked and hypnotized the men that the next in line had not taken advantage of the intermission to give their underclothes a final inspection. A dozen or so lice were captured and their owners, one after the other, went to the stool. The inspection went on accompanied by the thud of the rubber hose, the yells and the moans, but the lice became rarer and rarer, and there were no more crabs in their stubbly pubic hair. Boredom began to overtake the Kapos, who had come for the whipping party with the firm intention of having a good time. They had to come up with some other pretext to send people to the stool. Bullseye found it. His idea must have been a routine at Mauthausen because the inspectors didn't even have to confer. Their new game was called a cleanliness inspection. *Schreiber* the interpreter ordered each man to pull back the foreskin on his penis. Woe to him who had too much foreskin or whose penis wasn't clean.

"*Schweine*," all the pseudo dockers would scream together. And as the miserable fellow made his way toward the stool, he could think only of covering his wretched member with his hands, as it became the object of the unleashed clubs.

Paulo was no prude and in three months he had learned not to be surprised by anything. All the same, he just couldn't get over a show like this. How degrading for these men, grandfathers included, to be forced to present their tackle to this panel of excited poofs. This was something he wouldn't dare tell his Pigalle friends, if he ever got out of here; they wouldn't stand for it. And yet he had gone like the others, tackle in hand, and rolled back his foreskin in front of all these voyeurs. He promised himself he would slice them up with a razor. Later. For the moment at any rate, he had escaped the twenty-five strokes on the backside and that was the main thing.

The inspectors must have had other blocks to do because already they were packing up, and the tattooed sailor who had been at the party escorted the nudists back into the dormitory with the aid of his length of piping. When everybody was inside, he yelled:

"Schlafen, los, und morgen früh alle aufstehen vier Uhr. Ruhe."

Silence. This last order prevented those in neighboring beds from any exchange of thoughts. Besides, they had no real desire to talk: they were disgusted, disheartened and more and more sickened at the treatment to which they were being subjected. "No point trying to understand" was now the evening prayer for those who had lost faith, and there ware a lot of them that first night in the mystery camp.

Paulo was trying to work things out before he went to sleep, and he kept coming back to the same conclusion: they had not been installed in this mountain backwater just for prick parades. They were there to sweat, and he was anxious to know exactly what sort of work was waiting for them. With their convict's uniform, it couldn't be anything but breaking stones. On the road probably. "Good chance to make a break for it," he thought. And with this hopeful prospect in mind, he fell asleep.

Again he was jarred from his dreams by the rubber club, and as before, the dreams had been euphoric. But this time Paulo didn't even try to reconstruct them. He had no more time to lose. In his head, cleared by the blow, there was room for only one thought: the road. And he started to gallop down between the bays, knocking over some slugabeds who had failed to grasp the urgency of Sailor's alarm clock. They were standing wondering whether they ought to go to roll call in shorts or in full uniform. Shorts was the right answer, and Sailor administered a triple ration of the club to the hesitant ones before explaining that he didn't like prisoners who stank, and that each morning he would personally oversee the ablutions of the men in his block. Opening the door, he finished with:

"Alle Waschraum, schnell!"

The *Waschraum* was one of the joys of the SS. Even in this miniature camp huddled in the mountains, where the disposition of the blocks must have been calculated down to the inch, they had considered it essential to build a real washroom.

Obviously it bore no resemblance to the luxurious Turkish-style baths of Mauthausen, where the main fountains were in mosaic and the shitting pans were equipped with a vertical stream of water which efficiently replaced shit paper (strictly forbidden). But the *Waschraum* here did at least exist.

Sailor had known only one procedure, Mauthausen's. And so, as soon as they reached the washroom, he charged the first four men to enter with the scrubbing of those who followed. In the house style: great sluicings of icy mountain water on bare backs, and his club encouraging the sleepy ones to get right under the nozzle. Clearly even in this minor camp, they were not keen to abandon good traditions. Four o'clock in the morning: an icy shower, then a beating to warm up the prisoners—it looked like things were off to a good start. And as at Mauthausen, the prisoners had to dry themselves with their only shirt before going back in rows of five to Block 3 for coffee, a clear bowl of piss. It wasn't even black like the disgusting surrogate made from grilled chick-peas. Fortunately, this quart of dishwater was hot, and the warmth it produced in their empty stomachs made the prisoners forget that their breakfast was served without bread.

"Roll on the midday soup," thought Paulo, blowing on his last mouthful of coffee.

In the open air at four o'clock in the morning he was already famished. And noon was eight hours away. It was going to be hard to wait until then.

Much harder than he thought. Sailor, who had downed in front of the famished men an *ersatz* chocolate bar and three hunks of bread and margarine, had just called for silence to announce the day's schedule. He began his spiel in German and then, seeing the majority of his audience understood better the language of the rubber club than Goethe's native tongue, he fetched his length of piping, yelling:

"Dolmetscher! Wer spricht Deutsch darin?"

Pozzi had already stepped forward. But not altogether sure of his German, he hesitated. Berck, the little pimp from Alsace, beat him to the job:

"Ich spreche Deutsch, Chef!"

"*Gut!* Translate precisely for these animals what I'm going to tell you. I won't say it twice."

Berck turned toward his comrades and began to translate with some difficulty the chief's orders. This traitor spoke German, but not French. "You will go immediately to the dormitory to get dressed except for the overcoat, which will be folded at the head of the mattress. Three minutes for that and assembly immediately following in front of the block, in rows of *fünf*, for muster. After muster, work till noon. Half hour for lunch and back to work again. Six o'clock at the camp, another coffee with bread."

There was nothing dramatic about the schedule, and it would have been welcomed with relief if it weren't for Sailor's rubber club, which continued to swing worryingly at the end of his long sinewy arm. The chief had not finished talking. Berck continued his translation:

"The chief says if you think you can go to bed after dinner you're in for a real surprise. That's when he's going to devote all his attention to us. After the work outside, it will be time to work inside until the evening bell at eight o'clock. This time we will be working for Karl. The chief wants his block to be the smartest. He's counting on us, but since we are all slackers, like all Frenchmen, he says he's counting even more on his hose. Dismiss. In three minutes everybody outside, dressed!"

There was a general rush for the dormitory, avoiding the need for the hose. They had gotten the message. Every movement on the double, that seemed to be indispensable in this small camp. Folding his striped coat, Paulo made some calculations: "From five o'clock in the morning until eight at night minus an hour for lunch, makes exactly fourteen hours of hustling a day." For a dilettante like him who had never worked, it didn't mean very much. But it was a dramatic change for the unionized workers accustomed to a forty-hour week. "And what are they going to give us to eat for that kind of work?" Paulo asked himself, pursuing his mental calculations. "If we don't get any more than we got at Mauthausen, we'll all be gone in a week. I have the feeling that fucker Bullseye wasn't kidding: *alle kaputt Franzosen*... like the Spanish pioneers of Mauthausen."

This pessimistic view of the future hadn't stopped him from getting on with things. He dressed on the run, arriving among the first for the roll call in front of the block.

The day had clearly dawned, and Paulo took advantage of being ahead of time to inspect this mountain camp which Kapos and SS had surrounded with so much mystery since leaving Mauthausen.

What immediately struck him was the intelligence of whoever had discovered this spot, ideal for torturing and exterminating *in camera*. No prison in the world could afford walls like this. North, south, east and west, the mountain was everywhere. And what a mountain it was! No gentle slopes for grazing, but sheer rock face, enough to discourage the hardiest mountaineers, and clinging to the crags were pine trees which were even more inaccessible. There was only one exit from this deadfall: the bootlace of a road which the previous night Paulo had taken to be a dead end. In fact, the road ran parallel to the camp, a hundred yards or so from the barbed wire, and continued to wind laboriously toward the summit. Most of the road was visible from the quadrangle of the *Appelplatz* where Paulo was standing. It was fairly certain that the SS guards, perched high in the watchtowers, could see every foot of it. One would have to be infinitely clever to go unnoticed on that white, almost phosphorescent road set against the purple rocks and the bottle-green pines.

"There's going to have to be another way of vanishing, besides the road," murmured Paulo disappointedly. And he tried to take an interest in the area fenced in by the barbed wire. The camp was really tiny, a hundred yards by a hundred yards at the most, mainly covered by five or six wooden barracks, which must have been built the day before their arrival on a bumpy and uneven clearing, dotted every five yards by holes and tree stumps. The whole area was on a slight incline, enclosed by a double row of immense poles strung with particularly murderous barbed wire. There was a watchtower every fifty yards equipped with a machine gun and a floodlight. It was enough to put down the best-planned revolt. But even these precautions were insufficient for the good men of the SS. They had thought it more prudent to set up their own camp a few yards from the lower blocks, just on the other side of the barbed wire. They could even see the slaves from their beds. To fear a mutiny to such an extent, they must have known, the bloodthirsty brutes, that life was going to be impossible for Kommando X. At any rate, they had used the available land efficiently: there wasn't a square yard to stand on, apart from the road and the area which had been cleared for the barracks housing the guards and prisoners. This glimpse of what his world was going to be from now on didn't suit Paulo at all. On the road up, he had stupidly decided that it would be child's play to break out of this annex camp. All of a sudden, he realized that it was almost as complicated as escaping from Mauthausen. In other words, impossible.

Demoralized and depressed, he was anxious for muster to begin. The first muster might bring something new. Something, anything, to prevent him thinking. Thinking was becoming unbearable.

Paulo should have known better. First of all, the muster brought blows. The doyen and the block chiefs had to demonstrate their goodwill to the SS, who hardly knew them. For a good hour, they let fly with their fists, feet and rubber hoses to get the troops to stand at attention, lined up within half an inch of perfection. Not one of the three hundred prisoners escaped a beating. And finally, when the pig-faced officers of the general staff made their entry, the formation of prisoners was so perfectly foursquare that even the Kommandant himself could not suppress a grunt of satisfaction.

"Good work," he mouthed to the doyen, who puffed up with pride. "Your men look robust and I think the company will be satisfied. The selection made at Mauthausen was good."

Turning to a young NCO who was hanging at his heels like a poodle, he said:

"*Rapportführer*, prepare a letter of thanks for me to Kommandant Ziereis."

The head of the mystery camp appeared to know his job. Like a slave trader, he couldn't have given a shit that the men he had received were not trained. His experience had taught him that the Mauthausen rationale could extract from the clumsiest of intellectuals a level of production superior to the output of a Russian miner. He didn't even want to know the percentages of students, pimps, office clerks and good-for-nothings which made up the livestock he had been delivered. The club would determine their areas of specialization.

The sight of his shaven-headed men, stiff as ramrods, seemed to fascinate him. He walked around them three times, and having satisfied himself that the uniform physique of his Kommando was not disgraced by a single swelling, malformation or potbelly, he climbed nimbly, in spite of his fat stomach, onto a sort of dais. The deportees anxiously awaited his speech.

"*Heil Hitler, Arbeit,*" barked the Kommandant, making the fascist salute.

"*Heil Hitler,*" answered his subordinates.

That was it. The Kapos, visibly reassured by the positive reaction of their seigneur, wanted to lay it on thick. They had to show the indulgent Kommandant that no one could wait to start work. The clubs made the striped statues take an immaculate left wheel. *Im gleich Schritt Marsch, links, zwo, drei, vier, links*... Toward the exit.

The barbed-wire gates opened wide, but on the road they were also ready and waiting. Seventy SS, almost a company, were standing with rifles at rest. This really was an expensive turn-out, considering the less than distinguished levels of productivity they could expect. The day's work was going to cost the Hitler administration dear.

In ranks of five and flanked every six feet by an armed SS guard, the pressed men began to march up the narrow road which snaked away to the summit, to the unknown. The pace was regulated at the head of the column by a medal-wearing sergeant major, the *Kommandoführer* and some NCOs. Ten yards behind the last prisoners was another group of young Nazis, submachine guns at the ready. Bringing up the rear was a last NCO, blond as a field of corn, with six enormous Alsatians on a leash. They were German too.

With such an escort, it wasn't easy to pretend they were off to gather edelweiss. Any move out of line was corrected by a firm butt in the ribs. "Forward march" was the order. This time, however, they were allowed to look at their surroundings, which were even more hostile and inhospitable than they could have imagined down below. The mountains seemed higher and more impossible, the pine trees more towering and grim, the farther they climbed. They felt that even the road was an enemy. For a start, its number—333—indicated by little markers every hundred yards along the edge of the ravine, was improbable. Doubtless it had been invented by the Machiavellian SS to reinforce the unreality of their situation in this godforsaken place, where there couldn't possibly be 333 numbered roads. Not a single house to be seen, not even a log cabin. And yet the air had to be utterly pure at this altitude and it was odd that it had not occurred to any local inhabitants to live here. Unless, of course, the SS had cleared the region before erecting their clandestine encampment.

It was a steep climb, and the convicts began to wonder whether the SS up front intended to take them right over the ridge they could see looming high in the distance. With the meager rations in their bellies, this was no sport. The ranks' breathing was becoming more staccato and they were no longer marching in step. Happily they were almost there. The work site must certainly be that little clearing on the mountainside, just around the next bend, where a group of men in gray-green uniform seemed to be expecting the column's arrival. Another two hundred yards and the prisoners would at last know the reason for bringing them such a distance.

But not before a small episode would remind them that, mountain or no mountain, they were still at Mauthausen.

On the right-hand side of the road, against the rock face, a little chapel with a Gothic bell tower had just come into sight. The believers in the procession saw in this a symbol: God was about to watch his martyrs pass by. This chapel represented another stage on their Calvary, one of the Stations of the Cross. They crossed themselves. It was just what the SS were waiting for. They had spotted the signs of the cross and their gun butts went straight for the faithful.

"*Scheisse Katholiken,*" they yelled, and to show that the thunderbolts of the Day of Judgment did not frighten them, they began to spit one after the other on the Slavic chapel.

Even Paulo the unbeliever couldn't hide his revulsion at this sacrilege.

"They've even more insane than those priest-floggers at Mauthausen," he blurted out in a low voice.

It was not reassuring. Even out walking in the country, the little bastards didn't forget their Nazi catechism. And religious persecutions were only a short chapter. It boded ill for the future.

When the thirty SS on the right of the column had done with hawking over the Good Lord, the column was allowed to halt. It was not yet six o'clock, but on the first day of work there was not to be one second's delay. The men were rapidly divided into groups of twenty, each under the command of a green-triangled Kapo. A blast on the whistle, confused shouts in which the words *Arbeit* and *Schnell* were unmistakable, then a flurry of sparrows toward the clearing, each group running after its Kapo. By the time Paulo and his comrades reached theirs, they were on all fours. The last men to arrive had hardly picked themselves up as the Kapo began to yell his orders.

"You see those two tree trunks up there? Carry them down to the edge of the road. And quickly. And when you've done that, go back up and get two more. Go!"

The trees were enormous; even well-fed professional lumberjacks would have balked at such a burden. Alas, complaints could not be registered here. Paulo, who was certainly one of the sturdiest in spite of being so thin, thought he would burst when he felt the weight of the pine on his shoulder; but he quickly realized that because of his height, he was carrying virtually the entire tree on his own. Some of his lazy workmates were cunningly bending their knees, and one short fellow even looked as though he was actually hanging from the trunk. Paulo was incensed and he yelled at his companions:

"Find another sucker, you bunch of fairies!" and he let himself slip as if he had stumbled, taking care to sprawl well to one side. By doing this he avoided the tree trunk, which, no longer supported, rolled down the slope, almost mowing down the shirkers. General chaos ensued, and all those still sprawled on the ground collected a beating from the panic-stricken Kapo. Except Paulo, who had quickly regained his footing and was savoring his sweet revenge. He had won. The dull-witted Kapo had now realized that it might be a better idea if the ten men carrying each tree trunk were arranged in order of height. For the remaining trees Paulo only carried his share. But he carried it often, all mornning, for six hours. The pace was diabolical. On the way down, the Kapos refrained from beating the prisoners because the SS, who formed a tight cordon a few yards above, yelled in chorus each time a tree trunk broke loose from its carriers. It was essential to maintain productivity, and an untimely blow could upset the whole team and its load.

On the way back however, with prisoners scrambling up on all fours, blows were authorized. For the sake of variety, the rubber clubs had been swapped for supple young branches which landed with a whistle on their backs. Backs which were bare, since they had been ordered to take off their jackets with the first rays of the sun. This was not intended as a punishment, but it was June, and working at this relentless pace made even the most skeletal prisoners sweat. On each body the sweat soon began to mingle with the blood which trickled from wounds inflicted by the branches. At noon when the Kapos assembled them for muster, the prisoners looked like a shipment of wounded men. There was no one in this wilderness to be moved by the scene; no one to stare at the even more surprising scene which followed. Each convict had taken his place in the ranks carrying an enormous stone on his back. When the column moved off at the whistle blast, the impression was of a wall which had just been set in motion; a wall three yards wide and a hundred yards long, moving at a good pace down the road toward the camp. Rocks, not pebbles, the Kapos had ordered, and there were some who were so nervous that they had picked up the heaviest they could find, to the point of actually having themselves loaded up by two comrades. Paulo, as always, chose the middle course. His stone looked impressive, but it wasn't heavy, just rather flat. He had had the time to see that two or three smart fellows had just caught some useless blows for having chosen stones that were too light. For these men the Kapos had been obliging enough to fetch other stones themselves, enormous ones, almost boulders. And so by the time the column came within sight of the camp, a good number of these worn-out wretches were on their knees. They were weeping, but they held on to their rocks. Even a convicted murderer at Cayenne would never have been treated like this. It was only possible to compare their rapid descent of the mountain road, loaded so heavily after a morning of forced labor, with the toils of the Pyramid slaves.

Had a witness known that the slaves buckled under a mountain of stones were Frenchmen, deportees far from their own country, his only conclusion would have been that these martyrs must be seething with patriotic revolt against a barbarian enemy. He would have been mistaken. The martyrs were indeed of one mind, but it was neither hatred nor revenge which united them. It was something much less noble, much more down-to-earth: the craving for food. An intolerable craving which had lasted for three months. But after six hours of superhuman effort at more than 3600 feet, the deportees of Kommando X had been transformed into real animals. They had only one thing in mind: soup. What would it be like? Dishwater? Or would it be thick with potatoes and perhaps meat? For the moment, soup was the only preoccupation of the three hundred stone-bearers. Moments of self-pity could wait, so could resistance to the Germans or thoughts of loved ones back in France who couldn't even conceive of their situation. When the gates closed behind the formation and the rocks had been stacked in an impressive pile at the entrance to the *Appelplatz*, three hundred pairs of eyes focused eagerly on the door to the kitchens. But the Krauts had to maintain discipline even for a quart of soup. An interpreter announced:

"Assembly by fives in front of the blocks."

At attention, obviously. And with their thumbs on the seam of their striped trousers, the three hundred starving men had to wait more than a quarter of an hour for the arrival of the soup cauldrons. The soup looked strange; it was red, almost purple.

"It's beet," volunteered a farmer in the last row, and no one dared question his competence.

The beetroot soup was a change from the hot fluid they had had at Mauthausen and, moreover, it looked thick. So there was no need to debate whether it was best to be served from the top of the vat, in order to get some of the floating rutabagas, or from the bottom, hoping for the potatoes which had sunk. Sailor had a way of filling the mess bowls without spilling a drop. He even went too quickly, and in the rush his ladle filled the bowls unevenly. A few unlucky fellows found themselves with half as much beet juice as their friends. Of course no one dared to claim his fair share, but a few of the greedier ones were so disappointed that they couldn't help lingering in front of the vat, hoping the chief would notice his measuring error. No such luck. His ominous glare made them retreat smartly, and there was nothing they could do to avoid a beating but back off with their pint of soup, with a bitter "*Danke schön, Chef.*"

The tactics of these dissatisfied prisoners had begun to annoy the tattooed bully. When the little old man who had caught the *fünf und zwanzig* at the opening of the crab hunt and who must have suffered from the extra beating more than the others, waited timidly for his bowl to be filled up, Sailor lost his temper completely.

"You want another spoonful, you greedy bastard? Here you are!"

And without warning, he hit the old man in the face with the iron ladle. Blood spurted from his open mouth even before a second and third blow landed on his shaven head with tremendous force, each one making a deep cut. Rather pleased with the terror he had just caused among the men of his block, Sailor didn't even bother to wipe the bloodied ladle before plunging it back into the steaming cauldron, where the blood mixed with the reddish beet juice.

Karl must have deliberately calculated the filling of the bowls according to the face of each customer. When the eighty detainees of Block 3 had all been served, there were still a dozen or so helpings in the bottom of the last vat; and the convicts who had just polished off their bloody soup without spoons, as they stood in line, enviously eyed the unlooked-for extra. Perhaps the chief was going to call out numbers, lottery style.

It didn't work out like that. The chief already had his favorites, and the first one called was Pozzi, the collaborator-caretaker. Bullseye must have put his colleague in the picture. Much less sheepish than in the freight car, Pozzi ran for the extra soup, with a litany of "*Viel danke, Chef, viel danke.*"

And off he went to gorge himself on the contents of his bowl, filled right to the top this time, under the jealous, even murderous eyes of the whole block.

The next ladle was for pimp-interpreter Berck of Alsace. Then Sailor called:

"Friseur, komm her, Mensch!"

A small dark fellow stepped out of the ranks. Paulo had not noticed him before, but when he saw his spiteful weasel-face he realized this loafer must have had his barber's lessons inside. He was no more a barber in civilian life than Paulo was a driver, but he had nonetheless risked giving that as his occupation, and after all, given the hairstyle in vogue at the camp, his chances of getting kicked out of his profession were slim. The barber went to guzzle the soup in front of them all, but there were still a few quarts left in the bottom of the vat. Everyone was wondering how the rest of it would be divided. Sailor deliberately kept them guessing. He looked over the ranks with his expressionless gaze.

"Du, komm her," he said looking at Angel Belloni, who dived forward with his mess bowl.

"Du, du, du," Sailor continued, pointing his leathery chin at the men in the first row, the smallest.

His voice was not completely random. Paulo noticed that the lucky ones chosen were all very young. To the uninitiated, Sailor's choice might have been dictated by his warm heart, by a desire for justice, systematically distributing the extra soup to those under eighteen, growing lads more undermined by hunger than their elders. Paulo, however, with his nose for vice, had immediately understood that the Kapo's motive was not one of compassion. The real reason was that the tattooed man, like all his fellow common criminals, was queer to the core. And in his own way he was busy making advances to the potential fags in his block.

Angel Belloni must also have understood the chief's intentions, but this time he didn't give a damn about losing face in front of the older crooks. He was too hungry.

Sailor continued calling them forward, and as the young and fuckable filed past the vat, bending their knees so that their bowls would be better filled, the procurer in the docker's cap lost his rough edge. He no longer seemed anything other than what he really was: a vulgar piss-house queer. His pointed tongue licked his thin, almost nonexistent lips. The dumbshow of his eyes, made up for life by a prison tattooist, gave him a strange likeness to the anytime Annies enticing clients from behind their windows in the reserved quarter of Hamburg, his hometown.

Suddenly, his whorish expressions ceased. In seconds he had reassumed his usual mask of terror, and the ladle on the end of his long arm swung through the air to land squarely on the head of one of the extra-helping candidates, a naïve soul convinced that one of the *dus* had been intended for him, who had come forward with his bowl, all smiles. The poor fellow hadn't looked at himself recently. He was certainly small, but he was not at all the fag type. He was at least twenty years too old. But even if he had wanted to, he would have had no chance. The Mauthausen Kapos, spoiled by the Russian and Polish children saved from the crematorium at the age of fourteen, only went for young flesh.

Paulo finished licking the last drop of beet soup from his bowl and wondered how these youngsters would respond to the advances of the queermaster. The little foreign faggots he had seen develop at Mauthausen seemed to find it to their liking, but they had been taken much younger. With the skirt-chasing Frenchmen, it was touch and go. These kids faced an agonizing problem: to have their cherries broken, or to be beaten to death. Paulo preferred not to think about it. In any case his underworld appearance put him out of danger. He looked too much a man to give the block chief the horn. Unless that heap of shit decided to play the girl as well . . .

"That really would be the limit," thought Paulo, promising himself to disguise his good looks. The whistle snapped him out of his immodest thoughts. Lunch hour was over and it was already time to get back to slogging.

"With a feast like that, the climb won't be too difficult," joked Paulo, marking time in front of the gates. But he thought privately that the beet would not weigh heavy on their stomachs if the little game with the trees was to continue at the nightmarish pace of that morning.

There were not enough trees left to keep them occupied until six-o'clock muster, but the *Kommandoführer* had anticipated that. There were other things to carry: enormous blocks of stone which littered the clearing had to be piled on pallets, *Trage* in German, and dumped a little farther along a line marked off by two stakes. They would probably be used to build a wall, but the site foreman didn't bother to explain this to the workers. The club served once again as interpreter, and the column set off to the sneers of the SS.

"*Alle kaputt,*" the pimps screamed. "*Franzosen alle Syphlitiken alle krematorium. Nicht zurück Frankreich, immer Arbeit, fertig Fräulein.*"

And, just to drive the point home, they pretended to be jerking off. Such insults, the same for three months, no longer bothered anyone. On the other hand, the convicts, loaded down like mules, were less tolerant of the way in which these pimps punctuated their sentences with small rocks, and gun butts for those within range. And a short while later, the pallet bearers were rivaling each other's cunning by loading their stones as far as possible from the cordon of sentries. The NCO with the dogs was the only one, apart from the Kommandoführer, allowed to stroll on the work site; it didn't take him long to discover the trick. He unleashed his animals. Stupidly, because in their pain the men dropped their *Trage* and the stones rolled down the slope. Productivity was slowed considerably while the men went to pick up the stones, bring them back up the slope, load them and set off again. It was idiotic, but the whole exercise, carried out with blows from clubs, proved that for the SS the men's training was as important as their productivity.

There must have been something good about this combined method of beating and hustling, because when the evening assembly was sounded, the clearing was as clean as a whistle and the beginnings of a wall jutted out near the road. Paulo was not particularly gifted in civil engineering, but he realized immediately that the SS intended to clear a flat area at this point on the mountain. To do what? Mysteriously, the workers had not been informed. At any rate, it wasn't to build another camp. It would have been illogical with the other one so close. Nor a road, because one already existed.

"We'll see," Paulo said to himself, "but I'm not going to be around for when they get their level ground."

If only he had known, this apprentice laborer, how wrong he was.

In record time the level ground would be ready, and then there would be another level, and yet another, and many more. Paulo was right about one thing only: Kommando X would not be around. But in the meantime the indefatigable builders marched down in rows of five to their little camp, carrying their large slabs of rock on their backs. The stone crocodile wound its way down the narrow road, covering its full width. But there were no stray tourists to be surprised by this strange phenomenon, no more so than in the morning.

After a day like that, the stones seemed even heavier than before, and this time dozens of convicts collapsed before reaching the camp.

As they fell with their loads one after another, they were groaning, "I can't go on, I just can't make it."

But they did go on, and they did reach the camp, even with their stones on their backs. A little late perhaps, just late enough for the tail-enders to get another beating, as the ranks closed up to fill their empty places. But the beating overcame their weakness, and five minutes later, despite their cuts, they charged just as fast as their workmates to the blocks for the distribution of coffee and dinner, a tiny slice of bread less than half an inch thick. This stale black crust spread with a speck of greenish margarine could not possibly give the convicts the strength to start all over again tomorrow. There were two alternatives: either the SS really wanted the work done, in which case they were wrong to feed the work force so badly, or—what was more worrying—they just wanted to kill everyone off, and the work was only a pretense, a waste of time.

Paulo was beginning to get the hang of the SS mentality. He was convinced there was no point hoping that the food would improve in the days to come or that the pace would ease up on the site. Quite the opposite. It wasn't funny. Paulo could see only one solution, and it became more and more imperative: to get out. At any price.

"But how am I going to survive till I get the chance to make a break?" he asked himself, in despair at having swallowed his crust of bread almost without noticing.

It was six-thirty, and the next meal was eighteen hours away.

A blast of the whistle put an end to his efforts to forget his hunger. It was the signal for the end of dinner, and as Sailor had said, it was time to work for him or, more accurately, for the block. In two hours it would be dark, just enough time for the chores devised by the block chiefs: clearing the unsightly tree stumps and filling in all the holes around the barracks. As on the work site, the Krauts persisted in their mania for flattening the mountain. Soon the little camp looked like an anthill. Picks, shovels, wheelbarrows and sleds were prodded into action by the first blows of the club. And this time the chiefs gave it all they had. Each of their reputations was at stake, since a block with poorly maintained surroundings meant a bad mark, and a few of those could cost the Kapo his stripe. No question of Karl risking a reprimand from his SS bosses: he had too good a job. The poor beggar had become a happy man the day he had been solemnly presented with his stripe, docker's cap and regulation length of hose. In civilian life he had had to do without food; here he could stuff himself until it made him sick—meat, bread and potatoes galore. Having had to rely on dog ends in times of poverty between two jail sentences, here he suddenly had as many cigarettes as he wanted, even cigars. Here he could pickle himself on cheap schnaps or the cognac filched from the belongings of the new arrivals at Mauthausen. At last, this overtattooed queer, whose past was one long story of failed café pickups, suddenly found himself in charge of a harem of young boys who couldn't say they were meeting somebody.

It was the life of a pasha, and Karl knew it. He wouldn't have accepted freedom for anything in the world. His tattooed belly shook with laughter when he compared his lot to all those poor suckers, mobilized in the defense of the Fatherland, who would end up as cannon fodder. He didn't even have to worry about air raids, because of course concentration camps were always far away from towns. Being a Kapo was like heaven on earth, and Karl certainly intended to make it last till the end of his days. Even if he was to go up in smoke when he became too old to benefit from this perfect life. He was now an elder, a founding member of this new camp which promised to be particularly agreeable. The SS seemed lost in this mountain outpost, and they would obviously need him for little jobs. No need for cash in the camps. A few gold fillings knocked out with a good right hook would provide the necessary small change—cigarettes by the carton. And cigarettes bought everything: steak, dripping, chips, schnaps and love.

Sailor rejoiced at the thought of the good times ahead, and he congratulated himself on volunteering for Kommando

X. He had already marked out a few potential customers whose false teeth were mounted on a gold base, and his rapid estimate of their value delighted him in advance.

The men in Karl's block, however, did not share his bliss. They were beginning to wonder whether they hadn't done something really stupid by showing off the last of their muscles on the Mauthausen *Appelplatz*. More than ever before they were dead with hunger and exhaustion, and in this camp where they got no more to eat than at Mauthausen, the beatings never stopped. By this time at Mauthausen, they would already have hit the sack. Like sardines of course, but at least in quarantine no physical effort was required, and by conserving their strength they might have hung on. In this new prison, the hell just went on and on. It was no use running around with wheelbarrows or carrying slabs of stone, because they got the shit beaten out of them anyway, simply because Karl and his pals wanted the camp to be spotless.

The fun lasted until eight-thirty. Whistle, assembly, *alle schlafen*, the day was over. They had been up for almost twenty-four hours on the trot, running, carrying, getting beaten. Theoretically, the convicts should have fallen into the deepest sleep as soon as the lights went out; but they found it difficult. They would have gladly shared their anguish with each other, but the fear of disobeying the strict order for silence was too strong. They had to be content with brooding or praying. Paulo and his kind were ruminating, but there was no real difference. On every mattress the collapse was the same—iron in the soul, more painful than any physical pain.

V

It took ten days for the men of Kommando X to find out what they were doing in this godforsaken place: the SS were counting on them to dig a tunnel. A tunnel a mile long, right through the Karawanken Mountains which formed the natural, and troublesome, border between occupied Yugoslavia and German-annexed Austria. German manpower must have been tied up elsewhere for such an important strategic mission to be entrusted to a team of unskilled barebones. If this tunnel ever saw the light of day, the Panzer divisions would have ready-made all-weather invasion access to Trieste and the Adriatic. The Nazis' confidence in the men of Kommando X was beyond belief, but there was no longer any doubt. They were there to dig a tunnel, a real tunnel. Everything pointed to it: the large area they had cleared on the mountainside at the edge of the road, the barracks full of mining bars and pneumatic drills, the cases of dynamite and the small compressor which a truck had just delivered. Shovels, picks and sledgehammers were all ready for the order to attack the mountain.

The prisoners were ready too, but they didn't share the Germans' impatience. The ten days they had just lived through had put them off working at high altitudes for good. All of them, without exception, now missed Mauthausen and its quarantine, where there was no work, where, above all, one could escape notice. In this cursed place—Loibl Pass was its name—it was impossible to remain anonymous. Even the most insignificant faces had been picked out of the crowd, in spite of their identical uniform and their billiard-ball heads. With one SS to every four men, plus the Kapos, it was impossible to escape an individual beating for more than two hours. Since the starvation and the beatings would soon kill everyone anyway, they might just as well have died at Mauthausen without noticing it. This depressing line of reasoning had overtaken the whole Kommando and Paulo was no exception. His nightmare of ending up grilled had returned when he saw that the men who were too weak to keep up with the pace had been put in a temporary *Revier.*

Now he was sure of it. The executioners were waiting for the infirmary to be full before sending the weaklings back to their fate. But as there had to be a certain number to justify the expense of a shipment to Mauthausen's hungry chimneys, there were few volunteers for the last beds. As for the "patients," they gained a few extra days, which they spent fast asleep. He who sleeps forgets his hunger, they reasoned, trying to ignore the foolish risk they had taken, but unable to hide their anxiety at seeing their numbers swell every evening. The others managed desperately to hang on. Their unbelievable resistance was a testimony to the care taken in selecting them on the day of the slave market. The Germans had not been wrong to dismiss out of hand nine tenths of the material from Compiègne. The ones who remained were worth it. The tunnel was off to a good start.

Why, then, beat the hell out of them and continue to let them go so hungry?

Reasoning it all out in cold blood, Paulo could see only one explanation: the Fritzes were anxious to build their tunnel, and their only concern was to get the work completed at top speed. The sickly might slow down the pace. This must not happen. The process was simple: tunnel, *Revier*, Mauthausen, crematorium. In the other direction, Mauthausen, tunnel, *Revier*... It was a vicious circle. Take another lot and start all over again. After all, there was no difference between the shaven heads as far as the SS were concerned. Their registration numbers were insignificant. Europe was full of workers.

Yet even if one wanted to die by reporting sick, there were difficulties. There was only one way into the *Revier*—on a stretcher. The unfortunates who turned up after roll call with their heads split open were entitled to a few stitches before returning to work bandaged up with strips of paper. But the soft ones who came with split lips, smashed noses or shins torn by the fangs of the camp hounds were kicked out by an NCO with a whip. His jacket bore the red cross, which indicated that nursing was his specialty.

It is impossible to give an adequate description of the events which took place during those ten days at Loibl Pass. Only a camera hidden in a hole in the rock could have recorded the hysterical atmosphere of speeded-up action like an old silent movie. But a film director seeking authenticity would never have gone so far. It would have looked false. This was supposed to be a prison, but it was more like a pastiche of prison life. The pace was so hectic, the beatings so numerous, the guards so strident. From dawn to dusk, on the work site and then at the camp, the camera would have seen nothing but a mad merry-go-round of frightened zebras pursued by yelling monsters with rubber clubs. Fourteen hours on the trot, running with blocks of stone, tree trunks, wheelbarrows. Fourteen hours swinging a pick and wielding a shovel at the speed of a cartoon. Fourteen hours protecting one's head from the Kapos' whipping and hiding one's calves from the dogs, who were madder still. And the cartoon image of a prison was reinforced by their horribly emaciated bare torsos, already tanned by ten days of a mid-June sun, particularly strong at 3900 feet. It was Cayenne ten times over.

That, at least, was the opinion of an inmate from Block 5, Jo from Oran, a connoisseur who had just completed ten years on the banks of the Maroni and, using mobilization as an excuse, had managed to return to France in '39 to fight against the Germans. He had had all the punishment he could take, but in this new kind of war he couldn't fight back at all. He could only moan, recalling the good old days when he was moldering away on hard labor.

"Give me life in Cayenne rather than a year here," he kept on repeating like an old dodderer. His homesickness moved no one, but they all believed him.

The phase of sleepless nights and secret anguish was over. It was now rare for the detainees to hear the doyen strike his cast-iron pipe with a hammer at eight-thirty to announce lights out. Most of them, dead tired, were already asleep. The others, whose painful wounds prevented them from stretching out comfortably, hid under their covers trying to make these moments of calm and silence last as long as possible, the only moments of the day when they were no longer pursued by savages.

Exhausted, they couldn't fight sleep for long, but their last thoughts before dozing off were far, very far from Loibl Pass. They all thought of France, *la belle France*, civilized, happy, carefree. They thought of love and tenderness. Under his coat, each man built himself a world of friendship and kindness. Even the villains, who suddenly registered the absurdity and cowardice of playing the hard guy in their peaceful country. Under their coats, the gangsters could finally hide their shame at having had to drop their heavy disguises. For three and a half months, and especially for the last ten days, they had shown no signs of being any more "men" than the others. Like those they called straights, like the bourgeois who surrounded them, they had taken the beatings without protest, presenting their naked backsides to the rubber clubs of the queer block chiefs, running to work like zealots.

Without question, it was the Resistance fighters and the communists who came out best at this time of lonely contrition. They knew why they were there, and there martyrdom even inspired a certain pride in themselves. Huddled on their mattresses, they didn't weep. They only regretted that their atonement should last so long, because their courage, too, was beginning to falter. Every day they prayed a little less for the death of the martyred patriot. The well-planned regime of the *Konzentrationslager* was having its effect, even on the real heroes. The harder his life, the more the deportee clung to it.

For thoughts of shame or pride or just for sniveling, bed was the only place. And so, in the evening before lights out, the prisoners avoided barracks-type discussions from bunk to bunk. In this hell where tenderness had no place, their bed was their only refuge.

It must be said that for these men who had lived through the nightmare of the sardine nights at Mauthausen, from which one was never sure to awaken, having a bed each was a surprising luxury, which didn't fit in with the rest and was certainly not going to last. It was important to take advantage of it. Paulo, like the others, looked forward all day long to this blessed moment of going to bed. Not to wrap himself up in tender thoughts or to indulge in self-analysis, but to sleep. Physically, he was at the end of his tether. He sank into sleep each evening a little quicker, almost instantaneously, avoiding the brooding which he found futile. Every night he waited impatiently for Sailor to beat the flock toward the dormitory, and he would go to his bed without saying a word to his neighbors. His one thought was to sleep, hoping that the next blow would be the one which woke him the following morning, not the one which interrupted his deep sleep for a midnight crab parade. The consequences of weakening frightened him—the ovens were still fresh in his mind—for in spite of the work, which was daily more frantic, they were no better fed than before. A quart of fluid and a slice of bread . . . The only variation was the piece of *ersatz* sausage which every other day replaced the margarine. That might have been all right at Mauthausen but here, combined with the hard labor, it was intolerable. In ten days the men had become frighteningly thin. Yet this was only apparent in the morning when they went naked to the *Waschraum*, or at night during the cock inspections, for the mountain sun had perfidiously tanned their torsos and faces, and the whole crew had lost their deathly pallor. With the mountain air, by day the skeletons looked almost healthy.

Alas, the bracing air of the Karawanken Mountains also aggravated their hunger. In any other prison in the world, such hunger would have caused a rebellion. Here another solution had to be found, and for several days now, everything had been good enough to eat, even grass and dandelions. It filled them up, but it didn't give them any nourishment. No more than the live, slimy snails which they ate raw, or the sap snatched from the pine trees, which had to be munched for hours like chewing gum before it could be swallowed. The result of these gastronomic orgies was a gigantic case of the shits throughout Kommando X. The day began with a continuous procession to the work site's open-air crappers and it continued in the evening to the oil barrels in the blocks. In both cases, the Kapos administered the same medicine for the dysentery sufferers: the rubber club. Going to the crapper several times during working hours was called sabotage, and the price was twenty-five strokes. At night, the barrel might overflow and dirty the block. That was sabotage too.

The diet of raw salad, dysentery and rubber club soon reduced the men to shadows, but chewing whatever came to hand was their sole means of appeasing this obsessive hunger of theirs which would eventually drive them mad. The deportees of Kommando X thus continued to stuff themselves with all kinds of filth: grass, snails, slugs, bark, anything they could find, only to run the gauntlet of the Kapos as they were forced to relieve themselves almost immediately. It was in this deplorable physical state ten days after their arrival that they prepared to attack the rockface.

Paulo had been allotted a pickax and he was anxiously eyeing the *Kommandoführer,* who was to give the signal for work to begin. It was not in the best interests of Number 28,214 to cry off today, because he was to be one of the central attractions for the SS. He had been assigned to a team of fifteen, who would carry out the first blows of the pickax. What an honor! Normally on these occasions, only ministers are granted the pleasure of accomplishing this symbolic gesture. But the Loibl Tunnel workers were hardly presentable and work methods were so unusual that the SS had favored a quiet ceremony, with only immediate family in attendance. Anyway they were sure to keep a close watch on the operation and Paulo was growing increasingly more anxious. His fourteen companions cut equally sorry figures. Almost all of them belonged to Block 3: Pozzi, the Campana brothers, the whining peasant, the history teacher and his friend the gymnast, Jo from Oran, Angel Belloni and others who seemed to have been chosen for their slightly less debilitated physical appearance. Not a single miner among them, apart from the *Arbeitskapo*, who was anxious to show the assembled SS that this was not his first tunnel. The brute positively bristled with impatience, and at the solemn blast of the whistle, he dropped his club and grabbed Paulo's pick, pretending to show him how to go about it.

"I must be thankful for small mercies," Paulo thought to himself, counting the strokes and subtracting them from his own work load. His eyes widened with hypocritical admiration, urging the Kapo to continue, and it was only when the dimwit was completely out of breath that he decided to hand back the pick. The demonstration had lasted a good quarter of an hour. Paulo laughed inwardly as he retrieved his pick.

"Let's see you do as well, good-for-nothing," the Kapo said to him, wiping away the sweat which was running down his polished skull. The SS had seen him working, that was the important thing. "*Arbeit, schnell,*" he shouted hoarsely, picking up his club, and he immediately set upon the wheelbarrow men who had not managed to clear away the earth and rocks which he had enthusiastically dislodged.

When he returned to Paulo five minutes later, it was clear to him that his pupil had little talent for demolition work. His progress was completely unsatisfactory. The tall thin prisoner was obviously using a pickax for the first time in his life, and at this rate the war would probably be finished before the tunnel. For a moment, Paulo thought he was going to benefit from a second pickax lesson. Unfortunately, behind his back, the *Kommandoführer* in charge of the work must have also reached the same conclusion. He came running with his whip. And his target was Paulo, who continued to chop away haphazardly with his pickax.

The whip whistled down onto the back of his neck. The pain made Paulo drop his pick and he put his hands up to protect his face. The little mustachioed *Kommandoführer* could just as easily have beaten his arms or back, but he must already have begun to worry about his tunnel. If he leaned too hard into the only prisoners still capable of lifting a pick, he would never accomplish the mission entrusted to him. This was probably why Paulo got away with minor injuries. His neck was bleeding and one of his eyes was cut, but he could still hold his pickax.

The discipline he had just received galvanized the demolition team into action. Nevertheless, an hour later, it would have taken a lot of imagination to make out the little hole they had attempted to carve into the mountain. Moreover, that hole had been made by Pozzi almost single-handedly. The double ration of soup to which he seemed permanently entitled gave the little sneak strength. He worked all out to show that he, too, was an old hand at demolition. And it was true. He must have worked for a demolition company before playing informer on the rue Lauriston, to have learned to swing a pick so efficiently. His productivity caught the attention of the *Arbeitskapo* and all morning Pozzi was exempt from the club. He even earned a few approving grunts from the *Kommandoführer* who still wasn't inclined to leave them to it. Jo from Oran, the ex-lifer, didn't seem to care for his continued presence, and he kept moaning over his shovel:

"This Kommando is no bloody hideout, with that fucker standing there staring at us."

He was right. The attraction of the first pickax blows made this a very bad hiding place indeed, and soon quite a crowd had gathered in front of what would be the entrance to the tunnel. Even off-duty SS had strolled up from the camp to see how things were going. Two or three noncoms were even taking photos. Paulo, acting on an old criminal's instinct, tried at first to hide his face from the lenses, but then he began to smile at this precaution. It would have taken a casino bouncer to recognize the hood inside these faded pajamas whose grayness blended with the gray tones of rock. So he allowed himself to be photographed, but he already knew that he would never see any proof of this tableau. A strategic tunnel, prisoners in convicts' dress—that kind of photograph was bound to be classified information.

"Pity," Paulo said to himself, "I'd have liked to see what I would have looked like in this costume."

Over the last fourteen weeks without a mirror, Paulo had been lucky enough not to see the change wrought in his appearance. He wouldn't have liked his picture. Handsome at the time of his arrest, he had become unrecognizable. With his curly hair cropped, his dirty eight-day-old beard, his hollow cheeks and his sunken eyes, he looked just like his unfortunate companions, like an old tramp. His broad shoulders had shrunk and, like them all, he ran around constantly bent over, like the nine-to-fivers at home afraid of missing their Métro.

In any case good looks were of little use in this prison. Except of course for getting yourself sodomized. It was just as well for Paulo's morale that there were no mirrors lying about in concentration camps. If he really wanted to know what he looked like, he had only to glance at his neighbors. The likeness was as faithful as any mirror. But that was not a comforting thought, and Paulo preferred to think that he was less seedy-looking than the others. In fact, he was almost ready to play the young blade to the photographers, who continued snapping action shots of the excavation team, when some of these uniformed pricks took it into their heads to borrow pickaxes and have themselves photographed doing their bit of rock-breaking. Gorged with soup, they piled on the pace and Paulo, short of a pick once more, spent a good twenty minutes watching them tussle with the rock. Two breaks were worth a good deal in a morning's work, but unfortunately the SS photographers' spree was rather irregular and before long they had disappeared, much to the regret of the prisoners. The only one left was the *Kommandoführer*, who seemed rooted to the spot. The shit wanted to make up for lost time.

"*Arbeit*," he yelled, running after an overflowing wheelbarrow with his whip.

It was Angel Belloni's wheelbarrow, which a panic-stricken shoveler had piled high with enormous stones. Even a peasant working on his own land would have hesitated before pushing that cartload on the furrowed ground. Belloni's naked torso, reminiscent of an undernourished child, was helpless despite the whipping he was getting; the wheelbarrow would not budge. Paulo, standing fifteen feet away, wondered how the scene would end. Things could turn out badly, with the *Führer* enraged that this weakling had managed to slip into his shock troops.

"Get on with it, you French bastard, you lazy good-for-nothing cripple," he cried, punctuating each insult with the riding crop.

Making a superhuman effort, Belloni tried once again, but suddenly he dropped the wheelbarrow and turned around to face his tormentor.

The *Kommandoführer* was not prepared for this reaction. Disconcerted, he threw down his crop and swiftly drew his gun. But Angel Belloni's intentions were neither belligerent nor desperate. He had simply decided that, lacking muscle, he'd have to talk his way out of it.

"Ich will arbeit, Kommandoführer," he let fly. *"Ich will arbeit* but wheelbarrow *zu viel* full. *Besser zwei* wheelbarrows. *Zwei kleine* wheelbarrows *für schnell arbeit. Ich kann arbeit mehr schnell!"*

The SS was completely flabbergasted. He had never encountered such gall from a prisoner, and the few seconds that it took him to react saved Belloni. Coolly, Angel began to unload the huge rocks which were unbalancing his wheelbarrow, and when the load reached normal height, he took off like a rocket.

Paulo heaved a sigh of relief. He had feared the worst for Belloni and the scene which he had just witnessed proved that, in spite of his own problems, he was still capable of feeling. He had really felt for Belloni when the SS pulled out his pistol and pointed it at him. Paulo had imagined the boy taking the bullets courageously, point-blank. Now that the crisis was over, and Belloni was returning unharmed to pick up the overflow from his first wheelbarrow load, he felt like hugging him. Such a display of emotion would have looked odd under the circumstances, particularly as Paulo was not used to letting his feelings show. So he contented himself with abusing the coward who, frightened or eager to please, was filling the wheelbarrow to breaking point. Everyone should know that Belloni was to be considered Paulo's friend. His target was that peasant from the Sarthe, the man who had sapped everyone's morale, the inventor of the phrase "No point trying to understand." Hardly surprising, really.

"You heap of shit, you fucking turd," hissed Paulo. "Keep on ass-licking and filling up the wheelbarrows like that, and you'll find your face rearranged with a pickax."

"Mind your own business," replied the peasant, somewhat

surprised. "It's not you who'll get smashed up if I don't fill up the wheelbarrows. And I don't stick my nose into your work, you big lazy bastard."

He was too stupid for words. Paulo let it go. Anyway, he would never have been crazy enough to hit him with the pickax. He had bluffed, but his threatening look had made its point. The loads became normal and Belloni was able to lift his wheelbarrow. He threw Paulo a grateful smile. A smile in this hellhole was unexpected, and Angel Belloni must have been very moved for his sad childlike face suddenly to brighten. He was particularly in need of friendship in this jungle because even at night, when all his exhausted workmates were asleep, oblivious to their misery, there was no rest. It was official now: the tattooed Karl lusted after him. At first the chief of Block 3 had tried the second-helping technique, and Angel Belloni had taken temporary advantage of the misunderstanding. But when the horrible specimen came to prowl around his bed, the boy from Cannes had felt obliged to announce there had been a mistake; he only liked girls. Convinced that everybody on earth was queer, Karl took it very badly. It was a personal affront to find that he didn't appeal to Belloni. For several days, mad as a dog, the chief had mounted a seduction offensive; at night he got dressed up to the nines, with his beard and head closely shaved, dousing himself with eau de cologne and sporting shirts with a real civilian collar. He even had his striped trousers tailored to show off his buttocks. If the surroundings had been less sinister, his queer-in-heat performance might have been funny. But it wasn't good enough for Angel Belloni, and Karl's love remained unrequited. The boy became more and more upset by the ambiguity of the situation. To make his position clear, he had already had to fight on two occasions with sneering prisoners who began to bait him.

It was Sailor himself who put him out of that misery. Furious at having been made a laughingstock, he suddenly dropped his mask. In a flash, the *fille de joie* turned back into a bloodthirsty bully, and he mounted a new campaign of assault, this time with boots, fists, ladle and stick. At morning muster, midday soup, evening coffee and at night, three or four times a night at the slightest pretext, he forced him out of bed for twenty-five strokes on the backside. He was so enraged that it was difficult to know if he was avenging his failure to seduce Angel, or hoping by this treatment to bend the resistance of his young prey. For Angel Belloni, however, things were now much clearer. The blood which pissed constantly from his wounds, and the blue, yellow and green marks that the club left on his back and buttocks, proved to all that he knew how to behave like a man. To establish this reputation, which he had not had the time to do in civilian life, was the only thing he cared about, which was why the support of a respected character like Paulo was so important for the abandoned boy. He now looked transformed as he pushed his wheelbarrow loads. The hard labor on the work site would become the high point of his day. He would forget his jealous scourge waiting for him down below in the block, club raised.

Paulo understood the reasons for his friend's momentary optimism, but they couldn't much affect his own situation. Each hour of work saw him a little more gloomy, a little more depressed. The blisters on his hands had literally exploded when he touched the handle of the pickax. His fine white idle hands were nothing more than an open wound. He was hurt and demoralized.

"And there's no reason for it to stop," he thought, watching his neighbors running, hacking, shoveling. "This shit could go on for months and months, even years if these maniacs win the war. No one knows we're here. They can torture us, kill us, fuck us, no one will ever know. How did I ever get myself into this mess?"

His workmates couldn't give him the answer. Neither the peasant, the Campana brothers, Pozzi, Jo from Oran, the little Breton with his Basque friend, nor any of the others arrested for a thousand different reasons could possibly know why they united in the same destiny, at the mouth of this diabolical tunnel. After all, there were plenty of guys in France and in Europe who didn't agree with the Germans, and they didn't all spend their time in pajamas, nose to the grindstone eighteen hours a day without eating. The prisons were full of these Hun-haters, so were the POW camps. And they had an address, they got letters and little parcels, and if they fell ill it was the sanatorium or a trip home. Not the oven.

"Why pick on us rather than the others?" Paulo continued to himself, swinging his pickax more and more feebly.

"Christ, it's not worth the death penalty just to want quietly to be a Kraut. Especially as I didn't even know that my Belgian was a Kraut!"

He was losing his grip. He was ready to accept the punishment, but for the others, the terrorists, the Reds, the Jews. Not for himself. What he had done didn't deserve more than three months in the cooler. It was a pity he had not been given time in the Cherche-Midi to get a lawyer. Things were going wrong inside his head, for he had just come to the conclusion that the tunnel was a trap. They were cornered like rats, these handpicked workmen. Not the remotest chance of escaping, of even risking a break between sleeping guards, under the pretense of fetching a rock or a tree trunk in the distance. For the tunnel Kommando, there was only one direction: the mountain. You had to go forward, because behind you there was a semicircle of guns, clubs and watching eyes. A real ambush.

Angel Belloni might perhaps have thought that Paulo was sticking it out better than the others. But the former villain had no illusions. He knew something had given way inside.

"I really am going off the rails," he murmured. "I'm thinking too much. Only the stupid have a chance of surviving. That fellow from the Sarthe has it straight: there isn't any point in trying to understand."

And he swung his pickax a little bit harder, wondering whether he was the only one to be troubled. The Campana brothers certainly weren't. They looked like two wild beasts in a zoo, and it was evident from their murderous looks that they were dreaming up the worst possible tortures for their keepers. But that didn't stop them from getting on with it, and from being damn careful to hide their bloodthirsty fury from the guards. Without their guns, they didn't frighten anybody anymore. Not even Pozzi, who now indulged in a little sniping at the clumsy way they handled their shovels. For the two Corsicans, Loibl was just a reform center, and the thoughts in their minds must have been the same as those of reform-school kids.

As for Pozzi, his mind was so bent on ass-licking the SS and Kapos to avoid beatings and get his extra soup that he pretended to be passionately interested in his work. With this tactic he was certain to come off better than the others.

That was enough for him. Belloni had his own problems, and his moral crisis was already enough to cope with. If he could only manage to escape being raped, he would have time to think about the future. The peasant, as always, was moaning, but then he had probably done so from birth. He hadn't tried to understand why he was there, and with nonstop beatings to contend with, he was even less keen to know. Working eighteen hours a day was something he had known all his life, and he saw no difference between shoveling cow shit and stones. It was only the lack of food which made him desperate. The only effort that his brain accepted was the search for ways of gathering dandelions, snails and potato peelings. That was where his mental activity ended. It satisfied his only need: to fill his belly. Anything was better than the gnawing in his guts which drove him insane from the moment he woke up.

"He's got the right attitude," thought Paulo, watching him work like an ox. "I'll go mad trying to analyze it all. We've had it. I might as well give up."

But it overwhelmed him; he couldn't get over what was happening. He wanted to understand, and yet there was nothing to understand. He would wear himself out if he continued looking for a reason, instead of following the example of his mates: working all-out to avoid thinking. Even Jo from Oran, who was a rebellious type, had stopped moaning. He was splitting rocks, albeit without enthusiasm, but his small, purposeful, rapid blows with the pickax left no time for self-pity and nostalgia for Cayenne. Paulo's companions, without exception, appeared to have accepted their sad lot without protest. There was internal protest of course. Paulo didn't expect anything else, but their passiveness mortified him. He felt like shouting out loud:

"Stop, you bunch of idiots! Don't you see that you're digging your own graves? The tunnel is just a trick, it's to bury you, all of you."

He didn't shout out, of course, but he began to hate violently all the poor wretches, himself included, who were naïvely attacking the treacherous mountain. It was incredible that none of the fifteen had understood the macabre intentions of the Fritzes. This tunnel was the end for all of them. They couldn't seriously imagine finishing the job with their transparent little biceps. They would die well before, from hunger and exhaustion. It was inevitable. In a few days, or a few months, it didn't matter because they would immediately be replaced by others just as proud at having escaped the Mauthausen crematorium. There was no one who seemed to understand that in an SS tunnel you couldn't escape, your screams wouldn't be heard, and you could only die. It was an SS brainstorm—a crematorium without fire.

Paulo was rushing things. His thoughts were becoming morbid and it was just as well that incomprehension prevailed around him. If he had been able to explain the reasons for his anxiety, he would have caused general panic. The unfortunate fellows who had been slaving at his side for almost six hours could do without that. The whippings and the yells were quite enough to create an atmosphere of insanity. Paulo kept his dark thoughts to himself, but now he resented his companions for their fatalism almost as much as he resented his executionars.

"And they call themselves men!" he hissed as the history teacher went by lugging an overloaded wheelbarrow without a murmur.

The old man looked at him strangely as if he had guessed that Paulo was not quite himself. He didn't reply but, confronted with his strange look, it was Paulo who lowered his eyes, ashamed.

"I'm the one who can't be called a man," he realized. It had suddenly dawned on him that the Basque didn't need him to point out that the tunnel they had started on would be the death of them all. In his historian's mind, he too had hoped for a partisan attack, and must be suffering. But the difference was that the teacher knew how to suffer in silence. He probably knew how to die like that too. In a way, he must have expected this end, on the field of honor, whereas Paulo, by conning his Belgian, had never imagined a punishment so out of proportion.

A look had been enough to dissipate Paulo's aggressiveness toward his fellows, but he had yet to return to an even keel. Now his resentment was directed against himself. He was tormented by remorse at having been pinched for a peccadillo. If he had only known, instead of being all smiles as he relieved the collaborationist crooks of their cash, he would have dealt with them once and for all. The punishment would have been the same, but at least he would have known why he had been stuck in a convict's uniform before being dispatched. What a fool he had been!

He suddenly felt less scorn for those he had rather hastily labeled suckers. The teacher and his friend the gymnast, for example. The real sucker was Paulo himself. He envied the relaxed way in which the small Breton was filling his friend's wheelbarrow. He looked athletic, and each movement of his shovel was executed with style. The gym teacher worked sparingly, without wasted or exaggerated movements, like the tennis champion who knows that the match is going to last all afternoon. His method was an intelligent one, and after a day of exercise the Breton seemed ten times less exhausted than his neighbor, the peasant, a shoveler too, but who exerted himself like a madman with lesser result. The gymnast's relaxation was not simply muscular. His face, too, seemed calm, almost rested. And yet he must have known that this tunnel was going to bring them disappointment and suffering. He saved his strength and prepared to suffer a little longer, in order to stay to the end, like his companion the Basque.

In civilian life, Paulo had already met plenty of heroic fighters and patriots, but he put that kind of courage down to sheer bravado, and their tales of daring exploits always made him laugh quietly to himself. Here, in this arena, it was another story. Being decorated and mentioned in dispatches was not a part of this deal; good conduct didn't impress the audience.

His train of thought stopped dead at the yells announcing the end of work. He put away his pickax and ran to find a good-sized slab of rock before taking his place at the head of the stone crocodile.

VI

The news which had been going around the camp and the work site for some time was confirmed toward the end of June. Now it was no longer a vague rumor; the doyen had announced it to the block chiefs. It was official. Mauthausen was sending in reinforcements. Nobody knew whether to be pleased at this new turn of events, but they all hoped life would change, that this would be a relief force; they were said to be coming in strength. Would the newcomers be arriving straight from France, or would they see some of their fellows who had missed the first convoy? Precious few of the two thousand left behind were likely to be alive, given the capacity and speed of the ovens. At least they would have recent news of Mauthausen, and perhaps of France; for here, in the hermitage of Loibl, nothing got through. In the tunnel, on the site, in the blocks, in the crappers, they could talk only of the new transport, and as no one had any real leads, speculation was rife, sometimes optimistic, sometimes anxious.

In the *Revier*, stuffed fit to burst after the terrible first month, the patients had no illusions. The premises would be evacuated since they were no longer even good for pushing wheelbarrows or carrying rocks.

Among the rest, on the other hand, the news had triggered off tremendous excitement. In the places where they could talk, tongues wagged nonstop. Paulo had ended up modeling his conduct on that of the Breton, suffering in silence and trying to keep clear of compromises and ass-licking, but he too was overcome by the desire for information.

"D'you think this new shipment's a good thing?" he had asked Riton.

"That depends who for," the Montparnasse pimp had replied. He was fairly well informed since Bullseye, pleased by his knowing the ropes, had promoted him dormitory chief of his block, Block 2.

"I don't mean the guys in the *Revier*," Paulo interrupted, anticipating Riton's explanations. "I mean for us."

"For us, it won't change very much except that they're sending new guards and Kapos with the workers. From what Bullseye says, they don't sound much like nursemaids. He's expecting a friend of his, Fritz, who he thinks the world of."

"I get the picture," concluded Paulo.

And he dropped Riton, who was dying to pursue the conversation, looking for an opportunity to justify his nomination as dormitory chief in the eyes of a "man" like Paulo.

For some time now Paulo had fought shy of talking to his former crooked friends. He found them comical, these small-time toughs who volunteered to shine the block chiefs' boots and, on occasion, to wash their underclothes. Their ridiculous attempts to keep their reputations as villains made these "men" forget the unwritten code of their background. They thought themselves smarter than the others because from time to time they earned a cigarette or an extra mouthful of soup, but to whitewash these tainted charities, they had to behave as if they belonged to a sort of Criminal Brotherhood. In fact one of them, Maurice from the Bastille, a young pimp of twenty, stretched the Brotherhood's solidarity a bit far. He slept in Bullseye's bed, quite shamelessly. He didn't seem to mind at all, the fairy, and if ever he got out, he certainly risked being the laughingstock of the little night spots on the rue de Lappe. From now on, he'd be better off looking for a new specialty. But in the meantime, he was shoveling in food, smoking and enjoying exemption from all chores at night after work. Bullseye only asked one thing of him: to decorate the block with flowers. It was unbelievable. This youngster who not too long ago was swaggering about the place, airing the fact that he was already a pimp, was now busy gathering marguerites, poppies and daisies, right under the nose of comrades staggering beneath the stones and the blows. And the funny thing was, this faggot procurer had taste. The arrangement of his bouquets was most harmonious, and Bullseye was overjoyed when his protégé came back with an edelweiss or a four-leaf clover among the flowers. It was turning into a story of true love. Maurice didn't seem in the least embarrassed by this public show of feelings. He tried to impress upon anyone who would listen that Bullseye was the girl.

"I pimp for him, he whores for me," he would say, to explain away the dishes of fried potatoes which Bullseye prepared lovingly for him before they said bye-bye.

Unfortunately for the terror of the Bastille, his sodomy sessions had had a witness: a young fellow from Burgundy called François, an unintentional voyeur. From his bed, the first in the dormitory, he saw through the door—which was always left open as a precaution—one of the chief's bedtime parties. And he had seen all of it, in detail.

"With my own eyes," he recounted again and again, "with my own eyes, I saw the chief giving it to Maumau."

The scene had surprised young François so much that he had had to repeat the story to everybody. That same evening the whole camp, from the *Revier* to the kitchens, knew that Maurice from the Bastille had lost his virginity. However, nobody dared call him a hustler. Sarcastic comments were dangerous, because Bullseye was very fond of his sweetie. He was even wary of his block chief colleagues who began to leer in Maumau's direction a little too closely for his liking. They hadn't all had Bullseye's luck. In some blocks they had had to resort to force to procure love. Some of the boys approached had resisted the tyrants' advances as heroically as Belloni, but others had capitulated after two or three bowls of soup, and still others after the first beating.

Yet no one thought of reproaching these young kids, mostly under twenty, for having given in. The mad month about to end encouraged indulgence. The toughest, the oldest, the weakest, the most honorable, all knew at the bottom of their hearts that they, too, would have been raped if the chief had so desired. Defending one's honor was solely a question of standing up to the beatings. And not everybody took those like Belloni. Consequently, apart from Maurice in Block 2, who was universally despised (how bizarre to have chosen the profession of pimp so young), the hustlers were regarded more as victims. Even Paulo found excuses for them, and he was rather strict when it came to queers. He sincerely pitied one of them in Block 1, a fellow from the north and a young father of two children: "He's got to eat if he wants to see his kids again," he said drily.

For himself, Paulo preferred to stick to his new policy of self-effacement. He pulled his cap as far down as possible about his ears to protect himself from the Kapos in heat who might find him attractive. And he also avoided talking big like Riton and ending up compromised into block chief's pet in the name of Criminal Brotherhood. He knew that Sailor only respected delinquents, but although Paulo felt big enough to put a creep like Karl into his pocket, for the last two weeks he had chosen to melt into the mass. And he stuck to it.

Paulo found this strategy difficult because it was always the mass, the army of nonentities, who got beaten, systematically. He calculated that not one day since he arrived had he escaped a beating. Not once had he come back from the site without blood running down his face, and several times in the block at night, he had gone to the stool for the *fünf und zwanzig*. This acceptance of physical suffering produced excellent moral results, however: Paulo knew now that it wouldn't be his mind which gave way. But there was still his body. At first glance, it gave him cause for concern. The skeletons who had survived Mauthausen were still skeletons after a month, and he couldn't see, given the work and the home cooking, how a layer of fat would ever again cover their miserable frames. How much longer could these skeletons, despite their tan, endure the diabolical pace? That was a question which none dared ask. Except for their SS employers, who were meticulous when it came to statistics.

For them nothing dramatic had happened so far, apart from the 10 per cent drop-out rate (the good-for-nothings in the *Revier* whom Mauthausen would be delighted to salvage), because the French dogs were not a disappointment. On the contrary, the biceps handpicked on the *Appelplatz* seemed to have been a definite success. The selected *Franzosen* were working better and better, and faster and faster. But their skinniness? An excellent thing, which had been foreseen and calculated. There was a fine line which should not be crossed in either direction: of course detainees who suddenly lost weight ended up all too quickly in the crematorium; equally, those who became bloated with soup turned into fat slobs, lazy and short of breath. An experiment conducted at Mauthausen where rations of synthetic sauerkraut were distributed systematically for several months among the men of Block 16 had had disastrous results. The guinea pigs had all become distended water-skins incapable of movement. The SS at Loibl, armed with this knowledge, worked at keeping their slaves thin. The thinness had reached the ideal level for good production. Improving on the norm could only be prejudicial. Like conscientious trainers, they supervised the weight of their colts. The latter, convinced they had reached the furthest limit of physical resistance, felt their only salvation lay in more food. Yet they had to face the facts: in spite of the rations, which remained as scanty as ever, almost everyone was holding out. Their stomachs were no more hollow than two weeks before, and their shriveled muscles, snatched from the quarantine, even seemed to have developed from all the pushing, carrying and rock-breaking.

Paulo was more surprised than most. A complete stranger to manual labor, he couldn't get over having slaved a hundred hours a week without a break, emerging after a month with a minimum of aches and pains. His blisters had hardened, his cuts from being beaten had closed naturally and the horrible back pains of the first days had completely disappeared. He was still dead tired in the evenings and he was still ravenous, but he felt that he was coming out on top. Gradually, he regained the indestructible optimism he had paraded on his departure from Murder Incorporated at the end of May. Looking back he felt ashamed of the self-indulgence of his minor depression that morning at the foot of the tunnel. That bout of low spirits could have led to the *Revier*, with all that that implied. Fortunately, he had pulled himself together and chosen the only sensible method to survive in this lunatic camp: deliberate self-debasement. He no longer gave a shit about paying so heavily for his misdeed, nor did he care about his reputation as a tough, the esteem of his peers, and the contempt of those who knew why they were there—all the things he had turned over and over in his too-rational skull when confronted with the blackness of the tunnel. He was not even so afraid of the cavity which bit into the mountain a little deeper each day. He felt an almost masochistic pleasure when running automatically, like the others, for stones, tools and soup, at the blast of the whistle. At last Paulo had found peace of mind, and the news of the convoy from Mauthausen with the smell of the ovens still clinging to it couldn't snap him out of his mental retreat. Without too much effort, he had succeeded in becoming a simple beast of burden. The only discussions he allowed himself now exclusively concerned food. Usually about the consistency of the soup or about the margarine or sausage which accompanied the evening slice of bread.

In fact, although Paulo wouldn't admit it, he was rather proud of having become a half-tidy workman in less than a month. He had learned how to swing a pickax, and he began to show interest in handling a sledgehammer. It amused him to look for the vein of a rock and tap it neatly and accurately in just the right place, rejoicing when the rock began to crumble. Gone was the brooding of the previous week. His air of self-satisfaction when a boulder had turned into a pile of stones infuriated Pozzi, the peasant, and a few others. They were manual workers from birth and had pretensions to superiority. They no longer even had the satisfaction of needling him for his clumsiness or of calling him a slacker.

It was now more and more evident that the Germans believed in their tunnel. It was the reason why they had come here, and those who did not disappoint them would earn a reprieve from the flames. Paulo had worked out that a year was the minimum time before the motorized divisions could cross the Karawanken without freezing or overheating. It was an awful schedule for the convicts, but at least they knew where they stood. Paulo knew it would be a terrible year, that their rations would not increase and that the beatings would not diminish. But he also knew that there was no point in the SS assassinating them *en masse* or making them drop like flies with starvation. It didn't take a university degree to understand these things. It was obvious from the volume of dirt dug out daily at the camp and in front of the tunnel that the construction site at Loibl Pass was of major importance. Wooden barracks sprang up like mushrooms. In the camp alone there were three new ones, of which two were blocks big enough to house two or three hundred jailbirds with room to spare. In the SS camp the number of barracks had literally tripled; the general conclusion was that the prisoners in the new shipment must be particularly vicious. One good sign was that the kitchens were being extended: a truck had just unloaded five huge ultramodern pressure cookers, enough to feed a regiment. Paulo was right. The Germans would have to have a good year to set off investments like these. But this hive of activity was nothing compared to what was going on around the mouth of the tunnel. A realistic contractor would never have believed that barely a month ago the mountain had been intact. Three or four sections of road were now in place, and stone walls, workshops and barracks had been built. Obviously they had had to tear out hundreds of trees and shift tons of rocks, quite apart from the digging of the tunnel itself. The best foreman in the world would never have dared promise such results in so short a time.

It was risky all the same, to have bourgeois, students, peasants and gangsters digging a full-scale tunnel. There were certainly a few villains—among them an architect, a contractor and an engineer—who had tried their hand at digging a tunnel under the patrol path at Compiègne, but when they got to Loibl, they had carefully hushed up this exploit. Anyway, a mousehole dug by hand was nothing compared to the gigantic operation commanded by the Wehrmacht general staff. What they needed was an engineer.

He arrived on the site in the early days of summer, and one might have thought that the macabre performance which he was witnessing at first hand would upset his civilian conscience. Not at all. This mathematical genius, Austrian by his accent, must have been used to it, and he displayed no emotion when he saw a poor fool almost lynched for breaking his overloaded wheelbarrow on a stone. It seemed as if SS and Kapos were happy to reveal to this important personage the secret of their being ahead of schedule, and clearly, this misbegotten shit in the green hat would not be the one to hold things up. Having probed the rock in various places, he immediately began to issue instructions to the *Kommandoführer* and Hanz, chief of the *Arbeitskapos*. Even in a reserved occupation, he was chasing his Iron Cross. The prisoners had naïvely hoped that the beatings would stop with the appearance of the first civilian on Route 333, and some greedy fools had even imagined that the SS would quickly stuff them with soup and *Kartoffel* to disguise their repulsive thinness. Too bad, the engineer was a trusted member of the Nazi Party.

Paulo interpreted the arrival of this loathsome character as further proof that the Germans did indeed mean business with their tunnel. Visions of the oven faded, and the registration number sewn on each jacket over the heart was not necessarily a death certificate. Only a few idiots who had swallowed the Kapos' stories believed that there were camps where life was easy: Buchenwald, for example, known by the block chiefs as a "sanatorium"—report sick, and you might well be transferred there. These trusting children dreamed of such idylls where the Kapos devoted themselves to the prisoners' every need like nurses, where a spoon stood up in the soup, where Red Cross packages arrived by the truckload and where the long-stay patients were allowed to go and raise their ropes in the brothel.

Sadly, these fairy stories did find an audience, and five or six innocents out of the thirty *Revier* residents were there on purpose. Their hearts filled with hope, they waited impatiently for the arrival of the reinforcements who would signal the end of their misery. For them, it was simple: they would be packed off immediately to another center. They could not possibly be taken back to Mauthausen because they had already done their quarantine time and, besides, there was no work there.

The problem for the others was how to conserve their strength, and plans were cooked up on the work site for slowing down the pace. The crapper was crowded to its maximum. It was the one place where the workers could sit down for a few minutes. The trick, quickly uncovered, led to the usual repression, but it didn't slow the procession of diarrhetics. They knew that going to the cans would cost them a few cuts, but they went all the same. To sit down, even at that price, was the only way to hold out one more day. The Kapos had realized this too, and they did not forbid entry to the shithouse. They saved their fun for getting the prisoners out. Their excitement reached its peak when all the places in the latrines were occupied. They crept up to the building on tiptoe, always in pairs, careful to avoid being seen. Charging in, yelling, from the two entrances, they struck out with all their might at the shaven heads of the men crouched down, either shitting or just pretending. The chase continued outside, and nothing amused the SS sentries more than to see a Kapo chasing a prisoner torn between trying to protect his head and pulling up his trousers to cover his bare backside. The price for a few moments of rest was high, but everyone accepted it because, in addition, it was the only place to chat, safe from indiscreet ears. Consequently the naturally talkative French had not delayed in turning the shithouse into a speakeasy.

In these conditions it was hardly surprising that the Kapos didn't seem keen to discourage the comings and goings to the crapper: it allowed them to corner large groups of malingerers all at once and, more important still, it forced the adults in their care to behave like naughty schoolboys. To be forced at the age of forty or fifty to hug one's stomach and pretend to have the trots gave even the most dignified a guilt complex. Just what was needed for those who thought they didn't deserve the concentration camp. The mere fact that you were in the camp proved that you were bad, and any way of making you recognize your guilt was justified. A few more weeks and even the most indomitable would be ashamed of their lies, their diarrhea and their laziness.

Paulo had not yet come to that, but these minor annoyances, the "Sir, may I be excused," really began to get on his nerves. He felt that he, too, would end up having to play the whining little truant. It made him furious to see that practically everyone in the blocks was happy to play the Kapos' game.

"They're a real bunch of bums here," he said to himself, looking around for someone he could confide in. But it was tricky to confront characters like the Basque or his friend, proper patriots, face to face. For them, he was only one gangster among many others. Hadn't he already stressed that fact on the way here, when he had been only inches away from getting into a fight with the gym teacher? Since then, the two inseparable companions had seemed to be suspicious of him.

It would be easier to approach his own kind first, and immediately he thought of Belloni. The boy had proved his dignity, and he would immediately understand the point of what his idol had to say. By saying no to extra soup and by accepting the extra beatings, he was ideal material. In fact, it was he who, refusing to play the flower girl, had been the first to set the example.

"I've got to support young Angel, tell him he's doing the right thing," Paulo thought to himself. "I've got to explain to him that the only way to get out of this is to carry on putting up two fingers to the Krauts. If they get the order to send us to the crematorium, they won't make any distinction between the hustlers and the others. So it's just stupid getting fucked if we're going to die anyway."

Refusing to give in when one was unlucky enough to attract a block chief was exactly what Paulo understood by resistance. He no longer wanted the crook's halo which had made him respected during the first days at Mauthausen and still followed him here. A villain's visiting card in this strange world run by the vilest bastards imaginable was no more than a certificate of shame. On their poor showing of the last month some of the villains had been condemned in the eyes of the crowd, patriots or not, more finally than by any pitiless criminal jury. Paulo felt that nobody would take his theories of resistance seriously if he didn't break with his past once and for all. He must sever immediately his ties with the mob, with Riton the procurer-*Stubedienst*, with Berck, Maumau and the other thugs—to hell with gangland solidarity! With the exception of those who knew how to behave, like Belloni, or even the Campana brothers, still looking as murderous as chained-up wild animals, but remaining fiercely determined not to be taken for queers.

The ace gunmen's reputation had reached the ears of the block chiefs and it would have been easy for these two old lions to get friendly with their associates in crime. Via, as always, the Criminal Brotherhood. But the two Corsicans preferred to go hungry and take their beatings, so fierce was their hatred, and it was perhaps the most revealing spectacle of the whole camp to see these two terrors standing at attention, receiving vicious punches to the face without flinching. No one in the world could ever have even imagined inflicting such brutality on the two brothers. It seemed they too were biding their time, and Paulo could count on them. It would be easy to talk to them because, like Belloni, they belonged to his block and his work team. In the underground recess of the tunnel, he could risk holding forth. Paulo decided to begin his propaganda campaign immediately. One of the Campana brothers was just arriving with his empty wheelbarrow, and judging by the speed at which his brother prepared to fill it, he was going to be there for a fair while. Paulo took advantage of this:

"Riton told me—" he began.

He didn't finish. With one voice, in the same deadpan tone, the two brothers cut him off:

"Don't talk to us about that fucker."

This terse judgment fitted in nicely with what Paulo had prepared to say.

"Fuckers don't come worse than Riton, but he gets his information from Bullseye and it's worth hearing. He told me the biggest bastard of all the Mauthausen Kapos was arriving with the convoy. Someone called Fritz. That's promising."

"They're all fuckers."

They had a limited vocabulary, these two. Paulo persisted.

"Things aren't going to get any better when that queer arrives. We've already been pretty spoiled with the last bunch. These Kraut pimps aren't my idea of fun, and they'd better steer clear of me if I ever get out of this fucking mess. I can't believe there are shits who actually lick their asses. And they call themselves Frenchmen—so-called fucking Frenchmen."

Paulo had said all he wanted to, and in the right sort of language, but clearly the brothers only knew one word:

"Fuckers," they spat out.

The wheelbarrow was full, they separated, and Paulo judged it useless to prolong the discussion. He wrapped up his lecture and quickened the pace of his pickax as he glimpsed the ominous silhouette of the *Arbeitskapo* at the mouth of the tunnel.

He continued to break up the soft rock and began to mull over the position he had taken up in deciding to play Don Quixote all of a sudden. It was going to bring him nothing but trouble. He was going to have to be bloody careful. No danger with the Campana brothers, at least. They were perhaps somewhat narrow-minded, but they weren't natural chatterers, still less telltales. Paulo had nevertheless made his point and it was a start. He would have to go on trying, to detect the strong-minded men and, little by little, to sift out the rotten ones, like Berck, Maurice or Riton, who could only cause trouble. Against the grayness of the rock face, Paulo tried to sort out which of the pickaxers and shovelers could be trusted.

Jo from Oran? Not a chance, he had been too long in vice school not to slip back sooner or later into his dirty little Cayenne habits. He had taken it into his head to play the old convict, the one who knows the ropes. While in this new prison where there were no two ways of getting by. That kind of mentality was best left well alone. He would have to be put aside. Like Pozzi, too, who still spent his time pushing for promotion, and giving the tired and clumsy ones a hard time in front of the *Kommandoführer*. The old history teacher had already gotten it twice, thanks to this miserable sneak, and Pozzi would have to pay for that breach of loyalty. Paulo would have liked to explain to the Basque that he would take care of Pozzi, but that subject would have to be broached when the occasion arose. Unfortunately, the old man seemed even less inclined to talk than the Campana brothers.

The appearance of Belloni wearily pushing his wheelbarrow was a relief. At least with him, Paulo would not have to wear kid gloves. Putting his pick down, he blocked the path of the boy's cart. Surprised, Belloni looked sharply behind him, but seeing that the *Arbeitskapo* had disappeared from the entrance to the tunnel, he dropped his cart.

"What's up?" he asked.

He was worried by the abrupt way his friend had stopped

him. For several days, Paulo, who had been hewing rock from morning to night like a lunatic, without a word or a look for his workmates, had seemed to be avoiding him completely. His sudden change of attitude was odd, and Belloni was eager to know why.

"What's up?" he repeated.

"Nothing," answered Paulo. "I felt like chatting."

Not taken in, Belloni smiled slightly. Paulo certainly had something important to say, so he gave him the opportunity.

"I can't stand up straight anymore. Tomorrow I'm going to drop a rock on my toes and wait in the *Revier* for the next chapter."

Paulo took the bait: here was a chance to preach his gospel.

"You're off your head, kid. In two days the whole *Revier* will be packed off back to Mauthausen with the reinforcement escort, and I don't suppose you need to be told what happens after that."

"Look, Paulo, I know, but I've had about enough of this shit. I can't even walk straight anymore. I'm finished."

"Come on, for God's sake, pull yourself together! You're not going to give in now. Listen, I've got an idea."

"There's only one, and that's to get out."

"No," Paulo interrupted. "No chance of making a break. Not a chance, we wouldn't get a hundred yards. No, my plan is to stay here, to the end."

"You can't be serious, Paulo," answered Belloni, stupefied. "We're all going to die at this rate, you know."

"Possibly, but here things *can* drag on, whereas at Mauthausen you're cooked, if you'll forgive the expression. There's no choice, you've got to stay here, you've got to hang on."

Belloni had succeeded: by playing forlorn and desperate, he had managed to drag Paulo out of his unnatural silence.

"Tell me," he said, anxious to know.

"It's quite simple," continued Paulo. "They want their tunnel and they're not going to kill us until it's finished. I want to finish it. I know it'll take time, but it's our only chance of getting out of here. A tunnel like this will take over a year to finish, and the war might easily end before then. So that's it."

"It's not exactly brilliant," exclaimed Angel, after a second's thought. "I thought of that too, you know, but I also reckoned that whether the war ends or not, they'll never let us go back. We know too much."

"Right, but we might as well not get roasted now. It may not look like it, but they're not keen on that either. It would mess up their schedule. I tell you, we've got to stay, whatever it costs. If we can survive for a few more months, we'll be more difficult to move. We've got to get organized now; because the day they start packing it all in, we'll know why. Then we really can risk our necks. That's the day we've got to prepare for: the day of the big break."

"So your plan's a mutiny? You think you're in Sing-Sing? Only one guy in four is a man here. The place is crawling with informers—"

"Exactly. It's the informers we've got to take care of. There are more men here than you think, they don't have to be crooks. To get through, all you need is dignity. First, to hang on, and secondly to avoid going back to Mauthausen."

Dignity! To give himself time to answer, Belloni grabbed the handles of his wheelbarrow as if on the point of leaving. Paulo held him back, then whispered almost in his ear:

"Yes, dignity. Like yours—telling Sailor to go and fuck himself."

That struck home. Belloni, flattered, straightened up again and, just for form's sake, made one final objection:

"Your 'dignified' men just think about their mess bowls. They'd eat each other if they weren't afraid of getting beaten. I don't believe in your idea. There's only one worthwhile thing here and that's a friend. You're my friend, the only one. The others can go to hell."

"Wrong, Angel. If we want to get out, we've got to get out as a team. We've got to dig ourselves into this place, make ourselves indispensable. So that they won't replace us before the end."

"It's not going to be easy," said Belloni, still a little shaken. He had managed to make Paulo spill the thoughts he had been brooding over for some time, but now he knew what it was about, he was bewildered. All this business of obeying the rules was not in his nature, no more so than in Paulo's. What on earth could have brought about this change?

Paulo must have read his thoughts because he offered an explanation:

"Listen, Angel! I'm just like the rest. I almost went to pieces when I saw that we were starting this hole, and the first day I had the same lousy idea of the *Revier* as you. It was that little Breton fellow busy shoveling down the end who made me think. He doesn't act like a fairy, does he, and yet he's holding on. Look at him, he's relaxed, he's not that thin, and if we were to go for a big break-out, he wouldn't be the type to turn chicken. It's with guys like him that we'll be able to keep going. That's how we'll find a way out. Not with shits like Riton or Berck. Haven't you seen that I've kept myself to myself for the last two weeks? It's good tactics not to get yourself noticed. I know your case is special but Sailor's fancy will go, and you've just got to last out. We'll close our ranks and we'll get the Krauts by wearing them down. But first of all, we've got to cut out the bastards. Criminals or not. I don't know if it's this camouflage we're wearing, but I don't see it as the straights and the rest: it's the men and the rest."

"Perhaps you're right," shrugged Angel Belloni. In fact, he agreed entirely, but he would never have dared champion such a theory himself. Until now, only the nobility of the criminal had existed for him, and the code of honor of the underworld. This new way of looking at things in his senior was destroying a whole education. Belloni tried to dismiss it with a joke:

"Hey, Paulo, what do you call your plan? 'Resistance'?"

"That's right, friend, it's resistance, but not the fucking patriotic Resistance. I don't give a fuck about their war, I'm a pacifist. My resistance is to the crematorium and I can't do it on my own. If we carry on behaving like nuts sniping at each other, and just thinking about reporting sick, we'll all be sent back to roast. I'd look pretty silly playing the tough guy all by myself. Wht we need, I tell you again, is something together, some kind of solidarity, so that they'll let us finish the tunnel. Afterward, we'll see. Do you think I enjoy this landscaping work? I wasn't born stupid, but with these madmen, it's the only way out."

"You may be right. But if I've got this straight, there's going to be a whole lot more of this shit. I wouldn't have minded risking it with you. But talking to all the straight guys? Don't like that idea for a start. I'd sooner beat in the heads of those bastards who take the piss out of me when Sailor works me over."

"Yeah, I know, but I'll take care of them. If you want to help me, start by explaining to the guys you trust that they've got to pull their fingers out and, whatever they do, avoid reporting sick. And no sabotage, no sulking, on any account. Let's look happy about this fucking tunnel."

Belloni had understood. He had needed guidance, and the instructions which Paulo had given him surprised but also pleased him. He was less lost, he had a goal. He was almost humming as he took up his wheelbarrow.

Paulo was also pleased. In three sentences with the Campana brothers and five minutes of conversation with Belloni, he had straightened things out. To remain friends with Paulo in this penitentiary, people were going to have to work hard and forget about vice.

Such an attitude could have made people scoff. But coming from Paulo, the good-for-nothing hood, it just might catch on. It had to be spread quickly, because each passing day saw the deportees of Kommando X sinking a little deeper into submission and slavery.

In less than a month, they had indeed become slaves, but they were not fully aware of it.

Yet even the blindest among them must have had some idea of it the day the SS assembled everyone for their latest trick, the *Autobahn*. And even the dullest fellows should have realized that they had ceased to be men when they got their scalps divided in two by a wide shaven furrow, like livestock on the way to the sales. But, curiously, it made the whole Kommando laugh. Even the glummest had been amused to see their friends disfigured by such a mortifying haircut. Three fingers wide and extending from the forehead to the back of the neck, it looked just like a motorway through a forest. The *Autobahn*, as the Kapos called it, was very much in the German spirit. But this highly original style was practical as well, because it saved spending hours and hours each week cutting three hundred heads of hair which paid no heed to the rules and kept on growing. Moreover, a broad strip down the middle of the scalp would also cool the enthusiasm of escape candidates. Which is why, instead of splitting their sides, the deportees would have done better to worry a little. A style like that would take six months to camouflage, and it was on the cards that patrols in the area had received orders to bare the heads of any suspect ramblers they found.

But escape was not on anyone's mind today. The other cause for anxiety, which was Paulo's preoccupation, was more immediate. Above all, the *Autobahn* was supposed to be degrading. Like the stripes and the numbers replacing surnames and forgotten Christian names, it meant that the shaven men of Loibl from now on were just cattle. The *Autobahn* was the definitive mark of their slavery. This had registered with the Kapos as well, for in spite of the order, they had all gotten the best barber to shave them an imperceptible stripe which would be easy to hide. They did this partly out of homosexual vanity, but above all to avoid being confused with the riffraff.

The shaving session was unfortunately only one episode in the pursuit of humiliation. But since it took place on Sundays, just after reveille, it seemed to herald the start of the carefully planned entertainment of the day. A day of rest, the Kommandant had announced. Only the bastard had omitted to mention that the rest was for him and his tired soldiers. Not for the *Haeftlinge*, whom he turned over to the tender care of the doyen and his aides for twenty-four hours. With such conscientious deputies, the SS could drink themselves under the table without worrying. The gentlemen *Blockführer* did a good job of replacing them. They awaited this exciting day with impatience and set about enjoying themselves so thoroughly that after the first Sunday the whole Kommando was unanimous: "Christ, let's get back to work!"

Every Sunday the fits of madness began with reveille, and they were allowed to do only two things: either to trot or to stand at attention. Right up until lights out. Trotting to go to the *Waschraum*, to assemblies, to fatigues; standing frozen at attention for searches and cleanliness inspections. It was forbidden to walk, to sit down, to talk, to obstruct or duck blows, and it was compulsory to understand orders and speeches and to laugh at jokes in German.

Paulo was humiliated and angry at being forced to parade naked ten times a day, to present his prick for inspection every three hours, to square and resquare his bed, to wax his shoes with grease like a cadet, to wash his clothes without soap, to darn his socks and to mend his clothes like a girl. But he did these petty debasing tasks all the same. And he did them smiling. In order to go unnoticed, according to his plan. The dignity which he had talked about to Belloni was difficult to sustain in such ridiculous postures, but in any case he would have lost face if he had complained, because at Loibl lack of keenness meant twenty-five strokes. And to be whipped in public with your bum in the air was something of a handicap to preaching respectability. It didn't take Paulo long to realize that he would have to find a day other than Sunday to explain to the others what was going on in his mind. It was a pity, because on Sundays everyone was together, whereas during the week, his audience was limited by the separation of the work Kommandos. Especially in the tunnel's narrow thoroughfare.

One fine morning, Paulo swallowed his pride and decided to have a shot at talking frankly to the little Breton, one of the few in his crew to whom he could talk without danger.

The young man had had orders from the *Arbeitskapo* to pile up at the tunnel mouth the largest stones cut from the rock face at the tunnel mouth. As one of the pickmen, Paulo was supplying him. The Breton had to stand around doing nothing until the chunks to be carried were of a decent size. Ideal for broaching the matter. Paulo began:

"With me, you've got it easy. You won't have to worry about straining yourself; I won't give you big rocks."

The other didn't reply, but his look was encouraging. Paulo decided to spill the beans.

"I hope you don't still hold it against me for what happened on the train. We were all going crazy in there, and I didn't know Bullseye would take it out on you."

"That's okay, forget it. I've been hammered since," the Breton answered. "For Frenchmen to fight among themselves would be a pity. You probably think the same."

"That's right, but there are some Frenchmen I'd like to get my hands on. Real bastards. Pozzi, for example."

Paulo was getting straight to the point. The Breton was about to agree, but he hesitated: a villain running down another villain? It was suspect. Paulo immediately understood the reason for his hesitation, and he decided to get things straight without wasting time:

"Listen, my friend. Stop being suspicious. It's no good staying in a corner by yourself. We're all in this shit together, and we'll never get out if we keep on sulking. I trust you. I like you, you're a man. Like your friend, the old fellow. It's rare to find men in a cesspool like this. Obviously, you think I'm just a crook. But there are some here who could tell you that even before I was arrested, I always kept certain standards. And here, for the last month—"

"You don't need to go on, I know. You're right, there's no point in being resentful. But I might tell you, trusting people cost me a lot sixteen months ago."

The Breton was unwinding. He set off with three rocks of a ridiculously small size—which Paulo had managed to extract from the rock face while talking—and came back almost at a run. Paulo went on:

"Did somebody crow?"

"Crow?"

"Squeal, that means. Denounce, if you like."

"Not me personally, but my group. We were all arrested. Thanks to a would-be Englishman, a Gestapo agent."

For the first time, a fellow who was not a criminal dared to admit that his arrest had not been a mistake. The Breton must have definitely changed his opinion of Paulo to be able to talk to him so openly, because the rule in the camp was that you kept your mouth shut about your past, with the exception of burglaries or holdups. At Loibl, specialists in those had a tendency to exaggerate. Paulo kept his surprise at the Breton's frankness to himself, and laughed.

"A phony Englishman? Hey, that's funny. For me, it was a phony Belgian. Not for the same reason, as you can well imagine, but the result was no different and here we are, like a pair of idiots. What's your name?"

"Le Goff, Joel Le Goff. And you?"

"Chastagnier. Paulo, to my friends."

"I know. Your name's gotten around."

"That doesn't help much. Look, I'd rather talk to you than to those so-called heavies who spend their time saying 'I know him, he's a friend of mine.' They'd walk all over me to pick up a crust."

"Yeah, it's pretty mixed in this camp, isn't it? I leave the shits alone. I've got one friend, the teacher, the 'old fellow' as you call him. Believe me, he's all right, and his friendship's important to me."

"That's great, but it's not enough. I've got friends here too, but unfortunately it doesn't get you very far. The problem is to break out of this dump and we're not going to do it by just chatting about the good old days. Listen, I've had an idea."

Joel was preparing to carry off his next load, but he stopped dead:

"Idea for what? Escape?"

"Slow down, friend. It's more a line of reasoning than an idea. I figured there was another way of getting out of here—other than risking some stupid escape. But it depends on more than just me, and that's why I'm talking to you."

Joel Le Goff looked terribly disappointed. Sadly, he went off with his stones to the tunnel entrance, and when he came back to Paulo his excitement had gone. It was now more out of politeness that he listened to the young crook explain his theories about resisting depression and putting down roots, becoming indispensable:

"This tunnel," Paulo went on, "is our chance, our only chance, believe me. Don't do anything crazy like trying to run for it. You'd get picked up in no time with that mark on your head. We can only get out of here all together, but for that we've got to have patience and organization."

Joel heard him out and his impassive athlete's face did not betray his thoughts on this philosophy lesson. He set off again with his methodical step, a stone under each arm. He didn't want to know any more, and Paulo was relieved. He had finally spoken to the Breton. Little Joel's dignified attitude had given Paulo such an inferiority complex, and now Joel no longer despised him. Paulo suddenly felt less handicapped by his reputation as a criminal.

VII

The arrival that night of the Mauthausen reinforcements was very quickly going to disrupt Paulo's plans for caution and staying in the background. The workers in the tunnel, christened miners now that the hole was more than sixty feet deep, had quite calmly dropped their shovels, picks and wheelbarrows. Taking advantage of the absence of the

Arbeitskapo who had gone to get the latest news from the SS, they gathered around Pozzi and fired off a barrage of questions.

"How many are they?"

"Are there many Kapos with them?"

"Are they all French?" and so on.

No one had any details. The convoy had arrived well after the evening bell when they had already been asleep for two hours. But Pozzi knew a little more than the others, for that morning, just before muster, he had managed to interview Bullseye.

"Look, I didn't see them either," he was saying cautiously. "All I know is that those new boys got quite a reception. Bullseye was all in. He came back with his club, puffing and wheezing, at two o'clock this morning."

"Has his friend Fritz come?" threw in Belloni, already worried.

"Yes, Angel-face, he's here with the rest," replied Pozzi, deliberately adding, "He's already made inquiries about the specialties of you French hustlers. You've got a chance . . ."

Angel paled at the insult. He walked menacingly toward Pozzi, but he was forestalled. Paulo had just shut up the caretaker with a lightning backhand swipe. After a month of forced labor, his hand had become more calloused than a professional navvy's. Blood instantly ran from Pozzi's split lips.

"You filthy bastard," mumbled the ex-caretaker, holding a hand to his mouth. "Just because there aren't any Kapos around."

It was quite true. Paulo had jumped at the opportunity. Somebody had to teach this misguided collaborator a lesson, and quickly. The slap on the mouth was his first warning. Pozzi's dirty innuendos stopped, but his shifty expression clearly indicated this wasn't the last they would hear of the affair. Paulo had no illusions about what was in store. Beatings would be coming his way in the days ahead, and doubtless Belloni would have his turn too. Anxious to recover face, Pozzi went to retrieve his pick, and the rest followed suit. The press conference was over.

For the next five hours the only sounds to be heard in the dusty tunnel were the creaking of wheelbarrows and the scraping of shovels. No one dared to speak, but Paulo knew that inside their shaven skulls they were all thinking about him. He had just taken a big risk, but it was necessary. The business of the slap might perhaps encourage a few of the men. They might stick it out, and the more they stuck it out, the less the SS would try to replace them. Other reinforcements might come, but it wouldn't be to relieve them. In any case the SS would hardly be able to make a relief team out of the specimens the men had finally seen at the roll call following soup distribution. The new boys didn't look as if they were up to much. They were as emaciated as the others, but a ghastly white color, like aspirin tablets. Like phantoms. They looked as if death had stroked them a little too closely at Mauthausen. Their pupils were abnormally dilated and their eyes glittered. The eyes of shocked hostages, of terrorized men. Some of their mouths were half open, like dead men's mouths, still gaping because no one has had the time to do them the last service.

And yet these shadows of men must have had uncommon powers of resistance to have lasted out a month longer in the hell of the quarantine.

In fact here and there one could make out a few survivors of the train from Compiègne. Out of two thousand, of course, it wasn't a lot. Barely a hundred or a hundred and twenty at the very most. The other half of the contingent looked as if they might be Polish, but how do you tell a man's nationality when his head's shaven and he only weighs ninety pounds? On the other hand, the Kapos, even without their caps, were easily recognized by their girth. One in particular was as wide as he was tall, and he was whirling over his head his own version of a Kapo's life preserver—a long length of light-green garden hose. Paulo realized immediately that this must be the terrible Fritz, whose reputation had preceded him. Sailor was like a dog with two tails at being reunited with his friend.

"Allow me to introduce you," he announced to the men gathered at attention in front of his block.

This was one joke they didn't feel like laughing at. In Block 3, as in the other two original blocks, everyone's thoughts were elsewhere. They were thinking of when they would finally be able to talk to the newcomers, to hug a friend they thought they had recognized, and above all to get some news of the war, perhaps even of France.

But first they had to wait for Fritz, escorted by the doyen

and the full complement of block chiefs, to meet all the prisoners, both veterans and novices. There were now almost six hundred heads. Handshakes were replaced by the green hose, but this was tolerable because when the doyen arrived at the last row of Block 1, he yelled at the top of his voice:

"Dismissed! Assemble for general muster in twenty minutes!"

Belloni and Paulo pushed their way through the crowd of pallid ghosts whose striped uniforms were still tainted with the smell of the crematorium, trying to find a friendly face. Without success. It was obvious that their only contacts in civilian life, the crooks, had been unable to tolerate their re-education; their ashes were now probably sprinkled on the banks of the Danube.

"Well, in the end I suppose that's justice," Paulo shrugged, by way of a funeral oration. "Judging by the way the others are carrying on here, those guys wouldn't have been much use. We're better off with a few eager yokels."

Belloni suddenly tugged at his sleeve.

"Look over there, don't you recognize him?"

Paulo looked across the sea of striped caps.

"Look, there he is, it's old Pépé," and Angel threw his arms around the neck of a skinny old man, who wept with joy.

"Angel, my boy, you look well," said Pépé. "It looks all right here. And Paulo, you're here too, you rogue. This camp must be like Mégève, you're all tanned! And what's the food like?"

"Same as where you've come from," answered Paulo. "Only here you sweat it before you can piss it and you get beaten into the middle of next week every day. There's only one good thing about it, everyone's got his own bed. That's the only reason you see us still standing up. Not everybody, though. Some are going to take your places at Mauthausen, where they'll be nice and warm. Let me give you just one bit of advice: dig yourself in."

"You can count on me," replied Pépé. His haunted look had returned. "I saw them turn their toes up one after the other, Joe, Pablo, Gaston, Gégé, young and old, everyone, they made a bonfire out of the crooks. If we ever get out of here, we certainly won't be short of jobs."

"And what about the fucking war?" asked Paulo, quite indifferent to the list of associates who had gone up in smoke.

"It goes on. Everywhere, in Russia, Africa, Asia. There's no end to it."

Pépé, who had knocked about quite a bit, was better in geography than in history. Military campaigns were not a great specialty of his. That was all he knew. Paulo dropped him there and he and Belloni went off in search of news.

"Did you notice?" remarked Angel. "Pépé's still got his golden ivories. Must be worth quite a bit."

No doubt about it, the apprentice crook was still as down-to-earth as ever. Of course Paulo had noticed. After all, such a sunny smile could hardly go unremarked; all the old fellow's teeth—canines, incisors, and molars—were in twenty-two-carat gold. Of course Belloni was right, it was surprising that Pépé had managed to keep his teeth after four months in the citadel, but it was not the sort of problem that was exercising Paulo at the moment.

"The jokes obviously weren't funny enough to make him grin. That's why they didn't spot his nuggets," he answered. But Angel had let him down, and he felt like sitting on him.

"You're beyond hope, kid. Instead of trying to find out what's going on in this fucking war, all you can think about is Pépé's golden ivories. If he wants to pawn his nuggets he doesn't need you. Sailor will make friends with him, and that's that. Stop dreaming."

Smarting from the rebuke, Belloni pretended to have spotted another associate and he left Paulo to continue his newspaper chase on his own. Just then, Paulo noticed a group of men standing near Block 3, deep in conversation. Among them were Joel, the old Basque and three newcomers whom he thought he vaguely recognized.

"Weren't you all in Block Seventeen?" he asked, to break into the conversation.

"Yes, I was," answered the youngest-looking of them. "You too?"

"Yes," said Paulo, "I remember you now."

He didn't remember him at all, but he didn't care. He hadn't paid attention to anybody at Mauthausen, he hadn't cared if his neighbors died. But here anybody might be useful, and it was just as well to be friendly to Joel's pals. It didn't look as if somebody had made a mistake in arresting these three. You could see real determination beneath their pale, drawn features.

"Are you from Paname?" asked Paulo, feeling awkward in the silence which had greeted his arrival.

"No, man," Joel cut in. "They're all from the country. Us Bretons have got thick skins. Haven't we?" and he grabbed his three friends in a bear-hug, butting their shaven heads with his own.

"They've got guts," thought Paulo. "We could do with a few more like them," and trying to fall into step with them, he said, "Tough nuts like you don't crack easily, but between ourselves, your sort's thin on the ground. Good thing you came."

"According to what we've heard, it's no holiday camp here," said the oldest of the three.

"Maybe not," answered Paulo. "But at least time's on our side here. Digging a tunnel takes longer than shithouse duty."

"That's true," Joel added. "Paulo's right, we're lucky to have a tunnel to dig."

"It doesn't seem to be making you very happy," the youngest of the three remarked. "There must be a catch to your paradise. Give us the whole story."

As Joel remained silent, Paulo felt obliged to explain a bit more. "The catch is, you've got to be able to run, and to stand up to beatings. In fact, Loibl Pass is just like a boxing ring."

They all began to laugh, which saved Paulo from having to add that the SS of Kommando X didn't tolerate any deadwood and that those who couldn't keep up with the rest would be chopped off instantly. It was hardly the right moment to explain that kind of detail to these men. They had just had a miraculous escape from the "bone mill," as the Spanish veterans used to call Mauthausen. For the three Bretons, Loibl was a sort of reward, a free pardon even. To come out alive after four months in quarantine seemed firm proof of divine mercy—as if the clumsy executioner had missed their heads on the block. Paulo took care not to destroy their illusions. Besides, he had not joined the group to sow the seeds of panic, unlike some ignorant inmates who were delighted to frighten the new boys, by proudly showing off their livid backs and their split eyebrows, adding comments like "It's ten times worse than Cayenne."

Well, of course it was ten times worse than Cayenne, but the newcomers would find that out for themselves all too quickly. No point in sapping the morale of these fellows, who had come to put their shoulders to the wheel, on their first day.

"The bastards! Stupid cunts," thought Paulo, and he deliberately took the opposite tack.

"They're putting it on. Don't listen to those loudmouths. They're real creampuffs. Before they got here, three quarters of them had never had anything worse than a slap from the wife. Twenty-five strokes on the bum is a bit of a change from a rolling pin, but these softies seem to have suddenly forgotten where we've all come from. In this place, when you turn on the tap in the washroom, you know it's water that's going to come out, and not gas. There isn't any here. Surely it's worth suffering a few extra beatings for that. Don't you think?"

"Yeah, he's right," Joel and the Basque chimed in together, who alone had noticed that Paulo's optimism was a little forced. The three newcomers had been completely carried away by it. The tall man with his unshakable morale reassured them, and this Yugoslavian copy of Cayenne could not be as dreadful as they had heard.

They had only five minutes to go before assembly and Paulo, now that he had played his part in showing them the brighter side of things, felt it was time to see what he could do about raising his own spirits. Nonchalantly, because everything hinged on the reply, he asked in what he hoped was a casual tone, "How are things in France? Have you heard anything recently?"

"The Germans have had it. Peace will be signed before Christmas," replied the youngest of the Bretons, the one they called Dédé. He had spoken the last words quietly, but with such conviction that it sounded like an official communiqué. Paulo stiffened. Before Christmas! The morale booster had just met his match, and the new man seemed to know what he was talking about. "It's all over on the Eastern Front," Dédé was explaining. "According to what I last heard, the

Russians are attacking all along the line from Leningrad to the Black Sea. And it's only a matter of days before the Allies invade."

He spoke unequivocally. And while he filled in the background to each of his claims, Paulo looked at him closely. A fellow who could seriously predict demobilization before six months were out was worth a second look. Either this fellow had gone completely around the bend at Mauthausen or he really was intelligent and objective, in which case what he said changed everything. Was his high forehead a sign of a superior intellect, or was it just that his head had become swollen with the blows of the clubs?

"The German generals are trying to make contact with the British in Sweden and in Switzerland, to conclude an honorable peace," continued the Breton with the sage's head. He had lowered his voice, looking around in case anyone was eavesdropping. Paulo wasn't listening anymore. He was miles away, calculating furiously: before Christmas . . . in six months, perhaps five months . . . ?

"Madness . . . this boy's insane," thought Paulo, his heart beginning to race, but the more he studied the boy, the less mad he seemed to be. The optimistic Dédé was quite normal. He showed no excitement as he dropped his bombshells. It didn't even seem to make him particularly happy. To hear him talk, you would think the chips had been down for a long time. Apparently the war wasn't news, it was history.

"He really doesn't look crazy," Paulo said to himself, still unable to get over someone saying these fantastic things in such a detached way. The destruction of Germany, peace in a few months' time: it was the commentary of a BBC announcer ensconced in an armchair in his London studio. Coming from someone who only two days ago had still been at Mauthausen, it struck a strange note. Yet there were no two ways about it, this Breton called Dédé was quite serious. His friends, at any rate, certainly didn't seem to consider him a practical joker. Nor did the old Basque. Paulo didn't know how to take all this. Should he yell for joy? Feign the skeptic to find out more? He preferred to keep both his excitement and his questions to himself. He felt positively out of place as soon as he found himself among people who were neither thieves nor pimps. He suddenly felt like slipping away quietly, without a word, to go and find Belloni or Pépé, or anyone else with whom he would be more at ease than with these strange types who were discussing war and peace as if there were something they could do about it.

"What am I doing among these choirboys?" he thought. "I'm letting myself get carried away by their bloody nonsense. The Russians, the Yanks, peace, what do they know about it all? Even Hitler doesn't know." Abruptly, he broke into Dédé's lofty discourse.

"You're going a bit too quick, friend. The Krauts here in this camp can't have heard all your secrets, or they'd be a bit friendlier."

The Breton didn't answer, and his friends pretended not to have heard. Paulo immediately regretted his hasty remark. He had said it without thinking, to try and find out the truth. He was more than happy to hear, for the first time in a long while, words of hope, even if they were only hot air. In his and everyone else's situation, good news could not do any harm. He gave Joel a hearty slap on the back and burst out laughing.

"He's terrific, your pal. We'll have to fix it so that he works with us in the tunnel. We won't get half so pissed off; it'll be like we were knocking back a few drinks in the Café du Commerce."

The Breton strategists didn't seem to have a sense of humor. They carried on their discussion without paying any attention to Paulo.

This time, the young crook felt distinctly uncomfortable. He would have liked to hear the whistle blow for assembly, to rescue him from his embarrassment. But SS and Kapos from the two convoys must also have had a lot to tell each other. The rest period went on, and Dédé with the big head was able to continue his military lecture unhurriedly.

"The Germans made a mistake in wanting to occupy the whole of Europe. Now they've succeeded in seizing it all, they'd do better to withdraw. The number of their troops immobilized everywhere is stretching them to their limit, and those troops have lost the fighting habit; they're getting spoiled by too much contact with civilians. They're going to need those men elsewhere. Quite soon, believe me."

That wasn't so stupid. Paulo hadn't thought of it, but was beginning to see that everything Dédé said was logical.

"What the hell does this kid do for a living normally?"

wondered Paulo. "He's younger than me, he must still be a student." And he examined the lecturer even more closely. The boy was definitely going to get himself noticed very quickly at Loibl. For a start, his sententious volubility. Then, his registration number was too easy to remember: 27,000 exactly, three zeros. Bad luck when you're held prisoner by illiterates. With that tag on his wrist and on his jacket, he'd be easy game for all duties. The Breton intellectual was going to find himself constantly emptying barrels of shit, and he'd be in for more than his fair share of beatings.

"While we're on the subject," thought Paulo, "I know somebody else who'd do well to watch out."

The arrival of the newcomers had made him completely forget what had happened that morning. Where was Pozzi? The traitor was not to be seen among the groups standing around. Obviously a double-crossing bastard like him couldn't have that many friends, and that was surely why the squealer hadn't hung around on the *Appelplatz*. But it was highly likely, too, that he had taken advantage of the break to go and make his report to Bullseye.

"I bet there'll be some action before long," Paulo said to himself. Already, he saw himself over the stool. That was worse than anything. He'd far rather get the riding crop on his neck or the boot in his stomach than this queer's idea of punishment for public schoolboys. He could no longer stand having to take his trousers down in front of a hundred men.

"I should have left Belloni to settle his own affairs. What a cunt I am, a real cunt," he grumbled to himself.

He had perfected a plan for survival, and now at the very first provocation, he was losing his self-control. He was a fine one to preach underground resistance! Paulo Chastagnier was not grown up enough to play at being network boss. He'd better leave things like initiative to Dédé and his friends. They would know how to avoid getting involved with informers. Looking back, he realized his scuffle must have appeared to people like the Basque and perhaps even Joel as a crooks' wrangle: "I got the insult, you get the fist." Nothing more than that.

"And all that, just for Belloni," he complained bitterly to himself. He no longer heard Dédé's comforting news, which had so encouraged him only a little while ago. He could only think about his immediate problem, the twenty-five strokes and the rest which was certainly in store for him. Going against his rules, he had gotten himself noticed by sticking his neck out to defend the honor of that little creep Belloni, that louse already written off by everyone, screws and jailbirds alike. The petty crook from Cannes was a dead loss. He had to be dumped overboard and quickly, now that Armistice Day was a more likely prospect, a clear outline on the horizon. If he only had to wait six months longer, it was even more imperative to melt into the mass, to stifle his feelings and to blend completely into the background. Whether or not it was because he had been impressed by Dédé's logic and maturity, for a few moments now his desire to play the morale booster had subsided. He felt diminished by these men whose problems hadn't changed: at liberty to fight underground or imprisoned at Mauthausen and now at Loibl, it was still a question of war, and resistance. Right from the start, one thing only had motivated them: the fight against the Germans. The floggings, the torture, the starvation diet, the execution squads, the crematorium—all everyday things for men who cared passionately about the war. At the moment of reckoning, a man like that would shout "*Vive la France*" or try to break into the "Marseillaise," whereas even the bravest criminal has nothing to shout for. Paulo had thought up his own exit line, in case they decided to shoot him or hang him from a meat hook like the Yugoslavs at Mauthausen, but his line—"Bunch of fuckers!"—wasn't altogether satisfactory. An insult like that spurs on the executioner without troubling his conscience. It's no no use. Paulo had just realized that even in death he would not find release. "I'm hardly unique, though," he said to himself, "here alone, there are six hundred of us. They're not all shining heroes in this bunch. Not by any means. There's a whole load of jerks and tramps who don't give a shit about the war. What would those guys yell before they were knocked off? '*Vive la France!*' or 'Bunch of fuckers!' It'd be interesting to see."

But Paulo was not stupid. He knew perfectly well what each one's reaction would be. There would be a handful of men who would stand stiffly at attention and look straight down the gun barrels; there would be others, who still hadn't understood anything, begging on their knees for mercy. And finally some, like himself, would search for the vilest insult in their vocabulary, or spit in the faces of the trigger-happy firing squad. Out of these three ways of dying, which was the finest? The first way of course, but to win a death of such dignity he ought to have done something about it sooner. Too late again, Paulo.

In the end the men to be truly pitied in this upside-down world were the villains. Traditionally they write their own rules in prison, and if one morning they climb onto the scaffold, they have to put on a good performance. They take their time and shout: "Long live anarchy," "My head to the executioner, my heart to Mother, and my prick to the whores," the old prison chorus. In SS prisons, this sort of line was a guaranteed flop. Nobody believed in tigers in striped pajamas anymore. They had fallen much further than the bourgeois deprived of his slippers and his fireside comfort, further than the officer in ragged uniform, than the peasant with his empty stomach, than everybody. By stripping them of their one strength, their talent for frightening people, the SS had reduced them to being good for nothing, utterly inept and miserable, shits who could be slapped, stripped, even fucked. A bitter and hopeless end.

The whistle for assembly snapped Paulo out of his depressing thoughts. Followed by Joel and the Basque, he ran to take his place by the perimeter fence near the exit. Pozzi was already there in the first row, just in front of Angel Belloni. When he saw Paulo arrive, his perjurer's face lit up.

"The fucker," thought Paulo. "He's already squealed. The reprisals will start any minute now."

Sure enough, it was not long coming. Bullseye was also there, lining them up, and he took Belloni as his scapegoat. A backhander with his fist in the boy's face, followed by a short hook to his ear and a good right in his gut to make the boy double up, leaving the back of his neck open to the real work of hammer blows all over as Bullseye bellowed his anger. Paulo held himself more rigidly at attention, not daring to look. But that didn't make any difference. The line-up was only a pretext and soon he took over from Belloni. This time the rubber hose was used, because Paulo was too tall for Bullseye's fists. He didn't flinch under the ever-stronger hail of blows and the diversion might have gone on for a long time if the barbed-wire gates hadn't opened at the same time as the order to march was given. The tunnel couldn't wait, and Bullseye's empire stopped at the gates.

"Till this evening, *mein lieber Mensch*," hissed the cyclops, putting away his club.

There was no longer any doubt, it was official; Pozzi had gone over to the enemy. He was more dangerous than a Kapo, more dangerous than an SS officer, because he was always going to be around, at work in the tunnel, in the blocks, listening, reporting.

"I'll get rid of him myself," Paulo swore to himself in a low voice. But he couldn't stifle his fury and as soon as they were on the road, he leaned toward the traitor and spat in his ear:

"You filthy son of a bitch, I swear to you, you'll never get out of here alive."

He instantly regretted his ill-judged reaction. He had to shut up right to the end. He'd get his revenge, and he would have six months to savor it all the more. Now he had his reason, he'd found a motive for being in this prison: he had nothing to envy his Resistance friends for. If they shot him now, he knew what to yell: "Pozzi is a fucker." The others could take this as his last testament. In the meantime, no more slip-ups. No matter how extreme the provocation, Paulo would not react.

It wasn't long before he was put to the test, for hardly had the Kommando arrived at the tunnel when the concierge-collaborator brushed past him to fetch his pick and hissed with a smirk on his swollen lips:

"You stuck up really well for your fairy friend in front of Bullseye, didn't you?"

Paulo hadn't expected an attack quite so soon. In spite of his surprise, he managed to control himself, but he had reckoned without Belloni. The kid had heard every word, and he ran forward, shouting:

"Fairy! I'll show you who's a fairy!"

Paulo saw that a fight was inevitable if he didn't step in. Already Angel was moving in fast with his fists up. Paulo hauled him back just as he got to Pozzi.

"Leave me alone! I'm going to teach that queer a lesson," cried the boy. But Paulo had pinned his arms, and Pozzi used the delay to run off. Paulo let go his grasp only when

Pozzi had reached the rock face at the end. Belloni was beside himself.

"What's got into you?" he demanded, almost sobbing with rage. "You're mad. He was shitting on me, I'll kill the fucker, he's mine, I'll kill him."

"Don't you ever learn anything? Can't you remember the thrashing you got just now? And what's waiting for us when we get back? Do you want your funeral today? I'm not in any hurry. I'm onto Pozzi too, and I'll get him someday. I'm going to slice that filthy scab into little bits. Paulo's word on it. I'll wait a year if I have to."

"What about me?" demanded Angel, calmer now and feeling foolish after what Paulo had just said.

"Just pipe down. You're doing one lunatic thing after another. Either you listen to what I tell you or you find yourself another mate. I've had enough of hotheads, of pipsqueaks who think they're still in Pigalle. You can't see it, can you? Settling hash is out of date. I don't want to hear any more about you and your gangsters. D'you hear? Instead of hanging around with old Pépé, you'd have done better to listen to the Bretons who've just arrived. Now they've got guts, but they don't use them for brawling."

Paulo was exaggerating on purpose. The Bretons had not affected him to that extent, but he felt it was essential to sit on his young friend, to get him to keep his mouth shut. The kid went off dejectedly with his shovel to load Jo from Oran's wheelbarrow. Paulo seized the chance to approach Joel, who for once was separated from his Basque friend. The *Arbeitskapo* had kicked him out of his élite corps. The old man was working outside in the sun now, with the tree carriers, the unskilled workers—favorite targets of the excitable SS.

"Mind if I team up with you?" Paulo asked.

"Don't be stupid," answered Joel and, seeing the marks left on Paulo's cheeks by Bullseye's club, he added: "Is that because of Pozzi?"

"Yeah, but it's not important. I don't feel them anymore. And anyway, it may be useful. Now everyone knows they've got to watch it with that shit around."

"He'll have to pay for it on the day of liberation," replied Joel flatly.

"Speaking of liberation, do you believe all those things your friend Dédé said?"

"I have to, to some extent. He knows what he's talking about. The war's his field. He's reassuring to have around."

"Well, if what he says is true, we'll have to keep him with us. Is he a student?"

"Yes, a science student. At Rennes, like me. I'll tell you about him someday. We've got a lot of shared memories, us two. Do you know the hotel Lutétia, on the boulevard Raspail in Paris? I'll tell you about that, too. Dédé and I are like brothers."

Paulo would have liked to know a bit more about the astonishing Dédé, who had given him new hope. But he felt that Joel already regretted having said so much, and to put his companion at ease he changed the subject.

"Don't you get the feeling we're going to have an easy afternoon? It's been quite a while since we've seen any sign of a Kapo."

"You're right, they must all be with the newcomers. It's typical of them to want to put the wind up the new arrivals. Remember the frantic reception they gave us on our first day at Mauthausen? I thought for a moment it was a joke, that it was Mardi Gras and that the guys already there had gotten themselves dressed up to give us a laugh."

"That's true, I'd forgotten. For a good two hours after we arrived I couldn't stop laughing, and I wasn't the only one. When I think that already it's four months since all this started, four months of this crazy life where you run around like frightened rabbits from morning till night. I feel as if this merry-go-round could go on forever. Don't you?"

"Oh, it's not that bad. What's happened to you, Paulo? I thought you were made of steel. You're putting me on."

"I've been thinking. I've noticed that you and your buddies are making a better job of hanging on than me."

"Well, we all have our good moments and our bad moments. I'm not proud of myself all the time."

"I'm ashamed of myself day and night. It's because I haven't got anything to fight for that I feel so damned awful. Whereas you've got something to hold out for. I don't honestly give a fuck about your patriotism and the war. But I have to admit that it seems to be good medicine. When your Basque friend gets a beating, you'd think he was a Christian martyr."

"Etcheverry? A Christian! Good Lord no, Lenin's his god. He's been in the Party for thirty years."

"You're joking. That old man a commie? And you and Dédé—you commies too?"

"Certainly not, but we think the same way as Etcheverry about many things: the war, the Resistance, those things you say you don't give a fuck about."

Joel had gently rebuffed Paulo and the young crook couldn't help but acknowledge it.

"Sorry," Paulo replied. "I didn't mean to annoy you. But I'll always be amazed to see guys like you sticking their necks out for the sake of rotten bastards who can only think about lining their pockets."

Paulo's voice had risen almost to a shout.

"Not so loud! Calm down," Joel interrupted him hastily. "But refusing to fight hasn't got you much further. You're no better off than me now."

"Maybe, but at least I've had the satisfaction of making marshmallows out of a few of them before I got caught. I had a great time for two years. If I don't survive, at least I'll have had some fun. There are a few who'll miss me when I'm dead, like the collectors of *louis d'or,* whose lovely cash bought me my food and my good times."

"I had my satisfactions too, but of a different kind," Joel cut in, drily.

They were on the point of a quarrel. But Paulo, for one, didn't want to argue. He was too happy to at last be talking about something other than soup with one of the few men he could respect in this mass of nonentities. A little earlier, he had begun to admit that he was worried about his own standards. By standards, he meant his conscience, and he knew that the gym teacher had understood the nuance. So why did he, once again and so clumsily, have to cross swords with the idealistic Joel by claiming out of sheer bravado that he was proud of his past as a gangster? What good could that do him since, deep inside, he knew what he really thought about things. If he had been less arrogant and less prone to showing off, he would simply have said to his workmate: "Listen, friend, I've got a confession to make. I'm unhappy, and I know why: it's because I've done nothing with my life."

Such a total confession, even with no one else to hear it in the half-light of the tunnel, was beyond him. He couldn't bring himself to do it, but neither should he pass up this unexpected opportunity on a quiet afternoon, to make Joel and his friends understand that they could count themselves one extra. Paulo swallowed his pride, and pretending not to have noticed the clipped and final tone with which the Breton had cut him off, he continued as if nothing had happened.

"Just look at us standing here chatting, and getting worked up about things, and we haven't even noticed that for a good hour they haven't been in here once to check up on us. Don't you think that's good news. Instead of arguing about stupid things, we should be congratulating ourselves. Nice tunnel, very shady, an easy life."

Joel remained silent. Paulo persisted.

"For the first time in four months, we're doing okay. That's all that matters. You know, I understand your kind of satisfaction, but I'm still looking for something to achieve. I've got to understand what I'm doing here. For you it's straightforward. You knew what was coming to you, and now you accept it. I'm trying to accept it too, but since I didn't really ask for it, I have to invent my own reasons and I fall back on my memories. Thinking about the faces of those rotten bastards I screwed makes me feel better. Now and again, I burst out laughing when I think of their mugs. It does me good."

"Okay, laugh away," answered Joel, unconvinced.

"Come on, Joel, you're not going to sulk," Paulo continued, ready to make all kinds of allowances. "What a face! Unwind a bit, say anything you like, but at least talk while you can. Think about the others who are scurrying around outside in the sun, in broad daylight where they're easy targets. I'm enjoying this. I'd be quite happy to spend the next six months here in the dark. Even with a bundle of fun like you."

Paulo was almost softening. Joel couldn't help smiling. Realizing that he had won, Paulo continued.

"You don't have to take everything I say literally. After all, I can't really spit on my past simply because I get punched from the train stop to the front door and have to go without pudding. If I suddenly began to think like a rosy-cheeked boy scout, I'd look like a fairy. No, I don't regret anything I've done. I only regret what I haven't done. Do you get me?"

"Yeah, I get you, but I was still right earlier. What I've

done, what you haven't done, any way you look at it, we've come to the same point, as far as the future goes at any rate—"

"Yes, the future," interrupted Paulo. "That's just what's worrying me, and I have to admit that since your optimistic friends arrived, I'm much more cheerful about it. Now I feel I'm not the only one who wants to do something constructive. It was about time that they showed up, your Breton friends, because apart from you and your old fellow, I've found hardly any men with any determination. I don't think much of Belloni or those Corsican brothers anymore. They follow the leader, like everyone else, and there's no room in their brains for anything except soup. It's depressing."

"You're hard on people, Paulo."

"Hard on myself too. I have some awful moments but at least I don't just think about filling my mess bowl. Those grabbers spend all their time thinking about stuffing their faces. Not me. My dreams are about women, and freedom. For the first time it's all becoming clearer. I'm on my feet again. I'm doing all right, and I can't understand why today of all days you look as if you're going to a funeral. Things have changed, don't you see?"

"I don't see how."

"You don't see? You must be blind! The difference is that since this morning, I know where we are. If the gunfire stops before six months are out, we're saved, d'you hear? Saved. When the Armistice comes, she'll find us right here."

"Armistice is 'it,' not 'she.'"

"He, she, it, I don't give a fuck," answered Paulo, whose enthusiasm was irrepressible. "When the Armistice comes, I'll be in great shape. I feel so confident about it I could go without food for six months and dig this tunnel on my own. They're bound to keep us here now. Their tunnel has become too important for them to retreat from Italy, or maybe they could even hide out there if the Cossacks advance too fast. The worse things get for them, the more they'll need us. Oh, I'm going to look after their tunnel as if it were my own, believe me."

There was no stopping Paulo now, and his enthusiasm was infectious. Joel couldn't sulk anymore. Instead he remarked ironically:

"You make Dédé look like a prophet of doom, Paulo. I think I'd rather do my six months with you."

"No need to take the piss. We're all going to do them together. The more optimists we are, the better it'll be. We'll leave the rabble to carry on chasing soup and we, my friend, will become professionals. Paul Chastagnier—twenty-eight thousand two hundred and fourteen, profession? Miner. Joel Le Goff? Miner. Dédé . . ."

"Ménard's his name," interrupted the Breton. "No need to worry about a specialty for him, he can turn his hand to anything: physics, chemistry, electrics, explosives, radio transmitters, you name it."

"Be better if he kept quiet about all that, but an electrician is useful to have around. The SS love that kind of thing. What a pity we'll all be out of here before the tunnel's wired up. We'll have to find something else for him to do. Bricklayer wouldn't be bad. We'll need a few of them. I can just see him at the head of a cement mixer, calculating the mixture of sand and cement down to the last grain. Blacksmith too, they're always handy . . ."

This last image made Joel guffaw, and Paulo joined in. Had a Kapo come into the tunnel at that moment, he would have been amazed to see these two prisoners doubled up with laughter. "They must have gone off their heads," he would have thought.

But the Kapos were working too hard outside, and the two convicts hadn't gone off their heads at all. It was just that they were happy with their findings, especially Paulo. His idea stood up to scrutiny. The Krauts would certainly think twice before sending a good tunneler or bricklayer back to Mauthausen. On the other hand, reserves of barbers, cooks, chambermaids and boys for rent, were overflowing. If this was a representative cross section, all half of Europe did was cut the other half's hair or cook its meals.

"There's only one hitch," said Joel, sobering up. "These gentlemen are soon going to discover that we're complete beginners. We'll have to compensate for our lack of training by being eager—in other words, working twice as hard as the others. And with the little they give us to eat . . ."

"We can compromise. Between ourselves, there's nothing magic about digging a hole. I noticed immediately that you, for example, manage very well. You must get it from being an athlete. Your pickax looks as well balanced as a javelin. In fact, I've been copying you and it works: I'm using ten times less energy. I'll tell you something else as well: if it weren't for the other shit that goes down here—the food, the stool, and the hounding—I'd quite like being a laborer. I find manual work quite satisfying. I've never tried it before."

"You're a strange fellow, Paulo. Your friends would be amazed to hear you talk like this. I thought the hard labor was what they hated most at Loibl. Even more than the punishments and humiliations."

"My friends can go to hell," Paulo answered, annoyed that Joel had mentioned them. "They don't feel strongly about anything anymore. Even getting fucked."

"Not all of them. You're being unfair, Paulo."

"Okay, not all of them. There are some who are still all right, but you see, their attitudes get me down. I have nothing to say to them, whereas with you I can discuss things, it's constructive. I feel alive again since this morning."

It was evident that Paulo had come to life again. He was talking, joking, making the most of things. He looked animated, his voice had changed. It was as if he had rediscovered the youth which he'd had to grow out of too quickly. But his liking for Joel, which seemed to be returned, could not alone explain his sudden good humor. There was something else. There was Dédé and what he had said during the lunch break, the great news of an early end to the war, and all the agreeable and exciting prospects it brought with it. Paulo began to think again of Dédé, that prisoner turned good prophet, who was at this moment outside, getting to know the local SS better with each blow on his skinny back.

"Let's just hope they don't knock him off," he said out loud.

"Knock who off?" asked Joel, surprised. He hadn't followed Paulo's complicated train of thought, but he quickly guessed whom Paulo was talking about: "You mean Dédé?"

"Yes, I'm worried that he's not in this gallery with us. If he gets too beaten up he's so slight he's bound to be sent to the *Revier*."

"He's not very well built, I'll admit, but when it comes to endurance he can take care of himself. Seriously."

"A guy like that amazes me. At first, I thought he was a

bit cracked. It didn't seem normal to be able to smile in this miserable dump. I haven't seen you smile for a month, Joel."

"You're right—my morale has taken a bad blow here. It's ridiculous, but even at Mauthausen I found things less gloomy. Perhaps I just didn't see what was going on. I think I need Dédé even more than you do. You see, even if things get worse, he won't give up, he'll keep smiling right to the end."

"That'll cost him extra clubbings."

"He doesn't care. You don't know him. It's not extra soup or extra beatings, it's his hunger for life that counts. I try to forget that we shouldn't be here, but Dédé remembers and counts every second."

"I count the seconds too, but not in the same way. I'm only interested in how many are left. I don't give a shit for the past."

"You're wrong, Paulo. Don't you see that this is extra life for you too, because they need roads and tunnels. Otherwise you'd still be in the gasworks. And if you get out, you'll have to tell the story of what you saw there. It's your duty. You've got no right now to say that you don't give a shit about the past. Your recent past, at least, isn't something to blush about."

It was a bit overdone, but the forced tone suited Paulo. Besides, there was some truth in what Joel said: to come out of Mauthausen alive, to have escaped the barbaric slaughter, gave you some rights. And Paulo was fed up with feeling guilty that he couldn't wear his past with as much pride as Joel and his friends. He was tired of conversations where his past faults were continually dragged out from under the carpet. From now on, his past, as Joel said, began at Mauthausen. At the first snip of the clippers or the first smack of the riding crop, it didn't matter.

"I agree," he exclaimed, "Mauthausen was no piece of cake. They'll have to decorate us when we get back. Pimps and all."

"You can joke, but I'm serious. The ones who get back, shits included, will see life in a different light. They'll have redeemed themselves without noticing it. Holding out against the crematorium is a mark of honor."

Rights and honor? Joel was sounding pompous. What kind of mark of honor? Proof of patriotism? All the same, thought Paulo, these courageous Bretons who had taken every risk were hardly of the same stamp as the mediocre civilians arrested on the doorsteps of their shops, like that butcher from Lyon who had arrived at Mauthausen with his apron still spattered with blood. The famine-monger had barely had time to throw down his meatax, and Lyon housewives certainly wouldn't miss him much. He'd had it coming to him, the onetime fat slob who had moaned and proclaimed his innocence incessantly after he arrived at Compiègne.

Another who deserved what he got was Serpette, a retarded farmhand from Mayenne who had been nicked even more idiotically. He had literally begged for his punishment, the dimwit, but at least he didn't complain. This pantomime seemed rather to amuse him. His story was so farfetched that in spite of the forbidding atmosphere at Compiègne, they had all told each other the story again and again, and everybody knew it. And at the time, it had made them helpless with laughter.

Serpette had been hanging around Laval station when a large group of civilians disappearing into the station buffet had attracted his attention. Buffet, in his pinhead, meant grub. And obviously such a rush meant grub without ration cards, courtesy of the National Relief Society. He was so hungry he failed to notice that the civilians were being propelled into the buffet by gun butts, and that in front of the door, slammed shut on the last man in, two mean-looking *Feldwebel* in helmets, with submachine guns at their waists and grenades at their belts, barred the way. Serpette had pleaded with them, tears in his eyes. The irritated guards' shouts of "*Raus*" failed to shake him off. He'd even taken out his ration card to persuade them that everything was in order, that he too was entitled to the free handout. Bad luck, the door didn't open. *Raus* and *weg* meant nothing to the illiterate Serpette, and he was so insistent that eventually one of the exasperated sentries had grabbed him by the scruff of his neck and sent him flying into the middle of the room. So Serpette had gotten his free meal—but only two days later at Mauthausen, after he had been shaved, washed, deloused and given, as a bonus, a nice striped pair of blue and white pajamas. His first pair ever.

That was his story of resistance. It was simple, but it didn't seem fair that the poor fellow and his friend, the "I'm-not-involved-in-politics" butcher, and all the others, pimps and bookies, picked up on their own premises, should undergo the same fate as the spies, the saboteurs who derailed trains and the cowardly terrorists who pitched grenades into German barracks. There was no justice anymore. And the innocent men were liberal with their insults at first: at Compiègne and in the livestock cars they spat at the bastards they held responsible—"If you hadn't been so fucking eager to meddle, we wouldn't be here." Before leaving Compiègne, these easy consciences would have liked to denounce the commies and Gaullists who had brought them such misfortune. Like schoolboys threatened with a caning for the whole class, elbowing the troublemakers toward the headmaster, so that he would punish only the culprits.

And now it was the turn of these dog-in-the-manger communists—who had been avoided like the plague, and sometimes even denounced, by people who didn't want trouble in their apartment building—to have the last laugh. Sweet revenge for these pariahs to find themselves camouflaged, and hidden in the crowd which proclaimed itself innocent. Unhappily for the whited sepulchres, the Krauts could not be bothered to get the files on the communists sent on. They preferred to think the whole group guilty of the same grave misdeeds.

Only for the few known communists, that who at five o'clock every morning had tensed with fear at the sound of boots echoing in the prison courtyard, and keys grating in the monstrous locks of the cell doors, was the terror over. At Loibl, everybody was in the same boat.

The equal share of honors allowed to everyone by Joel, decent fellow that he was, had been more coldly worked out by the less generous Paulo. His apportioning had been hard on many.

But not on himself, because he felt he belonged in an intermediate category, with the men of independent action. And when the whistle blew for the end of work he had so convinced himself of his categories being right that, seeing the men of the demolition Kommando already assembled with their rocks on their right shoulders, he couldn't help saying aloud:

"This life must be hard for a man with nothing on his conscience."

VIII

If Paulo had been allowed to stroll along Route 333 on the other side of the barbed wire, he would have given up trying to classify his partners in misery as good, bad or dangerous. Seen from the other side of the fence, from the SS point of view, personalities counted for nothing. From a hundred and fifty feet away, nothing distinguished Joel from Pozzi, and Dédé didn't look any more an intellectual than Serpette. Seen from the road, the butchers, the peasants, the teachers and the habitual criminals were as alike as brothers. More than brothers: they might have been a new species.

Yes, you had to be on the other side to know what was really going to happen to this bloody Kommando. Only their keepers were in a good position to predict that future. All they had to do was open the shutters of their prefabricated barracks. The hive of industry, the noise of the picks overlaid by the frantic scraping of shovels and the squeaking of wheelbarrows, all this extraordinary activity was more than a clue. The Germans didn't need to waste time looking for volunteers. From the other side, it was apparent that everyone, without exception, would do their bit for the tunnel. It was quite obvious.

If the SS had been able to read Paulo's thoughts, they would have had a quiet laugh. The flock of zebras which had been handed over to them without previous employers' references suited them very well—all of them, innocent as well as guilty.

So, in the early days of July, now that the work force had been knocked into shape, they decided to concentrate their efforts on the technical side. Civilian specialists like the engineer turned up from all over the place, on foot, by car and in trucks. Austrians or Yugoslavs, without a doubt. Conscripts or volunteers? It was difficult to say because the crowd of civilians had brought with them a fairly substantial company of *Feldgendarmes*, either as guards or as protectors.

Housing this great crowd posed a problem. Obviously, any camp for free men would have to be built some distance from the barracks of the pest-ridden. On the other side of the road of course: this meant felling hundreds of pine trees, shifting tons of earth and digging big holes. Work fit for slaves, work for Paulo and his friends.

On the opposite side, the shaven heads were peering optimistically at their next building site. To see civilians close at hand would make a change, and perhaps they would be able to glean some news from these Yugoslavs, who might be as sympathetic as the ones they had met at Trzic station. They might even be offered some bread or cigarettes.

Unfortunately, the SS had also considered these possibilities, and it was the civilians who built their own nice little private camp. Helped by the accompanying gendarmes, they rolled up their sleeves and, two weeks later, without shouting or commotion, a village had sprung up. The slaves on the other side of the road were left with nothing but their dreams. The order to keep the vermin at a distance had once again been followed to the letter.

In the first few days of July, Loibl Pass quickly came to resemble an anthill swarming with life. To begin with, there were the 600 convicts, who were now very tanned. Under the glaring sun beating down on the prison, sweat trickled down their shoulders and over their skinny rib cages, and they glistened so much that their numbers seemed to have multiplied. There might have been 3000 men there, but 600 was already a goodly number. Added to the 50-odd civilians and 50 gendarmes, plus 120 SS and the Kapos, the total figure was not far off 1000—the population of a decent-sized parish. Quite an achievement for this remote part of the world where, only a month earlier, there had been nothing. The only things missing were a church, a cemetery and a football field.

They could do without the football field, because, as Paulo had said, the whole of Loibl was just like a stadium, and they already had a church, too: the little Slavic chapel was prominent on the road, looking much bigger than it really was because of its disproportionately large gilded bell tower, in the Kremlin style. Each day, it was sullied a little more by the SS freethinkers, champions at spitting. If a stray Allied pilot had flown over this perfect mountain hamlet, not marked on his charts, only the absence of a cemetery would have caught his attention. He would probably have come back, hedgehopping this time, to photograph this curious, overpopulated village whose inhabitants never died. And he could have come back ten or even twenty times without ever locating the cemetery. Those who were seriously ill, condemned men, had been shipped back just in time, before their graves needed to be dug. They had gone quietly in the trucks which had brought the reinforcements, a few hours after the arrival of the newcomers. Even a wooden cross bearing a registration number was too good for these unhappy men who had given up their last ounces of strength. Only in peacetime are the names of workmen who die in the course of their duty inscribed on a marble plaque. Hardly likely here, this touching tradition dear to all miners. Twenty dead in a month, twenty dead for thirty yards, was too many. The only real solution was to send those who got in the way to be killed elsewhere, to Mauthausen, where the voracious ovens would make quick work of them. Twenty extras would have little impact there. What a waste of space twenty graves would be in this overcrowded valley.

The twenty pioneers had gone now, at dawn, with neither flowers nor wreaths, helping each other to the trucks without a word of farewell for their fellows, who were busy greeting each other. It was only that evening that everybody noticed they were missing. By then, it was too late to feel sorry for them.

But this hushed departure had left an unpleasant taste. All the members of the Kommando, new and old alike, began to understand the risks involved in playing sick. Going back to the fold at Mauthausen with a temperature of 104 was unmistakably the end, in smoke.

Even the most hard-bitten shivered at the mere thought of this quiet repatriation. As a result, everyone suddenly felt stronger, more eager to work. They all began to take a genuine interest in the bustle of the construction site, as Paulo had already done. At the first opportunity for conversation, in the crapper as a rule, it was professional things which were discussed. In low voices, they talked about rock, wooden scaffolding and vaulting. Talking about the war, about France, about memories or about the future could only sap morale. They were much happier estimating the length, the width and the height of the tunnel, and the time it would take, now that they were there in strength, to reach the other side of the Karawanken chain. Had the Kommandant put his ear to the wall, he would have been delighted. With such goodwill, the work would forge ahead. Thanks to these halfwits, easy promotion would be his within a year. Then he would send them back, all of them this time, to his friend the big boss Ziereis, to be grilled or to build another tunnel. As for him, with his new stripes he'd have himself transferred to France. *Gross Paris*, gay Paris, was even more enjoyable as he thought of these idiot Frenchmen who were going to build his beautiful tunnel.

The big black cavity consumed all thoughts and energies. It meant hope. Even for bums like Sailor and his block chief friends who, unlike the Kommandant, wanted it to drag on for years. That was Maumau's firm hope too. He had realized that he would not easily find another daddy like Bullseye, and that if he wanted to stay in good shape for his comeback to the world of pimping, he would have to go on accepting the triple rations of soup. Too bad if his bum wore out before he got back. His girls weren't going to see it. Paulo could step down from the pulpit; the tunnel, and nothing but the tunnel, dominated the thoughts of all, French, Poles, Germans, Austrians and Yugoslavians. Each new piece of information, each detail which had something to do with the tunnel, interested them all. The shaven heads were constantly on the lookout. They kept a close watch, and no detail of life on the other side of the barbed wire escaped their attention. Thus, one fine morning at coffee time, an incredible piece of news ran like wildfire through the camp: two girls had just arrived, real women in skirts. They had been seen by more than one; they were not a mirage caused by the blinding sun. They were real, this was serious.

What was even more extraordinary was that these good ladies appeared from a distance to be both young and beautiful. They had spent the morning of their arrival strolling up and down the road between the SS and civilian barracks, as if there were a minor problem of where they would be lodged. So, they were going to stay. They hadn't just come on a day trip like wantons excited by the idea of giving nine hundred brutes a simultaneous hard on and then taking off the same evening, leaving them frustrated.

No, it was official. These two dames were going to settle in, just like everyone else. They were attracted by the tunnel too. Obviously, it was a major attraction. But who on earth had had the idea of inviting these sweethearts? It would have been understandable if they had been whores—a Mauthausen tradition. But now that all the convicts, heading for the daily grind, had seen them a little closer—no more than three hundred feet away—they had to admit that these girls didn't look at all like whores. They were simply good-looking girls with good figures, one blond and the other brunette, appealing to all tastes.

What the hell were they doing in the midst of these savages whose only thoughts of assault were directed at the mountain? Who would end up on top of these pretty girls? The SS or the civilians? At any rate, the shaven heads knew they weren't in the running; hairless, cashless and dressed like clowns, they didn't have a chance. But they were interested, and would have liked to know more. The arrival of the women was quite a shock for men who had not seen any skirt for months, and some for years—apart from the fleeting glimpses of the little Slav girls at Trzic station.

For Paulo, it was exactly seven months: three at the Cherche-Midi jail, three at Mauthausen, and another solid one here. He had worked it out, but only mechanically because he couldn't have cared less about these two bitches who had come to flaunt themselves here. They were of no interest to him, they were not going to make the work go any faster. On the contrary, these ladies threatened to create havoc on the construction site. The civilians wearing their pricks on their sleeves were quite capable of fighting for the right to screw them, and that would leave fewer biceps and brains around. No, Paulo had made up his mind. The two tarts weren't worth a single glance.

The following Sunday, toward the middle of the afternoon, he was forced to give them the glance which he had considered pointless. At least to one of them, the blond one. And almost close enough to touch her, the lucky fellow.

Fritz had stormed into Block 3, shouting:

"Zwei Mann, schnell, zwei Fahrer."

Paulo jumped up. *Fahrer,* driver: he remembered the profession he had given. This might be his chance, better not miss it. And he ran after the Kapo to the sentry post, followed by Jo from Oran, the second driver. It was only when Fritz doubled up with laughter as he pointed to a stretcher used for carrying stones that they understood the bastard had done a dirty on them. The Kapo with the green hose was still laughing as he walked out of the camp gate. Paulo and Jo found nothing to laugh at. At best they might have resigned themselves to the cheap trick, but less amusing was the fact that the *Rapportführer* and two fully armed SS were waiting on the other side of the fence.

"Forward march," the officer had yelled, and the small formation began to march along the road.

What was the significance of this escort? Four Germans, three of whom were armed to the teeth, against two unarmed and almost naked Frenchmen. Fortunately, there was the *Trage*. Otherwise, in spite of the time—it was noon—and the brilliant sun, the excursion would have been disturbing. Jo, quick to panic, had already begun to complain, in slang so that the Krauts wouldn't understand.

"They're going to rub us out, we're going to get knocked off."

Paulo turned toward him and although he did not utter a word the message in his look was clear: shut your face, you cunt, now's not the time.

After a hundred yards, the *Rapportführer* who was leading the formation left the road and, followed by everyone, veered off to the right, behind the blocks of the SS encampment. When they reached the last barracks half concealed in a small larch wood, they found the explanation. It wasn't the treacherous shot in the back that the ex-lifer had feared. The reason for the assignment was the blonde thirteen feet in front of them, whom the *Rapportführer*, clicking his heels officiously, had just addressed as Frau Martha.

She stood there, quite close, smiling. Her smile was for the young *Rapportführer*, but Jo, who was just behind him, took it for himself. He had been so scared that he smiled back at the pretty girl. Luckily for the ex-convict, the stretcher which Paulo had hoisted on to his shoulders hid most of Jo's scarecrow face, and no one, not even the *Rapportführer* or Fritz, noticed the frightful grimace meant for the blonde.

He was lucky, because under the dumb-blonde exterior, there was something disturbing about the woman. Frau Martha was neither Yugoslavian nor a whore, as the French had assumed a little too quickly. She was thoroughbred German stock, down to the marrow, Aryan for generations. Jo the Algerian didn't realize that his many long years of hard labor had made him look like a little rat. Doubly lucky that nobody had seen his sacrilegious Arab smile, his attempt at charm which was about as subtle as indecent exposure. But all five men, prisoners and guards alike, had eyes only for the blond apparition, the first vision of freshness in this brutish world. Paulo reacted just like the others, in spite of his efforts not to dream, to keep his feet on the ground in his present world without women.

The *Rapportführer* didn't seem to be in any great hurry. He walked up and down the length of the barracks, beside the blonde. Paulo had to admire the graceful body, from the front and back, which brushed past indifferent to him. However, this female display wasn't a particularly serious provocation. After seven months without an erection, you lose the habit. The African from Cayenne must have felt the same; famine dispels all thoughts of love. But Fritz, stuffed with fried potatoes, had a problem of a different kind, and if he was feeling horny at that moment, it could only have been out of desire for the elegant *Rapportführer*, like the fine queer he was. On the other hand, the remaining witnesses to the scene, the two young soldiers, flowers of German youth, were suffocating with excitement inside their death's-head helmets. The wanton prick-teaser, German like themselves, was perfumed like a Parisian, and she was going too far, strolling back and forth in front of their bulging crotches. The lower ranks must have been cursing their superior. What dashing figures they cut with their guns and heavily loaded cartridge belts, in front of this German woman who was well aware that Loibl was not the Russian front. How they must have envied their senior in his light summer outfit, armed only with an elegant and artistically plaited riding crop. Naturally, he was the only one of the bunch who could hit it off with her, and he knew it. He was taking advantage of his luck by making his little chat last as long as possible.

Paulo would have given anything to be somewhere else, not to have to see this flirtation between two people of his own age, which upset him more than anything he had had to endure so far. For the first time in his life, Paulo the lady-killer was a spectator. Hadn't she noticed that he was still good-looking in spite of his ten-day beard, his convict's shirt, and his gauntness? The *Rapportführer* wasn't bad-looking, admittedly, but he looked less masculine, with his wide almond eyes and his mop of curly brown hair. There was even something a little feminine in the details of his features: his nose was too small and straight, and his rosy mouth and full lips, as if painted on, belonged to a girl. Nor did his body redeem him in Paulo's eyes, because of his narrow waist, squeezed tight by his belt. Engraved on the buckle were the words *Meine Ehre heisst Treue,* My honor is fidelity! The motto of a fag...

"What a tart," thought Paulo, "a real mincing faggot. In Paris he'd make straight for Place Blanche, hanging around the men's bogs with his tapered waist, his tight buttocks and that pouting mouth." In the meantime, things were not going badly for the "tart." He had linked arms with Martha and, ignoring the others, he accompanied her as she paraded up and down. Fifty times she went past Paulo, the beautiful Martha, without noticing him, without so much as a look, even a look of scorn. To her he was just shit. Of course she was German, she belonged to the race of the conquerors, and he was French, beaten, a prisoner, a convict. But she was a woman too. She might have given him a look, just one look. Paulo hadn't suddenly aged by twenty years, they were about the same age, give or take three years. Naturally he was emaciated, but his tan made up for that in small measure. What was it then? His pajamas? His *Autobahn* haircut? His stubbly chin? She must have been able to sense that there was something else under his disguise. His eyes, for example, were the same as before: fine blue eyes, very clear. And his mouth, which had pleased so many in the past, had not changed. Obviously, he was more attractive when he smiled, and he would have liked to show Martha his splendid white teeth, which had helped him a little on the day of the selection to get out of Mauthausen. But she persisted in not looking. And his hair? That swarthy bastard with his curls could go stuff himself. Paulo's hair, before the clippers, was proper hair. And finally his nose was something else, a proper nose, full of character, not just skin and cartilage. Paulo bettered Madame's SS in every respect, from head to toe.

Give him a tailor-made uniform and a razor, give him back his sixty-five pounds and his former muscles, and then let the undiscriminating slut make her comparison.

Paulo was seething with rage. He had been taken for a ride. The bitch had to notice him, otherwise he would die of shame.

Now, each time she went by, he looked at her straight in the eyes and kept on looking. She was bound to sense this man's presence. Even from behind, women like that have a sixth sense about an interested male, even without seeing him. And Martha really looked the part, an easy lay with her big tits thrusting against her low-cut blouse, and her cherry-shaped bum which she swung deliberately to right and left with each step. She must certainly have felt Paulo's aggressive glare.

"A fore-and-aft Fanny like that would take some satisfying, and she's hardly going to get it from that SS mannequin," he muttered between his teeth.

In just ten minutes he had forgotten everything—Mauthausen, the tunnel, his hunger. Nothing else existed except for himself and that girl . . . and the *Rapportführer*, who had, for some time, been aware of Paulo's killing looks. At the risk of wrecking his own show, he abruptly dropped his tart's arm and walked straight up to Paulo.

"Was willst du, Dreckmann?"

Shit-man. Exactly what Paulo needed to hear to stop his filthy fantasies on the spot. The base insult saved him from the irreparable idiocy which was boiling up inside his head.

Had things gone any further he might have thanked the *Rapportführer* for his intervention, but his thanks would have been slightly out of place, for a second later the riding crop lashed out at the side of his face. On his mouth made for kissing, a blow to the right, another to the left, one to each eye, his beautiful irresistible eyes, and on his virile nose, a blow for each of his fine features, even on his head of hair, which wasn't at all provocative. The jealous SS had quite simply set about disfiguring his rival, coolly taking his time. He stopped and waited patiently for Paulo to lower his arms, then he started whipping again. He used his crop like a tennis racket, forehand, then backhand, and only when he had thoroughly opened Paulo's all too handsome face did he wipe his riding crop on his boots and take Martha's arm once again.

The indifferent beauty had not missed a single detail of the spectacle, and this time she had certainly noticed him, Paulo was sure of it. But the sweetheart's emotions didn't seem very strong and Paulo would doubtless never know what she thought of him. Was he better- or worse-looking than his tormentor?

The punishment just handed out to Paulo was quite unpremeditated. There was a fatigue to complete, and Fritz the Kapo was beginning to get extremely bored. He was not really into women at all, and all he wanted to do was get off back to his friends, the other block chiefs, for a bite to eat. Ungraciously, he interrupted the courtly promenade.

"*Herr Rapportführer*, do you want me to get another man to do the moving?"

"No, Fritz, he'll do," replied the SS, having cast a quick glance at Paulo, who was mopping up the blood running from his wounds with an already red piece of rag.

Even without the distraction of the riding crop, the fatigue which was the root of all the trouble would have been no Sunday stroll. Jo and Paulo worked that out right away. The suitcases and packing cases which they had to pile onto their stretcher weighed as much as the rocks from the tunnel. What could there be in these packing cases? Paulo didn't even bother to hazard a glance. He had learned his lesson: a look, even at some packing cases, was dangerous when these lunatics were around. So, at the risk of sprawling headlong with all his load, he stared fixedly at the tips of his shoes for this first trip.

Dead tired, he advanced more and more slowly with his load. Fritz saw that it was his turn to play a part, so on came the hose, not for Jo, but for Paulo, on his back this time. Unnecessary to whip both men to get a load like this moving, the leading man was enough and, probably by chance, Paulo was leading. Unless Fritz, combining his talents for ass-licking with psychology, had thought that beating Paulo would give the *Rapportführer* greater pleasure. Or Martha. How could you tell with a woman made of marble?

The afternoon was almost over. The sun had disappeared behind the mountains, and a cool wind had just come up.

Blowing down the valley off the summits, it made the two volunteer removal men shiver, as the sweat on their bodies began to freeze. Martha, too, started shivering in her summer clothes. The *Rapportführer*, sensitive to her every need, noticed, and with the gallantry characteristic of the German Army, he ordered Fritz to step up the pace. The last two loads were carried at a run. The prisoners' burdens were lighter, but rather strange: medicine bottles, syringes, cases of surgical instruments—scissors, surgical knives, needles, boxes of bandages—a real doctor's surgery.

"She can't be a doctor, that bitch," Paulo said to himself. "If she was, her boy friend wouldn't have called her Frau, he'd have said Doktor, or Professor. But then Frau isn't the same as Fräulein—it means Madame; so the tart must be married, and hubby must have come with her, because you don't go around with other men's women in this part of wartime Germany. The doctor must be Martha's husband."

His guess was correct. Frau Martha was the wife of a doctor sent to Loibl by the Mauthausen authorities, who had deemed it essential to assign a doctor to the Kommando given the importance of the work force there. And judging by the amount of stuff which the medical household had brought with it, one could deduce, once again, that there were people, and in high places, who believed in the tunnel.

"So much the better," Paulo concluded. "It's handy, you might even say reassuring, to have a doctor around."

The little packages of sticking plaster, marked with a red cross, could be used right away, after the riding crop's furious volleying session. They could stick a yard of it on his face alone. The idea made him smile.

Paulo was an astonishing fellow. He had just had a punishing of appalling brutality, his face was an open wound and his back was not much better. He was staggering with exhaustion under inhuman loads over the bumpy path which led from the SS barracks to the one set slightly back from the road, which the civilians were busy erecting for Martha and her doctor. And he could still smile. Most men in his shoes would have begged for mercy or tried to run for it, hoping that a burst of gunfire in the back would cut short their martyrdom. But no, Paulo stuck it out. Blinking through his own blood, his ears pounding, his skin raw, he still found the strength to think about what was going on and to find a ray of hope.

He had gotten himself into a nasty mess, however, by provoking the all-powerful *Rapportführer,* who ranked only below the Kommandant, and whose duties required him to spend his days among the detainees. All day long, at work or at the camp, Paulo would have him on his back. There weren't many tall, lanky fellows like himself, and the little jockey with his crop would have no trouble picking him out from the ranks. And all because of an instinct for vanity, of wanting to convince himself that he was still an attractive male. He hadn't been very clever, and it was hardly in line with his strategy of disappearing into the crowd. The unforeseen appearance of this haughty female only a few feet away had been enough to shatter his fine resolutions. But, as always, after taking a bad knock, he got a grip on himself again and put his mind to work on getting together a quick plan of action. For the moment, there was only one thing to do: to stick it out to the last packing case. But in the future, the rule was absolute. When a Kapo asks for a volunteer for fatigues, keep your mouth shut, especially if he wants a volunteer who knows how to drive.

As was to be expected, once the disdainful Martha was settled in she had not so much as a word or gesture for the two who had almost killed themselves lugging her field hospital around. Not even, ungrateful bitch that she was, for Fritz, who had, after all, helped things along with his hose.

It was only the *Rapportführer* who earned a sugar lump, her grudgingly proffered hand to kiss, which spurred him to a sensational click of the heels, accompanied with a flourish by:

"*Meine Huldingung, Frau Ramsauer.*"

"*Danke schön, Helmut,*" she answered.

Time for them to leave. "Back to camp, *schnell,*" barked the *Rapportführer,* looking at his watch. He had taken a bit too much liberty this afternoon, stretching his pleasure a little too far, and they would be expecting Monsieur the *Rapportführer* for roll call at the camp. *Schnell*.

"Tell me, Helmut," Paulo would have liked to ask, relieved of the weight of his litter, "didn't anyone ever tell you that doing this in public just isn't done? Only peasants do it." It made him laugh now to think about the two young lovers he had cursed so bitterly earlier on. Helmut and Madame Ramsauer—and Dr. Ramsauer—nice snippet of information for his friends. It would be easier to refer to them by name: Helmut the ballbuster and pain-in-the-ass Ramsauer, instead of *Rapportführer* and *Sanitätsführer.*

The small group set out briskly along the road. They had already passed the civilian camp and in five minutes everyone would be back home. Fritz, who had had to go without his four-o'clock snack, was thinking about the plate of potatoes he was going to get down him. The prospect lent him wings. Paulo and Jo were longing for their mattresses, where they would be able to stretch out their aching limbs, and this last burst of speed suited them too. But just as the civilian camp was disappearing from view, all three thought their dreams would be shattered.

The *Rapportführer* had just stopped and was gesticulating wildly. Who the shit was it who had slowed them down? The three inmates all turned to look simultaneously. Fritz was furious, Jo and Paulo were worried. The cause of the disturbance, unbelievably, was the other girl, the brunette! She was climbing a rock above the road, about fifty yards away. You couldn't see her face very well, but her silhouette gave her away. The ridiculous thing was that, like Martha, even more so than Martha, she looked stunning. What a cruel day for Paulo! For a man who had resolved that he was through with women to be obliged to tolerate the sight of girls who, by the unkindest chance, were beautiful, much more beautiful than most, and a lot better than many of the women he used to pick up in France, in the days when he had everything going for him, it was too much. Unhappily, he had not lost his eye for attractive women; with the brunette or the untouchable Martha on his arm he would have been the envy of many in the clubs of Montmartre.

How were such things possible, such good taste among these boors whose reputation for bad taste had spread far and wide? Unless they had improved their stock from the collection of countries they had annexed. For Paulo, and certainly for plenty of other young men at the peak of their sexual drive, the presence of these two girls with their perfect figures was going to be yet another trial. It was perfectly obvious that the bitches would deliberately hang around the camp, showing off their bums and tits to arouse the famous Gallic lust; to make these Frenchmen wank themselves to death as their last ounces of strength trickled away. An original way for these Aryan maidens, spoiled by nature's gifts, to help Germany and to serve their Führer.

"She can go and get herself watched somewhere else, I won't look at her, I've learned my lesson," said Paulo, turning his back on the skirted climber.

Nevertheless, he'd had time to notice that the beautiful brunette wasn't the smiling type. She had acknowledged the wild arm-waving of the *Rapportführer* with a small, scarcely polite movement of her hand, and resumed her climbing.

The cool reception he had received visibly annoyed Helmut, and he ordered them to march on. Paulo breathed again. For a moment, he had feared that the agitated poodle might resume his imitation of the Marquis de Sade's seduction technique. But the brown-haired girl was no Justine; she seemed to prefer nature to vice.

"I prefer that type," thought Paulo, lengthening his stride. "And anyway she's better-looking."

His sentiments were hardly sincere for he hadn't seen much of the small brunette, but he was so delighted that the posturing SS had not made a hit with her that he was quite ready to accord her every favor. He had even gone so far as to decide—rightly—that the girl must be Yugoslavian, or at worst Austrian, but certainly not German. She had quite clearly shown, by the abrupt way in which she had turned aside, that she did not appreciate the sight of soldiers, armed to the teeth, driving skeletonlike prisoners before them.

"She can't be friendly with that Madame Ramsauer," Paulo said to himself. "Otherwise, she'd have been settled in the SS barracks. She'll be staying in the civilian camp. But what can she be doing here? Maybe she's come to cook for them, or she might be a typist, or a plain whore. No, that can't be right. A conscientious hooker would have made a pass at Helmut."

Soon they would arrive back at the camp. Paulo was weighing up the afternoon so rich in incident. In a couple of sentences he would put his pals in the picture. The arrival of a doctor, the behavior of the two women, Helmut's character, the stretch of road they couldn't see from the camp, the path cutting through the larch wood, it was all information which could be useful to the community. Paulo had picked up a lot today.

"It doesn't matter one way or the other," he finished just as the guard on sentry duty presented arms to the *Rapportführer.* "That little turd isn't going to make any friends here, given the way he sets upon his friends' women. The doctor probably wouldn't care for anyone sweet-talking his floozy behind his back. I've just got to find a way to tip him off about that wife of his."

Paulo smiled, thinking about the nice mess he could stir up without any risk, such as a little note under the *Revier* door addressed to Herr Ramsauer, Doktor: "Your wife is sleeping with the *Rapportführer,*" signed "An anonymous well-wisher," or simply "Sailor" or even "Fritz." Two birds with one stone.

Paulo was grinning so much as he imagined the consequences that he didn't realize he was parading in front of the whole camp, Kapos and detainees alike, all of whom had been standing in formation for a good hour, waiting for evening roll call. Six hundred striped pickets, block chiefs as well, literally devoured him with their eyes. Lost in thought, Paulo was completely unaware of the tragic effect of his entrance and the deathly hush caused by the sight of his flayed head, so precisely sliced open by the riding crop. His shaggy beard and his naked chest streaked with blood from his battered head, and the long stretcher which he carried like a cross on his bruised shoulder made him look like Christ on the way to Golgotha. And Jo from Oran following behind, looking more like the bad thief than the good one, didn't spoil the holy image.

The procession was quite a sight. Surprised by the anxious looks his slow pace provoked, Paulo stopped smiling. He straightened up, gravely, proudly. Never before at Loibl had a prisoner been worked over like this. By concentrating on striking only Paulo's face, the *Rapportführer* had achieved his desired effect, and now Paulo was achieving his own. What he cared about most of all was his reputation as a tough. And that reputation had just climbed dramatically in the eyes of the whole crowd, especially those, gangsters or otherwise, who had had doubts.

When he got back to the men of his block, he could see,

through his horribly swollen eyelids, Joel and Dédé standing side by side. Their expressions seemed to be saying, "Well done, Paulo, your country can be proud of you." Behind them, Angel Belloni's eyes were filled with tears, and Paulo was afraid he would burst out crying like a kid, like the little boy he really was.

But for heaven's sake, wasn't Loibl a camp of frantic egotists? Were there still men capable of trembling for a life other than their own? Paulo was very moved. He went to put the stretcher against a barrack wall, and took his place in the ranks.

That evening Paulo felt less scorn for the sea of skulls which the Kapos had got lined up to within a hair's breadth, using the humiliating *Autobahn* haircut as an axis. The men who had held their breath in a kind of homage as they saw him go past deserved to be reconsidered.

"Perhaps we can get something done all together," he murmured, heading for the *Revier* to get his face stitched up. A little later, in the darkness of the block dormitory, he answered his neighbors' questions without irritation, almost kindly. His contact with the outside world and his walk beyond the barbed wire had not produced any cheering discoveries, but he was careful not to say so, seeking instead to mention anything which might raise morale. Even if only for one night it was a lot for these unfortunate men.

"It's my opinion," he summed up, "that now these civilian guys have arrived and set up camp, things will be better. In theory, we ought to get beaten up less. There are too many witnesses now."

In the dark none could see that Paulo had rolled his jacket, trousers and shoes up into a ball, which he had stuffed under his shoulders to keep his poor cauliflower head up in the air. In his present state there was something courageous about Paulo's attempts to raise his comrades' morale, so that they should get a good night's sleep.

IX

Paulo was not to retain his title as the most scarred man of the camp for long, nor his record for the maximum number of stitches. He lost them both on Bastille Day, the Fourteenth of July.

The French should have known to expect something out of the ordinary that day. The block chiefs had gathered them together the day before to make a surprising announcement.

"*Franzosen, morgen ist Bastille Day.* Tomorrow we're going to celebrate your national holiday, *on va vous faire votre fête*."

The shits had learned that last sentence by heart, in French, so that the humor would not be lost on anyone. It probably hadn't been easy for their thick skulls to take in those six words, three of which began with a V, a letter which Germans can't pronounce. It came out as "*On fa fous faire fotre fète*." But that was funnier still and most of the listeners almost cracked up on the spot. Only the real villains didn't appreciate the joke. They knew the expression "*On va te faire ta fète*" only too well; it was always the prelude to a fight. So what bastard had been giving these illiterates French lessons? It must have been a crook, most likely Pozzi or Berck.

The preparations for the national holiday had been meticulous. The whole team of convicts had scratched away in the tunnel all morning, and nothing abnormal had occurred. Back at the camp, they had licked their bowls quite clean and were quietly waiting for the signal to get back to work, and still nothing happened. Except that this lunch break lasted longer than usual. A good ten minutes longer, or so it seemed, but obviously no one had a watch and they could only guess at the time. However, the bell didn't ring, and the SS remained hidden in their barracks. It was all rather odd.

"Must be because it's Saturday," joked one or two bright sparks. "They're giving us the English working week."

This idea appealed to the prisoners, and it put them all in a good mood. The funniest part of it was that the men who had come up with the idea of the English working week were right. The doyen had blown his whistle to reassemble his men on the *Appelplatz*, and then he had confirmed it. An interpreter translated as he spoke.

"There will be no work in the tunnel this afternoon and every Saturday afternoon from now on."

Thunderous applause would have greeted this wonderful announcement, if such a thing had been permitted. A half-day of rest! What a godsend for the worn-out workers! They would be able to have a snooze on their bunks, and the liter of fluid they had just swallowed would stay in their stomachs a bit longer. It would be the first luxury they had had in four and a half months. No one could believe his ears. But the doyen hadn't finished.

"The company which employs you, the *Universale* of Vienna, is a humanitarian enterprise, like all National Socialist enterprises. It respects the sacred rights of workers, especially those who are working for Europe like you, for its future and for its defense against the forces of evil, pluto-Judaic-Masonic . . ."

"*Kommunisten und Syphilitiken*," concluded Sailor.

These jokers were going over the top. They hadn't come up with all that by themselves. It was Nazi catechism they were reciting, because with their green triangles marking them as thieves, everyone was well aware that politics was not their business.

"I thought as much," Paulo whispered in Joel's ear. "They're taking us for a ride. Just wait, we'll soon find out how they plan to celebrate our holiday."

The doyen was just coming to that.

"But it would be a bad idea to let your muscles go rusty. I have decided, therefore, with the agreement of Herr Kommandant, to devote this afternoon of rest to physical training."

This time everyone got the picture. There was no need to spell it out. Trouble was brewing.

The physical training involved the usual tools: shovels, picks and wheelbarrows, but no axes or sledgehammers. The order was to dig a small ditch in front of each block and carry the earth to the top of the camp, on the right behind the

Waschraum. With almost six hundred ditchdiggers, it shouldn't take more than a couple of hours. Hardly enough to stop the muscular atrophy, but not quite a five-and-a-half day week either. In spite of their disappointment, the whole camp set to work without too much fuss. But the pace slackened very quickly because block chiefs and *Arbeitskapos* had vanished as if by magic. One of the men had seen them enter the doyen's hut straight after the speech, at least half an hour ago, and they were still there. Under the circumstances, there was no point in the men straining themselves. The intervals between pickax blows lengthened, and the wheelbarrows weren't getting filled up. In the baking sun, they'd all taken off their shirts and the prescribed physical training seemed more like a cure in the sun.

"They're letting us laze about on purpose," someone was saying just as the door of the doyen's hut burst open.

Clubs in hand, the block chiefs descended on them, yelling like Sioux Indians. Hard on their heels were the doyen and four *Arbeitskapos*, including Fritz who clutched an empty bottle of schnaps in the other hand. The brutes were pissed out of their minds, paralytic. Real monsters.

Those who hadn't seen them heard their roars, and as if a magic wand had waved, picks were lifted, shovels flew and wheelbarrows rolled simultaneously. The prisoners all kept their heads down, waiting for the inevitable blows. But today was the Fourteenth of July, no ordinary day. To honor France, these gentlemen Kapos had thought up a proper military strategy. This was not to be a simple everyday beating. What the cowards wanted to pull off was a commando raid, against prisoners. The first group they got hold of was captured in front of Block 1, thirty men at once, three to each attacker. Forward march up toward the prison, Block 5, the most isolated block.

"What's going on?" Paulo wondered. "They can't be going to screw all thirty of them? With queers as drunk as that though, anything's possible."

He found out quickly enough. From half a mile away you could have guessed what kind of session was going on behind the wooden walls of Block 5: a *fünf und zwanzig* jamboree. Obviously the Kapos had gotten themselves into teams, for the screams of men squealing like stuck pigs were coming from several prisoners at once. In any case, five minutes later the door opened and the thirty wretched men of Block 1 came running out, hitching up their striped trousers, and that proved that to get the thing done so quickly, it must have been a team effort.

So this was the fiesta promised to the French. This was their exercise and sport. At this rate, everybody would get a turn—astride the stool, bum exposed.

The Kapos were playing a game of soldiers, and offensives were mounted against one block after another. Paulo was rounded up at the same time as his friends Joel, Dédé, Belloni and poor old Etcheverry. A stool each and two clubs per stool. The first few blows are terrible, when you know how many you've still got to come. Paulo almost missed the *Rapportführer*'s distinguished riding crop, and had to grit his teeth to stop himself from yelling. It would have done him good to yell, but he didn't want to give the fuckers any additional pleasure, so he stayed mute till the end, and got up unaided at the twenty-fifth stroke. Next to him, Etcheverry was lying unconscious. He hadn't emitted a sound either, but it was too much for a grandfather of his age, and he had fainted. And the bloodthirsty doyen was bringing him around by kicking him in the stomach while Fritz doused him with buckets of water. Murder gleamed in the eyes of Paulo and Joel, but what could they do? Nothing. And the misbegotten Kapos knew it too, had known it for the ten years they had spent in the camps. No prisoner had ever done anything to stop a friend being massacred. Or if he had, they died together.

Their little game had been going on for almost two hours now. More than half of Kommando X had already been to the stool. Almost as many remained to be whipped, it was all going nicely according to schedule, but the sadists had not counted on getting tired. They had hit the bottle too hard and their arms weren't obeying them anymore.

"Break!" screamed the doyen, withdrawing to his block with his whipping squad.

For an hour the prisoners heard them bawling obscene marching songs. "If only they would fall asleep," was the thought in everyone's mind. But just the opposite seemed to be the case; the more time passed, the louder they bellowed, and their second sortie was more terrifying than the first. Monsters before, now they were hellhounds unleashed, as if they had been given pure alcohol to drink.

In preparation for the second attack, Paulo turned around, so that the weals on his back were clearly visible. If these madmen wanted everybody punished today, they'd better not grab the same ones twice. He had gotten it right. He caught half a dozen passing blows on the back of his neck, but the mob went on to corner a group of men who seemed to be convinced that if they shoveled and scraped like fury, they might just earn a reprieve. Off to the torture chamber with them all, including those, like poor Etcheverry, who hadn't reacted quickly enough in turning their checkered backs to their torturers. One young man, caught for the second time, dropped his trousers just as he was being taken, so the Kapos should see that his bloodied buttocks had already been through the mincer. Unfortunately, they dragged him off in the crowd to make up the numbers.

In spite of the element of error, almost everyone had had his ration by the end of the afternoon, and for twenty or so of them, there had been a double ration: *fünfzig*. It had completely finished old Etcheverry the second time, and the efforts to revive him were unsuccessful. Unconscious, he was carried off to the *Revier* on a stretcher.

The doyen had really overdone it and perhaps the sight of the half-dead old man would calm him down. So they all thought. Once again they were all wrong. Clearly, these naïve young deportees still believed in Santa Claus. They imagined there were limits to physical resistance. By the end of that evening, they would be amazed to find themselves still standing upright. It was fortunate they weren't entrusted with the administration of the camp; that would be quite something. Time to give them some exercise, all of them, good-for-nothing weaklings with their clogged-up muscles.

This time the game was more sophisticated. "*Gymnastik*," the doyen yelled. At the peak of excitement, his assistants had taken up the chant: "*Gymnastik*." At the sight of their faces flushed with anticipation, you could tell that this new thing was going to be a winner.

Paulo now remembered having heard all about this famous *Gymnastik* from the long-serving Spanish Republicans at Mauthausen. So this was it. Sailor, Bullseye, Fritz and the other boys had not forgotten how it went. They picked out about twenty men here and there, fellows who seemed in better shape than the real skeletons like Dédé and his Breton friends. These men were the pick of the first convoy.

One by one the twenty gymnasts were beaten into the room adjacent to the *Waschraum*, the *Schneiderei*, the tailor's workroom. That particular tailor was unlikely to blow a fuse trying to develop new styles. One kind of cloth, one style, what a varied job! But today the tailor, a Parisian, was out front with his fellows, and in any case they didn't need him to clothe the physical fitness freaks. Mauthausen-style gymnastics weren't done in track suits or running shorts. The rules were clear: each detainee had to don a minimum of three pairs of trousers, three jackets and two overcoats. And if you could get more on, so much the better.

The emergence of the twenty Michelin men from the *Schneiderei* should have made their comrades guffaw. But after what had happened since lunchtime, no one had the heart to laugh. Yet the twenty men were more grotesque than one would have thought possible. They were shapeless lumps, like striped human punchballs, each wearing at least four pairs of pajamas. Hustled along by the Kapos, they lurched like robots toward the *Appelplatz*, and the block chiefs were so confident of the effect of their act that they ordered the whole camp to lay down their tools and gather round so that no one would miss the show.

Perched on a stepladder, the doyen put them under starter's orders.

"*Eins, zwei . . . eins, zwei . . .* five laps, faster."

Every twenty yards there was a Kapo with a club to keep the race going. A prod for each of the slowpokes as they lumbered past . . . one, two . . . one, two . . . faster.

Among the twenty star performers there was a real professional: Joel. In different circumstances Paulo would have bet a fortune on him, but here his sense of decency directed his thoughts elsewhere. And anyway, the five laps around the course were only a warm-up. The doyen had just cried "*Halt!*" to explain the next event.

"On the ground, *los* . . . on your stomachs . . . Line up, then crawl; go, *schnell* . . . No hands, you bastards, *schnell* . . ."

Joel was well in the lead, but he was about to be caught up because suddenly the back markers began to sprint forward like crocodiles, the reason being the lengths of piping stuffed with sand or electric cable which made a hell of a noise as they crashed down on the men's heads. Hitting their padded bodies would have had no impact.

Joel still reached the finishing line by the doyen's stepladder first. But he hadn't won the race yet. Back they had to go again, still wriggling without using their hands. At this pace their midday soup had long since been sweated into their overcoats. One more race, and the sausage-men were sufficiently loosened up to tackle the next event: the high jump. There were no records to be broken, a foot was high enough, just enough to clear the nine hoses arranged at six-foot intervals like hurdles with Kapos for stanchions. Only these hurdles had a tendency to jerk upward, ballward. By the ninth hurdle, the twenty competitors were streaming with sweat and half-asphyxiated by their bundles of uniform; it was all they could do to clamber over on their knees. The Olympics must surely be over now; either replacements would have to be found, or they would have to stop altogether. But the doyen was hell-bent on completing his pentathlon. Another flat race, to get their breath back, before he outlined the final event.

"Down on your stomachs and push-ups in time. *Eins, zwei, drei, vier, fünf . . . zehn . . . zwanzig.*"

Once more Joel was the champion. He only collapsed on his twenty-fourth. The others had given up long before. In spite of the maddened hoses, their small biceps refused to flex under the triple layer of clothing.

The effete Frenchmen had met their Waterloo. Just as in the Berlin Olympics, they had proved that as far as sport was concerned, they were a dead loss. The Kapos had had to concede that they could not be budged. Never mind, let them lie there, let them die, there was always the spectators.

"*Arbeit, alle,*" screamed the doyen, clearly on top form today.

A hundred picks buried themselves in the ground as one, tearing out great lumps of earth, which the shovelers piled enthusiastically into the wheelbarrows. Less than five minutes later the Kapos intervened.

"*Nein, nein,*" they cried. "*Kein* picks, *fertig* picks. *Zustopfen Lochen*, fill up the holes, *Schweine Franzosen.*"

So it was all a hoax, digging trenches in front of the

barracks, it was just part of the PT, part of the muscle oiling, and now it was time to fill them in again. It would take at least an hour to repair the damage, the hour the marauders in dockers' caps had set aside for the grand finale to their fireworks. More than the wholesale flogging, more than *Gymnastik*, this hour must leave all the prisoners with an unforgettable memory, one which would mark them for life. The theme for this spare hour went by the name of a "corrida."

Repeating the performance of earlier on, the savages charged in wave after wave, but this time nobody was taken captive. The game was to bring the enemy to his knees. Club blows to the head, punches, boots in the stomach—it was no holds barred. In front of each block, the men dropped like flies, still holding their shovels and wheelbarrows. In the face of such bestiality some of them panicked, thinking their final hour had come, and scattered in all directions, dropping their tools. They couldn't have made themselves easier targets if they'd tried. The savages had banked on their panic, and they'd have a field day with these runaway chickens. They stalked the prey in threes or fours, suddenly cornering their man to pursue him alongside the barbed-wire fence, yelling "Geronimo!" Up in the watchtowers the duty SS, beside themselves with excitement, shouted encouragement. The fugitives couldn't make it very far; very quickly, one after the other, they collapsed, out for the count. Such was the corrida. There was no *coup de grâce*, but it was a close-run thing.

A lot of blood had been shed in the arena since the beginning of the afternoon, and although it was impossible to count the wounded, Paulo could be sure that after this pogrom he had lost his claim to be the most wounded man in the camp. All the detainees, without exception, were bleeding somewhere, even the Kapos' friends like Riton, Pozzi and Berck, even their young pets, who were more used to dropping their trousers for sport of a different kind. The chiefs must have drunk one hell of a lot to go as far as beating their protégés. In their drunken stupor they must only have been capable of seeing silhouettes—they wouldn't have done it otherwise—but all the same it was nice to know that Pozzi had been in the soup too. Paulo regretted not having seen it with his own eyes.

At long last the sadists' bonanza had come to an end.

About fifty men were lined up in front of the *Revier.* Not a pretty sight. Dédé Ménard was among them, his large head swollen to almost twice its normal size. Belloni wasn't bad either, with his broken nose and his lips split open. As for Etcheverry, nobody had seen him; the orderly must have kept him back.

Yet the following Saturday, and the ones after that, the same thing happened again. Same program: stool, *Gymnastik,* manhunt and so on. As a result, every Monday morning saw increased absenteeism at the tunnel. Not a clever idea, the corrida.

X

With the first days of August the timid hopes which Paulo had cherished went up in smoke, the first smoke to be seen at Loibl Pass this blazing summer, smoke which looked and smelled like the smoke at Mauthausen, the smoke of men burning.

The Kommandant with his death's-head badge hadn't been able to resist it. He wanted his very own crematorium, on his doorstep. The sick and wounded in the infirmary weren't quite ready to die, but one fine morning he decided to inaugurate it anyway by arbitrarily murdering two men, a Frenchman and a Pole.

The lottery took place at midday roll call just before the departure for work. The doyen was in the picture, he knew which men he was going to have to extract from the striped mass.

"*Acht und zwanzig tausend . . . sieben und zwanzig,* step forward," he articulated emphatically.

Everyone strained anxiously to hear the last two digits of the numbers being called. Even the most dull-witted were now capable of recognizing the complicated combinations which replaced their family names, and two men had already stepped out of the ranks before the doyen repeated the numbers. Prodded by four Kapos, they suddenly found themselves on the platform just six feet away from the Kommandant.

"*Ruhe*, attention, face your comrades and listen, you *Schweine Franzose, Schweine Polak*."

The big boss looked thunderous and his words, screamed out by two interpreters, resounded through the whole valley, bouncing off the mountain and back to the *Appelplatz* in a chain of echoes. It was quite impossible to shut your ears to the uproar.

"You are all degenerates, a danger to society. My mission is to re-educate you and I intend to do so. Beware all idlers and saboteurs. These two animals you see in front of you on this platform will be severely punished. This morning, one of them concealed himself to avoid going to work, and the other deliberately spilled his soup over his uniform. This is called sabotage. Dismiss, *Arbeit*."

It was indeed time to return to work, even for the two who were to be punished. They were at the tail end of the column, and hardly had they crossed the threshold before they began to pay for their deplorable behavior.

The Kommandant hadn't made it up. The Pole had indeed spilled spinach soup on his jacket, that is to say spinach juice, nice and green, so that Sailor had immediately noticed the stain. He had lost no time reporting it to the doyen, who, since that morning, had been on the lookout for two wrongdoers to fulfill a confidential mission. Hanz, the chief of the *Arbeitskapos*, had already unearthed another, a work-shy Frenchman from the second convoy. With the soup-stained Pole they had what was needed, but if Fritz continued to thrash the Pole with such vigor on the way up the hill, they would no longer be able to accuse him of having stained his nice striped tunic green. With the blood pouring from his smashed nose, red was already the dominant color, and red stains were tolerated at Loibl.

As they marched, the convicts tried to fathom why the Kommandant had gone over the top for such a minor transgression. What a performance, all that fuss on the platform just for a fellow who had been messy about drinking his soup. It wouldn't have happened if they'd given him a spoon. Anyway, you only had to take one look at his eyes, dilated by a continued longing for food, to see he hadn't done it on purpose. Sabotage? The boss must be joking! But why all the uncalled-for paraphernalia?

The explanation came long after they had given up trying to find the reason: two short bursts of machine-gun fire, the first exactly a quarter of an hour after their arrival on the work site, the second two hours later. The condemned men—condemned before they climbed on to the platform, but nobody, including themselves, had realized—had paid the penalty for their sins.

Paulo and about fifty others working a hundred yards down the tunnel were the only ones not to hear the shots, which were covered by the din of the pneumatic drills. They continued their work, without suspecting anything, until the evening. But the five hundred-odd men who were working outside in the sun spent an afternoon more horrible than any other they had known since their arrival, including the afternoons of corrida. The cold-blooded murder before their very eyes of culprits no more guilty than themselves left them rigid with fear, silent, shocked, disbelieving. All the men had seen it, down to the last detail. The *Kommandoführer* had made certain that everyone should witness it.

It was the shouting which first attracted their attention. Then three Kapos, Fritz among them, began to take care of the Frenchman, a tall man with a long hollow frame, a body so frail that in itself it was a justification for refusing to work. The brutes had given him a wheelbarrow and then they did the job of filling it up themselves, until it was overflowing, of course. When they couldn't squeeze on even a single pebble more, the men exchanged their shovels for hoses. Seconds away, round one... Empty out the contents of the wheelbarrow against a tree at the perimeter of the work site. Round two: Come straight back for another load. With three rubber hoses in play, the work went very quickly, but by the tenth load, the purpose of a pile of dirt and stones at the foot of an isolated tree seemed more and more obscure. It's just punishment, everyone thought, no point trying to understand. The wretched man was bound to collapse, ready to be carted off to the infirmary, the classic story.

Classic, that is, until Fritz, pointing his hose at another tree ten yards beyond, ordered the man at his mercy, completely finished by now, to empty the eleventh wheelbarrow there. It was just as he got to the tree that the first burst of fire rang out, or more precisely the first two, one fired by an SS sitting twenty yards to the left of the tree, the other from his opposite number, on the right and slightly closer. It was a neat, tidy crossfire, just like firing practice.

The *Kommandoführer* approached, revolver in hand, but the *coup de grâce* was superfluous; the young men from Mauthausen had good aim. The French slacker, twenty-eight thousand something, had had it. He had died without even knowing it, shot in the back.

To see one more comrade die should not have been a great drama for the hardened survivors of Mauthausen quarantine. And yet this time, all five hundred witnesses were shocked. It was not as if the fellow who had just been struck off the register was a sick man. He was a man like them, he had been handpicked to work, to last. And his execution was legal: the second tree was beyond the cordon of sentries. By going so far, the man with the wheelbarrow had "crossed the line," a line invisible to him, merely hypothetical; but for the SS, it might as well have been marked out with white paint. The murderers used the first tree as their boundary mark.

It was a monstrous sham, blatantly premeditated, but there could be no protest. The body lay beyond the perimeter of the work site. The evening report would write up the incident as attempted escape, and in the column opposite, the victim's five-figure number would be entered with his nationality: *Franzose*.

All of a sudden, the convicts could think of nothing but this line, which they couldn't see but which was everywhere. It cut across the road, along the edge of the rocks, passing behind the tool sheds, through the wood and along the paths to the piles of rubble. The line had become more frightening than the electrified barbed wire. At least that was visible, and therefore avoidable, and even if you were beaten toward it, as at Mauthausen, you could still hope that the current might be off. Whereas with this invisible boundary line, one step in the wrong direction and your number was up.

So now every prisoner, especially the tree carriers and the discharge details, the men with pallets and wheelbarrows, were frantically trying to fix the fatal line. Killers must be lying in wait everywhere, well camouflaged, fingers on the trigger, amd as a little while ago, their only warning would be a shot in the back.

Continuing today's program was the other "attempted escape," the Polish soup saboteur's, and down the length of the line every *Posten* was hoping that the ambush would be set up in his sector. But the *Kommandoführer* was quite happy with the little tree standing on its own in full view of the whole work site, so he ordered Fritz to organize his wheelbarrow game at the same spot. This time no one was taken by surprise. Everybody knew what was going to happen, not least the unhappy Pole. Stubbornly he continued to empty his wheelbarrow against the tree on the edge of the line. Fritz pushed him and hit him, pointing to the second tree. But in vain. He would go no farther. The pool of blood marking the spot where his comrade had fallen seemed to be warning him: "Stick to it, don't go, don't cross the line." He was right to cling to his tree, for the disciplined SS didn't even bother to raise their weapons as long as he remained on the right side.

It wouldn't have made any difference anyway, they could have shot him on the line itself, since the Kommandant had condemned him to death; as from that evening he was no longer to appear on the work-force register. But no, the Krauts had their orders, it had to be an escape. Naturally prisoners try to escape, and if seen they are shot. Even the civilians, engineers and others, had to bow to the wisdom of that.

All they had to do was to ensure that the escapee looked as though he were making a break, just in case one of the civilians happened to be looking.

The Nazi bastards had thought of absolutely everything. They had even anticipated the desperate reflexes of men who didn't want to die, like the courageous little Pole. For almost an hour now he had been clinging on to his tree like a shipwrecked man clinging to his life belt. Two rubber hoses were powerless to make him go any further. He was covered with blood, but would not budge a step more. How much longer could this horrible game last?

"Run, make a break for it, instead of wearing yourself out for nothing," his closest compatriots seemed to be saying to him. One of them had made the sign of the cross, though with what hope God only knew. But the small fellow thought differently, and to bring it to an end, Fritz changed his tactics. No more blows, no more yells. That the Polack should empty his wheelbarrow was all that was asked of him. Did he think he'd been let off the hook? That a counterorder had just arrived, or that they had just wanted to scare the shit out of him? Difficult to know what he thought, but in any case he looked very happy that the beating had stopped. He was going freely back and forth with his wheelbarrow now, emptying it against the tree almost at a run, then scooting back for another load. Fritz approached casually, watching him and smiling, as if to say: "Good work, pint-size, you've got guts."

The little fellow thought it wise to acknowledge the smile and before turning around to get his wheelbarrow going again, he glanced at the man who had been beating him. Just what Fritz had been waiting for. Deftly, with a neat sidestep, he nudged the Pole's right shoulder hard and sent his victim sprawling on the ground six feet away. It was far enough, and the SS opened fire, emptying their magazines. The little Pole's struggles had been in vain. Death was instantaneous. But the wheelbarrow which he had tried to hang on to with his boyish hands until the end had remained by the tree. It hadn't crossed the line.

A second murder only a few hours after the first was so terrifying that not a single deportee dared open his mouth until the whistle blew for evening assembly. Each man retreated into himself, thinking about the youngster shot down because he had ventured to soil his humiliating uniform. Of course it was only an excuse, but to have chosen an excuse like that made it even more loathsome. The kid was bound to have a mother in Warsaw or somewhere similar who must often have clipped his ear in the past to teach him how to eat his soup decently. One could only hope she would never know that her son had died for that very reason. It could only make her regret her attempts to bring him up properly, and she would die of remorse.

When he emerged from the tunnel at six o'clock with the rest of the mining team, Paulo was still ignorant of what had happened outside. Happy for his hard day's work to be over, he went almost merrily to collect his daily stone. It was only when he joined the ranks and saw the downcast expressions of his neighbors that he began to get worried.

"What are you all looking so glum about? Corrida?"

"No, worse than that," whispered a voice at his back. "They shot them, the two guys on the platform."

"Shot dead?"

"Yes, they're dead. The bodies are already down at the camp."

Shot dead! Paulo couldn't believe it. What was it supposed to mean? The Kommandant must be mad. And what about his tunnel? To get rid of the sick was just about understandable, but to kill two able-bodied men was a terrible blow. What possible reason could there be? To lose your life because you spilled your soup was absurd; absurd, too, for refusing to work (as if that were possible). What then? Paulo would have liked to know more, but no one around him seemed at all keen to tell. Talking in the ranks was about as harmless as a spinach stain on your jacket.

There was no way Paulo could break the resolute silence which had descended, for as the forced laborers set out down the road, they noticed a thin ribbon of smoke rising from the valley behind the *Revier* block. Even without smelling it, everyone could tell it was the afternoon's two corpses. The men marched down the road to the camp in deathly silence. Anyway, now Paulo didn't need to know any more.

"So it's come to that," he said to himself bitterly as he took his place for muster. "Loibl Pass has christened its own crematorium. From now on, we might just as well be at Mauthausen. No need for the expensive parcel service to send back the dying. Only a short walk from the *Revier* now, a few splashes of diesel, a few logs, put a match to it and stand well back."

Scarcely six hours before Paulo had seen the two guys who were going up in smoke at close quarters, still alive, and they hadn't looked too worried. He remembered their faces very well, faces like the others, like his own. And now there was nothing left of them, no body, not even bones.

The whole business seemed unreal. The ruthless Kapos, with Fritz at the head, walked back and forth between the rows of shaven men, counting and recounting as if they hoped to find the two who were missing. The monsters were doing it on purpose, keeping them all at attention so that they would have to fill their lungs with the treacherous breeze blowing across the *Appelplatz*, tainted with the sickening smell of charred flesh. They must have agreed among themselves to drag things out and wait until the shadow of the mountains darkened the square. Then in the twilight the French and Poles would clearly see the flames consuming the bodies of their fellows. Would you not behave yourself after that, *Mensch*?

Lost in thought, Paulo failed to see the rubber hose aimed at his head, but he was indifferent to the blow. The blow to his morale was far more serious, because now it was not enough simply to hang on. Survival was a question of luck too. And luck was the province of the Kommandant, the *Rapportführer* and the block chiefs who were in sole charge of its distribution.

The days following the first auto-da-fé merely confirmed his pessimistic outlook. To come out alive would certainly be a question of chance. That chance had already been missed by some. It became rare, as that summer drew to an end, not to see smoke rising from behind the *Revier* in the evenings. Whether they were Frenchmen or Poles, gunned down on the work site or dead from exhaustion on an infirmary bed, the funeral ceremony was always the same: four SS, Herr Doktor Ramsauer, forensic pathologist, two dogs, a litter, a Kapo and five prisoners. One for the cans of diesel, the others to carry the body, stripped naked like at Mauthausen. A prisoner's clothes, even stained with blood, torn and burned by bullets fired at point-blank range, were too precious to destroy.

One evening it was the turn of Dédé Ménard and Paulo to play pallbearer. It was no accident that the man to be burned was one of their dormitory mates, a Pole called Pavlovski. Sailor had thought that by making them watch the cremation ceremony at first hand, the sight of an empty bed next to their own would have greater impact. For some time now Ménard had been the black sheep of his block. The young man, who looked neither crooked nor queer, annoyed the Kapo prodigiously with his air of self-confidence, and Sailor had vowed to use his influence with the SS to get him pursued across the invisible line. In the meantime, to get him in the right frame of mind, it would do no harm to put him on the crematorium detail. Soon see if he still had his fine manner of assurance on his return.

Sailor had gotten the wrong man. When he came back

half an hour later, Dédé hadn't changed. He simply looked a little more serious, his face more set. The dead man hadn't been his or Paulo's friend. In general French and Poles were at daggers drawn in the blocks. On two or three occasions in the rush of the nocturnal inspections, Pavlovski had gone for the smaller Dédé, and Paulo had been forced to intervene. They had never come to blows, but it was close. Fortunately the conflict had been confined to insults; otherwise Paulo and Dédé would have felt rather more uncomfortable as they watched their quarrelsome blockmate burn.

Paulo thought about these narrowly avoided fights as he looked at Pavlovski's stiff corpse lying facedown on the litter. He couldn't take his eyes off the three little black holes in the middle of the man's back, nicely grouped bullet holes as if on a rifle-range target. Yet every day at Mauthausen, in Block 17, he had seen dozens of dead men, and when the corpses suddenly stiffened, staring upward, he had not felt very much emotion. For the death of these men had, to some extent, been booked in advance. Several days before, when they had begun to take on, like cancer patients, an expression of irredeemability, it was clear that they had had enough, that they accepted their fate. In that situation, there was no reason to feel pity. But to see this boy, with his youthful complexion and his muscular, albeit thin body suddenly lifeless, was too unjust. His young frame cried out his refusal to die. Confident of his youth, for months he had accepted everything, enduring blows, hunger and shame, and doubtless he thought he had played the game well.

So why had they killed him? There was no answer; he had neither spilled his soup nor refused to work. It was all just chance. They wanted another death today and it was his number that had come up at roll call.

Paulo was trying to relate all this to his own situation, telling himself that things were going rapidly downhill. It was idiotic to pick men off without taking into account their physical condition, utterly ignoring the usefulness to the tunnel project of a wiry fellow like the little Pole, who had boundless reserves of energy. "Tomorrow it'll be me," he thought, and he imagined himself stretched out on the litter in his turn, with neat round holes below his shoulder blades, like the twenty-year-old boy who would soon go up in smoke and whose Christian name he didn't know.

What was Ménard thinking, at the other end of the litter? Undoubtedly the same as Paulo, but being less hardened by life, he must be on the point of tears. Paulo glanced at him. The Breton didn't look in the slightest as if he wanted to cry. His eyes glistened, but their brilliance was not due to tears which he held back; there was no room in his expression for anything but hatred and revenge. Paulo was stunned. Enough whining, it wasn't his style either. What he had to do was follow Dédé's example and open his eyes wide, to etch on his memory the features of the murderers escorting them to the crematorium.

Loibl's Kommandant hadn't bothered about a prize-winning design for his crematorium: it was a trench six feet long and two feet wide, just enough room for one body, in the dry bed of a mountain stream. There were four piles of bricks on which iron bars had been laid crosswise and lengthwise. It was less impressive than the Mauthausen factory ovens, but this griddle at the bottom of a ravine, shaded by larch trees whose trunks were already blackened by the fire, was just as sinister.

In any event, the human barbecue was cleverly concealed. No civilian or rambler would ever come across it, so cleverly hidden by trees in an old riverbed, which was, moreover, in a restricted area a few yards away from the guards' patrol path. The smoke could be seen from the road, but seeing it rise almost every day would not provoke surprise. Doubtless they thought in the civilian camp opposite that this was where the Germans dumped their rubbish, and that, as they were fanatical about hygiene, they set fire to it regularly.

The murderers thought of everything. The guiding principle at Mauthausen was that you left no traces. And none would be found here either. What could be more commonplace than this neat pile of carefully sawn logs, next to a rustic barbecue? And yet it was the sight of the stacked wood which overwhelmed Paulo even more than the frightful procession, or the dreadfully simple crematorium. The long crisscrossed logs, the armed soldiers, the naked body laid out on the bier—suddenly the sacrificial scene reminded Paulo of an illustration from a child's picture book of Joan of Arc at the stake. And here he was, an accomplice. He felt ashamed of his helplessness. When the Kapo poured the diesel into the trench and lit a paper torch, Paulo shut his eyes, too cowardly to watch.

Dédé and the other pallbearers, two Poles, had done likewise. None of them had the courage to look at the burning pyre. But they couldn't avoid hearing it and, above all, smelling it. They recognized the dismal crackling and the horrible stench which for months had tainted them at Mauthausen, and which tonight, only three feet away, was stronger and more repellent. Astonishingly, the SS didn't force them to open their eyes. Paulo took advantage of the thick smoke which obscured Pavlovski's already shriveling body to look round, and what he saw was more foul than anything he could have imagined: Herr Doktor Ramsauer was taking close-up photographs.

"I suppose it's to excite his bitch of a wife," Paulo said to himself. He had thought that she had enjoyed it the other day, watching without a shudder as his face was cut to ribbons, and he'd been right. Close-up shots of flames licking at a dead man's face would certainly interest her. What a pair!

It was the first time that Paulo had seen Ramsauer so close. And they call that fucker a doctor? So young, and already a captain? That number of stripes must have been earned by burning a fair number of Germany's enemies, and inoculating a lot of sick men with his syringe.

"Christ, and I thought the arrival of a doctor was reassuring," he went on. "The man's obviously a complete lunatic." And he vowed never to report sick. Ill in bed at the mercy of that twisted pervert—Jesus!

Paulo was now sure that what old Etcheverry had told him when he got out of the *Revier* after the first corrida session was true: 30 cubic centimeters of benzol injected into the heart. According to the two French orderlies working in the *Revier*, Ramsauer had already treated five or six incurable cases in this way since his arrival. At least, incurable had been Ramsauer's opinion and, again according to the orderlies, on his first case it had taken him three shots before he found out exactly where the man's heart was. This medical officer's training must have been brief. Even the benzol-filled syringe must have been a new experience for him. To kill men one by one when, where he had come from, lowering a lever was sufficient to asphyxiate three hundred people a minute, could not really be called a job. It was the work of a skilled craftsman. He must have had to adapt to the circumstances, which explained not only his ignorance of basic anatomy but also his clumsiness with the syringe.

What a nightmare, thought Paulo, as he watched him caper about. The madman was now taking a general shot, since there wasn't much left of the barbecued Pole. The foul creature wanted to finish his film for Martha, so that she could file the complete sequence in her folders without getting it mixed up with the others—the sequences of hanged men with their tongues hanging out, of hands stuck to high voltage wires, of shrunken heads, of skin peeled from tattooed chests, of dead men frozen at attention, all the atrocities which had been described to Paulo during his first days at Mauthausen. Now he believed.

Military executions were nothing new. But what had never before been seen in an army were doctors who murdered. Genuine doctors, who had studied to preserve life, and who now made it their business, through either cowardice or preference, to destroy life. For Herr Doktor Ramsauer was not unique. There were plenty like him in every camp, thousands of them, professional killers, qualified handlers of benzol vaccine. . . . How shameful for an army to authorize its health officers to replace the wand of Mercury on their uniform with a death's head. *Totenkopf:* a skull and two tibias, which was exactly what remained on the Loibl crematorium grill of a twenty-year-old Polish boy, taken in war.

Climbing back up the steep path with the empty stretcher on his back, Paulo couldn't get Ramsauer's disturbing features out of his mind. The face danced in front of his eyes, illuminated and distorted, lengthening and shrinking in the leaping flames. His demonic features were no mask: the doctor was mad. So were the *Rapportführer,* the Kommandant, the SS and the Kapos. All rabid, bloodthirsty lunatics.

"It's like a lunatic asylum inside out" had been Paulo's immediate reaction at Mauthausen. At Loibl Pass nothing had belied this truth; but in this smaller camp where life was led on the double, there was so little time to think that he had forgotten it. What he had just experienced in the grim riverbed plunged him brutally back into the state of panic which had gripped him six months before, when he saw the mound of men on a cart being taken to the huge chimneys. His own phrase sprang to his lips again:

"It's all over, we're finished, we're all going to die."

XI

Sailor had scored heavily when he assigned Paulo to the funeral detail. The empty bed next to his own scared the shit out of him.

He would have liked to rouse his snoring neighbors and make these ignorants share his fear. He would have liked to explain to them that one by one they would all turn into smoke, into a few black flakes which would swirl away over the Karawanken Mountains like Pavlovski and company.

He had to find someone to talk to, urgently. Rudely he shook Dédé, who was closest to him.

"Don't tell me you're asleep after what we've just seen. You've got a bloody thick skin."

"I wasn't asleep," answered Dédé, turning over. "I was thinking."

"Me too, and I bet we're thinking the same thing. We're all going to get done in—isn't that what you were thinking?"

"No, I was thinking about Pavlovski."

"That's what I mean. We'll all end up like him if we don't try something soon. Your Armistice in six months, that's a joke. Bloody smoke in six months, that's what it'll be. Can't you see they're killing us off man by man?"

Paulo's voice had risen.

"Not so loud," warned Dédé. "Sailor will hear you."

This counsel of caution restrained Paulo, but he wasn't letting Dédé go. He continued, this time in a whisper.

"You know exactly what I mean. This just can't go on, we've got to come up with some way of escaping. You and your big head, can't you come up with something?"

Paulo waited anxiously for a reply. He was badly in need of a few words of encouragement. Otherwise he'd toss and turn all night, and be left without the energy to scratch away at the mountain again in a few hours. That alone was sufficient cause for another empty bed next to Pavlovski's tomorrow night.

Unfortunately "bighead's" strong point was stoicism and the reply he gave was not going to help Paulo's insomnia.

"I've examined all the options," he said quietly. "To escape in our present situation is absolutely impossible. Escaping from the camp is out of the question. On the road up to the tunnel we might make ten yards before they got us. No chance on the work site either. The work teams are too heavily concentrated around the tunnel mouth and the sentries can almost touch each other. All we can do is wait. A tunnel had to be dug from both ends, and they'll have to lay on track at each end to get out the stones and earth. The area under surveillance will then be much bigger, which will alter everything. I'm going to wait, and I advise you not to try anything stupid. At the moment, you have exactly one chance in ten thousand of succeeding."

One chance in ten thousand. There was an authoritative ring to Dédé's last words. It was intentional and Paulo, silenced, found no reply. So Dédé, seizing his chance, turned over and disappeared under his sacking blanket.

"You've lost your nerve, go on, admit it," Paulo said after a few moments. But only to have the last word, because he knew quite well that Dédé's odds of ten thousand to one were absolutely right. Quite pointless trying to delude himself with dreams of escape. He had to stay, waiting and waiting like Dédé, the most intensely resistant of them all, who had waited patiently for nearly six months.

"Six months . . ." he said out loud.

For lack of a listener he was reduced to talking to himself to clear his thoughts. Perhaps in the end he'd be able to talk himself to sleep. He felt completely at sea. Patience or escape? It was terrible to confront the choice alone. The new generation of Krauts was less gentlemanly than their fathers in 1914. The Nazis didn't tolerate escape. But with their massive invasion of Europe and the huge numbers of prisoners they had taken, it had become difficult to police every corner of their new territory. They'd had to find a speedy alternative to a patrol force: just get every deportee to decide for himself not to escape. The bastards had achieved this aim without having to ask any prisoner's word of honor. Everyone knew what to expect if he bungled it. You didn't get a second chance with the Krauts, as you might at Cayenne.

But there was another excuse for giving up the idea of

escape which Paulo hadn't perhaps understood. What he had yet to see was that by suffering every minute of every day, by witnessing the horror, men merely became more determined than ever to stay alive. In the end, his brooding was of little use to him in this upside-down world. Forcing him to watch flames devouring his Polish neighbor had swept away five months of superhuman resistance. All he could do now was weep, hoping that at the next assembly his number would not be called out from the platform. Once more, Paulo the tough, the man with nerves of steel, was cracking up. Tonight, not one of those stupid men who were deafening him with their snores had reason to envy him. In fact, he was even more to be pitied than them for, quicker to weigh up situations, he had believed in something. He had believed in the tunnel. He had even become accustomed to the daily autos-da-fé and the smoke which was part of the scenery. But what had not fully sunk in, because before Pavlovski he had never seen it firsthand, was the atrocious end suffered by the men brought down from the construction site on stretchers with their bodies riddled by bullets, the end suffered by the ghosts spilling out of the infirmary with their hearts punctured by Ramsauer's deadly syringe. Now Paulo could see them all, laid out naked on the grill, doused with diesel. Now he knew how they suddenly caught fire, like torches, with a muffled explosion. The worst was knowing that that's how he would go.

"Tonight was a rehearsal of my funeral," he murmured very low.

If he continued thinking like this, Sailor wouldn't need to give him the standard early-morning call. He'd find him wide awake anyway. But he'd have to get some sleep if he didn't want to end up on the review platform as a saboteur. It was his first sleepless night since his arrival at Loibl. Clearly, he was in a bad way, a very bad way. And still there was nobody to talk to. In the dormitory of Block 3, everyone was snoring. It was sickening; even Dédé was fast asleep.

Deep in the tunnel, safe from informers' ears, Joel had dropped all suspicion of Paulo and spoken at length about his Breton friend. Paulo had learned that before Dédé's arrest he had occupied a very important position in the Resistance network throughout the whole of Brittany. He had been in prison since January 1942, almost eighteen months. He had spent more than a year in solitary at Fresnes, submitted to weekly interrogation. Dédé hadn't talked, and that was probably why he hadn't been eliminated. With a track record like his, Joel had asserted, he had earned the firing squad many times over: parachute drops, sabotage, radio transmissions, intelligence, all more than qualified him for execution.

Paulo tried to recall everything the small gym teacher had quietly disclosed. Ménard had been arrested in his parents' small house in Rennes, tapping out the news of his network chief's capture right up to the last minute. He had known for an hour that a radio detector van was circling the house; he could have shut down and gone underground. He had chosen to stay at his post, like the captain of a sinking ship, and, "thanks to his sacrifice," Joel had declared, "the fight against the Germans still goes on in Brittany."

Joel had also spoken about himself in a modest way. He too had a pedigree well worth an appearance on the red *Bekanntmachung* poster for all to see: Name Le Goff, Joel; Age 22; and underneath in small letters, as if to reassure the general public, Occupation Terrorist. Joel still bore on his forehead the marks of twenty sessions with the SD, the super-Gestapo, in the basement of the Edouard VII hotel. His shaven skull bore the imprints of the gun butts which had left him half dead one spring afternoon in 1942, lying on the pavement of the boulevard Raspail by the Hotel Lutétia. He had tried to escape from the Mercedes which was collecting him back from the torture sessions. Ménard had been with him and their friendship dated from that time. "There must be something wrong if guys of that caliber won't try a break," thought Paulo.

With the arrival of the second convoy, a lot of fanatical anti-Germans like Joel and Dédé had appeared at Loibl. Firstly, the communists, Etcheverry and the small group of new men who seemed to be supporting him after his spell in the *Revier* so that he didn't falter ("Courage, comrade, we're behind you"). All of them inflexible militants to whom, back in France, life was cheap, whether it was their own or that of people who got in the way of their chosen course of action. There were others too, of good French families, who knew that by joining the Resistance they were putting their lives on the line, like the two farmers from Morbihan who had arrived with Dédé and were survivors of his group, or the wizened white-haired lawyer, chief of the Resistance in Limoges, or the crazy young man from Burgundy, who at the age of eighteen was shooting at the Krauts with his grandfather's revolver, or the others who had just allowed themselves to be caught up in it. Altogether, there was quite a crowd of these volunteers for death, almost a company. Formed into a squad and well armed, they could have wrought havoc pitted against the Wehrmacht, and especially against the SS. They would have given no quarter, and taken no prisoners. And even the rest of the bunch—the ones rounded up at random, who'd done nothing, who didn't try to understand—could have swelled the ranks and played their part, following the mass like sheep, as they usually did. Count in the crooks, who would have ample opportunity to prove their belligerence and practice their talent for killing, and what a force they wouvd make!

Paulo was forgetting the nightmare of the crematorium, but this vision of the whole Kommando armed and merciless, let loose upon the enemy, excited more than calmed him, and he was set for a sleepless night.

His vision had its good side, too. For a little while now, he had resented his sleeping neighbors less; they were all elements of his imaginary avenging army. Sitting up on his bunk he counted his "comrades," and row by row, bed by bed, his glance lingered on each man, brushing aside his worst traits: ass-licking, greed and other dirty little tricks. He chose to remember what he had willfully ignored until the last few days, and what everybody else, especially those who had most to gain, had forgotten—that they ware all here for the same reason. For a good majority, this reason was courage. These men who had suffered for months the most humiliating degradations, who had been brought so low that they began to despise themselves—these men were the valor of France.

Running around eighteen hours a day with a hose on your tail took away all your strength, it drained you. Every evening, five minutes after lights out, you couldn't fight off sleep, you didn't have time to think, you didn't have time to remember why you were there. You had to have a whole night without sleep, like Paulo, to retrace your steps so far back into the past, to the mainspring of it all, to France.

But what in God's name was France up to in the middle

of August 1943? She certainly wasn't trying to find out what had become of her four hundred children, miraculously snatched from the flames of an extermination camp. And what of the Red Cross, what good were they doing? Their investigating committees weren't very effective. The Frenchmen at Loibl could stuff themselves with snails, grass and bark, they could die. Nice parcels weren't coming their way; it was far easier to address them to the fat bums in POW camps.

Joel, Dédé and Etcheverry were officers, weren't they, or at least Resistance leaders? Why weren't they in a POW camp? Dédé would have liked a library where he could pursue his studies, and a little sports ground for Joel, even behind barbed wire, would have kept him in shape. There was enough material at Loibl to get together basketball teams, bridge clubs, amateur dramatic groups, choirs and a lot more. What sort of a spineless France was she who could line the stomachs of men who had surrendered her, and deny those who had tried to save her?

She must have been aware that they were being burned in the tens of thousands: schoolteachers, mayors, priests, workmen, farmers and students, shipped off each week in freight cars from Compiègne; because these departures were rarely unscheduled. Paulo even remembered seeing news cameramen at the station. It was obvious that on that day the German and the Vichy propaganda ministries had collaborated to arrange for a train overflowing with repatriated prisoners to pull into the same platform as the train scheduled for Mauthausen. It chuffed slowly into the station, so that they'd get some good film. Each car bore the same inscription in huge letters: "Long live the Relief Troops!" Drunk as lords, the heroes of 1940 had waved their arms in thanks to those who were going to take their place in the factories of their new ally, the Reich. They believed it all, these artless repatriates, but they had clearly been taken aback at being cold-shouldered by the twenty-five hundred replacements in the train opposite when, thinking they were doing the right thing, they broke into the "Marseillaise." Only then did they realize at last that something had changed at home.

"Shut your fucking mouths! . . . Fuck your Relief! . . . Death to Pétain! . . ."

That finally shut up the *Kriegsgefangene*. Back home in their villages, they couldn't have talked much about what they had seen and heard. Otherwise Vichy might have tried to find out what the Germans really intended to do with the replacement work force, which heavy-handed *Feldgendarmes* were thrusting into the train with their rifle butts. A hundred men sealed into each car with no air and no water.

Of course France must know by now what went on in the death trains, whose escorts fired at random through the partitions to silence the screams. Some prisoners had managed to jump, Paulo had seen them with his own eyes. They must have told their story. So, was France just going to stand back? Would she make no protest? Didn't anybody know about the ovens waiting at the other end? After all, a camp the size of Mauthausen with its disproportionate complement of guards, and the columns of civilians who went in by tens of thousands but who never came out, surely must stick out a mile. Of course the French administration knew the score, but they were keeping quiet, in order not to rock the boat.

"*C'est la guerre*," Marshal Pétain must have shrugged when he learned what went on. For a man who had known the slaughter of Verdun, with fifty thousand, a hundred thousand dead, this was a trifle.

But what the sublime statesman forgot a little too easily was that among these new-style combatants boarding trains for the east were women, children and invalids, and that those to whom he had extended his old man's hand were waiting impatiently to exterminate them.

Even at Mauthausen Paulo had never thought that the old soldier could be held partly responsible for the systematic massacre of French citizens unloaded each month, neither tried nor sentenced, and often simply scooped up by chance. But at that time, Paulo had only thought of his own skin, and he hadn't made the connection. For him Pétain had remained a pleasant memory. He was the respected buffer who had elevated rationing to the status of a religion, giving the sharpsters an unexpected boost to their trade. Had Paulo not arrived at Mauthausen with this disgraceful attitude, it would not have taken him five months to realize that the buffer-Marshal laid himself wide open to some pretty nasty allegations. Paulo had seen the proof with his own eyes in Block 16, which was full of communists whom the Republic had thrown in the slammer for security reasons in 1939. Pétain had quite simply handed these wicked Frenchmen over to Hitler, and those who had survived didn't mince their words: he was a murderer.

If he had cared to, Paulo could also have listened to what the Spanish founder members of *KL* Mauthausen had to say. The French Head of State had sold out twelve thousand of these "refugees"—perhaps his most contemptible act. The two thousand Spaniards of Mauthausen had reason to bless Franco's friend, for they had been spared by Hitler to build his beautiful fortress there. Ten thousand deaths is quite a responsibility, especially the deaths of men who had just fought like tigers against the common enemy of Fascism, and those men had believed themselves protected by a generous France who had welcomed them with open arms. Paulo had often heard the dreadful saying: "Under each stone at Mauthausen lies the blood of a Spaniard."

But his memories of Mauthausen remained nebulous. The whirlwind of phantoms, of identical shadowy men who arrived with the same air of bewilderment to burn in concert, hadn't aroused his emotions. He hadn't seen them clearly, the thousands of red triangles, will-o'-the-wisps in an immense cemetery, who danced on the stage for a while and then disappeared, leaving him uncertain whether he had seen them at all. And then, Mauthausen was like a Tower of Babel, a hodgepodge of many races, of people whose language he didn't understand: Dutch, Danish, Czech, Hungarian, Bulgarian, Rumanian, Greek, Luxembourgeois, Russian, Yugoslavian, Polish, Romanies and other stateless people. All these foreigners were a far cry from his narrow world in Paris. The skulls, the pajamas, the mixture of nations, the huge annihilation factory, was all too vast to grasp, too unreal for anyone to do anything about.

Loibl, on the other hand, was a place worthy of at least France's attention. Here on the other side of the Alps, less than six hundred miles away, were several hundred of her missing sons who were not yet dead, who could still be saved. Alas, all trace of them had been lost in the smoke screen at Mauthausen. Kommando X was a military secret, it had been whisked away in the night. And now, pinned to the foot of this mountain, were old men who could take no more and boys being beaten to death by homosexual guards. There was no hope for them. France would never hear their cries of agony.

Would their mother country have taken up arms again if she had been aware of their plight? For this kind of suffering was far worse than death. Such an insult to the finest of her children (Paulo was thinking of the others, not of himself) was unacceptable to a country so scrupulous on matters of honor. How could they let her know? How could they get through to the military careerists with desk jobs who were waiting out the end of the war on both sides of the Mediterranean without getting their feet wet? How could they tell the Marshal: "Your sons are being martyred, they're being murdered, they're being raped, do something . . . ?"

Paulo was becoming more and more agitated, completely forgetting who he was, why he was there. He was identifying himself with the others, with the good guys, the patriots.

"Loibl *is* France's affair," he continued to himself, unrestrainable in his new train of thought. "And being in this death hole is, as Joel said, equivalent to an act of resistance."

It might only be the resistance of your backside to the riding crop, but never mind, the idea of struggle remained the same.

Paulo's emotions were at last stirring. But he was perfectly well aware that France's patriotic fervor would hardly be aroused by the picture of this army of tramps who all around him were snoring louder and louder. He knew that if the shaven heads from the Karawanken Mountains were suddenly dragged through the streets of Paris, the crowd would turn away with the same air of embarrassment they had shown on the return of the crippled veterans of 1914–18. The legless and the maimed are pitied, but people avoid them and cross over to the other side of the street. No hope in that direction; France could not be relied upon, she never had liked deformity. The only person you could rely on was yourself.

Paulo would have been wrong to regret his sleepless night, because he had made some progress. In a few moments, when his sleeping neighbors were beaten back to reality by the rubber hose, they'd carry on believing blindly in luck, God and France, being very careful not to raise a finger for fear of thwarting the march of destiny. But he had struck Providence from his program, for it only made you look heavenward when it was more useful to watch out for, and perhaps avoid, treacherous gun butts or the fatal burst of machine-gun fire. He had indeed made progress.

"You can't be helped, you bunch of wet rags," he concluded.

This time his voice had risen to a shout and two or three sleepers in the bunks below began to stir. One more word in that fierce Kapo's voice, and in two minutes everybody in the block, although numbed by sleep, would start running out to the *Appelplatz* in their shorts. A potentially dangerous initiative. Not spiteful to quite that extent, Paulo shut up. A little reluctantly nonetheless, because a general beating was the only thing that could have compensated for his turbulent night spent trying to find the best way out of this mess for the others, for all the imbeciles who wouldn't listen.

In his agitation, he was forgetting the main thing. It was he who needed the friends, not the other way around. In order to wake up France, to confront her with her shame and get her moving, there would have to be more evidence than the sorry tale of a crook. There were a few people in Paris who would have paid a lot of money to hear Paulo's yells of "Help! We're being murdered!" And as for the previous chapter of his nocturnal ramblings, the avenging army in stripes, it was certainly not his place to lead the crusade. There were men more qualified than he to set the tattered army on its feet. He'd be lucky if they just took him on.

Paulo now wanted to be among the foolish idealists. He needed their warmth. If he criticized them so loudly, it was mostly because his cries from the heart for human contact when unanswered.

Paulo didn't know it, but it was his heart that had been moved at the sight of old Etcheverry lying senseless by the torture stool, at the sight of Angel Belloni being belabored by the big tattooed queer, at the sight of the flames consuming the naked body of a twenty-year-old boy. In these awful moments Paulo, probably for the first time in his life, had forgotten to think of himself. On several occasions he had had to hold back the tears which welled up in his eyes. And that was a new experience for him as well; even at Mauthausen, shrine of cruelty, he had not felt like that. There must have been something unusual about Loibl for an unsentimental tough like Paulo, usually so impassive, to soften.

"Come on, you bitch of a bell, why don't you ring?" he cried in his exhaustion.

He sat on the end of his bed and calmly and quietly began to slip on his clothing. He would have liked to get fully dressed, put on his shoes, go and have a pee, do something to take his mind off his gloomy thoughts. But dawn was already breaking through the windows, lighting up the block, and a morning walk, fully clothed, through the building before the appointed time would certainly have aroused Sailor's wrath. Paulo stopped dressing, and to prevent his depressing introspection from taking hold of him once again, he began to count: one, two, three, ten, a hundred.

Had he known that his future was not so clearly mapped out as it seemed to be, he would have continued to devote the few precious minutes of calm and silence before muster to contemplation. He wouldn't have just counted sheep like a child trying to get to sleep. Had he known, he would have marked with a cross this third month in Yugoslavia which was coming to an end, to help him tell its story later in greater detail: the tanned skeletons with their zebra stripes, the crocodile of stones, the corridas, the *Gymnastik*, the lottery on the review platform, the line being crossed, the stack of logs, the doctor, both voyeur and carrion crow, and his well-matched wife. He'd need precise details if he wanted to be believed. Otherwise such an improbable story would be dismissed out of hand: "Come off it, what d'you take us for?" Even those who were living through this tragic merry-go-round had not stopped saying "It's unreal." Paulo heard the phrase a hundred times every day, in the camp or in the tunnel. There was no other way to describe the unprecedented hounding ("Get killed or get fucked, take your pick!"). At peak hours, when the madness of the Kapos and the SS reached its height and blood flowed everywhere, and when the cries of the wounded could be heard above those of the tormentors, each prisoner would beg the heavens for a witness to record the medieval tortures and fly to France to proclaim the truth to parents, friends and Pétain. Not so that France would take up their cause—there was no point in dreaming—but simply that she should know what was going on. By the end of August, that was all the condemned men of Loibl were asking. They all thought they would surely die, and the only message they wanted to get through to their dear country was one final testament: "Everything you have been told about Loibl Pass is true." The wretched men lived with the anguish that they might be called liars one day, even posthumously.

It must have been utterly unheard of anywhere for men in such misery to have to add to that misery the fear that no one, ever, would take their story seriously. It could have been precisely that childish concern to see their calvary verified and confirmed which stopped them imagining what would come after. When you reach that point, you're scarcely in the land of the living. So it was normal for Paulo and his comrades not to feel, in the dreadful passion play they were being forced to enact, that there would be repercussions.

Ding, ding, ding, the bell at last. *Alle raus, schnell, Waschraum*. They were off again. Paulo jumped out of his bed, but he had to put a hand out to steady himself. His legs were weak and he was feeling lightheaded after his sleepless night. He began the new day at a sprint, a day which would not end for sixteen hours. It couldn't go on like this.

XII

"*Kein Stein heute, Mensch. Stein fertig.*"

Paulo snatched his hands back, leaving the stone and just avoiding a nasty kick from the old fossil of a new *Kommandoführer*, who seemed the cantankerous kind, but his absurdly short legs were slow in reacting to the commands of his brain.

What cupboard had they dragged him out of? With his Iron Cross, his handlebar mustache *à la* Bismarck against his yellowed skin, small and wrinkled, he was a real relic. He continued braying orders, slapping the fat holster at his belt.

"Christ, he still thinks he's at Verdun," Paulo thought to himself, backing off sharply. "What's got into the SS to make them recruit old farts like that from 'fourteen-'eighteen?"

The appointment of the old boy to the important job of *Kommandoführer* seemed like a practical joke, but what was much more interesting was the command croaked out by the senile old codger: "No stones today, *fertig* stones."

What was behind this order which cheated the SS of

their favorite entertainment? It must certainly have come from above, direct from the Kommandant since he called the tune, but it wasn't quite in his line, nor was it his mission to husband the strength of men who were supposed to be squeezed dry. Before being posted to Loibl, he must have done his compulsory stint at the sinister Mauthausen quarry with its 186 steps. So what did lie behind the first treat he had handed out to his slaves in three months?

Yet although the crocodile was without stones for the first time, the news which spread through the striped column like wildfire, that the measure was permanent, was not greeted with great enthusiasm. The men must have been lamentably conditioned not to perceive that the tunnel, the object of their fear, was their ally. It was the tunnel which was the real Kommandant, and its great mouth open in the pinkish rock seemed to be warning the murderers:

"Slow down your massacre, otherwise there won't be a tunnel, and it'll be you, you German bums, who'll have to explain yourselves."

Nobody got this message, and the order, *Steine fertig*, was greeted with the traditional "No point trying to understand." Certainly everyone thought: "So much the better," but that was all. Kommando X had learned not to believe in anything that came from the SS anymore, especially not in anything good. Suspicion was the rule. And of anything that looked like good news, they were extra suspicious.

It was not surprising that such skeptics needed a good week to realize that a further order had stopped their slow march toward the crematorium even more effectively than the one to spare their strength. The second order put an end to the game of pushing prisoners over the line, unless it was justified by a valid professional reason. In short, murder on the grounds that a face didn't fit was now prohibited.

This time the prisoners had to admit it: they owed it to the tunnel, and the tunnel alone, that they no longer had to witness the horrible column of black smoke which rose every evening by the small larch wood. If occasionally it still appeared, they knew that they were only burning the incurables who had been injected with benzol by Ramsauer's syringe.

The *Arbeitskapos* had quickly changed their tactics: their manhunts were no longer directed toward the death line, but toward the tunnel. There were two openings now. The first one, fifteen feet wide and six feet high, was at ground level. The second was just above and much narrower. Paulo was intrigued and immediately made inquiries of a newcomer, a French-Pole, who was obviously a miner to the core. It was more than likely that this shadow owed the privilege of being chosen for Loibl to his coal-ingrained face. Hacking away all day at the rock reminded him of his life in the Pas-de-Calais pit from which the *Feldgendarmes* had extracted him. Almost like the good old days!

Stanislas was delighted to display his knowledge, and in his best northern accent he gave Paulo a lecture on tunnel building.

"Two holes is the Belgian way, the 'descent' method. It's used when the rock isn't hard like here. When the rock's hard, you use the German 'ascent' method. That is, you begin at the bottom and move upward. Here, the bottom hole will just be fitted with rails for the mining wagons. The real work will be done in the little hole at the top of the vault. It will be enlarged sideways, then shored up with pilings, a wooden frame will be built and brickwork will follow. All the rubbish will get slung out through trap doors into the wagons in the gallery below. The place to be is down below. There's nothing to do while the wagons cart the material outside."

"Hmm, you seem to know quite a bit about it," exclaimed Paulo, partly to flatter the amiable Pole, but mainly so that he carried on.

"A tunnel's just plain sailing compared to a mine. The only problem is your lungs getting filled with rock dust, which is very dangerous. If we get out of here, we ought to be X-rayed."

This extra treat hadn't occurred to Paulo, but in any case, it wouldn't be tomorrow they got their TB checkups. In the meantime, there was the vault to be getting on with, the rails to be laid, trap doors to be installed, all the woodwork, the masonry and the whole bag of tricks. It was truly a major operation which was going to take quite some time. All of which was good news.

"It's going to take a good while, then?"

"Depends on the length of the tunnel," the northerner answered. "The height and width I suppose will be twelve by twelve for the big trucks to get through, twenty-tonners and more. Have they told you how far it is from here to Austria?"

"About a mile, it seems."

"A mile..." the Pole muttered to himself, rubbing his coal-furrowed forehead. "A mile... a year, easily, to get through to the other side, and then widen it. After that, it'll have to be cemented. It could go faster if the Austrians have bombs under their asses like us. Didn't you know? They've got prisoners on the other side as well."

Oh hell, Paulo had never even thought about the other side. Obviously there must be guys attacking the mountain from the Austrian side, otherwise the Yugoslavian team could be at it for years, digging a rather circular tunnel in the heart of the Karawankens.

"They must be deportees from another camp," replied Paulo, not wishing to appear ignorant. But he would have liked to know, just for his own information, exactly what the score was on the other side of the mountain.

That same evening Paulo and the whole camp knew the answer. Less than fifteen minutes after muster, a contingent for Austria had been bludgeoned into volunteering. Forty pioneers, who seemed to have been chosen at random, found themselves formed up in front of the kitchen block. Those who had been recommended were forbidden from that moment on to enter the barracks or to talk to the men who were left. On pain of the usual. A separate dormitory had been prepared for them well out of the way near the clothing store, and they were put to bed immediately because in a few hours they were going off on a hike. They'd have a bird's-eye view, no less, from the col of Loibl Pass (5091 feet exactly), which they would scramble over like mountaineers. But without rucksacks, because like the thousands of unfortunate men who had been through Mauthausen, they had no possessions whatsoever. Not even a spoon to eat their meager soup with, not even a spare shirt or a handkerchief to cry into.

Old Etcheverry was among them, which prompted Paulo to remark that chance was not the only factor. The list of "volunteers" for what they called Nordfeld had been carefully drawn up by Bullseye, Fritz, Sailor and all the other block chiefs. There were very few young or sturdy men in the exiled Kommando, except for about fifteen new arrivals, almost all Poles, who had not yet been allocated to a particular section. Even the Kapo, Willy from the Saar, who wore a green triangle and had been promoted chief of the new camp, didn't appear to be in the authorities' good books. It was obvious the sneaky coup organized by his fellow Kapos had taken him by surprise, and to put a brave face on it, he began to strike out viciously at the unhappy prisoners who were going to share his penance on the Austrian expedition.

It was still pitch-dark the next day when the northern team set off for the col, and a few hours later on the *Appelplatz* Joel looked terribly subdued without his inseparable companion, the old history teacher, next to him. Paulo knew how he felt. He too was affected by the departure of this brave and intelligent man, who maintained his dignity through all the suffering and humiliation. The old man set an example to all. Even with his ass exposed on the stool or in the scuffle for extra soup, he had never lost that dignity.

"After all, one way or the other," Paulo whispered in Joel's ear, "your friend couldn't have held out very much longer. Don't think about it any more. Tell yourself it's good news they're setting up a site on the north side. It proves that Kommando X is responsible for the whole tunnel. They need us, and they're going to go on needing us for a long time. Do you see? Come on, forget your old friend, and anyway perhaps we'll see him again when the tunnel is through."

Joel's gaze was distant and he didn't seem to have heard. Paulo could have sworn that the tough little Breton was praying. Such tenderness in this brutal world was a fine thing, but since Compiègne, there had been so many good friends, childhood friends, brothers, fathers and sons whom destiny had cruelly separated that it was impossible to sympathize each and every time. And besides, Paulo had difficulty disguising his satisfaction at the events of the last ten days in this blessed hole: the end of the useless fatigues and the capricious executions, and above all the daily arrival of more civilians, engineers, surveyors, drivers, explosives experts and their retinue.

New barracks had sprung up around the tunnel mouth: workshops, tool sheds, a carpenter's shed, a forge and even a refectory with benches. But no one was under any illusions; the refectory was the product of expediency, to avoid wasting time going to and from the camp, and to be able to assemble all the workers together during the lunch break, so that the face workers and the surface Kommandos could be duly counted and recounted, one by one, at the entrance and the exit. So, during the midday break, the SS could leave their posts along their famous line. But for security's sake they had stuck their own refectory directly opposite the door of the other. Thus, with a single machine gun leveled in the right direction, they could all shovel in their sauerkraut without worrying.

At the same time, the camp's attentions had been focused on the north side. Over the last few days there had been a second and a third departure, but the third one was made up of deportees straight from Mauthausen: more Poles, some Czechs or Hungarians, and about a hundred Russians, who were merely rushed through the camp's main avenue.

As two block chiefs had been attached to the company going north, Mauthausen had immediately sent down two more: an Austrian by the name of Sladek, hideous, toothless and green-triangled, who inherited Block 4, and Eddy, a pure German, but at first glance apparently quite agreeable. His supple and muscular body, which rippled beneath his striped but overtailored uniform, compensated for his small size. He radiated strength and health, but this Kapo's most unusual features were his freckles and his enormous green eyes. Very feline. He was queer, of course, like his colleague Sladek, but he didn't appear to be the butch kind. With his shapely body, and his eyes whose long lashes he fluttered like a silent-movie actress, he must have been the other kind. Just so that no one was left in any doubt, the SS administration had stuck the pink triangle of the homosexual below his registration number—which didn't seem to bother him in the slightest.

The arrival of a Kapo who was mild and soft-spoken and who swung his hose without conviction made the men of Block 4 green with envy. They had had no luck whatsoever because the other new Kapo, Sladek, seemed quite simply to have been let out of an asylum. His fits of rage were equal to those of Bullseye and Sailor put together; he almost foamed at the mouth when he yelled and lashed out. His eyes were more protuberant even than Hitler's, and they darted about in all directions, making him a very dangerous customer indeed.

It was impossible to know who was the target of his

abuse. You only knew as the blows from his feet, fists and hose landed on you. And they hurt like anything, because the psychopath was also very well built.

The doyen, homo-in-chief of the south, had nonetheless managed to keep back a Russian for himself, a young boy of nineteen who was very thin but very handsome; and he had immediately christened him Sebastopol, after the boy's hometown no doubt. It was quite interesting to have in the camp a Soviet who could tell them about the battles of the Red Army and whether its advance was continuing.

Sebastopol was quite irrepressible. He had had a rough time for the last two years as a partisan before being captured, and presumably afterward as well, but that hadn't dampened his fervor. The first thing he did when he arrived was to tell everybody that he was a member of the communist youth group of his town, and that the invading Fascists had lost the war. Theoretically, the Kapos ought to have drawn the attention of the SS to this young wolf who was in danger of subverting the rest of the flock. But Sebastopol was so good-looking and had such beautiful eyes that the old queer of a doyen, casting prudence aside, refused to pay any attention to telltales. Since Herr Lageraltester, who went by the dashing name of Otto, let things be, there was no good reason not to hear the Marxist gospel. The young Russki had been attached to Pozzi's spearhead Kommando, to the vanguard, as Stanislas the Polish tunnel Ph.D. had labeled it, where they needed strength, and Paulo was delighted. With Dédé in the next bed at night and Sebastopol as his teammate by day—both of them optimists whose most frequent topic of conversation was along the lines of "The Krauts are in the shit"—Paulo could count himself a very lucky man.

Their neat summary of the military situation was in any case quite adequate, because in the upper and more important of the two galleries (the Belgian method) which had been given to Pozzi as a favor, there weren't many natural breaks which would allow lengthy discussion. They had to catch up at all costs with the team below, which had penetrated to a depth of over three hundred feet and was already beginning to lay the railway track. With the help of the rubber hoses, of course. It was far too good an opportunity for the Kapos to miss, since the men's hands were taken up with track laying and they couldn't protect their heads. Besides, there was nothing else to hit in the tunnel: it was now virtually forbidden to lay into miners like Paulo and his companions.

The pneumatic drills began their infernal din at six o'clock every morning. Gone were the little hand hammers first used to chip away at the sandy rock. In their place were enormous drills powered by a deafening compressor which made a one meter fifty mining bar look like a knitting needle and took two men to hold. These siege engines shook you to pieces, and Paulo would have liked to beg off, but he was less emaciated than many and Hanz, chief Kapo of the tunnel, had noticed him: *Du gut Mineur.* It would have been very unwise to duck such a compliment.

Every three hours on the dot, at nine, at one o'clock after lunch, four and seven, the mining bars were supposed to be three feet deep in the rock. Ten minutes for a trusted civilian to stuff bundles of dynamite into the holes and light the wick; then, *Alle raus*. At which they had to shift to get to the exit if they didn't want to be hit on the head by falling rocks. Especially as the miners didn't have helmets, another of the mining directors' original ideas. The Krauts must have felt that scalps worked over with clubs were as tough as steel plate. In any case, the helmets were needed elsewhere, at Stalingrad for example, where, according to the little communist fanatic, the gray-green army had lost three hundred thousand of its best soldiers. At a pinch, one could understand an economy drive on helmets, and anyway for the moment it wasn't exactly raining slabs of rock. But what was much more unpleasant was the lack of masks for the shovelers, who, exactly five minutes after the explosion, were forced to go straight back through clouds of gas to clear away the debris. At top speed, so that their colleagues on the pneumatic drills could keep to the schedule.

The first few times, taking a big risk, some half-asphyxiated men had dared to come back out again. Coughing, spitting and puking, their eyes as bloodshot as rare beef, they tried to clear their lungs in the fresh air while waiting for the clouds of gas to subside. Such initiative was termed sabotage, and hardly a week ago it would have earned them a trip over the line. But today, clearly each man was recognized as useful, and the saboteurs got away each time with a few gun butts on their backs which prodded them relentlessly back into the depths of the tunnel.

But all this to-ing and fro-ing in the galleries wasted a good quarter of an hour after each explosion. By the end of the day, it amounted to an hour for each gallery. In other words, including the two galleries on the north side, it added up to four hours a day. Herr Putz, the chief engineer, saw this delay as pure folly and took the matter into his own hands. All the men in the tunnel were issued with a cheap little mask of his own design; it was just a sponge which you moistened before you clamped it over your mouth, to allow normal breathing without inhaling gas. But Putz was a practical man and his sponge wasn't just a wad of absorbent material. He had designed it with strings which knotted behind the head to hold it in place. As it left the men's hands free, there was no need to wait for the screen to dissipate before starting work again. Of course, for the first ten minutes their unprotected eyes suffered badly and streamed with tears. There was a good chance that some of these wretched men, who had held back tears for months, were taking advantage of the situation to shed real tears.

When all was said and done, it had been a stroke of luck to get the sharp-witted Putz as their chief engineer. The SS would never have come up with the sponge idea on their own, and the fact that they allowed this humanitarian solution was yet another indication of change.

The real boss of Loibl was now Putz. Or more precisely, Universale Hoch und Tiefbau Aktiengesellschaft of Vienna, the company which had assigned to him the job of seeing the tunnel project through. Herr Putz had posted the name of his firm all over the work site, as proof that it was possible to serve the causes of both the National Socialists and the capitalists at the same time. The hourly wage being what it was, the Universale must have been making a tidy profit.

An announcement at roll call that, as of that evening, there would be a night shift did not provoke any sulks. For the French, working around the clock meant three shifts of eight hours as in the good days of the Popular Front. But when it was explained to them that they would do just fine with two teams working twelve hours each, they all wisely refrained from comment.

It took a week of night-shift work for the miners to realize that they had been duped into trusting the new system. For the simple reason that Putz had reckoned without the block chiefs. For the past three months the brutes had found time hanging heavy in their domain, deserted from five in the morning till seven at night. They couldn't contain their joy at seeing the night-shift miners return just as the others escaped their clutches. Every morning at six-thirty on the dot the full company of bastards in docker's caps waited at the gates, eyes glued to the road. Their life preservers hung by their sides and their heads were full of ideas. The little darlings marching shakily down the road after an exhausting night were theirs, all theirs, until evening when the rest of the troupe returned. It was going to be Sunday every day from now on. For miners covered in dust the routine was a thorough scrub to start with, followed by a cock inspection and general search, all of which was a good two hours' worth.

That sort of timetable made the night shift's week a long one, and Putz was quick to notice that the miners were not putting their backs into the drilling, and that each new explosion lost a few inches more. "The Frenchmen are not standing up to the change in working hours," he said to himself. "We'll have to fatten them up." And he ordered a large spoonful of drippings to be distributed to all the night workers, to be taken each morning—under careful supervision.

These pounds of fat had an unfortunate effect on some people. Firstly on the block chiefs, who felt ill at the sight of a hundred good-for-nothings gobbling up all those precious reserves of fat every morning. It was far better used for crisping their *Kartoffel* or browning bits of meat whipped from the bottom of the soup vats and mixing them with onions. What a waste, and yet another perfect reason for taking it out on the *Schweine Franzosen*!

If discipline at Loibl had been slacker, the drippings might well have been responsible for a number of deaths. The first time it was distributed, the entire camp began to hate the privileged miners who consumed their spoonful of fat each morning under everyone's nose with as much lip-smacking as if it were caviar. They had all had the same idea for making the treat last longer: they saved up the slice of bread from the previous evening's snack. These starving men must have had great will power to restrain themselves for the whole night from eating their one crust of bread a day, but the pork fat gave their stale bread such a wonderful taste that it seemed like cake. For a good quarter of an hour they almost wore their tongues out, licking their crusts like lollipops. And all the others who had to stand and watch them eat felt like strangling them. But there was only one way to get a taste of these damn drippings; you had to worm your way into the night team. For a few days at Loibl, everyone was obsessed with plotting his way into the night and, once there, with staying put.

Paulo knew that he didn't have long to enjoy the revolting pudding coveted by so many envious volunteers. And in the end, he didn't give a damn, for despite the well-being which the early-morning greasing spread through his poor dried-out body, all he really wanted, more and more, was to be outside breathing the pure mountain air. With all the gas and stone dust he swallowed during the shift, with the unholy vibration of the pneumatic drills, and with the sleepless nights, it was goodbye to any health he had left. So Putz could take his drippings and he could stuff them.

XIII

Paulo had no time to devise a way of getting himself kicked out of the tunnel, for toward the middle of September a piece of news broke which pushed his own problem right into the background. The Saturday corridas had been canceled!

It was incredible, it would change everything. Apart from a few incurable pessimists who greeted the news with the characteristic "They're up to something!" the majority of prisoners who had not believed in any of the previous indications now admitted, a good while after Paulo, that the Germans wanted to make them last. Right down to Serpette, the village idiot.

"They're fu-fucked . . . because of the tu-tu-tunnel!" he stammered with joy.

And yet SS and Kapos went out of their way to keep the prisoners in the dark. By midday assembly on the first Saturday, nothing had leaked out. The prisoners hurriedly downed their soup, staying on their feet, and every man tensed his buttocks, trying to look as small as possible. But as a whole hour passed, and still no sign of the matadors, they all began to wonder what was going on.

It was Maumau of the Bastille, closely linked to Bullseye (very closely linked), who first had confirmation of the news. It was official: "Bullseye wouldn't have dared lie to me. The corrida is over."

By three o'clock the Kapos had still not made any attempt to disperse the men standing around in groups. The prisoners had to concede that the authorities were probably up to something, but that of course didn't stop them from being rooted to the spot by a sort of panic at not knowing what to do with themselves. Should they go into the blocks and stretch out on their mattresses? Out of the question. Should they sit down outside? That was out as well, they would never dare. In truth, it was their empty hands which troubled these convict professionals the most. They couldn't just stick them in their pockets and stroll around the *Appelplatz* like well-behaved pupils in a school playground. They were all stricken by a feeling of guilt, almost of shame, longing for an order, any order, to put an end to their confusion.

Sure enough, Sailor and Max, the chief of Block 5—a Czech with a green triangle, queer as a nine-franc note and a lunatic to boot—started yelling. Instinctively, before they'd even understood the German orders, the entire camp formed into ranks, block by block.

"Who asked you to line up, you bunch of greasers? Why so eager all of a sudden?"

It was obviously some kind of trick; even the *Dolmetscher* couldn't get over having to interpret this crass outburst. Listening to the chief without being lined up, without standing to attention? It all smacked of a nasty joke. The faces the two bastards pulled in feigned surprise at their squared-up flock were very appropriate for men who had spent the greater part of their lives beating up the thousands of heads, noses and ears which marred the harmony of their assemblies. The pride and joy of these idiots and their favorite maneuver was to achieve a formation so perfect that from either the front or the side only one man could be seen per rank. All Europe's deportees knew that perfect formation was obligatory when they were addressed in German. So Karl and Max really should have known better than to tire themselves out with furious yelling which only sounded false. But in the end they had to be obeyed, and everyone broke ranks to gather round and hear what they had to say.

"Today, *Menschen*, you're going to take French leave. No work, no corrida, the Kommandant and the Universale Company want you nice and fresh for work on Monday. A shame, because your PT lessons were giving good results, but the tunnel is more important. We must finish it quickly. Then we can build another one, and then another one. Until you all end up as worn-out old fools, only fit to be boiled up for soup. But don't worry, you won't be missed. All right, bums, dismissed."

Sailor and Max seemed rather put out by this order from above which deprived them of their weekend entertainment. But from his bungalow behind the SS barracks the Kommandant had a bird's-eye view of the camp through his binoculars, and Putz, the real boss, was certainly going to keep a weather eye out from the other side of the road. It was most likely he who had demanded a stop to the pointless death race which beat his precious miners into the ground every weekend.

Even so it must have been quite a show for the civilian camp over the last two months; the club gala must have looked like a Roman circus and some, such as Mère Ramsauer, must have had quite a thrill. On the other hand, many like the little brunette and her Slav friends must have been sickened by it. Had they perhaps protested? In any case, it was comforting to think so.

The good news had added significance for Paulo. He no longer needed to get mixed up in all that preaching of dignity, solidarity and resistance. Nor did he have to force himself to be friendly with Joel, Dédé and the others, anti-Krauts up to the hilt. They were becoming a little tiresome with their fixed ideas. From now on, all that mattered was to get by on your own, to take care of yourself, to try and work less, eat more and not get knocked around unnecessarily. Paulo's new approach quickly took shape as Sailor continued ranting to mask his disappointment.

Each man for himself, just like Paname. It was even worth getting back in with those who were well placed, the Ritons and Bercks of the camp, or Bullseye's little boy friend, who was visibly putting on weight, and not only around his buttocks. Henceforth the most pressing need was for food.

Paulo was busy contemplating this fine resolution when a

word from Sailor caught his attention. *Küche*, yelled Karl, kitchen. He was looking for volunteers for a duty in the holy of holies.

In two bounds Paulo was back in the first row with a group of other hungry fellows. They only needed two men per block and Sailor's choice was made with a great slap on the cheek. Paulo caught one, but he didn't mind, as it sent him flying in the direction of the kitchen.

Two minutes later, cap in hand, he reported to the kitchen Kapo, accompanied by a young peasant who had also had the benefit of Karl's open hand.

"This guy looks all right," Paulo thought, announcing his block and registration number. In fact, in spite of the thieves' green triangle which decorated his tunic, the chief cook didn't look like much of a villain. There was even something refined about this German. He was in his early forties and quite handsome; his cheeks were smooth and his crew-cut hair was peppered with gray. The regulation *Autobahn* had to be looked for. In its place he had an impeccable parting, lightly touched by the razor, which showed off his silvery head. He was immaculate from head to toe: his jacket and trousers didn't have so much as a wrinkle or stain, and he wore a tunic collar and leather shoes which shone like burnished copper. Paulo felt almost embarrassed to present himself, grubby as he was, to such an elegant man. Particularly since the gentleman-cook smelled good too. Well, maybe he'd overdone it a little.

"But at least he's the type who folds up his clothes before he goes to bed," thought Paulo, unable to find this queer disagreeable.

As if welcoming houseguests, the *Küchenkapo* stood to one side as he ushered in the ten men of the detail. He almost seemed to want to give them a guided tour of his show kitchen. For that's exactly what it was, as polished and as perfumed as he, sparkling clean. The ragged little group couldn't understand what on earth they were doing in this hygienic laboratory where there was nothing to clean. All they could do was make the place filthy with their muddy boots and their pajamas covered in tunnel dust.

Monsieur le Kapo, who spoke French with a legionnaire's accent, explained their task: he had asked for them because he wanted potatoes to be taken from one unit, peeled and put in another.

"You may sit down if you wish," he finished.

The volunteers didn't know what to make of it. They weren't being beaten or insulted; they felt horribly ill at ease and not one of them dared move.

"Come, gentlemen," urged the Kapo gently, lifting the lid of a huge pot and distributing a knife to each man.

Paulo thought he would faint when he saw the mountain of potatoes they were supposed to peel. "Christ, who's all that for?" he wondered, grasping an enormous *Kartoffel*. "We haven't seen half that many in our soup vats in three whole months." Obviously they were for the SS troops, but just looking was incredible.

With their eyes starting out of their heads, the prisoners set to. The potatoes were hot, white and floury. It broke their hearts to have to chuck them, when peeled, into the cooker. Paulo was the first to take a chance. He cut one in half, stuffed the bigger piece into his mouth and swallowed it whole. Red in the face and half-choked, he glanced around to see if he had been spotted by the Kapo. No reaction. He could risk another.

The small peasant from Block 3 who had come with Paulo hadn't seen anything either. His particular brainstorm was to stuff his pockets with peelings. What a feast the poor sucker would have tonight!

Paulo preferred to take things on account immediately. It was risky, but this kitchen chore was pure provocation, worse than the torture of Tantalus. So fuck the consequences! He was too hungry, likely to go mad from a hunger which hadn't let up for a single day in the past six and a half months. An opportunity like this was hardly likely to come their way again, and soon the ten barebones were stuffing themselves to the bursting point, throwing all caution to the winds because the Kapo had just been called to the door.

Half the *Kartoffel* taken out of the first cooker were fast disappearing into the concave bellies of the starving men, when Ernst—that was the gracious kitchen chief's name—came to resume his supervision. Paulo, who was by now full up, began to study him.

Ernst hadn't been taken in, that was quite certain. He

probably knew to the nearest potato how many the detail had gobbled up. And still he said nothing. He stared at all his potato peelers in turn, but it was obvious that he was miles away, far from his cooking and far from the camp. Although he must have been moldering away at Mauthausen or with Mauthausen Kommandos for years, it didn't seem to have marked him: there was no vulgarity, nor any meanness or brutality in this fellow. A romantic before being collared, a romantic he had remained, despite his ignominious badge. A poet in this key position was a pleasant surprise and Paulo would have liked to make friends with him. You never knew, they might need an assistant in the kitchen now and again.

When Ernst rested his glance on Paulo, the latter tried out a little smile with a touch of the coquette about it. If he was queer, it might do the trick. Nil response: the handsome Kapo was wrapped up in his dreams again.

Paulo was disappointed, and by way of consolation he popped another potato into his mouth. But he had no room left in his distended stomach; as at the end of a black-market beanfeast, he had to admit defeat. And every single man of the detail was in the same state. Satiated, crammed to the gills with potatoes, they were all only a belch away from vomiting. Had the little scene taken place in a less forbidding kitchen, they could have been taken for kitchen boys who'd helped themselves to a little too much Beaujolais. Blinking muzzily, feeling lightheaded, they had the classic symptoms of drunkenness. Getting stone drunk on fistfuls of *Kartoffel* was certainly unusual, but then things always were a little different at Loibl.

"Perhaps they'll want all of us back the same time next Saturday," thought Paulo dizzily.

He must have been off his head because you don't hit the jackpot twice. Particularly since competition would be fierce once the news of the potato orgy spread through the camp.

The *Kartoffel* bouncing from one cooker to the other would never be seen again. In a few hours they would have disappeared down the gullets of the greedy SS. "Unless we put a few on one side as a little reserve to last us till next Saturday, till the next peeling duty," thought Paulo. "That might be pushing our luck: however easygoing he looks, we can't be sure the Kapo will let that pass. He might even have warned the others to search the whole crew on our way out.

It's too risky to trust a German." Paulo had yet to meet a good German. Best to be cautious on the way out. Even the chief engineer would be powerless to prevent that fatal crossing of the line, faced with such a heinous crime as robbing the SS of their food. "It's too bad, I can't bear all this handling of quality spuds, and we're nearly at the end of the pot. Ah, I've got it," Paulo said to himself.

Casually he bent over to tie his shoelaces, but instead of tightening them he undid them completely. Then he tugged on his trouser bottoms and stuffed them under his heels. He finished up by pulling his laces hard and winding them around his ankles before securing them with a double knot. He had just made himself a real pair of ski pants, or rather two enormous kangaroo pouches, with enough room to stash away a good six pounds of potatoes between heels and flies. Loosening the cord which served as a belt, he slipped the last of the unpeeled *Kartoffel* down his trousers, two or three at a time.

The Kapo had disappeared again, so there was no immediate danger, but Paulo's companion peelers were alarmed by his boldness. He was taking a risk with a capital R, thieving such an enormous amount. A potato in each pocket, fair enough, you might get away with it, but several pounds was bound to warrant the maximum penalty. The rest of the men would dearly have liked to make him abandon his folly, but all of a sudden the tall prisoner with the mean look in his eye and his idle peeling knife frightened them as much as an SS. The whole scene had something of a holdup about it, the only difference being that this bandit was not scooping up dollars or *louis d'or* in front of his petrified audience, but common or garden potatoes at a cent a pound.

Audacity pays those who are born under a good sign. Paulo was a Sagittarian. He was the only one who got through on the way out. Most of the men, following the example of the little peasant from Block 3, had stuffed their pockets with potato peelings.

"Turn out your pockets," the Kapo ordered each one, "and go and put that rubbish in the bin." But he said it nicely, half smiling.

Two or three braver men had risked a whole potato, which earned them a slap. But the Kapo slapped them without conviction, lightly and almost affectionately, as one would a spoiled child. What a world of difference there was between this reluctant Kapo and his colleagues. When Paulo went past him, having turned his pockets inside out without being asked, the Kapo placed a hand gently on his chest to stop him. But his mild look showed that this inspection was just for show. You could tell he wouldn't search you, a little like the customs officer putting the statutory question: "Anything to declare?" to the smuggling tourist, and hoping that the answer will be no. It makes life simpler for him.

Paulo would have liked to run back to his block as fast as possible and hide his booty. Not the easiest thing in the world with a sack of potatoes around each leg, not to mention the one in his stomach, which was beginning to gurgle ominously, making breathing difficult and half suffocating him.

"Hope to God they don't blow the whistle right now," he muttered as he inched forward, bowlegged so as not to crush his potatoes. Everything was going well, but he had to find himself a larder quickly. It wasn't going to be easy with the mean-minded Karl blocking the doorway to the barrack, which was his only possible hiding place. Typically, Karl had chosen these few minutes before evening coffee to get himself titivated in the open air. A gaggle of young boys were running round him in circles, cutting off the entrance to the block. First there was the cute little barber, razor in hand, and behind him bustled his aides with shaving brush, jug, bowl, towels, bottles and mirror. They were already dreaming of the extra soup they'd have tomorrow . . . if Sailor recognized them. Which was why the sweeties were kicking up so much dust, in the hopes that the chief's memory might be photographic. It was impossible to creep into the *Schlafenstube* with all these obstructions around, quite apart from the wicked blade of the razor which was being whisked about the master's face. By an unlucky chance the session promised to be a lengthy one because Sailor, unlike his colleagues, had given up his center parting. His current brand of vanity was to have his whole head shaved bare every day, then polished and oiled with margarine, the bastard, and finally dabbed with revolting German eau de Cologne.

"Never mind, I'll wait for assembly," Paulo resolved, hoping that Sailor wouldn't decide to kick him in the shins, in his lovely spuds. His fears were unfounded. Karl must have liked what he saw in the mirror for he was clearly in a good mood. The club blows which he had to dole out so that his squad was presentable at roll call were relatively lightweight, and the ritual which normally accompanied the distribution of coffee was just as half-hearted. But this wasn't the reason why Paulo for once appreciated his bowl of clear liquid. This time, it didn't slop away through his empty intestines but lingered instead in his stomach, blocked by the mound of mashed potatoes. How good it felt in his purring belly! It was almost like having two blowouts in one day. But like a squirrel which has to think of winter, he must find a safe spot for his hoard.

Instead of walking up and down in front of the block with his friends, Paulo headed straight for the dormitory. Hitting the sack before the evening bell was now permissible and today there was very little chance that Sailor, all dolled up as he was, would bother to make a trip into the sleeping quarters. Passing in front of him, Paulo ventured a quiet "*Gut Nacht, chef,*" just for good measure. "Good night, bum," the other answered in French. How very cordial.

Now all he had to do was find a safe niche. Putting them under his mattress would be a real giveaway. Likewise stuffing them down the side of the bunk. Indeed, the farther away from his bed he hid the spuds, the less he would be suspected. But choosing any other bed was equally risky, because they might be stolen. No, he had to look for somewhere neutral and isolated. But there wasn't much spare room in this overcrowded nest.

"That's it, I've got it," Paulo exclaimed a moment later. The crapper. No one would dare put their paws behind the crapper—certainly not Karl with his manicured nails!

The nighttime crapper at Loibl Pass had not of course been installed by Thomas Crapper. It was just an oil drum, full stop. No flush and no drains. The barrel overflowed every morning and Paulo had staggered under its weight more often than he should have, to empty it into the cesspit under the main lavatories. The throne was about four inches from the partition, and, luckily, there was a little play between the last two floorboards behind. Paulo bent down and, by pulling with both hands, he managed to widen the gap at the first go, just enough to slip in a medium-sized potato.

"The others I'll break in half," he decided, straightening up.

He had to get cracking, because his fellows were beginning to head for their beds.

Lying fully dressed on his bunk, he decided it would be prudent to wait for lights out before carrying on his storage operation. But he couldn't resist the pleasure of counting his little darlings again and again, feeling them in the dark through the rough material of his striped pants, until the bell sounded. There were eighteen of them, real whoppers, three a day until next Saturday.

"And we'll do that again each week," he congratulated himself.

An hour later the eighteen spuds were safe and sound, lined up against each other under the floorboards behind the barrel of shit. As a precaution, Paulo had wedged the planks back together, so as not to tempt an inquisitive pisser, and especially so that the diarrhetics wouldn't splash his nice boiled potatoes with shit. Toward the end of the week, being so close to a barrel which was rather on the small side for a hundred men would detract from the heavenly flavor Paulo had so enjoyed in the kitchen. But after all, he had no right to be fussy, after six months of famine. The delicious rumbling in his guts which had gone on all night must equally have tickled his fantasies, giving him sweet dreams, for when he got up, he didn't have that feeling of fright which seized him by the throat every morning as his feet touched the ground.

The next day was Sunday and it, too, went well for him and the others: there were a few fatigues, of course, assemblies, reassemblies, a prick parade, and a volley of impromptu backhands, but nothing tragic. Nothing like the fourteen diabolical Sundays they had just lived through. A few more relaxed weekends like this, and the forced labor in the tunnel all week long would become bearable.

Not before time, because they weren't up there on the construction site for recreation. On the contrary. Now that the Sabbath had resumed its original meaning, all hell was let loose on Monday morning, and sticks and gun butts rained down on their rested backs. But now it was not really for enjoyment's sake that the SS and Kapos beat them. It made sense as a means toward maximum productivity. The whole bunch joined in, as if the outcome of the war and the destiny of Germany depended on it. The most frequent targets were naturally the miners in the vanguard, for every minute they lost was relayed back down the whole chain of workers, and things could get really out of hand. So . . .

Paulo quickly caught on. Goodbye to the drippings, it was a matter of urgency to get himself slung out of the tunnel and to find himself a replacement. Nothing could have been easier with all those greedy pigs queuing up for it. Before the week was out Paulo found himself transferred to a new earthworks Kommando on the outer edge of the site. This was all thanks to Sailor, who wanted to put pressure on a young fag eager for a spoonful of drippings.

By coincidence the month of September 1943 seemed determined to break all records for fine weather. The sun blazed hotter than in June, there was no wind and the air was dry. Being outside in weather like this, stripped to the waist instead of freezing your balls off in the darkness of the tunnel, which was lit only by the lurid glow of hurricane lamps, was ten times better than drippings.

Things at Loibl Pass were definitely looking up for Paulo. In fact, for two weeks, two glorious weeks, Paulo enjoyed the good life; after the horror film of the last six months, he'd almost gotten himself a rest cure.

In this new outpost Kommando, you could see the *Arbeitskapos* and the old fossil of a *Kommandoführer* coming from a long way off, and you had plenty of time to survey your surroundings far from the punches and the rubber hose. And from the very first day, Paulo made the most of his opportunity. He could see the whole construction site: the tunnel entrance, a long stretch of road above and below it, the forge, the carpentry shed and the refectory. By moving to one side he could even see part of the camp down in the valley. It was something to focus his mind on, something to occupy his time more pleasantly than being behind a pneumatic drill.

Of course he still had to put his back into it, for if the job wasn't done each evening, there'd be trouble. But the new Kommando's task wasn't too demanding. Their job was to make a cutting following the contours of the mountain to the left of the tunnel. Once they'd leveled the ground, tracks were to be laid. These were the famous tracks which would carry the little train described to Paulo by the Pole with the Ph.D. in tunnels. The railway track had to be solid enough to withstand the wagonloads of rock which the workers on drippings were extracting from the tunnel at ever greater speed. For the moment, it was up to a hundred of their fellow prisoners to cart away all this material in wheelbarrows; these men were the butt of everyone's wit. And so the laying of the railway track entrusted Paulo and his workmates was both vital and urgent.

The first morning of their new assignment, the men felt elated as they followed old Fossil, who led them unaccompanied toward the south, toward Yugoslavia, far from the tunnel. He had explained their task to them and then left them, without a Kapo. They all felt quite giddy: this quiet spot was an open invitation to escape.

But the canny old warrior had anticipated them, for on closer inspection they noticed that the guard around them had been reinforced, in fact doubled. There was a sentry with a menacing submachine gun under almost every tree and behind every rock, watching. As bad as the frontier, so in that respect nothing had changed: they wanted to hang on to the good French workers for a little while longer.

Before he left them, old Fossil had taken the precaution of nominating a foreman with overall responsibility, and although there was only one Pole among the twenty-odd laborers in the Kommando, he was the one to receive the awesome honor. To be a Kapo without a stripe was the worst possible position to be in, but nevertheless his promotion seemed to electrify the Pole and he stiffened smartly to attention, which pleased old Fossil. It was manifestly obvious that he didn't care for the French at all. Verdun still rankled; he had not forgotten their barbaric tactics and one could well imagine how he must have blessed Corporal Hitler, his comrade in the trenches, for allowing him twenty years later to avenge himself on the sons of the men who had given him such a rough time.

"*Scheisse Franzosen,*" he had said, swearing in his auxiliary Kapo.

And he had departed, confident of having once again humiliated the hereditary enemy. The old clown was mistaken, because his Pole had reserves of hatred just as bitter and much more recent. His alacrity was a sham. He wasn't about to collaborate with the murderers who had bled his country to death. As soon as he had assembled the men for instructions, he set the record straight.

"Don't worry, comrades, I have no intention of becoming a Kapo. Get yourselves organized as you like. This is a people's republic. Let's have the strongest men on the picks and wheelbarrows, but let's get things moving. I mean really moving, because if we want to hang on to this soft berth, we've got to get the work done."

Although he made his announcement in broken French, his sincerity was plain to see. He was indeed a responsible fellow, but not in the way old Fossil would have liked: he was of the same breed as Dédé, Joel and company.

Paulo immediately had confidence in him and had he played the game honestly, he would have rushed for a pick. He chose a shovel, or rather, he snatched a shovel from a wretchedly skinny old man. The Pole had seen it all and Paulo was on the verge of handing back the shovel when he saw his look of reproach, but it was too late. The unwilling pickaxer seemed utterly resigned to his fate and was already chopping away at the knoll.

"I hope the dumb ox dies," Paulo muttered angrily to himself. "He's in better shape than me, and anyway he's obviously used to it."

He knew quite well that it wasn't true, and that it was up to him and the younger, less worn-out men to take up pickaxes, if they wanted, as the Pole had said, to shift enough earth by the end of the day to avoid having to explain themselves. Besides, his selfish instinct turned out to be pointless, for after ten minutes of feverish activity the men had already put down their picks, waiting for the shovelers and the wheelbarrow men to cart off the results of their labors. It was the Pole who had called the break, by simply putting down his pick without a word. For although he could have twiddled his thumbs and merely supervised the work, he too had taken up a pick. In fact, he had even taken it out of the hands of a young man. Quite the opposite of Paulo.

The wheelbarrows had come back empty and the picks should have gotten moving again, that was the routine. But curiously, without any conferring among the men, the break continued. Not a sound could be heard on the site; the tools had fallen silent, the men stood motionless. Suddenly, the same idea crossed everybody's mind: they could talk. Out loud, about anything they liked, without the order for "*Ruhe*" and then the hose clamping down on them. For three months, apart from the miners in the vanguard, it had been virtually impossible for the men to talk on the work site. But even the miners couldn't really talk because there was always the compressor which powered the noisy hammers. And since talking in the ranks on the way up and down from the camp was also forbidden, the twenty privileged prisoners were experiencing quite a new sensation. They all began to talk at once like a bunch of old women let loose in a tea room. They were all seized by verbal diarrhea and nobody could finish what he was saying.

Yet they had lots to tell each other after three long months of silence, three months of keeping to themselves their fear, their disgust and, for the last few days, their hope. They were so overwhelmed by the need to talk that they had forgotten the extra cordon of sentries guarding them. Luckily, the malicious SS were out of earshot, old Fossil having judged it wiser to leave a good distance, a no-man's-land of over a hundred yards, between the guards and the prisoners, in case all twenty of them decided to run for it at once.

A small haven of liberty had just been created within Loibl's impregnable walls, and in spite of his joy at being part of it, Paulo couldn't help thinking that the other men would cast envious glances at the relative freedom of the Kommando. "It won't be out of love for drippings," he thought, "but we're soon going to have smart-Alec volunteers on our backs."

"Listen, you guys," he burst out. "If you want to be here again tomorrow, you'd do better to shut up and get grinding." And he set about raking up a pile of stones which the wheelbarrows had missed.

The babble stopped dead; as if they'd just received an order, the chatterers picked up their tools as one. The one who was most surprised was the "foreman"; it should have been him who set the example. He had been thinking about it for ten minutes, but for fear of being thought overeager by these bolshy Frenchmen he had hesitated. Paulo's intervention had solved his problem.

Just before he sounded the whistle for midday soup, the Fossil came to check up on them, and from his complete lack of criticism it was clear that the Frenchmen must have done a good job. He even favored the Pole with a *"Du Gut Kapo,"* as he went past.

How misplaced was his flattery, what an insult it was! But everyone, including the "Kapo," heaved a sigh of relief, for clearly that meant the same good little team would be back tomorrow to break rocks in the same relaxed atmosphere.

Work, then a break, then work again; they'd gotten nicely into the swing of things, and by the end of the afternoon everyone was surprised by the amount they'd achieved without rushing, without beatings and almost without getting tired. Perhaps if they were to let the prisoners organize the work in their own way, they might see the light at the end of their tunnel more quickly! But it would be a trifle difficult to explain that to the champions of European security.

As Paulo had feared, by that first evening everyone in the camp was in the know. The team was extremely lucky that Fossil-Face had a say in things, otherwise Bullseye's and Sailor's pets would have found themselves whisked, as if by magic, into the Kommando where the sun shone all day long. Five o'clock in the morning when the shaven heads were lined up in work crews on the *Appelplatz* was when they'd have to watch their step. One smack in the mouth, and you might find yourself back at the tunnel, trapped between a wheelbarrow and a rubber hose. Fossil-Face must have struck terror in the block chiefs' hearts with his pistol, which never stayed long in its holster. The next day, the lucky gang of laborers was the same as the day before.

The weather hadn't broken either, and the sun warming the torsos of the workers' cooperative was an additional bonus. In any case it was much better to be tanned in this colony of queers. Not, that is, to arouse interest, but simply that the worse your health, the more cadaverous your appearance, the more you got beaten up. Because blood spurting from milky skin was more exciting for the German perverts.

As they waited for their suntans to reach perfection, Paulo and his mates took maximum advantage of their corner of Paradise. A spontaneous bond had sprung up between them and when one fellow wanted to rest, or even to sit down (they hadn't sat down for three and a half months), no one objected. They would even cover him so he wouldn't be seen by the guards. What the good Pole had achieved with Paulo's support was an agreement that there would always be enough men on their feet to break the rocks, pick them up and cart them away. And those who had taken things easy would work twice as hard when they took up their tools again. The result was that on the second evening Fossil-Face seemed even more satisfied after his little inspection. With such efficient organization he had no cause to change anything or anybody at all. The gang of twenty were drawing closer together and each man found less and less fault with his neighbor. They were fast becoming friends—well, almost all of them.

Paulo had chosen to team up with two fellows who were a bit brighter than the rest. It helped conversation along. As chance would have it, his two new partners were a couple of ne'er-do-wells: Angelo Baroni was an Italian from Marseilles and Pierrot Martin was a Parisian. Choosing such men as friends just went to show how much Paulo was subject to his changing moods. When he was convinced they were all about to die at the hands of the Germans, he hung on the Resistance members' every word of hope, even that of the commies, such as old Etcheverry; but when things seemed to be going better, back he went to his own kind.

Before being picked up, Baroni had been famous for his particular brand of justice, stiletto-style. Take one look at his set face—it was all rehearsed, but as he closed one eye you shook in your shoes—and you soon coughed up. He had managed to hold on to his knife at Compiègne, and everyone fell over himself to be friends with him. It was only at Mauthausen, with the first fist in his face, that he opened his second eye, and since then, with both eyes open, sideburns missing and unarmed, he hadn't frightened a mouse. Seeing him arrive meekly at Loibl with the second transport had given rise to a snicker or two and Paulo, who still bore him an old grudge, couldn't resist a small dig: "A word in your ear, Angelo; don't close it. Even with two, you won't see them coming."

The scourge of Marseilles didn't reply. Since his one-eyed trick was a flop these days, he had tried to salvage his dignity by playing dumb.

Paulo's other partner, Pierrot Martin, was a self-styled boxer, and he had enough conversation for two. This fellow was a Parisian born and bred, inexhaustible on the subject of the Vel-d'Hiv, on sport in general and horseracing in particular. He knew another side to the turf, too: the Panier Fleuri on the rue Grégoire-de-Tours, where he eked out his thin times. After landing on his ass at the Central in the first round, the madam's assistant at the brothel had felt sorry for him and taken him under her wing. Since then, he'd never been short of a story—or three.

"Don't worry, Paulo, with me around, time'll fly past," he joked.

He couldn't have been more wrong. Paulo didn't give a shit about Paris at the moment, and he soon got sick and tired of hearing the pugilist-pimp drone on all day long about the same old thing.

"What class did you fight in?" he set him up one morning.

"The roughest, the middleweight," Pierrot boasted.

"Well then, you're in luck. When you get back, with that skinny body you can move into the flyweights. There'll be less competition."

It was below the belt, but it did shut up the undernourished boxer. He was furious and he would have liked to lash out, but he didn't even have the strength to swing his nasty right hook. Paulo was in about as much danger as the little peasant collector of potato peelings, who had dared to insult Angelo Baroni.

The latter was getting ready to set off with his fully laden wheelbarrow just as the young yokel was returning from the dump with his own. He let go of his empty wheelbarrow a bit too soon and it bumped into Baroni's full one, knocking it over and spilling its contents.

"Sorry," said the boy.

"You'd better pick that up, you little cunt, and quick!"

The boy was so happy in the friendly atmosphere of the Kommando that he thought Baroni was joking.

"No need to shout, Angelo, I'll help you pick it up."

"Just pick it up, you fucking peasant!"

Baroni had closed one eye. Realizing this was serious, the peasant turned on him.

"Well, if you want to take it like that, you can pick up your own fucking stones, you lousy small-time crook."

Baroni's eye flashed.

"Just say that again, you filthy peasant . . ."

"Lousy small-time crook, do I have to say it twice? Go fuck yourself, you lazy cunt!"

The little fellow was on the offensive now and a fight seemed inevitable, particularly as all the other men had downed tools and gathered around the two wheelbarrow men. The ball was in Baroni's court. Wrenching Paulo's shovel out of his hands, he spat a final threat.

"You say that just once more, you little shit, and you get this shovel in your face."

"Lousy crook . . . lousy crook."

The shovel stayed where it was. The Marseilles villain backed out of the confrontation with an "It's lucky for you I don't have my blade," and under the mocking gaze of the whole Kommando, he bent down to fill up his wheelbarrow with his own hands, the hands of a killer who was past it.

To see Baroni climb down in public when, for the first time, there had been no danger of intervention or reprisal from Kapos or SS quite disgusted Paulo. The two associates he had chosen for himself were really terrific. They were ruining the first good times he had had in six months. He'd have to dump them, but how?

His problem solved itself. As more and more earth and stones were piled up at the tunnel mouth, they began to spill over on Route 333, forcing the few trucks which ventured into this wilderness dangerously far out on the bends. Despite the rate at which the wheelbarrow men plied back and forth from the tunnel, the backlog of material had gotten out of hand. Would they ask the miners to slow down? Quite absurd! There was only one intelligent solution, which was adopted instantly: slap as many men as possible into the plate-laying gang. So Paulo's crew became top priority, and Putz asked Fossil-Face to triple the work force.

Among the volunteers assigned to the express track were a few familiar faces apart from Joel and Belloni. There was Pépé with the golden smile, François from Burgundy, the Corsican brothers (together of course) and some new men from the second convoy: Jean Leblond, a sailor turned over to the Gestapo by the French police for having blown up three Doriotists, the two Bretons from Dédé Ménard's network, and Lagrive from Marseilles, an ex-boxer too but, unlike Pierrot Martin, a good sort. After hanging up his gloves he hadn't scrounged from prostitutes, he'd gone out to work. With a mask and a gun. His masterpiece, which was an open secret at Loibl, had been the attack on the Paris–Marseilles express.

In other words, the men who had managed to slip into the back-up team were not just choirboys, and what was more, they were all more or less French. With the exception of Sebastopol, but with balls like he had, they had no choice but to count him in. .

Fossil-Face was so pleased with his first team that he didn't even bother to explain to the new men the kind of work he expected of them. He was content to delegate that responsibility to the willing Pole, the man to whom he thought all credit for the good progress was due. But he was uneasy at the thought that his "Kapo" would be in charge of sixty men now, not twenty, so he decided to give him an assistant. Without hesitation he called forward the tallest and least skinny man he could see: a Frenchman who knew only one word of German apart from his registration number—*Jawohl*.

"*Du Kapo*," Fossil-Face simply said.

"*Jawohl!*"

And this was how Monsieur Marcel, a truck driver from the Vichy region, was sworn in as Kapo.

With Marcel as Kapo his French fellows would have no problem, because he already had a reputation as a weak-kneed wretch. His new appointment scared the living daylights out of him, but it was his own fault: he shouldn't have been so sturdy-looking. Of course he couldn't help his height, but even after the Loibl diet he still had a layer of fat, which went to show that he must have been enormous when he got to Mauthausen. That's not normal when you live in a country under rationing, bled dry by the occupying forces. Unless . . .

Collaboration, black market or Resistance? Well, no one was going to quibble now. Marcel was there and like everybody else he was paying the price. The only thing that mattered was that his promotion and the gentle Pole's reappointment meant the Kommando was not under the evil eye of Fritz or one of his ferocious *Arbeitskapo* colleagues. What the rest of them had to do was help the two acting officers fulfill their duty. But hardly had Fossil-Face turned on his heels when the sixty prisoners, paying no heed to their "chiefs," arranged themselves in groups of friends. Without asking anyone's permission, Paulo took Joel and young Belloni to one side.

"Over here, you two. Shift yourselves, or Baroni and Pierrot will be on my back again. Let's team up together... you Joel, get hold of that pick and start chopping quick."

In a few brief sentences, Paulo undertook to explain all the advantages of this job to his new workmates.

"First of all, nobody can see us. But we're not stupid, we work like there was a Kapo about. Luckily, Fossil-Face hasn't noticed the rock here is as soft as sponge cake, it's practically sand. When he comes around in the evening to check progress, he thinks we've been working like blacks. Not true, of course. Anyway, hold it, it's break time. Every half hour, fifteen minutes' break. Okay, down tools, chat time."

Joel was extremely reluctant to put down his pick. Skeptically, he looked around at the old hands like Paulo sitting on their wheelbarrows or squatting on the ground. They were all chewing the fat. It looked as if Paulo really meant it.

"I can't believe it!" said Belloni. "This is the first time in four months that I don't have to run around like a madman. Why does Fossil-Face put up with it? There must be a catch somewhere..."

"There's no catch," Paulo interrupted. "I told you, we've got it sorted out. When we work, we work. Then we stop, we chat, then off we go again. That's what we do, all day, every day. There are no goof-offs around here. Look, all the Krauts want is that we get on and build their little railway for them."

"But it feels really strange to be emptyhanded and have nobody shouting at you. It's like being at the seaside with all this sun. Aren't we the lucky ones!" Belloni chattered happily.

Paulo was delighted his guests liked his place so much. At least they were showing appreciation as they ought to, and they weren't going to get up his nose with boring anecdotes.

Joel was lost in thought, not daring to sit down, so Paulo turned to him.

"What's the matter? D'you still think there's a catch?"

"No, not at all. Just give me time to appreciate it all. This peace and silence is so strange."

"Well, go ahead, talk, have a laugh. Sing us a song if you want!"

"Don't get carried away, Paulo. You know as well as I do, this cushy number can't last for very long..."

"Hey," interrupted Belloni, "how many days is it going to take us to lay the track, d'you think?"

"Two weeks exactly to level the bed. You see that big tree on the bend? That's where we're going to stop. There wouldn't be any point in going any farther because below that tree the ravine's as deep as it gets. There's enough room to tip the whole tunnel down there. That'll be the end of the line, right by the SS cordon."

"And what next?"

"Well, then we lay the rails, of course. In fact we'll do that at the same time, because they're in a bit of a hurry, as I understand it. So that makes two weeks, boys, no more."

His calculations were correct. And by the first of October precisely a splendid railway track a thousand feet long, almost straight, emerged from the tunnel mouth and expired at the foot of the big tree. Just in front of the buffers—a big pile of rocks—the track curved, which meant that from the tunnel and even from most of the barracks, the train would disappear from view. That could be interesting...

Hardly had the last few feet of track been laid when a shiny new *decauville* locomotive appeared out of nowhere and was already rolling, to check the gauge. A civilian they'd never seen before, probably part of the same delivery, was at the controls with Putz the engineer beside him, and on the footplate stood the old fart Fossil-Face, proud as a peacock. The old boy was thrilled, behaving as if he thought he was the engine driver. Even before the locomotive set off back along the line, he had jumped off the moving train at the risk of falling flat on his face, and blown his whistle to assemble the plate-laying Kommando. For Paulo and his friends, sunbathing was a thing of the past.

"Down the tunnel," the senile old fool had rasped.

Not one of the sixty men was surprised, but over the past days, which had been so unlike the daily drudge of life at Loibl, they had deliberately avoided thinking about what would happen afterward. It was only now, as they marched in columns of five toward the ominous and frightening black mouth, that they realized the full extent of their loss.

Paulo was surely one of the most bitterly disappointed. But during the idyll he had just lived through and which was now almost over, something had occurred which should have reminded him that he was still shaven, disguised and numbered, a prisoner.

Even a mangy dog would not have been treated with such contempt. It was a blisteringly hot afternoon; Fossil-Face had finished his siesta early and had walked up to the work site, his bandy legs creaking. Sweating profusely into his wilting uniform, he had sat down on a wheelbarrow to mop his skull with an enormous black-and-white checked granny handkerchief. As he was getting his breath back, he had explained the reason for his visit to the Polish "Kapo." He was looking for a volunteer for a small outdoor duty which would take up the rest of the afternoon. But as the duty would be a pleasant one—a stroll, he had called it—he wanted a fellow who deserved this reward. The good Pole, thinking he was doing him a good turn, had immediately suggested Paulo. He had taken a liking to the tall prisoner since noticing his good influence on the Frenchmen in the Kommando. Pleased to be able to repay the debt, he asked him to drop his shovel and report to the *Kommandoführer*.

The duty really was a stroll, skirting around all the work sites, following the line of the sentries.

The SS guards were dying of thirst and they had asked their chief to get them something to drink. Not beer, but cold water, the icy mountain water which trickled out of a spring. At the foot of the spring a canvas flagon and a Wehrmacht beaker were waiting for Paulo. In his German dialect Fossil-Face had ordered Paulo to fill up the flagon with water, and when that was done, he sent him off with a shove toward one of the duty SS on the road.

"Alle Posten trinken, jeden nach ein ander, schnell, Mensch."

Such elementary German wasn't hard to understand.

"Gevorten, Herr Kommandoführer," Paulo replied as he headed toward the thirsty soldier. The bastard nearly swallowed the flagon too; he drank seven or eight beakers in a row.

"If they're all as parched as him," thought Paulo, "this fountain lark'll turn me into a fucking yoyo. Not half as easy as I thought."

Handing back the beaker, the Fritz had pointed to one of his friends, as dried out as he, who was waving frantically from his perch on a rock about a hundred yards from the tunnel entrance. Another shove and Paulo found himself on the other side of the road. For a second, he had been seized by terrible doubt: hadn't he just crossed the death line? "I've been had, Fossil-Face's water duty was all a sham, that guard's going to shoot me in the back," he panicked.

It wasn't bullets but yells which whistled past his ears: "*Schnell, Mensch, Scheisse Franzosen.*"

Phew, that wasn't quite so bad. Paulo scuttled over to the second *Posten*. Just like the first, this one had slaked his thirst, belched noisily, then shoved him toward a third SS who was already bellowing how thirsty he was in the same agreeable manner: "*Schnell, Scheisse Français.*"

The third SS was a good way off and Paulo had wondered how they could let him wander about unescorted on this mountain where freedom, with a head start, was only seconds away. Fossil-Face must have had his binoculars trained on him. However, when Paulo had turned around to try to spot the old fellow, he had encountered a very alert gaze, or rather seven alert gazes: the *Hundenführer* and his six awesome hounds, who were growling and straining dangerously at the leash. It was pointless to daydream: the great escape had been postponed. "Still," said Paulo to himself, "might as well look on the bright side, it's not too unpleasant playing Gunga Din in this heat." Each time he returned to the fountain to fill up, he managed to gulp down two or three mouthfuls, taking good care to turn his back on the SS with the dogs, so that he shouldn't see this vermin putting his unclean lips to an Aryan beaker.

There were easily thirty sentries to be quenched, the majority of them on the south face, backs to Yugoslavia. Fossil-Face must have chosen the meanest men to guard this baking spot; the first in line had started by smacking Paulo in the mouth as he proffered him the full beaker.

"Attention!" he had ordered, as he lashed out. "*Komm her,* nearer, *Franzose syphilitik.*"

Not only did the bastard desire Paulo's heels to touch as he was drinking, but he was also of a suspicious nature: before he drank he rinsed the half-pint mug out twice and then, like his friends, downed a good five or six beakerfuls. But the last proved to be one too many. What Paulo hadn't foreseen was that the son of a bitch standing directly in front of him would spit out the last mugful right in his face, twenty inches away.

"How—how dare he!" he stammered to himself, shaking with hatred. "That little shit's not even out of nappies. I could strangle him and he wouldn't even have time to take aim. If he knew who he was talking to..."

Obviously the little shit didn't know he was dealing with a gangster, neither did anybody anymore. Paulo looked more like a scarecrow, with his ribs jutting out against his tanned skin and his long thin biceps. Had it come to a fight, it wasn't certain that he would have gotten the better of this well-fed youngster. Seeing his joke hadn't been appreciated, the coward actually did it again, this time rinsing his mouth out properly as he sought to include with his jet of water the bits of sauerkraut which had gotten stuck in his teeth at lunchtime.

Three times right in the face. Paulo had had to endure his humiliation not only without saying anything but standing at attention as well. Everything he had had done to him over the last seven months looked like a Sunday-school outing compared to this latest insult.

After he had exhausted his joke, the pimply SS burst out laughing and patted his belt. His neighbor, the next in line, followed suit. He was so eager for his French spittoon that he had completely forgotten his thirst. And the scene was repeated ten times along the tight cordon of SS sentries. Paulo was soaked, with water, saliva and bits of meat and cabbage. Tears of rage mingled with the disgusting paste, but that, at least, the foul SS hadn't seen.

It was only after he had served the last hawker in the line that Paulo collapsed. Clutching the empty flagon in one hand, he bit his lip until it bled to stop his tears. Fortunately nobody, apart from the other SS bastards, had witnessed the degrading scene.

Now, with hindsight, he confronted the matter squarely: "What would a real man have done in my place? To react would have been certain death, being so close to the line. I did well to take it without a murmur, I'm still alive. I've got to stay alive, so I can knock them all off. Every single one of them."

Thus he came to an agreement with his conscience and basically he was right. Joel and Dédé would certainly have acted as he did, and so would all the heavy brigade, even the Campana brothers, those superannuated terrors. That's what Loibl Pass was like: they could do anything to you, puke all over you, shit in your face, fuck you, anything, absolutely anything. And not once had anybody protested, not once would anybody protest.

Paulo couldn't wipe out the memory of this unpleasant incident. And yet, set against the magnificent days spent with the railway gang, it wasn't dramatic enough to cancel out the good side of things. He found himself in much better shape, he was as bronzed as a starlet and he had lasted out ten months—four months at Loibl, three at Mauthausen, three at Cherche-Midi, almost a year. Surely this bitch of a war couldn't last forever.

"I've got to hang on a little bit longer," he murmured as he marched. "Just a bit longer, then I'll get my own back."

Where was he going to end up now? Probably in the tunnel, for thanks to the new track, dumping would be swift and efficient. That's where men were needed most urgently, to fill the wagons and empty them. Not a happy thought.

He couldn't help saying his bit to Joel and Belloni, who flanked him as if they were afraid of losing him, afraid to see him transferred to somebody else's group.

"We've missed our chance, we'll never get another. Instead of sunning ourselves, we'd have done better to cook up some way of making a break. We're going to regret that."

He had a nerve coming out with that, he who had swanned about a whole afternoon with one foot in Austria and the other in Yugoslavia. If anybody had had an opportunity, it had certainly been him. Maybe Joel would not have passed up a chance like that.

As the Breton hadn't replied, he changed his tune.

"Maybe we did the right thing. The SS cordon had been doubled where we were, there was one every sixty feet. We'd have been sitting ducks."

He was better informed on this subject than the others, having had to spend three hours playing waiter to the SS sentries. But if he began to give them any more details, he'd also have to tell them about his ignominious bath. And that secret he was going to keep to himself.

What was the point of dragging it out into the open? It was the voracious mouth of the tunnel a few yards away which was making him talk nonsense. Fortunately Belloni, anxious to have his say, stopped him from putting his foot in it any deeper.

"It's my opinion there's been too much shit for us to have risked it. It wouldn't make sense to get killed now."

The boy had voiced what everyone was thinking: they'd been through too much together in this blind alley at Loibl to quit it one by one.

XIV

After an animated discussion with Putz, who was making his case for the tunnel, Fossil-Face had conceded less than half of his crack demolition gang. The others, among them Paulo, Joel and Belloni, were to stay outside because manpower was needed for a new construction project. They were to build a concrete-mixing plant.

Paulo, who had convinced himself that the black hole would swallow the gang in its entirety, breathed again.

But, for the sake of convenience, the engineer wanted his fine cement plant within easy reach, right by the tunnel entrance. No need therefore for binoculars to spy out flagging workers. And with no nice mound of earth to sit on during the breaks, and no breaks anyway, the men became the hub of the work site, the center of attraction for idle Kapos. A hell of a difference to the Kommando of beach boys.

And since troubles always come in pairs, the wonderful potato-peeling racket ended almost at the same time. Paulo was well aware that it couldn't last indefinitely, but given that the handsome kitchen Kapo had continued each Saturday to turn a blind eye, it would have been stupid not to have taken advantage of the windfall.

But Paulo had not foreseen that the *Küchenkapo* was going to close his dreamy eyes forever. And in an unexpected way.

One morning, to everyone's surprise, Ernst took his place in the column setting out for the tunnel. Not at the head, nor at the rear with his colleagues, but right in the middle, like a common jailbird. What had the good man done? Perhaps it was on account of his lenience on the prisoners, or maybe the SS had noticed the potato thieving and he was paying for the thieves? Paulo was only half reassured. That bastard Helmut with his Gestapo methods was quite capable of making his compatriot talk, and of getting to the bottom of the story—and finding Paulo. He'd better be on the lookout.

It was odd, nonetheless, that Ernst had kept his docker's cap. It clashed with the sea of striped prisoners' caps. The black peaked cap of Mauthausen was almost an officer's kepi, which you were only stripped of as a grave punishment together with your stripe. And Ernst still had his stripe. Something was wrong.

The convicts didn't learn the whole story until that evening, when the drama had been played out. And once again it was only through the indiscretion of one of the hustlers that they knew the details. Ernst, the Kapo with the silvery hair, had been madly in love with a young SS sergeant, who as his direct superior was responsible for the mess arrangements.

So it was the sergeant who must have been on Ernst's mind when he stared unseeingly at Paulo, while the latter slipped pounds of potatoes down his trousers. Even then, things couldn't have been going smoothly between the two turtledoves. The chief cook must have been brooding over his desperate move for a long time. How pathetic at his age to fall in love with a kid! It was not difficult to guess the pattern: "If you leave me, I'll resign from the kitchen." The little sergeant must have been thoroughly fed up with his old sucker, because he let him go. Yet he must have been surprised to see him in the ranks, along with the riffraff; his status as Kapo entitled him to be transferred to a block. Or, queer that he was, to the laundry.

When they reached the tunnel, Ernst asked Fritz to give him a job outside, "to enjoy the beautiful autumn weather," he had said. Since the concrete-mixing plant was the most important area, that was where he ended up.

"He's nuts! To give up a cushy number like that to come and muck around with us is sheer perversion!"

At the start of the day, Paulo still didn't know the intricacies of the story. He knew that Ernst had volunteered to join the work gang, but he put it down to his romantic nature, a one-day whim to perfect the tan on his torso.

"I ought to have a word with him," Paulo decided. "He

was nice to me, it's a good opportunity and there could be many more fine Saturdays to come."

But Ernst was even less inclined to talk than among his pots and pans. He seemed alone, completely alone, in the midst of all the activity. As soon as his wheelbarrow was empty, he placed it in front of Marcel the driver, who was his shoveler, and stared at the sky. When the wheelbarrow was full, he set off again, still looking up at the sky like an idiot. Even Marcel, ass-licker par excellence, had not managed, despite repeated efforts, to shake him out of his reverie. Paulo had a shot at smiling and winking—but nothing doing.

By lunchtime you would have thought Ernst might have begun to thaw. No such luck. He had sought refuge at the back of the refectory, well away from the conversations of which he was the sole topic. Although he had queued up for his soup ration, it was only to empty it into greedy Marcel's bowl. So ass-licking paid.

After lunch, Ernst took up his sky-and-wheelbarrow act again, and since he still shunned all contact, they lost interest in him. It was only by accident that Paulo, straining upward at the top of his swing, was the first to see what was happening. He grabbed Joel's arm and whispered urgently to him.

"Look! He's gone mad, that Kraut of mine. He's going the wrong way, the crazy guy's heading straight for the line!"

Paulo was right, Ernst was making for forbidden ground, dragging his empty wheelbarrow behind him.

"We've got to warn him," said Joel. "Go on, shout, Paulo. You've got a loud voice, quick, or it'll be too late . . ."

"No, shut up. He may be trying to make a break for it, in broad daylight. Just pretend you haven't seen anything."

If the kitchen Kapo had really wanted to escape, he hadn't come up with a terribly discreet plan. Already he had been spotted by one of the *Posten*.

"Halt, Kapo, halt. Zurück."

Ernst didn't hear. He had dropped his wheelbarrow and was walking on, not toward the sentry who had challenged him, but straight ahead between him and another SS. Now the two of them were yelling at him to turn back. Without success; still looking heavenward, Ernst was advancing at the same slow, almost mechanical pace. On the site of the future factory, an agonized silence had replaced the sound of shovels. They had all realized that Ernst wasn't going to stop.

The two SS guards were in a dilemma. They knew the German well, because for months now he had stuffed them like pigs. He was harmless, and surely he wasn't going to desert after spending so many years in the camps? And anyway, where did he think he was going? He was half naked, wearing only his striped trousers and without even his cap. To gun him down was a difficult decision to take; he might only be going for a pee, prudishly looking for a private spot. All the same, he was going a bit far. No, Ernst had lost his head; he was going to cross the line! The sentries left their posts and began to move toward him, shouting louder and louder, entreating him to stop. Their cries fell on deaf ears. Still staring up at the sky, Ernst had by now crossed over the fatal line. If only it had been a Frenchman or a Pole, there wouldn't have been any problem. They had to make up their minds. . . From behind them the order was rapped out.

"*Feuer!*"

It was the *Kommandoführer* who had given the order and shots rang out almost instantaneously. On the kitchen Kapo's brown back the holes made by half a dozen bullets were almost visible. At any rate, the horrified convicts all saw the blood streaming from his body, like soup from a leaking pot. The poor cook! Even more heart-rending and unbearable, Ernst walked on a little farther with the same dignified step, more than ever a stranger to this loveless world he had decided to leave.

Suddenly his knees buckled and he slumped onto the ground. It was over, and without a word the gunmen went back to their posts. Fossil-Face approached to confirm the "attempted escape." With a disdainful boot, he turned the body over. Pointlessly, he held his fat pistol to the dead man's temple and administered the *coup de grâce*. The sentimental Kapo's dreamy eyes still stared at the sky.

The macabre scene had deeply distressed the convicts on the cement-block site. Only the senile *Kommandoführer* was unshaken. All he had seen in the incident was an opportunity to fire his gun. Into a dead man, but he wouldn't put that in his report.

For the morale of the prisoners, it was far better that

Ernst should have died for love. They weren't far off in declaring him a hero! But that would have been a bad idea for a German, and a Kapo to boot.

The flames from the crematorium lit up the barracks of the camp at dusk, but were greeted with supreme indifference. Paulo had not mourned the fate of the unhappy cook any longer than the others, but the crude jokes which some prisoners indulged in over the tragedy of homosexual love failed to make him laugh. He felt that all around him things were deteriorating. Ernst, the potatoes and the sun had all perished at the same time, as if preordained. Overnight, in fact, the sun began to melt into a grayish blend of fog and cloud which chilled the spine. Perhaps the vain kitchen Kapo might have hesitated if he'd had to make his exit in such a gloomy setting.

The sun had beaten down pitilessly almost every day for four months on the shaven heads and burned their raw backs, and now it had suddenly abandoned them. Just as suddenly, all the prisoners began to pray for its return, because without it, the bower of Loibl seemed to have returned to the ice age. No one had seen it coming, no one had ever thought that winter would also come to Loibl.

Fooled by the memories of films like the one where Chéri-Bibi and company in similar striped garb had sweated buckets over their rocks, the men had forgotten the other type of prison: the freezing, Siberian type, even more nightmarish. With the war still dragging on, they would soon get to know the second type without leaving their seats.

It was this joyless prospect which had given Paulo the impression that everything was deteriorating. Precisely three days after the death of the sentimental Kapo, Paulo had his first taste of the way these gentlemen were going to go about protecting their livestock from inclement weather.

It was not quite eight o'clock in the morning and with the cold spurring them on, the work on the cement-block site was forging ahead. Suddenly the dense black clouds which had been gathering low over the mountain since the night before decided to break and the workers felt their first drops of rain. It was a new experience, and for a quarter of an hour the rain distracted rather than bothered the men. "If the rain carries on like this, Fossil-Face will send us in to the refectory or the tunnel," they thought. How naïve they still were!

They were kidding themselves; they'd been too spoiled recently. It was crucial for the tunnel to get its lining blocks; otherwise the vault which their mining friends were cutting out with their pneumatic drills would not hold. No time to lose, *Schnell*! Shoulders to the wheel, rain or no rain.

So pickaxers, shovelers and wheelbarrow men all stayed at their posts till nightfall. Soaked to the skin, the miserable-looking band had worked harder than ever in the hope of warming their dripping bodies. And the picture was the same on the other open air sites. "Let's hope it rains tomorrow," Fritz, Fossil-Face and especially the productivity-mad Putz must have said to themselves.

The following day did bring more rain, but it made little difference to the convicts, because they had already been through the worst of it at four o'clock that morning. They had had to put on their meager clothing, which was sopping wet, but they had been forbidden to wring it out, doubtless for fear it might shrink. It was dreadful, when you were half-asleep, to slide a soaking shirt and trousers next to your skin. Everyone had slept naked, but their clothes hadn't dried much, for of course it was forbidden to hang them up. "A block is not a washhouse," Karl had chortled.

And the next day the rain began to fall again, as if trying to make up for time lost during the summer. This filthy weather was to last for three whole days.

Putz, good soul that he was, had certainly asked that they be given their overcoats, but unfortunately these were made of the same cheap cloth as their jackets and just soaked up the water, so that after an hour, the coats stuck to the skin with everything else like a filthy and clammy poultice.

"If we ever get out of here," an experienced old fellow pointed out, "we'll have rheumatism for the rest of our lives. It'd be better to go naked."

Working in the raw wasn't such a bad idea, and during the lunch break, a young Polish peasant attempted to explain to one of the *Arbeitskapos* what the farmhands did back home when caught in a cloud-burst. At the first drops, they stripped off and put their clothes somewhere dry. Then they carried on working as before. "As soon as the rain stops, they get dressed again," the Pole had explained. "That way nobody catches cold."

"Try telling that to the old fossil yourself, you halfwit,"

the Kapo had replied. And there was an end to it. But the idea had appealed to the young peasant from the Sarthe, the one who had bravely stood up to the terrible Baroni. It pleased him to have learned something out of the ordinary, and he chuckled to himself as he pictured the reaction of his pious neighbors seeing him cut corn in the nude. This Polish-style striptease might surprise some of the local women, and you never knew, with a gimmick like that, he might do very well for himself. With this in mind, he took the rain and its unpleasantness in good part, unlike Paulo, who couldn't help thinking that after the rain there would be snow. Like all true Parisians, he detested snow. Foolishly, he wanted to impart his fears to his teammates Joel and Angel.

"We've got plenty of time to worry about snow," interrupted Angel. "Right now we'd do better to protect ourselves against this unending flood. I know a trick to stop the water from getting through. You make yourself a lining of old cement sacks and you put it between your coat and your jacket. It stops the water, and because it keeps you warm it'll dry your shirt. And as a bonus, it'll deaden the blows. There are heaps of those old sacks behind the refectory. I'll go and pinch a few at lunchtime. Don't worry, Paulo, you'll be all right when it starts snowing."

The tall man couldn't think of anything to say. He was sickened by the drenching he had had to endure for three days. He couldn't accept being forced to stay outside for so long in such a deluge, especially as the raindrops stung like hailstones as they fell repeatedly on the same parts of the body, on his hands, his shoulders and his head.

Thanks to Belloni's ruse, when the heavens opened on the fourth day, life was bearable for the three friends. On the fifth day the rain ceased, and had the good Lord been sympathetic, he would have sent back the sun to repair the damage. But no, Yugoslavia couldn't have been in his good books: after the rain, it was the wind he hurled into the cursed valley.

Being thoroughly soaked for four whole days and then feeling a chill wind cutting through your clothes ought to have been enough to send the whole Kommando to the *Revier* with bronchitis or pneumonia. However, no one dared risk a visit to evening surgery. The thought of finding oneself at the mercy of the quack whose answer to a dubious diagnosis was a quick jab with his syringe put off even the worst afflicted. The pure air at this altitude restored all wounds and killed bacteria, and Ramsauer found he had run out of fuel for his infernal fire. Especially since he had been forced over the past few weeks to comply with an order from the Kommandant and allow two small "deliveries" to leave for Mauthausen. These were men who were not yet ripe for inoculation, but still too feeble for Loibl Pass. He felt ill at seeing them slip through his fingers.

To offset the expense of a one-way trip, Mauthausen had sandwiched a few Russkies and half a dozen Frenchmen among the sacks of grub. To everyone's astonishment, one of the latter was a Parisian Jew.

What on earth had made the Mauthausen SS preserve this specimen? It was a mystery. At any rate, Eli Katz (he hadn't even taken the precaution of disguising his name) had gone with his brothers to the camps equipped with factory furnaces. In blissful ignorance, he was quite unaware of the fantastic luck which had landed him in a camp of "subversives." His face with its cherubic smile seemed to be saying to the astonished inmates: "Of course I'm a Jew. You can see I'm one. So what?" Eli was one of life's optimists.

As for the SS at Loibl, they were simply delighted to have netted a Jew, their very own Jew! "*Schwein Jude, komm her,*" they would yell from all over the camp. They had dispensed with his registration number; "*Jude*" was enough to identify him since there was only one in the camp. This unexpected delivery had delighted the Kapos too, and for several days they amused themselves stripping the newcomer, fascinated to see whether he'd really had his prick snipped.

The merciless ragging he got made all the prisoners feel sorry for little Katz. In fact, life didn't look as if it was going to be too bad for this survivor, and furthermore, by arriving so late at Loibl, he had missed the murderous lunacy of that summer. What a perfect target, he would have stuck out like a sore thumb! Eli must have been under the protection of the prophet Elias, because on top of it all, before his arrest, he had given the Krauts a lot of bother. He hadn't been rounded up with the rest of the herd by the French cops. He was a clear case for the Gestapo. He was a spy, no less. Thanks to that complication, he had been shunted off to Fresnes instead of Drancy, and it was this mistaken switch which had temporarily saved his skin.

At Mauthausen he had announced that he was a tailor by profession, and as they were short of one in the SS workshop, he had stayed there a good six months, six months of grace. But he had caught a fair number of beatings during that time. For Eli had an obsession: he collected things. Everything he found lying around he picked up and popped into a sack of his own making, fashioned out of the house cloth in gray and blue stripes, which he hung from the cord holding up his pajamas. The sack followed him everywhere, to assembly and to the shithouse. He even slept with it, so that no one would pinch his pathetic treasure: bits of wood, pieces of soap, thread, paper, safety pins, a whole pile of things which were completely useless in this upside-down world. But it always got the better of him, he absolutely had to possess something. Ten times the Kapos had confiscated his rag bag, ten times he had gone to the stool. It was a complete waste of time and energy. Every time he managed to build up his miserable capital again, with some variations, and it was clutching an eleventh sack stuffed with rubbish that he had arrived at Loibl, enormously pleased with his achievement.

The tenacious Jew was a good recruit. He was an optimist, always smiling, his eyes always alert, even if you didn't take into account that the luck which seemed to have followed him since the start of his adventure might be infectious. After all, if this lucky little Jew, dispatched in error to the lion's den, had come out alive, why shouldn't the others? At the end of October, Paulo thought he saw proof of this in his own escape from the worst of underhanded tricks, an accusation of sabotage for which there was ample evidence, despite the fact that it was unintentional.

One evening an hour before assembly Pozzi, carrying an ax on his shoulder, had come to find him. Paulo was to take the ax and chop out a tree stump which the pickaxes had failed to shift. The roots of the stump were solidly embedded in the ground, blocking the path of the wheelbarrows. The job had to be done quickly if the work site was to be cleared before muster. And Pozzi, who had just received his Kapo's stripe, the ultimate disgrace for a Frenchman, was counting on him. He hadn't chosen Paulo to make him pay twice over for the split lip, he had simply picked on him because the big fellow with his long arms was more capable than the others of getting to the bottom of the troublesome stump. Never in his life had Paulo had the opportunity to use an ax, but since he managed pretty well with a pick, and even better with a sledgehammer, he found this new game intriguing. With the style and panache of an Italian woodsman, he set upon the stump.

Unluckily the ground was stony and Paulo, who was swinging his ax like a madman to impress Pozzi, didn't realize that by the tenth stroke the beautiful new ax was only fit for the scrap heap.

"Just look what you've done, you idiot, you useless bastard!" Pozzi screamed, grabbing the tool from him. "Look, it's completely fucked up, it's had it... That's called sabotage. You can explain yourself to the *Rapportführer.* Stay there, don't move, I'm going to fetch him."

And that is exactly what the bastard did. Two minutes later, Helmut arrived with the ax under his arm. He stood squarely in front of Paulo and running a delicate finger along the chipped blade he asked in an ominously quiet voice: "Was it you who did this? You do know what we do to saboteurs here, don't you, *Dreckmann*?"

Paulo had turned green. Of course he knew how saboteurs at Loibl Pass ended up. He had seen a few fall across the line, and for mere trifles: being late for muster, or laziness. It was more serious to have broken an expensive tool like an ax.

"This time I deserve it," he thought. In his distress he forgot to curse Pozzi the traitor, this "Frenchman" who had just condemned him to death by squealing on him. He lowered his eyes and, trembling with fear, he listened to the insults: "*Dreckmann*, shit-man." He didn't see the ax coming. It landed, the flat of it, right on his head, and Paulo had the impression that Helmut had deliberately dealt the blow with the wrong side. Which was lucky, because a cut from the sharp edge would have been beyond Ramsauer to stitch up; he would have messed around with a needle and cotton out of sadism, and very soon he would have fallen back on his syringe. You might just as well die on the spot, shot in the back. What was the *Rapportführer* waiting for?

Paulo was mistaken. The *Rapportführer* had no intention

of finishing him off, even for such a serious crime. "Attention!" he yelled. "Don't move!"

The attack came as a surprise to Paulo this time too. He was staring at the ax at his feet and stoically waiting for the *Rapportführer* to pick it up. But Helmut had something else in mind: he drew back his foot and kicked Paulo as hard as he could in the balls. For a moment, Paulo thought that the iron toe cap of his mountain boot had gone right through his nuts and they had burst. With a strangled yell of pain he rolled on the ground, but Helmut had no intention of letting him off yet. With vicious kicks he laid into the prisoner's groin, and Paulo, having finally gotten his breath back, tried in vain to protect himself. He was a fool not to pick himself up. Never stay down, was the most important piece of advice which the old boys gave the new arrivals at Mauthausen. He knew it, but the pain was too excruciating and all he could do was shuffle away clutching his balls. Helmut didn't even bother to go after him. He called to Pozzi, "Kapo, go and get him, and make him piss."

And he disappeared in the direction of the forge, taking the ax with him.

It wasn't possible that Paulo had been let off so lightly! He must be having trouble with his hearing. It couldn't have been the *Rapportführer* who had ordered that he be made to piss!

"I must be dreaming," he said, but he pissed all the same.

If he still needed proof that his death interested the Nazis far less than the work they anticipated from him, this should have been enough to convince him.

From now on, Paulo had no more right to doubt, nor to continue pestering everyone with his unjustified anxieties. And since there was no longer any need to fear death as the ultimate penalty for sabotage, surely it was better to get on with living, to sit up and take an interest in what went on. It would kill time in a far less depressing way than laying bets on the future.

If he turned his attention to the civilians, for example, either in their camp or running about the work sites, it could distract him from the hypnotic stripes of the prisoner's world. There were plenty of newcomers among these people who were allowed to dress normally. For a start, there was a man called Gruber, the second engineer, who was completely mad. Every time he passed a Frenchman he drew a finger across his throat shouting "Snip, snip!" all because his *Mutter* had brought him up from the cradle with tales of the atrocities committed by the French against the Senegalese. That was as far as his threats went, but with the little witticism he earned the nickname Snip-Snip, and it would follow him wherever there was a Frenchman around.

A concrete specialist had been appointed third chief engineer and he arrived at the same time as Snip-Snip. There was no need to come up with a nickname for this one: he was called Goebel, which was a very sticky label, and one that could hardly be improved on. That said, Herr Goebel didn't seem to have anything in common with his hysterical namesake. He was calm, almost polite; or perhaps he was just indifferent; but not once had they heard him raise his voice on the concete-factory site of which he was in sole charge.

Paulo had discovered that taking an interest in the civilians was an excellent thing. In the space of a few days, his haunted look born of frightening himself with thoughts of winter had left him. By stubbornly focusing his attention exclusively on men out of uniform, he had unconsciously in a small way left his prison.

Two other civilians, both engine drivers, intrigued him. One was a swarthy handsome Italian youth in charge of driving the *decauville;* it didn't seem to be to his taste to have to slog away all day in the dark tunnel. The other was Yugoslavian, a young man too, whose job was to act as guard for the hoppers full of rubbish as they trundled to the tip. He didn't look overwhelmed by job satisfaction either. Paulo found it difficult to understand why these two guys who were bursting with health should accept to live in this dump. If they were labor conscripts, STO, or prisoners on parole, they had countless chances for escape: they hadn't been autobahned or uniformed, they had complete freedom of movement and plenty of marks in their pockets. On the other hand, if they were volunteers, why on earth did they look so glum? Their uneasy manner must be hiding something.

Apart from these four newcomers, the other civilians, specialized laborers or truck drivers, were of no great interest. It didn't raise Paulo's spirits much to look at their oafish workers' life and their unenviable and doubtless well-deserved future. Paulo chose to look at a much more inspiring sight: the mysterious dark-haired girl who had arrived at the same time as Frau Ramsauer.

At first, he had to make a strenuous effort to remember her, to make his image of her real and then assign her a role in his daydreams. What he remembered was very sketchy, because after his famous brush with the *Rapportführer's* riding crop—his reward for staring at Martha—he had purposely turned his back on her. Since then he had made up for lost time, devouring her with his eyes every evening between muster and the bell. But from such a distance, more than two hundred yards away among the barracks of the civilian camp, even with the best will in the world, it was difficult to construct a novel out of her tiny silhouette. Until the day when the *Rapportführer*—him again—had come to find Sailor. He needed ten strong men to repair a retaining wall which had just given way on the path leading to the civilian camp. The timing couldn't have been better; it was Saturday and the tunnel wouldn't suffer. Dédé Ménard, who always pricked up his ears when he heard German being spoken, immediately tipped Paulo off.

"They're going to get a detail together for the civilian camp. They want ten volunteers right away. We'd better jump at it, it's always useful to get the lay of the land. Go and hang around Karl."

Paulo didn't need to be told twice, and five minutes later he walked out of the camp gate with Dédé and the eight shaven men rounded up with a rubber hose. Helmut, his riding crop in hand, was at their head, followed by three SS with their submachine guns at the ready. Four guards for ten prisoners was a little more than the statutory requirement, but for a walk in the open, prudence was advisable.

"Tell me, Dédé," Paulo exclaimed in a low voice, "d'you understand Kraut? You never told me that. Do you speak it too? Why didn't you let us in on it when you arrived? You could be a *Dolmetscher,* that's a soft number."

"Whatever you do, forget it. Don't talk about it. Ever. Even to friends."

"What a guy that Dédé is," thought Paulo, "what a great guy." But for the moment there were better things to do than to find out why Dédé was so adamant about keeping his secret. He ought to be getting an eyeful of all the new discoveries which this ramble afforded. To begin with, he had a view of the camp from the other side of the road. From this far away, his pajama-clad fellows, who were strolling around the blocks or up and down the *Appelplatz*, deep in conversation under the watchful eye of machine guns, looked like genuine madmen let out of their padded cells for their daily constitutional.

"Christ, is that what we look like to the civilians?" Paulo couldn't help exclaiming. "It's not surprising that they keep clear of us in the tunnel. I'd be frightened too."

There was more than a grain of truth in that, judging by the lack of enthusiasm with which the civilians greeted the gang come to repair their wall. Only two or three out of the fifty had deigned to come and watch them. But . . . there she was, smiling and pretty as a picture.

Paulo had the shock of his life. If he had been able to, he would have run away and hidden; then he would have thrown his humiliating get-up into the bushes. His embarrassment was absurd, but that was Paulo all over. In front of this vision, so feminine, so fresh, so improbable in this filthy dump, Paulo was appalled at his own appearance and at his dirty, unshaven, vulgar jailbird friends.

The girl of his dreams had certainly taken him by surprise. He had completely blown his first date. Now she was seeing these striped creatures, these tramps, close up, she would get a strange idea of the charms of the French.

Was it patriotic pride or just plain pride? Paulo's embarrassment had overtaken his companions too. The poor bastards didn't know where to put themselves.

Happily, they hadn't been fetched just for introductions. The fall of stones which they were to clear gave them the chance to recover their sangfroid. "*Arbeit*," Helmut had yelled, before turning around to extend a hand to the chief of the civilian camp. He made a slight bow to the girl, looking a little tight-lipped as if to make it clear that he hadn't gotten over the flop of their first meeting. This time the little Yugoslavian made the first move.

"*Gut Morgen, Rapportführer*," she called, with a brilliant smile. She seemed delighted by the visitation and not at all inclined to leave, for the very good reason that it was her quarters which had suffered the most from the cave-in. The rubble was blocking her front door and windows, where her washing was hanging up to dry. Not the striped regulation underwear, but delicate pink embroidered things. Briefs, petticoats, bras—all the intimate apparel of a pretty Yugoslavian girl—fluttered in the wind like so many flags of Liberty, Civilization and Love.

They weren't indecent thoughts which sprang to Paulo's mind while, bent over his shovel, he literally devoured the pretty civilian with his eyes. He was just fascinated by her grace and her natural, rather shy elegance. Everything about this girl pleased him: her face, her body and even her voice. The German language became tolerable when she spoke it. He stored up every detail to be able to recall each one that night and every other night when he lay in the awful dormitory, trying to escape his callous world by drifting into dreamland. Of course, to conjure up a fantasy, he could just as well have brought on some of the girls he had known in Paris, who were beautiful, scented, better dressed and good lays. But like almost all the wretches caught in Loibl's trap, Paulo had long since buried his memories. This girl, alive and close enough to touch, was a reality. He wouldn't be able to get her out of his mind now, even if he wanted to.

The *Rapportführer*, clearly still smarting, had not stayed long in Yanka's company (Yanka was how he had addressed her as he took his leave). He'd excused himself with a bow on the grounds that he had to conduct an inspection, then he'd disappeared with the camp chief, leaving his three underlings in charge of getting the job done quickly. After a quick conference, the three numbskulls arranged themselves in a triangle and started up the usual chant: *"Arbeit, schnell, schweine Franzosen."* These three couldn't give a damn about revealing their true colors to Yanka.

"What a lovely name," thought Paulo. "Yanka, that's very pretty. It's soft, ideal for her."

For some minutes now, he had been sure the slim Yugoslavian had noticed him—which was hardly surprising, considering the boldly admiring glances he had been casting in her direction. But she must have felt a little embarrassed, for she soon disappeared behind her cabin. But not for long, for her front door would soon be cleared and she seemed anxious to go inside, if only to whisk away her provocative underthings, the symbols of her femininity. When she did so, a few moments later, it was with quick, hurried movements like a laundress. She had blushed at the curious stares of soldiers and convicts alike, who continued to watch her with interest. And when the clothesline was bare, she smiled her most charming smile at all the spectators as if to apologize for blushing in public.

Paulo of course thought that her gaze and smile had lingered longer on him than on the others. And he was not mistaken, for five minutes later, Yanka approached him with a small package in her hand, and when she was close enough to his earth-laden shovel, she threw it down accurately and discreetly in front of him. He was taken by surprise and didn't even have time to thank her, doubtless because he had acted on an old prisoner's instinct and, before anything else, had made certain no one had seen the package land. The rapid glance he swept over the three gray-green slobs reassured him. But now it was too late to say thank you, for Yanka had disappeared.

Coolly, Paulo scooped the package into his shovel, and from there into his pocket. Running a hand swiftly over it he could guess at its contents: cigarettes, several packets of them, three or four by the feel of it, a precious stock which he would be able to trade for bowls of soup, or bread, or drippings.

The guards may not have seen anything, but his friends had seen it all, down to the last detail. It would be difficult to hide his manna from heaven for very long. Especially from Dédé right next to him, the main witness.

"If it weren't for him being here," thought Paulo, "how I'd love to tell those gluttons to go and get stuffed."

Those gluttons couldn't take their eyes off his bulging pocket; they were waiting for an explanation, and he'd better get there first.

"So they're smokes," he said abruptly. "There's enough for everybody. But lay off with your vulture impersonations. Will you get on with your work? D'you want to get us into trouble?"

He thought he'd done rather well, but Dédé, who'd been keeping a close eye on him, wasn't taken in.

"How many packs?" he asked.

"Four."

"Well, you keep half, and we'll split the rest."

"Sounds like a good idea," Paulo agreed, delighted with

the deal. "I'm quite happy just to hand out a couple, on the condition you and I share the rest. A pack each, okay?"

The thrill of being given cigarettes out of the blue had not made Paulo forget whom he owed them to: "She's got to come back," he said impatiently, "so I can say thank you . . . I mean for all of us."

And he tried to figure out how to go about it. The *Rapportführer* was bound to be there when it was time to say goodbye, and with his nibs around, smiling at girls was an expensive hobby. "What am I going to do?" he groaned to himself. "Hey, Dédé, you haven't got a pencil on you, have you? I've absolutely got to say thank you to her. It's impossible to talk to her with that hysterical Helmut around, and just smiling at her would be even worse. Once was enough."

To Paulo's amazement, Dédé produced a stub of pencil from the hem of his jacket and held it out to him.

"Here, will this do? Ask, and you shall receive," he added with a grin, rather chuffed with his conjuring act. "I knew it would come in handy one day. But what d'you want to say to her, and what language are you going to say it in?"

"In Kraut, you spell it for me. It won't be much, just 'Thank you, mademoiselle.' No need to waffle on, and anyway I know what to say. *Danke schön, Fraulein*. How do you write *Danke schön*?"

"D-a-n-k-e s-c-h-ö-n, two words, and *Fraulein* . . ."

"No, that's horrible, *Fraulein*. She'd be really annoyed . . . Here, bighead, how do you say *mademoiselle* in Yugoslav?"

"*Gospodicna*, spelled like you say it."

Paulo went straight toward the barracks where he had noticed a bit of light-colored paper, and turning his shovel over, he scraped it back to his feet. Then he bent down, pretending to tie his shoelaces, and scribbled out his "DANKE SCHÖN GOSPODICNA" in capital letters. Since there was a little space left on the paper, he drew a heart and signed it: Paulo 28,214.

It was a good thing he hadn't wasted any time, because the *Rapportführer* was coming back with the camp chief, and Yanka was with them. It was going to be difficult for Paulo to deliver his love letter. Hastily, he folded it in fourths, put it on his shovel with some earth and spaded the whole lot into the doorway of her cabin. Right in the middle of the passage; she couldn't fail to see it.

Antreten, assembly. It was time to go, but unfortunately, Yanka apparently wanted to see the gang off before she went inside. Paulo would leave without knowing his message had been found. As she was still smiling, regardless of Helmut, and Paulo was sure this time that her smile was addressed to him, he decided it was worth taking a risk. Before that pig of a *Rapportführer* gave the order to march, he wanted to see her pick up the scrap of paper. By nodding his head and pointing his forefinger discreetly at her doorway, he contrived to guide Yanka's gaze in the right direction. Surprised and even a little worried, she hesitated a few seconds. What did he want, this tall nice-looking fellow? Did he want her to hide him? Under her bed perhaps? The Frenchman was going a bit far. Then she caught sight of the folded note, and she lowered her eyes to show she had understood. Paulo breathed again. Now he had a friend here, an accomplice, someone who could put a name to his anonymous pajamas.

As Helmut still had a few words to say to the civilian chief, and the Slav girl was apparently keen to stay and watch the departure of the men who had so quickly cleared up the damage caused by the cave-in, Paulo was able to study her at leisure. She really was rather gorgeous: not very tall, but her hips, waist and breasts were in perfect proportion. There was no mistaking all this through the cheap dress she was wearing. Her face was even more attractive, framed by long, shining black hair which fell gracefully on to her shoulders, emphasizing her large light-gray eyes and her full red lips. Her features were as serene as a madonna's, but this madonna was sparkling with good health as if she had stepped from her picture frame to spend a holiday in the mountains. "She's a real beauty," Paulo said to himself again. "It's incredible in this wilderness. What the hell is she doing here? It doesn't look as if she's got a boy friend here. Yanka, you're messing up your life, your youth. You'd do better to clear out of here as fast as you can. I'll just have to manage."

But for now, it was he who was clearing out. *Eins . . . zwei . . . los . . .* Helmut closed in behind, and Paulo had had his last look. For him, Yanka would once more be a tiny speck in the distance, whom he'd watch out for every evening after coffee. But now that he had seen her up close, he didn't regret having made a vague silhouette into the leading lady of his dreams.

Heading back to the camp, reality got the upper hand. There really were four packs of cigarettes in his normally empty pocket. Twenty butts just for him. That meant ten bowls of soup. Paulo knew who he could fence them to, without getting nabbed: to the hustler in the laundry, the only decent queer, who gave extra rations to his compatriots, even those he only knew by sight. Paulo must have been very hungry not to think twice about trading his smokes; once, he had smoked forty a day. Apart from a few butts picked up on the work site which he had greedily smoked down to the mouthpiece, he hadn't smoked a whole cigarette in eight months, and he had certainly never had the pleasure of lighting one up.

"Still, I think I'll treat myself to one this evening to celebrate the day," he resolved. "And I'll do it on the quiet, so that I don't get any scavengers coming to beg a drag off me. I want to smoke a whole one to myself."

After the distribution of coffee and the bread, which was as meager as ever, but even blacker and bitter as bran, he made for the *Waschraum* with Dédé, to split the cigarettes. Hot on their heels came the eight others from the afternoon detail. To make quite sure they got their fair share of fags, they had suddenly turned friendly, not to say greasy. "Hey, Paulo, you've scored a big hit with that civilian dame," said one of them, voicing the others' thoughts. "Even half bald, you've got her where you want her."

"Mind your own business, you can all take your cigarettes and piss off. And I wouldn't say too much about them, otherwise you might not get any more." He couldn't see how there would ever be another opportunity, but it amused him to surround himself with mystery and superiority.

In the eyes of a few he had just stepped out of the ranks of the tramps, thanks to that pretty girl. They would rush off to waggle their smokes under their friends' noses, and like gossipy old women they would tell the whole story about the girl, about Paulo's way with women, and his billet-doux. But he wasn't too eager for the Kapos to hear about it, for more than ever at Loibl it was better to be envied than pitied. The main thing was that he'd been able to attract such a pretty girl when his head was shaved and he was in rags, and she was surrounded by fifty healthy and eager males. It was quite an achievement; he found it flattering, and it was well worth the three packs of cigarettes he'd had to hand over.

Rather pleased with himself, Paulo left them all to it, including Dédé, and disappeared in the direction of the kitchen block, the one nearest the road. Two minutes later, he'd sat himself down against the wall of the barrack and was pulling on his first cigarette with relish. It was the Yugoslav equivalent of a Gauloise, a drava, rolled with black tobacco, Paulo's favorite kind. Thoughtful Yanka must have known the tastes of the French. Christ, it was good! What a pleasure it was to feel the smoke reaching down into the depths of his stomach! Paulo exhaled slowly and carefully, so that the smoke shouldn't blow away in the wind, but instead cling to his face and eyes, intoxicating him. He surrounded himself with it, then drew it in again through his nostrils and sucked it into his lungs. Two drags on the same puff!

"Fuck the soup," he said, as he felt the butt burning his lips. "I've got time for another before the bell. God, how good it is here, all by myself."

Paulo smoked his second cigarette in the more usual way. He had calmed down, and his thoughts automatically turned to the girl to whom he owed this unhoped-for pleasure. From where he was sitting, he could see the whole civilian camp, but he couldn't quite make out which was Yanka's cabin. Night was falling, and it was too dark.

"Well, I've got to get back, the bell will be ringing soon," he said, getting up. "Tomorrow I'll come back earlier. I can afford to treat myself to one more."

All set to smoke away his extra bowls of soup one by one, he wasn't going to put on any weight. To hell with desires for food. For him, spiritual nourishment was more important. And so he came back the following day, and every evening for the rest of the week. He got through all his cigarettes, much to the regret of the pansy in the laundry, who had heard of Paulo's stock through the grapevine and already advanced him a bowl of soup.

"Well, thanks for that," Paulo said, accepting the soup. "I'll bring you the butts this evening."

He had meant it, and he intended to keep his word. But once the coffee had been handed out the temptation was too much. So he ran to his vantage point behind the kitchen, where, far from everyone and everything, he satisfied his craving with one cigarette after another. Goodbye soup!

Out in the open in these surroundings, was an even better way of escaping than lying in bed. From where he sat at the higher end of the camp, he could see over the top of the barbed-wire fence. He couldn't see the watchtowers and still less his striped fellows who were strolling about in the camp behind him. There was no one else on earth except for him and the girl opposite.

It was sad that she didn't know her amorous convict was there, looking out for her each time she left her cabin. In a whole week, he had seen her perhaps three times, no more, and even then only for a few seconds out of the two hours he kept watch each day.

But this long wait in isolation and silence, far from adding to his depression, made him see the future less bleakly. Not because he hoped something would develop between him and Yanka; he had no illusions about that, she would always be unapproachable, and the detail with its wonderful windfall of cigarettes was an unrepeatable stroke of luck. No, the future seemed less bleak simply because, by occupying his thoughts day and night, the Yugoslavian girl prevented him from thinking about anything else. Although it got a little colder every evening, he even got to the point of forgetting about the frightful winter ahead.

And yet winter was fast drawing in, and soon the first snowflakes fell, mingling with the raindrops. They melted when they touched the ground, but it was clear to everyone that winter would not wait for the twenty-second of December to make its appearance over the col at Loibl. In spite of the continual icy rainfall, Paulo's uplifted spirits had persuaded him that autumn would make a big comeback. November was often sunny in the mountains, wasn't it? If only to help the migrating birds on their way. Wasn't it a familiar postcard scene? With the reddish leaves on the trees reflecting a sun which was redder still, nature was warm and mellow at this time of year. According to the experts, the painters and the poets, autumn is the most glorious season.

And yet it looked as if the sun which had dogged them all summer had left this cursed valley for ever. By the second of November, it was all over: snow had fallen in the night, covering everything: the camp, the road, and the work sites. Nearly a foot had fallen, soundlessly, without anyone realizing it. Apart from Otto, the doyen, who must have been having a sleepless night; at two o'clock that morning he blew hard on his whistle to rouse the block chiefs.

Five minutes later all the sleepers in the camp were up and dressed, each man holding a shovel to start clearing away the snow. First they had to clear the immediate surroundings of each block, then the *Appelplatz*, and lastly the road, where all the SS on day duty were waiting with their guns at rest. The Kommandant was there too. He had decided to direct the operation in person, for the snow had caught him by surprise, and he'd made no preparations for it. Who would be blamed if the tunnel was a day late, at least fifteen feet short on each side? It would be his neck on the block.

Working up the road ten abreast, the convicts were a human snowplow. The first wave of men cleared the top layer, followed by ten others behind who scraped the remaining snow to the sides of the road, and the last team pitched the whole lot into the ravine. The Kommandant had warned his men and the Kapos: "If you're not in the tunnel by six o'clock . . ."

Everybody knew what to expect, and the hoses took up their old tune in the wakeful night. This turned out to be very effective because the prisoners could go in one direction only, if they were to avoid the blows: forward. And to move forward, they had to scrape away like fury. The men of Loibl Pass, who considered themselves the world's fastest workers, were in the process of smashing their own record.

Snow is not as heavy to shovel as earth or stones, but working at this rate exhausted them just as quickly. The Kapos realized that it was in the general interest, and in their own above all, to replace the leading men every quarter of an hour. Which was no great problem, for the bulk of the gang was just marking time in the rear and the Kapos had to draw from the stock in sets of thirty. So the work continued at the same backbreaking pace until dawn, and at the exact hour appointed by the big boss, they were at the tunnel.

The sites too were cleared at lightning speed, and well before eight o'clock they set about their real work on the hard ground. They were barely two hours behind, which was nothing considering they had ten hours in which to catch up.

By nightfall, the objectives set by Putz and his assistants Goebel and Snip-Snip had been achieved, and the tons of rubble extracted from the hole had disappeared down into the dump with the same regularity as on a normal day.

With organization like this, the snow was almost a diversion for the spotty SS youths on duty. As soon as they knew the lost time had been made up, they amused themselves by throwing gravel-filled snowballs at the convicts. Even in this recreational atmosphere, the prisoners obviously couldn't throw snowballs back. By the end of the day, the workers were sick and tired of being bombarded in a one-way battle. Why didn't the snow hurry up and melt!

But instead it began to fall again more thickly, even before the day shift, already thoroughly fed up with the frightful day the snow had given them, had reached the gates of the camp.

"I bet you we'll be up again at two o'clock tomorrow," Paulo whispered in Joel's ear. "I was right, this winter's going to last six months, and it's not even cold yet. It'll be far worse in January. What a vile hole! If we don't want to be frozen alive, we'd better get back into the tunnel, and it's just too bad about our lungs. In any case, with all the shit that lands on our backs outside we'll get TB just the same. So we might as well not freeze our balls off."

He wasn't given the time to act on the decision. During roll call, as he searched fruitlessly for the best way to get back into the hole, he thought he heard his number being called—*acht und swanzig tausend zwei hundert vierzehn*. No, his ears hadn't been playing tricks on him, they had definitely called out his number. What did it mean?

Thoroughly rattled, he stepped out of the ranks, and was propelled forward by Fritz with one hand on his cord and the other at the scruff of his neck, the classic jailer's grip. He found himself catapulted straight into the middle of a group standing to one side, made up of numbers read out from the lists which each of the five block chiefs had handed in turn to the *Rapportführer*. Helmut paused as each man passed in front of him, and looked him over carefully before resuming his agonizing roll call: *Acht und swanzig, sieben und zwanzig*... When it was Paulo's turn, Helmut, who up till then had stared with disdainful indifference at the men he was extracting from the formation, was unable to suppress a smirk of satisfaction.

"This new Kommando doesn't look like it's a promotion," was Paulo's immediate reaction.

Helmut offered him a few helpful hints. "The Nordfeld ought to do you good, you great pimp. You won't find any women to leer at there!"

Paulo grasped only two words of this charming little speech, pimp and Nordfeld. He didn't need an interpreter. Pimp was hard to take coming from this perfumed tart, but Paulo had learned to shrug off that kind of insult. The second word, Nordfeld, was more ominous. The north was regarded with terror by them all, SS and Kapos included, as a sort of transportation colony, a cooler for the hotheads. Nobody knew what went on there, nothing had ever leaked out, no one had ever come back. And worst of all, the other side of the mountain was in Austria, part of the Great Reich. The route back to Mauthausen was direct, there was no frontier to cross. Paulo was stunned; he couldn't believe his ears. Even at the height of his anxiety he had never even considered a blow as bitter as this. Why him? He was a founding member. Who had leaned on whom? There were only two possible candidates: Sailor and Helmut. The former because of Belloni, out of homosexual jealousy (he would have been the one to write "big pimp" by Paulo's number). And the latter for the incident of the blunted ax—unless Helmut, too, had been motivated by jealousy. But of course, he was the jealous kind... And anyway his *Dolmetscher* had translated: "You won't find any women to leer at there." That must be it. But Paulo was hardly in the best position to let the elegant officer have it in the balls. The spiteful bastard had nothing to fear. But it must have displeased him that a *Haeftling*, and a Frenchman to boot, had twice wanted to show the only two women in the place that he was still a man.

The snow was falling more and more thickly and Paulo was anxiously listening for the order to return barracks. Before he went he wanted to say goodbye to Joel, Angel, Dédé. The others could go hang, they were no more important than the men surrounding him, all of them strangers to him and nonentities in any case, apart from François of Burgundy from Block 2. This fellow was anything but a bootlicker, and despite his youth—he was only nineteen—and his good looks, he had managed to evade Bullseye's shaft. He, too, was the victim of jealousy. It was bad luck for him to be caught up in this dirty deal, but for Paulo it was something of a consolation.

The order to disperse was finally given, and there was a general rush toward the blocks to get out of the snow. Except for the twenty unlucky men who would henceforth be attached to the north camp. The Kommandant had ordered that the departure take place within the hour, for if the snow continued to fall like this, the road would become impassable.

Get going, forward march . . . *eins, zwei*, toward the gate. Paulo and his companions were spared painful scenes of farewell.

With empty hands, empty pockets and no baggage, they walked out of the place where they had nearly all spent five months. That was the big difference between prisoners anywhere else in the world and Nazi deportees, who had no rights, possessed nothing, not even a bar of soap, a spare shirt, socks or a handkerchief. They owned nothing, absolutely nothing. At a moment's notice they could be ferried from one camp to another, brought back, sent off again, dispatched like common bales of cloth. They were less important even than the clothes they wore; clothing, after all, was left outside crematoriums. Not to be destroyed, but to clothe the newcomers. The *KLM* tatters were more precious than some of the bodies they covered. Even at Loibl, if you looked closely enough, you could see that quite a few of the numbers sewn just above the red triangle had been restitched several times.

By the side of the road, in the light of the combined searchlights from two corner watchtowers, was a large group of detainees standing at attention and guarded by ten armed SS. No one in Paulo's gang had seen them assemble.

"They're the men who've come to take our places," someone said. "Some more Mauthausen newcomers. Why didn't they send them straight to the north? They wouldn't have needed to send us then."

The truth was that these fellows were also going north. They had indeed been sent by the mother camp as reinforcements, but to avoid confusion the SS had made them wait well away from the barracks. Judging from the thick layer of snow covering their coats and caps, they had been hanging around for some time.

These men had no baggage either, which proved they had been through Mauthausen. Yet these unknown characters must have come a long way, a very, very long way. They were Chinese, with yellow skin, flattened noses, and slanted eyes.

"The Krauts can't have gotten as far as China!" Paulo panicked for a second. "They can't have, they're retreating everywhere. So where on earth have these chinks sprung from? Good grief, the Gestapo must have raided all the Chinese restaurants in Europe, from Naples to Amsterdam. Christ!"

The explanation was more simple. The newcomers did indeed originate from the Chinese continent, but they were Mongols, in other words Soviet citizens. They still didn't speak Russian or German, let alone French. When the two groups finally merged, the only phrase the newcomers managed to utter from between their thick and frozen lips was "*Nye panimayu*, I don't understand," in a kind of muffled growl. It looked as if conversation might be sticky.

The arrival of these savages, who seemed to communicate with each other like a troupe of deaf-mute acrobats, had made Paulo forget that he was accompanying them on the path to misfortune. It was only as they drew level with the civilian camp that everything came flooding back: Yanka, the cigarettes, the potatoes and hope. What he was leaving behind was nothing special, but he'd been through so much at the beginning, he had suffered, he had bled, he had been so afraid, that he couldn't accept losing it all so suddenly.

Over on the other side of the mountain, at Nordfeld, he would have to start all over again.

XV

The Mongols who flanked Paulo in the column marching north wore their caps in a curious way: yanking down the snow-sodden cloth below their ears and right over their eyes, they crammed their heads into them as if they were night-caps. Tugged about like this, the caps were less esthetic than usual, but they offered better protection from the snow, the wind and most of all from his whining neighbors who the moment they left the camp had begun to bemoan their fate as if they had just quit Paradise on earth. Paulo followed the Mongols' example, so that he wouldn't have to hear the moaners either, and with his cap squashed firmly onto his head, he was indistinguishable from the group of slant-eyed men as he arrived at Nordfeld.

He would spend six months there, from November to April, and during that time the snow wouldn't stop falling, the ground wouldn't thaw, and death would continue to strike. Six dreadful months, worse than anything he could have imagined, but at the end of it all he would come out alive, without really knowing what had happened. Hunched up under his cap, he had said, mostly for his own benefit: "I can't go on, I don't want to see, I don't want to know. This is the end."

At the top of the col, Paulo already knew what was in store for him on the Austrian side. The snow had stopped, but it was still deep on the ground from two days before. The vicious wind from the Reich whipped it up off the road to chase it back in squalls as hard as hailstones onto the faces and the hands of the prisoners, who struggled manfully onward. Even the SS guards, warmly dressed in gloves, woolen hats and fur-lined boots, began to curse the weather. They'd been taken for suckers, too. The officers at Loibl had gotten rid of them without warning, as if they were lepers. They'd pay them back for being double-crossed, and they'd start with their gun butts on the shivering *Haeftlinge* who were the cause of all their misfortune.

It was during this nightmarish climb that Paulo decided to give up the struggle; or, more precisely, when he arrived at the summit and caught sight of the four or five miserable barracks, crouched against the snow-covered rock face down below, which were pompously referred to as Nordfeld.

This site, which was exposed to a wind so glacial it must blow straight off the Baltic, could only be described as a cold storage. Before hurling itself against the cursed mountain, the wind seemed to want to blow its worst, without pity for those who had been departed to this uninhabitable place; as if it, too, were in a hurry to see the tunnel finished, so that it could rush in with the whole German Army.

"Just what I was afraid of. We'll have to begin all over again. I won't survive."

Had Paulo thought things through a little more carefully, he wouldn't have talked like this. There was nothing to begin all over again in the north. They hadn't sent him there to be disciplined—they had already done that extremely thoroughly—but to make him work, because for lack of seasoned labor, the tunnel on this side was behind schedule. This was demonstrated to him the following morning at roll call.

"*Alles mineurs*, all miners!" the head of the detachment had announced by way of an introduction to the newcomers.

On the same evening Paulo found himself holding a pneumatic drill. It was the hardest kind of work, but the infernal noise the machine made was also the best way to ensure that no one would come to annoy him. The one thing he no longer wanted to do was talk. And so that no one would pester him after work either, he had chosen a bunk in a corner right at the back of the block, so that he would only have one neighbor to put up with. By chance, it was one of the Mongols.

After several days, some of the men who had known Paulo in the south camp began to get worried.

"Something's up with Paulo," François of Burgundy remarked. "He's cracking up." And he tried to bring him out of his shell by cracking a joke or two.

"Don't upset yourself, old man, you'll see Paname again. Don't look so glum. Come on, talk, say something, anything, it helps."

"Piss off," was all Paulo would say. He would have nothing to do with François, the youngster with the indomitable morale, the most boisterous of all the Frenchmen in the Kommando, the boy who could take twenty-five strokes without a whimper and get up smiling. Nor would he have anything to do with the old history teacher, and yet several times in the south camp he had sought him out to prop up his failing morale. Etcheverry, who lugged his old carcass around with more and more difficulty, would surely have liked to talk to him; there weren't all that many Frenchmen in the north. No, Paulo wanted to be left alone in his icy tower.

Everything, past and future, war and peace, had been

swept from his mind by the hellish climate. From December to March there was two meters of snow on the ground, and half the time the temperature dropped to 30 degrees below zero. Compared to his obsession with the cold, even food became a secondary problem. How could you avoid freezing on your feet when your socks were pieces of cement sack, your wooden-soled shoes are full of holes, and your coat was cut from rough cloth worn threadbare by torrential autumn rains? You had to be young like the boy from Burgundy to endure it.

François had kept his childlike eyes open, but since he thought himself still at school, he was oblivious to the gravity of the situation, and it was his mischievous streak which made him the star of Nordfeld. On the men's return from work one evening, an *Arbeitskapo* who had been irritated by François's defiant expression, had demanded that the doyen, Willy from the Sarre, administer a public punishment. Only too happy to oblige, Willy had had a stool and his thickest club fetched on the spot. He had begun the usual whipping session in front of the assembled camp. But the first strokes made such a peculiar noise that on the fifth, he stopped.

"Drop your trousers, *Franzose*."

The chief had just realized that the little comedian had slipped something between his buttocks and his trousers, but he still didn't expect what he found. It was a shovel, the blade of a laborer's shovel, which the kid had slipped down his strides. And to crown it all, he held up his shield with a cheeky grin, doubtless hoping the doyen would appreciate the joke. Only a kid would have thought of a trick like that and have the audacity to try and carry it off. In the ranks everyone trembled for him. How would the doyen take it? Badly—there were too many witnesses who, with lowered eyes, were inwardly mocking him.

His face paled in anger and humiliation, and everybody knew that, far from appreciating the humor, he had taken the joke very badly indeed. Suppressing his rage, he walked up to the impertinent boy and quite gently placed him back on the stool in the house position, facedown. Then, in a deceptively friendly voice, he commanded, "Take off your shorts, for all your friends to see your pretty pink bum."

As he said this, he had winked conspiratorially at the crowd of prisoners. For a second they even wondered whether the whole shovel incident and the armored backside hadn't all been staged by the queer doyen himself. Alas, this was not the case. The bastard resumed his malicious look and added, screaming this time, "Double or nothing, you lost, *Scheisskubel*. You get fifty instead of twenty-five."

With the help of the cold, the youngster's skin readily split open and the blood ran. Even Willy must have been sickened by being spattered with blood at each new stroke. But he didn't want to lose face in front of all the men: he had said fifty strokes and fifty strokes it would be. "Get up, you little bastard, take off your jacket and shirt."

And he systematically set about the boy's back, his shoulders, even the back of his neck. At *fünfzig*, the kid's body had been reduced to an open wound. His face contorted with pain and biting his lip, he had nonetheless found the strength throughout the entire ordeal to stifle his screams of agony in his throat.

The young boy's unbelievable resistance to this open-air flagellation in such sinister surroundings and such bitter cold had stunned all the spectators. That day Paulo had been forced to open his eyes, and his ears had heard and counted the blows which lashed his comrade's back. If he was left with only one memory of Nordfeld, it would be this, particularly as the fifty strokes were only the beginning of François of Burgundy's story. As was to be expected, his shovel ruse quickly went around the camp; all the SS and Kapos, in fact anyone who had a club or a gun butt handy, soon adopted the rebel as their favorite target. He must have come from Mauthausen in fantastically good shape to still be alive after all these beatings. Granted the boy was mad, hadn't he just demonstrated it? But according to a onetime communist Kapo who had spent years in the camps, nobody had ever seen a prisoner with nerve like his. And the old Kapo had added that François was well on the way to breaking the all-time record for beatings in any *Konzentrationslager* anywhere. Not counting men who had been beaten to death, of course.

François's courage was almost a source of embarrassment for the other detainees, and he knew it. But with the arrogance of youth which made him want to scare his fellow prisoners or put them to shame, every day he went one better.

Paulo remained aloof. Hunched up under his coat like a specter, with his *Mütze* jammed down over his ears like a cowl, he still refused to see. The fate of the boy from Burgundy didn't hold his attention any more than two other incidents which were, nonetheless, going to disrupt the lives of all the detainees in the north: the linking of the two tunnels, and the unusual circumstances surrounding the deaths of two of Paulo's blockmates, a harmless Frenchman, and a Pole who was tougher than seemed humanly possible.

The fourth of December was the feast day of St. Barbara, the patron saint of miners. Chief engineer Putz had chosen that day to dynamite the last few yards separating the two tunnel teams. At both ends of the tunnel the men were working double time, having taken on trust a rumor that if the schedule were met, the *Universale* was to invite every single miner to an enormous feast of drippings, sausage, jam and above all the famous goulash, which made their mouths water just talking about it.

It was the team on the south side who were the first to drill through. Putz had come to Nordfeld to direct operations, leaving the other side in the hands of his second-in-command, Snip-Snip. Putz was proud of himself: his calculations had been precise, he was bang on target, give or take four inches, and on schedule.

He himself had set the dynamite charges in the holes made by the drills, and he was longing to detonate them. But the Kommandant had demanded that they wait for him on this historic occasion. After all, although nobody had asked Yugoslavia's permission, this was a new frontier opening up between the two countries. To contain his impatience, Putz began to dance up and down in front of the section of wall about to be blown up.

Completely indifferent to the engineer's euphoria, Paulo merely viewed the ceremony as his first chance since arriving in the north to put down the deafening pneumatic drill. He knew that the following day he'd have to take up his bone-shaking tool again to attack the upper gallery, which was hardly begun. So he didn't give a shit about St. Barbe. Nobody had celebrated his name day or his birthday. He had completely forgotten it anyway. It had been only four days before, on the thirtieth of November, and if Putz hadn't been such a stickler for tradition, trumpeting to the world that today was the fourth of December, Paulo would never have realized that he had just turned twenty-four. For him, birthdays only meant he was a year older, but for a good many others at Loibl, fathers or beloved sons, birthdays must have been another source of pain. Putz's own birthday was definitely St. Barbe. At the time appointed by Winkler, he lit the fuse and shouted to everybody to stand clear.

Boom, boom-boom! Two out of ten for fireworks: the breach was hardly big enough for a football. Big enough, however, for the Kommandant to pop his beaming face through almost immediately.

"Well done, Putz, *schöne Arbeit*! Heil Hitler!" he hollered.

He must have been disappointed there wasn't enough room for him to put his arm through as well, but one could easily picture the fool saluting the rock from the other side.

Some of the men had thought that the joining of the tunnel would open the door to the sorely missed south camp, and relieve the unfair exile of the men in the north. It was not to be: as soon as the passage was cleared, it was barred by a large door made of planks, and two SS guards were posted on either side. A sort of border post separating the veterans of the south from the lepers of the north.

But the rickety partition was not big enough to block the whole gallery, and a draft worse than the cold outside whipped through the tunnel day and night. This was something nobody had foreseen. It froze the backs of the men in the tunnel, and turned the water sweating from the disemboweled mountain into icicles. Which meant that the helmetless miners no longer had to contend only with regular rockfalls, but also with slabs of razor-sharp ice which broke loose without warning. Winter, Paulo's constant nightmare, had managed to pursue him into his last refuge in the heart of the mountain.

So that was the real change which the opening of the tunnel had wrought upon those who were its principal makers. They had no reason to jump for joy like that fat idiot Putz who, needless to say, had not kept his promise of a feast for everybody. You don't give goulash to animals, even on a day of rejoicing.

The second event which jerked the north camp out of its stupor was the execution of Pierrefeu, a French businessman from Nancy. Right up to the last minute, nobody believed it was anything more than a parody of an execution dreamed up by the block chief to scare the living daylights out of the poor fellow, who had treated himself to a second helping of bread by queuing up twice.

It must have been a fit of madness due to his terrible hunger which had compelled Pierrefeu to take such a risk. A polite family man with three children, he had always been timid, and he regularly lost out in the scuffles for extra soup. He was the exact opposite of an opportunist. It was certainly the first time in his life that he had ever stolen anything. Many of the men even wondered if the chief's allegations hadn't been a complete frame-up. But no; the poor man had publicly confessed to the crime and hardly made a murmur when the *Schreiber* hung around his neck a placard describing his wickedness: "I stole my comrades' bread."

After that, things happened very quickly. Pierrefeu spent a night standing at attention outside in 10 degrees of frost without a coat, facing the block so that from their beds his mates should see his placard clearly. Just in case they might have the idea of copying the self-seeker. Then *fünf-und-zwanzig* for morning coffee, and special instructions issued to the chief of the *Arbeitskapos*. By the end of the day when he came back from the tunnel, his lacerated head was like a football, and his skinny legs, which had managed to support him for twenty-four hours in a row, looked as though they wouldn't carry him for much longer. It wasn't over yet; they were waiting for him at the gate of the camp: the doyen was there in person, with several Kapos and an SS officer. The theft had been reported to higher powers and it was evident that the matter would not rest there.

The Loibl convicts ought to have been used to it by now, but every time the Kapos joined forces to lynch one of their number, their hearts were wrung. In the column marching toward the barracks, there must have been many praying for Pierrefeu. Their prayers were fitting, for a scaffold was being constructed opposite the barracks. They had never had one at Loibl, even in the south, and this one must have been hurriedly put together during the day by the night shift. Even only fifteen feet away, the angular scaffold towering above them had a slightly stagey look about it. The convicts didn't know what to think. It had been some time now, more than three months, since able-bodied workers had been executed at Loibl. The gallows must surely be just for effect, another of their tricks to frighten the prisoners into obedience.

The disbelievers didn't have long to wait for the answer. Assembly had been called and the block chief, perched on a stepladder, slowly recited his prepared speech. A *Dolmetscher* began to translate in an expressionless voice.

"One of you, a Frenchman, good for nothing like all Frenchmen, is guilty of stealing bread. I could have punished him myself last night when he confessed, but here, as at Mauthausen, punishment is conducted in the proper way. A thief is not a soldier, we don't shoot him, we hang him. You are going to watch him die so that you know how saboteurs end up. By stealing the bread of one of his comrades, this despicable man deprived his fellow of the ration calculated for a day's work. His comrades' output in the tunnel will doubtless have been lower than the established norm. That is sabotage, and it deserves the death penalty."

As they listened to this professional thief with his green triangle holding forth so outrageously, the convicts were mystified. Output...calculated ration...established norm...he must have been rehearsing his speech all afternoon. It smacked of a bluff, and yet the joke had gone too far to be taken lightly. Doubt had given way to anxiety in the ranks, and all eyes were focused on Pierrefeu. What did the accused man think about it all? But his battered face gave no indication of his feelings. The suspense was becoming unbearable. Let's get it over with, everybody was thinking.

It didn't take long. Two Kapos grabbed hold of Pierrefeu and led him to the scaffold. They tied his hands behind his back and hoisted him onto a table. A third man was already in position holding the rope in his hand. He slipped the noose around the Frenchman's neck and jumped quickly to the ground. In the instant before the block chief pulled away the table, all the prisoners had time to see the questioning look Pierrefeu gave them through half-closed eyes. He had believed even longer than his comrades that it was just a sham.

His last imploring look shook even the most callous of the men, and it snapped Paulo out of his numbness. Only a short while ago he would have cursed the whole world to see such inhumanity, and would have sought some act of cruelty to pay for this latest crime. This time he just trembled for himself. In retrospect, because he realized he'd deserved ten times over the fate of the amateur thief whose already stiff body was swinging grotesquely in the dark, a few feet away.

Indeed, for the last month, unconscious of the seriousness of his action, he had developed the habit of queuing twice for soup. He had done it without thinking, like a starving animal. It wasn't even his own numbed brain which had come up with the idea. He had seen a Russian do it and had followed suit, instinctively. The only reason Paulo hadn't been spotted was because the Russky's strategy was shrewd and simple. He was always one of the first in the line, and having gotten his soup, he would disappear to his bunk at the end of the block to gulp it down in one swallow. Then he would slip out of the window next to his bed and rejoin the line, which stretched the whole length of the block. With a handful of snow, he did his dishwashing, and a few moments later he held out to the block chief a soup bowl so sparkling clean that it couldn't arouse suspicion. And as the Russians at Nordfeld all looked like brothers, with the same deep-set gray eyes, stocky figures amd medium height, and there were almost fifty of them in the block, the wily little Russky could continue treating himself to a double ration quite happily for a while longer. For Paulo it was a different story. His height (he was six foot two) was emphasized by his thinness. The Kapos called him "*lange*" because he was one of the tallest men there. He was therefore easily spotted, and he would be wise to drop his subterfuge immediately. Pierrefeu's death had brought him to his senses just in time, but that was all it meant to him.

Nevertheless, it did mean something else, something which took them back to where they had started: execution for faces that didn't fit. Had Paulo remained as lucid as he was in the south, he would have slipped back into his brooding anxiety. But here, for the first time, he was content to dismiss it all with the phrase which had so often angered him: "No point trying to understand."

They had made an example of Pierrefeu, but the subsequent victims were not hanged. They were shot down on the line, without explanations or speechifying. They were Russian for the most part, but it was not only because they were more numerous than the French or the Poles. There was another reason which would have struck Paulo immediately if he would only open his eyes to it: it was obvious things were going very badly on the Eastern Front, and before opening fire the SS made no attempt to hide the fact. "One Ivan less," they declared, then they shot him down and reloaded their submachine guns. It was a pity that Paulo's frame of mind prevented him from realizing that their absurd fury smelled of defeat.

One afternoon in mid-December, Paulo went beyond all bounds in his selfishness. A murder took place under his nose and he was intimately involved in the macabre scene which ensued. An *Arbeitskapo* had shaken him out of a deep sleep for a small duty outside the camp. Accompanying him were a Pole and a very young Russian whom he had never seen before. The latter was not supposed to come back alive. Those were the Kapo's orders, and the matter was dealt with in the usual way: "Go and get that plank, Russky"—no need even to beat him, the plank was beyond the line. The other two had been detailed to bring back his body.

It had all taken place very quickly, but Paulo had time to catch the SS executioner's abuse before he fired: "You're going to pay for Stalingrad!"

So they still hadn't gotten over Stalingrad. In any case, it proved that they couldn't have had many chances since then to blot out the memory of that first setback with other victories. Not so long ago, such telling abuse would have given Paulo new courage and an even greater desire than ever to hang on until the end, which was obviously imminent. But he paid no attention whatsoever. The only thing he cared about was the almost new shoes of the dead man whom he was carrying with his Polish helper.

"Put him down behind the block and go back to bed," ordered the Kapo. "We'll burn him tomorrow. He's not likely to rot in this weather."

Paulo didn't go back to bed. Hurrying, in case the Pole had had the same idea, he went back to the corpse to swap the Russian's shoes for his own. Unmoved by the tortured body he turned it over and over, looking for anything else he could steal to replace his worn-out rags. Unfortunately, the boy was even thinner than Paulo, and then there were all the holes made by the bullets, and the bloodstains. It was too risky. On the other hand, he could whip the boy's belt, nobody would recognize it. And what did he have in his pockets? Nothing, of course; Paulo should have known better.

What he was doing was inexcusable, but he didn't even

know it. The pantomime he had just experienced would be only a blurred memory of the north camp. He would never be able to remember the features of the boy whose glassy eyes stared at him as he went about his vile business of looting the body. Small wonder that he would be unable to remember all the others shot down on the line. Even the abominable murder of a Pole called Max would leave him cold.

Like Pierrefeu, Max was married with children, and he too had made the mistake of lining up twice for bread. The agony of the Frenchman and the public example they had made of him couldn't have had much effect, because it was less than three weeks later that he took the same risk. It must be said that Max was one of the hardest of the toughs. His reputation had followed him first to Mauthausen, then to Loibl and finally to the north, where the colony of Poles held him in the greatest esteem. He had become their natural leader, unchallenged except by a young queer, who was the block chief's official lover, and who was put in an embarrassing position by Max's inflexibility and moral superiority. "I'll have you tried and stripped of your Polish nationality, Yeboni, you little fucker," Max snarled every time he came across him. On two occasions, he had gone as far as punching him.

It was ill advised, for to continue to profit from his privileged position without feeling ashamed, the panic-stricken little queer saw only one way out: he would have to grass on his tormentor to his lover. With good enough reason never to have to see him again. Since he spent his time watching Max carefully, to trip him up, he was there when his scourge presented himself for a second bread ration. He whispered in the chief's ear, and disappeared, lacking the courage to bear the gaze of the man he had just condemned to death.

Even without the bread theft the Polish leader would have died: the SS had marked him out since discovering he had been an officer in the Polish Army, one of the kind who had attacked their armored divisions with lances in August '39. But in fact he was less chivalrous; it was with a Molotov cocktail that he'd gone after the Panzers. Refusing to surrender, he had taken charge of a Resistance cell near Krakow. One day a detachment of SS tanks moved in to smoke out the partisans from their lair, and he had succeeded in setting fire to two of them. But a third tank had literally mown him down with its machine gun. He was so badly wounded that the Krauts left him for dead and didn't take the precaution of finishing him off. He was picked up by his men, and patched up in an underground hospital, before spending a year convalescing in the forest. Then he resumed his command, and his grenade attacks on German convoys.

Wounded again, but less seriously this time, taken prisoner, interrogated and tortured, he found himself at Mauthausen. Like the little Jew who had dodged the ovens, Max had had a charmed life. In every desperate situation, a stroke of luck had saved him at the eleventh hour.

And so, after the latest risk he had taken, while the infuriated block chief was telling him that he wouldn't live to see another day, Max must have been wondering how the hand of fortune would set about extricating him from trouble this time.

He was wrong to do so: his nine lives were over and he was going to die—but not at the end of a rope like his thieving predecessor. He was to die the dignified death he had always courted as a soldier: he would go down in a burst of gunfire.

That's what the block chief had promised him, omitting to mention that before he was shot, he would suffer. As a prelude, he would get an all-out beating at the hands of the Nordfeld Kapos, not with their clubs, but with heavy pine staffs.

"Carve him up as much as you like," the doyen had said; "we don't need him in the tunnel anymore."

The flogging far exceeded the brutality of anything witnessed at Loibl so far. The SS had given the green light for the terrorist they had twice missed, so the Kapos could really go to town. They smashed his skull and broke his hands, which were not needed for work anymore. That evening when the day shift returned, it took two men to carry his inanimate body to his bunk.

Four hours later in the middle of the night, the whole block was roused by the sound of boots: three SS, including the *Rapportführer*, had come to see how he was doing. The Pole must have interested them enormously for them to go to all this trouble at such a late hour. It was also unheard of for them to enter a dormitory. They walked through holding their noses, so as not to smell the stench of the slaves, and as they went through, they spat on the prisoners who anxiously raised themselves up. They went straight to Max's bed.

"Get up, you pig Polack," ordered *Rapportführer.* "We're going for a walk."

The Pole was conscious now, but he was quite unable to get up, still less to walk. Two Kapos lifted him and managed to stand him up straight, before pushing him down between the rows of beds to the door of the *Schlafstube*. It was the first time at Loibl that someone had been taken away in the middle of the night. No one dared move or make a sound. In a deathly silence, all the convicts strained their ears for the sound of the shots, which would come as a relief.

For the present, all that reached the dormitory was screams. Not the screams of the man about to die, but those of his killers. One phrase was repeated over and over again.

"Underneath, get underneath, you Polish shit!"

The *Rapportführer* had had an idea: he would make the condemned man scale the barbed-wire fence and have him shot when he got over it. Between the three of them, they couldn't possibly miss him, quite apart from the *Posten* in the watchtower who had turned on his floodlight and already had his machine gun trained. The only problem was, they had forgotten that their "escapee," after the Kapos had finished with him, no longer had the strength even to stand up, let alone climb. Which was why they were all three yelling in unison: "Get underneath!"

But that didn't work either. In spite of the boots kicking him under the barbed wire, Max had wrapped his arms around one of the fence posts and was desperately clinging to it, determined that only death would make him let go.

The *Rapportführer* had thought his plan was foolproof, and here was this near-dead man making a song and dance about dying. The whole affair should have been wrapped up in a couple of minutes, and still he was keeping the whole camp awake.

"We'll try again tomorrow," he said to the block chief. "Take the scum away and take him off work."

Before leaving for the tunnel a few hours later, the Poles on the day shift filed one by one past the bed of the man who, ever since Mauthausen, had set them an example of dignity and courage. They had all wanted to pay their last respects, but none of them could find the right words.

Holding back his tears, each man simply took Max's hands in his own, those hands which were swollen almost beyond recognition by the blows from the pine staffs. It was difficult to lie to Max now, he knew it was all over; his last-minute luck had finally deserted him, and he accepted it. To each of his countrymen in turn, he whispered:

"They're going to kill me this morning. Make them pay for it. Death to the Fascists! Long live Poland!"

When his comrades returned from the tunnel that evening, Max had been burned. But he hadn't died in the morning as they'd expected, he had managed to hold on till lunchtime, stubbornly refusing to cross the line and frustrating his executioners to the bitter end. The junior SS officer who had been charged with liquidating him was a beginner who went by the book. As his second-rate Kapo had failed to get the prisoner across the line, he hadn't dared give the order to fire.

At the sight of his Pole coming back alive at lunchtime, the *Rapportführer* almost had a fit. After lunch, he took charge himself and within the next hour, it was all over for the indomitable resistance fighter. But before he died, he made one last brave stand. Facing his killers as he had once faced their tanks, he spat in their faces and cried:

"Death to the Fascists! Long live Poland!"

The hero had at last fallen. The Panzers had not managed to wipe him out; he had been betrayed by one of his country's sons, a son who had been so afraid and so hungry that he had lost all sense of right and wrong. The boy had accepted everything—informing, thieving, being raped and being vomited on by his brothers—rather than having to start all over again with the hunger, the beatings and the freezing cold. And in every block in every camp, there were many like him. To fall so low when nothing in your character leads you to it was certainly food for thought for men with any perception left. But not for Paulo. Anything which might distract him, or force him to think or reflect, was stubbornly ignored. He talked less and less, listened to nobody and heard nothing; he wanted only to be forgotten.

"Well, Paulo, how was Nordfeld?"

"We froze our balls off. . ."

"What did you get up to all that time?"

"I froze my balls off. . ."

As far as Paulo was concerned, nothing had happened in the north. He had been shoved into cold storage and nothing happens in cold storage except that you freeze. And on one particular morning he nearly did, in fact, freeze to death.

Emerging from the tunnel at dawn, the night shift, dead tired, had been detailed to clear a small road swamped by a huge snowdrift about half a mile from the camp. It was exactly 35 degrees below zero, but during the rapid march along the uneven road, no one knew the temperature had dropped so low. It was only when they got to the drift that things began to go wrong. In vain the prisoners flailed with their shovels and stamped their feet; the icy air attacked every exposed inch of their bodies. Hands, noses, ears and even lips, froze in turn. Not to mention their bare feet in wooden-soled shoes. It was fortunate that the SS were getting it full in the face as well; it was one of them, an absentminded man who had forgotten his woolen hat, who saved the detail from certain death. His face had turned black and although he rubbed it, trying to bring the blood back, it was too late: his nose was so numb he couldn't even feel it. The other stroke of luck was that he was the one in charge of the detachment and, at the risk of being hauled over the coals, he gave the order to return to camp. Seeing his team return well before they were expected made the duty officer very angry at first, but as he took in the extent of the damage, it dawned on him that he had almost lost the whole night shift in one fell swoop. He quickly changed his tune and began fussing over them like a mother hen.

"Into the blocks with you all, hurry up and get warm, but don't get too close to the stoves. Rub yourselves where you're numb. Inside with you, don't stay out here in the cold."

Not one of the men had escaped. Paulo's own count was three dead fingers, frostbite on part of his nose, and on both his ears. For the others, it was mainly their lips; they couldn't close their mouths. When the medical orderly came running to ask them where they hurt, they could only answer in a comical gibberish.

For the first time that winter the block chiefs had been forced to let the riffraff get near the stoves. The heat was a brand-new sensation for them, and it felt so good that in the end nobody regretted freezing their balls off in the middle of a snowdrift.

The men had formed a tight-knit circle sitting cross-legged around the source of heat: Paulo would not forget this moment for a long time to come. What wouldn't he have given for the chance to stay in this cozy room until Armistice Day! They were lucky, all those barbers, *Schreiber,* hustler and all the rest who spent their nights here. Now he could understand why the little fairy had not hesitated to squeal on his Polish brother. And the warmth wasn't the only advantage; there was the food too, and what food! Real sausages which the fairy in question had just laid on the red-hot stove. Was he doing it to provoke them, or simply because it was time for one of his many snacks? Either way, by preparing his food in public, he showed that he couldn't have cared a tinker's cuss what the others thought of him.

The mouth-watering smell of grilled pork made the convicts forget the pain of the blood returning to their frozen skin. They would all have liked to kill the little bastard who was gobbling sausages under their noses. The selfish little pig was eating them without bread, to let everyone know that they were just a starter; the real meal would be served a little later. His protector had had a fucking nerve talking all that shit in his speech to justify the hanging of Pierrefeu, when he accused him of having deprived a comrade of bread by lining up twice. He was ripping off bread by the loaf, the community's bread, to fatten up his harem!

"So why are the slices getting thinner and thinner? It's because of all the bastards like him," hissed one of the envious prisoners in the front row of the circle, voicing the opinion of them all.

The display of gluttony and the aroma which filled their nostrils made no difference to Paulo. He was so content with the warmth which flooded his body that he asked for nothing more. Everything in good time, and for the moment, enemy number one was the cold. He savored every minute of being by the stove. For the first time, his clothes would dry out. It was one of his recurrent nightmares to have to punch his overcoat into shape before he could put it on. It froze so much in the night that by the morning it was as stiff as armor. He had come to hate the snow, and the mountain; and even

Christmas, which he spent lying alone on his bunk, watching the snowflakes cluster round the window panes, while his comrades were putting together an improvised "recreational evening" with the chief's blessing, singing carols interspersed with dirty songs. The Russians, who still kept to themselves, had gathered around a comrade's bed and were singing too, but in three-part harmony, in melodious and solemn voices. Their songs were sad ones, but much more to Paulo's taste than those coming from the other end of the block, "Nini Peau de Chien," "Le Père Dupanloup," and other bawdy songs. The Russians were probably singing of snow-covered steppes and frozen rivers, and ultimately that was more appropriate to their present predicament. It was better not to dream of Paris and its women; disillusionment would only be harder to bear in a few hours.

The SS were joining in in their own way. From their barracks came the well-worn notes of "Lili Marlene" played on a strident accordion. It was a song that Paulo had once rather liked. It was the best of its kind that the Krauts had composed, all Paris was singing it and apparently it had even crossed the Channel. But since then, like all the others who had heard its strains accompanying the march to the gallows at Mauthausen, Paulo couldn't stand it. Blocking his ears, he buried himself under the covers. For him, Christmas was a thing of the past.

He woke up shortly before dawn. Silence had descended once again on the block, but outside there was a real fireworks display going on. From the sentry posts and in the watchtowers, the SS thugs were letting off their guns and yelling abuse. Their string of insults encompassed France, Russia and Poland. Now and again they stopped firing, and Paulo could hear them vomiting from their perches their Christmas goulash which they had washed down with champagne and Bordeaux.

The sight of the bottles of wine which had arrived the previous day had distressed the Frenchmen; not because they were jealous—they would have fallen down dead if they had had to drink the stuff—but because of the labels stuck all over the cases spelling out in large letters the name of the sender: *Frankreich*. Had the French wine growers known what sort of monsters were going to swill their lovingly prepared nectar, they would have slipped arsenic into it. Seeing the cases of wine, every single Frenchman in the north had been instantly transported back to his homeland. Depending on how old they were, they began to think about their wives, their children or their parents, hopelessly torturing their spirits by imagining them weeping together in front of the Christmas tree. What would their loved ones have said, how they would have wept, if they had been able to see how the men the Gestapo had snatched from them more than a year ago were spending their Christmas. If they listened to the tales which the noble dodderer and his Prison Ministry served up daily on the radio, they might even believe that the cases of wine being shipped off to the east were destined for their missing sons. A whole world separated France from these her children, and even if one day the horror were to end, she would not be able to believe that it had really gone so far. That was too much to hope for.

Paulo was not upset by the noise of champagne corks which the drunken SS were popping between rounds. He kept going back in his mind to his obsession, and all he could think of on this Christmas night was that the snow hadn't stopped falling and would have to be cleared.

"If I ever get out," he groaned over and over, "I swear I'll never set foot on a mountain as long as I live."

He might just as well have sworn never to drink soup again, never to sleep in striped pajamas, never to cut his hair, any one of which was just as much a mark of his ordeal.

Nevertheless, it was regrettable that a man of Paulo's caliber could get to the point of seeing only the trivial details of his extraordinary experience.

Obviously there was nobody waiting for him by a brightly lit Christmas tree somewhere in Paris. There was no reason for him to make a fuss about it, but all the same, he had seen enough examples of heroism during thus winter in the north for him to forget his physical suffering for a while. But there would be no way of knowing whether the snow and ice were the only causes of his abject state, until they melted in the spring.

The weather began to change toward the end of the second week in April. Snow still fell from time to time, but it had lost its dazzling whiteness, and soon it stopped altogether, giving way to rain and taking with it into the gulleys the snow which had covered the ground and the barrack roofs for over six months. The camp was finally rid of its shroud.

How would Paulo take this? Would he emerge from his self-imposed exile? Would he turn again to his brothers? Find his tongue again? He didn't get the chance; no sooner had the incredible departure of the detested snow roused him from his torpor than something totally unforeseen cut right across his gradual return to life.

Jumping down from his bunk one morning, he gave a yell of pain. He thought he had broken his leg. Happily it wasn't so, but neither was it exactly good news. It was a sort of seizure of the joint which had suddenly paralyzed his knee, doubtless caused by the shock of landing heavily on it. He had managed somehow to get to his place in the column leaving for the tunnel, but he was pushed and shoved to one side by the men he was holding up, and soon he found himself limping along in the last row.

"Stop!" the *Arbeitskapo* yelled, before the first men in line had reached the camp gates. "You there, what's the matter?"

"I can't bend my knee. It happened suddenly when I got up this morning."

"Let me see, you lazy bastard. Drop your trousers, and roll up your long pants. If I find out you've been lying, you're really going to be in the shit."

The cunning guard knew very well that at Loibl there were no slackers, but he had a right to check, and Paulo complied with the order. His knee was inflamed and swollen. The Kapo's curiosity was satisfied.

"Go and find your block chief," he said. "You are excused from work, but if I were you, I wouldn't jump for joy about it."

"What's all that crap supposed to mean?" thought Paulo, limping back to the block.

What it all meant was, quite simply, that Paulo's time at Nordfeld was over. He would be leaving for the south in a few hours, together with four or five spent workers who were no good for anything.

Paulo was flabbergasted. How could he be released like that, at a moment's notice? He was going to leave this hell just because of a tiny scratch, when he had had beating after beating which hurt far more. It couldn't be true! Unless—and suddenly he sobered up—unless the inflammation of his knee was really very serious, incurable even. That changed everything. Maybe his departure for the south would be his last journey.

Paulo must have felt that he would come out on top, for when he passed through the gates of the diabolical camp later on, inglorious but alive, he had almost forgotten his knee. Miraculously, it was much less painful. The old Paulo was coming back; he was alert, optimistic, voluble. His mind had suddenly thawed, and he desperately wanted to talk to the stragglers who were heading back to the other side with him.

Etcheverry, the history teacher, was among the men being sent back, but Paulo hesitated before striking up a conversation. A rigorous militant like the old communist couldn't have been very impressed by his selfish behavior. In the event, it was Etcheverry who caught hold of Paulo's arm, as much to help him along as to support his own feeble body.

"Well, this can't be bad," Paulo began. "I couldn't have stood another month. Where are you hurt?"

"Nowhere and everywhere. I'm finished. I'm too old for them. But I don't care if they stick a needle in me, I know they've lost and that's the only thing that matters. I did what had to be done, now it's the others' turn."

"Hey, come on, cheer up," Paulo urged him. "They're not going to pack us off to Mauthausen, there's a *Revier* in the south. That's where we'll be going, the doyen told me so. Come on, old man, you'll get all your strength back in there."

Paulo was getting ahead of himself, he didn't have the slightest idea what would happen to them in the south. And then, if they stayed in the *Revier*, there was a good chance that Ramsauer and his syringe would still be boss. If that were the case, the old man clinging on to his arm had every reason to fear the benzol shot. But Paulo couldn't tell him that. After all, wasn't it up to him to try to raise his companion's morale? What a dramatic change this was from the man of a few hours ago. He was quite himself again, as if the six months spent in cold storage had been only one bad night, a brief nightmare from which he had awoken without any aftereffects.

The small group of sick men and its SS escort were now entering the tunnel. After spending these last months scraping in the upper gallery, Paulo was genuinely amazed to see the progress which had been made by the teams below. The partition dividing the two camps had been done away with, and the railway now ran the whole length of the tunnel. He was so excited as he drew nearer to the south that the shooting pains in his knee completely disappeared. But a mile in the dark was still quite a hike and the SS, seeing that their captives were having trouble keeping up, ordered a short break.

"When I think we dug all this on our own! I can't get over it!" Paulo said, sitting down. "We're heroes!"

He was trying his best to distract Etcheverry from his gloomy thoughts, but the communist didn't seem very happy with Paulo's air of satisfaction. He replied in a rather weary voice,

"We've got nothing to be proud of. My only consolation is that I won't live to see their tanks making use of it. We've behaved like sheep. Now what we have to do is sabotage the tunnel. Think about that, my friend, otherwise you might be ashamed of yourself when you get home."

Sabotage! As if there weren't enough risks already! Paulo would have liked to bring the teacher back to earth, but he reckoned it was the man's despair which prompted him to make such harebrained remarks. It was better to change the subject.

"Let's wait until we know what the war is doing. They must have heard something in the south, and we'll be there in less than an hour. Come on, up you get, Grandpa. We're going."

The day shift had just left when they reached the south face, and the night shift hadn't quite arrived. On the road a thousand feet from the camp, looking like two giant snakes, the two teams were about to pass each other. Marching five abreast, this blue-gray crocodile of nearly five hundred men was an impressive sight.

Paulo would have liked to catch up with them, ask them a thousand questions, slap them heartily on the back crying: "Hey look, I'm back! I'm still alive!" But the escorting officer must have had his orders, for he waited until the night shift were at their places in the tunnel before taking to the road with his little group of cripples. Less than half an hour later, as night fell, the barbed-wire gate of the south camp closed quietly behind them, almost as if their return were a secret. They were forbidden to talk to anyone, they were to go straight to the *Revier:* those were the orders, so that the wretched rejects from the north didn't spread their filthy diseases to the hale and hearty men of the south.

A small windowless room at the back of the *Revier* had been cleared as an isolation ward for Paulo and friends.

"Good night, gentlemen," a Polish orderly had said, allocating each man a bed. "Tomorrow morning a Major Ramsauer will examine you."

And he went out, double-locking the door from the outside.

Paulo still wasn't worried, despite the disquieting evidence: the enforced quarantine with its ridiculous precautions, and the fact that Ramsauer was still master of the house, couldn't reduce the optimism which had come flooding back the moment he found himself on the right side of the tunnel again. A little earlier, he had carefully counted the buildings on the work site, and had been delighted to see that their number had more than doubled. He had immediately recognized the cement-block factory which had been only a hole in the ground when he left. Next to it was an even bigger building, a sawmill by the looks of it, then more and more new barracks, as far as the eye could see, right down to the dump at the end of the railway track.

Paulo lay in bed counting up all this new wealth, as pleased as if it were his own property. These new developments proved one thing: the south needed manpower. So there was no reason for them not to keep him, once his knee was healed.

"An inflammation of a joint isn't even contagious. In a few days they'll put me with the others," he said, burying himself under the covers. He was as excited as a schoolboy at the end of the summer vacation, and it was a long time before he got to sleep.

XVI

Paulo had been awake for a long time when the bell clanged at five in the morning. It wasn't the excitement of being back in the south and all that it promised which had woken him so early. It was something much less pleasant: he had a raging temperature.

Well before midnight he had begun to feel that something was badly wrong with his knee. It felt as if it were in an iron clamp which gripped tighter and tighter with every hour. The pain was too strong for Paulo to go back to sleep, and neither could he make plans for the new life awaiting him. For the present all he wanted was for the orderly who had wished them good night to come back in a hurry and examine him.

Next to him, Etcheverry had stirred when he heard his groans, but the old teacher seemed so weak and so overcome that Paulo couldn't bring himself to say anything to him. In any event, it would have been useless; what he needed—and now it was a matter of urgency—was someone on duty in the building who knew what to do, who could give him a compress, some tablets or an injection. It didn't matter what, as long as it took the pain away.

Finally, a key turned in the lock.

"Morning, northerners," cried an orderly as he pushed open the door. "How are you all feeling this morning? Any of you French?" It was not the same man who had locked them in the night before.

"There are two of us," answered Paulo, thinking, "A French orderly, that's okay! Looks as if yours truly will be taken care of right away."

It was still too dark to make out who the man was, but he thought he recognized his voice, by the Parisian accent. Better still.

But when the orderly turned on the light, Paulo's relief subsided. His savior was Daniel, certainly a Parisian, but no more a nurse than Paulo was a driver. Diplomas and identity cards had disappeared on the way to Loibl, and cunning Daniel, caught unawares the night he arrived, must have made a snap decision to call himself a nurse. That was eleven months ago, and it was remarkable that he had managed to hold on to his soft job for so long. Maybe he had acquired a few notions of medicine by dint of working in the crowded infirmary? Thinking about this, Paulo was slightly reassured.

"Come and look here, Daniel," he said. "I can't move my knee anymore, it feels as if I've got a wooden leg. You must have picked up a bit since you've been here. What do you think it is? Water on the knee?"

Wisely, Daniel didn't answer. Instead, he rolled back the covers and spent a good minute looking at Paulo's knee, which was now the size of a balloon, hmmphing from time to time to give the impression he had diagnosed the root of the problem. The would-be nurse played his part so well that Paulo was on the point of saying, as in the old French song:

"Tell me, Doctor, is it serious?"

The "doctor" was not a complete charlatan and he admitted that, in all honesty, he didn't know the answer. But so that Paulo would be reassured, he was quick to assume an air of authority.

"First of all, we'll take your temperature. Sit up and put this thermometer in. Not up your ass, they don't like that here. Put it in your mouth, it'll give just as good results. Then I'll get out my stethoscope."

Paulo's temperature was just under 105. Daniel was unable to suppress a little grimace of anxiety: Ramsauer had decreed that all patients with temperatures over 103 were to be dealt with by him in person. Before he made his rounds, it was absolutely imperative to get Paulo's temperature down.

"I'm going to stuff you full of aspirin," he said. "Does it hurt when I press on it here?"

"Oh, Christ, stop!" Paulo yelled. "I almost fainted."

"All right, all right, I'll go and get Jaryk, the Czech doctor. Don't thrash around, whatever you do, otherwise your temperature will go up even more."

And Daniel went out without seeing to Etcheverry or the other survivors from the north.

For once, thought Paulo, being born in Paris had been useful.

Less than five minutes later, Jaryk came into the ward accompanied by another detainee who must have been the second *Revier* doctor. Paulo was acquainted with the latter. He was a Polish refugee from Paris called Jérôme who spoke perfect French, thanks to which he had saved a good many men at Mauthausen, where he had also been a doctor. There he had seen a bunch of malingerers the day they arrived, who had come to him with all sorts of exaggerated aches and pains. They were hoping to be repatriated on the spot, like common POWs.

"Don't ever say that here, you misguided fools," he warned all those complaining of a history of tuberculosis or syphilis whose treatment had been interrupted by their arrest. He set them straight about Mauthausen, whispering almost without moving his lips, like a ventriloquist. This was so that the SS doctor who decided which category they fell into should not register them in a separate column with small crosses by their names. To be registered there meant their death was sealed, and it was the only column they would have been written in if the good doctor hadn't taken the initiative.

It was marvelous that this high-minded man was at Loibl Pass. Immediately Paulo began to feel better.

"Let's see your leg," said Jaryk, who spoke French as well, "and tell me how it happened. Did you fall? Did you get hit there?"

"No, it just happened by itself when I got up yesterday morning. They kicked me out of the north camp, and I was able to walk back through the tunnel all right. It's only since last night it's been killing me; it feels like I've got my foot screwed on the end of a wooden leg."

"How long have you had a temperature?" asked the Pole.

"I don't know, they only took it this morning. They say it's over a hundred and four."

The two medics exchanged a look, which Paulo fortunately didn't see because he had turned over onto his side to ease the pain in his leg. Otherwise, his temperature might have shot up even further.

"It's not water on the knee," said Jaryk after a pause. "Your knee is too inflamed. But it's not good news either: you've got a real infection."

"How come?" Paulo asked. "I've never hurt my knee, except when the hounds took a lump out of my leg. But that goes back six months. There weren't any dogs in the north—"

"No, my friend, it can't be that," the Pole interrupted. "It's internal, it must be an old complaint which has decided to come to the surface. It's chosen its moment badly. Rest a while and let me have a word with my colleague. You're a lucky man to have two doctors to yourself!"

And they went and sat down on an empty bed at the end of the room. Paulo couldn't hear what they were saying, but the conversation went on too long for his liking. When they came back to him several minutes later, they seemed to be in agreement. It was the Pole who broke the news to him: "You've got purulent arthritis of the knee."

"Is it serious? How could I have got it?"

"A dose of gonorrhea which was badly treated, probably. Did you ever get the clap when you were young?"

"Well, maybe I did," answered Paulo.

He knew he had, but it embarrassed him to admit it to these two men who, despite their shaven heads and convicts' uniforms, still had the slightly superior air of men of science. Seeing the two of them bent gravely over his bed, one taking his pulse and the other prodding his bad leg, suddenly reminded him of the Boucicaut hospital. He had been born there, and he had wound up there again twenty years later to the day, following a fight during which a vicious blade had severed three tendons. This nasty coincidence had shaken him badly and left him with an abiding fear of hospitals, operating tables and surgeons. And the two men examining him looked just like surgeons. They no longer seemed like convicts, like him; they were real doctors, the only breed of men who had ever impressed him. Without realizing it, he became very formal with the Pole.

"Are you going to have to operate, Doctor?"

"No, but we are going to have to lance it. Can you stand pain?"

"Oh yes, no worries on that score, I'm used to gritting my teeth. But who's going to do the lancing? Not Ramsauer, I hope. You won't tell him, will you? Do it yourselves, right now."

Paulo wasn't at all keen on the idea of being cut open without any preparation; his knee made him yell with pain at the slightest touch. But he was resolved to endure without a murmur the sharpest scalpel they had, because he had finally understood the seriousness of his situation. If his knee stayed locked, it was goodbye to the tunnel, to Loibl, to everything. A lame man can't work on a building site, and a man who can't work anymore is no longer a deportee. You liquidate him, you turn him into smoke and ashes. Either here in the nearby larch wood or in Mauthausen's furnace. There were no two ways about it.

That's what the two medics must have been discussing when they went off into a corner. Paulo had to know.

"Tell me, Doctor, will I be stuck with a trick leg after you've lanced it? Don't put me off, I've got to know."

"Of course not, my friend," Jaryk answered. "Your kind of arthritis heals very well. Don't upset yourself, just relax and let the leg rest. We'll come and see you again in a while."

And they had departed, apparently not at all worried. One of two things was possible: either Paulo had made a mountain out of a molehill when he saw them conferring, or since they were so used to seeing men unfit for work—that is, condemned—the two doctors had concealed the truth out of kindness.

Paulo had been so happy last night to be back in the south camp, and now he told himself that maybe he'd only come back to die. To have been put through the mill every single day for a whole year just to end up here was horribly ironic; it just wasn't possible. Tears welled in his eyes, but they weren't the tears of hatred like those he shed on that humiliating day at the end of summer when he had been a target for the SS to hawk at. They were tears of despair.

Now he understood how the thousands of hapless men before him must have felt at Mauthausen and other camps when it suddenly dawned on them that they no longer had the strength to lift their wheelbarrows, or swing their picks, or, worst of all, to stand on their feet. Just like him. All these fellows, in tens of thousands, even hundreds of thousands perhaps, had watched each other die by degrees, hour by hour, all terribly alone, abandoned by their brothers who averted their gaze so they wouldn't be next. No one had ever given a thought to the awful moments which had to be endured by men who knew, without a shadow of a doubt, that they were going to die. Even more bitter was the knowledge that theirs was not a fatal illness like cancer, cirrhosis, or heart failure which was pushing them in waves to the crematoriums. All they had was a fever or a weakness of some sort, mild ailments which any country doctor could have cured in less than a week. They must all have known this before they died, and it was unquestionably the most revolting aspect of the whole barbaric Nazi enterprise to feel that you were being pushed into the role of a dying man. It was only now that he was trapped by his stiff leg that Paulo registered all these things. Oh, if he ever got out alive, how carefully he would look after his health!

There was virtually no risk of an epidemic at Loibl, by virtue of the small number of prisoners, the relative comfort, especially with a bed for each man, and the high altitude. On the other hand, the continual outbursts of brutality could, at any moment, leave you with an arm broken by a gun butt or a leg crushed under a runaway hopper. That is precisely what had happened to an Italian just before Paulo was sent off to the north. Faced with a broken leg and an open fracture, Ramsauer went completely to pieces. First, he had tried to stick the bits back together, but a week later the wounded man's temperature was still rising and he was in more and more pain, so Ramsauer had thought he had a case of gangrene on his hands. Without asking the opinion of his shaven colleagues, he decided there and then to amputate. And before his patient woke up to discover he had only one leg, he had emptied a syringeful of gasoline into the man's heart.

Obviously there was no room for a one-legged man in this prison full of athletes, but even so this Ramsauer character had an odd idea of euthanasia! As if that weren't enough, the second-rate Frankenstein then tried his hand at an autopsy, and made his orderlies scratch about for hours among the poor Italian's most interesting bones, which would undoubtedly join the photos of Pavlovski in his archives of horror. Had Mussolini known how his mustachioed ally was treating his countrymen, the court jester might perhaps have changed sides, but unfortunately no one would be going to tell him about Loibl, for the simple reason that nobody was allowed to leave unless they were dead.

"It's accidents that I'm really going to have to watch out for," Paulo exclaimed, as he suddenly remembered how abominably the Italian had died. Nobody had had the time to learn his name, for between his arrival at Loibl and his exit in pieces, there had been only a week.

For Paulo to be thinking about accidents meant that he could already see himself back at work, so he was obviously feeling better. Indeed, the aspirin tablets Daniel had given him seemed to have stopped the pain, and now he was no longer frightened of entrusting his knee to the syringe which would drain off the pus. On the contrary, he was getting impatient.

"Hurry up and come back, you medics!"

The door opened, but it wasn't the medics; it was Dédé Ménard.

He had changed so much that Paulo didn't recognize him at first. He had put on at least twenty-five pounds since last autumn. His face had filled out and his broad forehead no longer looked out of proportion; his gray eyes were even brighter than before and they sparkled with mischief and good health. He was almost unrecognizable, and his nearly new striped uniform, without a single stain or darn, emphasized the transformation even more.

"Surely he can't have turned queer, being such a dyed-in-the-wood Kraut-hater!" thought Paulo. "But who the hell gave him permission to swan around unaccompanied in a restricted area like this, when all his comrades are busy slaving away in the tunnel?"

Dédé must have anticipated Paulo's astonishment, for his first words were an explanation.

"Hello there, Paulo, I've come to change a light bulb. I'm an electrician now; it's really hard work! You see, your physics at Loibl is just as useful as your physique. How were things in the north?"

"Sheer hell. Next question?"

"What are you doing in the *Revier*? You're all skin and bones. Me and the others will soon fatten you up. You'll see some changes around here. You didn't by any chance pick up a dose of pleurisy in the tunnel."

"No, it's more serious. It's an infected arthritis in my knee. And problems with your joints are frowned upon here. I'm pretty worried about the whole thing."

Dédé sat down on the bed, and for a second Paulo thought he was going to take his hand, as people do in hospitals when they don't know what to say to the dying. That would have been the limit. But no, Dédé wasn't the weepy sort. He came straight to the point.

"Has Ramsauer seen you yet?"

"No, but it won't be long."

"Right, we've got to get you out of this room right away. I'll go and talk to Jaryk about it. In the general ward we'll have time to work something out."

Paulo cut him short. "But I've already seen him. He was with the other one, the Pole, and they left me here. They talked about lancing it and now I'm waiting."

"Sure, but they can do you just as well in there. They probably didn't think of it. I'm on my way."

He departed, after casting an anxious glance at Etcheverry, who was impervious to the comings and goings of that morning and still hadn't opened his eyes.

An hour later Paulo had been transferred to the general ward. With Daniel's assistance, Dédé had managed to lug him to the one remaining bed. When Ramsauer showed up presently, he would take Paulo for a fellow from the south and wouldn't give him the thorough going-over he would probably give the mangy creatures from Nordfeld who had stayed in the quarantine ward and were sullying his model field hospital with their filthy diseases.

The chief electrician had come up with just the right answer, and Paulo didn't know how to thank him.

"Okay, okay," Dédé interrupted. "All that matters now is that you get better."

"I'm feeling much better, it must be the aspirin."

"I've spoken to the medics about that. Before they cut your knee open, they're going to try something new, sulfonamides. Technically they're reserved for the SS, but the orderlies managed to lay their hands on a few boxes and Jaryk has agreed to give you a dozen tablets. They'll try that before they lance you. You've got three days' grace, three days to take it easy in your comfortable bed. All right, I'm off. I'll be back this evening with Joel after coffee."

"Hang on a minute," protested Paulo, catching him by the jacket. "I want to know what this thing's all about, these sulf-sulfonwhatsits. Will they save me from the operating table?"

"Yes, of course, that's what they're made for. They go straight into the stomach and into your blood to attack the germs. Let's hope your germs don't like them."

"Oh Christ, I hope it works!" thought Paulo, with a rush of hope. But one thing was worrying him. Why had the two medics, who had seemed to want to look after him so well, not mentioned the miracle cure? He needed to get to the bottom of it all.

"Just tell me, Dédé, if I understand what you've said, this little favor's being done for you. Your medic friends have got their favorites, haven't they, and if you don't want to end up on the operating table, a spell in the Resistance is a help."

"Are you crazy?" Dédé cut in, furious. "You ought to be ashamed of saying things like that. Those guys are real doctors, and the only distinction they make between their patients is the seriousness of their condition. We're all the same to them—you, me or even that collaborationist Pozzi. They treat the sick man, period; they're not interested in who he is or what he's done. The Hippocratic Oath still applies in the camps, except for the German doctors."

Paulo realized he had blundered badly and he didn't dare say any more. Dédé went on:

"As for the sulfonamides, if they didn't talk to you about them, it may have been because they weren't absolutely convinced they would be effective against arthritis. Your case isn't very common, it's a civilian ailment. They told me that, generally speaking, cases like yours aren't treated with sulfonamides. So they were quite justified in hesitating before wasting such precious drugs. In any case, it wasn't me who influenced them, they'd already made up their minds before I talked to them about you. All right, I'm off now. See you tonight."

"Thanks, thanks for everything," Paulo shouted at him through the window.

Dédé had looked after him like his own mother for the last two hours, giving him new hope and possibly saving him from the operating table with all that it implied. Paulo hadn't been fooled, Dédé must have worked on the medics.

"God, I'm lucky to be back in the south!" thought Paulo. He felt easier in his mind and decided to have a little snooze while he waited for his miracle pills.

Two hours later Daniel had to shake him awake. His bed had to be straightened out quickly, for Ramsauer was expected any minute, to hear how each of his precious charges was getting on.

"Here, swallow these," the orderly said, surreptitiously slipping two small white pills between Paulo's lips, "and hide the rest, because they search this place too. Listen, don't take more than six a day, and drink as much as you like; it's best if you piss a lot with these pills."

"That guy Daniel's pretty friendly too," thought Paulo. "What a difference from those apes up in the north! Back to civilization at last!"

There was more than a grain of truth in this. Being in

this white and peaceful room where nobody yelled and there was nobody to beat you was not like being in prison at all. All these men sitting up or lying in their clean beds didn't look in the least like convicts. They wore no uniform here, apart from their shirts and their long pants, but even striped versions of these could be found in any hospital in the world. The only thing which was a little unusual about the room was that all the patients had a shaven strip down the middle of their heads. But that was a minor detail. It was true to say that in Dr. Ramsauer's clinic, you really weren't at Loibl at all.

"This is just a dream, this *Revier,*" Paulo said to himself. "You don't have to work, you can sleep all day long, you can talk . . . it's like a dream come true!"

He might have added, ". . . for men who aren't ill," because for the others, with that maniac who had just made his entrance, it was more like a nightmare than a dream.

"Attention!" Daniel had shouted, flattening himself against the wall. For those who couldn't get up, standing at attention meant sitting at attention with their arms crossed over their chests. They all had to stay in that position for the time it took Ramsauer to do his rounds, the dying as well as the others. Nobody was dying today, but like everyone else at Loibl Paulo had heard of the vile doctor's idea of forcing the dying to attention. How ingenious. It couldn't be done in the other camps where the patients were piled up five to a bed, but in this cottage hospital where each man had a bed, it was quite feasible. This sign of deference was very important to the madman. It delighted him to look straight in the eyes of the men who would shortly have their hearts pumped full of gasoline. Furthermore, he didn't mince his words in letting them know what would happen. *Kaputt*, he would say whenever he saw a man who was dying. He wasn't generally mistaken, he merely cut short the agony a little.

Ramsauer hesitated in front of Paulo's bed. Turning to Jaryk behind him, he asked, "A new man?"

"*Jawohl, Oberarzt.*"

"What's the matter with him?"

"A little bump on the knee, *Oberarzt*, it's not serious."

The *Oberarzt* became suspicious. He approached Paulo's bed and roughly demanded,

"Show me your leg."

It was manifestly obvious that this dunce had never seen arthritis in his life, or he'd have been a bit more careful about pressing on the inflamed joint. The quack put his whole fist in it.

"Inflammation of the synovial membrane," he said in French in a tone which brooked no questions. "Give him compresses twice a day and send him to me before the end of the week."

Then he went on to the next patient, who was racked by a fit of nervous coughing and couldn't stay at attention.

Paulo had made a superhuman effort not to yell. All he had said was "ouch," so that the ignoramus shouldn't pursue his probing. But when Ramsauer had started talking about compresses, he felt an uncontrollable urge to yell at him.

"You're pathetic, you haven't got any idea; what I need is sulfonamides, like the ones which were stolen from your dispensary, and which are fizzing in my stomach right now."

Ramsauer had said only one important thing: "Send him to me before the end of the week." That sounded ominous.

It was a little early yet to know whether the germs or the sulfonamides would win the day, but when he woke from his afternoon siesta one thing was certain: the pain had almost completely gone. Paulo tried tentatively to bend his knee; there was progress there too. He didn't push his luck, but decided to take another two tablets immediately. Ramsauer's glittering eyes told him he'd better hurry things up.

Seeing that his neighbor had also woken from his siesta, he addressed him.

"Listen, friend, our chief doctor doesn't get any better, does he? I haven't seen him for more than six months, but he still scares me stiff."

"That's right, he's the one who's sick," answered the other, a particularly skinny man in his late forties. "He's heading for complete insanity, and we'd do well to be clear of his tender care when the storm breaks. I'm getting out of here tomorrow. But aren't you the famous Paulo?"

"Looks like it, how did you know?"

"Who doesn't know? My name's Rambaud, I'm from Limoges."

"Ah, the lawyer."

"Correct."

How absurd such formal introductions were in the

crematorium waiting room, but they helped pass the time. Paulo went on.

"What happens to guys from the north when they're cured?"

"Theoretically, they're supposed to go back there, but up till now they've generally gone back to Mauthausen."

"Jesus!" exclaimed Paulo. "I hadn't thought of that. It's the last thing I want to do. There must be a way of staying; there's plenty of work up on the new sites here."

"It should be possible, but you'll need to pull strings."

"I'll find strings to pull, believe me."

He was now so sure of recovering that he utterly dismissed the idea of getting sent back to Mauthausen, and just to prove it to himself, he tried to bend his knee again. The joint was definitely loosening up; he was right in thinking Mauthausen could do without him.

"By the way," he said, "have there been a lot of return trips in the last six months?"

"Not all that many, but there are a few gaps all the same. Among the youngsters especially, kids who are under twenty. They're the ones who crack most quickly, what with not being fully grown and not getting enough to eat . . . How old are you, Paulo?"

"Twenty-four."

"That's the best age for Loibl. You'll come out all right."

"When I woke up this morning, I wouldn't have believed you, but I'm feeling much better now. If Ramsauer wants to burn me, he's going to have to use his gun to do it. Hey, tell me, have they started up what they used to do on the work site last summer? Just recently in the north things were getting very bad, they were sending them across the line for nothing—the Russians especially."

"It's the same here. They've obviously got their orders, but they haven't only been shooting Russians here. Every country has had its casualties."

"They're mad. What must it be doing to their tunnel?"

"It doesn't seem to be slowing things down much. You must have seen that when you came through."

Sadly, the lawyer was right. A few bullets here, an injection there, was hardly going to change the course of things. Seen in that light, it was pretty obvious that the south camp was no holiday. Paulo had worked himself up a bit too soon, and seeing him suddenly fall silent, his neighbor tried to pick up the threads of the conversation.

"Tell me what they're up to in the north. Is the tunnel coming along well there too?"

"Yes, quite well, or at least as fast as it is here. But as for all the other news and gossip, I've forgotten it already. It doesn't interest me."

"Sure, I know what you mean. It's not worth going over old ground, it's pointless getting upset. Let's talk about something else," said the lawyer agreeably, as if he'd guessed the score.

But the news that they had started picking off random targets in the south again had dented Paulo's optimism. He had to get the lawyer to tell him the details.

"When did they knock off the last one?" he demanded anxiously.

"Less than two weeks ago. I was already in here and I didn't see how it all happened, but I did see the end from this window, with the rest of the *Revier.* It was more horrible than anything you could imagine: they took him to the crematorium alive. We all saw him move his arms and try to sit up; he had to watch them prepare his own funeral pyre. It was Ramsauer himself who finished him off with a boot in his chest, or at least he thought he'd finished him off. We'll never know whether he was dead when they burned him. But the brutes were taking photos as usual. It was a despicable crime which none of us must ever forget."

There was no need to ask the lawyer why he had been arrested; he was the same kind as Etcheverry, Dédé and company. But what still surprised Paulo was that these fellows, who were teachers, lawyers and students, and who wouldn't have hurt a fly in civilian life, far from recoiling from such scenes of horror, seemed rather to thrive on them, as though the atrocity cemented their convictions. Any doubts they may have had about the justice of their cause when they took up arms against the Krauts again were now cleared up for good; they hadn't burned their fingers for nothing. "No two ways about it," thought Paulo, "these Resistance guys stand up to it better than the others."

"Tell me," he said to the lawyer, "was this man who was burned alive one of your friends? Was he French?"

"No, he was a Russian, from the Ukraine. But he was a

friend of mine, a friend to many of us. He was a war hero wounded in action and taken prisoner; then he escaped and began picking off the enemy one by one. He couldn't conceal his hatred for the Nazis, they noticed it and eventually dealt with him. Shooting prisoners in the field is dishonorable enough, but to do it after a man has spent months at Mauthausen and then here defies description."

"When's it all going to end?" thought Paulo. "The butchery can't go on forever." It was now the end of April '44, there must be some news.

"And what's happening in the war?" he questioned.

"It's taking its course, but in the right direction. Your friend Dédé will tell you about that. I can't explain why, but he knows these things."

So they talked the afternoon away, and it was time for evening coffee. Dédé would shortly be here, and maybe he'd bring Joel and Belloni, for visits were authorized.

Indeed, they all turned up on the dot, and the scene around each bed was the same. There were no chairs, so the visitors stood and chatted with their sick friends. The *Revier* was suddenly buzzing with life. Just like the Boucicaut hospital, minus the good sisters. Some fellows had come to shake Paulo's hand, which pleased him; they remembered him in the south, and thought well of him. It couldn't be denied that during his first five months he'd conducted himself well, and nobody here had seen his deplorable conduct in the north, apart from poor Etcheverry, who was languishing in the isolation ward. Things seemed so well organized and almost comfortable in the south, that in spite of the cold which must have been just as bitter, he might in all probability have continued to act decently, to be the man all these fellows shaking his hand thought they knew.

Unluckily for Paulo, his friends had come to hear about Nordfeld, which the Kapos held over them all day long as the worst possible punishment.

"Listen, you guys," he said to the trio standing around his bed. "Just compare your faces with mine. You all look like cherubs compared to me. I look like a rat from the sewers, and that says it all. What you've got to do is figure out how to keep me here. I'd rather die here than go back to the north."

Cherubs was a slight exaggeration, especially in the case of Joel, who seemed hardly to have put on any weight at all. Belloni did seem to have filled out a little and even to have grown, which was only natural for a kid of his age.

"We can fix it so that you stay here," said the latter. "Sailor and I have declared a truce. It's not what you might think; I'll tell you about it later. Dédé and I'll have a word with him, we ought to be able to get you transferred to Block Three."

"Dédé? You're not in with Sailor too, are you?" Paulo was astonished. "When I left, he didn't seem at all keen on you."

"All thanks to electricity! I made him a bedside lamp . . ."

"To light his screwing parties . . ." Angel chipped in.

"This is neither the time nor the place to talk about love," interrupted Paulo, making his three visitors burst out laughing. "I'd rather you told me what exactly you're going to say to Sailor so he takes me back."

"There's only one way," Belloni said without hesitation. "We're going to tell him you're a pimp. He'll be thrilled!"

"Wouldn't it be better to tell him I run a queer shop in Paris?"

"If you like. We'll tell him you do both. The main thing is to make him realize you're a crook, not one of the political prisoners, because he's got a real down on them these days."

Dédé and Joel had listened in silence to Belloni's edifying suggestions, and as they continued to say nothing, it seemed that they approved. Sad to say, Loibl was no ordinary camp, and one's best recommendation to the camp administrators was a criminal record.

"We'll talk to him this evening," said Dédé, getting ready to go. "We'd better be off, the bell's about to go. By the way, Paulo, don't let your sulfa drugs go down the wrong way. Even if Sailor believes you're a pimp, he'd never dare snatch you away from Ramsauer. Okay, sleep well, we'll let you know tomorrow how we make out."

It all seemed like a practical joke, but the three cronies seemed so sure of themselves that Paulo had no alternative but to trust them. All that mattered now was whether the sulfonamides would do the trick. Paulo took the precious sachet from its hiding place under the inside sole of his shoe, and immediately swallowed two more tablets. Now all he had to do was sleep, with the covers right up over his head to sweat out the fever. If his temperature had dropped by the morning, then he'd have every right to start planning properly.

Already this evening he was certain it had fallen several degrees. Partly because for the first time since waking up he was hungry, and also because his knee seemed much less red and swollen.

As Daniel went past his bed dragging a broom, Paulo called after him: "Hey, nurse! Give us the thermometer. I'm sure my temperature's dropped, and I want to know what it is this evening so I can compare it with tomorrow morning."

"Can't do that now, I'm afraid," said Daniel, placing his broad, jobbing nurse's hand on Paulo's forehead. But then he added, perceiving that Paulo's skin was much cooler than in the morning, "You're right, let's take a look." His temperature had dropped to about 100. Considering it was getting late and that he'd just had the excitement of a visit, there was every indication that the fever was abating. Greatly relieved, Paulo fell asleep immediately.

When the bell rang at dawn he thought for a split second that he'd woken up in the north: he felt unpleasantly cold and damp from head to toe. But it was simply that he had sweated so much during the night that his shirt and long pants were wringing wet. He had slept for nine whole hours, quite dead to the world, and now he felt as light as a feather, ready to spring from his bed if he was ordered to do so.

"Quick, let's have the thermometer," he said to himself. "I think that's it, I'm completely better."

He sat bolt upright in bed and began cautiously to draw his knees up to his chest. Fantastic! Both knees were bending in perfect unison.

This time Paulo bent them right up. He wasn't dreaming, both knees responded to his commands without his feeling the slightest twinge. He threw back the covers and pushing his long pants down to his calves, he looked at his legs as if trying to see which was the bad one. It was a miracle!

Which was exactly what Daniel thought a few moments later when he had taken Paulo's temperature several times and found that the mercury wouldn't climb higher than 99.

"I'll go and tell the medics," he said. "They'll be amazed. Between you and me, they were pretty worried about you yesterday morning. You scum seem to have guardian angels too."

That might have been meant as an insult, or it might have

been affectionate. Paulo was so happy he didn't bother to take issue. He waited patiently for Jaryk and his colleague to come and witness the miracle. They too had to believe the evidence: the swelling and the fever had disappeared as if by magic.

"I'm amazed," said Jérôme, the Pole. "Yesterday you had a classic case of purulent arthritis, without a shadow of a doubt. Today there's absolutely nothing wrong with you. How many sulfa tablets did you take?"

"Six, three lots of two."

"They can't have done it, you didn't take enough, and sulfonamides take much longer than that to act. No, my friend, your arthritis must have cleared up on its own, there's no other explanation for it. The chances of that happening are one in a hundred. You've been extraordinarily lucky. When do you want to be discharged?"

"This minute, Doctor," cried Paulo excitedly.

"That's impossible," replied Jaryk. "You can only be discharged this evening; Ramsauer will have to see you beforehand. Talking of which, don't forget to ask the orderly to stick a compress on the knee before he does his rounds. We don't want to upset the major."

When Ramsauer appeared just before midday, Paulo uncovered his leg to let him see that the prescribed treatment had been adhered to.

"How is the knee this morning?" asked the *Oberarzt*, flicking off the compress with the tip of his riding crop.

"*Fertig*," replied Paulo, hypocritical as can be. "*Kompresse gut. Danke schön viel, Doktor.*"

Before Paulo went too far, Jaryk interrupted him.

"This man appeares to be cured, *Oberarzt*. Doubtless because of the compresses... We shall discharge him this evening, with your permission."

"*Ja. Schnell.*"

"*Schnell's* the word!" thought Paulo. "It's in the bag this time." Ramsauer would have to find somebody else for his autopsies.

But his heart had skipped a beat when the German dandy tickled him on the knee with his riding crop as if he had suddenly caught on to Paulo's conspiracy with the two convict doctors to make him look like a fool; there had been nothing in the way of an inflammation, and his clever idea of applying compresses had given them all a good laugh. If the vampire only knew what a perfect opportunity he had just missed to get out his scalpel! There must be a God up there somewhere . . .

Less than an hour after Ramsauer had authorized Paulo's discharge, Daniel slipped Paulo a note from Dédé: "All clear, Sailor's enrolled you in his block. I'll come and see you after muster."

"Come on, up you get, make your bed," Daniel added as he tore up the note. "The old man who came from the north with you is going to take your place."

Paulo had completely forgotten the poor old Basque. It was understandable, even excusable, that he hadn't spared a thought for Etcheverry over the last two dramatic days, but it was inexcusable not to have told Joel that his old friend was back, and in a dreadful state.

Daniel must have had to enlist the help of another orderly to carry him from the isolation ward, for there was no question of the old fighter being able to stand on his own. He had spoken the truth when he said to Paulo, as they walked back through the tunnel, "I'm finished." The atmosphere in the south camp which had inspired Paulo couldn't touch him; he had sunk too low, it was too late.

Like thousands before him, he would die without even being ill. He would die of exhaustion as a result of years of being dragged from prison to prison by oppressors, both French and German. Heedless of his age, they had beaten him, tortured him, worked, starved and frozen him to death, but it had taken them almost five years to be rid of him. It would have been better if they had shot him in a ditch on Mont Valérien,* like his comrades. Given the choice, he would probably still have chosen his protracted martyrdom, although it led him, drained of all life, to the syringe of a sadistic doctor. At least he could feel proud of having prolonged the struggle, of "having done what I had to do," as he had explained to Paulo, adding, "It's the others' turn now." It seemed very likely these would be his last words, for he

---

*A fort built on a small hill in a suburb of Paris, where the Germans had many members of the French Resistance executed. Nobody knows for certain, but it is thought that close to ten thousand died in the Mont Valérien ditch, many of them women and boys of less than twenty.

appeared to have fallen into a coma. They said everything. His own life was of no importance, the only thing which mattered was that the torch be taken up after him. Like Max, like the Ukrainian, like the men at Mont Valérien. All the communists died like Roman martyrs, almost gladly because their faith was intact. Which ought to shake the men who had applauded when Daladier and then Pétain had thrown them into jail.

Paulo felt it was time for the bell to ring for Dédé to come and fetch him, because the sight of the old man who had taken his place in bed was beginning to cloud his joy. He couldn't help imagining Etcheverry trying to sit at attention as Ramsauer would callously demand during his rounds tomorrow morning, sniffing out prospective customers for his syringe like a jackal.

"Got to get out of this mortuary now," Paulo muttered between clenched teeth.

The door opened as he spoke and a crowd of convicts surged in, led by Dédé Ménard. He grinned reassuringly at Paulo; everything had gone without a hitch. Phew! Farewell, *Revier*!

XVII

The write-up Dédé and Angel had given Paulo must have been extremely appetizing for Sailor to come over to meet them as soon as he spotted the three friends emerging from the *Revier*. It was almost as if he feared that another block chief would kidnap the rare bird described by the two accomplices.

"*Komm hier*, pimp. Welcome to Block Three," he hailed Paulo.

His lascivious grin illustrated better than words the pleasure he felt in inviting a genuine pimp into his band.

In the eighty feet between the *Revier* and Block 3, Paulo had made himself as small as possible, walking timidly along behind Dédé Ménard and Angel, like a pupil expelled from school being taken by his parents to see the headmaster of a new one. Now he straightened up: he mustn't disappoint Hamburg's queen of queers. Hamburg was, after all, Europe's vice capital. Staring him straight in his glaucous eyes, he greeted him with:

"Hello there, Karl. Thanks a lot for enrolling me in your block."

By being so familiar, Paulo had started as he meant to go on. If by any ghastly chance he hadn't yet been enrolled, he certainly was now.

"Come with me," said Sailor, clapping Paulo heartily on the shoulder. "My *Schreiber* will take your number."

When he stepped into the chief's HQ, Paulo was dumbfounded by what he saw. A group of shaven heads were clustered around the stove on which a dozen potatoes were sizzling, others were sitting around the big table taking enormous drags on a communal cigarette with the ecstasy of opium smokers, while five or six youngsters were sprawled on the beds chattering. And all this under the complacent noses of two *Arbeitskapos* who were Indian wrestling at a corner of the table, egged on by two pansies whose full rosy cheeks explained better than a pink triangle that they were getting it both ways. Dédé Ménard was right: things had changed at Loibl Pass.

They all got to their feet when the chief came in, but it was all very relaxed, nothing like the rigid Mauthausen posture. It was more the conspirator's mark of respect for the good boss who tolerated these sociable comings and goings in his place. Without even glancing at the others, Sailor sat down at the table which doubled as his desk, and invited Paulo to sit down next to him.

"While we wait for my *Schreiber* to come back from the *Rapportführer*'s, let's have a chat," he said, pushing half a loaf of bread and a plate piled high with black pudding and margarine toward his guest. "You hungry, fellow? Don't be shy, dig in."

What on earth had Dédé and Angel told the big thug to make him so attentive to Paulo's needs? "They must have laid it on really thick," thought Paulo. "But what exactly did they say? I'm bound to say something out of turn, and then it will be curtains. Too bad, here goes."

Sailor's personal interpreter had appeared and Paulo got his spiel going.

"First of all, say thanks to the chief for the snack. And ask if he wouldn't mind letting it pass that I spun him a line back in June when I told him I was a driver. I didn't want to risk giving pimp as my profession: it's not particularly useful when you're building a tunnel."

When he heard the enormous guffaw which greeted the translation of what he'd just said, Paulo knew he'd scored a hit. Sailor was doubled up, choking with laughter. When he finally stopped laughing, he leaned over to his interpreter.

"Tell him he's quite wrong. Nothing is more useful here than a decent pimp. Look at me. It's thanks to me the tunnel's getting on, I pimp for them all: the *Haeftlinge*, the civilians, the SS, everybody! It's Karl's block they deliver all the sausages, cigarettes and loaves to—"

"Your pussy-pennies," interrupted Paulo, taking advantage of the way the conversation was going to show his inside knowledge.

"*Was*, pussy-pennies?" queried Karl.

The interpreter was completely stumped, he'd never heard of the phrase "pussy-pennies." The good man's background was in banking, so despite his many months in prison, his ignorance could be excused. He did, however, manage to get the sense of Paulo's expression across to Sailor by paraphrasing it. The latter dissolved into more vulgar laughter than before.

"*Ja, ja*, pussy-pennies . . . pussy-pennies . . ." he repeated over and over, as if he wanted to learn the phrase by heart.

Paulo seized the opportunity to gulp down a piece of black pudding at least four inches long, and nonchalantly picking up the chief's knife, he spread a triple helping of margarine all over the hunk of bread. Karl had said to dig in.

Karl had calmed down again, and he tugged at the *Dolmetscher*'s sleeve.

"Ask him his name."

"Chastagnier," Paulo answered, beating the interpreter to it. "In Montmartre they call me Paulo . . ."

"Montmartre, *schön*." Sailor seized on this, very impressed. "Do you know the place Blanche? Tell me about it."

Obviously for this great queer, Paris and Montmartre were summed up by the place Blanche with its pavement urinals and its drag queens. Paulo didn't dare ask the banker to translate that, he preferred to skip over it.

"The place Blanche is finished. It's all organized now, the nightclubs have taken over. When you come to Paris after the war, Karl, you'll be my guest. You'll be treated like a king!"

"He'll get what's coming to him," thought Paulo as the interpreter translated this deplorable conversation in a deadpan voice. But Karl wouldn't let it stop there. Courtesy for courtesy, he continued.

"If I'd known all this, I wouldn't have had you kicked out to Nordfeld. We'll hang on to you this time, Paulo."

So the bastard admitted it! To get his own back for his six nightmarish months, Paulo grabbed the rest of the margarine and cut himself another slice of bread. But this wasn't the time to nurse grudges. On the contrary, they were going to get along just fine; Paulo was going to stay in the south. The great fool was calling him by his first name, inviting him to his table and stuffing him with food and promises. Belloni's outrageous idea of making him pass for a pimp had turned out to be a stroke of genius!

Sailor waffled on inanely, talking about his hometown, Hamburg, repeatedly running his pointed tongue over his wide lips as he described the matelots, the window displays, and prostitution row. It was sickening. Paulo had noticed that every time he opened his mouth, it only started Karl off again with his filthy stories, so he decided to shut up. Fortunately, there was some bread and black pudding left; with his mouth full, he had a good excuse, and above all it stopped him from dropping any bricks. To do that before the *Schreiber* had officially enrolled him in the block would have been too stupid for words. The *Schreiber* finally arrived with his notebook under his arm, sparing Paulo Sailor's latest theory on the advantages of putting whores in shop windows.

Still conscious of his responsibilities, Sailor stopped in midflow. He grabbed his secretary on his way through and said to him, "We've got a new player in the team, *Schreiber*. Take his number and get him assigned to the cement-mixing gang, or the sawmill, but not in the tunnel, he needs fresh air."

"*Jawohl, Blockaltester*," the *Schreiber* replied, looking faintly astonished, and letting Paulo know that it was rare for Sailor to go to such lengths. The *Schreiber* was not the only one to be surprised: in the games room, conversations had gradually tailed off and everybody was trying to figure out what their maestro found so special about this big scarecrow from the north. Even Paulo had begun to have his suspicions about Karl's sudden surge of affection for him. It was a bolt from the blue.

"The fool might have shown his hand a bit sooner." Lost in thought, Paulo didn't even bother to work out what Sailor was telling the *Schreiber* now. However, they were still talking about him: the chief had taken it into his head to fit him out with a new uniform from head to toe. What a model nursemaid Karl was.

"Go to the store and get him a complete new outfit," he said to the *Schreiber*, who had given up trying to understand. "Jacket, trousers, underwear, shirt, and a new *Mütze*. Shoes, too, if you can find some."

Then he turned to Paulo, adding: "I want you to do my block proud. Take your clothes off."

Paulo hesitated. All of a sudden, he realized he might have been taken for the biggest ride of his life. These protestations of friendship from one pimp to another had probably only been a well-staged farce; Karl's interest was centered on his buttocks. It was too much! Before you could say Jack Robinson, Paulo would find himself appointed official rent-boy, and worse still, in front of fifteen witnesses he could already hear snickering. He had an overwhelming desire to spit the black pudding back in the other false pimp's face.

"Come on, get undressed," Karl had repeated. "Everything off. I don't want my block infested by lice from Nordfeld."

He said it gently, almost in a whisper. It was so unusual for Loibl's number one loudmouth to speak in that tone that this time there was no other interpretation possible for Paulo: the chief was after his arse.

"I can't believe Angel would do the dirty on me like this," he seethed inwardly. "And I walked straight into it, like a real idiot! How the hell am I going to get out of this one?"

He must play for time. He had an idea.

"It's a bit chilly this evening," he said. "I'll wait till the *Schreiber* comes back with my new uniform."

Sailor found it hard to understand that someone should make such a fuss about taking his clothes off.

"Get undressed," he repeated more insistently. "Go and stand by the stove if you're cold."

There was no getting out of it. Shit! He was going to have to parade his bum in front of fifteen voyeurs! As an extra-quick way of letting the whole camp hear about it. Oh, no. It'd be far less degrading to stand naked in the corner, next to the table. With a heavy heart, Paulo resigned himself to his striptease, cursing himself for having gone along with Angel Belloni's idiotic little plan.

"I should have known there'd be some kind of slip-up with that little wanker involved. He's really landed me in it this time. If I'd known all this, I'd have stayed in the north!"

Paulo was being too sensitive; it wasn't as serious as all that. There were nice pansies in the world too, and it wasn't their fault if they were delectable.

That brought him back down to earth again. Delectable wasn't exactly how he could be described at the moment, naked as the day he was born. Perhaps Sailor would have second thoughts when he found out Paulo was so filthy, emaciated and generally seedy. There was better talent in the way of young flesh at Loibl! And yet Karl was lingering over his anatomy with a persistence which was making him more than uncomfortable.

"He couldn't possibly have such bad taste," Paulo tried to reassure himself, hollowing in his chest as far as possible, dangling his arms, making himself knock-kneed and pigeon-toed to appear hopelessly twisted and put an end to Karl's sadistic lusts once and for all.

Paulo was quite wrong to go to all this trouble; Sailor wasn't partial to beanpoles. His particular bent was for small men, five feet four at the most, and just then his great love of the moment, a young boy with girlish rosy cheeks, appeared in the block doorway. This little fellow couldn't conceal the fact that he was a hustler. His clothes, which were clean, well cut and perfectly pressed, gave him away even more than his face. Like the block chiefs, his shirt had a civilian collar, and over the red triangle on his jersey a capital letter L showed him to be from Luxembourg. Poor kid. On the other hand, nobody forced him to stitch that pretty little pink heart on the lapel of his jacket. It was an open invitation. He was only getting what he deserved, whereas Paulo . . .

But the crisis had blown over. Karl had suddenly put on his excited old queer's expression and the languorous gaze he cast at his little sugar bore no resemblance to the professional eye with which he'd sized up Paulo's nakedness. Paulo had gotten the wrong end of the stick.

The whole matter was cleared up when the *Dolmetscher* came back with a complete convict's issue: Karl's promise had not been idle, he really didn't want the men in his block to look like tramps.

Paulo's thankful "*Danke schön, chef*" as he seized upon the smart striped outfit was not lacking in sincerity either. And he added to himself "Since he's going to keep his hands off my arse, there's no reason we shouldn't get along fine."

Feeling far more comfortable now he had some clothes on his back again, he told himself that Sailor had simply wanted to find out what a French pimp's dick looked like, and didn't that prove that behind all his friendly overtures, the clothes and the grub, there was nothing sinister, no ulterior motive? What a shame Belloni hadn't had his idea eleven months ago!

While Karl was billing and cooing with his Luxembourg lover, Paulo slipped away to mingle with the convicts who were warming themselves by the stove before hitting the sack. The men who knew him welcomed him enthusiastically.

"Good to see you, Paulo! We thought you were dead. How did you escape from Nordfeld? Was it really bad over there?"

He'd expected questions like this, but instead of getting needled, he answered politely with a vague explanation, so woolly that it aroused no interest whatsoever.

"Nordfeld isn't a camp, it's just a dormitory," he said to each man in turn. "You grind, you go to bed, you grind again, you go to bed again. That's the whole story, except that there's half the grub and twice the beatings. For six months I didn't see anything, nothing happened except that a few got themselves killed. Talking about Nordfeld is just a waste of breath. That's it, forget it."

Given the number of prisoners who'd come to hear his news, in a short space of time the whole block, and the next day the whole camp, would realize there was no point pumping him about what went on in Nordfeld.

The latecomers were hurrying toward the dormitory, for night had fallen and the bell for lights out would soon be rung. Among them Paulo saw Angel and Joel, but Sailor had also spotted them. When they stopped by his desk to wish him a *"Gute Nacht, chef,"* he got up and gave Joel a resounding slap which sent him sprawling into the doorway leading to the dormitory. Joel picked himself up and made off into the darkness between the rows of beds. Karl didn't bother to follow but instead turned his anger on the knot of men around Paulo. Each one got either a slap or a backhand in the jaw, except for Paulo, in spite of him having caused the gathering. Paulo was so unused to getting off scot-free that he automatically raised his arms to protect his head. It wasn't very nice of him to show such a lack of confidence in the man who had just extended him a hand of friendship. Sailor was surprised, even put out, and he thought he'd better make things clear: "I don't want those stinking oafs hanging about my room. The *Blockführerstube* is for Karl and Karl's friends."

So Paulo had had it spelled out to him; he was one of Karl's friends. From now on, the thrashings would pass him by without his having to raise an arm. It was almost embarrassing, but in the end, what good did it do to get beaten when you could avoid the blows?

Karl had turned back to attend to his pet with the embroidered heart, and Paulo felt it was time for him to go to bed. He climbed into the bed nearest the door and hence nearest the stove—another of Karl's little favors.

He would have liked to talk to someone before he went to sleep, to find out more about the south camp which had welcomed him so warmly, but his nearest neighbors, the other favored ones, didn't seem to be particularly talkative. Anyway, most of them weren't French, and when he put himself in their shoes, he realized it couldn't be much fun to have a starving wreck from the north with an appetite multiplied by six months of famine arrive in their midst to compete for the chief's handouts.

"If they start resenting me, I'm going to have to watch my step," he noted as he stretched out on his mattress.

His blow-out of black pudding and margarine rumbled in his stomach and he was seriously worried that his guts, which had been swilled out with watery soup for so many months, might not be able to cope through the night with this sudden massive invasion of fatty substances. His eyes had been too big for his stomach, and his hour-long binge might end up sending him running for the crapper at regular intervals. He clenched his buttocks together to hold in his precious vitamins and managed to control the urge, but the effort put an end to his chances of going to sleep. Since no one wanted to talk, all he could do was dream, or draw up a balance sheet, as he had done in the past. At last he could give free rein to his imagination. The speed with which events had altered the course of his destiny was a good omen: in the space of a few days he'd gotten out of his tight corner and now he had a handful of trumps for the final game. There was no longer any doubt in his mind: the end was in sight. All the good things which had been showered on him—the miracle cure of his knee, Sailor's welcome, the black pudding, the new outfit and the useful friends he had rediscovered—had arrived in the nick of time. Eleven months ago, they wouldn't have been any good to him at all. It was now that reserves of strength and a winning hand were essential.

He didn't appreciate that luck had never really deserted him. It had been luck which had opened the gates of Mauthausen for him, while over three quarters of his twenty-five hundred fellows from Compiègne had left Mauthausen via the chimneys. It was sheer luck too that he hadn't been sent back there as a useless invalid. He could have caught a fever or dysentery on a hundred different occasions and been the perfect case for the syringe. Or his leg might have been crushed, like the Italian who had been sliced into little pieces by Ramsauer. Helmut might have had him shot after he'd sabotaged the ax, or he could have drawn Paulo's number in the line-crossing lottery, instead of packing him off to Nordfeld. And even there, wasn't it simply luck that he hadn't been caught and hanged like Pierrefeu, for queuing up twice for soup? Really, it would have been dishonest of him to claim that Fortune was only now beginning to smile on him. On the contrary, Fortune had not let him fall from her grasp for a single day during the whole of this terrible year. And to crown it all, he had hit the jackpot with his arthritis, which had heralded his death far better than any obituary notice, then suddenly cured itself, flying in the face of all the laws of medicine.

The black pudding hadn't gotten up to any tricks, but recapping the past like this had taken Paulo well beyond midnight. Tomorrow he'd have the concrete mixer to contend with, and he'd better bid his ruminations good night. He disappeared under the covers.

He was in fine fettle several hours later as he marched up to the tunnel. Just before they left for work Sailor, on the pretext of inspecting it, had quite openly slipped a sizable bread and dripping sandwich into Paulo's mess bowl. His night of passion must have gone well, and Paulo's first day in paradise regained looked promising. Particularly as the early dawn brought with it no clouds to mar the clarity of the sky, and there was not a breath of wind. Within the hour the heavens would have lightened to a cloudless blue and by nine o'clock, the sun would have risen to warm the new day.

"What luck to have hit on weather like this my first day back!" Paulo enthused.

He was more lucky than he knew to be outside enjoying the spring sunshine, because without Sailor's having come up with the brilliant idea of the concrete-mixing gang, he would have had to spend the first sunny day of his prodigal's return in the dank blackness of the tunnel. Everything was going his way. And it must have shown in his face. At the camp before assembly earlier on, and now in the ranks, everybody who had known him to any degree at all had waved. They were intrigued and attracted by a fellow who smiled and marveled at the way of things and the atmosphere. Paulo would be the center of attention if he kept up his sunny smile. Of course, these guys from the south couldn't understand the reason for it, they didn't know what it was like on the other side of the mountain; neither did they know what it felt like to be in the *Revier* with a stiff leg.

The first few rows of men must have reached the work site, because the whole column had just come to a halt. Before they dispersed into small gangs, the SS were going to count their *Stücken*. Paulo had a good five minutes to examine in more detail the little work settlement he had cursed so bitterly last year. Today, like the prodigal son rediscovering the home of his youth after a long absence, he felt almost sentimental.

He spotted the concrete mixer. In fact there were two of them now, one on either side of the tunnel, only a few yards from its mouth. This was doubtless to ensure that the concrete they produced had no chance to solidify. It wasn't an ideal place for chatting, but perhaps there would be slack moments when the wheelbarrow loads of concrete left for the tunnel.

Each of the concrete mixers was run by about fifteen men. There were the usual Kapo, four men to fetch the sand and sacks of cement, two men to carry buckets of water and pour them into the machine, another two to make the mixture with shovels, and the rest to load the liquid cement onto wheelbarrows and carry it off into the tunnel. And all this at top speed, for the masons couldn't be left to twiddle their thumbs in front of their shuttering; they had to line the vault with concrete across the final width of the tunnel.

"Seems to me you guys have been pretty busy around here," remarked Paulo to the man next to him while they waited for the whistle to disperse the Kommandos. The man had just explained the whole system to Paulo and filled him in on how the schedule was going. He seemed rather proud of what had been achieved and didn't rise to Paulo's remark. Paulo pressed the point.

"Look, what I'm trying to say is you're going a bit fast, it's not a very clever idea. Surely you don't need me to spell it out to you."

The other man was an old acquaintance of his, Marcel the truck driver. But Paulo wasn't aware that the Kapo in charge of the concrete mixer, the man Sailor had asked to take Paulo on, was the very person he was talking to. Kapo in a manner of speaking, for Marcel still had no stripe; but since he'd had the chance to show off his eagerness in the plate-laying gang, he'd been reappointed as acting Kapo on each new work site. And each time it happened, he was delighted. Paulo gave up trying to explain that it was because of ignorants like him that the tunnel would be finished before the war. He was a hopeless case, he'd clearly been born stupid. Still, better to have him than a Fritz or a Pozzi.

"Come along with me, Paulo," said Marcel, gathering his gang together. "What can you do?"

"Nothing. And I don't get along with wheelbarrows."

"Right, you can go and mix. That's no sweat."

Better and better. The honorary Kapo was easygoing. Sailor must have had a word with him.

On the mix there was already one guy busy with his

shovel, as if he had known that Paulo would turn up: it was the wily little Angel Belloni.

"Terrific," said Paulo. "Now you can tell me everything. You and Dédé didn't give much away when I was in the *Revier.*"

"We wanted to wait till you got out. You were in a bad way and it wouldn't have helped matters if you'd had to go back to Mauthausen knowing what I've got to say to you."

"Come on, give," interrupted Paulo.

"Hang on," Angel continued, "one thing at a time. First of all, you tell me how things went with Sailor. Pretty well, it seems. You might at least say thank you."

"Fantastic, thanks. But why did you two push off when we came out of the *Revier*?"

"To be honest, Dédé and I weren't sure it would work. If Karl got cross, there was no point the three of us getting it."

"Charming! But it's done now, and it didn't just work, it took off like a rocket. Look, he's given me new togs, crammed me full of food, and he calls me Paulo. But there were ten very nasty minutes when he asked me to strip in front of everybody. I thought you'd played a dirty trick on me and he was after my ass."

The thought of that made Angel cackle delightedly. Paulo went on.

"Fortunately, his darling showed up. Barely in time. I really thought I was going to end up as the houseboy the way he was eyeing me all over. In the end I caught on, he only wanted to see my prick. But the filthy old queer ought to know it by now after all the prick parades he organized last summer. By the way, what exactly did you tell him?"

"It's quite simple," explained Angel. "I told him you were queer."

"What!"

"Yes, queer. But an important one. That is, that you ran the biggest queer shop in Paris."

"And he believed that shit?" demanded Paulo skeptically.

"Seemed to. Of course, I added that you were impressed by his way of doing things, by his personality, and that after the war, since you were going to reorganize your business, you would need a strong director like him to get the transvestites into shape."

"Oh! Great! You really went to town," exclaimed Paulo. "But does that fool really think that when it's all over we're going to walk out arm in arm? He's in for a big surprise . . ."

"Sure he believes it, and he's not the only one! You'll see this evening, in every block it's the same story: Eddy, Max and especially Bullseye. They've almost got to the point of signing contracts. With Maumau and that shit Riton they're dividing up the girls and their patches in Pigalle between them."

"I can't get over it. When I think about the shit they laid on us last July, it's incredible!"

"Don't fool yourself, that hasn't stopped. There are less than ten crooks and fags in each block, they've still got four hundred to beat up, and they pay for the rest. They're not interested in peasants or factory managers. They can't stand the idea of working. They're hoping to get themselves fixed up with the crooks, or so they think. So they deliberately fatten them up and lay off with the hoses."

As Belloni listed all the gangsters under the block chiefs' protection, it was dawning on Paulo that he had gotten himself into a very odd situation. He had managed to stay clean for a year, longer if you counted the three months at Mauthausen, and in the space of twenty-four hours, he found himself trapped in exactly the same situation as the men he despised. It was obviously the false picture of his career which allowed him to stay in the south, but now that he was enrolled perhaps it would be a good idea to backpedal a little. For example, he could go and confess to Sailor that his queer's business was a lot of moonshine. It would be a nasty moment, but it would be better than having it thrown back in his face one day.

Angel couldn't have thought of that. Paulo cut him short.

"Listen, Angel, in a few days when I'm back in shape and settled in here, you can go to Sailor and put him wise. I don't want to wear this hat forever. I refuse to be taken for one of those professional shits. I'd still rather get beaten and starve."

He really meant it. He had loathed the flabby vice boys for too long now. He certainly didn't have as long still to go, so it was pointless and shabby to play the turncoat so late in the day.

Surprised by Paulo's suggestion, Angel could find no

reply and he stared at his friend as if he hadn't heard right.

"Forget it, Angel, I was joking," Paulo said, breaking the silence.

But it rang false, Paulo wasn't joking in the slightest. His scruples were genuine, he was truly ashamed to find himself on the side of the degenerates; but at the same time, he had just remembered the doorstep and drippings in his mess bowl waiting to be scoffed. It was hard to refuse such gifts. There must surely be a solution somewhere between taking advantage and betrayal. Angel was always so full of ideas, maybe he'd know. In any case he was doing nicely himself. But under which umbrella? With his baby face and his boyish build, he could hardly pass for a pimp. As for his past crooked exploits, even the most dull-witted of the block chiefs would never have been dim enough to believe them. That left the role of hustler, but Paulo himself had seen the kid furious at that suggestion, and prepared to be carved up rather than be counted as one of their number. So just how did he get to eat so well?

"Explain something to me, Angel," Paulo demanded. "When I left for the Nordfeld, things didn't seem to be going very well for you. How did you get around Sailor? In the *Revier* you said you'd tell me all about it."

"Nothing to it. I held him off like you told me to, and he got fed up. Queers have their pride too, and he wanted me to fall for him. If I had become his pansy, it would have been all around the camp that he'd had to rape me. It's as simple as that."

The explanation stood up to scrutiny, but it still didn't explain a year's subscription to extra soup. Angel sensed that Paulo was only half convinced, and he elaborated a little.

"I should tell you as well, that it was thanks to yours truly that he found his pretty boy from Luxembourg, and the one before him. I don't mean to, but I do seem to attract youngsters. Probably because of my age. They're fed up with being pushed around by the dried-up old bastards who seem to resent them for being young and see them all as budding fairies. So they band together, and as I'm the oldest they come to me. It didn't take Sailor long to catch on, and we quickly made it up: smiles, extra soup and finally supper at his table. With all my friends . . ."

"I suppose it's possible," thought Paulo. "He must be

the type of old queer who entertains all his boy friend's pals just to be friendly."

Angel was continuing his explanations.

"... And anyway, I make Sailor laugh, I teach him Parisian slang, he can't get by without me now. I'd like to have seen them at my age, those old has-beens who look down their noses at me."

Belloni was touching on the very problem which was worrying Paulo.

"Yes, and what do the others think, the ones who don't get any extra helpings? Do they make snide remarks?"

"Less and less these days," replied Angel. "Apart from the two or three old graybeards I was telling you about. On the whole, everyone understands, and that's the big change. There isn't any jealousy at Loibl anymore. Before, those who didn't have soft jobs felt like strangling the men who had. Today, it's the opposite. Whenever somebody, by which I mean a Frenchman, manages to land a plum, everybody's delighted. Because don't forget, the hoods and the fairies are not the only ones with cushy numbers. It's the same in the tunnel and on the work sites. Even here with that big simpleton Marcel, who, by the way, has been letting us chat for a good hour."

The real reason for their respite was that the cement had only just arrived. The acting Kapo brusquely interrupted the interesting conversation the two friends were having.

"Belloni will tell you what to do," he said to Paulo. "Be careful, don't put too much cement in, the sacks are counted, and I don't want my concrete fucked up."

"His concrete! What a fool!" thought Paulo. "He may not be a fag, but he's not much better."

As the truck driver had said, the work wasn't too strenuous and between shovelfuls Angel and Paulo could carry on with their little chat. That weedy Marcel could hardly stop them.

Paulo wanted to clear up what was on his mind once and for all.

"As I see it," he continued, "the men don't make any distinction between different kinds of soft jobs. Is that right?"

"Exactly. The difference is in how you make use of the job. If a guy plays dirty—if he squeals, for example—there's no two ways about it. Everyone avoids him, and he gets isolated. Or if he's a guzzler who keeps all his grub to himself, that doesn't go down well either; but it doesn't happen very often. Usually, anyone who gets special treatment manages to help out one or two friends. Take Olivier in the cookhouse, he virtually runs an orphanage, a really good candidate for the Cognac prize. The funny thing is sucking up to the block chiefs isn't taken badly at all; in fact you could almost say it's encouraged. It's a different story with the work Kapos and the SS. So there's no need for you to worry about Sailor having a soft spot for you. No one will take exception. Quite the opposite, you'll find you've made a whole lot of new friends. But be careful with Karl. He's a real prima donna: capricious and fickle. He could turn you out overnight. You'll know you've had it when you get your first slap in the face. In the meantime, make the most of it."

Angel's description of the change in attitude among the prisoners in the south was so astonishing that Paulo couldn't quite believe it, unless the end really was any day now. The funny thing was, Belloni seemed reluctant to talk about how the war was going, although that was the most important thing. Belloni must tell him everything he knew.

"Where does the war come into all this? Aren't you going to tell me about it?"

"Victory's around the corner, that's for sure, but it's impossible to know exactly what's going on. It seems to be a case of who's best at bluffing. The SS get the ball rolling by deliberately spinning the Kapos a line. Then they spread their own version of the news, spicing it up a bit. One day they tell us that we'll be here for another twenty years; the next day they get pissed, start getting melancholy and let the cat out of the bag. But it's all so muddled you can't rely on anything they say, except that we're friends of theirs and we'll be doing business together as soon as we get out. You're a prime example. Luckily, to help sort out fact from fiction, there are the Yugoslav civilians, who get their information from the partisans, but they tend to exaggerate in the opposite direction. In the end, nobody really knows anything and it's best to be like me and ignore it."

"That's just what I did for six months at Nordfeld," retorted Paulo, "but I can't do it here. Things have changed so much that there's almost a smell of freedom in the air. And when freedom comes, believe me, it'd be better to know about it a bit beforehand."

"Maybe you're right," replied Angel. "But I'd rather not daydream. In any case, if you want real information, there's another way of getting it—from Dédé. He won't talk to me. He thinks I talk too much. Why don't you try grilling him? You'll probably have more luck than me..."

"The lawyer hinted at something in the *Revier*, in a hush-hush sort of way. What's all the mystery about?"

"I've got a good idea," said Angel. "But you'll have to keep it under your hat. Promise?"

"It's a promise, I swear. Come on, out with it," said Paulo excitedly.

"Well, look, I'm not sure, but I think Dédé has put together a radio set with bits and pieces from the ones he mends for the SS. I haven't told you anything," he added quickly.

"I might have guessed, that guy's 100 per cent nerve! He only ever thinks about the war, it really gets him going. But thanks anyway, what you've just told me is really important."

"I've told you nothing," Belloni interrupted sharply. "It's only a feeling. I don't know anything. Go and ask Dédé, maybe he'll tell you. Some guys are in on it, but not me."

"Who's in on it?"

"Joel, I should think, and the commies. But it isn't easy to get on with the commies, they drive you mad with their bloody principles. They only accept the proles and the men arrested for Resistance activities, and not even all of them. They don't trust the bourgeois and the Gaullists. Only Dédé impresses them, because he's even more anti-Nazi than they are. Besides, his electrician's job means he can go anywhere, and it give them ideas. As far as me and the commies are concerned, I'm up against a blank wall. They give me the cold shoulder, and they can go to hell. Paris won't be any more fun if the Reds replace the Krauts, you'll see."

What Angel was saying was not all that stupid. The only problem was that you had to get back home to find out, and that wouldn't be tomorrow or the next day. But in all fairness things weren't turning out badly. The fellows in the south seemed to have got themselves intelligently organized. They looked nothing like the frightened and obedient sheep that Paulo had left at the beginning of November. The most irritating thing about it all was that the change had taken place while he had given up in despair at Nordfeld; he who had been the first, or so he thought, to challenge the general fatalism and upbraid all those who were proud of not trying to understand.

More than ever before, he heaped curses on Nordfeld, his second deportation, which had stopped him being present at the resurrection of hope, and, worse still, stopped him from taking part in it. They hadn't waited for him, it had all gone on without him, and all he could do was tag along. It would be easy with Joel and Dédé, who had known his thoughts at a time when nobody had dared express theirs. They would count him in, even if the commies decided to cold-shoulder him as well. He had longed too much for the grand finale, when they'd be able to settle accounts with every single one of the bastards, to be left out in the cold. No one would stop him from being there.

Quite carried away by the strength of his feelings, Paulo had forgotten Belloni. Beneath his devil-may-care exterior, the boy had just shown that he took a keen interest in everything. Far from blocking up his ears, as he made out he did, he kept them attuned to the slightest whisper, just as he kept a razor-sharp eye out for anything that looked interesting, especially if it was forbidden. As he seemed to have forgotten about being stupid, his ferreting meant that he grasped the situation better than anyone else. The picture of camp life he had just painted for Paulo was very sketchy, but he had got the essentials across, with the headline news of the radio set. What a shame those sectarian communists wanted nothing to do with him. He pretended not to give a damn, but he must have been hurt by their suspicious attitude. Perhaps, like Paulo, he regretted not having done anything to deserve this prison. He too must be wondering whether he hadn't been on the wrong track when he tried to get on in society with a crowbar, confusing crookedness with honor. "The poor kid may have been born into it, but he shouldn't have to pay for it for the rest of his life!" thought Paulo with genuine regret.

"Don't worry, Angel," he said. "Now that I'm here, things'll be different. Just give me time to put on a bit of weight and we'll organize our own little Resistance cell. We haven't let anybody down, there's no reason why we shouldn't have a say in things. I'll go and speak to Dédé this evening. And you know what we'll do if the commies turn their noses up?"

"No." Angel was intrigued.

"We'll split, won't we?"

Paulo had said it off t' e cuff, without thinking, wanting to raise his friend's spirits, but the effect was instantaneous. Angel was so taken aback he dropped his shovel and just stood there, waiting to see what Paulo would say next.

"Well, we'll try anyway," Paulo went on. "I've always been against it, but from what I can see, things have changed a lot. Now the snow's gone, it's worth considering again. Give me a little breathing space, though. I don't want to risk a noose around my neck if the Armistice is only two months away."

In the past Paulo had thrown out the idea of escape; but as he was speaking, he told himself perhaps it wasn't so crazy after all. They had been chatting for almost two hours and nobody had come to bother them so far. Discipline seemed to have become very lax, so the idea of escape might well be worth pursuing.

"We'll talk to Dédé and Joel about it. I know them, they'll certainly be game."

Angel was transfixed; this was more like the Paulo he knew.

"It's about time you came back. I've been sitting around getting fat and lazy," he laughed.

Fat Marcel's falsetto voice suddenly poured cold water on his high spirits.

"You two'd do better to do some work instead of standing around giggling. We're falling behind because of you and the *Kommandoführer* will be here in less than ten minutes."

"Shut your face, you grind," retorted Belloni, very cocky now that Paulo was around.

He'd gone too far.

"Well if that's your attitude, you lazy so-and-so, you can get on the wheelbarrow right now," Marcel retaliated angrily.

"Let it go, friend," Paulo intervened. "We'll speed things up. Don't worry, you'll have your concrete."

But the provisional Kapo wouldn't listen. He wrenched the shovel from Angel Belloni's hands, and screamed right in his face, "It's no good speeding it up now, my mixer doesn't run on your daydreams! Now pick up that wheelbarrow and start carting the mix to the men in the vault. Next time, you'll think twice about calling someone old enough to be your father a grind."

"Okay, okay, stop spluttering, grandpa, I'm going." Angel gave in, seeing it was useless to resist.

The acting Kapo wasn't a vindictive man, he wouldn't have reported the boy to Fossil-Face, but in the end his yelling would attract just as much attention.

Paulo had two hours to kill before soup, but there was nobody to talk to. Belloni's place had been taken by a Russian who was as friendly as a bear and about as chatty as a brick wall. However, the hours passed quickly because Paulo was so excited by what Angel had just told him. Joel was looking out for him in the refectory at lunchtime and he would tell him more about it.

The Breton was amazed that Paulo had already heard of Dédé's radio set. At first he pretended not to know anything about it, but he was soon reassured and lost no time in confirming the news.

"Yes, it's true," he said, "but you must keep quiet about it. Especially you, Angel, with all those young kids you hang around with. If it gets out, Dédé's done for, and everything will have to be started all over again."

"What do you mean?" asked Paulo.

"Subversion. It's all to do with the morale of the Kapos, the *Feldgendarmes*, even the SS. They don't believe German radio anymore, but they don't dare listen to other stations. Dédé has managed to get Lausanne, and virtually every night he brings us up to date so that we can plant the information in certain quarters. It reaches the ears of the Krauts in scraps without them having the slightest idea where it's come from. We've got the organization down to a fine art. No one suspects anything, and the only reason I'm telling you is because I find myself faced with a fait accompli. Who put you in the picture, Angel?"

"Nobody, I swear. But I don't walk around blindfolded and, between ourselves, your game's not very subtle. All I did was put two and two together."

"I'm sure you're right, we're not as careful as we should be," Joel replied, looking Belloni in the eyes, as if he wanted to be certain that that was all he knew. "But I ask you, you too, Paulo, to keep this completely to yourselves. I'll still have to tell the rest of the group that you know what's going on."

"Who is this group?" demanded Paulo, a little annoyed to see that Joel wouldn't have let him in on the secret, had nosy little Belloni not sniffed out the communists' nest.

"It's made up of the Loibl Resistance," Joel said after a moment's hesitation.

"Well, that's quite a crowd. Not surprising Angel spotted your game," Paulo scoffed.

"I mean the real Resistance," Joel went on. "Actually, there are very few of us, but we're gradually widening the circle, and I hope you'll both join forces with us. Everyone will have a part to play when we get the go-ahead."

Angel and Paulo were struck by Joel's serious manner. He was talking about the Big Day, D-Day, like a Resistance boss wanting to place the men to be enlisted in his network squarely before their responsibilities. Even if you were still active in France, his instructions would have been chilling. So here, in the lion's den, it was not so much boldness as sheer madness. Were it not for the business of the secret radio set, Paulo might have thought Joel was just living out his fantasies and scaring himself with his grand schemes. However, the ex-gym teacher didn't look as if he was playacting, and as he elaborated, it all got more and more frightening.

"What we've done is get together a command group, regardless of political ideology. I'm not going to tell you who they are, but you'll have guessed that the communists make up the largest part. Which is only to be expected, since they engineered the whole thing. Furthermore, their good relations with the Russian and Polish party members here have enabled them to liaise with the partisans outside. Given those two things, it was difficult not to let them take charge of the operation."

Paulo was dumbfounded to learn how far things had gone. And he was disappointed, too, that the communists had taken over the leadership of the movement. They had achieved what his own rebellious spirit dreamed of last summer, when he thought that all around him everyone had given up. What a fool he'd been. He'd have to learn his politics all over again. Swallowing his resentment, he said to Joel,

"What you're saying is terrific. I've dreamed of it so

much that it makes me sick I wasn't here while it was all going on. All the same, I'm not keen on the commies. I know their sort. They're real puritans, and they'll never want anything to do with me or Belloni—"

"Slow down, Paulo, there've been some changes in that direction too. Dédé will tell you what's been going on in France among the maquis. There the word Resistance is a sacred bond and that's how it should be here. Anyway, we call our group the Front National, so we're no longer communists, Gaullists, Socialists or guys who aren't anything at all. Being a patriot is the only qualification. Obviously, there are plenty of Kraut-haters at Loibl, but we can't take everybody on at the beginning. What we're going to need soon is guys with real guts. Which is why, like I said earlier on, I hope you two'll come in with us. For the moment, I must ask you again: don't breathe a word. Angel half guessed and I've taken it upon myself to tell you more, because I trust you. So you keep your mouths shut. Promise?"

"You can count on us," said Paulo, "we'll be discreet. But while we're being open with each other, tell me honestly what you think about me being friendly with Sailor. Your Front National won't take kindly to that. When we're free, you'll all throw it back in my face, all the extra soup and snacks which that great queer seems to want to give me—"

"He's so obstinate," interrupted Angel. "I've told him once. Why don't you tell him, Joel?"

"Honestly, we don't give a damn," Joel confirmed. "In fact, it's good tactics. Remember the Spaniards at Mauthausen? They had the whole camp in the palm of their hand. Nobody could do without them. Some of them even became Kapos. They ate as much as they wanted, but they fed others too. Many others, regardless of nationality, and those men will be standing on their own two feet at the final showdown. The skeletons in the *Revier* are of no interest, I'm afraid."

It was a brutal thing to say, when Joel's best friend, the old Basque, who was even more of an idealist than him, was at that very moment lying in the *Revier* on his deathbed.

Such ruthlessness was frightful, but Paulo decided there was no point in reproaching the young Breton, who continued describing the situation at Mauthausen.

". . . If the Spaniards had refused the cushy jobs and the compromises, they would all have died, twelve thousand instead of ten thousand. The men who survived don't need to be ashamed of their bonuses, they did a good job. They saved thousands of us. But to do it, they had to be utterly unsentimental, unafraid of the stink from the crematorium, the crematorium which ten thousand of their countrymen had inaugurated. There's no room for sentiment in war. I've learned a lot here; we were just children in France. Loibl has given us the chance to lose that innocence."

Paulo was hardly the type to run from danger, but Joel's inflammatory ideas were beginning to make him edgy. Yet there was no holding him back.

"There are some who won't like our going after the soft jobs, but that's too bad. When we arrived at Mauthausen we were suspicious too. The Spaniards seemed to kow-tow too much; they were well dressed and they'd swap your watch for a bowl of soup. But it was the right thing to do, because those watches turned into soup, and more soup meant less men dead. What we want to do is achieve here what the Spaniards achieved at Mauthausen. So don't worry about Sailor's hand-outs. I know why he's doing it. It's very funny, but there's nothing unworthy about it. It's in line with our motto: Grab what you can. Provided, of course, that the whole community benefits too."

"Let's make a start here and now," said Paulo, fishing out his bread and drippings from under his jacket. "Here, Joel, you take half and I'll split the rest with Angel. With any luck Karl will have the same good idea this evening and make me another."

Joel's eyes widened at the sight of the sandwich, but he hesitated. He felt an irresistible urge to take it, but on the other hand, he was afraid the others might think that he'd only made his fine speech about solidarity out of self-interest. Paulo chuckled at his embarrassment. "Don't make such a song and dance about it! I've thought about sharing it with you since this morning, Resistance or not. Go on, eat it, we've got to get back to work."

As he left the refectory Paulo, momentarily distracted by all the unlikely news, headed automatically for the tunnel.

"Paulo!" called Angel. "What do you think you're doing?"

"I was thinking about what Joel just told us," answered Paulo, retracing his steps.

"And what do you make of it? It scares me to death."

"Me too, I have to admit. If it falls through, we'll all go up in smoke. But on the other hand, it's fantastic to think we could do the Krauts in on the spot. But I don't see how, unless the Yugos attack the camp. Joel didn't mention that unfortunately, or the war, for that matter. This evening we'll have to think of a way to get Dédé to talk. Then tomorrow we'll see things more clearly. Having said that, there's going to be big trouble if those fools try anything."

"Yes, it would be a real waste to get ourselves killed now," Angel agreed. "Your idea's a lot better, Paulo."

"What idea's that?"

"Making a break for it, of course."

"Oh yes. Er, I'd forgotten. Making a break probably is less dangerous than a running battle. But why don't we wait and see if they want us in their Front National?"

"Even if they do, I'm not interested. Those commies get on my nerves a bit too much," Angel said huffily. And he took off abruptly with his wheelbarrow full of cement. Paulo's eyes followed him until he had completely disappeared into the darkness of the tunnel.

For the first time, he wasn't frightened of the insatiable hole in the rock. He was no longer the only one who refused to let it become the mass grave of Kommando X. And if it did happen, through ill fortune, it wouldn't be without a fight. It was a pity Belloni had disappeared in high dudgeon. He would have explained to him that when you call yourself a man, you have no right to pass up an opportunity like this to prove it. You have no right to run away before the showdown.

In any case, whether Paulo resolved to run or to stay and fight, he wouldn't have to make that decision today. So, rather than worrying himself about it before time, wasn't it better just to thank his lucky stars that he'd been given the chance to choose? At Nordfeld less than a week ago, Paulo hadn't had that chance.

From now on, he saw one need as more urgent than all the rest: he must put on weight. The others could perfect their brotherly supply line of soup, if it made them happy, but Paulo was going to wait until he was less skinny before joining in. He would need a good month, even with Sailor's handouts, before he would be presentable. "After that, we'll see," he told himself.

He was still grinning broadly at the thought of the

respite he had just given himself when he joined the secret meeting called by Joel after evening muster behind the *Waschraum*. Joel had decided that since Paulo and his friend knew quite a bit already, rather too much in fact, the best way to keep them quiet was to get them into the organization without delay. But the communists wouldn't hear of it. "No crooks in the Front National," they'd said, adding: "If you trust Chastagnier, ask him for his word of honor not to say anything to anyone. The same goes for the other little vagrant, but we don't want to talk to them." The result was that apart from Joel, there was only Dédé Ménard behind the *Waschraum*.

So that they shouldn't needlessly annoy Paulo and his friend, the two Bretons refrained from mentioning their approach to the Reds and the rebuff they had received; but they both looked thoroughly fed up. It was Dédé, however, who broke the ice.

"Well, Angel, you're a sly one, you've started listening through keyholes from what I hear."

"And I hear you've been listening to something else," Paulo butted in. "Which is a lot more interesting. What's your latest scoop? I haven't a clue, I've just gotten here, I didn't get any further than Stalingrad—"

"Stalingrad!" Dédé snorted with amusement. "That's really old-hat, you're way behind the times. They've been at Kiev for six months—I mean the Russians, not the Germans. It's one tactical withdrawal after the other; the Krauts'll soon be back in Germany. It's a rout! Come and see me in my niche in the tunnel, Paulo, and I'll show you a thing or two. Then maybe you'll understand better."

"Did you get Lausanne today?" queried Joel.

"No, I couldn't, I was never alone for long enough. But I've got a bit of fun lined up: I'm going to pick up London."

Dédé was unbelievable. Listening to the BBC in the comfort of your own home was already quite daring enough to get you sent straight to Mauthausen. So doing it in the place where you've been sent for doing it was the final insult. And yet Dédé didn't bask in the glory of his exploits; he seemed to do it for fun. How easygoing he was compared to his Resistance comrade Joel, who shrouded himself in his mysteries and his principles, and before he'd even gotten out of the joint was talking about reforming the world. He was too righteous for Paulo, who felt far more at ease with the cheerful Dédé.

The feeling seemed to be mutual. Earlier, when they'd arrived, Ménard hadn't put on any airs when he asked the two ex-crooks for their word of honor. He'd broached the matter without any fuss.

"Now you're in the breeze"—the science student was beginning to pick up slang—"you'd better keep your mouths shut. The Krauts mustn't be allowed to trace any news they've heard via you back to me." And for form's sake, just to reassure his comrade, he added, "Give me your word of honor."

Why was Dédé so friendly to Paulo? Since the latter's return, everything he'd done was proof of his friendship. He'd taken up Paulo's cause with the doctors to get him sulfonamides, with Sailor to stop him getting sent back to the north, and now, in this very delicate affair, he displayed unqualified confidence in Paulo. In each case he'd acted so freely and naturally that it couldn't be taken as anything other than friendship.

Dédé clearly had a soft spot for the big Parisian villain, who was such a far cry from his university world of bourgeois and patriots. He was greatly amused by Paulo's slightly anarchic nature and his obstinate translation of even the simplest words into slang. It made Dédé feel he was in with a bad crowd, like the provincial who comes to Paris for a night out on the tiles. Every time Paulo came out with a new expression, Dédé would start giggling—which wasn't at all in keeping with the gravity of the situation.

Joel finally became exasperated with them.

"Knock it off, you two!" he said sternly. "This is serious business."

"You don't expect us to start crying after what your friend here's just said?" retorted Paulo. "When I left for the north and saw all those Mongols arriving, I really thought the Krauts had made it to Peking! Today he tells me they're on their way home, with a boot up their backsides. Don't you think that's funny?"

"You mean your bunch at Nordfeld didn't know they were retreating?" asked Dédé. "Well, if I have to tell you everything that's happened in the last six months, we'll be here all night."

"Just give me the fundamentals. What I really want to know is how much longer we're going to be here."

"Three months at the most. At the outside, till the end of summer. One thing I can tell you: there won't be another winter of war. And this time, I'll bet my house in Rennes against a pack of dravas."

"You're on!" said Paulo, slapping his outstretched hand.

"It's a deal. And how about another: there'll be a *coup de théâtre* in Germany with Hitler thrown out by his own army. It could happen any day now."

In spite of Dédé's overwhelming optimism, Paulo had trouble seeing himself on Civvy Street before the end of the week. But it was immensely encouraging to hear these things. "Go on, let's hear some more," he said excitedly to Dédé. "It's great when you get going like that, it makes me want to hug you."

Dédé laughed! "Where was I? Oh, yes! I was saying that a political upheaval in Germany is quite in the cards. The Wehrmacht knows it's beaten, and where to lay the blame. One fine day, the Wehrmacht officers are going to wake up. For us idiots—as you would say!—that would be the best solution."

"Don't you believe it," said Joel. "The Germans are a race of cowards. Otherwise, they'd have rebelled in 'thirty-nine when they were sent to what might have been their slaughter. What one sees as courage in a German soldier is exactly the reverse: it's fear, the fear of being shot. Rather than risk death, a Kraut chooses to fight, since at least that gives him a chance. Believe me, when a Kraut's on his own, he's a coward."

"Exactly," Dédé cut in. "When he realized in nineteen-eighteen that he'd had it, he hoisted his flag, deposed the Kaiser and started a revolution. That's what I was saying and that, I hope, is what's going to take place."

"You're forgetting," Joel answered, "that in those days there was no SS. This time around there are at least five hundred thousand of those maniacs, up to their necks in atrocities, and they have nothing more to lose. They can make eighty million cowards tremble, Wehrmacht included. Every German, whether he's on the front line or not, knows that the moment he stops thinking Nazi, he could be shot. So he toes the line—like we do. We're no cowards, but we still haven't rebelled. Why not? Because their methods of repression are too refined. The German nation allowed it to happen out of cowardice, and they will die because of it, but they won't do anything to destroy it. We may escape, because all over Europe there are other nations taking up arms who don't have the same fear of death. Don't count for one second on revolution within Germany. Our job is to get ready to disarm our SS when the partisans launch their attack."

"There he goes again," thought Paulo. "Instead of dreaming about freedom, that guy's always thinking about blood and guts and revenge. You'd almost think he'd be dead pissed off if he went home with his hands in his pockets after a minor *coup d'état* in Germany! My God, haven't the commies indoctrinated him. I don't think he likes life much anymore. Let's hope Dédé's right and the end will come as a surprise, before that extremist and his cutthroat friends have time to put their hair-raising plots into practice."

It didn't matter whether it was a nice surprise, as Dédé suggested, or the general free-for-all that Joel wanted, which opened the camp gates. It was much more important that they were talking about it as a real possibility. What it basically meant was that the German hordes had had a rough time of it while Paulo had been in his icy tower. He regretted missing that, but now his feet were on the ground again and his brain was working properly.

"And why don't they just get an Armistice?" he wondered.

He had spoken aloud, cutting Joel off in the middle of his monologue about the cowardice of the individual German.

"What's that supposed to mean?" he asked, furious at being interrupted.

Dédé intervened. "I know what Paulo meant: Why don't the Germans ask for an Armistice, is that right?"

"Yes, of course. Don't wars usually end like that?"

"With Hitler? You're off your head. Really, Paulo, what do you take us for?"

"No, he's quite right," Dédé went on. "We can't rule out the possibility of an Armistice. Obviously we can't count on Hitler to ask for it, but the army might. It's what I was saying earlier."

Joel looked despairing as he answered.

"You're so naïve! I tell you the Krauts are petrified of Hitler, they won't do a thing. They're even more frightened of the SS than we are. Besides, they're in a kind of concentration camp too, every single one of them. Ever since nineteen thirty-three, as prisoners guards."

"Tell me, you lot," Paulo interjected, "Armistice, *coup d'état* or liberation by the partisans, we're still agreed on one thing: it's not going to last much longer?"

"That, at least, seems obvious," Joel and Dédé both replied.

"Well then," Paulo went on, "perhaps you'd like to tell me how you're so sure of it. I still don't know where we are in this war. Kiev and Odessa don't mean a thing to me."

"Okay, I'll sum it up for you," said Dédé. "The last Germans left Africa a long time ago. On the other hand, there are plenty in Italy. But the Americans and the English are there, and—wait for it—a real French army too, more than a hundred thousand men from North Africa."

"Jesus, you're kidding!" exclaimed Paulo. "How far's Italy from here?"

"Not very far at all." Angel opened his mouth for the first time. "But there are some fucking big mountains between us and them."

"Which is exactly what's stopping the Allies from advancing any quicker, according to Swiss radio," Dédé continued. "What else do you want to know?"

"Everything."

"Well, the most important thing, which will clinch the whole affair, is the landings which are expected any day now. That will be the end of Hitler. He'll be caught like a rat in a trap on all fronts, even here in Yugoslavia. Maybe our tunnel will serve some purpose."

"Do you seriously believe the war will get as far as here?" asked Paulo, torn between joy and anxiety.

"Certainly. There are almost a million Yugoslav partisans in the mountains, organized and armed. They've got artillery and the whole lot. If Tito, their leader, starts to march on Austria, he'll come this way. The Krauts can't have thought of that when they made us dig their strategic tunnel. It would be fantastic if we've been working for the right cause all along, in spite of ourselves. If that happens, we won't have wasted our year here, and I do wonder whether we shouldn't try and speed things up a bit."

"That's quite a different matter," Joel objected. "You can't prove anything. The tunnel could also be used to bring in the Panzers to hammer the Yugoslav Resistance. Let's wait for the orders they're bound to send us. In the meantime, our brief is to slow things down and sabotage the tunnel wherever we can."

"You can count on me to slow it down," said Paulo. "After what you've told me, I'm less and less eager to kill myself on the job. What else do you know, Dédé?"

"You have the whole story now. Don't bother telling your friends, they know it all already. As soon as I hear anything new, I'll let you know. It'll be up to you to find a clever way of passing it on to Sailor. The most important thing is to undermine the enemy's morale. But remember, we've agreed that no one must know how we get our information."

"My word on it," Angel and Paulo said one after the other.

It was dark now, and the four friends separated. They were all from Block 3, and if they arrived in a group just before the bell, they might attract the attention of curious eyes. Joel left first, alone. Two minutes later Angel and Paulo followed, making a detour around by the kitchens.

"You don't seem your usual chatty self, Angel," said Paulo, quickening his pace. "You haven't opened your mouth all evening. Aren't you excited?"

"I knew most of it already."

"Doesn't it make you any happier? You're just like Joel, you're never satisfied."

"Course I am, but the thought of something going wrong at the last minute scares me. I'm telling you, Paulo, we've got to split."

"You're crazy! There's no point now in taking the slightest risk. Personally I want the end to find me here at Loibl. This afternoon I gave myself a month to think it over. But I've already made up my mind: I stay put, and I keep my distance from the extremists in the Front National."

"D'you mean that?" Angel was badly shaken by Paulo's air of determination.

"Yes, I do. There's only one thing to be done now, and that's to get into shape physically. It'll be essential if we're going to escape or turn on the Krauts at the last minute.

We've all got to put on sixty pounds and develop some muscles. From now on we've got to concentrate on grub, and working as little as possible."

As if he could read Paulo's mind Sailor, all smiles, had just thrust his ugly head out of the block window.

Grub, for the time being, was in his hands.

XVIII

It took Paulo less than a week to get himself thoroughly back into the swing of things in the south. Like an excited schoolgirl back from vacation, he went around questioning everybody he met to try to see whether they all believed as strongly as Dédé that their misery would be over in three months, or at the worst five. Most of the convicts were not in any doubt, but out of caution or superstition, none would name a date. "I'll believe it when we're back in France," was the unhelpful reply Paulo's survey usually got.

He knew better than to be taken in. By deliberately dodging the issue the men Paulo had canvassed merely confirmed what he was after: the end was not a pipe dream anymore. They were unrecognizable now; they had all lost their pitiful hangdog look. They held their heads high, a little too high perhaps. A few impetuous characters had overstepped the mark, and their baiting of Maumau, still Bullseye's number one fag, and Sladek's little Polish friend, had immediately turned them into punchballs, and they'd found themselves in the *Revier* on the waiting list for Nordfeld.

Paulo had had enough of both those wonderful institutions, and he had very quickly memorized the features of all the little chubby-cheeks. It wasn't that he was afraid of picking on one of them by mistake; he simply wanted to keep out of their way. Given the block chiefs' jealous dispositions, striking up a friendship with any of them was a bad idea. This was a shame, because most of the youngsters seemed to have taken a liking to the tall crook who neither went around with a long face nor felt obliged, like most of the others, to make snide remarks at every opportunity. What could be more natural than to keep him in soup and bread when they had enough to make themselves sick!

"With a meal ticket in every block, it wouldn't be difficult to put back the pounds these thieving Krauts have robbed me of," Paulo said to himself in a moment of weakness. "But I suppose Sailor might not take too kindly to it. It's too risky, I'd better stay clear of the bunk boys."

So he decided to hunt for his "chuff" elsewhere. Paulo hadn't heard this barracks expression, which applied to everything that was food, but he rather liked it. The word "chuff" had become part of camp jargon, and it was on everyone's lips from morning to night. Even the Poles had made it part of their vocabulary. All the same Paulo should have got this famous chuff out of his system by the end of his first week. Even if he had managed to discover another source, it was difficult to see where he would put it. His belly was stretched to the bursting point by Sailor's sandwiches. But Angel had warned him that Karl, fickle queer that he was, could shut the door on him overnight, and then he'd find all the other doors shut too. Before that happened, he'd have to find another source of chuff.

The obvious place to look was the kitchens, and it didn't take Paulo long to find something in common with Olivier, the sugar daddy there.

"Okay," the fellow from Marseilles finally agreed. "Just show up quietly for the peeling on Saturday. One extra won't be noticed. But don't bother about the soft soap. I'm only doing you a favor because you've come back from the north. When you're back in shape, you'll have to find yourself another nursemaid."

At this, Paulo realized Olivier had been enlisted by the nameless men of the Front National. The commies had quickly worked out that in this moneyless community, the tons of food in Olivier's charge since Ernst's suicide constituted the nerve center of the war. The cook must have been told that he was not to waste it fattening up the bums, and he made no attempt to hide the fact.

"Anything I can get out of here goes straight to the *Revier*, where the comrades divide it out among the weakest. I don't want any part in wangling or scheming."

There was nothing more to be got out of the mulehead. Paulo thanked him for the permission to join the peeling sessions, but he already knew that under Olivier's watchful eye the Saturday potato raids would be less fruitful than when Ernst, the poet, had been in charge.

The camp pantry was a real Ali Baba's cave with its joints of meat for the SS, its huge jars of fat and jam, and its endless strings of black pudding. It was all the more annoying to find its doors closed to him when Paulo had resolved to keep Dédé, Joel and Angel supplied with chuff.

He had been deeply moved by the utterly unselfish welcome his three friends had given him. He hadn't dared say so; he hadn't known how to, flowery speeches weren't his forte. But he'd been thinking about it for several days, and it had set his mind at ease to think that he would be able to repay them by sharing all his kitchen chuff.

There were many such clubs in the camp where two or three men were fed by a friend on the inside, and the Front National had no say in the matter. Foremost among them were the Russians, but nobody envied them much, for their stock of peelings and stale crusts of bread retrieved from the SS dustbins was not very appetizing. These primitives were never given soft jobs. From time to time they managed at great risk to improve their poor lot by filching from a block chief's cupboard; but it was safer if their raids were strung out over a period of time. Even if Sebastopol, the young angel-faced partisan, and his sidekick, a redheaded boy with steely eyes, were usually the ones to direct these forays. These Russians were such hard nuts that they put the wind up everybody, Campana brothers included. Loibl's Russkies didn't give a damn about collectivist discipline or solidarity with their foreign allies.

"Being a crook in Moscow must really put you in the hot seat if they're all like those guys!" thought Paulo.

As for the Poles, they managed a bit better, for the simple reason that they had at least one food-supplying fairy in each block. But that wasn't much of a spree either, and at the most only about twenty benefited from the block chiefs' little presents. The rest of the colony, more than a hundred scarecrows, continued to go hungry. Their only consolation was to refer to their privileged compatriots as *yebonis* all day long.

But among the French, by far the largest group in the south, the situation was reversed: it was the "assisted" who were in the majority. The word "assisted" had been lifted from the vocabulary of a long-serving criminal from Clairvaux prison, and like "chuff," it had immediately been adopted by the French community. "I assist you," "you assist me," "he assists me"; they conjugated the verb from morning till night. And they had good reason, for now there were a good many men who could afford to feed one, two or even three mates. And they were far from all being crooks or hustlers. In the twinkling of an eye, the mass of shaven men from France had turned into tailors, barbers, cooks, plumbers, electricians, carpenters, gardeners, translators and accountants on demand—in short all the skills necessary to make a town run smoothly.

Nothing was beyond the ability of the wily Frenchmen. They now held all the key positions in the camp, from the *Revier* to the kitchens, via the laundry, the showers and the *Schreibstube*, and nobody thought to oust them because they were so good at their jobs. What sweet revenge for these *Franzosen* who had been humiliated and downtrodden for months as if they were the very dregs of humanity!

"*Scheisse Franzosen, Dreckmann,* bums, spastics, scum," was how they'd been known for months and months. The Krauts had walked all over France and spat on her beyond belief. Suddenly, without her doing anything and despite her limping so badly through the World War, she was beginning to get noticed. Her three hundred children gathered at Loibl for almost a year were a perfect cross section, even more representative than a voting list. They included Frenchmen from all over, from town and country, from Paris, Brittany, the Midi, the east and even North Africa. Every guild was represented: professional soldiers, lawyers, journalists, notaries, merchants, artists, farmers, workers, students and even schoolboys. Not to mention the prodigious contingent of gangsters. It was truly France in miniature. But what was even more unusual about this group of men, which was not found either in the army or in the POW camps, was that ages ranged through three generations, from boys of seventeen right up to grandfathers well over sixty. Up until now, although they had lived on top of each other for so long, they had known each other only by surname or place of origin. Suddenly they began to tell each other all about themselves, their families and their jobs. In the little groups which sprang up, each man knew how many children his neighbor had left behind in France, his wife's age and Christian name, what she looked like, what her special talents were, and so on. They talked in minute detail about their work, where they'd been born, about their homes; but what they talked about most openly was the reason for, and the circumstances surrounding, their arrest. For the past year they had all kept quiet for the sake of caution. Apart from a few shabby characters who had invented tales of armed robbery to tack themselves onto the crooked elements, and who were now trying to backpedal, nobody else had anything to be ashamed of. So sure were they all of victory that they held nothing back.

As for Paulo, he wasn't at all put out by the turning tide. In any case, he didn't really know, with the spiel Joel and Dédé had given him, whether he was supposed to count himself part of the Resistance now, or one of the rest. It was irrelevant anyway, because he found his fellows in the south a pleasant bunch. What had struck him most in all this upheaval was that the atmosphere was a hell of a lot friendlier here than on the other side of the mountain. He went from group to group, eagerly joining in with conversations, and he was welcomed wherever he went. The north was relegated to the past, and no one questioned him about it anymore. They were all talking about their plans for the future. Since the end was obviously close at hand, their immediate concern was their homecoming, which they'd celebrate with an endless round of enormous feasts, and tables groaning with enough food to make you sick. They all thought up their own menus and compared notes: pâté de foie gras, sweetbreads, coq au vin, jugged hare, cassoulet and choucroute garnie, all rounded off with a Camembert ripe enough to walk away. The heaviest and richest food they could think of, washed down with the year's Beaujolais.

Their mouths watered and they drooled with anticipation, to such an extent that one day a particularly run-down old man from Bullseye's block became intoxicated with the catalogue of rich dishes going round inside his head, and threw up his midday meal. It was a miserable rutabaga soup, and his indigestion was genuine. He couldn't face it anymore, thinking about all those fabulous dishes and their aroma. When he got to the trifle for pudding, it was the last straw, and he couldn't keep his soup down. The squanderer had spewed the whole lot up in the middle of a group of gluttons, who had been transfixed by the description of his gargantuan feast. As he listened to the man reeling off his idiotic list, Paulo was reminded of his cellmate in the Cherche-Midi jail, who had outdone even him in gluttony. Equally obsessed by the need to fill himself up, he had unraveled his wool blanket and, strand by strand, as if it were vermicelli, he garnished his soup with it to make it thicker. His voice became hoarser as the days passed, and he began to cough and choke. He was rushed to the hospital in the nick of time, and the doctors were astonished to find enough wool in his stomach to knit a long-sleeved pullover.

The Loibl jailbirds hadn't gone to quite such lengths yet; but the obsession with food was beginning to get dangerously out of hand. By making life easier for the French, who had always been good eaters, the Kapos and SS were gently leading them down the path to madness.

At any rate, that was Paulo's conclusion when he saw some greedy fools pushing their idiocy to the point of copying out the most appetizing recipes on scraps of cement sacks. They swapped secretly and learned them by heart; whenever hunger gnawed more than usual, they recited them like psalms. It calmed the hunger for a while, but they were behaving like silly old men. Instead of dreaming about spurious menus, they ought to have been trying to find another source of food within the system.

In the camp itself every avenue seemed to have been explored. That left the work sites with all the Austrian and Yugoslav civilians loafing around all day long among the work teams. Now there was a place which might repay a little investigation, especially as the civilians now used the tunnel. They actually drove their cars through it, to go and do their shopping in Klagenfurt, the nearest Austrian town. They found this shortcut most convenient, and on both sides of the onetime frontier they must have been grateful to the men who in so short a time had bored through the Alps for them.

"The guys working in the tunnel will really strike it rich with all these comings and goings," Paulo mused, and his first thought was to get himself taken on as a miner again. But after some consideration he decided against it; he reckoned that being on the mixer gang against the southern entrance, like a porter's lodge, would be just as good for making friends.

And anyway, what could be better than this easy work in the spring sun, which warmed his back from nine in the morning onward, and turned the calories in Sailor's great picnics into muscles?

Angel agreed with him: "When it comes to the civilians, we'll be king. We'll have to grovel a bit, but they've got so many dravas they don't know what to do with them. We can set up a little tobacconist's."

"That's just what I was going to suggest," replied Paulo. "A stock of smokes here is as good as money in the bank."

They had hit upon just the thing to keep themselves occupied: butt-hunting was much more dignified than pleading with a bunk-boy for a spoonful of soup.

"If we can put by a bit on the side," Angel continued, "we could buy a couple of Pépé's ivories. A few grams of yellow should easily fetch us a compass and some climbing shoes around here. The Yugos are bound to like gold better than Deutschmarks . . ."

"There you go again," Paulo interrupted. "I've told you already, you don't make a move until you know how things are going to turn out. We agreed to put back some weight first, remember? That's what the butts are going to be useful for. Look at you and your puny chest, you still look premature twenty years later."

Angel was very aggrieved. "Just because I'm not as big as you are," he retorted. "Anyway, I'm much better off, being light, for getting out of here, for climbing and that."

Not having been through the hell of Nordfeld, Angel couldn't understand that his friend wanted above all to have a breathing space and not to have his life complicated with a fresh problem. He needed to get as much as he could from his first real break and put behind him the death race of the last year. How could he consider escaping now, when in the whole of his eventful life, he had never felt such a sense of peace? It would have been sheer madness. He was fed, he had been given a new uniform, working on the concrete mixer was a cinch, the weather was fine and warm, and everyone liked him. What more could he want? Angel's timing was as bad as ever.

Even if, by an impossible chance, they succeeded in escaping, what would he and Angel find in the war-torn mountains? Certainly not the quiet life they led here. No, Pépé could keep his golden smile and his 22-carat teeth. The civilians' smokes would be bartered for bread and soup.

The day after they'd come to this decision, they decided to buttonhole the young Italian engine driver. He had stopped his machine level with the two Frenchmen because one of his wagons had not been properly coupled and had broken loose, he was looking around for help.

"We'll give you a hand, friend!" Paulo called out, walking up to him with Angel in tow.

"French?" asked the driver. "*Bene*, I speak French. Get yourselves onto the edge of the coupling and lean on it so that I can slip the hook over the top."

In two seconds it was all sorted out and with a *grazie molto* the Italian was preparing to hop up into his cab.

"Not so fast, mate, you don't just push off like that," Angel said, grabbing him by the arm. "It's going to cost you some smokes."

The Eyetie's jaw dropped in amazement. It was the first time since he'd arrived that a prisoner had dared talk to him like that. It was more usual for the shaven wretches among whom he spent his days to smile at him ingratiatingly in the hope that he might deign to flick a burning butt in their direction. The manner in which these two demanded compensation for their trouble bordered on a threat, and it was unlikely they'd be happy with one cigarette between them. Caught off his guard and feeling uneasy, he looked around as if for help, but since there were no Kapos or SS on hand, he pretended that he'd only just understood what they were after.

"Ah, *capito*! Cigarettes? *D'accordo*, my friends."

And taking a pack of Nazionales from his jacket, he stingily pulled out two cigarettes.

"Listen," Paulo stepped in. "Do you take us for a pair of beggars? Angel, give the miser back his smokes."

The Italian was thoroughly rattled by now. He'd better get rid of these two horrors in a hurry; they seemed to have forgotten the respect they owed to a civilian worker. And his best way of doing so was to hand over the pack which he'd unwisely brought out. He chucked it crossly at Paulo's feet, and leaped back onto his engine with a bitter *ciao* which sounded more like good riddance. Opening the throttle hard, he steamed off toward the dump.

"He was a bit reluctant to let them go, wasn't he?" chuckled Angel. "Paulo, I think we can cross him off our list of benefactors."

"I bet you we don't. We'll fine him a pack a week; he'll fall into line, you'll see. I bet you he feels like a shit working as a free civilian in a prison, when only a hundred and eighty miles away, his country is up in arms against the very men he's agreed to do this dirty job for."

"Shame there aren't more of his countrymen around. We could make a few more of them uncomfortable," said Angel. "But quite a good joke, eh?"

Five minutes later the two partners were still laughing at their game by the concrete mixer when Dédé Ménard spotted them as he came out of the tunnel, a roll of electric cable under each arm.

"Well, you two seem to be having a good time. What's so funny?"

"We made friends with an Italian, the one on the engine. Look what he gave us," replied Angel, flashing the pack of Nazionales. "Do you know the wop we mean?"

"Of course. He's not a volunteer, he was drafted. But go carefully. So far he hasn't been of much help to us, and the other driver, the one on the *decauville*, is even worse. There's only one safe guy among the civilians, and that's Yanko. He's the right sort of Slav, if you see what I mean."

Paulo understood perfectly. In plain language, the right sort of Slav meant he was a partisan sympathizer. But that wasn't what had caught his attention. It was the Christian name Yanko, almost like Yanka.

He had completely forgotten about her! Banished from his dreams the day he had set out for the north, she had never returned. Such neglect was understandable on the other side of the mountain, bearing in mind the state he was in, but it was ten days since he had returned to the nest and he might at least have asked after her. But he hadn't given a single thought to the young girl who had so generously given him her cigarettes. And not in dribs and drabs like that Italian Jew. She had given him four whole packs, and her dravas were made of real tobacco, not straw.

"Hey, Dédé, is Yanka still around?" he interrupted impatiently.

"Still the same old Paulo! You liked her, didn't you? You're in for a disappointment, she's gone on holiday in the mountains. Quite near here in a little house the Krauts aren't too hot on."

"Has she gone to the partisans?"

"Yes, but keep that to yourself too, because she'll be coming back."

"Good news."

Dédé carried on talking—Yanka this, Yanka that—and Paulo remembered the place she had held in his dreams on the evenings when he'd been depressed. But the picture was so different now that, rather than waste time dreaming, he'd do better to imagine himself back in France where there must be two million women, deprived of it for four years, waiting impatiently for the return of their horny menfolk. Last year, it might have been all right to toss off for the only tolerable girl in the place. But now, the fact that Yanka was gorgeous was beside the point: Paulo was only interested in her return to the camp for the packs of cigarettes she'd bring back. Particularly as the little racket at the tunnel entrance had not yielded the expected results.

The Italian was determined to avoid payment of his one pack a week, and he persisted in roaring by the two tobacconists, sneering at them from the safety of his locomotive. If it hadn't been for the good Yugloslav, Yanko, who threw them the occasional pack as he went by, their harvest would have been poor indeed. And yet they put a lot of effort into increasing their spoils of war! Angel, like the bum who taps on the driver's window when he's stuck at a red light, systematically accosted every single traveler entering and leaving the tunnel. Even the mountain gendarmes, whose numbers around the camp had swelled, couldn't escape his ingratiating smile and his imploring look. His masterpiece had been to move a young Austrian SS, who looked as unhappy as him about being there. The young soldier willingly handed over his little offering every day and was only too happy to talk about the *Scheisse Krieg* which had made a prison warder of him. If he was hoping Angel would raise his spirits he had made a bad error of judgment. The little fellow from Cannes made free with bad news, and sometimes even false news: the

Yanks were in Rome, the Russians in Prussia. He was barely ahead of Radio-Ménard, but the Austrian lapped it all up. It couldn't have gone down too well in the SS barracks at night.

The militants of the Front National might well have revised their opinion of Belloni if they had gotten wind of his work, but Angel was oblivious to its political implications. His motives were purely personal: butts, more butts, and yet more butts to be stored away secretly in the *Waschraum*, not to be smoked and not to be traded for food, because from that point of view things were going well for the moment. And one fine day they'd flog the whole group for something really important. Angel's views hadn't changed; something important meant things for his traveling bag, with or without Paulo.

As the days went by, their savings increased. The two friends had developed a routine: *Zigaretten, bitte, bitte schön*, a big please, smiles, bows . . . and every smoke prised from the enemy thrilled them and made the hours pass unbelievably quickly.

One day, however, Angel's artlessness almost wrecked their nice little business. A truck from the valley below had just parked next to the concrete mixer to let its engine cool down before going through the tunnel. The driver, who looked as if he enjoyed the good things in life, got out, followed by two blond girls who could have been his daughters. The pretty things seemed delighted with the enforced stop, which meant they could stretch their legs and also get a close look at the dangerous Frenchmen everyone was talking about in the nearby towns. In their light cotton frocks they quivered with pleasure at the thought, and while their big daddy went off to find out whether he could go on through unhindered, they struck up a conversation in a mixture of pidgin French and German.

"Are you French? *Warum* you here?"

"Political prisoners," Angel and Paulo answered, pointing to the little red triangles decorating their jackets lying on some cement sacks. Why get lost in details? Far simpler to say political prisoner.

They hadn't even found it funny that they had both, spontaneously and independently, introduced themselves like that. In fact, the two men, who had been so cheerful for the last few days, suddenly felt very serious. They almost felt like putting their jackets back on, to show the inquisitive girls that they had the right to a red triangle marked with an *F* for *Frankreich*. In a way Angel and Paulo were political prisoners, because, as idealistic Joel had said, "Leaving Mauthausen alive gives you rights."

The two friends' emotion couldn't have been very obvious, or maybe it was just that the girls couldn't have cared less whether they were political prisoners or not. What fascinated them was that these two half-naked boys who were entertaining them were French, and everyone knew what that meant. They were content just to look, and didn't bother to pursue their questioning.

Irritated at being looked at like a monkey in a zoo, Paulo went to fetch his shovel and deliberately turned his back on them.

"Drop those stupid tarts," he said as he passed Angel. "You're wasting your time, they don't even smoke."

The boy, only too happy to find civilians interested in him, and female civilians at that, wasn't thinking about cigarettes at all. But he wasn't content to leave them alone either, and he was racking his brains for some way of holding their attention.

The greedy concrete mixer needed new supplies, and although it wasn't his job, Angel took it upon himself to fetch a sack of cement, then another, then another, to the astonishment of the Russian allocated to the thankless task. Bent double under his load, he trotted back and forth in front of the girls, convinced that the weight he was carrying showed off his tanned little biceps to good advantage. "This'll get those two dames going," he thought to himself. But he was wasting his time. They didn't know each sack weighed 110 pounds and that they were being treated to a feat of strength. Already they were looking elsewhere, at Paulo, who was much better built than his shrimp of a friend. By this time Paulo was furious to see Angel make a fool of himself. He went up to him, saying scornfully,

"What are you trying to prove to those bitches? Are you out of your mind?"

"Piss off. It's doing me good, I need the exercise." And with that, Angel went off to get another sack.

Unfortunately, Paulo's rebuke spurred him to go one better, and he asked the Russian, who was only too happy that this fool was doing his work for him, to load a second sack onto his shoulders. To try and carry 220 pounds when he couldn't have weighed more than ninety, even fully clothed, was sheer lunacy. The inevitable happened. His knees bent more and more with each step, until he finally sprawled headlong with his load at the feet of the two girls. The bags burst open, sending up a thick white cloud which enveloped them. They began to shriek in unison. Angel made good his escape behind the screen of dust which billowed around the girls without waiting to see the outcome. But the damage was done: 220 pounds of cement had been lost— clear case of sabotage. And at that precise moment, the stout truck driver decided to come back . . . together with Fossil-Face. You didn't need a crystal ball to see that there would be hell to pay.

Luckily, the old fool kept pausing and turning back to the tunnel, gesticulating to explain to the driver that his truck was too wide to go through. You could even hear him repeating, "*Zu weit, zu weit dein Wagen*."

Paulo reckoned he had about thirty seconds to get rid of the split sacks of cement down the concrete mixer's throat. It was ready and waiting; he set to, and in ten shovelfuls it was done, sacks and all. But he had no time to help the honeys dust off the horrible powder they were covered in. Actually it made them all the prettier; they were powdered like Louis XV duchesses, and realizing this, their shrieks turned into gurgles of amusement. Phew! That was a near-miss. Fossil-Face didn't even bother to find out where the cement, which was causing such hilarity, had come from.

Angel, rather crestfallen and still powdered like a harlequin, had surfaced by now and was waiting for the telling off he deserved.

"Idiot," Paulo said, shrugging his shoulders.

He left it at that. But he made a mental note that if he ever decided to break out, on no account would he team up with an eager beaver prone to such stupidity. But he refrained from saying so, because to be that blunt would have crushed the boy's high spirits. Angel's lively company, which helped the time pass so quickly, was too valuable for the time being. To show him he didn't hold it against him for having made such an exhibition of himself, he went on to talk about something else.

"Angel, is it true there's a cat in Block Two?"

"Yeah, that's right, one of the hustlers pinched it from the civilian camp and gave it to Bullseye on his birthday."

"How old's that poof anyway?"

"Dunno, he hasn't got an age."

"Yeah, you're right. He's an old man from that neck up, and young from the neck down. And, er, what does he do with his cat? Does he fuck it?"

"Dunno."

Angel was clearly not in the mood for such a silly topic of conversation. Paulo's attempts to show he'd already forgotten the cement incident fell on stony ground. He'd have to try something else.

"Well, I don't give a damn about his tomcat, anyway. Something much more interesting just happened. I bet you didn't notice."

"Here we go," thought Angel. "It's back to the two powdered tarts." But Paulo's challenge intrigued him.

"What didn't I notice?"

"That they can't get trucks through the tunnel yet."

"Course I saw that. So what?"

"So, it means we stay. That's the important thing. Because the day trucks and tanks can get through, then it's *zurück* to Mauthausen for us. Through the tunnel we've built for them, it's the shortest way. And on that day, take my word for it, it'll be farewell to the good life."

"The good life? Huh! Good for who? You can stuff your good life. As far as I'm concerned, it's shit from A to Z."

Obviously, they didn't see eye to eye on the matter. For the men who had never left the south, like Belloni, their present situation was quite normal. All the improvements had taken place gradually, too slowly for them to appreciate and enjoy. Like grasping employees they looked upon each new concession as their right, and always wanted more. But Paulo, fresh from the north, was much less demanding. The corridas, the midnight parades, and the "attempted escapes" were still recent memories.

Life seemed to be treating others well, too, for the worthy collaborators of the Universale company on the other side of the fence. If everyone continued to work so diligently, the tunnel for which they'd been contracted would be finished ahead of schedule. Which would stand their firm in very good stead with the powers that be, who all knew they had undertaken their formidable task without any skilled work.

Under less dramatic circumstances, there would have been an interesting wager to make: send the lot of them home, not only the engineers and foremen, but the Kapos, the SS and the gendarmes as well, and fix a meeting with the Universale company a few months hence. It would have been quite possible for the convicts to finish the strategic tunnel all by themselves. They had sweated blood over it for a year, digging it, shoring it up and widening it, so while they were about it they might as well see it through.

This was the kind of thing that occurred to Paulo whenever he measured the surprising progress made during his absence. The hoppers trundled in and out of the tunnel with the regularity of commuter trains, the two sawmills whined all day long, turning out miles of wooden shuttering, and the small factory didn't even wait for its cement blocks to dry before rushing them into the tunnel. It was an exciting race against time, but to go as far as betting on it . . .

Yet Paulo couldn't have been the only one to have this flippant thought. There were certainly others in the game who would have been disappointed if they'd suddenly been told: "That's it, men, go home. Thanks for all your help, but we'll finish your tunnel." They'd feel as if they'd been taken.

You had only to hear the conversations on the work sites which constantly revolved around the cash they'd claim from Universale . . . after the war. The Viennese company would have one hell of a lot of compensation to pay. Nine hundred workers at fourteen hours a day for over a year must be worth quite a bit. They worked out what they were owed, they talked about forming an association and initiating large-scale proceedings. The lawyer from Limoges would represent them . . . They were dead serious about it. So Paulo was right: to make absolutely sure they got their wages, some men were prepared to go on and finish the tunnel even after the end of the war.

What they didn't know was that Universale had already paid out their share to somebody else: to the SS, of all people.

In order to win the contract for the tunnel, the company had had to agree to a special clause: the work force had to be hired from Mauthausen itself. At a high price, of course, since the deal included the housing of the workers, clothing, food, medical care, health insurance and probably also funeral expenses. The generous SS took care of everything, but in return Universale had to pay cash. So the poor dreamers who thought the company was making outrageous profits out of them, which one day they'd be able to claim back, were having the wool pulled over their eyes double thick. The profits went straight into Himmler's money box. At a rough guess, 90 per cent of what the firm paid out—not a bad little nest egg!

But at the same time all this was reassuring, because even if the recruitment of the work force had cost nothing, its training represented a long-term investment which would have to be offset by not killing the workers for fun, as they had done at the start.

"Just look around you," Paulo felt like saying to Angel. "Everybody's happy: the SS, the Kapos, the guys from Universale, especially the locals, who never seem to get tired of going in and out of the tunnel. Loibl's become a day out, a tourist attraction. We're not on our own anymore and they can't do anything to us now. Why don't you cheer up and make the most of it?"

Angel was still fuming about his ridiculous performance, and he wouldn't have appreciated the lesson in optimism. Paulo had to talk to him in his own language.

"Listen," he began. "Exactly how many butts have we got in the stash?"

"Eight packs." Announcing this total, Angel couldn't suppress a smile of satisfaction.

"What do you think we could trade them for?"

"I already told you . . . for some yellow. Pépé's fangs. You can't go wrong with gold."

"I s'pose you're right," Paulo replied easily, ready to make almost any concession if only his friend would snap out of it.

But he remained deliberately vague about what they would do with the retired crook's precious teeth. Best not to offend the boy, but not a good idea to let him get carried away by his harebrained idea of escape either. Afterward, it would be too late to back out.

"Well, escape or no escape," he went on, "we won't get

very far with eight measly packs. For the moment, we'd better just work on increasing our stock."

"I'm right behind you," replied Angel, excited again.

This was how Paulo liked to see him, enthusiastic and eager to be useful. The art of butt-hunting, at which he was a past master, would occupy all his energies. Give him a job to do, and let everything else carry on improving. Each day Angel would have less reason to escape. Paulo was determined to survive, but to survive at Loibl. His dreams were now limited to the boundaries of the camp and the work site. The last fortnight had been too good to be true. To hell with the fault finders and the men obsessed with escape or insurrection! Why couldn't they let him enjoy himself a little bit longer, for God's sake?

It was not to be. Not everyone saw things as he did, and one Saturday morning as he stretched in his bunk hoping the doyen would ring the bell as late as possible, he felt as if the sky had fallen in. An incredible piece of news had flashed through the dormitory: some Russians on the night shift had battered in the heads of three SS, and escaped.

Within seconds, everything began to collapse.

XIX

Before they knew what had happened, the five hundred detainees in the south camp found themselves lined up on the *Appelplatz*.

"Alle raus!"

It was never a good sign, but this time the Kapos' tone was not just threatening. It sounded as if it meant every man for himself, as if the men who had given the order were worried about their own skins. With good reason, because half a dozen armed and helmeted SS had made an unprecedented entrance into the prisoners' enclosure. Pushing the Kapos forward with bayonets in their backs, they forced them to turn every block upside down as if hoping to find the missing men.

When the prisoners saw the faces of the thugs in docker's caps contorted with fear, they knew the entire camp was going to pay for the Russians' violent escape, with the Kapos in the front line.

The panic on the *Appelplatz*, where the convicts had instinctively formed into ranks, was the sort of panic which overtakes passengers on the bridge of a torpedoed ship or the cinema audience which has been trapped by fire. It was the terror of imminent death. For death was the only possible outcome, after what they'd just learned. Three SS were critically injured, perhaps already dead; nobody knew for sure. But what was clear was that the Russians had gotten away, for the alarm had just been sounded: three distinct rifle shots which echoed dismally across the valley.

In the SS barracks and even on the other side of the road where the gendarmes were quartered, turmoil immediately ensued. An army of Krauts came tumbling out of every barracks through doors and windows, some only half dressed, and half awake, but all with guns in their hands.

At last they might get the chance to distinguish themselves in action, despite the lack of an enemy, and they wouldn't have missed it for the world. Nevertheless, the Kommandant picked out only thirty of the medal-hungry warriors, and he led them on the double up the road to the tunnel. Helmut and Fossil-Face were in on the act too, as was the *Hundenführer*, of course, with his six dogs who, for a change, would be used for something other than snapping at skinny calves and backsides.

Watching the troops march off so determinedly, Paulo figured that beneath his fury the Kommandant must be delighted with what had happened. Shaven men wearing only pajamas and wooden-soled clogs wouldn't get very far in the high mountains. They'd be caught before nightfall . . .

And it was a good thing too, because back at Mauthausen big boss Ziereis would have difficulty understanding how his subordinate could have let loose men who would be quick to spread the news of what went on in his forbidden citadel. If Kommandant Winkler didn't come back with them, he'd find himself in hot water.

The men in the ranks were relieved that their Kommandant had taken charge of operations himself. It meant that there would be no reprisals until his return. A small mercy . . . but if he came back with the escapees, perhaps there wouldn't be any reprisals at all.

What were the five hundred hostages thinking deep down as they stood tensely at attention? Were they hoping that the Russians would be taken or not? They must have been horribly torn in their minds and even Paulo, while admiring the desperadoes' nerve, didn't dare commit himself. If they weren't recaptured, his quiet life, the good life as he called it, was over, and everything was in ruins. On the other hand, it was fantastic that a few unarmed skeletons had managed to knock off three SS. It had exploded quite a few myths; they weren't just miserable shits. Mauthausen's methods had come badly unstuck at Loibl. Paulo was still of two minds. Did he want to see them captured or not? It was a pity the prisoners couldn't talk.

But they could listen, and every single man was anxiously straining his ears to follow the trail of the search party up the mountain. If Paulo really wanted to know what his neighbors were thinking, he had only to look at them as the barking and shouting from the search party suddenly intensified. The tear-filled eyes of the prisoners said better than words what they felt in that awful moment before the kill. You could almost hear their prayer: "Oh God, don't let them be caught!"

They knew very well what would happen to them, however, if the Kommandant and his headhunters came back emptyhanded. They would be beaten like animals and the *Revier* would be filled with split skulls and broken bones, all excellent pretexts for Ramsauer's syringe. Winkler would not miss the opportunity of teaching them a lesson. He was covered by the pact made with the "volunteers" of Kommando X at Mauthausen: for every man who escaped, ten would be shot. How many Russians were there here? Not too many, one hoped.

The manhunt dragged on all day, and the sun had long since disappeared behind the mountains when the doyen took it upon himself to send all the prisoners back to their blocks.

"If any man attempts to leave his block, I'll strangle him with my bare hands," he threatened before dismissing them. "And no talking either. Break ranks, you bunch of murderers."

The real reason behind his initiative was that he was in a hurry to get his henchmen together to cook up his defense against the Kommandant's inevitable accusations. As doyen of the camp, Otto was in charge of all the *Haeftlinge*, and one of his responsibilities was to alert the camp authorities to trouble. He ought to have sensed there was something fishy going on, and put a stop to it. It was lucky for him that the escapees were from Nordfeld, but he was still uneasy. Perhaps they'd had accomplices in the south . . . his spies should have tipped him off . . . And so on. Herr *Lagerältester* knew he was in a very tight corner, and he would have given his eye teeth for the dogs to pick up the scent of the fugitives.

Time dragged on, and in the blocks empty of Kapos the order for silence had obviously not been respected. Bit by bit, the men were able to piece together roughly what had happened.

Three men had escaped, all Russian, and officers in the Red Army. Their leader was apparently a tall redheaded man, known to everyone in Block 3 because he'd been there briefly before going over to Nordfeld. Paulo remembered him particularly well, because he had suspected him one night of pinching from under his nose half a loaf of bread which he'd hidden under his mattress. He'd never been able to prove it and it hadn't gone any further. But he had been surprised at the man's ability to move about in the dark just as easily as in broad daylight. He had also noticed him in the tunnel, creeping along galleries dotted with trapdoors, without even bothering to light his hurricane lamp. It was almost as if he was in training, both to filch bread from those who had too much and to investigate possible escape routes. Paulo had also been very struck by the Russian's steel-gray eyes and their tigerish glare which deterred you from wanting to settle accounts. Had Paulo known what he was plotting, he would have gladly given the brave man his loaf of bread. It certainly didn't surprise him that it was this rough fellow who had instigated the plot, which, although risky, seemed to have been planned with the precision of a commando attack.

They had escaped a little before three in the morning, and as they weren't missed until six, they had a good three hours' head start. Perhaps even more, because the officer in charge of the SS guard, nicknamed Green Bean and as conceited as they come, had refused to believe the evidence.

He had lost another good hour counting and recounting the two hundred miners in the night shift.

"*Ein hundert sieben und neunzig*... one hundred and ninety-seven... three missing." The halfwit wouldn't accept it, and although he recounted ten times, it never worked out right. He had made the mistake of believing that his surveillance was flawless. He had five SS fanned out in an arc at each of the two narrow entrances to the tunnel. At night, with everyone working inside and nobody, under any circumstances, allowed out, it was understandably difficult for him to believe in the Russians' vanishing trick. Particularly since, for some unknown reason, the south camp hadn't sent up a night shift, which halved the activity in the tunnel. "If ever an escape was impossible, it was last night," Green Bean must have thought, which was why he so stubbornly refused to accept the facts.

The same went for the Kommandant. As soon as he arrived on the scene, instead of sending his posse up into the mountains, he'd forced them to search every foot of the tunnel in the hope of finding the three absentees asleep, waiting to be punished in the appropriate way. Two and a half miles there and back added up to another hour's lead for the fugitives. The Russians would certainly not have anticipated such a degree of stupidity when they made their plan. Winkler must have had enormous contempt for his prisoners to refuse to believe that three of them had dared to break out.

Now that they knew the story, it all seemed very easy. The three Russians had calmly boarded the diesel locomotive and headed south in the direction of Yugoslavia and the partisans. One small detail had escaped the unimaginative officer and his dull-witted Kommandant: the men had swapped their easily recognizable striped pajamas for SS uniforms, complete with insignia, skull and crossbones and all the rest. Instead of challenging them, the five idiots on duty at the southern exit had stiffened to attention, mistaking them for officers. It had all the elements of a real POW escape, like in war films which ridicule the Germans. But nothing at Loibl was the same as anywhere else: the three Russians weren't actors and they had gotten hold of their gray-green uniforms by attacking the SS with pickaxes and mining bars.

Although searching the tunnel had led them to the scene

of the crime, the three sleeping men they found were not the ones naïve Winkler had hoped to find. Instead there were three SS, dressed only in shirts and underwear, lying in a thick pool of blood. One was already dead, and his two colleagues weren't much better off. Their skulls were fractured and their backs had been hacked open by pickaxes. The Russians didn't take any chances. They had even taken the precaution of trussing up the two survivors with ropes they'd found God knew where. Even in the Kommandant's dull brain, there couldn't be any doubt now that the crime had been thoroughly premeditated.

The men had heard these grisly details from Sailor when he got back to his block. He was shaking with fear. Partly from shock, but perhaps also at the thought that the savages responsible were no different from the wretches he quite happily cuffed around all day long. And, moreover, he had certainly thrashed the three murderers, especially their leader, who had been temporarily in his block. And there were a hundred "wretches" just like him listening to Karl at this very moment. He had reason to tremble.

Out of prudence he yelled at them to go to bed, adding that they should stay dressed. Everybody knew they were in for a bad night.

From what the fear-stricken Karl had just told them, it was easy to reconstruct the whole story. But there was one detail in the Russkies' devious scheme which nobody managed to explain, even long afterward. How had they known that, for the first time, the southern team would not be working that night? It was a factor which made escape much easier: the guard was at half strength, and most important, there were no witnesses to hamper them at the southern end where the attack had taken place. Apart from this mystery, which only the Gestapo could have solved by poking around among the civilians, everything was quite straightforward.

The lynx-eyed leader had been shrewd to plan the escape for a Friday night—the SS's favorite day for getting pissed. Since there was no work in the tunnel at weekends, they made the most of the evening in north and south alike, knocking themselves out with glass after glass of slivowitz. For lack of women, they invited each other, and at the end of it all they weaved unsteadily back through the tunnel. The Russians had noticed the routine, and it had been the easiest thing in the world for them to overpower the three drunken thugs from the south who were tottering back home. But no one was able to say with any accuracy how many prisoners there had been to deal with them quite so thoroughly.

Paulo could easily imagine the three carousing SS walking down the railway track in single file and singing, as if they were strolling down the Champs Elysées. They must have had to leave the track to skirt a wagon standing under the first trapdoor, which was where they had been found. There was nothing unusual about the wagon being there, since the job of the men in the lower gallery was to load the wagons with the debris shoveled through the trapdoors by the men working in the gallery above. The three jolly drunks suspected nothing, and it was quite likely that as they went past the hopper, they had had to duck to avoid being hit by the falling stones. Crouched on top of the wagon, the Red Army comrades were waiting. Swinging the two pickaxes and the mining bar they normally used to clear the chute when it got blocked, all three suddenly attacked the SS on their heads and backs, from a good three feet above them. Judging by the damage, they must have set about them ferociously. Sailor had some justification for saying that the deportees were all just savages.

Even if each of the escapees had battered his SS opponent singlehandedly, it was hard to believe that their Soviet comrades had simply stood by and watched the attack. There must have been 100 per cent solidarity among the Russians. How else could it be explained that none of the fifty-odd men present had alerted the Nordfeld *Arbeitskapo*, who was less than three hundred yards away? Even more damning, they had left the wounded men lying in their congealing blood for three hours. From there it was only a short step to assume they had helped strip and truss up the luckless Krauts . . .

Hardest of all to understand was why the fifty Russian miners, already so deeply implicated, hadn't gone for a mass escape.

Paulo tried to ignore the comments which his blockmates were exchanging, and attempted in vain to draw a lesson from the affair. Humbly, he admitted to himself that beside these Russians, the escapees and the others, when it came to sheer guts he personally looked very insignificant indeed.

Even in films, you didn't often see escapes as successful as this one seemed to be as the hours ticked by.

But the episode which followed the bloodbath was more like a scene from a Western, right down to the comic interlude designed to relax the spectator. It was the Italian conscript on the *decauville*, the skinflint who only handed out cigarettes on elastic, who was the fall guy. Reckoning it was time for the wagons to be full, he started his engine and reversed slowly toward the first hopper. Paulo would have given anything to see his expression when the three bogus SS leaped onto the footplate of his engine. He probably hadn't realized at first why the man who appeared to be in command was ordering him to drive off in the opposite direction, without coupling up the wagons.

According to the five duty SS, the locomotive had charged out of the southern entrance at top speed with its headlights blazing. Somewhat surprised, they'd been on the point of stopping it when they caught sight of three reassuring uniforms surrounding the driver. Because the train was going so fast, they obviously hadn't seen the two fat revolvers, one at his back and one in his stomach, which sandwiched the flabbergasted wop. What nobody quite knew was whether he had gone freely with his guardian angels when they got to the dump, because he too had vanished. It may have been the fear of reprisal which had dictated his choice, but it was far more likely that his kidnapping had been a part of the Russians' brilliantly executed plan.

The most extraordinary thing about the whole escapade was that between the escape and roll call three hours later, none of the screws had raised the alarm. The *Arbeitskapo*, or any other prowler, might easily have seen the trussed-up SS or heard their groans. That again was proof that after the departure of their comrades, every man of the Russian team must have mounted strict guard to ensure that nothing was discovered before the end of the shift. On the other hand, the slackness of the five Krauts on duty was inexcusable. Why hadn't their suspicions been aroused by the locomotive going off by itself, and by its failure to come back from the dump for another two or three trips, as it usually would at that time of night? They, too, must have been hitting the bottle. And if Herr Kommandant didn't recover the three hit-and-run fugitives with their hostage, the *Posten* in the south would be ripe for the Eastern Front. They could not be forgiven for the negligence which had given the fugitives four hours' head start, ample time to reach the shelter of the partisans.

"They're not going to find them," thought Paulo as more and more time elapsed. "They've done it, they're free. It's incredible!"

What wouldn't he have given to be in the kidnapped Italian's shoes! But like everyone else in the camp, he was so dreading the inevitable punishing they would get the moment Winkler returned that he soon gave up imagining himself as the Italian, dramatically hurling his convict's clothes over the edge of the mountain.

There was someone else whose mind must have been working overtime that night: the escape-mad Belloni. The Russians' bloody escape must have knocked the boy sideways; he must be thinking that getting clear of Loibl was now going to be twice as tough, especially without inside help. The Russkies must have had outside help from the partisans too, otherwise Tito's men would certainly have opened fire on three SS officers appearing from nowhere. And up till now, apart from the three gunshots which had sounded the alarm, not a single shot had been heard in the whole valley.

The intolerable silence outside had penetrated the blocks and no one dared talk now. Each man was selfishly thinking of his own fate when, just before midnight, the muffled sound of marching became audible. They all knew that Winkler and his men were coming back emptyhanded. They hadn't even retrieved the Italian. They were coming back alone and silent, feeling foolish and ashamed, and certainly full of murderous intent. They passed their own quarters without stopping, and marched out onto the *Appelplatz*.

A single, furious shout from the Kommandant himself, *Alle raus!*, shook the blocks into terrified action and within seconds, the entire camp formed itself up faster and more exactly than ever before, the men standing more rigidly to attention than seemed humanly possible, with their buttocks tensed. Just as well, it would hold back the urge to shit, which not a single man in Kommando X was strong enough to resist.

Posted along the length of the *Appelplatz*, Winkler's thirty volunteers had their rifles trained on the front row of convicts, and seemed only to be waiting for the order to empty their magazines. The prisoners' fear was at such a pitch that nine out of ten would have passed out like weak-kneed Home Guards, in order not to have to live through what was to follow. Only that would have made things worse.

"You are all murderers," screamed the Kommandant, his lips flecked with saliva.

It wasn't an order, but it was taken as one by the doyen who, with a barely perceptible nod of his head, indicated to his block chiefs and *Arbeitskapos* that they could set to with a will, as a way of showing exactly whose side they were on, as one way of commiserating with the Kommandant. After all, they were Germans too, like the three SS so summarily dealt with in the tunnel.

The force with which the doyen's henchmen attacked man after man, row after row, with boots and hoses, would clear them of all blame. After such a spontaneous display of German solidarity, the Kommandant would never have the heart to find fault with them in the inquiry which would inevitably follow.

The SS had joined in, slashing through the ranks with their rifle butts, and the violence went on for nearly an hour, almost surpassing in savagery the July corridas. Then Winkler's high-pitched voice screamed again.

"All Russians step forward!"

Frightful to admit, the order was greeted with enormous relief by all those to whom it didn't apply. Their sighs applauded Winkler's decision to at last allocate the blame.

"A Frenchman would never have done such a thing, we're civilized people," the cowardly Ritons and Marcels (who had not escaped the beating) would have liked to assure the Kommandant, as a way of showing their approval of him singling out the chaff from the wheat. Their cowardice, and that of many other fags, greasers and natural ass-lickers, was so abject they couldn't see that these flayed Russian prisoners were giving them a rare lesson in courage. One by one, heads held high, they filed slowly past in front of the convicts, like proud victors stepping up to the platform for their prize.

They knew what kind of a prize it would be, but they looked grandly indifferent to it. Those Slavs were not prisoners like any others, and in the French ranks many lowered their eyes before such bravery.

Their majestic march past must have impressed even the SS, for just as everybody was waiting for the whipping to be concentrated on them, the order was given to leave them alone.

"*Weg Kapos*, stand back," Helmut and Fossil-Face must have said to Fritz and Bullseye, who had both come dangerously close with their hoses.

Since it had been decided to send all the non-Russians back to their blocks, nobody knew what Winkler had in mind, but in the dormitories the men's fear had subsided. If they really were going to shoot ten men for each fugitive, there were more than enough left on the *Appelplatz* for their needs.

Next morning, three hours later that is, they had even more to choose from. All the Russians at Nordfeld had been fetched in the meantime by a heavily armed escort. There were now a hundred and fifty men assembled in front of the kitchens in a tight formation, so that the machine guns in the watchtowers could mow them down in a single burst should they make the slightest movement.

At dawn the Russians were still standing at attention, because the SS and Kapos had taken care to revive those who had collapsed from exhaustion, or fallen asleep. The Russians stood there till the evening, with nothing to eat or drink. They were forbidden to talk too, but that was futile because all they would have said, had they been allowed, was "Death to the Fascists," like Max, the hero of Nordfeld. And they would probably have added, "Long live Russia," in preference to "Long live the Soviets."

Yet among them there were some unlikely patriots whom Sebastopol, the fanatical young militant, had openly insulted more than once. These were the Ukrainians or Mongols whose crime had been to enlist in the collaborationist army of General Vlasov. The Krauts hadn't bothered about such minor details, and had packed them off to Mauthausen for common crimes of theft, rape or murder, and the brigands were now redeeming themselves by rallying to their country's flag at the hardest moment, the moment of death.

For Mauthausen had reclaimed them all. They were to be burned with the maximum of publicity. The telephone had been in almost constant use for twenty-four hours, and the hot-line dialogue between Winkler and his superior was not hard to imagine.

"I am taking the matter out of your hands. Send them back to me immediately," Ziereis must have said. And that was why Winkler was afraid lest his impulsive Kapos went too far with a prisoner or two, and prevented him from delivering the full complement to Ziereis.

The departure of the Russian contingent coincided with evening roll call, as if Winkler wanted to show the remaining men, especially the French and Poles, who were the largest groups, that any subsequent escape would incur not ten deaths for one fugitive, but the deaths of all that man's countrymen at Loibl. Today Winkler introduced the expression "collective sanction" which he asked the *Dolmetscher* to translate into all languages.

"And discipline will be reinforced," he finished.

In columns of five with an SS flanking each row, the Russians marched toward the double gate, which was wide open for the occasion. They left emptyhanded without even a sandwich in the pockets of their miserable rags which, in less than forty-eight hours, the men of Mauthausen's special Kommando would collect from the entrance to the gas chamber.

Unable to hide his emotion, Dédé Ménard had dragged Joel and Paulo toward the kitchens. Before the column of martyrs disappeared, he wanted to salute young Sebastopol, who was so much like him. They were the same age, they were both students, both fanatical patriots, with indomitable nerve and an unfailing readiness to boost the morale of men weaker than themselves.

At the risk of being beaten, because obviously it was forbidden to speak to the "guilty," Dédé stepped forward and yelled over the wall of SS, "Goodbye, Sebastopol! We'll meet again soon. We'll get them!"

The young Russian, who understood French perfectly, turned around and smiled at Ménard, trying to mask his sadness.

"Don't worry, Dédé," he managed to shout back. "I shall die, I know, but it's worth it. Three of us have taken up the fight again—"

A gun butt in his back couldn't stop him. His voice rose above the yells of the SS who were beating him.

". . . We're no use anymore, a hundred and fifty for three isn't too high a price, it's better that way. Long live the Soviets!"

He had said too much, and a hose landed savagely across his mouth. It was Otto's, Otto the homosexual murderer with the black triangle. He wanted to make one last spiteful gesture of revenge on the boy with the beautiful face who had dared reject his vile advances. Had it been allowed, Otto would have pursued the swaggering young communist right to the door of the crematorium. But he could only hurl abuse from behind the closed gates. By the time he had turned around, still boiling with rage, Dédé, with Joel and Paulo, had disappeared and there was no one left on the *Appelplatz* for him to hit.

The following day Mauthausen informed Winkler that no more Russians would be sent to Loibl. It was not a good idea to have men like that working too near the border . . . and the partisans. It was much better not to have them work at all, but to keep them safely locked up in fortresses within the Reich, from which there was no escape. And if they were short of space, it was a simple matter to gas them, in order of seniority.

The Krauts at Loibl wished to hear nothing more about the bastard Russians, either escaped or burned. Before long, and prudently, they called off the mountain search party, and even the official confirmation of the hundred and fifty "repatriated men" having gone up in smoke as soon as they arrived gave them very little satisfaction. For them, the case was closed; now they could resume their quiet and easy life.

But the prisoners couldn't forget quite so quickly. They needed to talk about the escape, if only to congratulate each other for having gotten off so lightly.

"That was a close shave," they all agreed. But there the agreement ended, and the heated discussions in the camp began to reveal the true political colors of the prisoners. The picture had changed drastically from what it had been on their arrival at Mauthausen. Broadly speaking, they were now divided into two camps: on one side, nearly all the young men, whether from the Resistance or not, wholeheartedly approved of the bloody methods used by the Russians, while the older, more responsible men, of thirty or over, condemned them just as vehemently.

"After what's happened, we shouldn't even consider escape. It's the excuse the SS are waiting for to exterminate every last man here. Anyone who tries to run for it is a criminal."

"You miserable coward, you sound just like Pétain . . ."

To prevent the verbal abuse from turning into physical violence, the nameless men of the Front National had had to show themselves sooner than they'd expected. There was more than chuff at stake this time: this was politics. And politics was their business.

"Calm down, comrades . . . We must stick together."

Their interference came at a bad time, because even among their own members discord was rife. Depending on how old they were, both militants and sympathizers had opposing views on the justice of their Soviet brothers' escape. The Party ran the risk of losing its credibility.

Paulo was stirred by the way the controversy was developing. Without a moment's hesitation, he had aligned himself on the side of the young men, backing up Joel, Dédé, and of course Angel too, every time they clashed with the old sobersides. One day, he had even called an army officer squatting on the crapper an old piss-house queer when the man repeated for the tenth time to the other squatters that he would rather be killed on the spot than escape and feel responsible for the death of a single Frenchman.

The passion with which Paulo defended the Russians wasn't just to impress his three friends. His admiration was genuine and it made itself felt in his words.

"Shut your mouth. Men like that aren't to be judged."

Their cold-bloodedness, their toughness and most of all their success had impressed him enormously. He had often, especially since Mauthausen, looked for an exact definition of what the underworld phrase, "being a man," meant. The Russians had given him that definition. He had never met "men" like that before.

Nonetheless, his determination to stand apart from the others didn't trouble his conscience in the slightest. He didn't consider it at all cowardly, or even selfish; it was simply the most intelligent thing to do. What a pity his hot-headed young friends were too busy proclaiming their allegiances to listen to him. Yet it was absolutely vital now for Dédé and Joel to lie low. Otherwise, the investigation which was already underway might in the process uncover Dédé's radio set and Joel's role in the underground organization. As for Angel, his determination to escape was so plainly written all over his face that from one moment to the next, Paulo expected to see him shoot off from the concrete mixer and sprint up the mountainside. These three were hardly the companions to choose for a quiet life.

But Paulo was too fond of the trio to avoid them as well as the others, and he continued taking their side in their quarrels with the older men. But he swore that as soon as the excitement died down, he would bring them back to earth, one by one.

In any case, even if it had been fear which induced him to cool their ardor, events would soon prove him right. Contrary to Winkler's threats, two days after the escape discipline seemed to have been relaxed, as if all the hatred of the SS had been spent the moment they'd learned that the entire Russian contingent had been grilled. They hadn't exactly become friendly, but they weren't far short, and the *Dreckmann, Scheisskubel, Schweine,* no longer automatically accompanied their orders. *Franzosen,* was all the Germans said, without tacking on the usual curses. They had obviously received orders not to abuse unnecessarily the good workers who were going to finish their splendid project at Loibl without complaining. And the most valuable and indispensable workers were the French. Their numbers and their seniority made them suitable instructors for the replacement work force which Mauthausen was to despatch without delay. All the more reason not to call them every name under the sun.

The Germans' unexpected reaction put a swift end to all the arguments raised by the escape. As if by magic no more was heard from the men who had uncompromisingly defended it. And the communist leaders, who were beginning to fret about the responsibilities which would fall on their shoulders now that all the political commissars of the sister party had disappeared wholesale, didn't take long to realize that a week after the escape, nobody was in the mood to listen to any lessons which might be learned from it.

Hadn't even the Krauts shut the door on it? Given their reaction, it would have been madness to stir them up again by playing conspirators.

Prudently, the party leaders swallowed their words of wisdom, and disappeared into the shadows as quickly as they had emerged. But they were greatly distressed by the indifference of virtually the whole camp to the announcement, a few days later, of the death of their old comrade Etcheverry.

XX

Ramsauer had killed him with his syringe after muster one evening. Everyone was in bed and they only heard the next day when they came back from work. They hadn't seen any black smoke rising above the larch wood for some time now, and it had intrigued them.

"Who's burning?" asked someone in the ranks.

"It's the old man from the north, the Basque."

No one made any comment. They had all expected it, and the sad news did not halt the usual scuffle around the coffee urns. There weren't many that evening who bothered to wonder what the old fighter must have thought or said when the sadistic doctor approached with his shot of benzol. The deed had been done on the quiet after dark, therefore Etcheverry must still have been conscious during the day. And no one wondered whether he had seen his killer coming, or whether he'd had the strength to curse him and all his race before the needle sank like a dagger into his heart. Back in the blocks, they found other things to talk about.

Although Paulo had known better than anyone else that the old man would soon die, he felt a lump in his throat when he heard it was all over. To conceal his feelings from the others, he went quickly out of the block and headed for the *Revier.* Not to hear how Etcheverry had spent his last few hours, it was too late for that, nor to hear exactly how Ramsauer had operated. No, he felt he needed to revisit the cursed place to which he'd half carried the old man when they came back from the north less than three weeks ago. Lost in his thoughts, he didn't notice Joel among a small group of men coming out of the *Revier* with their caps in their hands.

"Come with us," Joel called to him, breaking into his meditation.

The others had already disappeared and Paulo realized that he had just seen together, for the first time, the communist leaders of the south camp.

"Are your friends scared of me?" He spoke mechanically.

He stopped as he noticed Joel's distress. The tough little Breton was badly shaken and he, too, was irritated that it showed. But he still needed to talk about his dead friend, with one of the few people who had known him a bit better than most.

"Tell me, Paulo, you spent six months with him in the north. When did he start going downhill? Was he in much pain? Did he get hit around a lot?"

"No, it wasn't that, he just got gradually weaker, he didn't even notice. He was worn out, too old for this lark, and he knew it. He just died of old age really."

"I suppose so, but I feel bad about not talking to him since he came back. He was too far gone, and I didn't want to tire him."

"You did the right thing. Remember, you saw him every evening, and he saw you too, which is why he held on for another three weeks, I'm sure," Paulo said, for the sake of saying something.

Joel had taken hold of himself again. After all, the death of his comrade in arms strengthened his own resolve. His expression hardened.

"Another thing to make the SS murderers pay for," he swore.

Paulo was tempted to tell him that making them pay for it was the last thing he had heard Etcheverry say, as he clung to his arm in the tunnel. It was pure chance that Paulo had been the one to hear him, and he should have told Joel; but it would only have aggravated the Breton's angry passion.

"Look at that smoke, Paulo, just smell it. The bastards! They'll pay a lot for that. Christ, his kind are rare! All his life he fought for freedom. Three years in Spain, twice wounded and barely out of the hospital before he was slung into jail in France. Thanks to Daladier, who handed him over to Pétain. And then? Clairvaux, Compiègne, Mauthausen, to end up here, put down like a crippled old dog. After eight years of fighting and suffering. The bastards, the bloody bastards!"

Paulo knew the man's history by heart, Etcheverry had actively chosen the lonely life of a revolutionary, and so he couldn't share Joel's anger. He had been more struck by the old man's resignation when almost every day he was on the receiving end of a Kapo's fist or the *fünf und zwanzig*. He had never heard him complain, still less curse his persecutors as Joel was now doing. He had kept his protest to himself. Had he seen the war won, it might have exploded then, but who could tell?

His lifelong acceptance of suffering told them he would not have wanted to be wept over. His death at Loibl, amid general indifference, was the death he would have wished for.

Paulo went back to Block 3 with Joel, passing here and there a few groups of shaven men who were talking about everything except the man being burned. "What the hell?" he thought. "These guys are heartless anyway. One of us dies, and they care less about that then getting no potatoes in their soup."

He couldn't say that to Joel either. It was better to keep his depressing thoughts to himself.

"All right, Joel, I'm exhausted, I'm going to hit the sack."

A few moments later, ensconced in his sagging bed, Paulo went over things again.

"The whole Russian incident's a blessing in disguise. The hotheads who want to escape will shut up now. They're not so blind they can't see Winkler's had orders to go easy on us."

This was confirmed by Herr Kommandant the following evening after roll call.

"*Haeftlinge!*" he yelled in his ridiculous voice. "The Russian vermin have been eliminated. I count on you to finish the tunnel which most of you started. The work will take a few more months. And don't forget that in doing this work, you are defending civilization, which is under attack by the barbarians and their Jewish-American allies. Saboteurs will be shot as a matter of course, and good workers will be rewarded."

Rewarded? That wasn't the way the idiot usually talked. What was behind it? The explanation was translated into French and Polish by Sailor's personal *Dolmetscher*.

"There are more detainees on their way to take the place of the Soviet murderers, and this time, I have decided to promote the best French and Polish workers to Kapo. I have asked the *Blocführer* to nominate them, and I hope that those who will wear the Mauthausen insignia on their jackets will do it honor."

Winkler had put on an expression of benevolence as he announced the good news. The hypocritical bastard smiled. For a brief second his civilian face had shown through. He looked just like the harmless fool of a gardener he was rumored to have been before applying for a job with the SS. His speech could only be welcomed by the men he had not so long ago threatened with a "collective sanction." So, appointing the French as Kapos instead gave them good reason to be relieved. And even to smile back at the big sheep in wolf's clothing.

Only when the replacement work force arrived would the promotion ceremony take place. It wasn't long in coming: the new men were delivered two days after Winkler's pretty speech. There were a few less than the deceased Russians, a hundred at the very most, but their appearance was a surprise. They were smiling, and their regulation striped pajamas looked more like fancy dress than a uniform on them. It was as if they had escaped the quarantine and only made a flying visit to Mauthausen, just long enough for a change of clothes and a top and tail shave. A quick dab of crab powder on their asses and under their arms, and straight off to work. These men, with registrations of ninety thousand and above, didn't know how lucky they were that Loibl needed manpower. Otherwise, a lot of them would have made their exit from Mauthausen via the chimney. Nine out of ten, in fact; the standard drop-out rate.

It was a boost to have men so unmarked by Mauthausen: for productivity, for the tunnel's future and especially for morale. They were still so close to civilian life and the liberty they had only recently lost. They would have reliable news about the war, and about France too, because another good thing was that they were mostly French. Mauthausen had finally begun to acknowledge the qualities of the French.

Just for fun, Paulo tried to spot a familiar face among these alert-looking latecomers. He was wasting his time; they were all railway workers, saboteurs, Resistance men and the like . . . Nobody of his kind.

"Joel will enjoy having these diehards around for his showdown," Paulo thought anxiously.

He didn't need to worry: the raw recruits were fully aware of what they had just escaped, and this sunny mountain outpost was greatly to their liking. Would they want to begin the war again here? No thanks, they had just left it behind. Unlike Joel, who was restless after his three years of inactivity in prison, they desperately wanted to forget. His demands for revenge would fall flat with these optimists.

"What beautiful scenery! What wonderful air!" exclaimed a very small youngster to everyone he saw, as he inhaled great lungfuls of mountain air.

The kid was right, Loibl was beautiful, but you had to be a recent arrival like him to appreciate it. The long servers, numbers 26, 27 and 28 thousand, had been knocked about so badly since their arrival that they couldn't stand the sight of the beautiful countryside, and found fault with it in every possible way. The ungrateful wretches wouldn't even concede that it was precisely the "wonderful air" to which they all owed their lives. Well, almost all of them . . .

The young boy's rapture was a bit overdone all the same. Paulo wanted to know the reason for it.

"Listen, little man, are you kidding? Don't you like this place? Are you trying to make monkeys of us?"

"Not at all, I really mean it. I think this place is beautiful. Purple peaks and bottle-green trees against a sky bluer than the Mediterranean . . . It's like a real painting, I've never seen anything like it. And this air's so pure, can't you smell it? You're all too used to it, you can't see how beautiful it is anymore."

The kid sounded so serious about his praise of the place that Paulo automatically scanned the panorama in astonishment. He found himself breathing deeply too, and fell right into the other's mood. Feeling rather silly, he remarked casually, "Better for you to take it like that, kid. Take your deep breaths, clean your lungs out before they get filled up with tunnel dust."

"Why? Does everyone work in the tunnel?"

"No, they don't. There is work outside. I work in the open, for example, on the concrete mixer . . ."

"Room for another one?"

"We'll see what we can arrange."

Paulo was bluffing. He wasn't a Kapo yet, and he couldn't decide who went where; but the boy seemed only too happy to have stumbled upon an important guy the first thing. Thinking his future was all sorted out, he was already introducing himself.

"My name's Jacques, Jacques Lepreux. From Savoy, Chamonix, to be precise. I was in the Resistance and taken prisoner less than two months ago. I ought to have been shot like my friends. I don't know why, but by some miracle I survived, the only one in my group. Now do you understand why I'm so happy to be here? I'm still alive. And I feel at home in the mountains too."

"I suppose," Paulo thought, listening to the boy's accounts of his battles as if the war was over, "I suppose he's right, and that's how you should look at things. He's done his time, he's a veteran, already demobed. He talks sense, I'll introduce him to Joel. Maybe he'll make that bloodthirsty fighter have second thoughts."

"By the way, how old are you?"

"Eighteen last month," Lepreux replied proudly.

Eighteen! Paulo suddenly felt terribly old next to this boy six years his junior. Life had already been hard on him, but it had left no scars on his fresh young face. His youthful enthusiasm was a breath of fresh air as pure as the alpine air, with which he carried on avidly filling his lungs.

Paulo definitely felt happier in the company of younger men, but like him, the ones at Loibl had aged enormously over the past months despite the air and the beauty of the place. Caught up in the crowd of older men, their youth had deserted them, leaving them bad-tempered and querulous.

"How many young guys are in your lot?" he asked, pursuing his train of thought.

"You mean the French? We're all young, and it's the same with the Yugos and the Poles. They were all with partisan groups too. For that kind of work, twenty is a good age. True?"

"True," agreed Paulo. "It's a good thing your group came along. It'll liven things up. It's a bit gloomy around here, you'll see. 'Bye for now, Jacques, I'm off. See you tomorrow. You won't have any problem finding me again, even if we're all dressed alike."

He wanted to see all these unembittered newcomers. Before the old grumblers got around to mocking their optimism, he wanted to point out to all of them that it was the chance of a lifetime to be sent to this nice little camp, and that they should make the most of it, instead of whining like the old dimwits, or wanting to escape like Angel. After what they'd just been through, their best bet was to treat Loibl as a joke.

In less than two days, he had met almost all of them. The young Savoyard had told the truth: the Frenchmen were all young, picked up in the country or trapped in city dragnets. Not one of the boys rounded up protested his innocence, and there wasn't a single criminal among them. You'd think that France was entirely made up of out-and-out Resistance members. Attitudes back home seemed to have changed a hell of a lot. Yet another sign, if one were needed, that the end was near.

The young maquis didn't all jump for joy like Jacques Lepreux, but none of them seemed worried about being there. "Not much longer... a matter of weeks...," they shrugged. Not because their experience in the mountains made it seem like child's play to break out of this camp 3900 feet high; the idea of escape didn't even cross their minds. No, "a matter of weeks" referred to how much longer the war would last.

Paulo was delighted. "Great! Let these babies keep their illusions! Let's hope their enthusiasm's catching, and their faith comes over loud and clear. There are too many of the old-timers walking around with faces as long as fiddles."

The Poles in the new shipment may have been just as optimistic as Lepreux, but it didn't show in their faces. If they had good news from the Eastern Front, they didn't give the impression of wanting to publicize it.

Paulo immediately realized he wouldn't get anything out of them. "They don't come more suspicious than the Polacks. They're po'-faced from birth, they always think they're being had, whether it's chuff, the job or anything... Of course, they've got some excuse with neighbors like theirs—the Reds and Krauts have been stabbing them in the back for centuries."

Happily, there were only a couple of dozen of these Polish savages, half as many as there were Yugoslavs. And the latter were lively characters who didn't whimper about their fate. They found it very amusing that the Krauts at Mauthausen had been stupid enough to send them back to their own country (most were from Slovenia), only a few hundred yards away from their partisan brothers.

One of these Slavs was called Tito. Paulo didn't know what the real Tito looked like, but this one didn't look at all like a fighter. He was more like a clown with his permanent grin and Perrier-bottle shoulders. He was a very strange shape altogether, and it made you wonder how he could possibly have shouldered his sniper's rifle before his capture. For, of course, he too had been in the Yugoslav maquis, but the thing about this young fellow, apart from his unfailing smile and his affability, was that he spoke fluent French. Being an arts student, the boy was delighted to have ended up in a camp where French was, to all intents and purposes, the main language. He certainly hadn't expected such an opportunity when, barely two months ago, he'd found himself packed off to the Reich. For him, Loibl was going to be a sort of summer school.

He hadn't stopped talking for one minute since he arrived, quizzing all the Frenchmen in the south one after the other, and getting them to spell words whose meaning he hadn't quite grasped. If he continued, at this rate the student would end up speaking a very odd sort of French. He'd get a degree in French slang when he got out, probably with first-class honors. The men all tried to outdo each other to explain to him that chuff meant food, and so on.

The poor fellow had to learn everything all over again, but it only seemed to make him more cheerful. He never stopped laughing, and within twenty-four hours his infectious chuckle had changed the whole atmosphere of the camp.

They could have done with dozens more like him, but although his friends were less extroverted, they were almost as good-natured as he was. Another student had caught Paulo's eye. He was quite the reverse of his comrade. He was very good-looking, built like an athlete, and as reserved as his compatriot was voluble. In fact he looked a bit like Paulo and they were naturally drawn to each other. They managed to communicate in a Franco-German dialect.

"*Mein name ist Karavic, Alexandre*. I'm a Serb from Belgrade. And you?"

"Chastagnier, from Paris. Everybody calls me Paulo. Are you a student too?"

"*Ja*, in medicine . . . and you? Your profession?"

"Oh, I, er . . ." Paulo stopped short, to avoid having to lie. If he'd said he was a crook, the medical student would have been shocked. He didn't want that, the fellow looked like a nice guy.

"And what about your pal who jabbers away in French, what's his name? Isn't it Tito? Or is that a piss-take?"

Pal . . . jabber . . . piss-take . . . ? The Serb dried up completely.

"*Nicht vorsten*," he said. "*You speak English?*"

"*A little*," Paulo answered automatically. And then he burst into a peal of laughter.

The situation struck him as hilarious: here they were, two convicts in rags, using the language of Shakespeare to get to know each other. They'd certainly catch it if there was a Kapo within earshot, but the Yugoslav didn't seem to give a damn.

"*I have not understand that you say*," he went on.

"*Your friend . . . what is his name? Tito?*" repeated Paulo, who was worried that his English was more Pigalle than Berlitz.

"*No, it's a surname, a name of war. His true name is Ugrin and his forename Grgo. In French, Guergo*."

"Oh, right."

Paulo was feeling a little out of his depth. He cut short the conversation with a passable "*See you later*," and went off to join the group clustered around the boy called Guergo.

A French lesson was in full swing, and it was the crooked Angel Belloni who was playing teacher.

"Queer, prick, nuts, pussy, fucker . . ." The whole catalogue of four-letter words came out, and each new one provoked gales of laughter. All these youngsters, French as well as Yugoslavs, seemed to have completely forgotten they were in a prison.

One thing was certain: Angel was not thinking about escaping at the moment. He had just caught sight of Paulo.

"Move over, you guys," he ordered. "Let Professor Chastagnier through. He'll teach you some more words. Paulo, tell them how you say *Abort* in French."

Paulo could do little else but join in the game.

"There are quite a few ways: crappers, bogs, shithouse . . ."

The laughter got even louder, especially from the Yugos,

who were just beginning to understand that they weren't picking up a very academic French. But that only seemed to amuse them the more. Anyway, it was easier for the Slavs to say "bog" than "lavatory" or "toilets"!

Paulo listened to them trying out each of the words in turn and was giving them marks out of ten, when suddenly he stopped short at the face of the boy opposite him. What an incredible face! It was unbelievable, only a girl should have eyes like that! Enormous green eyes with infinitely long eyelashes, an artist's dream. And everything else was just as good: eyebrows that looked as if he plucked them, a slightly turned-up nose, full red lips, and a mouth made for kissing. And it was worse still when he laughed, showing all his sparkling white and perfectly even teeth. It was enough to turn your head! The boy's parents had blessed him with a movie star's face.

Paulo couldn't get over it. He stopped playing teacher, and just stared. He wasn't going to try and pick him up? No, but it had given him quite a shock to see a girl's face in his coarse world. And what made it more ambiguous still was that the boy, who was obviously used to having this effect on people, began to look at Paulo provocatively, stealing sidelong glances at him from beneath his long, feminine eyelashes.

Paulo eventually came to his senses. He was not suddenly going to turn into a queer. Although it had never been considered dishonorable in prison for a highly-sexed man... To regain his self-possession, he said to Belloni, who had also noticed the beautiful boy:

"You seen his eyes, Angel? It's unbelievable! What a dame! The Mauthausen doctors couldn't have made a mistake, could they? They must have stripped it before sending it here? I can't believe it!"

"Yeah, I noticed, you'd think his eyes were made up and that he was wearing lipstick... The Kapos'll be falling over each other to get him into bed. Fortunately, he's a big boy and they don't like that. It makes them go limp."

"Yeah, you're right. They're real queers, that boy looks too much like a girl," agreed Paulo, telling himself that his recent emotion was quite normal in the circumstances.

Good-looking or not, the Yugoslavs were interesting and not just because of their cheerfulness and their youth. The most positive thing was that Loibl was in Yugoslavia, and Paulo and his friends were well inside these boys' own country. They would at last find out what exactly was going on, and what mischief their partisan friends had up their sleeves. The prisoners had never seen these famous partisans, but judging by the increasing anxiety of Winkler and his isolated garrison of troops, you could tell that they were out there, watching. It had been of the utmost importance to the long-serving prisoners to get some decent information on the question, but it was perhaps less important than the fact that there were now fifty Yugoslavs in the camp.

"That kind of information's bound to leak out pretty quickly around here," Paulo reckoned. "And the partisans won't sit back and watch if the SS start knocking the Yugos about too much. Another plus. It's obvious the Krauts are scared, they won't be keen to brush with Tito's men. They've been told to build the tunnel, not to chase *Banditen*."

This time he'd got back his morale for good. The troublemakers, problems, his conscience, and even the memory of past sufferings could all go to hell. From now on, he was going to see Loibl through the eyes of the newcomers, joking like them, breathing in the "wonderful" air and even singing. Why not? To the amazement of everybody, that was precisely what one of them was now doing.

"You don't sing on the *Appelplatz*! The boy's mad, he's off his head!" said the old-timers, certain that a Kapo's hose would soon shut him up.

They were mistaken. They had missed the whole point of the Herr Kommandant's little speech. They simply couldn't take in the fact that the Loibl summer had brought real changes. Was it really possible that the Krauts no longer wanted to do them in, that they only wanted them to work? It was indeed hard to understand. And if they wanted to sing while they worked, so much the better. *Kraft durch Freude*, the happy worker is a good worker, was a maxim that even Putz, the chief engineer, would never dare to adopt. Instead of running away from the singer, the men should have taken up the chorus, so that their massed voices echoed joyfully across the valley and back to the Kommandant's quarters, as a gesture of thanks for his friendly words, and his gracious pardon.

Sailor had just stuck his bullet head out of the block window. He was one step ahead of them, he had been quick to adapt to the new situation.

"*Bravo, eine andere, Mensch!*" he cried, applauding noisily, followed by his Luxembourg boy friend.

"*Danke schön, chef, danke,*" replied the singer, bowing like an old music-hall ham.

"You Spanish?"

"*Jawohl, chef. Voy a cantar 'Adios muchachos.' Te gusta?*"

This time, since Sailor had given it his blessing, there was no reason to hang back: the whole block, old and new alike, gathered around the dago. Those who knew the words couldn't help joining in the chorus.

Adios muchachos
Compañeros de mi vida . . .

How extraordinary that these jailbirds were sitting around like gypsies humming an old-fashioned tango tune on the *Appelplatz* which, less than a week ago, they had crossed in fear of their lives.

Gradually they shed their fear and the quiet humming swelled to a full-throated choir. Shivers ran up and down the veterans' spines as they heard themselves singing without either the Kapos or the SS in the watchtowers screaming at them to shut up. The Argentinian tango became their "Marseillaise," and they chanted it louder and louder like a revolutionary anthem, hoping that it might be heard beyond the peaks of their gigantic prison.

Sailor didn't understand the reasons behind their fervor, but he was just as carried away. "Adios muchachos" reminded him of his early days at Mauthausen when the citadel was run by the Spaniards. What wonderful evenings he'd be able to organize in his block with a singer like that, and how green his colleagues would be!

"Come inside," he said to the Spaniard. "Can you play the guitar?"

"*Jawohl, chef.*"

"Tomorrow, you'll have one, Karl's word on it."

And by the following day cunning Sailor had managed to dig one out from the civilian camp. There was no problem about payment: he had used the miners' drippings. "*Organ-*

iziert," he explained. Incongruously, *organiziert* meant stolen, implying stolen from the enemy.

And now every evening in Block 3 there was a fiesta. After muster, the block chiefs and their boy friends showed up from all over the camp with contributions of margarine, sausage, schnaps and cigarettes. Karl's block became a regular nightclub, for members only. Men whose faces he took exception to were kicked into the dormitory, leaving only those clever fellows who could sing, dance or do conjuring tricks.

Karl's shindigs were not much appreciated in the *Schlafstube*. It was impossible to sleep with the revelers taking up the chorus of every song; and even worse were the smells of potatoes, grilled sausages, alcohol and tobacco which hung in the air.

Paulo was an honorary member of the club. Karl wanted to shine in the eyes of his block-chief friends and he insisted on Paulo being there, to show he had good contacts.

"*Er ist ein* pimp," he confided to Sladek and Eddy. "He has a nightclub in Paris, we're going to go into partnership and we'll take on the Spaniard."

Paulo let him talk. He didn't give a shit about music or the Spaniard. The important thing was to fill his face, and on that score, things were going pretty well. He even had too much, but his full stomach didn't stop him from grabbing the sandwiches which the fags stuck in front of him, like hostesses at a formal cocktail party, and stuffing them into his jacket pockets. "One for Dédé, one for Joel," he thought every time he got hold of another.

Every evening the show ended with a song which everyone got to know very quickly by hearing it so often. "El Tatuado" was the name of this hit. At the end of his recital, the Spaniard would call for silence and then announce in solemn tones: "Now, as a tribute to our host, I shall sing you '*El Tatuado*.'"

The words were stirring. They told the story of a tatooed sailor, arrogant, proud and blond as honey, who was being looked for by his abandoned wench in the bars of ports all over the world:

Escuchame marinero
Y dime que sabes de El

Era arrogante y altanero
Era mas rubio que la miel . . .

The chorus, *Mira mi brazo tatuado*, sent the queer into raptures and he would strip to the waist to show that El Tatuado was himself.

As Paulo too joined in with the ballad of El Tatuado, it crossed his mind that the dago crooner might have invented this hymn to Sailor to ensure that he lined his stomach until Armistice Day. But that wasn't what made him burst out laughing when Sailor stripped. As he puffed out his chest to show off his galley in full sail and his big-breasted tarts in suspender belts, it reminded Paulo of Angel's comment the first time he had seen Karl strip off. "What a lampshade that queer would have made at Mauthausen!"

The evening sing-songs in Block 3 may have lacked romance, but they sparked off an impulse to sing all over the camp. The men who hummed their favorite sentimental songs on the work sites, in the tunnel, in the refectory, in the crappers or anywhere else were no longer taken for idiots. For men still in this living hell, singing was the first real sign of their hope for the future.

And so the nomination of French Kapos, which at one time would have been greeted with scorn or in Pozzi's case with thinly veiled threats, was treated as a joke in this new atmosphere. There was plenty to laugh at in the list of promotions: Riton, the pimp in Block 2, Bullseye's boy friend Maumau; Daniel the orderly, the banker-translator, Marcel the truck driver and a few other sharp fellows who had some knowledge of German. The new chiefs nonetheless looked awkward wearing their single chevron, which was identical to that of a Wehrmacht corporal. On the other hand, everyone agreed it was difficult to refuse. "It's better to have Frenchmen rather than Polacks or any of those other savages from Central Europe . . . We're digging ourselves in a bit more . . . We're becoming indispensable . . ." were the kind of excuses which helped them swallow these promotions.

Paulo didn't see things in quite that light. The stripe which Sailor had tried to put his name forward for would, he had said, have been like someone spitting in his face. In fact, what he was most afraid of was that afterward he would be faced with the contempt of the communists: "Your stripe is a mark of shame. It proves that you betrayed us and collaborated with the Germans," was the sort of accusation they would throw at him the day the war ended. He had no illusions about their present tolerance. The Ritons, Maumaus and Pozzis with their little black ribbons would be wise to watch out... Paulo was very lucky that the doyen had a Polish protégé whom he wanted to reward and so had refused Sailor's nomination.

"Otto has promised me you'll be in the next batch. You're at the top of the list," Karl said consolingly.

There was only one thing left for him to do, if he wanted to stay unpromoted: drag even more.

"The concrete mixer isn't a responsible job, I'd better hang on to it till my time's up," he decided.

For the moment, luckily, nobody thought of watching him to see whether he had any gifts of leadership, for during the days following the swearing-in of the new Kapos, the camp was in a state of great upheaval. Men coming back from Nordfeld, others going to take their places, SS being sent back to Mauthausen, new SS arriving, it made the camp look like a mainline station in rush hour. Herr Kommandant seemed to have gone completely off the rails. Except for the poor beggars transferred to Nordfeld, his administrative decisions didn't affect the prisoners much. At least until the day they heard that Ramsauer was also on the way out. And not of his own free will. Under orders like a common *Haeftling*!

The news was too good to be true. Everyone wanted to know why Mauthausen was reclaiming the murderer with the syringe. The details were not slow to follow since literally everybody, even the civilians, could talk of nothing else.

His fault had been his failure to understand why he had been attached to Loibl Pass. His brief had been to heal the workers, not to kill them. The men had been handpicked at Mauthausen to be kept alive, and he had no business to interfere. Winkler had given him several warnings, but it was to no avail. His psychopathic nature blinded him, he couldn't control himself and he went on injecting, conducting autopsies and sending men up in smoke. Moreover, when it came to tending the sick, he was useless. He made even the SS nervous. Winkler had been swamped by unfavorable reports.

"What really tipped the scales," Daniel, newly appointed Kapo, informed them, "was last week's case of appendicitis."

The new *Sanitatskapo*'s description of the operation may have been slightly exaggerated, but given Ramsauer's ignorance, there was certainly a good deal of truth in it. If it hadn't been for Jaryk, the Czech doctor, who stopped him just in time, the madman would have opened up the patient's left side, "the wrong side of the road," as Daniel had said, doubling up with laughter. Ramsauer was furious and he sent Jaryk out of the operating room to show that he was quite capable of conducting the operation on his own. The butchery had lasted for four hours, as Ramsauer kept leaving his patient to refer to a big surgical manual, open at the right page, as luck would have it, to find out precisely where the appendix was, what exactly he had to cut, how to sew it up again, and so forth. The patient, a twenty-five-year-old man from Périgord, had woken up at least three times, but seeing the vampire poking around in his stomach, he'd thought he'd better go back to sleep again. It was a miracle that Ramsauer didn't finish him off with a saw, as he had the Italian, but the story of his deplorable performance had nevertheless gone beyond the four walls of the *Revier*, and Herr Kommandant instantly seized the opportunity to dismiss him.

"You see, your friend Etcheverry has already been avenged," Paulo pointed out to Joel as soon as Ramsauer's recall was official.

"The bastard's not going to get away with it like that! Even if he's kicked out of the SS, it would be too easy! We'll find him someday, I swear we'll find him. We'll try him and hang him for the murderer he is. I promise you."

"I reckon you'll have your work cut out. They won't let him just walk away. You'll have to get him out of a loony bin . . . unless they use the syringe on him . . . that'd be a laugh! Just a minute, his bitch of a wife, that Frau Martha, will be going with him! I've got a score to settle with her. I'd lay that riding crop across her pink Aryan ass. You're right, we've got to deal with them. I know what I'd do with that slut. I'd stick her in a brothel, a brothel for niggers!"

The doctor who came to replace Ramsauer was unlikely to undermine the men's optimism. He looked like a real doctor, one of the new generation: he was athletic, tanned, smiling, sure of himself and his profession and bursting with health. He doubtless found himself in an SS corps because there was little opportunity elsewhere. You could see that he wasn't very happy about it, and that he must have been conscripted. He turned up for assembly the first evening sporting a fancy Tyrolean hat to make his independence clear. That day he had wanted to give everyone a thorough examination. Not on the *Appelplatz* as had been the case previously, but one by one in his surgery, like a real doctor.

"Are you in good health?" he asked each man in turn.

What a strange question. What were they supposed to say? Caution dictated that they say yes. They had learned the lesson at Mauthausen and it had saved many of the TB and syphilis cases. But this fellow didn't look the type to persecute sick men . . .

When it was Paulo's turn to strip naked, he felt at a loss. He racked his brains but he couldn't think of anything the matter, no aches and pains at all. His liver was functioning twice as well, which was only to be expected, and his lungs were working like forge bellows. He had never felt better. He was a little on the thin side, of course, but that deficiency didn't need pills to cure it.

"I'm in terrific shape, Doctor," he said with a smile.

"Good, keep on like that. Next man."

The next in line was Joel, looking as glum as ever. "There's nothing the matter with me."

"Turn around," the doctor said to him. "And again. Now let's look at your profile."

"What's the problem?" Paulo wondered, taking his time putting his clothes back on. He was beginning to get worried about his friend. Needlessly as it happened, because the cultured young doctor only wanted to admire Joel's anatomy. Granted, the ex-gym teacher had a good body. But all the same, unless he was queer, the doctor was going a bit far with all the fuss he was making, walking around Joel, measuring him in spans of his hand, making him bend his knees and stretch his arms, and then standing back to study him.

"Look, Dr. Jaryk," he said to his colleague. "Here you have the perfect example of the Greek ideal of beauty. This man is the exact double of the Apollo of Tiber. Less well covered of course, but the proportions are there, almost to the inch. Take a look at his bone structure . . . and look at his muscles . . . trapezius, deltoids, obliques, buttocks . . . it's incredible!"

Joel didn't know where to put himself. He was blushing like a young girl who can sense a man eyeing her; he stood rooted to the spot, not daring to get dressed.

"Psst, Apollo, are you coming?" said Paulo with a grin to save him from further embarrassment.

"You're just jealous!"

Joel was smiling for the first time in months. It was always nice to get a compliment, but what had really made the patriot's day was that the praise for a product of an inferior race had come from a Kraut, one in an SS uniform to boot.

"You see," he told Paulo, when they had left the *Revier*, "it all goes to show that construction work is as good as any other way of keeping fit. It's the ideal exercise for keeping yourself in shape. If I get out of here, I'm going to have to rethink my teaching methods. Of course, I haven't got an ounce of spare fat on me, and it makes all the muscles stand out better."

"Don't be so bloody modest. Stop making excuses for yourself. We all know you're the best specimen Loibl's got . . . But you can count yourself lucky that Ramsauer didn't notice, otherwise he would have pickled you and stuck you on a pedestal in his museum with a label saying: 'Aryan found in Brittany.'"

"It's all right to laugh now, we can afford to, because a doctor like him here means fewer men dead. That's the most important thing to remember. I reckon he'd even try to set a broken leg."

A broken leg! Paulo had quite forgotten that in this scrummage you could get your leg broken from one moment to the next. But when you worked on a cushy site like the concrete mixer, the risks were minimal.

"I'd better stick there," he said to himself, "and the only way to do it is to butter up Marcel, and not pull the fat idiot's leg about his stripe."

The day after the driver's promotion, Paulo said to him, "It's not really the thing to congratulate you, but I'm genuinely pleased. You're not a slave driver like that creep Pozzi."

"I'm glad you see it like that, Paulo. I didn't grovel for it, but I've never been afraid of hard work."

"Yeah, you're no bum. But you're a big boy and you

need your grub. Now that you're a Kapo, you'll be in for extra rations."

"Really?"

As if the greedy fucker didn't know he was going to get double rations from now on! He immediately suspected that Paulo had steered the conversation around to supplementary rations deliberately. Perhaps he thought he was going to twist his arm for half a bowl of soup a day—rackets like that were in his line of business. Drily he changed the subject.

"Well, Paulo, it's good to have you in my gang. Don't worry about the work, I'll look the other way. Just try not to let Fossil-Face see you. I'll be keeping an eye out anyway. Being in charge of the concrete mixer, I'd catch it before you."

"I knew we'd understand each other. That's just what I was saying to my friends: Marcel's no shit, I said, his stripe hasn't gone to his head."

The great fool was beaming! Paulo pressed home his advantage.

"I'm relying on you to get Belloni back on the mix with me. Now that my Russian's gone, I'm on my own. I've got another friend, Joel, you know, the Breton, who's shoveling away at the dump. You've got to get him into your crew too. But you needn't worry, he's a real worker, that guy."

"Okay as far as Belloni goes, it's as good as done. I'll talk to the *Rapportführer* about the other guy."

Paulo had played his cards right, catching Marcel off his guard by being nice to him before he had a chance to feel secure about his new stripe. Of course he was proud of it, but naturally he felt a bit like a shit on his first day. Paulo had timed it perfectly . . .

Sure enough, before the week was out the three friends were reunited at the concrete mixer. Time would not drag so much now. Particularly as Paulo hadn't been the only one to think Marcel's Kommando would be a good job. One by one, the main chancers turned up: Pépé with the golden smile, Pierrot Martin, Katz, the Jewish specimen who had recently been slung out of the *Schneiderei* for having made himself a waistcoat from scraps of material, and a few new fellows, like the famous Tito and his sloe-eyed friend, and François of Burgundy, whom the doyen of Nordfeld had given up trying to break and sent back to the south. With a team like that, the concrete mixer wasn't likely to seize up through over-production. And during the breaks, conversation promised to be interesting.

In this convivial company, the last days of May slipped by without Paulo noticing. The weather was still perfect, the sun beat down on their backs, and by ten o'clock all the men working in the open had taken off their jackets. Two hours after they started work, the light began to filter down between the two high peaks to the right of the tunnel mouth, becoming more intense by the second, brightening and then warming the whole bowl, dispelling the damp shadows of the night. It was somehow familiar to the veterans. They had already felt the sun's warm caress at this time of day. When? Christ, a year ago! It was exactly a year, to the day, that Paulo, Angel and the others on the first convoy had arrived at Loibl.

Belloni was the first to point it out:

"Hey, you guys, do you know what day it is today?"

There were no calendars in the blocks, and nobody knew the date, even to within a week. Anyway, what good would it have done to know the exact date? They couldn't have cared less. It wasn't as if any of them had any pressing engagements.

Undeterred, Angel went on. "Well then, I'll tell you: it is the first of June, nineteen forty-four. And exactly a year ago, almost to the hour, I landed up in this God-forsaken hole. So did Paulo. What d'you think of that then, you novices? A year! Not bad, eh?"

This triggered off all kinds of rubbish. Pierrot Martin was the first.

"It feels more like I've been here for ten years! . . ."

"Me too," Paulo chipped in. "To have had the shit that we've had, you'd have to live a hundred years by normal standards . . . And yet I can't really believe that we've gotten through a whole year here. If you'd said six months, or even three months, I'd have believed you more easily."

Their display of morale had made them the life and soul of Loibl, and in the refectory at lunch break, men gathered around their little group. Anybody who wanted to be cheered up or had a funny story to tell came to join them at the back of the big shed. There, well away from the SS guarding the door, they could talk freely, and they set to with a will. The silliest jokes were greeted with uproarious laughter. It was all a damn sight more amusing than Sailor's sing-songs.

What a different picture from barely two weeks ago. One day they'd started singing again, the next they were laughing and joking as if it were the most natural thing in the world. And still the SS and Kapos merely looked on, although you would have thought the men's good humor bordered on provocation. It was undeniable that a new kind of relationship was developing between guards and prisoners: they no longer regarded each other on the one hand with hatred and on the other with fear. At bottom everyone was sick of the brutality, the hatred and the fear, all pointless now that both camps knew they were going to live alongside each other to the end of the affair. But how would they part company? There were no guarantees, but as they waited for that glorious day, each man wanted to make some contribution: the Krauts by behaving like real soldiers, and Paulo and his fellows like classic prisoners. Just like a real POW camp, the only difference being that real POWs would have fewer stories to tell when they got back...

For example, the *Kriegsgefangene* would have been quite incapable of understanding stories like the one about Serpette's soup wager. The refectory was the scene of the incident; the boisterous atmosphere was catching and one lunchtime Fritz decided to play a trick on the good-natured peasant.

"Do you want another bowl of soup?" he asked him when everybody had had their ration, slyly dangling the overflowing ladle under Serpette's nose.

"Ja, danke schön, chef," Serpette replied in his inimitable Sarthe accent. And in four slurps he polished off the second bowl of soup, watched by three hundred prisoners pleased at his good fortune.

"Still hungry?" Fritz asked again after Serpette had licked the last drops from the bottom of his bowl like a cat.

"Ja, chef."

"Very hungry?"

"Fairly, *chef*."

"And if I gave you five more, would you eat them?"

Serpette may well have been the village idiot, but even he smelled a rat. Generally, Fritz kept the extras to fatten up his bedmates, hoping to make their asses bigger. But Serpette had never given anybody a hard on. He didn't know how to reply.

"Are you deaf?" Fritz demanded. "I said five more bowls, can you drink five more bowls? Right here, in front of your friends? But I warn you, if you leave a single spoonful, I'll send you across the line."

Serpette wavered, but it was already too late! Fritz was swilling the soup around with his ladle, scooping up potatoes and bits of meat from the bottom, then letting them plop back into the vat. Serpette had never had soup like this.

"Okay, *chef*, I'll eat them," he mumbled, his eyes popping out of his head.

"Bravo!" Fritz applauded. "Hold out your bowl."

The whole company felt sure the joke would turn sour. Given the capacity of the human stomach, it was a mathematical impossibility for Serpette to drink five quarts of thick soup after the two he'd just swallowed. Especially since a year of Loibl's diet had shrunk the men's stomachs. None of them could drink more than two quarts without throwing up, except for Serpette, whose gluttony, which had brought him here in the first place, was boundless.

Mauthausen had been a very nasty experience for him. The area around the quarantine blocks was paved and nothing could grow. There was nothing to assuage his maddening hunger, and it had almost led him to the crematorium. Loibl had saved his life. Dazzled by the vegetation, he had begun to chew grass, dandelions and pine bark, and from there he went on to snails, slugs and rutabaga peelings. The SS had found it highly amusing to see the Frenchman grubbing about for his food like an animal. To humiliate him even further, they had one day forced him to get down on all fours and share the hounds' soup. They were convinced he'd be eaten alive, but it was one of nature's mysteries that the dogs didn't even growl. They had accepted Serpette, allowing him to lap up what he could from their dainty scraps; they jostled him a little but didn't once snap at him. As the others wouldn't believe the *Hundenführer*'s story, Serpette had had to repeat the performance a dozen times. It was more than likely that Fritz had seen the show, and it was probably just to outdo the dog handler and get himself a bit of publicity that he had invented the seven-bowl trick.

But at the rate Serpette was downing his soups it looked as if the joke might rebound on the good *Arbeitskapo* chief. There were ten minutes left before they had to go back to work and the world's soup champion had already demolished three bowlfuls. Counting the two before the wager, that made five quarts swimming around in his belly. The entire refectory stood transfixed by the sight of his stomach, which was expanding like a football being inflated with a bicycle pump. With the sixth bowl, the football became a basketball, but Serpette wasn't giving up. His crimson face was swollen too, dripping with sweat, and there were tears in his eyes, but he held out his bowl to Fritz of his own accord.

"*Fünf,*" yelled the thug, drawing up another overflowing ladle.

"*Sieben,*" Serpette corrected him.

The number came out as a hoarse gasp. He looked drunk and was tottering dangerously, as if it were seven quarts of red wine he'd just downed. What a great help he would be at work this afternoon if he managed to find room in his belly for the seventh bowl!

It was unbearable to watch, but what could they do except hope that the poor clown would spew up his wretched soup right in Fritz's sadistic mug. It was surely only because God protects the innocent that Serpette finally won his bet—in the nick of time, just as the whistle blew for the work gangs to reassemble. In addition, the men's sympathy for the fool was wearing thin and men who felt his performance was unworthy of a Frenchman didn't wait for the ranks to form up before insulting him.

"You asked for it, you fucking peasant. I hope it kills you . . ." a particularly thin Parisian snarled at him, probably out of jealousy.

Joel stepped in. "Leave him alone. You don't take it out on him, the poor guy's just a victim."

Serpette was incapable of answering anyway. With great difficulty he had managed to zigzag back to his post at the cement-block factory, and collapsed onto a wheelbarrow. Despite his intoxicated state, he had chosen his spot well: three barracks hid him from Fossil-Face's HQ and the cordon of sentries. But he was in full view of the concrete-mixing gang, who were less than a hundred feet away from his wheelbarrow, where he lay sprawled with his legs apart as if sitting on the throne. The wisecracks began to fly.

"I bet you he'll shit his seven quarts into the wheelbarrow. That way he won't lose any of it, he can slurp it all back up again," guffawed Pierrot Martin, with his usual good taste.

It was an exaggeration and the image was rather crude, but there was a grain of truth in it. Serpette was obviously most reluctant to part with the soup which had cost him so much, and he had chosen this position to take the pressure off his stomach and let the soup circulate in the hope that it wouldn't come back up again. But seven quarts was still an awful lot of soup, and after three or four burps he had had to let the surplus go.

From where Paulo and his friends were, it was difficult to say exactly how many quarts he had parted with, but at a rough guess he had sicked up a good four bowls' worth. What a waste!

"It would be a real shame if he yelled it all up, including his own bowlful," remarked Angel, sympathetically.

He was underestimating Serpette. This possibility had just occurred to him too, and he had resolved the difficulty immediately: cupping his hands, he saved as much as he could and unashamedly poured it back into his mouth, arching his back so that it would go down and stay down.

Fortunately, the SS, and Fritz especially, had not seen any of this. But you could be sure, with the whole of Marcel's crew as witnesses, that his disgusting exhibition of vomit-eating would soon be public knowledge. It'd be good for any number of jokes in the refectory, and that, after all, was what was important. Serpette's escapade would boost morale by making them laugh, and he had unwittingly done the community a great service.

But there were other funny stories besides his. The one about Reboux the teacher was a good one too, in a different way—less crude and more dignified, but it had also made the men laugh a lot.

The teacher was by far the most senior of the detainees; he was at least sixty and a little wrinkled, but he was lucky enough not to have a single gray hair. This, in addition to his strong constitution, was the only possible explanation for his presence at Loibl. He must have fooled them on the day of the slave market at Mauthausen. But building a tunnel was asking too much from an old boy who had never handled anything except books in his life. It was not long before he resumed the look of an old classics master minus the specs. He was better off without them, considering the beatings that landed from all quarters. Now that Loibl was becoming more civilized, people remembered Reboux's age and it earned him a few concessions—a bowl of soup here, a hunk of bread there and light work at the sawmill. An SS subaltern, nicknamed Tits, had even taken a shine to him. Reboux spoke flawless German, and Tits frequently came over to get him to explain things to him. Judging by the stupid questions he came out with, you could be damn sure Tits hadn't been top of his class at school. But now that he had a real teacher all to himself, at his beck and call, he had a wonderful chance to catch up.

"Tell me, *Professor,* since you know everything, why do the Jews cut those bits off their sons' pricks?" Why this, why that, why the other . . . His questions were all rather below the belt, they centered on sex education, and the teacher needed every ounce of diplomacy he could muster to find answers which would satisfy the ignoramus. Because, to make matters worse, Tits was a mean bastard, one of the meanest. The day Ramsauer left, he'd had a slightly more original idea than usual.

"*Professor,* drop what you're doing and draw me a picture of the doctor and his wife. Here's a pencil and some paper."

"But . . . I don't know how to draw, sir. I'm a classics teacher, I teach Latin and Greek, not art."

"Teachers know how to draw. Come on . . . *schnell!*"

Tits was getting angry. In his tiny mind, *Professor* meant tutor, someone who teaches handwriting and who, therefore, knows how to draw. The old man must be lying . . .

"Take care, *Mensch*, don't make fun of me. Draw a portrait of the doctor and his wife, that's an order."

"But, sir, that's impossible, I can't . . ."

A sharp backhander sent old Reboux sprawling and he dropped the paper and pencil.

"Pick them up, you old shit, and draw. I'm telling you for the last time."

The poor old man picked up the paper and placed it on a

bench. Tits came closer, thinking he was going to start drawing, but no inspiration came and the paper remained hopelessly blank.

"So, you old bastard, you old fart, beatings don't have any effect on you anymore. But you're still going to do my drawing," Tits said menacingly. He unholstered his gun, and pressed it against Reboux's temple.

"Now, draw. Or I'll shoot."

And to make it quite clear he wasn't joking, he flipped off the safety catch.

Tits must have blown prisoners' brains out at Mauthausen or other camps for less than this, and the old man had to consider the threat real. Nevertheless, he still didn't draw. It was difficult to know whether he had decided to take advantage of the situation to put an end to his exhausting life, or whether he had decided the retarded SS was bluffing—in which case it was a dangerous bet.

The suspense lasted for five minutes, which must have seemed interminable to old Reboux, because he had indeed staked everything on Tits backing down and not pulling the trigger. And he had won the bet, standing his ground without flinching. His tormentor looked completely deflated. Without a word, he put his gun back in its holster and disappeared in such a hurry that he forgot to pick up his pencil.

No one had seen this episode. It was old Reboux himself who had related it, and everyone believed him. Some of them because they figured that at his age and in his weak physical state, he was too near death to want to lie or boast. Others, his Resistance comrades, because they knew that the Russian roulette side of his nature had made him take the wildest gambles in his underground career.

Tits' threat was right up the old man's street, and it must have been one of his greatest thrills ever!

"Why did you take such a risk, Reboux? Christ, you're perverse," Paulo couldn't help saying to him.

"Well, Paulo, you know, it was a calculated risk. Believe me, if I'd drawn his *Oberarzt* for him and it didn't flatter him, he would have been able to use it as an excuse to bump me off. Remember what happened to one of those Poles at Nordfeld? That was an even more stupid story. There was an SS who knew the Pole could see the future in the cards, and he asked him nicely, just as Tits asked me, to predict the future.

"'What do you want to know?' the Pole asked. 'When are we going to win the war?' 'I can't see that in the cards.' 'What can you see?' 'You'll lose the war!' That same evening he sent the Pole across the line, so you see, I was right not to fall into Tits' trap."

"You can't fool me, friend. We know you better than that. You didn't refuse to draw because you were scared, you old gambler, you just did it for the hell of it!"

Whether Reboux had been honest or not about his motives, the important thing about this wild story was that Tits had backed down. Like his boss Winkler, he must have lost his blind faith in the thousand-year Reich promised by their Great Dictator. Face to face with the stubborn Reboux, Tits must have wondered what would happen to him if they lost the war. He was beginning to understand that his return to civilian life depended to a large extent on the *Scheisskubel* like this obstinate old man who couldn't take a joke.

It didn't even occur to him that it might be a little late to mend his ways. And Helmut, that supreme bastard, was even less perceptive: he now smiled as he gave his orders! As if that would wipe the slate clean. The faggot was suffering from a bad case of wishful thinking.

At assembly one evening he looked almost moved as he announced some surprising news. You'd think he was overjoyed to be able to tell them they could write to their families.

Each man was immediately issued with a stamped and franked postcard. The postmark was that of *Konzentrationslager Mauthausen* in large capital letters; on the stamp was Hitler himself in profile beneath his peaked cap, as he had been at the height of his glory. The juxtaposition wasn't without a certain piquancy, but the most incredible thing was that some of the principal witnesses of Nazi horror were now authorized to write to their families. It was absolute proof that something had snapped in the SS machinery. Himmler too must have sensed the winds of change, and the bastard was altering course.

These postcards, the first he had allowed his deportees to send, were clearly an indication that he had decided to give back to their families the men he hadn't had the time to dispose of. But curiously, instead of shouting for joy, the assembled detainees felt anguish rising in their throats. Their families! For a whole year they had made a superhuman effort to forget them, and now this small postcard opened up the wound again. Their emotion could only make life more difficult for them. Besides, what could they say to their sweethearts or their mothers? They couldn't very well tell them what had happened. It was hardly the thing to write under Hitler's beady eye.

But as each man looked at his postcard a little more closely, he realized that the two short lines given to him ruled out lengthy messages. The most you could squeeze in if you wrote small enough was a single sentence. You couldn't even get around it by writing over the printed words, as you could in the postcards allowed between occupied and unoccupied France. She wouldn't have the truth this time around.

Paulo was only momentarily upset, because he couldn't think of anyone to send his card to. But most of his friends couldn't see how to make their message mean something. They would have to choose their words carefully, and most of them were jotting down their messages in rough on scraps of cement sack, like kids who don't want any crossings-out in their letters to Santa Claus. Still smiling, Helmut came to their rescue.

"No need to make a fuss. Just say that you're in good health. It's compulsory, otherwise your cards will never arrive."

"I am in good health." Five words, plus love and kisses, and your signature took up all the space.

"It's probably just as well," the men thought. They wouldn't admit it, but it made them uncomfortable to have to put their misery in writing. "I am in good health, as we all are," was good enough. Besides, it was true: they were bursting with health. Except, of course, those waiting in the *Revier* to return to Mauthausen's gas chambers, for although the new doctor was strongly opposed to the benzol treatment, he couldn't perform miracles. But as the postcards had been distributed to the entire work force, the specters in the infirmary, wounded, tubercular or just worn out, dutifully scribbled down the pious lie: "I am in good health."

Most of them would be dead before their messages reached their destination but new hope would be kindled in the hearts of their nearest and dearest who had had no news of them for the last fifteen months.

In the end the emotion aroused by the postcards bearing the Führer's stamp was short-lived. As with everything else, it was better to treat them as a joke and the clowns on the concrete-mixer Kommando set the tone.

"I touched up the Führer's mustaches, gave him a circumflex accent. It suits him much better, it makes him look like the Kaiser," declared François of Burgundy in the refectory the next day.

"I gave him a Jewish nose," said Katz.

Two days later, they couldn't have cared less whether the cards arrived or not. Thanks to the whole episode, they'd had a bit of fun, and that was the main thing. But Helmut had another surprise up his sleeve. At assembly the following week, each man was issued with a toothbrush and a comb.

"Hell," exclaimed Paulo, "they're going to let us out this week . . . they're trying to clean us up."

That wasn't quite why they'd had this unusual handout, but it had to be seen as a good sign, like the postcards. It was the good Tyrolean doctor's idea. He had decided to wage war against germs. He wanted to eradicate scabies and scurvy by a campaign of hygiene. As far as the Kapos could remember, toothbrushes were unprecedented in a *Konzentrationslager.* Loibl was turning into a model camp! The morale on the *Appelplatz* went up a notch, despite the admonition which Helmut had just had translated:

"You are responsible for the toilet equipment which has just been issued. If you lose or damage either article, they will not be replaced, but you will be punished."

Toilet equipment! The toothbrush was okay, but the comb looked as if it came from a joke shop. It was double-sided and each side had teeth barely half an inch long and so close together that they were useless for anything except scraping off ticks and scabs from the inmates of a kennel. It was a lice trap, that was for sure, but only for dogs! Of course, given the regulation length of their thatch, a barber's comb would have been quite useless, but what on earth were they supposed to do with this? It was just a joke. Maybe the SS had thought that Loibl needed entertainment! The block chiefs were helpless with laughter. A scab rake for each detainee! They'd never seen that in a camp either. But they at least might have had some use for it: vain queers that they were, they let their hair grow, against all the regulations. Not too much, one or two inches, just enough to hide the *Autobahn* by combing it over. In any case they had their *Autobahnen* done delicately, with a razor rather than clippers. As the months passed, it had become an elegant center parting, *à la* George Raft. Their fancy haircuts may indeed have made them look more obviously queer, but they didn't look like deportees anymore. Their cooperation was so necessary to Winkler for the running of the camp that he overlooked this breach of discipline, as he overlooked the tunic-collared shirts, the jackets tailored at the waist and the flared trousers.

He had also overlooked the possibility that Mauthausen's top brass would turn up with warning to inspect their Yugoslavian annex.

Ranking officers drove their cars through the tunnel almost every day and the unexpected arrival of Ziereis with a small *Totenkopf* escort went unnoticed. Nobody had recognized the boss; he had been satisfied to see them all working hard, and he hadn't hung about the tunnel for long. It was in the camp itself a little later that he had raised hell. His yells had woken up the night shift asleep in the dormitories. They all clambered onto the beds nearest the windows, and they hadn't missed a single moment of the show. On the immense parade ground where the *Haeftlinge* normally stood, Ziereis had had the block chiefs lined up. Stiff as posts, their buttocks tense with fear, they were being slapped and having their hair pulled by an *Unterscharführer* with powerful hands. Then Ziereis took over for him and thrashed the culprits' necks with his crop. The punishment had lasted a good half hour, and those of the night shift who understood German had had a wonderful time: *Dreckschwein*, *Scheisserei*, every insult under the sun which had the word "shit" in it. So the big boss in black also knew the repertoire, but what joy to hear this! Sailor was the only one to escape, for the simple reason that he had his billiard-ball skull shaved and polished every evening.

Mauthausen's jailer didn't trust his subordinate Winkler, and he had delayed his departure to ensure that the shearing was carried out. Down to the scalp, he had stipulated, not even enough to trace out an *Autobahn*.

That evening at roll call Otto and his henchmen didn't know where to put themselves. And when they had to doff their caps as the *Rapportführer* arrived, the three hundred prisoners in the day shift bit their lips until they bled to stop themselves laughing. What a shame that they hadn't been there to see their torturers get it; it was something they had all dreamed of for more than a year. And who had avenged the prisoners? Ziereis, enemy number one, chief murderer and supreme terror.

Contrary to the men's fears, in the days that followed none of the chiefs tried to take out their humiliation on their charges. Better still, Bullseye, Eddy and Sladek, making out that they knew how to take a joke, now had their heads shaved every evening by their respective barbers. To look like Karl. And everyone enjoyed the joke, as they'd enjoyed the onion affair, which was another well-meaning gesture on the part of Ramsauer's replacement.

Obsessed by his battle against scurvy, one Saturday he had called for a special-issue assembly on the *Appelplatz*. Square up, attention! And every man was given a large onion to eat raw, there and then.

"Extra rations . . . won't say no . . . thank you, Doctor . . ." the prisoners said to themselves, and at the order they bit hard into their onions. By the second bite, they were beginning to think that the gift wasn't such a nice idea after all. The damn things were impossible to eat on an empty stomach, they took the roof of your mouth off, they burned and how they made you cry! But there was no question of throwing away the horrid snack. The doctor had anticipated that move and he had given the Kapos and block chiefs strict instructions to watch the prisoners closely and make sure they left nothing. And nothing was left, but their eyes were still streaming with tears an hour later, as if someone had just announced to them that they'd been sentenced to life imprisonment at Loibl. To stop the tears, they rushed to the *Waschraum,* without waiting for the order, jostling each other to get to the taps and bathe their smarting eyes with icy water.

"What a mean trick, we're not used to it anymore," complained Serpette, who for once had not gone up for a second helping.

He was quite right. For over fifteen months, they had

eaten no meat, sugar, milk, fat or fruit. The onion was like a foreign body in their digestive systems, and it wouldn't dissolve. One of the side effects was that for almost a whole week the entire Kommando had an attack of wind.

The jokes were endless, especially after midday soup, because then the belching got better and more fruity, to the enormous delight of the whole refectory. "M-more mud in the mixer . . . oops, Germans lost that one too . . ." Every day they laid it on thicker. You would have thought they were happy factory workers milling around in their canteen. But it was odd that none of these captives drew on memories of civilian life for a funny story to make his friends laugh. Only ancedotes about life in the camp itself were appreciated, the most popular ones being those which made fun of the characters, SS or civilian, who had been given comic-strip names by the refectory mob: Green Bean, the Medal-Man, Perrier, Fossil-Face, Mikado, Mama Michèle, Snip-Snip, Tits, the Tart and so on. Each of the screws now had a nickname, even Winkler, who was christened Knock-Knees—for obvious reasons. The slightest incident went to embellish the prisoners' cartoon strip. None of their conversations, either in the refectory, the tunnel or in the dormitories at night, touched on anything outside the confines of the camp.

Apart from a few uncouth peasants, the men were all reasonably intelligent, and yet as soon as two of them got together, they chose to talk about Fossil-Face, Fritz, grub or work, rather than the war, their future and other more exalted topics. Their deliberate refusal to take an interest in anything outside their present sphere had been their saving grace when things were going badly. But now that the end was daily more of a reality, their attitude was no longer justifiable. They would be completely senile by the time they got out if their level of conversation remained so trivial. They were behaving as if they were afraid premature dreams would make everything crumble. At the first glimmers of hope, when the Saturday corridas and the daily "attempted escapes" had been forbidden, they'd come clean to each other about their past lives and it had done them good. Now, not a word more was heard about families, jobs or hometowns. Have you heard the latest about Green Bean? Oh yes, they pricked up their ears at that, and clustered around the storyteller so as not to miss a single line.

It was hard to deny that the latest Green Bean adventure was no sob story. The nut, the biggest nut of the whole SS garrison, must have been the only man not to have noticed the watch which Fatalitas, a Parisian with a colorful past and a veteran of the *bataillon d'Afrique*, had tattooed on his left wrist. One evening, a quarter of an hour before the end of work, Green Bean had asked him the time. Instinctively, Fatalitas had held out this tattoo, which was a proper work of art. It looked three-dimensional, complete with strap, buckle and red hands frozen for life at five to six.

"Five minutes before six, *gut*," said Green Bean. And he had blown the knocking-off whistle ten minutes early. It was only because Fatalitas had succumbed to the schoolboy atmosphere that he had played this prank, because he was fed up to the back teeth with his ticker. It had caused him years of grief, constant questions of "Hey, Fatalitas, have you got the time?" To which his usual reply was "Drop dead." However, he couldn't very well say that to Green Bean. At last Fatalitas had got the joke, and he never tired of recounting his trick. For once, his wristwatch, a rash mistake of his youth, was not to be cursed. The joke almost made him forget the tattoo on his forehead which spelled Fatalitas in red letters, and his doe eyes, which were made up for life. They were enough to make a starlet turn pale with envy: green eyelids, long and well-defined eyebrows, eyeliner above and below his lashes, a complete facial which had gotten him picked out of the crowd more often than was his turn.

But the prize for the best tattoos would not go to him, nor even to Karl. A young gypsy (the Krauts called him *Tziganer*) won hands down. Inscribed right across his forehead was "Child of Misfortune." Around his neck, the classic message to the executioner: "Cut along the dotted line." On his prick: "Love tap," with an arrow indicating the direction of the jet. And much more original, on his right foot: "I'm tired," and on the left: "Me too." It was lucky for Tziganer that the tattoos were spread all over his body and had no artistic value. The lampshade collectors at Mauthausen had let him go.

Tziganer, Fatalitas, Serpette, Reboux, there were dozens of these eccentrics who were always getting into scrapes, and the time spent hearing about their brushes with Tits, Green Bean, Mama Michèle, and the other cartoon characters made the days seem much shorter. These tales provided very little intellectual stimulation and, unlike their brothers in the POW camps, the young men were not likely to come back better educated than they had been at the outset. Loibl was no university: not a single book, not even a Bible, had ever been seen in the camp, but that didn't seem to make life any less tolerable.

XXI

"As of today, you are permitted to smoke. Each week you will receive five cigarettes. The Universale company has granted you this reward. The company hopes you will prove worthy of it by working better and better."

As he listened to the good news, bells began clanging furiously in Paulo's head. Cigarettes, thousands of cigarettes in the camp—as good as Deutschmarks for buying food! What else did he have to offer the wide boys to persuade them to give him margarine, sausage and jam? Nothing. He had nothing except his big smile and his gift of gab, which wouldn't buy you anything in the Loibl marketplace.

"Five butts a week, not even one a day. I can't see anything to get so excited about." Angel was surprised to see Paulo so jubilant.

"God, you're slow, little man. It's precisely the stingy way they're handing them out that makes it so good. You don't know what a smoker's like when he touches the stuff again. He's worse than a junkie. There's a vanload of men eating as much as they want these days, and they'll be caught by the habit again. Thousands of butts around the camp will drive them mad—and they're dravas, they taste like Gauloises. They'd fight to get their hands on more. And we'll supply them with more..."

"How?"

"Er, I haven't worked that out yet, but it's a minor point. The main thing is, Loibl's minting its own money. And then, you don't think it was Universale who decided on the miserable ration, do you? I'll bet they'll hand out at least a pack a week for each man and that swindling doyen will confiscate the rest. So, all we've got to do is find where he hides them."

"I'm with you. That's neat. But what I'd like to know is, what are you going to do with all the extra scoff, since you stuff yourself every night at Karl's place?"

"Ah, now that's another thing I wanted to talk to you about. I've had it up to here with your Sailor, and blowouts at the poofs' table. From now on, blowouts will be among friends only, at the concrete mixer. I don't like begging. I've always just taken people's wallets."

"But there's no point spoiling the party while the going's still good. Why don't you wait till Sailor throws you out himself?"

"No, no, look, I'm sick of smiling at his hustlers, at his barber and his *Schreiber*. The whole time I have to restrain myself from calling them fucking fairies and stuffing their sausage up where they like it. I can't stand it any longer, and anyway, fags or no fags, I'd have walked out on that queer by the end of this week. Because I don't want any dirty comments coming back at me one day. D'you see?"

"Yeah, you're right, I'm going to drop it too. Sailor can pick up his own sweethearts from now on. But how are we going to get out of it? We can't just pretend we're not hungry anymore . . ."

"Don't worry about it. We'll behave as if we're depressed or retarded or something."

By giving himself a week to ditch his benefactor, it was almost as though Paulo sensed something would happen which would allow him to make the break without having to go straight back to the dismal diet of soup, bread and gnat's-piss coffee. That something was another of the doctor's original notions. Ramsauer's successor was certainly not one to let the dust settle. He had sent for two of his eminent colleagues, both dentists and SS of course, to eradicate scurvy once and for all. According to Daniel, there was no evidence that there was any scurvy in the camp, but the new *Oberarzt* had a real bee in his bonnet about germs. Unable to force-feed his patients with vitamin C, he had asked his colleagues to attack the evil . . . by the roots. With forceps, but without anesthetics. Crack, crack! Out came any suspicious-looking teeth.

The fang-extracting session lasted a whole week, but

Paulo had hit upon his clever idea as the first batch of patients, men from Block 1, had emerged from the *Revier.*

"The bathtardths!" fumed Lagrive, pointing down his throat. He was lisping, and not only with rage: the marauding dentists had yanked right out of the middle of his jaw an eye tooth which had had the misfortune to encounter Bullseye's right hook a few months back, and had been a little loose ever since. The Marseillais's teeth were his pride and joy. He had managed to keep all thirty-two of them through ten years of professional boxing. Poor fellow, he hadn't had his mouthguard in against Bullseye.

"For forty yearth I've never had a thingle bad tooth," he raged. "Jutht look what they've done to me, I'm going to fucking well have to have a crown or a bridge . . . and in front! The fuckerth!"

Even if he had had his bridge, it wouldn't have stayed put. For these odd dentists, as soon as they found a tooth that was at all wobbly, considered it their duty, and a pleasure, to yank it out with pliers, like an old stump. All the better if the bridge was made of gold; it would swell Mauthausen's coffers. And you couldn't protest: "You understand of course that we don't have time to give you false teeth." Naturally not.

Paulo got the message. He himself had nothing to lose; the two molars he had lost in the corridas had been knocked out complete with roots. But immediately he remembered Pépé. He'd better warn him as soon as possible and come to some arrangement with him before the pillagers made him open wide his golden mouth. Without wasting any time, he ran to Block 2, the old boy's quarters.

"I like you, Paulo, but it wouldn't do to take me for a novice. You're slipping, my boy," the old man told him. "I'm old enough to flog my teeth on my own. Besides, I didn't wait for you. Look!"

Paulo couldn't believe his eyes. Pépé only had his back teeth left, four on each side!

"They won't steal those off me," he went on. "I could hardly eat my bread with a spoon!"

He was right the doctors wouldn't dare do that to him. But Paulo was extremely put out: someone had beaten him to it. Pépé certainly hadn't yanked all his teeth out by himself.

"That fucking Riton must have helped him, for smokes, the bastard! They're in the same block, they must have done it on the quiet one night and with Bullseye's blessing," Paulo told Angel, who was eager to know how the interview had gone.

Poor Belloni had so often converted Pépé's teeth into cigarettes for his dreams of escape that now he could have wept.

"Never mind," Paulo said consolingly. "Not everyone has a gold mine in their mouth like that old crook, but there are other possible clients. We'll have to do a little research, and quickly. Tomorrow's Bullseye's block, and the day after that, it's us."

"But where will you do it? And how?"

"Don't worry, I've thought of everything. The tunnel will be my surgery, and I'll borrow some pliers from Dédé. That should do it. What I need urgently is some volunteers. The fellows all know that anything shaky and shiny gets pulled out right away in the *Revier.* If you can convince two or three fresh faces that I studied dentistry before going down the slippery slope, they'll come running. Especially as we'll give them soup in return . . . every day for a week. You can promise them that, we'll more than cover our costs."

"Who's your fence?"

"I haven't got one yet, but that's no problem. Everyone's in the market for yellow. The Yugos would give buckets of Marks for a few grams. I've got Yanko in mind. There won't be any danger with him."

Angel was delighted to see his friend falling into his crooked ways again, and immediately he set about finding customers. Work had been under way for less than an hour the following morning when a tall beanpole of a fellow, a Frenchman, turned up at the concrete mixer. He had arrived in the very last convoy, so he only knew the two accomplices by sight. Just as well.

"I hear one of you's a dentist?"

"That's right, I am," replied Paulo, drawing closer. "What's the problem?"

"Well, one of my bottom teeth is loose, but not loose enough for me to pull it out myself. It's gold-based and I don't want to have to give it to those bastards. Can you take it out for me, *Monsieur le dentiste*?"

"None of that here, just call me Paulo. Let me see . . . Ah yes, it's loose, all right. You're not squeamish?"

"Less so since Mauthausen."

"Good. Then come back at ten o'clock sharp, but not here. Five hundred feet down the tunnel, there's an alcove on the right. Wait for me there. I'll go and get my equipment."

Fortunately, the hurricane lamp Paulo had borrowed from a miner gave only a feeble light, for if the tall beanpole had seen the so-called equipment, he might have had second thoughts. It was a common or garden-variety pair of pincers, generally used for drawing nails. They weren't rusty, but not far from it. By a stroke of luck, the tooth came out at the first tug. With a bit of gum and some blood, but the patient seemed quite satisfied.

"Now go and rinse your mouth out," said Paulo, mindful of his dental responsibilities. "I'm going to give your tooth to a civilian. In a couple of days you'll have a pack of smokes, not five, mind you, but twenty, and dravas too. If you handle things properly, they'll fetch you twenty soups."

His first client was simply delighted, and Paulo later learned that he had flatly disbelieved the malicious tongues who insinuated that his champion dentist, as he called Paulo, had done his apprenticeship with a jimmy. Unluckily, the story was too good. Within a day it had made the rounds of the whole camp and the Chastagnier surgery was forced to pack up.

"Better to play safe," Paulo told Angel. "There was a Pole at Nordfeld last year who sold his bridge to a civilian and was shot for it. They called it gold-trafficking. Yanko's a safe bet, but we'd better not push our luck. Besides, that sucker's tooth is quite hefty. Enough to feed us for a month, on decent food, not on their gnat's piss."

Paulo had miscalculated in assuming Yanko would leap at the opportunity. Once again, he was subjected to a lesson in morality.

"I fight in the war, comrade, I'm not a gold peddler," the Slav had stated, in reply to Paulo's offer. "I've given you cigarettes already, and I'll give you more, but I don't want your gold. It's a bourgeois metal."

He had, however, agreed to help Paulo out by pointing him in the right direction.

"Go and talk to the Italian on the locomotive, the replacement for the one who vanished. He's a fascist, but he's not above a racket—in fact, he manages the black market for the whole civilian camp. But tread carefully, all the same."

So the exchange worked out well in the end: Paulo got his carton of ten packs and the tall beanpole his twenty soups.

In the meantime, the butchery in the *Revier* carried on. All the teeth which were decayed or loose, or had lead or gold fillings, clattered into the dentist' basin, faster than you could count them. According to the orderlies, they pulled out an average of four per man, but it was old Léon, a decent peasant from Cotentin, who made history by setting a record to beat them all: they pulled out no fewer than twenty-three of his teeth. At one sitting and still with no anesthetic. Add the twenty-three to the ones he lost a year ago from the Kapos' rights and lefts, and he had no teeth at all. The sadists had left him with the toothless mouth of a newborn baby. Of course, his teeth were not all as good as Lagrive's; quite a few had been eroded to stumps by too much Calvados. But the treatment they handed out to him was barbaric. Old Léon must have needed the devil's own strength not to pass out as he heard the forceps crunch twenty-three times inside his mouth. But it was impossible to know what he thought about it. He couldn't begin to talk, his mouth was horribly swollen and bloody.

The *Rapportführer* was not in the least sympathetic; he had packed Léon off to work that same evening with a couple of Kraut aspirins. "Within an hour, you won't even notice it," he had said. The poor old fellow dripped blood onto his shovel all night in the tunnel, but at dawn he was still standing. When it came to enduring pain, Loibl had some real champions.

The butcher dentists at last took themselves off with their spoils. If Paulo wanted to stick by his decision to quit Sailor's table, he had to find another source of income quickly. To make matters worse, he had started smoking again, and the Italian's carton in the *Waschraum* cache was shrinking visibly!

What could they filch? was the question which came up again and again in conversation with the faithful Angel. They had considered every item which might be transformed into dravas without turning up anything specific, apart from the doyen's reserve; but that was an enormous risk. Suddenly an incredible piece of news was announced: Loibl had received permission to organize boxing matches between prisoners, beginning the following weekend. Just like at Mauthausen—and Paulo and Angel both knew what that implied: huge bets on the winner. And what did they bet with? Cigarettes, by the carton, sometimes at ten to one!

"Put it there, Angel," said Paulo. "No point in us racking our brains anymore. This is the jackpot. When it comes to boxing, I'm unbeatable. Vel d'Hiv, Central, Elysées-Montmartre, Wagram—I never missed a fight, we can't go wrong. I'll be bookie and you just bring me the pigeons."

Whether the boxing matches would make their fortune or not, they were at least one more proof that Loibl was officially recognized as a camp. Such an expression of confidence, such a reward for the men, could only be attributable to Ziereis' lightning visit to Loibl and his evident satisfaction with the way work was progressing.

At Mauthausen everyone had enjoyed fight days. The whole camp, guards and prisoners, excepting the exhausted men in the quarantine and the dying in the *Revier*, crowded around the ring to cheer on their favorites. The Krauts came because it filled them with glee to see prisoners willingly taking a beating; and the prisoners came because they hoped to see a detested Kapo boxer go down for the count. Afterward, generally speaking, he wasn't so eager to throw his weight around.

This passion for the noble art was one of the biggest surprises for new arrivals. "Any boxers, step forward," the Kapos would order, even before they called out the roll of newcomers in the blocks. Many were those who kept quiet the first day, out of suspicion, but they soon regretted it, because the organizers of Mauthausen's Boxing Club pampered their boxers incredibly. They got double rations of bread, as much soup as they could eat, margarine, sausage, they slept in their chief's *Stube* and their only chore was to train in a room specially fitted out for the purpose. The professional boxers found Mauthausen quite up to date. It was really no different from their humdrum civilian lives . . . except that they trained a little harder here, because when they looked around them, they realized they weren't fighting for a purse but for their own lives. This was why each block contained a good number of boxers. Curiously there were few lame ducks, firstly because the fools who bragged about their pugilistic prowess found themselves knocked out by clubs before they even got to the ring. And then, so many thousands of men ended up at Mauthausen, fearless fighting types as a rule, that statistics dictated there must be a fair number of boxers among them. Nevertheless, the number of champions was remarkable, enough to make you think the Gestapo in occupied territory recruited them deliberately in order to please their friends, the concentration camp chiefs. Paulo knew at least six of the champions either by name or from having seen them in Parisian rings. They made certain evenings at the Palais des Sports look like a golliwog's tea party by comparison. The only thing lacking was the golliwogs, a species unknown to Mauthausen. Ziereis probably didn't care for them much, good racist that he was. But there were quite enough white boxers to put on a good show.

They came from all over, just turning up in the convoys: Warsaw, Brussels, Amsterdam, Budapest, Paris . . . Germany too, which gave the Kraut population, jailbirds and screws, a chance to display their patriotism. The excitement heated up on the *Appelplatz* when a Kraut was pitted against a Frenchman, or some other representative of a backward country, but generally speaking, the fights were clean, and it was rare to hear the cries of "Fix!" which were regularly to be heard at matches in Paris.

Paulo had never seen a fight at Mauthausen, because he had only been let out of the quarantine to board the train for Loibl. But the camp veterans had talked so much about the boxing that he could confidently tell you who had beaten whom, in which round, whether it was a technical knockout or an injury, and so on, and he was never wrong. He also knew that one unexpected knockout could pour into the smart fellows' pockets the entire tobacco reserves of their block, and this was the real reason for his delight in the news that the game was coming to Loibl.

He didn't think for one minute that Mauthausen would arrange for its champions to be transferred to Loibl; he'd have to make do with local talent. But that wasn't so bad; they might have some fun . . . and a few bets. There were at least five pros among the Frenchmen: Lagrive, Pierrot Martin, Michel Pommier, a highly strung young Parisian whose right hook had wrought havoc in the Polish ranks, Templier, also very young and a genuine heavyweight from the provinces, and finally Perrimond, onetime hero of the northern rings and the Pas-de-Calais, whose flattened nose and cauliflower ears made you wonder if he had been right to abandon mining and its risks for the ring. Perrimond had neither the style nor the finesse of an Al Brown, but when it came to taking punishment, you couldn't find better. When Bullseye or Sailor hit him, he would complain that it tickled and double up with laughter.

With a line-up of professionals like these, amateurs like the madcap François of Burgundy were certainly not going to stay in the wings. In spite of his youth, François had some impressive titles to his credit, among others the August 1939 University World Heavyweight Championship at Monaco, on the eve of war. This was no mean feat and although he had dropped three classes since his arrest, a blowhard like Pierrot Martin, who was more of a pimp than a boxer, would have a few rough moments in store for him if chance brought them face to face.

François wasn't the only tough among the young men in the south. The Poles, Yugoslavs and Belgians of his age were eager to have a go too. After the punishment they had taken over the past year, they weren't afraid of having their looks spoiled. The qualifying rounds would definitely have to be carefully organized, in view of the excessive number of volunteers lured by promises of double soup rations, jam, margarine, and a host of other goodies.

"I know someone who'd beat the lot of them," mused Paulo to himself. "Joel. I don't know if he's ever boxed, but he's better built than the rest of them put together. He'd never done demolition work, but he picked up the knack right away, so he ought to pick up boxing just as quickly. I think I'll have a word with him. Christ, what an outsider he'd make!"

Before Paulo had finished working out his forecast, the ring had been set up. It was only a temporary one, for they were short of space, but there was nothing makeshift about it. Fritz had insisted that it should be regulation size. It had proper ropes too, taut enough to bounce back anybody who fell against them. The only thing missing was the padded mat to cushion the falls, but that was much more difficult to find in these remote mountains. In any case when it came to violent contact with the ground, the men of Loibl were superbly trained. They had also been trained to remain standing under a hail of blows, and when a fall was inevitable they had learned to get up before the count of ten to avoid the vicious kicks in their stomachs and balls. In fact for such hardened men, a boxing match by the book would be like a pillow fight.

That was why no one, neither the stiff-necked old men nor even the militants of the Front National, had criticized the volunteers for the first matches. So nothing stood in Paulo's way now, and he went to tackle Joel.

"Hey, Joel, I hope you're going to sign up. You heard what the doyen said? Double rations of bread and soup every day, and on fight evenings the winners get a feast of as much margarine and jam as they want. You'll need all the muscle you can get for what you and your revolutionary friends are cooking up, and this is your chance. Between you and me, you won't be letting yourself in for much trouble in your class, there isn't a single pro in it. Just a lot of farmers who've never worn gloves in their lives. I expect you've already tried your hand at it. Contact sports must be part of your job . . ."

"Yes, of course, I know the basics. I used to give boxing lessons. But I never went in for real matches, not even amateur ones. I used to fight a round from time to time in school competitions or maybe at local fairs, but really nothing very serious."

"Even better than I thought, you'll flatten them all. So you agree then?"

"Well, I'm quite tempted. I'm getting rusty and out of shape and I need some exercise other than shoveling and pickaxing. And then, even beatings don't bother me anymore. The only thing that does bother me is the idea of hitting a comrade, but come to think of it, they're pretty immune to it too . . . Okay, it's agreed, you can sign me up for Sunday. I don't know what I weigh now, but if you put me in the flyweights, somewhere between a hundred and five and a hundred and twelve pounds, you won't be far off."

"Well done, Joel, I knew I could count on you. I'll be your manager, Angel'll be second and we'll have a field day. We'll keep a close eye on your form, trust me."

The following Sunday, the day the ring was inaugurated, Joel, who looked so puny the crowd were convinced he'd soon be laid out, sent his opponent flying in the first round. A straight knockout. Even Paulo was taken by surprise. His odds of five smokes to one hadn't returned the expected yield, for this was only a qualifying round. The harvest still wasn't disastrous, he'd earned the equivalent of five packs, but the future didn't look too good, because everyone had had time to notice the Breton's clean style, his fast delivery, his feinting skill and, lastly, his punch. There was some danger that the odds might fall to evens at his next fight. Fortunately, the crowd had also realized that his opponent, a young Pole, had never thrown a punch in his life. He had set upon Joel as if fighting over a bowl of soup, and Joel had had to break away by hammering his face with a series of short straight lefts, two, and then three at a time—magic! It didn't calm his wretched opponent's hunger. He badly wanted the promised jam, but with Joel's gloves tearing his skin at each new punch, he looked as though he had a whole jar of the stuff smeared over his face. Doubtless wanting to put an end to the massacre, Joel finished him off with an uppercut in the solar plexus.

The other matches had yielded no surprises. All the pros, Templier, Perrimond, Pommier, even the hopeless Pierrot Martin, had easily bested their novice opponents. Only Lagrive, who still hadn't gotten over having his front tooth pulled out, had scratched. François of Burgundy had also won his match against an enormous Czech built like a wardrobe, who outweighed him by a good forty pounds. Several of the young men, not very good boxers but instinctive fighters, such as Leblond the sailor, had stood up to the test well. On the whole, it had been a good day's sport.

Otto the doyen was over the moon: his camp, which had been so despised at the beginning, no longer looked like Mauthausen's poor relation. The convicts were no less delighted than Otto: since all Kapos and block chiefs had stayed to the end of the fights, they had forgotten about the chores and usual annoyances. For a whole afternoon, Loibl had ceased to be a prison.

The following Sunday and every Sunday in June, the show was repeated: the ring was hurriedly set up in the morning, and after a short siesta, the sport began, with the Krauts in the front rows, seated on chairs or benches, according to their rank, and the riffraff behind them on the grass.

Loibl's Palais des Sports had it all—stools, basins, referees, points judges (Krauts, naturally)—and they even fetched the kitchen scales to weigh the competitors. It was every bit as good as the Vel d'Hiv, right down to the sponge, but you didn't throw it in here, it would have looked bad. It came in handy, though, for mopping up the blood, which flowed more than it usually did, from noses, foreheads, cheeks, even arms. The trouble was that the gloves were homemade. Out of leather? Of course not. They were made out of rough cloth, the only cloth there was, striped gray and blue.

The boxers who saw those ubiquitous stripes coming toward them soon abandoned any notions they may have had about this being the Vel d'Hiv. No hope of the jabs, uppercuts and hooks glancing off your skin. Even the slightest and most awkward thrust caught on everything it met, and it was certainly for this reason that the Sunday challengers, when they saw they were beaten, went down so easily. To the huge delight of the heavies in the ringside seats, who yelled in unison: "Finish him off! Kill him!"

Each successive Sunday saw the Loibl tournaments become a little more savage; it had degenerated into a Roman circus, yet actors and spectators were quite unconscious of it. Torn ears and eyebrows, broken noses, bloody mouths and knocked-out teeth were such an integral part of camp life that it seemed only natural for it all to continue under a different name. And the system was fair, for only those who asked for it suffered. Theoretically, it should have calmed the Kapos down. They were quite free to step into the ring if they really wanted to keep their muscles well oiled. Fritz, number one bully, the biggest thug of them all, had been unable to resist.

The problem had been to find him opponents of his own weight. Although he wasn't tall he weighed a good sixty-five to eighty-five pounds more than the least skinny of the prisoners. Undeterred by this minor point, he called for a list of the boxers and simply picked out those who suited him. The outcome could be seen a mile away and despite the fierce longing of the entire camp (Krauts included) to see Fritz thoroughly pasted, Paulo couldn't find any takers for a bet against the brute, or only at impossible odds. Fritz's first three wretched opponents stepped into the ring quivering with fright, and found themselves laid out with arms crossed. The bastard! He couldn't be allowed to get away with being supreme champion at Loibl! Or maybe that explained everything—it was only to be expected that someone so good at boxing should spend his days punishing men whose faces he didn't like. If he beat them all, even the pros, well, that would be that.

Happily his star began to fade the day he found himself face to face with Templier, the former heavyweight. You could tell that Fritz had done some boxing when he was younger, for his punches were well aimed, but what he had forgotten, during his long years of handing out blows to men forbidden to retaliate, was how to take them. At every right Templier threw at his face with no inhibitions whatsoever, he winced with pain, and by the second round Paulo was beginning to regret not having taken any bets. It would have ruined him if he had, for once again, Fritz carried the day.

As they came out of a rather muddy clinch just before the end of the third and final round, Templier, to everyone's astonishment, raised his arm to give in. It looked fishy, and those familiar with the tricks of the game protested noisily. They were in no doubt about what had happened: Fritz must have slipped a word in his opponent's ear when they were grappling together. Something along the lines of "Quit, and you won't have to worry about food," or simply, "You'll be sorry if you win, *Scheissekubel*!"

"It's becoming as bad as the Vel d'Hiv," grumbled Paulo. But at the same time it gave him an idea . . .

Joel, for his part, continued to win match after match. Nevertheless, he hadn't been fêted as a champion, for the flyweight class was filled with the starvelings, each man skinnier than the next. Seeing them display their miserable frames in the ring, you knew immediately they had no illusions about their future as boxers, but since they had been entitled to "boxers' rations" for a whole week preceding the fights, they couldn't very well get out of it. You never knew, one lucky punch and the scoff might last another week!

This was the theory upheld by the quarrelsome young peasant from the Sarthe who had caused the terrible Baroni to back down in public at the end of last summer. He must have been in pretty good shape when he arrived at Mauthausen—arms and thighs bounded by muscle, shoulders as wide as a barn door. Shoulders were all that was left of him now, or rather just the bones, for his muscles and fat had vanished. Time and again his farmer friends had warned him: "You're overdoing it, you can't take it . . . ," but it got the better of him. He had to work, he simply couldn't stop. With the result that he was wearing himself to death without realizing it.

Joel wasn't at all happy to learn he was going to meet this poor bastard in the ring. He had tried to talk him out of it, even suggesting that they fix the fight. Nothing doing. The peasant, typically obstinate, had dug his heels in. All he could think of was the chance of another week of extra food if he sent Joel out. The second the bell sounded, he went for Joel like a bull, head lowered and arms flailing wildly. But despite his headlong attack, his fists met only thin air, for Joel wasn't keen to counter the avalanche of blows and he had decided to dance around the ring, to lead him, the experts call it. The crowd began to hiss their disapproval and Bullseye, sole referee, felt obliged to warn the two boxers. But no sooner was the break over than the peasant started the same thing all over again.

"Oh, well, the idiot asked for it," Joel shrugged, and squaring himself up, he waited for the next attack. One-two, perfect, just like a professional, and it was all over for the peasant. He sailed through the air and landed back in his own corner, where his head hit the post with a dull thud.

Bullseye didn't even bother to count. "*Revier*," he shouted, puffing out his chest as if he were responsible for the model knockout.

It had all been rather painful, but even if the loser was off work the next day, one thing was sure: boxing was not going to be banned at Loibl. The Krauts enjoyed it too much, the best proof of this being that for the first time they mingled with their slaves without looking as if there were a smell under their noses. With no distinctions of rank or nationality, SS, Kapos and deportees crowded around the ring, yelling, laughing or applauding with one accord. It was irrefutable evidence that in the eyes of the SS and their green-triangled accomplices, the Loibl *Haeftlinge* had served their apprenticeship satisfactorily, like the Spaniards so envied at Mauthausen. Only a few months ago, the prisoners would have trembled with fear to see carpenters nailing together boards and ropes as they had just done for the ring, convinced that the planking must be a gallows to hang them from. Today, the strange ideas which occurred to their persecutors were for their entertainment! Otto was already talking of marking out a football field . . .

Paulo's take for these first matches had been disappointing, but, everything considered, this boxing business was turning out useful. As far as grub went, Joel had it made. "Boxer," the block chiefs all called him now, and they vied with each other to invite him in for a bite to eat. So, that meant one less mouth to feed. Better still, he would soon be in a position to stock up the team's supplies.

"No need for me to wait a single day more to tell Sailor and his harem to fuck off," Paulo decided. "The old queer's spoiling all my fun."

Karl, who was in the middle of an affair of the ass, took it extremely well. He needed a place at his table for a young Yugoslav innocent, and Paulo's excuse that he had sinus trouble which returned at the same time every day—coincidentally, at supper time—appeared to satisfy him. Paulo immediately chose for himself a bed in the farthest corner of the dormitory, among the dimwits.

Karl had wanted to be quite sure there were no bad feelings. "Come back when you feel like it, *mein lieber* Paul, treat this as your home. We haven't fallen out with each other, have we, you great crook? And it makes no difference to our plans for afterward . . ."

Jesus! So that turd still believed in their partnership after the war! He must be off his head to think he was going to settle happily in Pigalle once peace was declared, when the three hundred Frenchmen in the south vowed day and night to skin him alive!

"Dream away, my friend, that suits us just fine. Enjoy your fantasies," muttered Paulo between his teeth as he took his leave.

An enormous weight had fallen from his shoulders. He loathed being a favorite, terrified that from one moment to the next he might be labeled queer. And how could he have replied? How could he have refuted the accusation when that poison-tongue blabbed to everyone that they had a gangbang in his block every night? A reputation like that would follow you to Montmartre after the war . . . with or without Karl. Paulo had gotten out just in time.

All that was over now and he was free to come and go as

he pleased, to have a smoke with Dédé, Joel and Angel, with real friends, not the types Sailor had forced on him. How he was looking forward to strolling about the *Appelplatz* on hot summer evenings and chatting till the bell rang—provided, of course, that the gnawing in their stomachs didn't turn the conversation continually back to food.

Thanks to the smokes left from selling the tooth to the Italian, plus those reaped from a few fixed matches, hunger was something Paulo and Angel would not have to worry about for more than a month. As predicted, the smokers had indeed been hooked once more by their vice, a rich man's vice, a vice for the sharpsters with the soft jobs in the kitchens, the *Revier*, and the laundry . . . not to mention the ever-increasing number of barbers. These fellows still had to pass the time while their friends were out breaking rocks, and what could be more pleasant than having a smoke? Demand exceeded supply and the price of a drava soared. A single cigarette was now worth the full evening ration, bread plus what went with it, black pudding, margarine or jam on Sundays. The bowl of soup didn't even count, the smokers threw it in for free. "Go on, eat up, it's on me," they said as they gave their little present to keep deliveries coming their way.

Seeing all this had made Paulo virtually give up smoking. He allowed himself just two smokes a day and even that tiny ration caused him a few pangs. Two cigarettes meant two meals up in smoke, meals which might have been used to nourish a friend. Dédé Ménard, for example, that saint who never asked for anything.

If there was one person who deserved to be "assisted," it was Dédé. The whole camp, Frenchmen and the rest, ought to have carried his grub to him in his electrician's shack, because what Dédé gave in exchange, good news of the war, was beyond price.

He hadn't been very enthusiastic about the boxing matches in June; he must have found the sports Sundays very tedious, because they prevented him from tuning in to his radio. But on the morning of the sixth of June, he got his reward: the landings—after all the months he had spent hoping, swearing that they would happen.

With tears of joy in his eyes he dashed madly around the work sites, then through the tunnel, running along the upper gallery and coming back via the railway track, so that everyone should hear the news at the same time.

"They've landed, they've landed . . . this morning at dawn . . . in Normandy!" But he didn't stop as he called out his news, so the men shouldn't form into groups. Morale was dramatically boosted that day, in spite of the eternal skeptics and their moans. "That's the twentieth time we've been told about your landings . . . you're just crying wolf again. If it were true, don't you think we'd see it in the Krauts' faces?"

Certainly defeat was not written on their faces, that is, no more than on any other day. Nevertheless, they too had heard the news. Ménard hadn't actually told it to them direct, but the way he went about it was just as effective. Like a trail of gunpowder the news ran through the civilian camp and the Feldgendarmes to arrive, somewhat distorted and embellished, at the SS camp, forcing Herr Kommandant to give his soldiers an impromptu briefing. The wretched creatures had been strung along quite enough for two years; now they hardly believed the spurious communiqués which told them the Wehrmacht was still cutting the Red Army into shreds. How had the conquered forces gotten to Prussia? That had never been explained to them. But now that the Cossacks were about to screw their wives and mothers and deflower their daughters, they demanded information.

"Herr Kommandant, is it true that the Americans have landed in the west?"

"Tried to land, you mean. Marshal Rommel has pushed them back into the sea everywhere. Just like at Dieppe, if you remember.* They were only there for a few hours . . ."

Knock-Knees was exaggerating on purpose. It was naturally his duty to quash defeatism among his men, but over and above that, he was anxious to pour more cold water on the spirits of those *Haeftlinge* who were beginning to hold their slaves' heads a little too high for his liking.

Dédé knew, for God's sake, that the landings had been successfully accomplished, he shouted himself hoarse confirming it, but he couldn't very well cart his radio to Bullseye's or Sailor's block so as to shut up all the skeptics. Besides, as the

---

* An Allied Attack (mostly Canadian) in and around Dieppe in August 1942 was violently repulsed and resulted in heavy Canadian losses.

days went by, he, too, began to wonder a little. According to Swiss radio the Yanks weren't advancing very fast; anyone would think they wanted to spare their men. Not a patch on General Guderian's Blitzkrieg. They had advanced just a few miles in nearly a month, occupying a strip of land practically invisible on the map. And Normandy was one or two thousand miles from Yugoslavia! By the time the liberation got to Loibl . . . Dédé had to admit there wasn't that much reason to celebrate. Thank God for the Russkies on the other flank. Their advance looked impressive on the map, especially for those, like Paulo, who had heard nothing since Stalingrad. For he had finally seen the operations map kept so meticulously up to date by Dédé. It was the big surprise Dédé had promised him.

"Christ, you've got a nerve!" he stammered, breaking out into a cold sweat as he listened to Dédé's rundown. He had been returning his dentist's pliers and had found the Breton busy rubbing out the territory recently abandoned by the Krauts. That Red Army was like a steamroller, nothing like the tsarist troops! It had invaded all over the place: Bulgaria, Romania, Hungary, Czechoslovakia, Poland, not to mention part of the Great Reich itself. In front of a map covered with pencil shading showing each new Russian offensive, each one carefully dated, Paulo could only say stupidly, "Well, when you see that, it changes everything."

"That's just what I have to repeat to the others, day in, day out. Something's got to give, the Russians are hammering on all the doors. I only wish Eisenhower would do his stuff in the west. Look, here on the left, he hasn't taken very much, but that's France! It gives me the shivers."

"Christ, Dédé!" interrupted Paulo in a tone where panic mingled with excitement, "I hope you hide that map well!"

"Don't worry, no one could possibly find it in all this mess. But sometimes I think it wouldn't do any harm if one of the Krauts did stumble on it. He'd immediately go and tell the rest just where their Wehrmacht really is and it's important they should know, because if they did, they'd tell that lying Winkler to go to hell."

"I think we'd better keep it to ourselves, it's safer."

"But, Paulo! You're not going to start—to use your own expression—pissing in your pants? Wait a minute, it's nearly time. I've got something more important for you—the news on Radio Lausanne, in French! I gave up London and Algiers; they were too far, I couldn't hear them properly. I'd have to listen during the night. But in fact, it's better to listen to the Swiss. Being neutral, they don't exaggerate either way. It's only their broadcasts which give you the information essential for drawing up a realistic map."

Paulo was more than ready to take Dédé's word for it. He had one desire, to make himself scarce, but Dédé would have thought him a coward. So he merely said, "Just hurry it up before fat Marcel shows his face. He must be looking for me by now."

"We're almost there, we'll get the news in a minute. Go and stand by the grindstone near the window and look as if you're working. And keep your eyes and ears open. Right, here we go. Listen to this, Paulo . . ."

"In the east an army under the command of Marshal Rokossovsky has continued to strengthen its blockade of Warsaw during the night. In the north, the German defense of the town of Narva . . . On the Normandy front, the Americans are moving toward Caen, while the British under the command of Marshal Montgomery . . ."

"D'you hear that?" said Dédé. "And every day it gets better and better."

Paulo had stopped grinding, but he didn't take his eyes off the area around the shed in case one of those gray-green uniforms, routed everywhere, according to the announcer, should decide to come and spoil the sweet music ringing in his ears . . . "The garrison at Pskov has surrendered to the Soviets . . . the German troops have begun to withdraw toward Vitebsk and are digging in behind the Vistula . . ."

"They're fucked, they're really fucked!" repeated Paulo louder and louder, without leaving his observation post.

To hear news like that, live and in his own language, was just too much. It went straight to his head. Now he could understand the tense excitement of people back in France in their blacked-out apartments, gathering around the wireless to drink in, despite the irritating interference, the BBC's broadcasts of revenge. Not to have known the extraordinary thrill of this experience until now was another regret to add to his list.

But there was another thing about the crackling broadcast which stunned him: the elegant French of the Swiss announcer. The fellow spoke a different language altogether, no slang, not a single dirty word. There weren't many men at Loibl who would have understood him because the more he talked, the less one could understand his French. That was another thing sure to astonish a number of bourgeois families; their distinguished offspring would come home talking like working-class thugs. Take the Ménard family, for example...

The Swiss announcer continued in his emotionless voice: "We have just received a last-minute bulletin informing us that the city of Constanza in Romania has surrendered. And that brings us to the end of the news."

In two seconds, Dédé had folded away his operations map and dismantled the radio set, distributing the pieces around the shelves behind the rolls of electrical wire, old lamps and condensers. It would take a professional sleuth to find a radio set that worked in this shed: Dédé's bravery was matched by his cunning.

Now that the danger was past, Paulo was in less of a hurry to leave, but not because he wanted an explanation of what he had just heard. He had got the gist of it: "They're fucked" was the best summary of it all. No, if he was reluctant to go, it was because he wanted to tell Dédé that he admired him. Unable to find words for it, however, he just clapped him heartily on the shoulder and mumbled, "Dédé, you're a brave man, a braver man than me, that's all I can say."

It had been hard for Paulo to say that. Never in his life had he made such a compliment, such an admission. But already he'd recovered himself.

"Oh, I almost forgot! I didn't come just to give you back your pliers. Joel, Angel and me've decided to include you in our team, by force if we have to. Since Joel started boxing, even without Sailor—who I've just told to piss off, by the way—we've got enough chuff for four. So from now on you get a quarter of anything we manage to rake in. They asked me to tell you, you can't refuse."

"Thanks all the same, but I don't need it. I get by all right with the electrical jobs I do for them."

"No arguing, it's all fixed. It'll be a bonus if you scout out some on your own, it'll mean more grub for the community.

But I'm not sure I believe you. You're not as thin as you were, but I'm telling you, you're hardly smart enough for the Armistice."

When he got back to the concrete mixer a little later, Paulo was whistling jauntily.

"You're in a good mood," remarked Angel. "What's making you so happy? And where've you been for the last hour?"

"In Lausanne. You with me?"

"Christ! Well, go on, tell me about it!"

Paulo's summary of the news he had just heard was somewhat muddled, but as he accompanied every other sentence with an emphatic "They're really fucked!" Angel and the whole concrete-mixing gang, who had put down their shovels to listen, were quite willing to take his word for it. They took up their tools again in great good humor and somebody started singing "Mira mi brazo tatuado," which made them all chuckle delightedly.

Their jolly mood began to disturb the collaborationist Marcel. Of course he was pleased the Krauts were retreating on both fronts, but not so much that he was going to sing along with those bums, who were clearly going to make trouble for him. And the real troublemakers were Paulo and that cocky young Belloni. "I must get rid of them," he resolved.

Fat Marcel was scared to death of losing his foreman's rank, with all that came with it: double rations, no beatings, and no manual work. The selfish bastard was determined to hang on to his layers of fat, but fearful of having to tackle the two men himself, he had things fixed on the sly. Several days later, a Kapo friend of his, an Alsatian called Bayer who was in charge of the concrete-block factory, turned up at the mixer. He urgently needed two men to make up the numbers of his gang, "Healthy fellows who know the ropes," he said, nodding in the direction of Angel and Paulo. The dirty trick had been so well prepared by Marcel and so rapidly carried off that the two victims didn't immediately smell a rat. Paulo was even naïve enough to ask, "What sort of work is it in your factory?"

"Molding. It's very easy, you'll soon see."

"But we've never done molding, and we'd make a hash of your concrete blocks."

"Well, in that case, you can carry them!" retorted Bayer, with a snort of laughter.

Only then, when he heard the Alsatian's nasty snicker, did Paulo cotton on to fat Marcel's double-cross. The truck driver had assumed an expression of hypocritical dismay to give the impression he was heartbroken at losing two of his best workers. How very touching. For form's sake, mostly because he was afraid, he pretended to intervene.

"Wait a minute, Bayer. I'll check to see if there aren't two other men who might have done molding before."

But the other Kapo was already pushing Angel in front of him, and Paulo was obliged to follow.

"You fucking bastard, I'll make you pay for this," he had time to hiss at Marcel as he passed him.

He was wrong to take it so hard, because the concrete blocks were by no means a punishment. You still worked outdoors, like at the mixer, but with the added advantage that now that the factory was finished it was no longer the focal point of the whole work site. If they managed to sort Bayer out, Paulo and Angel would even be able to treat themselves to lengthy tea breaks sheltered by the fence surrounding the factory. Paulo was quickly consoled. "In fact, we're far better off here than with that sod Marcel," he remarked to Angel.

"If there weren't any concrete blocks to lug around. These buggers are heavy, I'm pissed off with them already."

Angel was right: It wasn't long before Paulo, too, was fed up with the concrete blocks. By the end of the first day, his back ached all over, his legs felt as if they were made of wood, and he could barely walk.

"I'm going to fix it so that bastard Marcel won't want to look at food ever again," he swore to his dormitory mates. He was seething with rage, but because he was so tired, he slept better than ever.

Again he was wrong to be so dramatic. The back pains which had frightened him completely disappeared after three days. It was the unaccustomed exercise, the continuous weight on the same shoulder, forcing unused muscles to work, which had caused the unpleasant feeling of paralysis. Anyway, he and Angel weren't the only ones lugging these blocks around; a good fifteen men, no stronger than they were, carted them around from morning till night and it seemed to suit them fine. Another reassuring note was that among them was

Pompon, who was as sharp as a razor. His presence was an absolute guarantee that the work wasn't too demanding. He had been delighted to see Angel and Paulo, and he quickly put them straight.

"I'm going to take you two in hand and we three'll have a good time. It's all *mañana* around here, you'll soon see. You and your nose for a good deal, Paulo! Trust you to land on your feet."

"That's one way of looking at it. I've had nothing to complain about for the last couple of months, but is it really that good here? The rate those paving blocks come off the molds gives me the shakes . . ."

"That's because you came at a bad time," interrupted Pompon. "The work goes in fits and starts, according to what the guys in the vault need. We've given them enough this week to keep them happy for a while, so we won't deliver any more till they've cleared another section of the vault. Got it? In a word, we work one week out of two."

"But the blocks are so bloody heavy, and they rip your hands to pieces," objected Angel.

"That's because you go about it the wrong way, you fathead. Look how I carry the blocks: flat across my shoulders. That way I don't feel it and my hands are free. I could even smoke on the job. Go on, you try it like that, little man."

His technique was sound, and after trying it that way, Paulo thanked him.

"You're right, it's less tiring than mixing cement for that fat turd Marcel. He can shove his mixer right up his ass, I won't miss it!"

"You see," Pompon continued, "it's always best to listen to the old hands. If the work was heavy, d'you think I'd have hung around all this time? And that's not all. The other handy thing is that the Kapo's a friend of mine. Pompon this, Pompon that, he can't get by without me, since I'm from Lorraine and he's from Alsace. So we talk about the old country, and while we do, I don't lift a finger. I'll pull a few strings for you."

"If you're from Lorraine, then I'm an Irishman," grinned Paulo.

"No, I'm dead serious. Mother and father came from Lorraine and I was born at Gérardmer. You're a Parisian, so you ought to know it's the provinces that produce the best Parisians."

The big city had certainly taught him a thing or two. From his dialect, which didn't sound at all Vosgien, you'd have taken him for a villain. But no. He simply worked behind the counter of his bar near the Bastille, carefully avoiding getting mixed up with the thugs who patronized it. The enormous biceps he had developed during a few rough years in a bakery made them keep their distance, and above all, Pompon knew how to keep his mouth shut. He never made any trouble and he had no time for the law; the villains appreciated that. Pompon's reputation had followed him to Mauthausen. The mobsters there hadn't done anything for him, but it pleased him all the same to know he was still respected.

For Paulo it was like a gift from heaven to work alongside this worthy fellow. He liked Joel, Dédé and the others very much and he admired their courage, but he couldn't stand their lofty principles and their choirboy mentality. If they were demobed tomorrow, he wouldn't celebrate with them; every man would turn to his own kind and Paulo knew he'd instinctively turn to the Pompons and Angels of this world. So he might as well stick to them now, to avoid any embarrassment later on.

Pompon arrived on the scene in the nick of time, because for several days young Belloni hadn't been himself at all. He didn't joke now, he hardly spoke except to complain. It was quite simply a bad case of depression, and he wasn't the only one among the boys of his age. Why were they all like this? The answer was that they were about four years too young. The hell had hit them at eighteen, nineteen or twenty, before they'd lived as men. They'd never held a gun, never voted or worked, hardly ever had a woman. The idiocy of their elders had nothing to do with them, and they had said so. The boys sent to Mauthausen shouted a bit too loudly perhaps, but the punishment they'd taken hadn't made them change their minds. They were still paying for the sins of others, for the older bastards who were in the mess with them.

The men of Paulo's age, between twenty-three and thirty, were much better prepared. They had seen the storm brewing since 1936: Spain, Munich, the mobilization, the absurd phony war, the invasion, Pétain, the collaboration. But their juniors had either just left school, blissfully ignorant of the ways of the world, or were still in the classroom. The camps were full of these kids and yet nobody, even those who suffered alongside them, felt any pity for them, least of all the men who could have been their fathers.

Paulo was well aware of Angel's distress, but all his efforts to distract him by joking, by cooking up new schemes for hunting extra food, were in vain. Even going back to the idea of escape, Angel's pet subject, did no good. As the end drew nearer, nothing seemed to matter anymore, not even his own fate.

Paulo was extremely worried about him. "I'm sure he's going to do something stupid, I can see it coming." He was afraid that one day Angel would crack and try to run for it in broad daylight, for the sheer hell of it, and his escape would come to an abrupt end in the larch wood. But Angel no longer had the heart for escape. He had chosen another way out, the *Revier*. If necessary, he would stay there forever, for he couldn't stand it any longer. He was sick to death of the work, the SS, the Kapos, and the tunnel, he hated it all; but not as much as he hated the older men around him, the bastard bourgeois, politicos and crooks who were all tarred with the same blue-and-gray brush, with shit on top. Paulo was the only exception he made, his only friend, as he had told him in the days when Sailor had been pursuing him: "I've only got one friend here. Fuck the others."

It still held good, which was why he felt the need one night to break his stubborn silence.

"I've got to tell you, Paulo. I've made my choice and nothing will make me change my mind. I'm going to report sick on Monday and go to the *Revier*."

"You're going off your head!"

"Yes, I am, and I've decided on the *Revier* to stop myself going completely mad. Either that, or I'll run straight across the line, I can't stand it anymore. At least in bed, I won't have to see anyone."

Angel's tired voice told Paulo that if he talked Angel out of his plan to report sick, the boy would immediately take the other alternative, perhaps that very day. In his present dangerous mood he'd have to handle the boy very carefully.

"I don't understand you, Angel. Things aren't bad here, we've got fresh air and we're getting our strength back before we go home. Of course the *Revier* is less dangerous now that that madman Ramsauer's gone, but you've still got to have a good reason. What are you going to tell the doctor?"

"An ulcer."

"Where've you got an ulcer?"

"Nowhere, but by Monday I'll have a beauty!"

"Oh, I see. The Jeanblanc method."

"Got it in one. It works every time."

"Oh, it works . . ." thought Paulo, "till the day it goes wrong and instead of the pus coming out, your leg goes septic and they have to cut it off." For the Jeanblanc method was to induce ulcers in the legs. He himself was on his fourth: once his leg was better after a fortnight in the *Revier*, he'd start on the other one. It was two months since he'd been seen at work. He was even younger than Belloni, so who on earth had told him how to do it? It must have been an old jailbird, for the trick was revolting. You put half a dozen large gobs of spit in a syringe and then pumped it into your calf or thigh just under the skin. Three days later, you'd have an inflammation and temperature in the hundreds. Then off to see the doctor, where the disgusting pus would move under his probing just as it was supposed to. An ulcer was the only possible diagnosis. And while you waited for it to run its course, there were hot baths and poultices and two weeks of lying flat on your back. Just what Angel was looking for. The following Monday, work in the factory continued without him, as he had so obstinately said it would. Jeanblanc had given him his shot so that his calf would be nicely swollen by Sunday. Over the weekend a number of men had been discharged from the *Revier*, and though Daniel wasn't fooled, he had admitted Angel without a murmur.

There were now a good half dozen of these cases in the infirmary, and the triumphant eradicator of scurvy was stumped. What kind of an epidemic was it which was ravaging the workers? As far as he knew, ulcers were not particularly contagious. "Of course," he said to himself, "the living conditions, overwork, malnutrition, and especially trauma and wounds from being beaten, must have created favorable conditions, but all the same, it's most unusual that some of these cases should develop another ulcer somewhere else as soon as the first has healed." He had already started to draw up a report supported by statistics when he noticed that the subsequent ulcers all developed in the same way, that is to say, they never turned malignant. Perplexed and rather unsure of his ground, he decided to sound out his convict assistants.

"Have either of you noticed that in all these cases we are dealing with circumscribed tumors, and never with diffuse tumors? I don't need to tell you that with the means of treatment available to us, septicemia would certainly follow in the case of the latter, and death would not be far away."

Jaryk and his colleague wisely kept quiet. Like Daniel, the Kapo orderly, and everyone else in the *Revier*, they knew what Jeanblanc was up to. Angered by it, they had hinted at the possible complications, but it was a waste of breath. The young fools continued injecting themselves. The older men refused to have anything to do with it; they had managed to preserve their poor bodies more or less intact, and they weren't going to be so stupid as to infect themselves voluntarily. Moreover, last winter a man had died from an ulcer. Nobody had known whether it was circumscribed or diffuse, to use the Tyrolean doctor's terms, or whether it had been self-induced or genuine, for Ramsauer had been in charge in those days, and he hadn't waited to see how the complaint evolved before administering his intracardiac injection. The ignoramus had taken this step as a simple precaution, to forestall the epidemic which he too thought he had detected.

The youngsters persisted in injecting themselves for all they were worth, and hearing their elders repeat this cautionary tale only aggravated them.

"So what?" they would retort. "You're just cowards, you'd rather die on the job, wouldn't you, just to keep the Krauts happy?"

The gulf between these angry young boys, of whom there were fortunately very few, and the more mature men of the camp, grew wider every day. The whole ulcer business was a reminder of the furious shouting matches which had followed the Russians' escape.

This time Paulo refused to take sides. "Let them do whatever they want," was all he would say to anyone who wanted to know what he thought, though deep down he totally disapproved of Angel's behavior. Over the last two months, he had gotten so used to having the boy at his side all day long that he felt as if he had just lost a younger brother. So that was what friendship meant.

Thank God Pompon was still around to talk to. Despite his easygoing exterior, he was not insensitive. He immediately guessed the reason for Paulo's low spirits, and he tried to console him:

"Cheer up, pal. In a couple of weeks, I'll get him reassigned to our crew. With old Bayer, that's no sweat. Fuck it, you make me cross, I'm here, aren't I?"

"You're dead right. I'm an idiot to worry about that stubborn little fool. If he croaks in the *Revier*, good luck to him. Come on, let's talk about something else."

"Okay," replied Pompon, "but remember, Bayer will have him sent straight back here. It's as good as done."

"Only if he wants to and doesn't go and inject his other leg when he gets out. I've a feeling we won't be seeing him again. He's lost his will to live, he's going to go under. It's all gone on too long for him. But we're soon going to be out of here, for God's sake, and he knows it. I give up!"

People find the depressions of others hard to understand, and even harder to excuse. Paulo was no exception, and in no time he struck Angel from his list of worries, only going to visit him in the *Revier* one evening in three, to take him his share of the grub. The boy scarcely even thanked him. He was miles away from Loibl, uninterested in anything Paulo had to say. To reach the point of thinking yourself elsewhere was what they all longed to do, but the disquieting thing in Angel's case was that there was no "elsewhere" and there was no afterward either.

Pompon had no such problems. On the contrary, he liked nothing better than to talk, about anything and everything. And none of it was dull. He had knocked around quite a bit, and had hundreds of adventures which he told with the timing of a born raconteur, so Paulo's days still passed quickly enough. While Paulo had always refused to talk about the future with Angel, he felt no hesitation in broaching the subject with Pompon.

"You going to go back to your bar when you get home, or are you going to start baking again?"

Pompon was amused at this suggestion. "Baking? Come off it, I'm not that stupid. I've done enough work here to last me the rest of my life . . . my bar, yes perhaps, if it's still there, if the landlord hasn't kicked my wife out. Even if he hasn't, I'll get someone in to run the joint, and I'll just come in to empty the till. All I'm going to do is go fishing. What about you?"

"Me?" replied Paulo, looking embarrassed. "Er . . . that depends on what I've still got when I get back, my apartment, my stuff, my woman . . . No idea what I'll do, but I can take care of myself, don't you worry."

It was during the long breaks, which Bayer tolerated between trips with the cement blocks, that Paulo and Pompon told each other their life stories. Their idle chatter took them far away from Loibl, and when one of the crew's gluttons rudely interrupted to get on to the subject of food again, they sent him away with a flea in his ear.

"Piss off, you jerk. You're out of date! We're talking about sex, not soup!"

For some time now, virtually everybody had begun to venture onto previously forbidden ground: the subject of their return to civilization. For two reasons: firstly because even the worst pessimists had come around to believing in the landings. This was thanks to two good Norman peasants whom Dédé had triumphantly informed that their villages, their homes, their wives, kids and cows had been liberated. As Sainte-Mer-l'Eglise and Cérisy-la-Fôret were confidential places, Ménard couldn't have invented them; they must have been mentioned on the radio. These precise details had finally done the trick. Something was definitely happening in France and the prisoners' return home was no longer wishful thinking. But what had really tipped the balance was the direct and positive proof which Loibl witnessed one fine sunny afternoon. With a deafening roar a squadron of planes had flown out of the sun and over the Karawankens heading northeast. Everyone had seen the markings, they were not German planes. Row upon row flew over in close formation for a whole hour without the Luftwaffe taking any action against their blatant provocation.

Dédé hurtled out of his shed and ran from group to group as he'd done on the day of the landings, yelling out, "Flying Fortresses! The Yanks are here, U.S. Air Force . . . Dakotas . . . Douglases . . . Liberators! They're going to bomb Vienna. It's started!"

The wretched deportees, particularly the French, could

scarcely take in this fantastic parade of lumbering planes flying past with their bombs clearly visible beneath their wings. They still vividly remembered the time before their capture when a German armada, with Goering at its head, had taken off to smash London. Their nightmare was nearly at an end, they could see it and hear it above their heads. So could the Krauts, who from now on would appear in a different light. The conquering heroes who had arrested them were now their conquered warders. Conquered like their friends in the Luftwaffe, who were incapable of stopping the bombers, which hadn't even bothered to take a fighter escort with them. It was a shame, because it would have given the convicts an indescribable thrill to see battle engaged above their shaven heads, a battle in which the Krauts would be shot out of the sky, nosediving fatally like the unfortunate Stukas which had once so terrified them in 1940. But there'd be no thrills today. Facts had to be faced: in the skies of the Great Reich there were no more Messerschmitts than there were angels.

"If you'd listened to me, you'd have known it, you bunch of jerk-offs!" yelled Dédé, whose excitement had made him vulgar. "In Normandy they haven't been able to get a single plane off the ground . . . they haven't got any, they're all on the Russian front, where Stalin's artillery's toppling them like ninepins. We're winning!"

The squadrons made such a din as they flew over the valley that the men in the tunnel, who'd been tipped off by the concrete-mixing crews, had stopped drilling to hear them go over. Some of them had even come out of the tunnel to set the beautiful Liberators sparkling like diamonds in a cloudless sky, without the slightest puff of antiaircraft fire. That the famous Kraut flak should not react, even in its own airspace, was the icing on the cake.

The SS soon recovered from their initial surprise. "*Ruhe, Scheisskubel! Arbeit, schnell!*" The men had no choice but to keep their eyes down, if only to look out for the Kapos' hoses and the gun butts of the nearest sentries. But it couldn't stop them from hearing the throbbing music in the sky.

The performance had been repeated the next day and the day after, and every day for the first two weeks of June whenever the weather was clear enough. The Yankee pilots must have been warned that they would come across deportation camps or POW camps every five or six miles, and even if they were as inept as they were reputed to be, they'd have to be complete cretins to make the mistake of dropping their cargo on Loibl. It really would have been too ironic for these poor bastards of *Haeftlinge* to get themselves wiped out now, and by their saviors. But they had nothing to fear. The gigantic mountains around Loibl made it ten times more impregnable than the Maginot Line, quite apart from the fact that in case of trouble, they could always take shelter in the tunnel. Surely Winkler couldn't be so cruel as to refuse entry to the men who had almost finished his tunnel for him with their own sweat and blood! However close the war came, there was no safer spot to await the end.

Paulo was not at all eager to be bombed, though he knew from Radio-Ménard that the Americans and the RAF were committed to an offensive which would raze Germany to the ground before Christmas. The bombing would be indiscriminate, that is to say, the Allies would be supremely indifferent to the plight of the poor bastards Himmler had dragged by force into Germany, and so Paulo appreciated the tunnel more and more every day.

"Seems to me we haven't been working for nothing," he remarked to Pompon one day, after they had distinctly heard explosions to the north.

"You're right, there's justice after all. But listen, it's getting closer, it sounds as if they're bombing Klagenfurt..."

"...or Linz, Hitler's town. It's not far from the border either... With their sense of humor, the English'd be quite capable of it!"

Compared to what was going on in the sky, the next installment in Pompon's life story seemed very dull. The only thing Paulo wanted to talk about was the war. No more about Paris, women or mad escapades. But the other Frenchmen in his gang looked like such idiots that he was obviously going to have to put up with Pompon's interminable stories.

"Did you know Fredo in Jo's dance hall on the rue de Lappe? Mm? Well, I've got a really good story about what happened one night when we were out on the town..." The man was inexhaustible.

Paulo was wrong to look down on him so much. It dawned on him the day he found himself on his own looking stupidly at his pile of concrete blocks. Goodbye to Pompon, he was leaving with Bayer, who had just been appointed timber Kapo.

"Can you split wood, *Kamarad*?" his countryman had asked him. "All right, you can come with me, it's for Universale's gas generators. A lazy guy like you ought to find the work right up his alley."

As he departed with Bayer, Pompon called over his shoulder, "Don't worry, Paulo, I'll ask him to get you along too, and we'll be able to go on chatting about Paname . . ."

Paulo was livid at being left on his own, and it was on the tip of his tongue to shout back, "You can keep your fucking stories to yourself, they bore me stiff!"

Bayer had been replaced by an Austrian Kapo who was obsessed with productivity. Since the vaulting needed more and more cement blocks and it had begun to pour with rain, the to-ing and fro-ing between the factory and the wagons soon became intolerable. But where could he go now? The concrete mixer was out, thanks to that bastard Marcel. Paulo scanned the work site, but his gaze kept coming back to the big black hole of the tunnel. They'd surely take him on there. There weren't many volunteers for it in the summer, despite the drippings, but getting out of it again was well nigh impossible. He hummed and hawed, unable to make up his mind, until one evening he saw a group of civilians disappearing into the tunnel and thought he recognized the graceful silhouette of Yanka.

"Am I seeing things? It must be her . . . I've got to find out right now."

Pretending to have a sudden attack of diarrhea, he sprinted to the crapper, came straight back out again, and headed for Ménard's hut. He was in luck: Dédé was home.

"Dédé, you've got to tell me, was that really Yanka who just went into the tunnel?"

"Might have been, she started work again yesterday."

"If she's been where you said she was, she's got a hell of a nerve! What is her job anyway?"

"Secretary to the chief engineer."

"You're joking!"

"What's so surprising about that?" asked Dédé. "I suppose you thought she was just a maid, that she did the dishes in the Feldgendarmes' mess?"

"Of course not," replied Paulo indignantly. "I could tell

the first time I saw her she wasn't that kind. I could see she had class . . ."

"That she had guts, you mean!"

"Certainly looks like it—but look, what on earth's she going to do in the north?"

"I don't know. Probably going shopping. Klagenfurt's less than twelve miles from here. It's a big town, you can find all sorts of things there—even partisans!"

"Christ . . . Partisans? In Austria?"

"And how! There's no border up in the mountains. Mobility is the maquis's best weapon, they always avoid direct confrontation. When the mountain police or the SS move in too close, they simply slip over to the other side, into enemy territory. It may not look like it, but Loibl is surrounded by them."

"Why doesn't Tito attack the camp then?" exclaimed Paulo excitedly.

"I'll tell you later, I haven't got time now. If you're in such a hurry to know, why don't you ask Yanka yourself? She'll be back tonight."

Paulo's jaw dropped. "How do you know that?"

"I know more than you think," replied Dédé, firmly pushing him toward the door. "Go on, out you go, it's closing time."

Not in the least bit sympathetic, and even less cooperative, his friends in the crew had left Chastagnier his full share of heavy paving stones. An enormous pile was waiting for him, but he set to with the smile he reserved for the good days.

"Take a look at me, you guys," he seemed to be saying to his workmates who were startled to see him shouldering his cement blocks with such a will. "Take a good look, because you're going to be doing this fucking job without me tomorrow."

After what Dédé had just told him, he wouldn't hesitate a second longer, and that very evening he would go and find the all-powerful Fritz to get himself transferred to the tunnel. No sweat, Sailor would fix it in no time. Too bad about the fresh air, the sunshine, the Flying Fortresses and the sweet sound of the bombing . . . he'd get the others to tell him about it. To be close to Yanka, to talk to her and hear from her lips what was going on in the rebellious mountains seemed far more important to him. She came back out of the tunnel just as Fossil-Face blew the whistle for assembly. One of the first to line up, as usual, Paulo managed to catch her eye. She recognized him instantly and acknowledged him with her most charming smile.

"She recognized me," he exulted. "So winter didn't mess up my looks too much." And he returned her greeting by comically doffing his striped cap.

If he hadn't changed too much, she, on the other hand, was unrecognizable. For the better. She was ten times more beautiful than before. She had put on just the right amount of weight, her face was tanned, her cheeks copper-colored; her jet-black hair had grown even longer while she'd been in the maquis, and it cascaded down her back, to just above her gorgeous backside. She was quite simply sensational.

This vision made Paulo more determined than ever.

XXII

Paulo's prediction was correct: his request was favorably received. But what he had not foreseen was that they were not taking on any more miners on the day shift, and he found himself transferred to a service crew which only worked at night—every night. As the civilians were restricted to their own camp after 9 P.M., he wouldn't have much chance of seducing Yanka. What a fucking awful timetable!

He could have kicked himself for not having made a few inquiries before going to find Fritz, but it was too late to back out now, especially since the fat thug had been particularly friendly to him.

"In a month you'll be on the day shift, *langer.* By then, there'll be work for everybody."

What was the Kapo talking about? Coming from an overseer like him, they could not be idle words, but—"work for everyone . . . in the tunnel . . ." when most of the work was completed? There was a catch somewhere, and it would have been a good idea to try and find out more. Paulo didn't bother, partly for fear that Fritz might find him overinquisitive and fly into a rage; then the only answer to his questions would be the rubber hose. In addition, he was much less concerned with what would happen in two months' time than with exactly what he was going to do to get out of the mess he had just landed himself in. Blithely volunteering for the only Kommando that never saw any civilians was the opposite of what he had intended.

He had every reason to be cross, but it was no good crying over spilled milk and by the following day, his anger had subsided. Every low was generally halfway to something good, he had shrugged to himself.

In fact, right from the beginning he realized that it was the miners in the night shift who benefitted most from the beautiful weather and the warm sun. The harassments, the useless duties and the prick parades which interrupted their sleep were finished, forbidden by Winkler. "Let them rest," he had ordered after Ziereis' visit, and the block chiefs had not only obeyed, they had gone one step further. Block organization had reached new heights of informality. No more lining up for distribution of soup and coffee, which they could now drink outside, sitting on the grass; no more set time to go to the *Waschraum* . . . it was amazing to see the effect that these Liberators, which had resumed their air raids, had on the way the Krauts thought, Karl in particular, who must have been thinking how little time he had left to perfect his plans for setting up in Pigalle. It was no joke: he was firmly convinced that he was going to start a new life in France! "*Hamburg kaputt . . .fertig für Karl* . . . long live Paris!" he would say, thinking he was flattering the Frenchmen in his block.

"That's something else I wasn't prepared for," Paulo said to himself, seeing the big slob welcome him like a lifelong friend.

There was no longer any question of cold-shouldering him. Sinus trouble all day long would not wash. No, he'd have to join in with the bastard's game again, and try to exploit the situation to its maximum.

So against his wishes, Paulo found himself a guest at Sailor's table for lunch every day. And he felt more compromised than ever, because this was lunch *à deux;* the pimp had pulled strings for the hustlers in his block, and they were all on the day shift, scratching away on some relaxing part of the site. But it wasn't so bad, because as Karl grew more and more concerned about the prospects of his new life in Paris, he became increasingly liberal with good food. There were potatoes, sautéed in drippings, fried black pudding, bread with margarine and jam—nothing was too good for *mein lieber* Paulo. And this was only the everyday offering. The real treat arrived straight from the kitchens twice a week: a goulash especially whipped up by the kitchen Kapo, a friend of Karl's, the man who had replaced Ernst after his suicide.

"Even Joel wouldn't turn this down," Paulo had said to himself, half ashamed the first few days. His conscience had soon cleared, for no one could claim that he actually deserved these favors this time. Nevertheless, he made sure that the intimacies were restricted to the lunch hour, and even then, as he stuffed his face, he did his best to avoid being at all grateful. He talked to his benefactor in arrogant and cynical tones:

"Listen, chief, the goulash isn't too hot today; you'll have to tell your friend in the *Küche*." And even: "Christ, you're stingy with the margarine, *Mensch*!"

The tattooed queer enjoyed all this tough talk, and every day there was more lunch on the table than before. It got to the point where Paulo, incapable of swallowing another mouthful, would quite openly get up and fetch his bowl to fill it up with everything that was left. "For tonight, in the tunnel," he would say, whereupon the soft-hearted Karl would delve into his reserves of margarine and sausages to make sure Paulo's bowl was full to overflowing. Their complicity had reached such a point that Paulo might just as well have admitted that these extra rations would be given that evening to Dédé and Angel, who was well rested and whose appetite had returned with his morale. But the tattooed queer was quite capable of getting jealous, and although he made out Karl was under an obligation to him, Paulo was extremely careful not to rub him the wrong way. In addition to the grub, Karl had allowed him one of those luxuries which are so hard to give up once you've tasted them: he had given him the go-ahead to take a blanket outside, so that after each of these lunch feasts he could grab a digestive nap on the grass behind the block.

Being able to sleep off a heavy lunch every afternoon, far

from the stale smell of the dormitory, easily made all the concessions, all the promises and all the declarations of "Karl, you're my pal" worthwhile.

There were no half measures either. Paulo's snoozing in the sun was done properly, in the nude, or more precisely in a pair of shorts, striped of course, which he had cut from an old pair of long underpants left behind in the *Waschraum*. Sailor couldn't get over Paulo's nerve, but since the SS in the watchtowers couldn't see behind the block where his protégé was tanning his paunch, he let him be. It was just as well that Karl was afraid of damaging his tattoos, otherwise he too would have come outside, to sprawl in the sun next to his "pal"!

Which Paulo wouldn't have enjoyed at all, for what he relished about these moments was the feeling of being completely alone. For almost sixteen months, there had always been—at work, at muster, or in the block—at least one guy, usually more, on his back. There was someone, every minute of the day, pushing and shoving, moaning and talking drivel, and it was an utterly new sensation to escape for a few hours, more of a treat than the most delectable goulash! Lately, he had been having a fairly good time, he'd had a few good moments, but here, alone and naked on his blanket, he was really in seventh heaven, as he had rarely been in his life before.

The young Savoyard was right! The Karawankens were beautiful, looked at from below, lying on your back . . . if you shut out from your field of vision the barbed-wire fences, the watchtowers, and the rest of the camp. Bounding from ridge to ridge in his imagination, like the chamois glimpsed from time to time on the highest summit, Paulo dreamed dreams of freedom, away from the Krauts and fellow prisoners who hemmed him in, and it did him a world of good.

His escapist fantasies were certainly influenced by no longer feeling the slave's uniform against his skin, but that wasn't why he stripped. He had made his comical shorts for only one reason: to get an all-over tan and become good-looking again, on the principle that it was best in this queer colony, to arouse desire rather than pity. So, methodically, he worked on his tan, half an hour on his back, half an hour on his front, even going as far as pulling down his brief shorts for his bottom to get its fair share of the sunbeams. He could lie out for hours without fear of sunburn—on the diet he'd been shoveling in over the last few days, his greasy skin would easily take care of him. His curiosity had not taken him to the point of weighing himself on the kitchen scales along with the Sunday boxers, but he estimated that he was only about twenty pounds short of his normal weight. It was not a bad performance for a former skeleton, and it was worth tanning muscles which he had paid so dearly for!

His progress was confirmed each evening when his friends returned from the day shift. They marveled at his transformation.

"Aah, there's nothing like the mountains," he joked. "I've decided to set up house in Mégève when I get back!"

But there was one thing which he kept well hidden from them. For the most part, his beauty cure had been inspired by Yanka, the girl who had picked him out, wretched and filthy as he was, from five hundred identically awful men. Whether out of gratitude or mere politeness, it was only proper that he should show her she had not erred in her choice . . . that he was indeed the most handsome man at Loibl.

Fritz had said it would be a month before he could go back to the day shift—well, so much the better. It was long enough for her to be shocked when she saw him again, stripped to the waist, as bronzed as a beach bum, clean, groomed and almost good enough to eat. Showers were allowed only on Saturdays, so he had gotten into the habit every morning after work of putting his whole body under the taps in the *Waschraum*. But it was his teeth he took most care of, probably because he knew that, since they didn't understand each other's language, his smile would be the best interpreter in his contact with the pretty Slav girl. As for his beard, Sailor's barber had promised to shave it twice a week, which only left his hair—and that was more complicated.

"I'll skip every other shearing session," he told himself. "I must be able to camouflage the *Autobahn* by wetting my hair and combing it over with the dog's comb. At least then I'll be able to say hello to her without her cracking up."

In the end Paulo's toothbrush and lice comb, the things everyone greeted with derision, had come in useful. Every day, he spruced himself up a bit more; you would have thought he had a date that same night, and that he was sure to finish up on top of his woman after she had licked him all over. But he was realistic, and if the idea occurred to him now and again that in the darkness of the tunnel . . . Yanka . . . a quick one . . . , he didn't linger on it very long. It was to women in general that his thoughts turned as he conscientiously washed his cock every day, to all the women he had had, and, more important, to those he was soon going to enjoy with his overflowing balls. Now that he wasn't hungry anymore, it was inevitable that girls would fill his thoughts again. It was also quite in keeping that while his less privileged companions were dreaming of the end of the war in the shape of an enormous blowout, Paulo saw it in the shape of a pair of well-rounded buttocks. A woman's buttocks, needless to say . . . because these days men's bottoms really gave him the staggers. Even a faggot who lived to be a hundred would never have the opportunity of seeing in his lifetime a tenth of what Paulo had seen and heard in a few months. Not to mention pricks. Fifteen nationalities, practically the whole of Europe, were represented at Loibl . . . a lot of comparisons to be made. However broadminded he was, Paulo had never managed to get used to it. This was another thing without precedent in a camp or prison; the modern generation of Aryans was a real bunch of bum bandits. In the end, dreaming about women as Paulo was doing was one way of resisting them.

In any event, even if it weren't patriotic pride which made his shorts swell as soon as he began his siesta in the sun, one thing was unmistakable: he had an erection again, for the first time. And there was no doubt about it: it wasn't brought on by needing to piss, it was the real thing. His rope was actually rising! It had caught him completely unawares the first day, and to make sure he hadn't been mistaken, he began to practice inducing it on demand, picturing more and more women to himself, each one dirtier than the one before. It worked like a charm.

"There's one or two that can start getting their bottoms ready," he rejoiced, like the TB patient who, as he feels his strength returning, swears he's going to make out with all the women in the world as soon as he gets out of the sanatorium. Paulo considered it a personal victory, as he watched his erect prick pointing up to the sky like the mountains which surrounded him. The Krauts had thought they could rob him of his virility, but they had made a big mistake—his prick was hard again!

Paulo had always shown a certain reserve in conversations about sex among his friends. He felt the smutty details were something for girls and queers to gossip about. But now he was curious to know whether there were others at Loibl who were absorbed by the question of their tools. There must have been. Every man who was eating his fill must have been in the same boat, especially the younger prisoners—although you couldn't attach much importance to them as a good many were well attended to by their cocksucking block chiefs. But what about the others—the older and scruffier men—who didn't get that opportunity? It was a rather delicate matter, asking a healthy man like Daniel the orderly if he didn't enjoy a quick wank now and again.

For the moment the question of grub was more important than sex to most of them, but it wouldn't need much to tip the balance—a slice of bread at lunchtime, perhaps, or some soup in the evening instead of coffee.

Given that Germany was crumbling, any improvement in the daily rations seemed out of the question. Nevertheless, that was exactly what happened in the first days of July. As if by magic, extra food began to arrive in the camp from all over the place. It started with a truckful of parcels from France, and the veterans who before Mauthausen had been rotting away in Pétain's prisons all jumped to the same conclusion: "It's the Quakers!"

But it was much better than that: the parcels were personally addressed, and not with the *KLM* registration numbers. The labels bore real names, surnames and Christian names written in the hands of their loved ones back home. By what miracle had they managed to trace them? The answer wasn't difficult. Some of the famous postcards with Hitler's mug on them, saying: "I am in good health," had actually arrived!

The distribution had a profound effect on the lucky men who were summoned to the doyen's hut after muster and half of them came back with tears in their eyes, overcome by emotion as they recognized their loved ones' handwriting and saw the loving way each item had been wrapped. But they were crying tears of anger, too, because—and they should have known—Otto and his acolytes, on the pretext of a search, had laid their hands on anything they wanted: tins of pâté, sardines, condensed milk, chocolate and other delicacies—leaving only the occupation biscuits, the rusks and the ersatz products like anchovy paste and barley sugars. In their hurry to rifle through the parcels, they had forgotten to remove the wrappings of the stolen tidbits, and some poor bastards had the additional grief of finding what they'd missed on an inventory in the bottom of their parcel.

"Yeah, it's like whipping a blind man's begging bowl," said Paulo, trying to console an old man in his block who was weeping bitterly.

"It's much worse," the man replied. "I know my wife, she went without for months so she could send me all this. Look at the list, all kinds of things . . . the bastards." And he began to sob again.

What Paulo hadn't realized was that he was going to be on the receiving end of some of the stuff which had been swiped, because of course Sailor had been as light-fingered as the rest, and now that his pantry was bursting at the seams, he obviously wanted to shower some of his wealth on his "friends." Paulo would not stoop to this, and he refused categorically:

"Give it to someone else, Karl. I'm not going to eat my friends' food, is that clear?"

In the end, he did accept the occasional slice of bread with sardines, or a pâté sandwich, but he drew the line at that.

"Just a taste," was how he justified it to himself.

He was wrong to be so high-minded, because none of the stolen parcels and their contents left the camp and eventually everyone benefitted from them. The block chiefs, their houseboys, fairies, barbers, and *Schreibers* were already crammed to the gills and quite unable to double their intake from one day to the next, so for lack of space in their stomachs, they were obliged to put their ordinary rations of soup, bread, margarine, etc., back into circulation. Finally everyone, the victims as much as the others, had a little more to eat. All things considered, it was fairer that way. It wouldn't really have been right for men who came from well-to-do families, or had loving wives or mothers, to gorge themselves under their friends' noses on blocks of chocolate, or cooked chickens.

Unfortunately, there was one good fellow in Block 2 who did exactly that, with tragic consequences. His name was Costampin, from the Jura, and he was no more a glutton than any of the others; in fact, his friends were agreed that he was generally a good sort. But he hadn't been able to resist one fine tin of food which had escaped the block chiefs' plundering, probably because it lacked an appetizing label. He had immediately recognized his wife's trademark, it was chicken and beans, his favorite dish. And so, for fear of not doing justice to the woman who had put all her love into preparing him this delicacy, he had decided not to share it with anyone, but to down the whole lot himself in one sitting. It was enough to give anyone the galloping shits when their intestines had been sluiced through with nothing but soup for a year . . . but too bad, it was worth the risk. How his old woman must have wept as she sealed up the container.

Even if she had decided that her chicken and beans was the best way of showing her greedy husband that she still loved him, she should have realized that air might get into the container. A few hours later, poor Costampin was flat on his back, but not with the shits—with a grave case of food poisoning. Anywhere else, quick action might have saved him, although he had gulped down all the bad meat and most of the beans. At Loibl, naturally, there was no antidote, and despite strenuous efforts, Ramsauer's replacement had had to admit defeat. The agony lasted four days and four nights, and it was an abominable experience for those who watched Costampin die. When he breathed his last, he was blind and swollen like a waterskin, unable to curse anybody for his misfortune.

To be poisoned at a distance by the one who loved him most was the worst end that the brave soldier could have come to. But the most sickening irony was that this terrible accident had happened at Loibl, a camp isolated from all contact with the outside world. The first link with the outside, with France, had brought with it the most appalling death. Of course, it was too much to expect that the thieving Kapos would be the ones to gorge themselves on the poisoned chicken. It would have been too perfect a crime! That was the conclusion everybody drew from the whole dreadful episode, but for several days, they all found themselves thinking inevitably about the poor woman from near Besançon who must have been wondering if her parcel had arrived safely. It would be hard to tell her the truth when they got back, and her grief would be even greater when she learned that there was nothing left of her dear husband—because of course, like so many of his fellows before him, they had wasted no time in burning him.

But at Loibl, no one could mourn for very long and the arrival a few days later of more trucks full of food, from Austria, was greeted with delight. This time it really was the Quakers. They had managed to stir the German Red Cross into action, but the things they had gotten hold of were much less exciting: a few joints of meat, a ton of spuds, and something new: dehydrated vegetables. There were boxes and boxes of this rubbish, which reminded them of the synthetic sauerkraut at Mauthausen, and since it was in concentrated form, they could be sure, even from this first load, that the supply of instant soup was guaranteed until winter.

At the start, everyone had found it delicious, with its aftertaste of celery, but in the long run it became monotonous, and those who were able to make other arrangements made haste to give it to anyone who'd take it. This meant that by the middle of July, the problem of hunger had virtually disappeared, because these dehydrated vegetables were arriving on top of the normal shipment of *Lebensmittel*, which Mauthausen continued to send since Universale was footing the bill. In other words, from one day to the next, the camp brimmed over with so much food that the block chiefs no longer took the trouble to preside over the ritual of soup distribution. No one bothered to slip to the back of the queue anymore in the hope of being served with the thicker stuff from the bottom of the vat. There were enough potatoes, chunks of meat, dehydrated vegetables—and maggots too—for everyone. Those who had any space in their bellies had only to raise a hand.

On such a diet, everyone quickly put on weight, blessing the Quakers for managing to pinpoint Loibl at the farthest end of the immense Alpine chain, and especially for making the SS administration relent.

But the truth of the matter was completely different, and once again Dédé Ménard set the record straight:

"How can you be so naïve? Hitler softening? Don't make

me laugh. If he has made any concessions—and it must be the same in all the other camps—it's for a very good reason. There has been a new development: For the first time, there are German prisoners in the Allied camps in France. The German Red Cross must have wanted to get in touch with them. Okay, they were told, but give and take, there are Frenchmen in your camps who aren't getting anything. Let our trucks through . . ."

This was not speculation on Dédé's part. He was only interpreting what Swiss radio had announced, albeit guardedly: the Krauts on the Western Front were proving to be much less tough than their compatriots in the east, who had been ordered to hold back the Russians. These were the twentieth-century Huns from whom they'd been told to expect no quarter, and now they were surrendering to the Yanks by whole companies. Everything had changed. The Germans' *Blitzkrieg* was over; they were having to learn diplomacy, and how to negotiate all over again. The French deportees, at Loibl Pass and elsewhere, had become a currency of exchange, worth even more now that there probably weren't many of them left.

Once the men were persuaded of the logic of Dédé's reasoning, camp morale soared even higher than it had been when the first squadrons of Flying Fortresses went over, with the difference that, as hunger was no longer the principal obsession, the war was once again the focus of all conversation. The Resistance men suddenly came to life everywhere, trying to make the others listen to them, as if they felt they would arrive in France too late for anyone to believe their stories. Their shadowy exploits necessarily went back to 1942 or even earlier, since by the beginning of 1943 they were already under arrest; out of the few witnesses who could authenticate their heroism, the dead must outnumber the living by now. They had good reason, then, to start talking about their pasts here at Loibl. If by some unlucky chance they didn't make it back, like Costampin, their friends would bear witness.

The others who had been rounded up, the crooks, and the men who had "not done anything," or not very much, might have been angry at this reminder which put them in their place, but no. On the contrary, they were generous in their support:

"You guys are right, you took risks, and you've paid for it . . . you shouldn't let them cheat you now."

Paulo went even further with Dédé:

"I never met any Resistance men before Mauthausen. It looks like there are millions of them today. It's really funny! Dédé, we're counting on you and your pals to make them shut their traps when we get back!"

XXIII

Paulo had ceased to be an exception as soon as they all had as much to eat as they wanted and were getting back to their normal weight. Every block now had its share of erections and in the evenings, at the far ends of the dormitories, they talked of nothing else. Sometimes, for a laugh, a young fellow would take out his stiff prick before he went to sleep, and shout, "Hey-hey, guys, what a whopper! Who's going to come and kiss it good night?"

It was a schoolboy's game, and had nothing to do with the sexual obsession that tortured Paulo, just a good atmosphere in the dorm and the last high spirits before lights out. The boys were enjoying the fact that their cocks were working again, and that's all there was to it. Who could reproach them for expressing their delight by playing with their reawakened pricks! It was a far cry from suspecting them of actually finishing the job off under the covers. Frenchmen are born womanizers and do not hold masturbating in very high regard, so it would have been out of character for the men at Loibl, so near to freedom, to let themselves go.

Some even thought it more respectable to get themselves sucked off, albeit by a man. They didn't shout it from the rooftops, but like jailbirds all over the world, they weren't ashamed of it, nor did it make them feel they had turned queer. Especially as those who did it for them—Bullseye, Karl, Otto, Sladek, and Eddy, the queen with the homosexual's pink triangle—what were they if not whores? The whole camp had agreed as much, even the more sober men. And shooting your load in their mouths was as good a way as any other of avenging yourself and humiliating them. Your principles were quite safe. Admittedly, there had been the odd case of a hustler getting pushed around by an impatient bully and agreeing to relieve him, but such incidents were very rare. Easily 95 per cent of the home sucking team were Krauts. "A real race of queers," was the general opinion.

And everyone tried to convince himself of it, putting the SS and the *Feldgendarmes* in the same bag as the Kapos. They had taunted the Frenchmen enough with *Fräulein fertig, fikfik fertig* during those first days as they pretended to jerk off. It was almost a confession of guilt. Since then, the prisoners had been unable to prove anything, as the SS avoided hanging around the camp, but even so, Ernst, the sentimental Kapo, had not invented the story about the NCO in the kitchens. Their love affair was public knowledge and it had gone a long way. The *Unterführer* was another example. He was one of the few SS who could easily get close to the prisoners, and everyone was aware that he had forced a young kid to let himself be sucked off by threatening to set his dogs on him, *mein Kamerad*! It was a small step from there to deduce that they were all doing it, that in the SS barracks they were all going around in circles buggering each other, and the Frenchmen at Loibl, as worthy representatives of the most antihomosexual people in the world, were swift to take that step. All the same, they had a skeleton in their own closet: a Parisian who was an inveterate cocksucker, and had let his vice get the better of him at the risk of getting himself beaten up by the chief of Block 1, who didn't like sharing. There was general amazement when this fellow, who was well over thirty and didn't look the slightest bit effeminate with his five o'clock shadow, showed his true colors.

"Let me do it for you," he'd say to the chief's boys. "You'll see what a blow job is when it's signed by Henriette."

He himself had asked them to call him only Henriette or Rirette, his *nom de plume* at the Porte de Champerret. What crime had he committed to be picked up by the Gestapo? He had probably been rounded up in a raid on a urinal, but it wasn't certain; he could well have been a member of the Resistance. Patriots were not recruited exclusively from the ranks of ladykillers. In any case, whether out of a genuine concern for the good name of the Resistance or not, he showed no desire to talk about the reasons for his arrest.

Once they had recovered from their initial surprise, the Frenchmen were the first to find it funny. This self-confessed queen in their midst could only instill respect among the top queers of the camp, who finally found something to joke about which was right up their street. Sailor above all; he went to quiz Paulo:

"How much does your pal Henriette make a day back in Paris?" He found it comforting to know that there were ways of earning his daily bread there in a rope and tackle shop.

"Ask him yourself. Why don't you team up?" answered Paulo, exasperated and ashamed for his compatriot.

Karl was beginning to wear him out with his continual questions about sex, but Henriette also contributed to Paulo's annoyance.

"A queer like that makes us look like fucking idiots!" he grumbled. "He'd better not get too close to me, the faggot... I've already got egg on my face because of that fucking Sailor."

Henriette made no fuss. "Don't worry, Paulo, you're not my type. There are others who are younger, and fresher... and more handsome. You jealous great thing!"

The things he had to listen to. But how had the poor bastard managed? No one had noticed anything for more than a year! It was simply that, like all his comrades, he had been frightened. Every hour of the day he had been frightened, of dying, of hunger, of beatings or of being hanged, and it had stopped him from thinking about anything else—including young boys. His sex drive and his thirst for pricks had ceased to have any meaning, although there were more here, within arm's reach, than he had ever dreamed of. Saving his own skin and staying alive was the highest priority and he had wisely kept quiet, even with his closest friends. Force of circumstance, and fear, had almost put him back on the straight and narrow, but now that the danger was past, he went mad.

There was another surprise in store for Paulo, along the same lines: the radical change in attitude of his friend Angel, who had come out of the *Revier* in top form. Paulo was thunderstruck when the boy admitted, without blushing—he was actually chuckling—that Eddy, the chief of Block 4 and his new jailer, had given him a blow job.

"I don't know what I was dreaming about, but I really

had a hard on! Christ, I felt randy. And all of a sudden, what do you know? There's a mouth there, sucking away like mad. By the time I realized what was going on, it was all over; what a mouthful. That's when I recognized Eddy's cap, he hadn't even taken it off! I couldn't very well hit him, could I?"

"Well done, Angel! Turned into a fucking fairy! If you've gotten to that state, you might as well have given in to Sailor last summer. It would have saved you a lot of trouble!"

"You're out of date, Paulo. Eddy's not interested in me. He goes around as if he'd never seen me in his life. What he likes doing is sucking guys off at random. He goes around the dormitory every night, row by row, and believe me, I've seen it with my own eyes, he hardly ever goes to bed without scoring. It was different with me—he took me by surprise."

Paulo was dumbfounded. It was just like in prison, like in Cayenne! There was no denying it: The men at Loibl were behaving more like convicts than prisoners of war.

Angel was right, Paulo was out of date; but fortunately for the conduct of the camp, he wasn't the only one. The commies weren't very pleased with it either and their reproving looks carried a lot of weight with the scatterbrained younger prisoners who thought that getting themselves sucked off was a sign of originality. It wasn't the first time that the Party members had appointed themselves as moral guardians, but up till now they had not had the opportunity to intervene in such a delicate matter.

"Delinquents, deviationists, you are undermining the workers' cause . . ." were the words they used to get it across to the horniest of the boys. At the end of the day their fooling would have to be paid for. Even being friends with a hustler put them beyond the pale, and a few young men who were true Resistance members, found themselves dropped from the Front National just for that. As the days went by, fewer and fewer young men were to be found bragging like Angel. Masturbation, even on your own, came to be regarded as a kind of betrayal. Their high-handed interference sent Angel into a rage, and he had no hesitation in railing loudly about it.

"Oh yes, it's going to be fun in a socialist paradise with guys like that! No screwing, no laughing, everything forbidden—worse than under Pétain!"

No point in his showing up on the rue de Châteaudun

when he got back. The communists weren't the only ones to feel that Angel was overstepping the mark. Almost everywhere people began to find it embarrassing that he persisted in recounting what went on in the dormitories or in the chiefs' quarters. Here, they could let him carry on about it, but later when everyone had gotten back home, it would look very bad indeed if he started describing Loibl, this bastion of antifascism, as a den of vice and debauchery.

What had happened to the Belloni boy who had been so dejected before he went into the *Revier*? He had come out completely wild, going on and on about nothing except bums and how big his prick was. Just to provoke people, as if he were only waiting for one thing: to be called a fairy by one of those who had snickered a year ago when Sailor had tried to get off with him. He was deliberately going over the top, clearly spoiling for a fight, and Paulo even wondered if his story about Eddy pouncing on him hadn't been a complete fabrication. It worried him.

"He's going off his head, heading for a breakdown," he thought. But Angel got worse and worse:

"Look at those long faces, they're already practicing their martyr looks. Okay, we've been pissed on, really pissed on, but let's not exaggerate—Loibl's been a piece of cake for the last two months. We eat enough, we can sing, we box, our pricks get stiff, and we jerk off . . . where's the shame in saying so, eh?"

"You're right, mate," said Paulo, trying to calm him down. "But keep it to yourself, keep it quiet . . ."

In his coarse way, Angel understood things fairly well, but the important thing escaped him: the men at Loibl had been crucified, tortured beyond belief, and now a resurrection was taking place without anybody's help. And it had all happened in the camp itself, with the SS still standing by. To hang on as they had done, when the situation was desperate, and then gain, day by day, at a killing price, their tormentors' respect—wasn't that more courageous than letting themselves go under like the sick man who loses his will to live? It would be ridiculous for them to blush now, just because their biceps were strong and their torsos tanned. You might as well criticize them for still being alive.

And there were other aspects of their behavior worthy of

admiration besides courage. Intelligence had played its part too. They had needed immense reserves of it to stand up to the two congenital bullies, Karl and Bullseye, and then to turn them virtually into their servants. Among the Frenchmen, at least, there was resourcefulness in abundance, a product of the combination of intellectuals and bourgeois who had been introduced to subterfuge by the Resistance members, by the natural cunning of the peasants, by the workers united in a common struggle, and all taught to make the best of things over the last year by the crooks' experience of prison ways.

The best demonstration of their solidarity was the way they had bagged every single soft job in the camp and on the work site, right under the noses of the Poles and others. Every man had played his part in getting dug into his spot, and had held on to it to everyone's satisfaction. Genuine bricklayers and carpenters, bogus tailors, nurses, cooks and barbers: the well-known ingenuity of the French, once applied, had inexorably overrun Loibl and its tunnel. The Krauts could no longer do without them.

Even the crawlers, like Pozzi and Riton, had contributed to the resurrection, without knowing it or wanting it. Fritz most of all and Bullseye too, dared not take any initiative without consulting them. Fat Marcel had helped in his own brutish way as well, since Fossil-Face had credited the concrete mixer's output to the French. There were many others, honorary Kapos, *Dolmetscher* and *Schreiber*, giving orders everywhere. They had all done their bit, finally, to make sure they would stop being taken for shits, right down to the hustlers who had given of themselves so unstintingly to mollify the thugs when things were going badly!

"The *Franzosen* are not a race of lazy shits—better to get on with them," the Krauts had concluded.

If it went on much longer, they were the ones who would be polishing the boots of the *Scheisse Franzosen*. Or handing over their rubber hoses, so the Frenchmen could whip them . . .

It was scarcely an exaggeration: in the ring one Sunday, Fritz got himself a real pasting at the hands of the irrepressible François of Burgundy. And the whole camp applauded, the guards as enthusiastically as the prisoners. It was an incredible scene, thinking about it afterward, to see a deportee pummeling his Kapo with his fists! And his friends were free to hurl insults at Fritz until he fell. That day at Loibl, France truly emerged victorious.

And there was another momentous occasion toward the middle of July: a big football match, which Otto had eventually been allowed to organize, resulted in his team of Kapos and block chiefs being roundly thrashed. It was a walkover—six to nothing, despite the fact that, with hardly any decent Kraut players, the doyen had imported a number of outsiders. Each nation had lent him its champions—there were Hungarians, Poles, Czechs and Yugoslavs on his side. But their hearts weren't in it, and that day the mountains echoed loud and long with the roars of *"Allez la France!"* which accompanied each new goal.

The going was nevertheless tough: The field had been laid out on sloping ground full of potholes. The doyen had had one of the goals set up against Block 3, and Paulo had tried his hand at a few practice shots, not to get himself picked for the team, but just to see exactly how rusty he was. Within fifteen minutes he was completely out of breath, and his legs felt like jelly; he vowed to himself that where football was concerned, that was it. He could not begin to understand how eleven men who were all about his age, and rather less fit than he, had managed to survive the full ninety minutes.

The explanation lay in what was at stake. The young players had realized that France must win this battle too, and they had run themselves into the ground. By the end of the match they were all on the point of blacking out, but how many times in this deportation camp had they not thought they would collapse under the weight of trees, rails or rocks? Perhaps, too, they were haunted by the memory of another sports session to which they had been invited a year ago, on the fourteenth of July 1943, by the same doyen. *Gymnastik*, corrida, the entire camp flogged. It was hard to believe that their opponents were the same men! The six–nothing score summed up better than anything how far they had come.

Otto was especially annoyed for he had appointed himself captain and center forward, and had played abysmally. His wingers, a Hungarian and a Czech, were both fairly good players, but he had missed every one of their perfect passes.

He could have kicked himself for going along with the idea of a match with France versus the rest of the world.

"As if these *Scheisskubel* aren't big-headed enough already," he railed, still smarting from the cries of "Get him off. . . useless. . . bring on the reserve!" which accompanied each goal.

"Football *fertig*. . . It's dangerous for your heart. Herr Kommandant has forbidden it," he declared, as a justification for not organizing any more games.

Nobody was deceived; he himself had made the decision, but it was just as well. At this altitude it was sheer madness to make men who had been wielding picks and shovels twelve hours a day for the past year run and leap about. Their muscles were hardened but specialized. It was like asking weightlifters to start doing *pas de deux*.

Boxing, on the other hand, still went on; it had become a regular feature of life at Loibl, and the boxers, even the losers, would have been the subject of universal derision if they had suddenly decided to nip off to the *Revier* to get a compress for their black eyes. Besides, no boxer had ever failed to turn up at the tunnel on Monday morning. And yet Otto must have been itching to put a stop to that sport, too, ever since the day his friend Fritz had been knocked off his pedestal by young François. He had been appalled to see the toughest Kapo of them all, the Max Schmeling of Mauthausen, who had a thousand knockouts to his credit, flat on his back. And by a little turd of twenty who was half his size.

That Sunday there was a rush for the good seats. Not a single pair of pajamas wanted to miss the unique opportunity of seeing Fritz getting thrashed. They trusted François implicitly; he wouldn't give anything away, for he had old scores to settle. But no one had thought for one second that they would see his hulk of an opponent spreadeagled on the floor. Except for Paulo, whose *Mütze* was overflowing with packets of dravas which the chiefs had bet on their colleague's chances—and he had just as many in his pockets: between three and four hundred smokes, an absolute fortune.

"I knew it! All he had to do was bend over, I would have bet my ass on it," he exclaimed as Bullseye, the referee, began the count, dragging out the seconds as if he hoped that his colleague would get up and carry on.

"Sie . . . ben, aa . . . acht, neu . . . eun . . . !"

"Zehn!" cried Paulo, beating him to it, and more quietly for his friends around him, "Phew, we've won!"

Saying "we" was no exaggeration, for François's knockout was in some measure his brainchild. François had merely been following instructions: "Go for his breadbasket, don't bother about the rest . . . give it all you've got, make him throw up his goulash."

At the start, François's straight lefts and rights all aimed at the stomach seemed like losing tactics to the unsuspecting Fritz and he kept his guard up around his face. By the second round François had closed in, still delivering his uppercuts and jabs in Fritz's stomach, and then it was too late. The prodding now felt like hammer blows to Fritz as his liver was squashed against his stomach. The hammering had lasted the whole round, and Fritz's fat belly was one immense bruise; he was gasping with the pain and he might well have raised his arm had the gong not sounded the end of the second round.

The sixty-second break gave him time both to recover and to realize what that bastard *Franzose* was up to. With new determination he tackled the third and last round by charging at François with his head down, his chin tucked in, and his guard to his ribs. He had only two alternatives: either he withdrew to put an end to the agonizing attacks on his belly, or he knocked out his opponent with a chance blow. As he couldn't raise his guard, he was relying on his head for that. He managed to push François onto the ropes, and twice his head thudded home, like a sledgehammer. The crowd began to hiss, but this did not, of course, deter Bullseye, much relieved for Fritz, from turning a blind eye to the irregularity. Even a boxer who'd been taking punches all his life would have been poleaxed by such blows, but not François. He had taken so many punches since Mauthausen, and more often than not from this same Fritz, that he didn't seem the least bit disconcerted. He'd had the best training available: a year and a half of punches, kicks, hoses, sticks and gun butts. Of course he knew how to take his punches, he was a past master at it, but he also knew how to feint, and nine times out of ten he wasn't where Fritz thought he was. François quickly realized that all he had to do was finish him off. A jab on his chin, twenty seconds before the end of the bout, and it was all over for the terror of Loibl.

Paulo felt very proud of his pupil, who had exceeded all his expectations, and when he went to congratulate him a little later, he told him in all seriousness, "You'd better not hang up your gloves when you get back, friend. You've got real class, and at your age you'll go a long way."

How good it was to hear that. A few months ago, François like all the ghosts who had come back from the north, might well have been advised to take to the *Revier* rather than the boxing ring to get back on his feet.

After this historic match, Paulo couldn't see how any subsequent fight could bring in as many smokes. The only reason he'd had such a harvest this time was because one of the champions was German. The elimination of Fritz, the sole representative of his country, considerably diminished interest in any future matches. Not that the bouts would be any less closely fought. In fact, just the opposite was true: all the outsiders, boxing for food, not glory, had been weeded out, but the passionate interest of the chiefs, the only ones who could bet high stakes, had died. The lousy Frenchmen were the only ones left in the running, despite Otto, jealous of this latest success, having brought over from Nordfeld the toughest Poles he could find. He had even set up a championship match, north versus south, France versus Poland, to rekindle interest. It was a complete fiasco; the Poles were wiped out in the opening seconds of each fight. So the French were still top of the class at Loibl in every subject. It made you wonder whether they mightn't be capable of taking over the entire administration of this new territory on behalf of the mother country.

Without going quite so far, they were still free to fix the fights. In other words, they could stop bashing each other up, by holding their punches and faking knockouts. They would pull a few faces to give the spectators their money's worth, and continue picking up the boxers' rations. It even struck Paulo that if they went through the motions cleverly enough, he might still relieve a few suckers of their dravas. He suggested as much to Pommier, who, as expected, had come out of all his fights with a smile on his face.

"Listen, Michel, you'll definitely be coming up against

my mate Joel, and he's never been beaten either. You'd win, no problem, you've got more experience, but just suppose—"

"Paulo, I can read you like a book! You want me to lose, right?"

"You don't have to go that far, but no one's forcing you to give it all you've got either. I could take bets on a points victory or a tie. If you're on, we'll go halves on the smokes. Okay?"

"All right by me as long as your pal plays the game. You just make sure it's all clear—he's got to watch his gloves too. I'm not going to be made a fool of."

"Don't worry, it's guaranteed. I'm going to put him in the picture right now."

Joel, who felt guilty every time he knocked one of his comrades around, agreed enthusiastically.

"It's a deal," he said, slapping Paulo's hand. "I like the idea of that. I'd have lost against Pommier anyway, so what's wrong with losing and making monkeys of Otto and Bullseye at the same time?"

They had to wait until the two champions had cleared the decks of opposition before they proposed the phony fight to the authorities. Pommier had no problems: the giant Tavernier, who had let himself be beaten in rather dubious circumstances by Fritz, crumpled at the knees without waiting to be asked. The following Sunday against François of Burgundy, who was still flushed with his recent victory, he was up against stiffer opposition, and the fight would certainly have ended bloodily if Paulo hadn't taken the Kapo-killer on one side for a few words of wisdom.

"I told you the other day and I'll say it again, you've got the makings of a champion. But I've had a lot of experience of boxing and believe me, Pommier's already a champion, a proper one. You don't stand an earthly. A word of advice: be satisfied with second place, and he's prepared to go easy on you."

For once François allowed himself to be persuaded, delighted to show the Krauts he wasn't the only Frenchman in the camp capable of beating big Fritz. Pommier's first serious right gave him his cue, and he went out like a light. It may not have taken François's breath away, but it certainly left all the Krauts gasping. They of course had blindly staked everything on him winning by a knockout.

"Put your money in here, please," cried Paulo passing his cap around.

He would dearly have liked to arrange Pommier's last bout, before he met Joel, with equal ease, but he had reckoned without Perrimond's sporting ambitions. The northerner had rebuffed his advances.

"Nothing doing. I've never cheated my public, get that into your thick skull, and I'm not going to start now at my age. Just for smokes! Who do you think you're talking to? You can tell your friend if he wants to win, he's going to have to work for it. We'll see which of us is better."

The veteran of the rings was clearly slow on the uptake. His boxing mania had taken hold again, and tirelessly he shadowboxed from morning to night as conscientiously as if he were training for the world championship. He would exhale noisily through one nostril, blocking the other with his thumb, so that like a real pro he would be able to snort his nose clear more efficiently. With his head down and his fists pummeling thin air, he would dance from foot to foot; nothing, not even the presence of an SS, could stop him from limbering up. In his own way, he too had made his escape from Loibl. But what he really wanted was to go home with the title of supreme champion of the Karawankens to add to his mediocre record. If he could manage that, he wouldn't have wasted his time here...

Alas, his hectic training program was not enough, and Pommier found himself champion of his class, the middleweights. In much the same way Joel had cleaned up in his class by getting rid of Pierrot Martin and Leblond the sailor in turn. Since they were the last two in the running, nothing more stood in the way of the big fight which Paulo was relying on to scoop up another sackful of dravas.

However, the whole thing almost fell through. Joel had little difficulty eliminating Pierrot Martin, whom he sent back into his corner at the end of the match with a pair of black eyes as big as flying goggles. But Leblond came as a surprise. The sailor had never boxed much by the book, but he was a first-class street fighter. In fact, the last brawl he'd been in, on the terrace of La Coupole, had involved three broken chairs on as many militia men's heads, and was the main reason for his being sent to Mauthausen. Maybe it was because they had worked over his scalp with whips before handing him over to the Gestapo, that he used his head to parry the punches; you couldn't tell, but against Joel, at any rate, the tactic was effective. Letting fly with a right which he hoped would prove decisive, instead the Breton felt as if his hand had been shattered. And yet he should have known that the man had a skull like concrete. Like everyone else, he had seen Leblond, either for practice or for fun, pound his head again and again with unbelievable force against the walls of the blocks. When he really felt in top form, he did it to tree trunks. The man was a real human cannonball. Every time he did it his horrified friends thought he would split his head open. But the more he banged it, the tougher it got. And so, far from looking upon him as slightly mad, they came to envy him, figuring that in the days when everyone was being beaten regularly, Loibl couldn't have been so hard for him. And Joel, instead of attacking from below with uppercuts or going for his body, had stupidly persisted in going for his face. He kept his distance, but every single one of his jabs, swings or hooks found the bullet head in its way. Leblond used it skillfully as a shield, dodging from right to left and countering attack from all angles. So a fractured wrist was the price Joel paid for his victory.

Paulo, who had spent the last round nervously wringing his cap, dragged him off to the *Revier* almost by force. There Jaryk, the doctor, confirmed the fracture.

"Two weeks' enforced rest. You went a bit far there, my friend. I've just seen your opponent. He's got a lump on his forehead the size of a tennis ball, I've never seen anything like it. Anywhere else, I'd put your hand in a metal splint. But that's too dangerous with Winkler; the boxing gets on his nerves, and he might well use it as an excuse to send you back to Mauthausen. I'd even prefer not to admit you to the *Revier;* we'll get around it by massage and a good strong bandage. Where are you working at the moment?"

"Outside on the wheelbarrows."

"Get yourself fixed up with a pickax job. You'll have to use it with your left hand, of course, it's the only exercise I can allow you. Boxing is out of the question for a couple of weeks or so, until the bones begin to knit."

Luckily for Paulo and his dravas, the rain came down in sheets on the Sunday fixed for the Pommier–Le Goff final, and the event was postponed for a week, just enough time for

Joel's wrist, well massaged and bandaged by Jaryk himself, to get stronger. The pain had been excruciating during the first few days on the pickax, and like an alarm signal, his broken wrist had reminded him, and Paulo too, that they were still at the mercy of an accident or some stupid injury, which could in no time make them good for nothing. Then Universale would have no more reason to feed them.

"This is ridiculous," said Paulo. "Let's stop it now. You'll have to scratch. In any case, against Pommier, it wouldn't make any difference whether you had two fists or one."

Even if it had been unintentional, he had just said exactly what was needed to stir up his friend's fighting instincts and Joel's hackles immediately rose.

"I'm sure you're right, but I like the idea of this fight. By Sunday my hand'll be better, and maybe I won't prove anything, but I'll give it a good go. For me, it'll be something to remember, and a chance to take Fritz down another peg. Me against the guy who beat the guy who beat Fritz! After this he'll think twice before using Frenchmen as punching bags. Don't deprive me of the pleasure."

Joel's enthusiasm was too genuine for Paulo to reproach himself for having pushed him into it. The only thing left for him to do was to make sure the fight went as well as possible. In other words, to make sure Pommier didn't get carried away at the last moment and forget to soften his punches. If the scrap turned into a serious fight, the Breton's hand would definitely be in a bad way. It was therefore of the utmost importance to know just how well and for how long it would hold, if it were well bandaged. To find that out, they'd need a number of training sessions in a quiet spot, but again that depended on the block chiefs.

You had to hand it to them, they were sporting fellows, at least when it came to fighting. It gave them a thrill to see men making each other bleed, and they could never get enough of it. In no time at all, they had ordered a room in the laundry to be cleared. Mauthausen couldn't have done better: sandbag, skipping ropes, kitchen scales by the door and the showers a few steps away. Bullseye was taking his role as referee more and more seriously and he'd made a particular effort; he was now to be found playing coach in the training room.

"Left . . . again . . . and again, and now with the right. *Links . . . links, rechts . . . gut, Mensch!*"

It had to be seen to be believed.

The enthusiasm Bullseye put into it made Otto change his mind about banning the boxing. He went one better: to please his one-eyed friend, he decided to take personal charge of the next match. He would make it a big occasion, and as the camp was out of bounds to the civilians, he would invite the *Feldgendarmes*. That way everyone in the area would hear about the healthy atmosphere of camaraderie which reigned in his establishment. But they would have to have top-class billing if the day were to be a success. He demanded a minimum of five or six fights, and as he failed to get a sufficient number of volunteers, he simply selected the opponents himself. And so all the runners-up, Tavernier, Pierrot Martin, Leblond, and so on, including Perrimond, who was only too pleased to oblige, had to make their way to the laundry.

It was worth more than all the other extraordinary sights to see ten shaven men return from an exhausting day's slog and start skipping like schoolgirls. And they were naked, what's more, because the tiny room was baked by the sun all afternoon and was like an oven. Such a hothouse atmosphere, coupled with the strong smell of sweat, inevitably attracted the queers, and the room quickly became the favorite meeting place of the block chiefs. Like the dirty old men who prowl around changing rooms masquerading as sportsmen, they made a mad rush for it as soon as muster was over.

"In a crowd like this," thought Paulo, "Joel's injury might go unnoticed." That was absolutely essential for the fraud he had set up, and every evening he mingled with the crowd of voyeurs to make quite sure. With the match three days away, he breathed again: his protégé, both hands identically bandaged, hit out at Bullseye's glove as powerfully and evenly with his right as with his left. His broken wrist seemed little more than a bad memory.

If the final had been a three-rounder like the others, Joel's hand would doubtless have stood up to it. But this was a sort of title fight, and Bullseye, without asking either opponent's opinion, had decreed that unless there was a knockout, it would go to six rounds. So the inevitable happened: the Breton's right hand couldn't last the distance. It broke again, but fortunately for Paulo, who had based all his bets on a draw, not until the end of the fifth round.

Pommier, however, had played fair, letting up when he felt his opponent falter and above all holding back with his killing right. Joel, on the other hand, had really had to push his talents to the limit to bring himself up to the level of such an artist. Using his intelligence he had managed it, countering each attack with a twisting feint in the classic style, which brought forth from the crowd, Krauts included, oohs and aahs of admiration. He had said he liked the idea of this fight, but it went deeper than that. He was glorying in being able to fight against a real boxer, a leading middleweight professional, in front of so many spectators. He came out with everything he had learned in the manuals, step forward, left-right, sidestep to foil a hook to the body . . . and especially his expert feinting. Obviously things were going well, he didn't even need to cover himself because Pommier was holding his punches, but their clashes followed so fast and furious, and the blows landed on target with such precision, that all the crowd could see was fireworks. It couldn't have been more perfect if they had rehearsed their fight like phony wrestlers. It was a gala match, a true exhibition complete with every punch imaginable. It was so perfect that Paulo began to get worried:

"What's gotten into them? They're mad to go on at that speed. They can't keep it up. One itchy fist with those unpadded gloves and one of them is going to end up on his ass! I can say goodbye to my smokes . . ."

Anxious to avert disaster, Paulo tried to cool Joel's ardor between rounds. Bluntly, he used the best argument he knew.

"Your hand, Joel! Watch it! If it goes again, it's back to Mauthausen," he yelled over the heads of the Krauts in the ringside seats.

It was no use. Egged on more and more by the crowd, who, like all boxing crowds, had sided with the small man, Joel didn't listen. Instead of relaxing to recover his strength before the next round, he was racking his Breton brains to come up with something even more dazzling to impress the crowd. And in the heat of the action, he inevitably forgot about his wounded hand, pushing it a little harder in every round.

He felt it break as he delivered an overenthusiastic right hook to Pommier's jaw, and he yelped with pain, but luckily the cry was muffled by the "bravos" which greeted the finesse of the blow. Even Bullseye in the ring didn't hear it. Neither did Paulo, but he had no need of his ears to realize what had happened. Joel's despairing look told the whole story.

"Shit! Shit! Fucking hell!" he cursed. "Didn't I warn him enough? They were even, there was no way we'd miss a draw, and now it's fucked!"

He had underestimated Joel. The first time he'd broken his hand, against Leblond, it must have been far more painful, but it hadn't stopped him from finishing the fight. So today, in front of all these enthusiastic supporters, he was even more unlikely to quit. Paulo had panicked too soon. For Joel had managed to drag Pommier into a clinch at the beginning of the deciding round and whisper in his ear, "Watch it, Michel, my right's gone, it's just given way again. Go carefully . . ."

"Okay, we'll close up, it won't show so much."

The fellow was either a real sport, or else his professionalism kept him from boxing for love and he was afraid that if he won, he'd get no reward in the way of butts. This latter must have been uppermost in his mind, for he started coming out with every crooked trick in the book, clinching shamefully, playing the exhausted boxer dead on his feet, but in fact supporting Joel in his arms as if afraid he might pass out with pain. In spite of his rather limited field of vision, Bullseye's one good eye spotted what was going on and Pommier picked up a warning.

So much the better, he must have thought, that'll even the chances, and he redoubled his muddying tactics. Their uninterrupted clinch and the way they were pummeling each other's ribs, instead of bringing jeers from the crowd, actually aroused its admiration. Every man watching was firmly convinced that the only reason the two champions were hanging on to each other like this was because they couldn't take any more, that they were both punch-drunk from the pounding they had given one another, like contestants at the end of the great fifteen-rounders in the Vel d'Hiv. Clearly such tremendous courage could allow of only one possible decision: a draw.

Paulo knew how to take his victories with decorum. Instead of rushing in with his cap to claim the winnings due to him as soon as the final bell rang, he waited patiently for Bullseye to raise in an Olympic flourish both boxers' arms together. However, Mr. Referee, sole arbiter, had other ideas. A draw? Certainly not. Did he just want to be different, or did he actually want to be labeled a bastard by a unanimous crowd, like that classic story about the goalkeeper who deliberately lets in goals just to hear the whole stadium roar "Who's your father?" Be that as it may, Bullseye raised only one arm, and it was Joel's.

Paulo was horror-struck. He couldn't even manage to boo with the rest of the crowd. Bankruptcy was staring him in the face. His entire fortune in cigarettes was going down the drain. But worst of all, how was he going to explain things to Pommier? He wasn't going to be at all pleased. The one thing he couldn't stand was being made to look like a fool. If that cretin Bullseye absolutely had to choose a winner, the least he could have done was pick the right one! Paulo had wisely covered himself against Pommier winning on points, but the reverse hadn't even crossed his mind.

He couldn't hold back his pent-up rage any longer and he yelled out, "You ought to be ashamed, it's disgusting! Bullseye, you're a fucker!"

"Bullseye *yeboni*." The cry was taken up by all the Poles, Czechs, Yugos and other Slavs in their various accents, but the decision was final. All that remained was for Paulo to go and console Michel, his unfortunate accomplice.

"We've been screwed," he began. "I couldn't have known this would happen, but you did a good job, Michel, and I'll pay you back. I don't know how, but you'll have your dravas, or my name's not Chastagnier."

"Drop it. I don't care about the fucking cigarettes. But what really gets me is that I've been taken for an amateur." His tone was bitter, rather than angry. Paulo, who'd been bracing himself for a furious attack, was relieved. He seized on Pommier's last word.

"Amateur? Who said you were an amateur? You must be deaf. Didn't you hear them yelling? Even the Krauts were complaining. They knew who the real winner was, it was you!"

"Yeah, yeah, carry on," Pommier muttered, only half convinced.

Thinking it over, he began to wonder whether Bullseye

hadn't been right after all. When he'd staggered about in the last round to stop Joel from falling, he'd boxed a bit too clever. The squinting referee might not have seen it in the same light as the crowd.

"No, it's my fault, I overdid it," he said.

He certainly was a good sport. He'd taken it like a man, and admitted his share of the blame. Paulo was touched, and thought he had found just the thing to soothe his wounded pride.

"Don't forget the return match, Michel. It'll be a real fight, and you'll win hands down."

He stopped short when he caught sight of Joel's reproving look. He'd come to join them, and his grimaces of pain made it clear that there wouldn't be a return match. Under its bandage his hand must be in a hell of a state. Paulo, who was the principal cause of the carnage, was appalled. "When I think that you both got done in for nothing, I'm even more disgusted with myself than you are."

"But we don't hold it against you at all," interrupted Joel. "Isn't that right, Michel?"

Paulo didn't give him time to reply. "Look, you two know how much I love boxing, but with the gloves we've got here, it's just ridiculous, it's sheer butchery. Why don't you all get together next Sunday, and refuse to fight? Go on strike, the Krauts can't force you."

It had dawned on him rather late in the day, but what he had said was quite true: you had to be completely around the bend to volunteer for something where you got your nose broken, your eyebrows split open and your teeth knocked out. Didn't they already live in a camp which must hold the world's record for beatings, and where there were so many guards that each one had only four prisoners to thrash? And now that after a whole year of thrashing the guards seemed to be getting tired, the convicts had relieved them and were taking it in turns to thrash each other! People had been certified insane for less.

Nevertheless, Paulo was full of odd contradictions. Every time he had an opportunity to put his crooked instincts to work, he jumped in feet first, but at the end of the day it was always his sense of camaraderie and his finer feelings which came out on top. This time, unfortunately, he was unable to repair the damage and he cast about for something else to occupy his mind. One evening at muster the doyen announced that boxing at Loibl was *fertig*, as were football and all other sporting activities which used up their strength. Not a day too soon, for there had been a rumor that track events were the next item on the agenda and some of the men had started training for that.

"Herr Kommandant has stated that Loibl is not a stadium," Otto had explained, "and you'd do better to work harder instead of boxing. He also feels you're getting into bad habits, especially you Frenchmen. All that is going to change. Discipline is going to be tightened up. And he says you're eating too much too, you don't deserve it. The good life is finished, you bunch of good-for-nothings."

The ban on boxing was no bad thing for the Frenchmen; they had had ample time to show that even when it came to brawling, no one could touch them. Without the ring, of course, they would never have had the chance to prove it. By now, the chiefs, and Fritz first and foremost, would think twice before they landed their pathetic punches on the *Franzosen*.

The only aspects of Otto's speech which really worried them were the brief mention at the end about discipline being reinforced and the reference to them eating too much. Why were they making these threats, when the Red Cross and the Quakers had just tracked them down? Didn't it undermine Ménard's apparent discovery that there were Kraut POWs in France?

Dédé, who spent more and more time tuned in to Swiss radio, was adamant:

"Don't take any notice, Knock-Knees is bluffing you. Every day there are thousands of Germans surrendering. There are hundreds of thousands of *Gefangene* now in France alone. I tell you, they can't touch us."

But the worriers persisted. "So what do all these threats mean?"

It took Ménard several days to come up with the answer, but it was worth waiting for: Hitler had almost been blown up, by a bomb in his bunker on the Russian Front! The Führer was wounded but alive. According to the news announcers, he had had a miraculous escape.

Before Dédé dropped his bombshell in the camp, he had wanted to make quite sure his information was accurate, because none of it was very clear. There had been a bomb and an attempt on the Führer's life, that much was official. Nazi radio stations didn't deny it; on the contrary, they used it to boost the morale of a populace impressed by their leader's incredible luck. But there were conflicting reports about what followed, about a Putsch within the army and fighting between the SS and the Wehrmacht. For it had been the generals decorated in the 1914–18 war who had rebelled, and not just within Germany. Tremors were felt throughout occupied Europe.

The lethal device had exploded on the twentieth of July, but luckily for Dédé and his Front National comrades, the radio stations had only gotten wind of it a few days later, when they were able to inform the world at the same time that the conspiracy had been crushed in its initial stages. Otherwise, in their euphoria and their ignorance of the outcome, they would have called for insurrection within Loibl.

The repression, both inside Germany and on all fronts, had been masterfully handled by the faithful SS. After a few hours of indecision, they had subdued the rebel garrisons and started the shooting. Since then, all had been quiet. The men at Loibl had just missed the most marvelous chance of seeing SS and *Feldgendarmes* gunning each other down.

"We were within a hair's breadth!" Dédé repeated excitedly. "They've taken to spying on each other now, which explains why Winkler's decided to put the screws on us. A camp which lets its prisoners laugh, box and take a hand in the running is all the Gestapo need to add the Kommandant's name to the list of conspirators."

All this was said lightly, but judging by the way all the Krauts started watching each other, Dédé's explanation must have approximated the truth. In the long run, the *Haeftlinge* were the ones least affected by the news and its consequences. Even the reduction in rations overnight could not dent their morale, for this time every man realized that the real battle was being played out far from Loibl. There might be another, better-timed bomb, for example. Everyone was more or less back in shape now, so going without food for a few more weeks would not have any dramatic effect. It was the last little sacrifice to be made.

The whole business had taken them well into August.

The fine weather was beginning to break, but even when the rain came down in sheets over the valley, the men took it in their stride. Everyone regretted not having any photos of their incredible summer. Joel had said as much to Paulo, but the only photograph he'd really have liked to take home as a souvenir was one of his fight against Pommier.

"I'd give away everything I possess, a year of my life even. The Krauts were filming me, I saw them; one gendarme even had a telephoto lens—"

"A snap of convicts hitting each other with the SS looking on approvingly is hardly going to make the front cover of *Signal*... Don't get too carried away, Joel," Paulo replied discouragingly.

"Too bad," Joel replied sadly, still seeing that moment of glory in his mind's eye. At least five hundred men had watched his performance in the ring, not counting those peering at him through binoculars from the watchtowers and the SS barracks. Some of the civilians had even climbed onto the roofs of their quarters. What a photograph it would have been! And just think how he could caption it! Good old Joel—it had certainly been his finest hour, despite his broken wrist. Paulo had never seen him so happy to be alive. It just went to show that his dedication to war and revolution was nothing so much as his nature.

XXIV

Winkler's announcement that in the interests of their common undertaking discipline would be tightened up had not been made lightly. But below him the block chiefs, the *Arbeitskapos*, and the civilian engineers on the work site, upon whom he ought to have been able to rely to enforce the order, were not prepared to share his point of view. Even the SS, who were in daily contact with the workers, had come to the conclusion that the tunnel had made much better progress since the atmosphere had relaxed and the men had gone about their work cheerfully. Slackening the reins had had the happy result of making each of the prisoners believe that the tunnel was in a way his own work, with Universale as his employer. Now that everything was ticking along nicely, going back to sanctions and the hose could only upset the routine. Fossil-Face, with his long years of experience, and Putz, the all-powerful engineer, had joined forces and managed to get this across to Herr Kommandant. Sensibly, he didn't insist; he could be brought to account over the tunnel, too. No doubt about it, Winkler was an apology for an SS, far more of a gardener than a *Hauptsturmführer.* This was the second time in less than three months that he had ranted and raved about discipline and then not followed it up; once after the Russians' escape, and now following the attempted assassination of Hitler.

"You're all mouth, Knock-Knees, you're not the real governor here any more," the detainees seemed to be saying, when he occasionally turned up on the work site. How could he answer them? He couldn't very well start beating them himself! The fool thought he would have his revenge when he heard on the radio one afternoon the strangled tones of his Führer announcing hysterically that the National-Socialist scientists had developed a complete range of secret weapons, based on flying bombs with homing devices, which would singlehandedly wipe out the Jewish and communist enemies.

"So, you upstarts, you've counted your chickens too soon," he thought gleefully. "You'll be here for the rest of your lives, for a thousand years . . . I'll announce the good news myself."

And he ordered the whole camp to assemble on the *Appelplatz* for a special communiqué.

"*Haeftlinge*, victory is close at hand." From his very first words, uttered in a voice shaking with emotion, the convicts realized that something had snapped inside his head. They had expected the usual diatribe on idleness and sabotage, and here was the old boy giving them information about the war for the first time, admitting the Wehrmacht's recent setbacks to make more plausible his tirade about the arms of vengeance given to the German people by the Creator. Like his leader on the radio a little while before, he was working himself up into a frenzy, and by the end of his speech, the men in the front ranks actually heard him sobbing.

"Even if there's any truth in his story and they have got guided rockets, they've come too late for the Krauts to win the war. They won't have any territory left to launch them from soon, they've retreated so much in the last week," said Dédé to cheer up the men who had been worried by the news.

Herr Kommandant's speech had about as much effect as pissing on a forest fire. For something else had happened on the outside. Something far more significant, far more of a deciding factor, to use Winkler's words, than the rubbish he had talked about secret weapons: Paris had been liberated! With such a shattering piece of news, the SS-gardener could scream himself hoarse, nobody in the camp gave a toss about his flying bombs! All the workers in the tunnel, not only the French, spontaneously broke into the "Marseillaise," as people must have done all over the world. Paris, mother of Liberty, liberated! Now that was something which was well worth sobbing about.

Even at Loibl, so cut off from the rest of the world, they'd been aware that it wouldn't be long before Paris fell to the Allies. Dédé Ménard had told them often enough that the Western Front was collapsing, but they had all waited for it to become a reality. Now they could give vent to their joy, laughing and hugging their friends, and in all the excitement even Bullseye and Karl came in for some hearty slaps on the back. Paris liberated! Incontrovertible proof that this bitch of a war was coming to an end. Hitler, who had pranced about in front of the Eiffel Tower in June 1940, would choke on this humiliation. He would have to ask for an Armistice, or, better still, commit suicide along with Himmler and all the SS—harakiri all around! It was so incredible, so wonderful, that they could well afford to include Bullseye and company in their celebrations. Especially as the naïve fools seemed as delighted as the rest of them. They drank to Liberation with great swigs of schnaps. "*Vive Paris! Gross Paris*!" yelled Karl drunkenly.

"*Vive Paris, Karl*!" chorused the Frenchmen in his block, adding quietly: "Now it's our turn to take care of you, you fucking fairy!"

They could count on Dédé Ménard to fan the flames. He was giving press conferences in the work site crappers during the day and in the *Waschraum* at night. It was thanks to him that they knew it had been the Parisians themselves who had liberated their city, and that the first troops to go in were French too, an armored division under the command of a certain Leclerc. And then de Gaulle had arrived. Things had been very hot for the first week, with widespread rioting and thousands of people killed, but now there wasn't a single armed Kraut left in Paris or its suburbs. For tens of thousands of them had surrendered and been marched off to prison or dumped in schools and sports stadiums. And perhaps it was the thought of all these Krauts who had just bumped up the human exchange rate which pleased the inmates of Loibl most of all. What sweet revenge! Their tormentors, Gestapo and militia, led handcuffed into the very same jails nearly all of them had come from, where they had been tortured more than a year and a half ago! And they felt proud too, at the thought that they had in some measure played a part in this Liberation, which the whole world must be hailing as a symbolic event. When they got home, the Resistance men would undoubtedly feel pangs of regret to hear others tell them of this historic battle which they had worked for in the shadows and, it must be said, in an atmosphere of almost total hostility in the early days. But since then they had suffered so much and been so afraid of never getting back that, despite mixed feelings, the thought which was uppermost in their minds at this time was they they were going to live again. Like proper human beings who are free to eat, love, screw—and let their hair grow.

"What a time we'll have! We'll live it up until we collapse from exhaustion! It's a new lease on life, they can't touch us now!"

New life, reprieve, these were their new catchwords, and they reveled in the idea. It was all they talked about, even the communists forgot their doctrines. All Loibl saw the Liberation of Paris as one long fiesta with girls galore. Wasn't that what Paris was famed for?

All of a sudden the men came out of their shells and talked interminably about the good things life had to offer, but that wasn't all. A sort of old boys' club had been founded from which the younger men, who had only known the restrictions, who had no idea what a real feast was like, were excluded. The young men retaliated by talking about nothing but sex, gangbangs and screwing girls doggy-fashion at monumental orgies.

As the generation gap widened a little more each day, another barrier, just as distressing, was being erected. You would have thought that social barriers had been destroyed forever on that first day at Mauthausen when they had found themselves shaven all over and decked out in identical clown's costumes. Since then, not once had an intellectual sought to display his knowledge, nor a bourgeois to snub his rustic neighbor nor a penniless worker. On the contrary, a sort of common language had evolved, mostly based on slang, as if each man wanted the others to forget his circumstances. Surely this slate wiped clean of all inequality was not going to be sullied simply because they knew that in a few weeks' time, perhaps in a few days, they would be going back to their own kind, to their own social class? Unfortunately it was. Paris, and France without the Germans, also meant that the hour had come to re-erect those barriers. There was no need to be brutal, it was done in a friendly way, but that was almost worse. How could you tell a lifelong loser that despite the road you had traveled together, he was still a loser?

"Come for as long as you like. Bring your wife and kids. We'll kill a pig... and we'll show you what an animal fed on chestnuts tastes like," a farmer from Morbihan was saying to a Renault factory-worker who had never set foot outside Billancourt except to come to Loibl.

The other man pretended to believe him. "That's going to cost you! I've got half a dozen kids and they eat enough for two dozen!"

The generosity of the invitations got completely out of hand. They were even fixing dates: "Better to come in October, we'll be able to hunt. Do you like hunting?"

It was turning into something of a *Tour de France* with immense sprees at the end of each leg. They swore they would never lose touch, but where they really went to town was when they talked about going into business together. Yes, there were already some men thinking about going back to work. How the money would come rolling in after they had elbowed out all those bastard competitors who had collaborated with the Krauts... there was no end to it.

"No need to lose sleep over what you do when you get older, kid. I'll take you on in my factory as assistant director..." And they gave themselves vast salaries!

Obviously, the dazzled proles tied themselves in knots trying to please the men who were going to rescue them from their miserable circumstances. By a strange coincidence, it was the fellows who held down the cushy jobs in the camp who were offered golden prospects. The promise of soup until the war was over, and the contract was as good as signed.

Alongside the bluffers, there were comics like the bank clerk who suddenly started being very formal with everybody, or the château owner who started sticking his nose in the air, when for the past year he could have been seen darning Bullseye's socks! The youngsters, who had nothing to offer, either now or later, were quick to squash them. "You stupid old fools, you haven't learned anything!" But it was said without rancor.

However, there was one group, the pimps, whose unholy joy was harder to swallow. The Ritons, Maumaus, Pierrot Martins and others had also banded together to discuss, man to man, they said, their shops where business must be booming again with the arrival of the Yanks in Paris. In dead earnest they totted up the dollars which their tarts would be salting away for their return. It wouldn't have been too bad if they had kept their sordid sums to themselves, but no, the whole camp had to know that their cash registers were jangling while they were still here. They couldn't have cared less about the future business arrangements within the camp which were making the bums drool, and they said so, loudly. Especially Riton, who had started opening his big mouth again.

"Just listen to those turds! They're not even out yet and they're already swearing undying friendship and talking about going into business. I've never heard anything like it. Haven't they done enough together here? They can keep their business contacts. My partners are my two women. I'll get by fine, my prick'll see to that."

Even that could be laughed off, but one Sunday in the *Wacshraum*, bolstered up by the presence of three fellow pimps, he overstepped the mark.

"It wasn't all milk and honey when the Krauts were around," he was explaining. "All that my tarts were bringing in (and mind you, they were going about it properly, two of them to one *Soldatenheim*) went in food and gear. *Deutschmarks* aren't worth a shit—"

"You'd better stop that," interrupted one of the young

communists who had overheard. "That kind of thing goes by the name of collaboration."

"Listen to the kid. The Krauts didn't jerk off up my ass, my friend. Collaboration! Take that back right now or I'll ram your teeth far down your throat . . ."

The Liberation of Paris was making Riton aggressive. It was the first time for over a year that Bullseye's favorite houseboy was showing his muscles! But the young communist was not impressed.

"I'm not taking anything back," he declared. "If you took money from Krauts, even by that route, then you're a collaborator and you'd better shut your mouth. You and your friends have been throwing your weight around too much just recently, much too much!"

If the boy had been on his own, Riton would probably have gone for him, but a crowd had gathered, Joel and several of his Front National friends among them. Paulo was there too, but it was the Breton's fists the pimp must be watching out for. Neatly, he changed his tune.

"Well, if we can't have a joke now and then," he started.

Joel interrupted him. "There are limits. What you're saying is provocation."

"It's got nothing to do with you, boxer. I was talking to this boy who can't take a joke. Listen, just to show there's no hard feelings, as soon as we're back in Paris, I'll introduce him to my girls and he can screw the night away, for free."

"Your girls," said Paulo, "ditched you a long time ago. And just in case they haven't, we'll take care of it by telling them you were a Kapo, and a queer's chambermaid. After that, it'll be them sending you out on the streets, you heap of shit."

Paulo had come out with the worst insults he knew. For a long time now he'd been waiting for a chance to tell Riton, whom he had always despised, exactly what he thought of him, in public.

"You haven't heard the last of this," replied the pimp, white as a sheet, and he left the *Waschraum* without even putting his shirt back on.

It wasn't so much his fear of getting beaten up which made him pale, as the panic which seized him when he realized that these men had risen in judgment against him, like a tribunal, and that tribunal would still be there the day the war ended to call him to account, and perhaps to sentence him on the spot. Seen in that light, the Liberation must have seemed a much less joyful prospect to him, for in the days which followed the confrontation, he made himself as inconspicuous as possible, skulking in the background so he didn't get mixed up in the groups discussing the burning issue of what they were going to do "afterwards." He knew what he was going to do: he was going to be fucking careful!

He wasn't the only one to have rubbed his hands too soon. The Liberation of Paris had not solved all the problems. The war was still going on, and Herr Kommandant made it his duty to remind his dear *Haeftlinge* of the fact. "The Wehrmacht has taken up a position on the Siegfried Line," he announced, "and no army in the world will be able to dislodge them." Dédé was forced to confirm it. Hitler and his stunted spokesman, Goebbels, far from capitulating, were exhorting their nation to defend the holy soil of the homeland to the death. They were mobilizing women and children, plus any old men capable of standing up, to turn Germany into an impregnable fortress. It could go on for years, the time it was taking the Yanks to get their second wind. With these Nazi bastards doggedly fighting on, the end of the war was not so cut and dried after all. Loibl was a part of that impregnable fortress, at the mercy of Knock-Knees and his hysteria.

For the time being, he was content with reducing their rations a little more each day, but it did them no harm to be forced to think about food again. It helped to take their minds off unfulfilled dreams. By the beginning of September, they had all retreated into their prisoners' skins. This time, before they started talking about Armistice Day, they would wait for the gates to be thrown open. The camp gates, not the gates of Paris.

Nevertheless, for a good week they had all thought it was over. They had rehearsed their exodus from Loibl again and again, exchanging addresses and forming into groups of men from the same area to travel home together. Even the youngsters had come to life, *en masse* leaving the *Revier* without waiting for their self-inflicted abscesses to heal. In the *Waschraum*, which had never seen such a throng, they were no longer reluctant to go and see what they looked like in a cheap mirror nailed to the wall.

"Haven't come off too badly," was the reassuring conclusion.

The maddest day of all had been Sunday, August 27, when the news of the liberation of Paris had become official. Singing broke out everywhere in the blocks, in the showers and in the *Revier.* Drafts, chess and packs of cards miraculously appeared, fashioned out of whatever they could find. Games were organized, poker being the most popular, and in all seriousness, they wrote down on pieces of cement sack the vast sums they owed each other, as if they would be settling their debts in a few days' time with real money. A few cautious characters had preferred to take a down payment there and then, and those men who had managed to put by some food and a few cigarettes parted with them quite freely. "What the hell! We won't be taking it home," they said rashly, and then raised the stakes.

For the Campana brothers, the villains had even organized a collection, as if the two Corsicans were the only men in the clink and all the others were outside. For over a year the two terrors had not been worth cultivating: they had no particular skills, no soft jobs, and they'd been forgotten. But now that they'd be rubbing shoulders outside, the whole picture changed. It would be better for Riton if they called him friend, rather than fucker. Otherwise it might end one's chances in the underworld for life.

That memorable week had also revealed the identity of the real communist leaders. There were two of them at the top of the ladder whose authority was unchallenged, and any men who didn't feel very comfortable about their performance as patriots had begun frantically to ingratiate themselves. The two commies, middle-aged men from the Parisian suburbs who'd been in the Party for twenty years, pretended not to understand. These sons of France were suspicious to the last. Accustomed to struggle and being out in the cold, they had been reluctant to drop their masks and in the end they had only resigned themselves to it in order to prevent the hotheads from pulling off an idiotic stunt like singing the "Marseillaise" on the *Appelplatz* or downing tools in the tunnel and going on strike. The worst had been averted thanks to their efforts, but they didn't carry enough weight to put a stop to the hopeless optimism. Besides, the two poor fellows must have half believed it was in the bag themselves.

What a disappointment it was at the end of that week to learn that the master stroke of Paris liberating itself had not changed *mein Führer's* mind! On the contrary, to punish the city of sin and to punish all those who had rung church bells all over the world to celebrate his downfall, he had decided to drag the whole of humanity down into the mire with him. He would be the loser, he no longer had the arms or the men, but it would drag on for many more months, unless the heavens, daily darkened by more bombers, had a hand in it. The main thing was to avoid being part of the holocaust. There was not much danger of being caught up in it at Loibl, and it could have been the ideal spot from which to watch the Reich crumble in the fine weather of June and July. Unfortunately, at 3900 feet the laws of nature are unchanging, and the rains of September soon give way to snow.

"Anything, but not this, not another winter," Paulo groaned. And he went off to find Fritz so he wouldn't have to see the downpour: "Listen, chief, you promised me that after a month I'd be on the day shift in the tunnel. It must be about time."

"You're right, *langer*. Next week we'll be starting on the galleries. But you look as if you're in a hurry, so don't take the night shift tomorrow. Go and register with the *Lagerschreiber*. Tell him I sent you, so that he doesn't make any difficulties."

Paulo thanked him and thought to himself, "Hey, he didn't call me a *Scheisskubel*. The beating he got from François has taught him some manners."

In his haste, Paulo had forgotten to ask him what he meant by "starting on the galleries." It must have something to do with his puzzling words of a month ago when he had said there would be enough work for everybody.

It was the Kommandant who revealed all, a few days later. Another occasion for a speech.

"*Haeftlinge!* The tunnel will soon be wide enough to accommodate motorized convoys, but don't imagine for a minute that you'll be going back to Mauthausen."

Paul grinned. "Cheers to that."

But this time Knock-Knees hadn't wound himself up to play his scratched record of hymns to the glorious *Führer*. He was talking about the galleries.

"We are going to dig other tunnels inside the main tunnel. Contrary to what some of you may have thought lately, you will be here for years to come. Don't forget it."

Years! If it hadn't been for the story of little tunnels to be dug inside the big one, they would all have died laughing. But little tunnels—what on earth for? To store arms and ammunition, of course. Tanks and guns, not food. In other words, Herr Kommandant intended to fight his own war here at Loibl. He didn't yet know whether it would be against the partisans, the Russians or the Americans, but one thing seemed obvious: SS, *Feldgendarmes*, civilians and prisoners would be taking part. They had a strange kind of Armistice to look forward to now.

Muster over, Paulo rushed off to find Joel and Dédé. They seemed as shattered as he was.

"You're thinking what I'm thinking," he said. "The maniac wants to make his last stand here, with us as cannon fodder to shield the SS! We've got to stop him before he turns Loibl into a bunker. Your partisan friends are our only hope. They've got to attack immediately, before the snow!"

"You're right, it's the only solution," Joel nodded. "What do you think, Dédé?"

"I'll tell you what I think. I think you'll have to come up with something else. The partisans would never dream of doing anything so foolish. It's not that they don't care what happens to us. They know what's going on and they feel sorry for us, but their orders are quite clear: there will be no assault on the camp."

"Tell us why, for God's sake!" Paulo interrupted.

"If Yanko's to be believed, there are plenty of good reasons, the best one being that it would force them to surround both camps simultaneously, and since there are more than three hundred SS and *Feldgendarmes* armed with automatic weapons between here and Nordfeld, they would have to bring in several battalions. And from a strictly military point of view, what would they get out of it? Nothing, except that if they won, they would find themselves with almost a thousand men on their hands to feed and arm, when they've barely got one rifle each, and they're short of food as it is. Not to mention that none of us is in a fit state to stay on the move day and night in the mountains, as Tito's men have to do."

"You're underestimating us," protested Paulo. "As far as fitness goes, we're all in fantastic shape. And as for not having enough to eat, I'll bet we could teach your partisans a thing or two about that."

"Possibly. I agree that our physical condition is not a good reason. The real reason is that they would suffer enormous losses from a frontal assault. Only one prisoner in ten would get out alive. It's just not worth the risk, especially for us."

Paulo was only half convinced. "But from what we know, Tito's men are not exactly sentimental. For them one man's life is neither here nor there. There must be something else. Tell me, Dédé, it's not because they don't trust the Polacks, is it?"

"I don't think so. At least Yanko hasn't said anything to suggest it. On the other hand, there is one thing that may have bothered them, and that's the composition of the camp, the different types of men, especially among us French. They know we're not all communists or Resistance. I suppose at a pinch that might justify their reluctance to get rid of the thorn in their side which Loibl must be to them, stuck in the middle of an area which they are otherwise completely in control of. But that's not good enough; the real reason they won't attack is because they're afraid of a bloodbath."

"So what are we supposed to do? Are they waiting for us to liberate ourselves?" Joel broke in.

"God forbid, the losses would be even greater. That's what's happening in Warsaw, where they've started an uprising without either the support or even the agreement of the Red Army."

"So what the hell *do* they want?" cried Paulo angrily.

"Perhaps quite simply to let things remain the way they are, so that we go on and finish the tunnel as planned. In a way, it's their tunnel too, and they're certainly counting on using it in the near future to cross over into Austria *en masse* if the col gets blocked by snow. Which, if you think about it, isn't so stupid. Besides that, they're probably telling themselves that, if we weren't here, there'd be three hundred more Germans on their tails. Stuck here guarding us, it's as if they were already prisoners." There was no answer to the logic of Dédé's arguments. Joel seemed even more disappointed than Paulo.

"So that's that," he said. "If we're to be of any use to anybody, all we can do is escape. But come to think of it, Dédé, perhaps they're against that, too. Yanko didn't tell you what kind of reception the Russians got, did he?"

"Yes, he did, and they were pleased. Any man prepared to kill an SS in order to escape is obviously going to make a first-rate fighter."

"Well then, a mass escape, a mutiny, ought to be to their liking. The men who got out would be the sort of men they're looking for. I just don't understand."

"Hang on a minute," Paulo rejoined. "You still haven't got it. Dédé just said it would either end in a bloodbath or, if by some fluke it came off, there'd still be the problem of mouths to feed. They don't want us, we'd get in their way. Now d'you understand?"

"No, I didn't say that," Dédé went on. "They wouldn't mind a few men here and there, even if they aren't very eager—and they're right. What can we possibly offer them? Information about the garrison? They know more about it than we do. Personally, I think the best way we can help them is to make some plan on the inside for the day the SS start packing things up."

"I'll say yes to that," said Joel. "But from what I can gather, although you're being very cagey, the Yugos aren't opposed to one or two individual escapes. It would depend on who escaped."

Paulo, who was clearly unwilling to discuss this subject, dug his heels in. "As far as I'm concerned you'd have to be an idiot to break out now, when we're so near the end. Have you forgotten what they did to the Russkies, Joel? The whole lot burned? A hundred and fifty guys is a high price to pay for three more partisans!"

"That's just why I'm in favor of a mass break-out," Joel interrupted. "I've even thought of a way of keeping casualties to a minimum. Every evening at half past six, the two shifts pass each other on the road. There's always enormous confusion when the two columns draw level. For those few seconds, we're three hundred against fewer than sixty SS. So we attack the guards with our hurricane lamps and mess bowls filled with rocks, and we take their guns. They'll be hemmed in by the ravine on one side and the mountain on the other, and they won't have any room to stand back and fire. I'll guarantee you if we set on them with our fists, we'd soon finish them off."

"Hold on, boxer, there's one catch to your scheme: what about the two escorts at the back of each column? If they open fire from only sixty feet, and they will, even if their own men are trapped in the middle, you can be damn sure not one of us would get away."

"But by then we'd have guns too. That'd give them something to think about. If the thing has to be bloody, it'll be bloody for everybody."

The gym teacher was slipping back into his extreme ways. Paulo brought him up short.

"What's wrong with you? You don't sound like someone who loves France. Don't you ever want to see it again? Christ, Dédé, listen to him, he must be crazy suggesting a full-scale battle with only a few weeks to go!"

But he left it at that. Winkler's intention to drag them all down with him into the mire, plus the partisans' refusal to help them get out, had robbed him of any desire to argue things further. His dreams of freedom had receded. They would be stuck here for some time to come. And winter was drawing on, bringing with it the hateful snow.

"Roll on bedtime, so I can shut my eyes and not think about it," he thought gloomily. Faced with this bleak outlook, he was forgetting the lack of food, which was once again the number one problem. There wasn't a single stale crust to be had in the whole camp, since in the general euphoria at the end of August all the men who had anything stored away had rashly distributed it. Nor was there the slightest hope of extra rations, for the chiefs had felt so acutely the rumblings of reprisals that they didn't dare pinch from the communal store anymore. Each man got his proper ration, and that was it. If they wanted food, they were going to have to get it outside, from the civilians. They too would do well to show some understanding if they wanted to avoid trouble after the war. Now that they could be spoken to as equals, there was no need to beg from them as they had had to in the bad old days.

Without further ado, Paulo confided these thoughts to Angel, who had been so successful at butt-hunting before the halcyon days of the boxing matches. The boy was quite himself again.

"This time, little man, we've got to put the arm on them for some decent grub, not smokes. Loaves of bread, bits of bacon, sugar. We're not beggars or slaves anymore."

"Couldn't agree with you more, but how are we going to make them cough up?"

"Oh, spin them a line of some sort. Tell them we've got some yellow stashed away somewhere, I don't know, anything. But it's vital if we want to get home in one piece. By the time they realize they've been had, the war will be over. You work outside, so you can pick out the pigeons and send them to me in the tunnel. I'll take care of the rest."

Angel didn't look very eager. "If you don't mind me saying so, Paulo, the civvies won't give you something for nothing. Even if it means a lot of work, I've got a better way."

"Well, go on!" said Paulo impatiently.

"It's very risky, but if it works, we'll have enough grub for three months."

"So get on with it! What's the job?"

"A spot of burglary."

"Don't give me that! Where are you going to do it?"

"Right here. In the sawmill, to be exact. We'll nick the belt, thirty feet of real leather. It's worth a fortune."

Paulo was silent. "You're right, it's risky," he said after a moment. But you could tell that the daredevil scheme appealed to him, and there was only one thing wrong with it: it hadn't been his own idea. But he quickly consoled himself by taking charge of operations.

"The two most important things are first to get the belt out without being seen, and second to stash it somewhere no one would think of looking for it. The job itself is child's play and, as for the rest, I think I've got it."

The success of his plan depended entirely on the speed of its execution. It had to be timed to the second. At five to six everybody on the outdoor sites and in the tunnel began to put their tools away, and they would have only five minutes until assembly at six o'clock. As a rule, the saw was switched off at half past five to give the men working on it time to sweep up the wood shavings, so there would be no need to engineer a breakdown in order to cut the belt.

On the appointed day and at the appointed time, Paulo emerged from the tunnel with a piece of cement sack prominent under his arm, and walked easily toward the latrines.

Given the daily diet at Loibl, attacks of diarrhea, even a few minutes before the end of work, were commonplace. Nobody gave him a second glance, and skirting around the *Abort*, he went into the back entrance of the sawmill. Angel was already there, waiting for him.

"There you are at last. We're lucky, they're all outside dusting themselves down."

"That's just what I hoped," answered Paulo. "Come on, let's get moving. Give me your knife, we've got thirty seconds."

It was plain sailing. Five seconds to cut the belt, twenty to roll it up and slip it into an empty cement sack, a few shovelfuls of sand on top, and Paulo had already left the scene of the crime. He set off at a trot as if he were afraid of being late for muster, and had barely reached the entrance to the tunnel before Angel emerged from the sawmill in his turn, briskly trundling a wheelbarrow with the sack of treasure in it.

Transporting it in a cement sack, the most common thing you could find on a building site, had been Paulo's first brainstorm. But the second, the hiding place, displayed even more subtlety of thought. That same afternoon, using a pneumatic drill, he had made a hole just big enough for one sack in the wall of the tunnel, very near the entrance—less than thirty yards down—for time was of the essence.

"Nice work, man," he said as he saw his accomplice's silhouette appear at the tunnel mouth. "We've done it. But get a move on, the first guys in the night shift will be here any minute."

At precisely one minute to six, the belt from the sawmill was in its resting place, and just to be sure that in spite of the darkness the cavity didn't attract the attention of prying eyes, the two friends blocked it up with a large flat stone.

Next to each other in the column going down to the camp, Angel and Paulo didn't say a word. It wasn't caution which silenced them; they could easily have discussed their deed and congratulated each other by talking in riddles unintelligible to the men around them. They were keeping quiet doubtless because the dangerous act they had just committed had not produced the same reactions in them, and they both knew it. For Angel it was just another job, and by not talking about it, he wanted to make the older man realize that their theft was peanuts to him, compared to what he was capable of doing, or indeed had already done. The reason for Paulo's silence was quite different. The theft of the belt was psychologically important to him, the most important thing he had done for a year and a half. He saw it as his first real gesture, it was the act of a man, and he was amazed to discover that it had taken him only five minutes to leave his slave's mentality behind, as dramatically as if he had pulled off an escape! If Angel had been older and more mature, he could have explained his feelings to him in a few words: Look at me, I'm no *Scheisskubel* now.

It must be said that what they had just done was a clear case of sabotage, the worst Loibl could suffer. Because of them work on the tunnel would be held up for several days. At six o'clock the next morning the theft would be discovered and there would be hell to pay. A general search, the threat of collective reprisals to force the culprits to confess, an investigation, the works. All good reasons for Paulo to go up in his own estimation. It would never be traced back to him, the operation had been too cleverly planned; it was Chastagnier at his best, as he'd been in his heyday before Mauthausen.

Fossil-Face would doubtless cover himself by insisting the sabotage must have taken place in the night, and he would be believed. The sawmill had been fully operational up to the usual time, and anyway a detainee would never be able to make off with a belt that size without being noticed, least of all one of the miners. They would be the last to come under suspicion. Looking back, it was a fine piece of work. But for five minutes, they had needed all the nerve they had. And it was that which mattered most to Paulo: he had become his old self again. His nerve had not once deserted him, either during the job or afterward. It was much more important than the luxuries he would get out of bartering the leather, which the civilian fools needed so badly to repair their worn-out boots.

Full of self-confidence, he began to get carried away. "If we weren't so near the end, I'd try a break for it in all the confusion."

That was something else he couldn't tell the hothead Angel. It was best just to leave him thinking that the theft was all in a day's work, and that nothing had changed. Besides, there was one more thing left to do which he hadn't yet worked out: they had to sell the belt.

"We lie low for a week to give the Krauts time to cool down," Paulo had stipulated. He waited patiently for the time to elapse, before accosting the Italian driver, who was even keener to do business than his predecessor.

"Hey, Luigi, you could do with some leather soles, couldn't you? Real leather," he began.

The wop was not taken in. "The belt," he said. "So you were the one who stole it. How much do you want?"

He hadn't batted an eyelid. Paulo breathed again. Putting on an air of injured innocence he protested, "I didn't say I did it, I'm only the middle man. It was the Polacks. Well, if you're not buying, too bad. For what it's paying me," and he made as if to go.

"Wait, listen, of course I'm interested!" cried the Italian, holding him back. The thought of the prize slipping through his fingers appalled him. "How much do your friends want for the belt, then?"

"The belt! Come off it. They sliced it up a long time ago. They've all got a piece hidden away. You'll have to buy it bit by bit."

Judging from the gleam in the Italian's eye, Paulo's precautions and the spiel about the Poles were quite unnecessary. He wasn't going to squeal, greed was written all over his face. But you never knew, a cheap crook like him might get the idea of double-crossing him after the goods had been delivered. So by selling it off in installments over several days they had him dangling.

"Okay," the wop said resignedly. "Bring me as much as you can tomorrow. What do your Polacks want in exchange?"

"They said no tobacco," Paulo lied. "They want food. Bacon, sugar, margarine and white bread. You'd better see to it."

"Fair enough, leave it to me."

The hand-over of the stolen goods went off as easily and happily as the job itself. Now the only problem for the two friends was to fill their faces without being seen. Food in the camp got more and more scanty every day, and it would have been unwise to upset hungry men by waving hunks of white bread under their noses. Where on earth had they gotten them, spread with all that margarine? In these thin times, it would not take long for the green-eyed and the sneaks to come out of their holes. Paulo was right, it would be tempting providence. "We'll put the wop's grub in the hole as it comes in, and we'll eat it on the spot," he told Angel.

Their buyer was as good as his word: it didn't look as if he had short-changed them, unless his leather had been even more of a hit than they had expected with the barefoot beggars across the way. But, despite Angel and Paulo eating two lunches and dinners a day, by the end of two weeks they still had more than half the belt left. And they had no way of letting Dédé, Joel and even the many other decent guys like Pompon and François have a share in their haul. Paulo had insisted that they shouldn't take the slightest risk. "We can't take anything back to the camp, not a single scrap. It'd be too stupid to get caught now."

Even putting on weight was dangerous enough, when the others were losing it just as fast. Paulo had been looking for a way of unloading the rest of the goods in one go for several days now, and one morning, when he saw his Italian furtively munching a delicious-looking ham sandwich, a brilliant idea occurred to him. The little capitalist had forgotten to mention ham.

"And what about us, you bastard! Don't we get any?" Paulo swore at him. "We've had it up to here with your ersatz margarine."

"It's difficult to get," the other said apologetically. "You have to buy the whole ham."

"Don't talk bullshit. How much does a ham cost?"

"It costs a fortune. A thousand marks, or more, I don't know exactly."

"This leather, if I give you as much again as you've already had, will you get me a ham?"

The startled Italian put down his sandwich. Counting on his fingers as if working out the official exchange rate for leather, he finally said: "We'll see. I can't promise you anything. I'll tell you tomorrow . . ."

The ham was there the next day, a good eight pounds of it. It hadn't taken the cunning so-and-so long to dig it out, and there again, he must have gotten a huge rake-off, but Paulo was relieved. It was becoming a worry to have to keep the compromising evidence, and every day's exchange multiplied the risks. This time they were rid of it. Even if a nosy Kapo ferreted out the hiding place, all he would find was a ham, hardly proof of sabotage.

"Whew!" sighed Paulo, when the Italian had carried off under his arm the bag containing the rest of the belt. He had been surprised to find that it was all in one piece, but it was too late now for blackmail.

Paulo felt proud of having concluded the affair so well, and especially of having stayed calm throughout the last two weeks fraught with danger and suspense.

Already his brain was hard at work looking for other crimes to commit. The only thing that made Loibl bearable was not behaving like a sheep. Nevertheless, he hadn't exactly behaved like a sheep since his return to the south, as least as far as food was concerned. The rubbish he had strung Sailor along with, the gold tooth he had stolen, betting with dravas, were all ideas which hadn't occurred to the others and had tided him over nicely. They weren't quite the same thing, however, they were just classic prisoners' schemes to make a bit on the side. With Angel, he had taken real risks for the first time. Doubtless the day would come when he would have to take others with far more serious consequences. The belt operation was a good training ground.

Working all day in the tunnel was ideal for discussing that big day. In the darkness, out of the enemy's sight and hearing, they could say what they liked about Hitler, Germany, and the fucking Krauts. They could insult eighty million Germans as loudly as they liked, promising them the direst of fates and inventing horrible forms of torture for them. They never tired of it, and the atmosphere had made Paulo feel right at home.

It was like the League of Nations. They put the world to rights, beginning with the camp, drawing up a list of traitors to be punished in order of priority. They also discussed how they would take control of Loibl as soon as the Krauts began to panic, and the communists were no longer the only men to have ideas. Others, who up until then had stayed in the background, now came forward with schemes for taking over. The minute there was a gathering anywhere in the tunnel, each crew would send a delegate to see what was being hatched and to raise objections if need be. The Party comrades were taken aback by their belated awakening but, safe in their beliefs and certain of their strength, they let the volunteers enlist. There would still be time afterward to change things. To show how broad-minded they were, they had allowed a few fellows who were a little crooked at the edges to join their ranks; they had even promoted one of them, a man from Dijon, to political commissar!

Paulo wasn't asking as much as that, but he was nonetheless very pleased not to be left out in the cold anymore. The highhats had come around to the idea that when the day came for action, Paulo could be more useful than a good many of the plucky youngsters who had been arrested for having slipped pamphlets through letterboxes.

Meanwhile, all these committee meetings were killing time very effectively. The teams on the upper level who were enlarging the vault, carpenters and masons for the most part, even allowed themselves the luxury of singing revolutionary songs. A quarter of an hour before lunch and again before the end of work, they sang songs like "L'Internationale," "La Jeune Garde," "Komintern," "Braves Soldats du Dix-septième," "La Carmagnole," and the latest ones from the maquis—the whole repertoire.

They could be heard proclaiming the revolution right over in Nordfeld. It was dangerous, but what a joy to hear. It stirred them all, even Paulo, who had been fed up with this kind of music at the time of the Popular Front when it could be heard all over Paris. Now he joined in the chorus with his mining comrades like a proper little Red:

> Nous sommes la jeune France
> Nous sommes les gars de l'avenir
> A qui travaille il faut du pain*

He didn't even find it funny; he sang out with conviction. Of course there was nowhere else in the world where the words meant as much as they did here:

> Debout les damnés de la Terre,
> Debout les forçats de la faim,
> Nous ne sommes rien, soyons tout . . .†

---

*We are the youth of France
We are the men of tomorrow
He who works needs bread

†Arise the damned of the earth
Arise the prisoners of hunger
We who are nothing shall be all

It did them a world of good to yell it out at the tops of their voices as they pictured the barbed wire a few hundred yards away, the *Revier,* the crematorium, Fossil-Face with his fat pistol and the *Hundenführer* walking his dogs along the death line.

The concerts may have served to boost the troops' morale, but far more significant things were going on in this tunnel of theirs. Sabotage was rife. There was no end to the derailed wagons, the full sacks of cement dropped through the trapdoors, the bent and useless mining bars, the picks and shovels buried forever in the concrete molds. "What a pity," thought Paulo, "that old Etcheverry died without ever seeing this." The acts of sabotage were not simply the work of a handful of fanatics; everyone did his bit quite openly, without bothering to hide the fact, as if a great bond of trust had suddenly formed between them all, like the maquis. In a way, Loibl's tunnelers had become just that.

Carried away by anti-German feeling, Paulo set to with a will and each day he went up a little more in the militants' estimation.

"Not that, comrade, they count those," one of the commie leaders had to tell him, seeing him about to pitch a pneumatic drill into some wet concrete. He was unquestionably one of them now. His crooked past, his little tricks here, were all forgotten.

Now he'd been accepted, his morale was at a peak, and he didn't have a hard word for anybody. He almost got to the point of sharing his ham with the whole tunnel.

He racked his brains for his own way of showing his appreciation to all these fellows who had given him such a warm welcome. He finally hit on an idea which immediately appealed to them. All they had to do was ambush the engine driver who on certain days brought the SS in the north their share of the goulash in covered vats. That kind of sabotage could be profitable.

"The wop'll be none the wiser," Paulo had explained. "When I say ambush, it's only a manner of speaking. I've got it all worked out. We'll derail his train, just enough to stop him. Then while one group helps him to put the wheels back on the rails, the others can open the vats, help themselves and put the lids back on. And we'll do it again every time there's goulash on. Of course we'll have to vary our tactics.

One day there'll be a rockfall in the way, the next there'll be planks of wood on the track, then a pile of stones, or someone could just pretend they wanted a chat with the Italian. I'll take care of it, I know him, we've got a little secret."

He seemed so sure of what he was doing that no one felt like arguing, and the first goulash holdup went off without a single hitch, as easily as the job in the sawmill. The Italian was at a loss to thank these Frenchmen who came running from all sides to help him set his little train back on its wheels. "Heave, heave," they yelled together, nice and loud so that the goulash-raiders wouldn't be heard opening and shutting the lids of the vats at the back. But where were they to put all this piping-hot stew when they had no bowls? Paulo had thought of that too.

"You fill up your *Mützen*," he had suggested. "They're a bit filthy, but they'll take a good two quarts. And take it from the bottom, use your fists . . . forget the gravy, just take the meat."

His friends had followed his instructions so faithfully that more than half the meat—twenty kilos at a conservative estimate—ended up in the striped berets. What a catch! In these cavelike surroundings, lit by the flickering glow of hurricane lamps which made their fearsome convicts' shadows leap and dance, they looked just like robbers counting up their spoils. But their joy at the idea of feasting on all this meat was as nothing compared to the delight they felt when they imagined the faces of the Nordfeld SS cursing the bastard cook in the south. It made them laugh so much that they couldn't eat.

"Terrific idea, Paulo," they said over and over. And since the Italian hadn't noticed anything, they all talked of doing it again.

Paulo was in his element. After all, joking, singing and getting up to no good was normal for his age. In his misspent past as a crook, he had lived a life bounded by false attitudes and twisted conventions. Living like an old man, inventing grown-up problems for himself, he had missed this kind of fun. He belonged far more to this group of mischievous boys whom Fritz and Fossil-Face—thinking they were punishing them—sent to work in the tunnel, than to the staid men outside, whom trainee Kapos like Pozzi and Fat Marcel he had assigned to the soft jobs in the hope of redeeming their past sins. In fact, why wasn't Joel in the tunnel with the rest of the impatient ones?

Paulo didn't have time to help repair this oversight. The tunnel complex demanded more and more manpower every day, and soon the Breton showed up, bursting with impatience to join in the fun. The crack boxer would take to this sustained atmosphere of revolt like a duck to water. He wasn't of course the ideal recruit for a lot of laughs, but quick-witted François and Jeanblanc, the brilliant abscess-maker, who was also from Burgundy, followed in his footsteps. They were both only too eager to join in the fooling they had heard about. Pommier the boxer had also volunteered, but more unexpected was the presence of Pompon. Given his pathological aversion to work and his genius for digging out the easy jobs, it was strange that he should have decided to join the tunnel crew. How had his pal, the timber Kapo, who took him along on every job, managed to part with him?

"What's happened to you?" Paulo asked him. "Did you fall out with your Alsatian?"

"Not at all, we're still friendly, but it was getting fucking cold outside. Cutting down trees in that downpour is enough to freeze your balls off and I always try to keep mine warm in the winter."

Winter, snow! Of course, they were going to be right in the thick of it soon. Paulo had quite forgotten that that was the very reason for his choice too. The reminder made him feel even more pleased with himself. Keen to convey his enthusiasm to the new arrivals, he immediately gathered them around him.

"Over here, you guys, you, Joel, Jeanblanc and you others, listen, we're going to have a good time. First of all, I'm going to fix you up with food. It's not a luxury, it's only what you need. Then we'll get ourselves organized into a commando. What we do is—"

Timidly, Joel interrupted him. "Bravo, Paulo, I'm delighted you finally see things like us, but aren't your plans a bit anarchistic? There are three hundred of us in the tunnel, five hundred if you count the men from Nordfeld. Don't you think it would be wiser to leave the planning of operations to the leaders of the Front National?"

"Joel, you're not with it! I'm an official member of your

Front National. Your colleagues have given me *carte blanche*. Ask them yourself."

His popularity in the tunnel was certainly not a figment of his imagination. It even had a good chance of going up a notch with fellows like François, Pommier and Jeanblanc around, who would follow him however mad his escapades. Dédé would have been no exception either, with the rowdy-student side to his character, but he was too useful outside listening to Swiss radio and using his electrician's climbing irons to ferret around all over the place.

As for Angel, on the other hand, they were better off without him. When he had stopped coming to collect his share of the ham, Paulo realized that his depression had taken hold again, worse than ever. The kid had again started railing at everybody, the commies, the queers and the bourgeois, as well as the villains. The nineteen-year-old boy was so sickened by what he had found out about the world here at Loibl that he was quite capable of killing himself the very day the war ended. He was probably right about many things, but it was better for his spleen to be carried away on the mountain wind outside rather than vented in the tunnel. The latest news was that he had started infecting himself again and was all set for the *Revier* as soon as his boil was ripe. Paulo would just as soon leave him to it.

With his black outlook, the poor boy wouldn't have fitted in, but it was still sad to see him destroying himself. He was playing a dangerous game with his syringe and he would find himself in the *Revier* sure enough—Mauthausen's *Revier*. And there, with four to a mattress, everyone knew that you gave up your birth certificate at the door. If he really wanted to gamble with his life, all Angel had to do was make a break for it, solo. Not so long ago he had almost driven Paulo mad talking about just that! He was a hopeless case. Allowing yourself to be depressed in an SS camp, when men who had arrived with much more complex psychological problems had gotten rid of them in the space of a few days, sometimes even as they stepped through the gate, was ridiculous. It was good of Paulo to be so concerned about the fate of his wretched friend, but really, with the state he was in now, there was nothing to be done for him. Adieu, Angel . . . unless his mood could be broken before. Dédé had managed to pick up some slightly better news recently. The Japanese had been driven out with flamethrowers from all the islands they had conquered in '41, the Reich was starving and completely blockaded, the Allies were bombing twenty-four hours a day and the Eastern Front was giving way from the Baltic to the Black Sea. It wasn't beyond the bounds of possibility that the gates might open at any moment.

Quite a few must have been dreaming of an end like this, a simple "Good evening, gentlemen, it's over, you can go home now." Fortunately, out of superstition, none of them dared voice these thoughts, at least in the tunnel. It wasn't in keeping with their mood, it might have undermined the spirit of revolt. The leaders had seen the danger and immediately countered with rumors designed to scare: "Winkler's received written orders to brick us up in the tunnel . . . to gas us . . . to blow everything up . . ." The means varied, but the end was always radical: they were all to be killed. And indeed, at this stage in the war, the whole business could just as easily end this way as the other, with the gates wide open and the SS vanished into the night. This bloody Kommando X would clearly be kept in suspense right up to the last minute.

This was the reason Paulo was careful not to dispute what the leaders said. He had a clear grasp of what they were trying to do, so he went one better, openly preparing for battle. He had sharpened a mining bar by pressing his pneumatic drill against a section of rail and had managed to fashion it into a proper cavalry lance capable of skewering two SS at once. Already some of the men around him had followed his example, making metal-tipped clubs out of pick-axes. Everything was well concealed under inconspicuous piles of stones, which could also be put to good use. The tunnel was fast turning into an arsenal, but not exactly the kind of arsenal that Winkler had in mind.

Even so, this was not a game; they'd better not push their luck. One morning, a Front delegation turned up and discreetly asked Paulo and his friends to moderate their war fever. Joel was among them.

"Paulo," he began, "the comrades are very grateful for what you're doing, and I'm sure you know the pleasure it gives me to say so on their behalf. I knew that one day you would join our ranks, and I'm proud of it."

"Come on, Joel, don't give me that," Paulo cut in.

"No, listen, let me finish. I mean what I say, I am proud that you're one of us, especially since you came of your own accord..."

"What are you getting at?" Paulo interrupted again. "Anyone would think you were going to give me a medal..."

"It's no joke. What I've got to say to you is serious. We think you're overdoing it. Your sort of freelance sabotage is not appropriate here. We can't endorse things like, for example, making pneumatic drills vanish into thin air... or playing basketball all afternoon with a couple of dozen cement sacks. From now on, you and your friends are not to take any risks unless they're approved by all the comrades, I mean by the leaders... If you carry on, we'll be heading straight for disaster; it'll wreck everything. You don't want that, do you?"

"That really does it," thought Paulo. "For a year, this hotheaded cutthroat has been boring me stiff with his revolutionary theories, and now he's the one telling me to calm down!"

He was just about to tell him so, when Joel, who had finished reading the riot act, wound up by being even more complimentary than at the start.

"Apart from being spokesman for the Front, I'm also talking to you as a friend. What I don't want is for you to get caught. You're a good man, I know that, you don't need to prove anything. But don't confuse Resistance with bravado—the two don't go together. What my friends like about you is not your big mouth but—forgive the word, but you said so yourself—it's your vice, like the goulash business."

Being reminded of that excellent affair restored the grin to Paulo's face. Joel was right. That kind of stunt was right up his alley. The other tricks—ripping cement sacks open with picks, dropping tools into the concrete mix—weren't so exciting anyway. If his union comrades disapproved of them into the bargain, he would be only too happy to call off these stupid, pointless and dangerous games.

"Don't worry, Joel," he said. "You won't have to tell me twice."

Luckily, the Front National had not mentioned the theft of SS food on its list of prohibitions, so Paulo, who never let himself get depressed for very long, consoled himself by devoting all his energies and cunning to it, setting up a real spy network to find out in advance the precise timetabling of the goulash trains, and getting Olivier, the dependable Marseillais sugar daddy of the kitchens, to lend him two big ladles which allowed them to fish out the meat from the bottom of the vats in record time. With this new technique, they didn't even have to stop the train. They now took their cut of the goulash on the move.

Each raid made Paulo more popular, but it was the reappearance of the pretty Yanka one fine evening which confirmed him as the undisputed star of the tunnel. As she was coming back from the north, he swept her off her feet, literally, in front of twenty witnesses. And he didn't just look at her. He gave her a kiss, a long screen kiss.

He was as surprised by his success as the men who saw him do it. The idea of snatching a kiss had been a sudden impulse, a flash of inspiration, while he was helping her—as he would have any other civilian—climb over a heap of gravel spilled from a wagon whose planking had given way. Work had just finished, and he was strolling back to the entrance when he ran straight into her.

Her way was blocked by the obstacle and she seemed to be looking around for help, reluctant to venture onto the pile of loose gravel. But Paulo's friends had such a deep-rooted complex about being the scum of the earth that they passed by her one after the other, without daring to offer a helping hand.

In the face of their lack of gallantry, Paulo stepped in. "Wait, mademoiselle, I'll help you. Put your arms around my neck."

And she did. In fact, she clung to him, so afraid was she of sinking in and losing one of her shoes, or both of them, in the filthy pile. Whether by accident or design, the way her rescuer went about it, she found herself wrapped in his arms with about as much chance of saying no as a young bride on the way to her marriage bed. Her groom hugged her to him, the better to feel her small breasts under her light blouse. Coolly, he had even leaned his head against hers, and still she did not protest.

It seemed that this cavalier abduction was to her liking, for once the gravel had been negotiated, the girl made no move to jump down. When she finally decided, after a good minute, to take her cheek from his, turning her head as if to say thank you, lips apart, Paulo seized his chance. It was the classic ploy which he had used a hundred times on his partners at the end of a cheek-to-cheek number. But today he was filthy and his chin was covered in stubble. The shy Yugoslav, unused to his technique, might not have taken it so well. However, it was just what Yanka had been waiting for, and later on the onlookers—there were now a good twenty of them, pretending to wait for Paulo to get out of the way—were able to swear to their incredulous fellows that Paulo had not stolen his kiss. The girl had kissed him back wholeheartedly, unashamedly pressing her pretty body against his humiliating convict's uniform and running her delicate hands over the scalp which the Krauts had shaved like a billiard ball, thinking they had made it repulsive.

It was inevitable that a story like this would be all around the camp within a few hours.

"That Paulo, what a man!" These hotblooded Frenchmen were pleased as punch when they discovered it was one of their compatriots who had landed the only woman in the place worthy of the name. Because, of course, they assumed the kiss was no chance encounter . . . the Yugoslav girl had been going with him in the tunnel for a long time now. There were even some who said they knew it for a fact, they had seen it. Standing up, doggy-fashion—there was no end to the lurid details.

Paulo left them to their fantasies. The important thing was not to screw the partisan girl, but to become her friend. She was his contact with the outside world, and that was beyond price. From that point of view, too, he could say he had succeeded. Next time he wouldn't need to whisper in her ear, "It's me, Paulo, twenty-eight thousand, two hundred and fourteen," as he'd had to do earlier to persuade her to be carried. In the darkness, she would recognize his touch.

XXV

It was flattering to have become the most famous prisoner in the camp, especially in this way, and Paulo lapped it up.

Everyone seemed to like the idea of his romance so much that he didn't even fear that someone would be jealous enough to tell the SS about it.

It would have been a pity if he had let it go to his head, and unfortunately, the self-assurance he displayed after each new meeting with Yanka—they had actually gotten to the point of arranging rendezvous like two lovers—was fast turning into pretentiousness. It was amazing how much cleverer and stronger he felt than the others, even feigning surprise in the evenings at the general grousing about the work, the cold, the hunger, and the never-ending war. Half listening to them, he seemed to be saying, "Why don't you do what I did?"

Although things with his girl friend didn't go beyond tender kisses, it made no difference to his self-respect. She had picked him out from five hundred shaven prisoners, a hundred civilians and two hundred *Feldgendarmes* and SS. He was Loibl's best, he was king. He couldn't have done better if he'd had his hair, and been shaved, dressed and turned out as he liked to be. Everyone agreed that his conquest was a *tour de force*, but what those who deep down envied him didn't know was that by seducing Yanka, he had avenged himself of the worst insult he had ever had in his whole life. He still remembered that mincing *Rapportführer* Helmut deliberately disfiguring him with his riding crop in front of Martha Ramsauer, out of pure jealousy.

Even to his best friends, he had never once in the past year confided the real reason for his beating. It was his secret, and more painful than the afternoon the sentries had spent hawking over him. With that bitch Martha looking on, it had been what he referred to as his personality which came under attack; in other words, the good looks which meant so much to him. He could hardly explain that to his friends; it would have looked like vanity. So he had kept it to himself, brooding about revenge for month after month. It would be a bloody revenge; he would tear that fucking Helmut's eyes out and smash his teeth in. He would shave his head and ram a poker up his ass—nothing was too cruel to pay back his humiliation. How had a man of his own age dared do that to him just to show off in front of a whore? And he had called him *Scheisskubel* on top of it all—not to mention the six months of exile in Nordfeld, which were also thanks to him. And all because Paulo was good-looking.

Paulo didn't expect to be able to have his revenge until the end of the war, but he had vowed that on that day he would demand an explanation from the man who had horsewhipped him; he would force him to admit that if he had been as ugly as Jo from Oran, who'd been with him, he would never have worked him over so viciously. Since his adolescence Paulo had been obsessed by the thought that someone could bear him ill will simply because of his physical appearance. The jealous malice of others had been the cause of endless problems and innumerable fights—"So you don't like my face?"—and the older he became, the less he could accept or forgive it. Obviously with Helmut, he had not been able to settle the score there and then, and so every time he saw him, in other words, several times a day, his rage festered. And now, thanks to Yanka, he had had his revenge, long before he had expected it. And in public, for many of his friends had seen Helmut making advances to the Slovene girl just as they now saw her throwing herself into Paulo's arms. They saw it only one way: it was the smart SS who had been cuckolded and humiliated! "We'll put him out to work on the streets with Karl and Bullseye when it's all over, that's about all he's good for!" they laughed. But behind all the joking it was clear that Paulo's chivalrous adventure flattered their egos. So the Frenchmen were champions in yet another sport.

This patriotic thrill was also felt by Paulo, but since he was the cause of it, he could hardly applaud. But how he longed to tell the jilted Helmut that it was he, the *Scheisskubel*, who had won the pretty Yugoslav. For the sake of his own safety, it was best to keep quiet. Anyway, the ironic smiles which greeted *Monsieur le Rapportführer* when he turned up for muster were ample revenge. Like all the others who had seen the Krauts march into Paris in June '40, tanned, blond, tall and strong, he had developed a complex about the whole German race. It almost seemed right that such men should have won the war and wanted to enslave the degenerate peoples of Europe. The effete intelligentsia of France had needlessly compromised itself by wanting to give the Krauts good publicity. After the spanking they had received, the whole country was behind Pétain and had opened its legs for these winged gods, these high-speed angels lovingly described by the bard of virility. As for the French women, the less said the better. They had instantly swooned at the sight of these booted men, so appetizing, so correct, *immer korrekt*. What a change, what an agreeable surprise were these blond pricks who marched in singing to take the place of their husbands and lovers who had departed with their ridiculous puttees and their old-fashioned helmets to spend the rest of the war playing cards behind barbed wire. How could anyone have wanted to pick a quarrel with men as attractive as these?

That was how Paulo, along with the rest of France, had felt when he had seen the Krauts settle in, he perhaps more than many. For their dominating presence made itself felt even more in his milieu of nightclubs and pleasure. Everything yielded to these Luftwaffe aces with their elegant ease, and these terrifying Panzer officers in their black dress uniforms. Mockingly, they had stolen his girls one after the other from right under his nose, from Paulo, the man girls couldn't resist! Admittedly, by 1943, before he had been picked up, their popularity had begun to wane. The finest specimens had disappeared to North Africa or Russia or in the skies above England and had been replaced by garrisons of slobs, but at Mauthausen, where Himmler had gathered the cream of the race, the feeling of inferiority had returned.

From the very first night, he had felt smaller than ever in the face of the Teutonic conquerors when, under the pretext of getting five men to a square yard in the dormitory of Block 17, they had walked on him, crushing him beneath cleated boots as if crushing a worm. He had just wiped away that insult too by taking Yanka away from one of the most typical and arrogant members of the race. Now he was cured of his complex, and the best thing about it was that he hadn't had to wait for Germany to capitulate to get rid of it. And he had managed to unshackle his virility ahead of everyone else, while they were all still slaves under the thumb of the Germans.

Alas, his liberation was only in his head and it was beginning to swell from so much self-admiration. The end result was that he started to wonder what the hell a man of his stature was still doing in this prison of fools. In less than three months he had proved himself in every way: he had made sure he had enough to eat in a time of famine, to the point where he was only a few pounds short of his normal weight; he had braved death by wholesale sabotage, by stealing and by dealing; and finally he had swept a girl off her feet with his charm, right inside the camp. There was even a good chance that he might soon go the whole way with her, as things were going. Maybe in one of the wagons—she didn't seem unwilling. That would be the crowning glory. But he didn't let himself become obsessed by the idea. It would only have been a fleeting climax. Since he succeeded at anything he turned his hand to, it seemed much more logical to him to focus his present efforts on the one thing which would solve all his problems at once: escape. If he failed, his fate would be no worse than if he had been caught stealing the belt from the sawmill, and he had accepted the risk of a rope around his neck before going into the sawmill job. All the same, freedom and a joint of ham were hardly in the same league.

"Okay, let's get this brain of mine working," he decided.

Now that he could see the Krauts at Loibl in their true colors, prison warders like any others, only more stupid, it seemed childish to bow before them. They were weary and flabby, looking as if they too were fed up with their sinister work, and it was possible that when the time came they would look the other way. Even if they did open fire, he would still have a chance of surviving by clever zigzagging. It had been months since they had had the opportunity to use their guns.

Making a break for it on the spur of the moment wasn't Paulo's style, and he didn't dwell long on the idea. Either his escape would be planned in meticulous detail or he wouldn't do it at all. He was easily the last man in the whole of Loibl to need to escape; his morale was higher than anybody's and he lacked nothing, not even a woman. So, gambling on a mad run for it was no good to him. There were other ways.

He hadn't decided on any of them, but he reckoned that his physical shape, his stocks of food, his reasonably new clothes, and the time of year—no snow yet but the nights beginning to lengthen—were all factors which ought to be to his advantage. But he had forgotten to include his trump card on the list: he would never have made up his mind without the good fairy of the Karawankens. Yanka had been far more than a catalyst and without her even saying or doing anything. In Paulo she had not sought to recruit a partisan whom she would have liked to fight alongside, but her look of disappointment after each tender meeting stung him more than a slap in the face. As her brave lover went to take his place in the column of slaves, kicked forward by the guards' boots, the intense expression of reproach in her beautiful eyes spoke for her: "Where are you going, my darling? You're not going back to sleep with those awful men? Stay with me."

Paulo was mortified. It was only the fear of looking a coward in the eyes of a girl which had set him thinking. All the rest—his logic, his sixth sense—were just excuses. One night he said to her, *"Ich weg mit du."* There was no going back.

The broken phrases they used to talk to each other had prevented him from going into any detail, but he was sure that she had understood and would play her part. Oddly, now that he had made up his mind, he began to think about the friends he was going to leave behind, and he reproached himself for being unkind and contemptuous to many of them on occasions. He had a sudden urge to ask them to forgive him one by one, Fat Marcel, Serpette and all those who were not fundamentally rotten whom he had jostled and insulted. "Don't hold it against me, I was at my wits' end, I like you a lot really." They would never have understood, unless he had added, "I'm telling you this because I'm packing my bags." But there was no question of telling them that; no one would be told, just as they hadn't told anyone about the ham. Except perhaps Dédé and Joel, and even they would only know at the last minute. It would give them a big shock.

It was Joel who had a shock in store for Paulo. One morning five minutes before they left for work, he said, "Paulo, let's go somewhere quiet before we have to line up. I've got something very important to tell you."

Once they were alone, the Breton went straight to the point. "I'm going to escape tonight."

Paulo started. His air of mystery and his caution had led Paulo to think that Joel was going to tell him about yet another tedious order given out by his Front National comrades, and he was half smiling as if to say, "If only you knew, I don't care a damn about that." Joel's disclosure wiped the ironic smile off his face, and small wonder. After tonight, it was Joel who wouldn't give a damn about Loibl. Paulo was amazed. How could the Breton, who only lived to see the camp rebel, abandon everything now that they were on the home track?

"Wait a moment, I don't understand. To say you weren't keen on escape is an understatement. Or were you just putting it on, you hypocrite?"

"You have no right to say that. You heard me talk about escape when Dédé told us the partisans weren't against small groups of determined men like the Russians trying their luck. And I'm not alone in this, there's a group of us. Look, Paulo, I haven't lied to you and the proof is that I'm letting you in on this. Better still, I'm asking you to come with us."

Jesus, that was really the limit! By running before he did, not only were they ruining his own plans, whether they were successful or not, but to make things worse, they'd call him a coward if he refused to go with them. He was caught.

"Joel, you've come too late. I've got a plan too," he was forced to say.

"What?" It was Joel's turn to be startled.

"Yes, it's as good as done. I've decided to escape. Does that surprise you?"

"You can say that again! Escape! Weren't you the one who couldn't bear to hear it even mentioned? But you're putting me on, you've just made that up because you're scared of going with us."

"Watch what you say!" snapped Paulo. "When I say something you'd better believe it." But seeing Joel was only half convinced, he decided to tell him everything.

"All right, I'll come clean. It's Yanka who's organizing things for me. So you see, I'm serious."

"Yes, of course, she's in a good position," Joel had to admit, "but that's when you get out. How do you propose to do that?"

It was an awkward question which Paulo dodged. "Don't worry, it's not for tonight. But I'm not at all happy about what you've just told me. We should have talked earlier."

"Paulo, I'm not the only one. All you've got to do now is come with us. The main thing is you've made up your mind. I must admit I hadn't expected it, I had really come to say my goodbyes. You and Dédé are my best friends, and I thought that if things ever went wrong, it would be safer if both of you could tell my parents one day that my last thoughts were of them. That's what I really came to ask you. Here, look, I had the address written down . . ."

His eyes filled with tears as he tore up the scrap of

cement sack with the address on it, but he quickly recovered himself.

"Since you're leaving too, there's no point. Dédé will have to go on his own. Or perhaps I'll be able to. I hope so."

"Christ, Joel, you don't sound very optimistic! From what you've said, your plan can't be perfect."

"Well, there will be one difficult moment . . ."

"And that's what you wanted to drag me into? Joel, you're mad! You shouldn't be taking chances when we're so near the end. When I push off, I'm going to do it nice and quietly with all the odds on my side. Come on, give it up. What's the hurry? I'll ask Yanka if she'll take you too."

"No, Paulo, I can't back out now. It's tonight, just before the end of work. Everything's ready, but calm down, we haven't just slung it together. It's been fixed, as you would say. So, it's goodbye, Paulo, if I don't see you before I go. And good luck with your plans too. See you in the mountains!" And he left smiling.

Joel had spoken the truth, his plan was very well fixed. Paulo went to find him just before lunch in the gallery where he was working, and got him to explain it. There were no loose threads, it was foolproof, and if they hadn't been set to leave that night, he would have gone along with them. But he couldn't do that to Yanka. He wouldn't see her until tomorrow, and there was no way Joel could postpone the expedition, for their whole plan hinged on him and his team taking advantage of a mistake which they knew the Krauts were going to rectify the very next day. In short, because it now got dark before the end of work, they were going to go back to the winter timetable, which meant pulling back all the outside crews to within fifty yards of the tunnel mouth after four o'clock. For the past week, they had worked the last hour in the dark, and despite the many lamps and searchlights at all the strategic points, it was more and more difficult to keep track of the striped silhouettes moving from one site to another.

It was this loophole which had decided Joel and his companions, but it was not their intention to make a desperate dash over the line. The leader of their team, a hotelier from southeastern France and a former football player, wasn't just relying on his reflexes; he was also an excellent strategist. At ten minutes to six, when he and his friends bolted, it would be completely dark. There wouldn't be a single light anywhere—for the very good reason that the current would be cut. That was their other stroke of genius. One lever to throw in the generator room, and there would be no power anywhere. All they had to do was run.

To create a diversion the hotelier had to call upon the Front National of which he had become one of the leaders, although he was not a communist. As the escape team were all trusted men—apart from him and Joel, there was a Parisian party member, a Pole who was also a communist and Tito, the young Yugoslav with the permanent grin who was going to act as their guide—the comrades had been generous in their support. They had ordered a few of their own men to position themselves at the entrance to the tunnel five minutes before the appointed time and find some way of attracting the attention of Fritz and a maximum number of *Arbeitskapos*.

Getting at the transformer wasn't quite so simple. Fossil-Face kept the only key on him, and to make matters more difficult, nobody had any business to be near it, except an electrician. And naturally the delicate job of attaching a string to the lever fell to Dédé Ménard. The string had to be strong enough and long enough to withstand a sharp tug from outside. In other words, Dédé had also had to drill a hole through the iron door. It was no small risk, but to help his friend Joel he had agreed immediately. By pure chance, the SS who had opened up the generator room for him to carry out some bogus repair job, had left him on his own for a good half hour. Too lazy to climb back up to it again, the SS had even left Dédé the key to lock up. Every aspect of the plan had been studied down to the last detail, and Paulo was speechless with admiration as he listened to Joel's explanation. He had only come to find Joel in the hope of pulling his plan to pieces, but now he was much less sure of finding a flaw which would make the escape impossible. Off the top of his head, he said, "But when you're gone, the Krauts will immediately suspect Dédé of cutting the current, maybe not in the generator room because it's locked, but by short-circuiting it outside."

"They may be stupid, but they're not that stupid. There's only one way of cutting the whole circuit, and that's by throwing the master lever. And where do you think Dédé will be when that happens? Chatting with Fossil-Face himself, so that he'll be the one last man they suspect, and especially so that he will be the one they order to repair it. The old fool will take him off to see what's going on, and there's a good chance he'll get out of breath and hand Dédé the key to save time. You see, we've thought of everything."

Paulo was stunned that these guys should have so much vice beneath their student exteriors. He tried to raise one last objection. "But if Dédé's off talking to Fossil-Face, he can't pull the string."

"Of course it won't be him. The communists have asked one of their men to do the job, and since he works nearby at the forge, his presence near the generator room won't look suspicious. We've already had a few rehearsals and they didn't notice anything."

In the face of such a well-oiled machine, all Paulo could do was wish him luck. "Bravo, it should work all right. I've got confidence in you now. See you with the partisans."

Joel was impatient for him to go. What he had deliberately kept from him was what happened after the site was plunged into darkness. That was the crucial moment when the success of the plan would hang in the balance, for their escape route was along the road. To make for the mountain direct from the work site in the pitch dark would have been madness, whereas along the tarmac of Route 333, despite their wooden clogs, they could sprint for the first bend which was on one of the gentlest slopes in the valley. Unfortunately, there was an SS on their road to freedom, and he had a submachine gun.

Since he usually positioned himself at the intersection of two small searchlights, theoretically he would be blinded for several seconds when the lights suddenly went out. His presence wouldn't have been an insurmountable difficulty had the searchlight on the central watchtower not had its own power supply. It was mounted high up, and there was nothing—no buildings, no trees—to stop it from sweeping the whole road with its beam. This was another thing Joel had omitted to tell Paulo. Naturally, the hotelier had thought of this damned searchlight, and Dédé Ménard was once again called in to help. He had managed to tamper with it on the pretext of giving it a clean, but not enough to stop it being a hazard—although, in principle, the job of the cretin operating it was to turn his back on the site so as to scan the mountainside for a possible partisan attack. The danger was that he was so used to being constantly on the lookout and to firing at anything that moved—generally wild animals for lack of an enemy—that his reactions would be fast and he would swing the light around as soon as the power was cut. And it was more than likely that he wouldn't wait for Fossil-Face to blast on his whistle. All this was extremely worrying, and had Paulo known how Joel and his friends had resolved the problem, he would have regretted even less not having embarked on such a perilous course.

For they were counting on the fact that the Kraut in the watchtower, from such a height and distance, would have no particular reason to shine his light straight onto them. They had calculated that since the work site was so vast he would grope about, seeking instinctively to illuminate the entrance to the tunnel. Unless the guard on the road heard footsteps around him and began yelling, or firing blindly . . .

They had talked only briefly about how they would overcome this last obstacle.

"By the time he's gotten used to the dark, we'll be on top of him. He'll only be ten yards away. It'll only take us two seconds to jump him, gag him, take his gun, and run." This was the hotelier talking, but Joel was against such moderation; he was all for braining the Kraut.

"I'll hit him on the head with a good hard block of wood. He doesn't have a helmet. That way we'll be clear down to the bend," he'd suggested.

As for young Tito, he would give no quarter. Out of his jacket he drew a long rapierlike knife and demonstrated exactly how he would carve up the troublesome *Posten*.

"Put that away, get rid of it, or you don't come with us," the hotelier had threatened. The youth was a danger to them, but they knew that up in the mountain later on they wouldn't be able to do without him. Joel had managed to reason with him.

"Killing a German doesn't bother me at all, but think of the reprisals against the friends we leave behind. It won't be so bad for them if there's no bloodshed. Someone must have told you what happened to the Russians . . ."

In the end they all agreed on the idea of knocking him on the head with a block of wood.

Paulo only got to hear about all these details the

following day, for that evening he was astonished to see that Joel along with the hotelier, the Pole, the Parisian commie and young Tito had obediently taken their places in the column going back down to the camp. At the last minute, they had all agreed to call if off. It was not because something had gone wrong with their plans: the string was trailing from the generator room, the Front National fellow who was to pull it was at his post, and the beam from the dangerous spotlight was as feeble as they could have wished. Everything was in readiness . . . except that the whole valley, including the work site, was blanketed in white.

The bastard snow had betrayed them! It had started falling shortly before five, as if by design. As soon as lunch was finished the freezing rain had started, which couldn't have pleased Joel's team but they must have found some comfort in the thought that the hounds which would be set on their heels would lose the scent that much more quickly. At four o'clock a fog had descended and by now they must have seen the filthy weather as a heaven-sent blessing. Suddenly, the drops of rain changed into snowflakes which fell more and more thickly and stubbornly refused to melt. After a week without sun the ground was cold and the snowflakes settled like confetti at a wedding, and within an hour the mountains, the buildings and the ground had disappeared under a blanket of snow four inches thick. Alas, so had the road. No longer was it the shadowy ribbon along which Joel and his friends had planned to vanish, it had turned into a ski slope which reflected and intensified the failing light. The lamps on the work site and the sabotaged searchlight cast only candlelight compared to this brilliant whiteness. The commie comrade could tug the string as hard as he liked, it would make no difference. It wouldn't be dark tonight.

Faced with this situation, the hotelier had wisely suggested cancelling, and they were all behind him, even the impetuous Tito. All that remained was for Dédé Ménard to go and retrieve his string. With the new timetable tomorrow, it would serve no more purpose. How bitter a disappointment it must have been for poor Joel.

"We should have gone ahead anyway," he said to Paulo, who had come to console him after coffee.

"Don't be stupid! You'd have been picked off like rabbits against that white road, all of you. And by now, you'd be on the grill! But cheer up, there's always the replay and this time you'll be my guest. I can tell you now, my way'll be less risky."

Holding out the prospect of another chance was the only way to raise his spirits. Over the past few days, he must have imagined himself outside so often, with a gun in his hand, and the red star of the partisans on his *Mütze*. It was impossible to get through to him on any other subject, including the struggle to be carried on within the camp, which until this doomed escape attempt had seemed the only thing which kept him going.

Now he had got him to listen, Paulo went on, "This fucking snow may be bad luck, but take it just as a warning. It's definitely going to melt, even in this rotten dump. September is still summer, for Christ's sake! We've still got a good month to get something serious organized. As I see it, the snow is going to get me moving. Feeling hemmed in like we are now will force me to hurry things up. Tomorrow I'll stir Yanka up about it, and you can take my word for it, you'll be coming with us. I know she'll agree, I've got lots of good reasons."

"But what's your plan?" Joel asked hesitantly. His hopes were beginning to rise.

Paulo still didn't have the slightest idea what his plan was. He decided to make something up on the spur of the moment. "What if she walked into the tunnel on the arm of a civilian, and came out an hour later—with me, dressed as a civilian. The real civilian just carries on down to the northern exit. That's all there is to it. All that's needed is for Yanka to carry in her handbag some clothes for the guy whose clothes I'll be wearing. We'd need a wig too, that's really important, with some glue to stick it on with."

"Terrific!" Joel exclaimed.

"Terrific, yes, terrific for one! But two civilians with two sets of gear makes the whole thing much more difficult. Yanka's friends would have to look a bit like us too, not too fat especially. No, there's no way we'll find two guys of our shape in this wilderness; but don't let that worry you, I've got plenty of imagination left. I'll fix it some other way."

He had risen to the occasion and come up with an escape plan, straight off the cuff, which bordered on the brilliant. What a pity he had already promised Joel to take him along;

otherwise, he would have sent his girl friend off the very next day to dig out a double, with all the trimmings!

High-minded as ever, Joel was already there.

"Paulo, you mustn't hamper yourself with me, I insist. Your idea's too good, you ought to see it through. It wouldn't work with two, but don't worry. If I stay here, I can be just as useful; I'm certain that if our expedition had succeeded, I'd always have regretted not being here the day the camp was ours. It'll only be another two or three months, it's not the end of the world."

"To hell with it, I'll go alone," Paulo swore to himself a little later before falling asleep, but his heart was no longer in it and it was obvious that he would continue to drag things out with Yanka. Only a few hours ago, convinced that Joel and his friends would make it, he had cursed his own plan—it was still so vague, and he had only himself to blame. This unseasonal snowfall, which had wrecked such a well-prepared scheme, had knocked him for a loop.

He was at a loss: should he go, or stay? It kept going around and around in his head without his being able to make any decision. Yanka had been amused by his idea of a civilian disguise, but she had been impressed too and was already pursuing it.

Any day now she might say to him: "Everything's ready, Paulo, we go on such-and-such a day." Just thinking about it scared him stiff, but there again, his feelings wavered between excitement and fear. Excitement at the thought that, if he succeeded in coming out of the tunnel without being recognized, freedom was only a minute away, and he didn't need telling what that meant, and fear that, despite the wig, he might seem familiar to the SS guard on the road: "*Halt, Mensch!* Come back!" It rang in his ears like a death sentence. It was good enough reason for him to hesitate—and take his time, which is what he did during the days that followed, slowing Yanka down in the most natural way he knew, by kissing her passionately the whole time they were together, so that she wouldn't say "Paulo, tomorrow's the day." If the girl liked their tender meetings and wanted them to last, she wouldn't want to hurry things up either.

XXVI

Less than twenty-four hours later, summer had reclaimed the mountains, even the highest peaks. Paulo had been right, the snow was only a warning, but instead of taking notice of it and setting a departure date with Yanka, or at least a time limit, he continued to prevaricate. So as not to disappoint his sweetheart when she mentioned the idea, he feigned great enthusiasm and a desire to improve their plan: for example, he suggested that the civilian whose place he was going to take should wear glasses. The result was that he complicated matters.

"But don't get me any sunglasses, they'd look suspicious. I want the large square kind bank clerks wear."

Every time they met he came up with something else. One day he wanted boots, the next day it was a false mustache. The pantomime he used to make himself understood made her laugh so much that she too forgot what was really at issue. As if to encourage their dalliance the days became warmer, the ground dried out, the leaves stayed on the trees and when night fell, the star-filled sky seemed to be saying: "Don't hurry, you lovebirds. Tomorrow, and the next day, and the whole week yet, the weather will be fine." Unfortunately, weather conditions were not the only factor. There was also the human element to be taken into account, and suddenly the Krauts began to turn nasty.

It had all started with a few brief bursts of fire between the *Feldgendarmes* and some stray partisans, but very quickly it had turned into sustained exchanges almost every night. Winkler, like everyone else, must have known that Tito's men were not looking for a confrontation, but since the first encounters he had bolstered up his own importance by clearing the decks for action and sounding full alert. He began to send out patrol after patrol to chase after shadows, and his men took a delight in shooting at anything that moved. Even in broad daylight, Herr Kommandant played at scaring himself, and to keep his men on their toes he had even ordered helmets to be worn at all times. In such a war-zone atmosphere, the easy life Loibl had led since the beginning of the summer could not last much longer.

It took the SS only two weeks to fall back into their vicious ways. First it was unprovoked yelling, then the pistol-whipping started, and finally, one fine morning, a luckless Pole had "attempted to escape" across the line. And they followed it with a public announcement that this was only the first of a series.

Paulo was shocked by this violent return to terror, and he despised himself for not having tried to escape. Now, in this explosive atmosphere, the ploy with Yanka looked pretty useless. Right after the first skirmishes the Slovene girl had disappeared into the mountains, probably recalled by her sector chief to report on the sudden and incomprehensible deterioration in the garrison at Loibl. She would certainly be back, for she was more useful to the maquis living among the enemy, and besides, she had left a message for Paulo saying so, via her friend Yanko—she would only be away for a short while and it hadn't altered any of their plans. That may have been so and she was evidently sincere, but Paulo didn't believe in Santa Claus. At any rate, he no longer believed he could calmly walk out in civilian clothes, with a salute for the SS on the road as he passed him, even if he did have a wig under his *Mütze*, bushy mustaches and bank-clerk spectacles. Besides, in this climate of fear, Yanka wasn't exactly going to fall over civilians who would agree to strip in the tunnel. Even if by some miracle she managed to set up the ploy as agreed, it would have to be done without further delay, because anything could happen now that their old brutality had gotten hold of the SS again. Yanka's defection was indeed a bad blow.

The only hope of her returning before the snow enveloped them lay in Winkler's receiving an order to call off his ridiculous war with the partisans. As far as Mauthausen was concerned, his mission was to complete the work in the galleries and finish the tunnel, not to play cowboys and Indians. But the onetime gardener in his Yugoslavian kingdom was going as mad as Hitler in his bunker on the Eastern Front. He felt trapped and, knowing as his *Führer* did that there would be no mitigating circumstances for him, he had decided to drag with him the whole of Loibl, even his own men, into disaster. His underlings had divined his intentions, and some who were opposed to them had been swift to confide in the prisoners. It was fitting that it should be in the tunnel, the core of Loibl, that the bond was first formed. A young Romanian SS, only recently arrived, made the first move. "*Scheisse Krieg*," he swore, each time he met a convict. It was difficult to disagree and the men picked up the habit of returning his "*Scheisse Krieg*" politely. But he might just as easily have meant it as provocation. The ice was only properly broken the day he turned up with some cigarettes and bread. *Danke schön, vielen Dank*. And as this unusual Nazi spoke a few words of French, the formalities were quickly dropped.

"You look like a good sort, *Kamerad*," Pompon began, typically one of the first to spot an opening. The other took the compliment well. Pompon was encouraged and he went on, "You can't be German. You don't shout and you don't hit us . . . Where do you come from?"

"Romania, Bucharest."

"I thought as much," Pompon lied. Unabashed he asked, "So what are you doing in the SS?"

The young soldier didn't really seem to know, or else he was too ashamed to say. Whatever the case, he wasn't angered by the question, and from them on, all suspicion of him vanished. Every afternoon, under the pretext of making his rounds, he would steal along to where the first main gang was working in the tunnel, about a thousand feet from the entrance, as if trying to become friendly with the greatest possible number of convicts. It took them a long time to understand what he was after; it was Joel, whom he seemed to find particularly approachable, who first found out.

"That Romanian is an idealist. He signed up with the SS when he was still a kid and he found out he'd been misinformed. The things he saw in Russia and then at Mauthasen started him thinking, and today he feels alienated from Germany. His great passion is Mediterranean civilization, he dreams of a holy alliance between Romania, Italy, France and Spain, but a fascist union. To think that now, in nineteen forty-four, beats everything! Between you and me, he's not all that bright, but leaving aside his obsession, he can be trusted. We've got nothing to fear from him, especially us French. He's a great fan of our seventeen eighty-nine Revolution. We mustn't disillusion him."

That they had nothing to fear was obvious; this SS comrade had had countless chances to raise the alarm. All he had to do was report the fervor with which they sang the "Internationale" at the end of work to mark the passing of another day. Like the newsreaders on the BBC, they counted the days: "Today is the fifteen hundredth day of the struggle against the Fascists . . ." They led their Romanian gently by starting with folk songs, "Aupres de Ma Blonde," "Le Temps des Cérises," which he would sing with them, trying hard to pronounce the words properly. Then, once they had him going, they moved on to revolutionary songs. And they ended up with him yelling at the top of his lungs, "*C'est la lutte finale . . . groupons-nous et demain!*"* Joel was right, the fellow couldn't be playing a double game.

Besides, he wasn't the first SS at Loibl to have his doubts. The Front National had won over another to their side in the strictest secrecy, a certain Zimmerman, as Austrian as Hitler. They hadn't needed to vet him, his references came straight from partisan headquarters. In Tito's army he even held the rank of captain. How on earth had it happened? Nobody knew, his past was shrouded in mystery, but it was probable that since he came from near the border, he must have felt more Slovene than German. According to Joel, all the maquis in the area were childhood friends of his. Unlike the Romanian, he didn't give food or smokes to his contacts in the Front National, but he did provide them with useful information about the local military situation and, more valuable still, he gave them a daily report on everything that was said and done in the SS camp. The news was not at all reassuring—like the confirmation of Knock-Knees' intention to gun down the whole of Kommando X when the galleries had been completed—but it was better that they should know. Strange to say, this charming piece of news didn't seem to depress Joel and his friends in the least. "Winkler won't have time," they said, "and anyway, since his men are surrounded, they'll refuse to commit such a massacre at the last moment."

Paulo wasn't at all happy at the prospect of an SS mutiny,

---

*"This is the last battle . . . unite and tomorrow. . . ."

because obviously not all of them would be against Winkler. Helmut for one, and then there was Fossil-Face and the other paranoiacs like Green Bean, Mikado, Tits or Medal-Man. They'd be only too thrilled to fire on SS who had betrayed the *Führer*, especially as among those likely to waver in their allegiance there were, because of Mauthausen's duty rota, more Romanians, Hungarians, Croats, Flemings and Alsatians than true Germans. What a hell of a mess it would be if they all joined in, the good and bad SS, the *Feldgendarmes* and the partisans, making the most of the situation! Unfortunately, in the free-for-all which followed there would be more than enough bullets for everyone.

The only men who might escape the bloody fireworks would be those bastard block chiefs. It would hardly be fair, but it had to be admitted that for some time now they had genuinely tried to be neutral. Whenever Winkler or Helmut said jump, they jumped, yelling, running and beating with all their old vigor, but as soon as these two had their backs turned, they made haste to put away their hoses, and were almost apologetic. They had never given a shit about the Fatherland, so they were hardly going to defend it now. Their low cunning told them who was going to win the war: the Yanks and the Britishers . . . and their French allies whom they had become so friendly with. And so they took good care not to hang around the tunnel where feelings were running high and a strong smell of gunpowder was in the air.

Herr Kommandant had gotten wind of the rebellious spirits of the tunnel workers and had sent for an *Arbeitskapo* from the north who answered to the gentle name of Herman. This monster was even more repulsive than Bullseye and he came from the Saar like his master, which was why he had been chosen. No taller than a large dwarf, but still as wide as he was high, he squinted dreadfully and was further disfigured by a cyst the size of a gull's egg in the middle of his forehead. He was a terrifying apparition in the tunnel, making sure they recognized his loathsome features by holding his hurricane lamp well above his head. He didn't care whether they saw him coming, he wasn't there to catch possible slackers, he was there to hit out at anything that wore stripes, and the bastard would smash his heavy steel lamp down on any backs and skulls within reach. Every day he sent a dozen men to the *Revier*. Paulo's solution was to sprint off as far as he could as soon as he saw the gnome rolling toward him, and when Herman had gotten about halfway through the tunnel, he would whip back past him at lightning speed. But it wasn't a real solution. What they had to do was to stop him from causing harm once and for all. The hysterical troll was behaving as if he thought the Saar would still be in the hands of the Nazis when he got out!

As Fossil-Face left him to it despite the doctor's repeated protests, the Front National decided to take care of him. They swore that the day the war ended he would be the very first one to hang, but something had to be done in the meantime. A madman like him on the loose was too dangerous with all the preparations being made in the tunnel. The moderates wanted to ask the engineers to send him back to Nordfeld, others simply talked of killing him first thing in the morning and sticking his body in the molding of the vault so that by nightfall he would be buried beneath a yard of concrete. Murder without a body. The trouble was that the Krauts would never believe such a good patriot had deserted. There would be an inquiry, and the tunnel would be searched—both of which had to be avoided at all costs. In the end, they agreed on a nice natural injury, a classic mining accident with a piece of rock dropping on his head without warning. Herman's docker's cap was hardly likely to stand up to the sort of blow they had in mind.

The whole thing almost fell through because a small group of headstrong men, among them the two unruly scrappers Pommier and François, didn't wait for the trap to be laid before setting on him. They jumped him from behind while he was pissing against the wall and the first punch knocked him out twice over. On the back of his neck he got a crashing right which would have felled an ox, and as he was thrown forward, his forehead, and its cyst, banged against the rock. A few kicks in the face as he lay crumpled on the ground hadn't brought him around, and he would never know who had done it. It didn't make any difference to him, the whole tunnel would pay anyway. He had plenty of time, and to be quite sure he would be free to settle his own accounts, he hadn't even reported the attack to Fossil-Face. That was his big mistake, for three days later, as he passed under a chute, the equivalent of a wagonload of stones descended on his head, and the SS put it down to bad luck, and even carelessness, because it was strictly forbidden to pass underneath the trapdoors. What his bosses didn't know was that some charitable soul had given the troll with the lamp a shove just as the men above sharply pulled away the planks retaining the stones. And Herman was in too much of a mess to remember.

The time it would take the good doctor to stitch him together again gave them a breathing space, and from one end of the tunnel to the other, his departure was hailed as a new victory. Paulo shared their delight of course, but the escalating violence was beginning to frighten him: "Tomorrow it will be something else," he thought, "and the SS are bound to come and poke around in the tunnel."

His fears were confirmed a few days later, when there was another accident, which upset them as much as the fate of the murderous dwarf had delighted them. The victim was a Frenchman, a young Resistance member called Felix, and he was one of the gentlest and best-liked fellows at Loibl. As in Herman's case, it was a trapdoor which caused the accident. Felix had been working in the gallery under the vault and, failing to see the chute in the darkness, he had fallen through it headfirst. Unfortunately, there were no mining wagons to break his fall, and he fell straight onto the rails from a height of almost twenty feet. His poor body was shattered and he lay on the ground unable to move his arms or legs. The first men who came to his aid realized immediately that he had broken his back. Helplessly, they resigned themselves to calling the SS guards at the entrance.

It was when the guards arrived on the scene that the horror began. First, they tried to make the wounded man get up by kicking him and calling him a lazy good-for-nothing. Then, seeing that he really couldn't move, they called him a saboteur. They did eventually decide to carry him off to the *Revier*, but lacking a stretcher, they ordered him to be put in a wheelbarrow and as they escorted him off, they started up the usual joke they reserved for injured men: "*Fertig . . . Krematorium*." Suddenly Felix made a desperate effort and raised himself up to spit in their faces, "SS fuckers!" in a voice throbbing with pain and hatred, which echoed the length of the tunnel. He knew how badly he was injured and that they wouldn't nurse him, so he told himself that before he died he would yell out what all the deportees in Germany longed to yell every second of the day: "You SS fuckers!

Hitler's a fucker! Himmler's a fucker!... Goering and Goebbels are fuckers," and so on down the list.

He made no attempt to vary his abuse but to make sure the message was understood he translated it: "*Enculati* . . . *Yeboni* . . . *Enculiert!*" One of the Fritzes, beside himself with fury, jabbed his submachine gun into Felix's stomach, but that only increased his frenzy: "Go on, shoot, you yellow fucker!" he taunted him.

Suddenly, with a last "SS fuckers!" more violent than all the others, his body stiffened.

Those were his last words, but he had survived long enough to shout them so many times that it was as if the hundred or so men who had watched his agony had taken up the chorus. Every one of them felt avenged, and overwhelmed to see such courage. He could have yelled "Help!" or "*Maman!*" before he died, but as an exemplary Resistance member he had summoned every remaining ounce of strength to go into action for the last time. He had hurled his contempt at his executioners like a grenade, and, judging by their ashen faces, it had gone home.

Paulo became more and more worried. The clashes with the partisans had virtually ceased, and he had hoped that Yanka would soon return. But with all these incidents in the tunnel, she would think twice before setting foot in it again! Already he was wondering whether it would be a good idea, before things deteriorated, to volunteer for work outside close to the entrance.

It would have been a mistake because the Germans outside were even more on edge and prisoners were dying just as shamefully. Less than five days after the execution of the Pole, which Winkler had warned would be the first of many, one of his compatriots was the next random victim of the assassins. Two young SS of the sort Winkler could certainly depend on, had vied for the honor of shooting him in turn. "Yours, mine!" they yelled, trying to hit him from behind the tree where he had taken refuge when he realized he was being pushed over the line to be "legally" murdered. As one killer shouldered his rifle, the unhappy man dodged around the tree, where the second rifle was waiting for him, and back again. It made no difference how fast he moved or how tightly he hugged the tree to offer less of a target; every time, a bullet tore at whatever was visible, his arms, his shoulders, or his thighs. He must have realized that by playing their game of hide-and-seek, he was giving his executioners an even greater thrill, for suddenly, between two rounds, he stepped away from his shelter. His striped pajamas hung in shreds, stained red with his blood. He took three steps forward, then stopped and stood grimly at attention, as if to say to the monstrous youths: "I'm not playing anymore," and to spoil their horrible shooting contest by forcing them into a vulgar murder in front of a hundred witnesses.

Startled, like the hunter whose prey unexpectedly appears in front of him, they couldn't shoot, and for a moment everyone thought the man would be spared. But these SS were in the great tradition of Mauthausen sadism, where killing demanded imagination, and even humor. Their fun had been spoiled, but never mind, they'd find some other way to finish off the *Schwein Polack* for whom death would be a deliverance.

"This dog's wasted too many of our cartridges," said one of them, and he took a pickax lying on the ground and smashed the point down on the Pole's head.

"Excellent!" the other guffawed, as if his colleague had just had a brainstorm, and in turn he used his gun butt to beat the man. "Yours, mine!"—the game could continue.

Their laughter when they had reduced their victim's skull to a bloody pulp told all the *Dreckmann* watching them that Loibl was still a Mauthausen Kommando. But at least they had been shown how to die.

That evening, when Paulo learned all the dreadful details from Joel, he lost all control.

"I hope to God, Joel, this'll make you change your mind about staying to the end. These guys are just vampires! I tell you, we've got to get out, and quick. I don't believe your theory that some of these bastards will change sides. Believe me, your decent SS won't stand a chance against guys like that!"

The subsequent murder of a German detainee with a red triangle called Rudolf, a hunchback employed in the SS kitchens, bore him out. Winkler had become aware of the uncertain element among his troops and this was his way of warning his compatriots.

"So perish all traitors to the Fatherland," he had Helmut announce in his report that evening.

The threat was officially addressed to the few German or Austrian *Haeftlinge*, political prisoners like the dead man, but Kapos, block chiefs, and SS present grasped its significance perfectly. They knew the course of Nazi history over the last ten years by heart, from the night of the long knives onward. German blood was no passport, and no excuse. Hadn't the first men in the camps, the first to be hanged, the first to be burned, been German? And if there had been a short respite because they needed their men to fight, it was over now that Germany was back home. It had been obvious as early as last July, after the attempt on the *Führer*'s life. Krauts had been tortured and shot, and had committed suicide in their thousands, and anyone who was even remotely German at Loibl knew it, whether they were inside the camp or not. If generals and whole armies had been helpless against the SS mob . . . Paulo was right. You certainly couldn't count on these poor shits, isolated up in the Karawankens, to pick a fight with the fanatics.

Probably the only reason Herr Kommandant had chosen the hunchback as a victim was that he wanted to force those of his men who were asking themselves too many questions into the open. Rudolf was a poor inoffensive fellow whose relations with the SS were fairly friendly, since he spoke their language and served them at table, and Winkler would soon find out if any of them were angered by his death. It would be a good way of discovering who the weak ones were on his staff.

Although the way the murder had been carried out was particularly vile, not one of his men made the slightest protest. The wretched cripple had been killed under cover of friendliness, and his murderers had joked with him in German. It was still the classic line-crossing ploy, but this time the two assassins, Medal-Man and the Croat, had had to resort to cunning and even exceed their orders in order for Rudolf, who had five years' experience in the camps, to be taken in.

"Let's go and get some fresh water from the stream, the stuff you give us at table is undrinkable," Medal-Man had suggested.

And they had set off like two old friends, down the path which ran alongside the SS barracks, the one balancing the bucket on his hump, the other armed only with his holstered pistol, his hands in his pockets. Medal-Man stopped when they got to the edge of the road. The stream was almost a thousand feet below.

"I don't want to get my boots dirty in that mud. You go on your own, Rudolf, and be quick. I'll wait here for you." Seeing the hunchback's reluctance he added with a loud laugh: "Don't think you can run off. With that hump of yours, you wouldn't get very far!"

His laugh had sounded so false that Rudolf was seized with panic. "If I obey," he said to himself, "he'll kill me." He had seen a hundred prisoners tricked into fetching water or wood. But on the other hand, he had done nothing wrong. If they had wanted to kill him because of his deformity, they would have done it ages ago. Uncertain, he played for time. "I don't trust you, I'm not going on my own." And he sat down on his bucket. If Medal-Man laughed and agreed to accompany him through the mud, then he would have no reason to worry. If, however, he got angry . . .

His executioner had allowed for this reaction. He neither got angry nor laughed.

"You're right," he said, "it's against the rules. I'll ask a *Posten* to go with you."

As if by chance, the Croat, his usual partner for this kind of job, was just approaching.

"Take Rudolf down to the stream, he's afraid to go on his own," Medal-Man ordered.

The poor hunchback's apprehension only increased, but this time, since he had stupidly said he would leave the road if he were accompanied, he was trapped. Picking up his bucket, he set off down the slope, turning round every few seconds to make sure the Croat was following him. No problem, the *Posten* was right behind, humming softly, and his rifle was still slung over his shoulder.

"What a lot of fuss about nothing," Rudolf must have thought when he reached the stream with his escort. All his suspicion had vanished and he knelt down to fill the bucket with water. The ideal position: still humming, the Croat lowered his gun without even taking the strap off his shoulder and fired a single bullet at point-blank range into Rudolf's hump.

As was customary, Helmut announced at roll call that evening that a detainee had been shot down attempting to escape. A German detainee, he emphasized, looking the block chiefs straight in the eyes.

Four deaths in less than two weeks was too many, and once again, they all began to fear for their lives, particularly the bastard Riton. For fear of going the same way, he was to be directly responsible for a fifth crime. This last, which followed an escape attempt, finally convinced Paulo that unless he decided to run within the next few days—with or without Yanka—he was done for. It wasn't only because of the renewed threat of sudden death in the camp or the tunnel; the worst thing was that too many men had abruptly taken it into their heads to escape.

Following on the attempt of Joel's team, no fewer than ten men, a whole Kommando, had put together a plan. If it hadn't been for that squealing shit Riton, it would certainly have succeeded. There were eight Frenchmen, a Yugoslav, and a Pole, and their way out was much less involved than the hotelier's scheme. In addition, it didn't depend on good weather conditions; in fact, it was because it had begun snowing again that the idea of escape had occurred to them, and they were praying it wouldn't melt as quickly as the first fall. Assigned to a temporary Kommando, the *Schneekommando*, they set off on foot every morning for the pass, clearing the snow on the road as they went, and only coming down to the camp at night. The snow wasn't very deep, but since there were only ten of them they were guaranteed enough work for a good week.

Seen from above, the camp looked so small and harmless in the shadow of these vast mountains uninhabited by Germans that from the first day their imaginations had run riot, and the idea of the whole gang clearing out together, which one of them had brought up as a joke, was quickly treated as a serious possibility. No one in the camp had ever been given such a fantastic opportunity. The chances of success were so great that the lousy Riton, Kapo of the Kommando, asked to be part of the expedition. It was far better for him that way, for if he should return to camp in the evening without his crew, it was more than likely that he would be barbecued before muster was over. Of course, he would have gotten out of it by undermining the courage of the weaker men, but two who had made up their minds were the Campana brothers. The savages had suddenly come to life, and Riton, who feared them more than he did the SS, knew that if he decided to stand in their way he would have made himself two enemies for life. He really had no choice.

It was difficult to know exactly what had been going on in his mind, but he pretended such enthusiasm that he managed to get the others to put him in charge of operations. At his signal, the strongest men would jump the two SS who accompanied the detail, in this case Green Bean and his underling, a real peasant by the name Augustin. The Campana brothers were all for killing the pair, but to do it swiftly and effectively would have meant using their guns, and that would naturally have alerted the duty SS on the col and in the tunnel. A more sensible prisoner, a notary by profession, persuaded them simply to knock out the SS and tie them up. Only then would they all jump down into the ravine and follow the Yugoslav, who knew where to find the nearest partisans.

The place for the attack had been chosen with care: it was along a short straight stretch of road between two hairpin bends, which couldn't be seen either from the col or the tunnel. In the event of a last-minute hitch—Green Bean stopping to piss, for example, and getting separated from his colleague—two other stretches, a little farther up the road, also out of sight of the col and the work site, had been selected.

The day arrived, and at the appointed time the ten convicts were waiting, feverish but confident that Riton would give the signal. "Forward, men," he was supposed to say, to trigger everything off. Everyone knew what he had to do. Unfortunately, just before the small group arrived at the first straight stretch, Green Bean had already jeopardized the plan by asking the notary to carry his heavy overcoat, which was making him sweat profusely as he climbed, despite the sharp air. By the time he had taken off his coat and folded it, the Kommando was no longer together. That imbecile Green Bean was at least a thousand feet behind them. We lose nothing by waiting, thought the escapees as they approached the second stretch.

This time everything was perfect: the first rank had slowed their step so much that the two Krauts could only move forward by kicking the prisoners directly in front of them. Ideal for turning on them, and yet they reached the bend without anything happening. Riton hadn't uttered a word.

"What the hell are you playing at?" hissed one of the Campana brothers menacingly.

Not in the least disconcerted, Riton replied, "It wasn't right, we slowed down too much. Green Bean didn't stop looking at me. Walk normally so that they forget about us. Get ready, we'll attack after the next bend."

It wasn't hard to guess what this Judas was up to; he wanted to foil their plans. And he would succeed unless someone decided to take things in hand. Unfortunately, it was a little late to improvise. All eyes were on him, and if somebody else shouted "Forward, men!" there would be confusion; they would hesitate, only for a second perhaps, but that second's delay could be fatal. They had no choice but to leave it up to their shit of a Kapo, in the hope that his fear of the Corsican killers would spur him into action. As they turned into the third and last stretch from which escape was possible that was what the little group was banking on, the eight Frenchmen at any rate, for the Yugoslav and his Polish neighbor had already started their escape in their minds. They had agreed in broken Slav not to wait for the doubtful signal from the French Kapo, who inspired in them no confidence whatsoever. They would jump straight after the bend.

They did just that, and luck was unbelievably on their side: Green Bean and his stooge, Augustin, had stopped to look through binoculars at a chamois which was scaling one of the peaks. Although the eight Frenchmen had lost a previous second before realizing what was happening, they still had time to follow the path of the two fugitives. Green Bean and his dull-witted private were now some one hundred and fifty feet behind them, but some absurd vestige of discipline made them all turn their eyes to Riton.

"What are you waiting for?" snapped the notary. "Go on, shout, give the order!"

Each man had gone right to the edge of the ravine so as to get over the side more quickly, when the pimp finally opened his mouth. But what he yelled stopped them all dead in their tracks.

"*Kommandoführer, Kommandoführer, zwei Mann weg!*" he started bawling. The traitor! It hadn't been enough for him to back out when success seemed certain: like the true snake he was, he had had to betray them as well, condemning to a probable death the two fugitives who, because the snow lay deeper on the slope, had not yet managed to reach the first trees on the other side of the ravine. What a target they made against this blanket of white. The first burst of fire found its mark. Both of them were hit, one perhaps mortally, because he stayed down, while the other struggled forward, limping. Reassured, Green Bean brought his attention back to the road.

"Everybody down, *Scheisse Franzosen*!" he yelled, punctuating his words with a burst over their heads. To be on the safe side, he ordered his subordinate to come forward and shoot any man who made a move. Now that he was free to continue the chase, Green Bean followed the footsteps in the snow and soon reached the wounded man on the ground. It was the Pole who, knowing what lay in store for him, threw himself on his assassin in a desperate attempt to grab his submachine gun. Cursing him, the callous subaltern finished him off with a bullet in his head at point-blank range.

Up on the road, Monsieur Riton couldn't have been feeling very comfortable. Had Augustin not forced him to bury his head in the snow like his fellows, he would probably have done so anyway, out of shame.

"You'll pay for this, you fucker! Like the Pole who's dead because you squealed," one of the Campana brothers managed to snarl at him.

The despicable bastard was certainly not going to get out of it this time. He had shown himself to be as contemptible as Pozzi, the other French Kapo. He too had just earned his German stripe, his traitor's badge. But the affair wasn't over yet and he might have a second death on his conscience, judging by Green Bean's sustained shooting. However, there was rather too much shooting for him to have caught the Yugoslav. It sounded as if he was firing blind, and indeed a quarter of an hour later, they saw him tramping back shamefacedly.

"*Er ist weg*," he growled for his colleague's benefit.

Unfortunately, the shots had been heard, and sections of SS were setting out from all points—the col, the tunnel and even the camp—to comb the mountain. The little Yugoslav would need every ounce of luck he possessed to slip through the net. But he managed it, Yanka confirmed it the next day. The dogs had followed his bloody trail, but although he had almost bled to death, a partisan patrol had reached him first. Wisely the SS had turned back, but to save face Winkler had Helmut report at roll call that evening that the two fugitives had been captured and executed.

"The bodies of the communist dogs remain in the mountain where foxes and vultures will devour them. May it be a lesson to you."

The French had indeed learned a lesson, but not a lesson of fear as Herr Kommandant had intended. It was a sense of dishonor which tormented them, as if each of them felt responsible for Riton's appalling behavior. Under normal circumstances, it would have been up to the Poles to settle accounts with him, but they had been subjected to so many underhanded tricks since 1940 that they had seemed almost to have expected this latest betrayal. Let the French wash their dirty linen in private, was their attitude, and that was worse, because their scorn meant they put the whole of France, going on the Frenchmen at Loibl, in the same category as Riton.

Condemning Riton posed no problems; eight witnesses were ranged against him, all agreed that he deserved death or, if he got back, life imprisonment, and a member of the Front undertook to inform him of his sentence. In the meantime, however, he ought to begin paying for his crime, and with the popularity he now enjoyed among the Krauts, that wasn't so easy to achieve. Riton had become their hero; his "*Zwei Mann weg*" had delighted Knock-Knees, who had told Fossil-Face and the rest of the Kapos that they should nurture and protect such a valuable auxiliary. So, although the whole camp wanted to get even with him, they were powerless.

There was only one thing they could do: they would dissociate themselves from the ex-pimp of the rue de la Gaîté entirely. Not one of the prisoners spoke to him now, not even his fellow pimps. There wasn't much the Krauts could do about it, but they were obviously furious, particularly Green Bean. He would have liked to follow up his *Schneekommando* incident with vindictive action, because unlike Riton, he hadn't returned to lavish compliments but to an official reprimand for having let the Yugoslav get away.

"Instead of ordering your subordinate to hold down the rest of the Kommando, you should have shot them all and taken him with you to pursue the escapees. Next time, you won't get away with it!"

It was Zimmerman, the partisan SS, who told them of Green Bean's castigation, and that was all Paulo needed to start panicking again.

"Next time? Christ! I might be the one next time to get mixed up in a double cross like that and they'll shoot the innocent prisoners just so the SS can chase the runners more easily. Jesus!"

Precisely two days after the Yugoslav's escape, he thought his hour had come. And with him nine other convicts began saying their prayers, so cleverly had the Krauts prepared their little intimidation exercise. It was the classic German technique of picking on scapegoats. Luckily they did it just to amuse themselves and the prisoners got off with a bad fright. But what a fright!

"Our Father who art in heaven . . . *Maman* . . . I don't want to die . . ." they moaned in the ten-man formation which Green Bean—him again—had prevented from entering the camp by suddenly ordering the gate to be closed on the last two rows of the column coming down from the tunnel.

"It's all over, Christ, they're going to finish us off!" Paulo remembered saying, as he saw six SS with rifles close in on them. Everything was set for it: the camp was closed, the soldiers were yelling and prodding them with gun butts toward the larch trees, toward the crematorium. They were going to the crematorium all right, but only to fetch wood for the SS kitchens. When he got to the grim trench, Green Bean broke into raucous laughter, joined by his men, who were delighted to have carried off the farce so well.

"Filthy bastards," cursed Paulo when he realized it had all been a joke.

But like the others, he was still shaking and dripping with sweat as he picked up the wood. More than half of the men had pissed their pants from fright and their legs were too weak to carry them. And yet they had to move because even if the macabre joke was over, they still had to cart the logs back up. Green Bean was not content to leave the joke at that, and he took advantage of the dusk, which obscured the detail in the larch wood from view, to settle a few old scores.

Breaking a supple branch from a tree, he lashed out violently at the head of each porter as they filed past. His underlings followed suit, and it was a blood-soaked group who entered the camp half an hour later after depositing their loads at the SS kitchens.

"God, there's no place like home!" someone said, expressing the thoughts of all of them, with the exception of Paulo. This time the warning had hit him between the eyes. The next time they seized him for a chore, it wouldn't be for fun. He had to get out quick, damn quick. Like the Yugoslav who plunged into the ravine heedless of anything else, particularly of his stupid fellows. *Eins, zwei,* go and fetch wood, go and fetch water . . . it was all starting again, the hounding of faces that didn't fit. Joel and company were crazy to think Loibl could end any other way. It was just going to get worse. The fear he had felt earlier at the crematorium would not be easily forgotten.

"They won't do that to me twice," he swore, seething with rage. "There's no place like home—they've got a nerve to say that, those fucking cretins! Well, good luck to them! My 'home' is on the other side of the fence, like that Yugo. After that kind of joke, there's no way I'm going to hang around for Yanka to say go. This time I swear I'm going to get out."

In his agitation he was forgetting that since he was stuck in the tunnel twelve hours a day he had little chance of being on one of the open-air details like the *Schneekommando,* with only two guards for ten prisoners. He would have to break out from inside the tunnel itself, as the Russians had done; but there had been three of them, quite apart from their accomplices . . .

He tried to reassure himself. "Shouldn't be difficult to find some takers." But what he hadn't found, at least since his sweetheart had disappeared, was an idea. If he didn't have a genuine plan, no one would be willing to go with him. Except perhaps a crazy kid like Angel . . .

The boy was in the *Revier* again, nursing his umpteenth abscess. By the time he got better and Paulo had arranged for him to work in the same team, the snow—which barely melted before it started falling again, with disturbing persistence—would have covered the whole region. However, Paulo didn't have to decide whether to wait for him or not, because before the week was out, the boy's foolhardy game had proved fatal. Much good spitting into a syringe had done him: he was being sent back to Mauthausen. They hadn't spotted his subterfuge, he wasn't being sent back as a punishment, but Universale considered that there were far too many people loafing about outside and especially in the kitchens, the blocks, the laundry, the workshops . . . and the *Revier.* The company was tired of coughing up daily for all these malingerers, these useless mouths to feed, who were exempted from the rough work in the tunnel by the obliging doctor, or—for reasons of a different sort—the block chiefs. A report, backed up with statistics, had reached Mauthausen and the reply had been short and sharp: all the parasites, the sick and the old, were to be assembled and prepared for departure. Ziereis must have made it clear that he didn't want any Yugoslavian lice or crabs in his fortress, for they were to be shaved bald and given the statutory delousing session. Annoyed by the suggestion that he ran a dirty camp, Knock-Knees requisitioned the oldest and most ragged uniforms for those who were leaving. Jackets, coats, trousers, underpants, shirts and even shoes had been swapped regardless of size. He was going to send his big boss a real bunch of beggars.

It ought to have worried the repatriated men to see they counted for so little; it didn't augur well for their future. But no, they found it quite in order that their clothes should be given to the others who were to continue working in this harsh country. They had done their stint, their next set of clothes would be some kind of civilian outfit. The main thing which had contributed to their deception was that in order to meet Universale's requirement that a hundred and fifty men should be sacked, Winkler had had to call on volunteers, as the maimed and the malingering were not sufficiently numerous. The twenty-odd volunteers necessary had stepped forward. They thought they had volunteered for an easy way out, following a wild rumor that the Red Cross had set up at Mauthausen to initiate the repatriation of the sick, and they looked so pleased with themselves that the men who had had no choice in the matter assumed their fears were groundless. When the time came for their departure, every single one of them was under the impression that he was about to be demobed, and among those left behind there were some who wondered if they hadn't let the chance of a lifetime slip through their fingers as they watched the convoy move off. But it was a dreadful sight, to see this column of ragged ghosts holding each other up. The whole *Revier* had been emptied, and the injured and fever-stricken staggered and shivered in the icy drizzle. Even without being pessimistic, it was hard to believe that they were all bound for the ministrations of the Red Cross, particularly as their stingy Kommandant had refused the gasoline requisition for their transport to Trzic. These men who had killed themselves to build him his tunnel were being thrown out to struggle nine miles along a slippery road, but he was rid of them, and the whole bunch could go up in smoke for all he cared.

Paulo had been very afraid that this was exactly how the journey would end and he fought tooth and nail all day to stop Angel leaving, petitioning Fritz, Sailor and even that influential queer, Otto. It was of no avail; as one of the *Revier* regulars, Belloni was top-priority for the shipment.

"Run for it before you get to the station," Paulo urged him. "It's your only chance. You've had it at Mauthausen. If I'd known you were going on foot, I swear I would have volunteered. You don't get a chance like that twice . . ."

Angel looked at him strangely. Could this be Paulo talking? Hadn't he always jumped on him whenever he mentioned escape? In the past, Angel would have retorted with a "That's rich, coming from you," but he was no longer the urchin with the quick wit and the sharp tongue. He was listless and vacant, as if he had been drugged.

"Too late," was all he said. "When it's time to go . . . *Adieu*. See you again, I hope, even so. If you manage to get out too . . ."

It was obvious that he wouldn't try to slip down the side of the ravine. As he watched Angel hobbling through the gates on his infected leg, among the last to leave, Paulo had difficulty holding back his emotion. But it was the boy's last words which upset him most: "if you manage to get out too . . ." Surely Angel couldn't believe that he had drawn the lucky straw?

This was the question in the minds of all the prisoners amassed on the *Appelplatz* to watch the "liberated" men depart. "Maybe there was some truth in the Red Cross story after all, and we're left in this death trap . . ."

Paulo's moment of weakness was soon succeeded by a rush of anger at the others. "You fucking hypocrites, don't pretend you believe it! You know well those hundred and fifty are the ones who've lost the race!" His anger had made him lucid and he had glimpsed another end to the Loibl saga which had been forgotten: Mauthausen might reclaim them in small random groups, and he for one was not keen on games of chance. He took Joel on one side the following morning, straight after reveille.

"This time I hope it's sunk in. Biy by bit, your Front National is going to get transferred to its Mauthausen branch and soon we'll find ourselves with two SS to guard each prisoner. You can say goodbye to all your fine schemes when that happens."

"You're right, it's a big setback," the Breton conceded. "We'll discuss it tonight at the meeting—"

"Discuss what, for Christ's sake! Haven't you almost gotten out once already? You can't start messing around again, you've got to get out. In the crowd at Mauthausen you wouldn't be any fucking use to anybody. Joel, don't be obstinate, let's go together; I'm working on something—"

"Yanka?" asked Joel, with a trace of irony in his voice.

"No, that's all off now. By the way, have you heard any news of her?"

"Yes, she's back."

"You're joking!" Paulo exclaimed, unable to conceal his joy.

It was true. She had come back to her job in the civilian camp, but her partisan chiefs had ordered her to stay at her typewriter. Her liaison missions were over, so there would be no more strolling in the tunnel, no more Paulo.

"Duty before love. Be brave, darling. See you soon," was the laconic message she had asked Yanko to convey to her tall villain the night she returned.

"What the fuck's that supposed to mean?" he fumed, as he read the bit of paper for the tenth time. "Be brave . . . see you soon . . . I get it, I've got to make my own arrangements."

Egotistical Paulo was utterly uninterested in whether their separation had made her unhappy. All he knew was that he hadn't missed the billing and cooing at all; he had had other things on his mind. Nevertheless, if she would only disobey her orders and see him again, he would give her her money's worth. "Just once, that's all I ask," he grumbled. "Just so that we can get something together. Or if only she'd send me a civilian with all the clothes and gear."

"Go and tell her that," he asked Yanko. He didn't add a single affectionate word, and it might have been better if he had, for her reply was equally terse:

"Impossible. Find your own way. Yanko will guide you."

"Hell!" Paulo exploded. "She's dumped me!"

Well, at least she hadn't said piss off, so he went to look for Joel, touching up the truth somewhat:

"Okay, Joel, they're expecting us. Yanka's got me a lead. Now all we need's the idea, and we can go."

Disappointed by the gym teacher's lack of enthusiasm, he threw in an idea off the top of his head.

"I thought Dédé might help. He could requisition us for some sort of fake repair job some lunchtime. Do you think he'd agree?"

"Possibly, you'll have to ask him. But you can count me out. We agreed on it yesterday at the meeting. We're going to stay until the end. We'll fix it so that our leaders won't be picked for any future shipments back to Mauthausen. From a military point of view this area has become significant and so has our work in the tunnel. We are in the front line now. Picking up a gun again is the only thing I care about."

"And I suppose you wouldn't be picking up a gun if you made it to the partisans, you stupid fool? We could be with them in three days if you'd agree."

"You know very well that Tito's men don't need us. They haven't got room. Let's face it, you're not escaping to fight."

In front of Joel, Paulo could hardly deny it. Furiously, he cut the conversation short.

"Well, that's fine by me. I'll go alone. But take my word for it, if you stay, you'll just go on losing your fucking war."

Those commies had really brainwashed the Gaullist. He had become disciplined and stupid, and nothing would make him change his mind. Clearly, what he longed for was to find himself with a commission in the Loibl Brigade. He was an army man now, individual action counted for nothing.

But going it alone was not to Paulo's liking, either, especially not from the tunnel. It could only be done in strength, by three or four men together. And out of the men he could fully trust, already two, Angel and Joel, had dropped out of the running. That left Dédé, Pompon, and possibly the two intrepid boxers, François and Pommier, but he wasn't at all sure whether they had any idea of escape in mind. On the other hand, those who had been in Joel's escape team, the hotelier and young Tito, would be certain takers. Before he sounded them out, he had to know what Dédé was up to. It would be surprising if that smart fellow, well placed as he was, hadn't done his homework and fixed up a very ingenious plan. Nor was there any need for Paulo to beat about the bush with him.

"Dédé, I'm going to escape," he announced. And so that Dédé didn't have any time to look surprised as Angel had done the day before, he went right on.

"Yes, I've finally made up my mind, and what I'm asking is whether you want to team up with me. Tito's men are expecting me, but that's all I can offer you. We've got to get out first."

"Was it Yanka who persuaded the partisans to cooperate?" Dédé inquired, smiling faintly as Joel had done.

"Sure, but I'd better tell you the whole story. Before things started getting warm around here, she'd fixed everything to get me out herself. But since she got back, the Krauts have been watching her too closely for her to do anything more than give me a lead for when I'm out. It's better than a kick in the ass!"

Dédé was looking so unenthusiastic that Paulo thought that he had said something wrong.

"I know you don't need me to set up contact with Tito's men, but since it's done at least you won't have to bother about it. You can concentrate on the other thing, the best way of getting out. I'm sure you haven't been waiting for me to study up on the subject."

"Of course not," said Dédé. But that was all he said.

By now it was clear he was ducking the question. And yet he was the ace underground radio ham, and he of all people knew how to take risks.

"Oh, I get it," said Paulo, "you're onto something already . . . ?"

He had hit the nail on the head. The student was unable to dodge a direct question.

"Well, yes, I am, Paulo," he admitted. "I'm getting ready to make my break too. I've just got to wait for the next snowstorm to bring down the telephone lines up on the col like last winter, and it'll be *adieu* Loibl! I've been planning it for months. Why do you think I wanted the job of electrician?"

"So you don't agree with Joel then? He says we have a duty to stay."

"His war is different. My place, my vice if you like, is at the transmitter. I only feel happy when I'm tapping the keys and in this godforsaken place, the partisans are the only ones who can find me a set."

"Apart from that, though," Paulo went on, wanting, if it was still possible, to convince himself that his own decision was the right one, "you feel like I do, that only a fool would stay?"

"Certainly, things are bound to go downhill. Yesterday's unpleasant exercise scared me, too. I only hope the snow comes, it'll change all that!"

"The snow..." thought Paulo. "That's the last thing I need. I've got to get out before it starts."

"Well, good luck," he said abruptly, shaking Dédé's hand. He was anxious to go and find the hotelier, or anyone else who would be willing to join him. Indeed, now that he knew of Dédé's imminent departure there was not a minute to lose. Escape was becoming a bit too popular at Loibl. First Joel's team, then the ten in the *Schneekommando*, and now Dédé, all within the space of a few days. Furthermore, despite the numbers of men intent on escape, his exit would have to be made without a single one of the three friends he had made in this hellhole. They all had their excuses, particularly Angel, who had been forcibly removed, but it was sad all the same that he'd lived with these men as brothers for more than a year and now found himself out on his own looking stupid, just when friendship and absolute trust were most needed. Of course there were other sound men to be found, like the hotelier, François, Pompon. They were no strangers to him and he knew the fiber they were made of. But it was nowhere near the same thing. Escaping with friends of his own age like Dédé, Joel and Angel, even from a death trap like this, would have been rather like playing truant from the barracks one night.

Since he had made the decision to escape and knew that nothing could cause him to back out now, he could allow himself to be sentimental. After all, wasn't he on the threshold of the most important moment of his life, perhaps the last? But instead of thinking, as most people would have done at a time like this, about the joys he had known—women, money and freedom—he kept coming back to his three friends at Loibl. He was finally able to admit it to himself: of all the people he had known in his empty life, they were the only ones he had loved. Only a short while ago, everything had suggested that all four of them would share the same destiny. The months had passed, their friendship had survived the severest tests, the war was coming to an end . . . but within a matter of days the band had disintegrated, each man playing his own dangerous game with destiny. Angel by almost volunteering to face Mauthausen, Joel by staying to cause chaos in the camp, probably with bloody consequences, Dédé by bringing down his irons on the skull of the SS who would escort him on his last job. Paulo didn't know yet what he was going to do, but he certainly wouldn't be staying up in the mountains for his health.

"How could it have happened?" he wondered sadly. "I suppose we didn't talk enough."

But the die was cast, and he'd have to accept it. If any of the four should fail to make it to the reunion banquet when the torment was over, the memory of their friendship would only be more precious. Anyway, old soldiers' reunions quickly bore you stiff. Choosing not to return home arm in arm with everyone else was more in keeping with their characters. The agonizing question was who of the four would make it home. The way things were going, if they all got home, it would really be a miracle.

XXVII

Both Joel and Dédé had been so firm that Paulo knew he had no hope of making them go back on their decisions. So the day after he had been rebuffed twice over, he set out to hunt for takers and met with a pleasant surprise. By that evening he had found his man: Pompon. What a reliable fellow he was! But he had his feet planted on the ground too, and if he had unhesitatingly agreed to the plan which Paulo had desperately dreamed up during the night, it could only mean that his scheme must be a damn good one.

Yet it was very basic; they would take the same route as the three Russians and use the train, the major difference being that it did not involve bloodshed. Their exit from the tunnel would go off quietly because the SS at the control post wouldn't see the escapees, who would be at the bottom of a wagon well concealed beneath a heap of earth and rocks. The Fritzes could prod away as much as they liked with their lances, but they wouldn't find anything, except perhaps the slight resistance of a false floor a foot and a half above the real one. For that was the gem of Paulo's nocturnal inspiration. A false bottom like the ones in the suitcases he used to lug his fake tungsten around the unsafe streets of Paris.

"Brilliant idea, man! Count me in!" Pompon had exclaimed.

Naturally there were a thousand details to be sorted out. How would they fix the false bottom in place? How would they get out of the wagon once they got to the dump, which was heavily guarded? Despite these difficulties, it would have been hard to conceive of a better way out than hiding in a wagon whose sole purpose was to carry the debris extracted from the tunnel far from the prison. The rest was simply a matter of organization. The first step was to get themselves transferred to the night shift. A word in the ear of their respective block chiefs sorted that out. By the following Monday, the start of the new working week, the two conspirators had taken their places in the column of night workers. They were over the first hurdle, and they would be able to spend every night in useful discussion, right up until the big day, if Pompon didn't fall back into his old habits and start holding forth about his past, his affairs and all his other wonderful exploits. Paulo needn't have worried, Pompon was a different man and he had given up playing to the gallery. But Paulo could hardly get a word out of him.

"It can't be because he's frightened that he's clammed up," he fretted.

But Pompon's radical change of attitude dated from at least a month earlier when of his own accord he had given up his idyllic life in the timber crew. True, it had turned chilly and, more importantly, there was a big trouble outside with men getting shot again. But with a bodyguard like his Kapo friend, it was unlikely that it would be he fetched one morning to be sent across the line. So why had he gone back to the tunnel without being told to? Paulo reckoned that he must have had a very good reason, but his motive certainly couldn't have been escape because his trips to the outermost edges of the work site to fetch and chop timber had made flight a thousand times more possible for him than for anyone else.

As far as Paulo was concerned, at any rate, Pompon was his last hope. Before considering the barman, he had approached three others with his false floor plan and one after the other, the hotelier, Pommier and even François had begged off, just like that. They all had good excuses, although it was astonishing to hear the tough Pommier, who had fought like a tiger in the ring all summer, say, "No, pal, cross me off. I've taken too much shit, I'm worn out."

As for the hotelier, Paulo should have known that he would hide behind the Front National, which, he said, couldn't do without him. There was some truth in what he said, for many of the noncommunist prisoners were pressing the respected citizen to stand up to the commies and prevent them from taking over complete control of the underground organization. So once again, Paulo had admitted defeat.

On the other hand, François's refusal, which had seemed far less probable, had greatly disappointed him, although the *fünf und zwanzig* champion had put forward his own very genuine reasons.

"I'm very tempted to join you," he had declared. "On the other hand though, I'd rather not be too far from the Krauts when the end comes. I don't want to leave the others the pleasure of beating them, one at a time." And bursting out laughing, he added, "Perhaps you didn't know, but the Front has promoted me to political commissar, and that's quite a responsibility."

How could he be blamed for wanting to live out the drama to the bitter end? Arrested at eighteen, he had known no other way of life. It was at Loibl that he had reached manhood and become a star at the same time. Asking him to escape was tantamount to depriving a bright pupil of his end-of-term prize. Paulo had not persisted and anyway, now that Pompon was coming along, he told himself he was glad he hadn't enlisted François or the hotelier. At some time or other, the Front National was bound to have wanted to shove their oar into a project which wasn't of their own making.

Paulo had made a point of not telling Pompon about the series of refusals, including Joel's and Dédé's, to prevent his having second thoughts. But suddenly, his doubts began to nag again.

"Even with Pompon, you never know. He's not one to panic at the last minute and he seems healthy enough, but he might go down with a fever or an attack of dysentery . . . or maybe a rock'll land on his head. Perhaps I'd be better off with two partners instead of one. As far as the plan goes, it's quite possible; the hiding place will easily take three. Shit, whose idea is it anyway! I'd be stupid not to give someone else a chance, any guy with some guts. A third guy'd be useful, there's a heap of things to get ready; and it'd be quicker with three of us. I'd better talk to Pompon about it. I can't pull any dirty tricks on him, he doesn't deserve it. If I tackle him indirectly, I ought to be able to bring him around to it without treading on his toes . . ." And he called Pompon over. "Listen, old friend, I've just been thinking. I'll bet you've never done any mountain climbing either, have you? How are we going to find our way once we're out?"

For an instant Pompon seemed surprised, but he knew Paulo well enough to realize that he hadn't asked such an idiot question for nothing, and he also knew that when you wanted to find out what Paulo was getting at, the best thing to do was to needle him.

"What do you think you're playing at?" he demanded tersely. "Are you trying to test me? When Pompon says yes, he means yes. My word's my bond. Nothing could stop me from running now, even if I had to go on my own . . ."

"Don't talk shit," Paulo interrupted. "You've got it all wrong. It's just an idea . . . it suddenly struck me, that's all. And since I'm not one to hide anything from you, I might just as well put you in the breeze right now. I was thinking that in the sleeping car of ours we could easily fit three, and it'd be stupid not to offer the third place to a fellow who knows the area or at least knows something about mountains . . . After all, we don't want to find ourselves ending up back at Nordfeld like a couple of idiots! What do you say?"

Pompon was delighted to have provoked him into coming clean, and he deliberately remained silent so that Paulo was obliged to tell him everything.

"Anyone who's lived in the mountains would fit the bill," Paulo went on. "I was thinking of Lepreux. That kid's like a chamois. Only three months ago he was still in the maquis. It ought to be child's play for him finding us a good way through these fucking Karawankens. D'you have anything against him?"

"You damn fool!" Pompon burst out. "It's been painful watching you going around in circles for the last quarter of an hour. Why couldn't you have told me all this the first day?"

"No, really, I only just thought of Lepreux. If you'd rather not have him, that's fine by me, I'll take it all back . . ."

"For Christ's sake, Paulo, stop telling me what I think. I never said I didn't want Lepreux. Quite the opposite. I like him a lot. If he wants to come, we'll squeeze him in."

Unluckily, Paulo's proposition didn't interest the highlander in the slightest, the reason being that he was on the verge of going out alone, like Dédé. The trick of the false floor had appealed to him. He had congratulated Paulo and, confidence for confidence, had revealed his own escape plan. It was very simple: he was just going to slop down the side of the ravine one evening as the night shift was trudging up to the tunnel. He was only waiting for the days to become shorter so that he could jump with all the odds on his side. "I'd be very surprised if the dogs beat me to the peak," he had asserted confidently.

Obviously a sprinter like him would have changed everything. "Damn," thought Paulo. But what he was far more concerned about was the mania for escape which had suddenly taken hold of Loibl. Now Lepreux had to be added to the list, and perhaps there were others who were keeping quiet.

"Up shit creek without a paddle is where we're going to be if we don't speed things up," he told Pompon, just as disappointed to hear that Lepreux wasn't game.

"Fucking egoist," Paulo was grumbling to himself when Pompon, who must have been thinking the same thing, suddenly exclaimed, "But I know another mountain type!"

"Who?" Paulo almost yelled, his morale quickening.

"The guy from Béarn in Block Five, for God's sake. You've probably never noticed him, seeing as how he hasn't opened his mouth more than three times since he's been here. It's all part of the Béarnais character. All the same I do know why the Krauts shipped him off to Mauthausen. It was dead simple, he had this job of getting American and British airmen who'd been shot down over to the other side of the Pyrenees! He was sent them in groups of ten from all over France, and even Belgium. Quite apart from the hundreds of Jews he helped over the border for nothing, just for the fun of it. He'd take your Lepreux to the cleaners. I tell you, he's a real pro!"

"And I tell you, Pompon, you're a real champion!" Paulo exulted. "The press gang will be knocking on his door tonight! Let's hope he hasn't got a plan up his sleeve too. By the way, what's the name of this rare bird?"

"Hegoburu. Hego or Buru to his friends. If I remember right, he comes from a mountain village south of Pau, about the same altitude as here."

Their luck had changed. The Béarnais had jumped for joy when Pompon had put him in the picture, and the color had returned to his cheeks at the thought of soon being free to scramble over rocks again. To be out in the mountains had been his dearest wish ever since he arrived.

"I feel as if I know the area as well as if I were born here. You two won't get lost with me. Oh, and thanks very much for thinking of me." As he was already in the night shift, briefing could begin.

"First, we've got to elect a leader," Pompon began. "Hego and I are unanimous, we nominate you."

"That's very kind of you," Paulo thanked them, although he didn't really see how it could be otherwise. "Good. Now listen, here's our program: First, we all get ourselves transferred to the gang loading the wagons. Second, we get together everything we need to make the false floor; it's got to be really high-quality stuff. We don't want to suffocate with a ton of gravel on top of us! So the first thing we've got to find is some solid, thick planks, about six feet long—we'll need four or five of them. We'll have to try several wagons before we decide on the exact length, because—I don't know whether you've thought about this, but we won't know until the last minute which one we'll be taking off in—"

"I'll take care of the planks if you like," Pompon interrupted. "My friend Bayer is in charge of the carpentry shop now, and I'll tell him I want to make a bed for myself in the tunnel. That'll tickle him to death, and he'll saw them for me himself, to the right length."

"Good, one thing less to worry about," Paulo approved. "So that's the floor taken care of, but we've got to work out how we're going to support it. I've thought about that too, we can put cement blocks at the four corners of the wagon. It'll reduce our leg room a bit, but they're about a foot and a half high. That should give us plenty of room to move and breathe, and there are hundreds of blocks stacked along the length of the tunnel under the vault, so we can wait for the big night, then put four of them on one side. But we won't bring the planks out until an hour before zero hour, which'll be about four in the morning. I've got a cache for all this stuff dead near here, in a hiding place I've used once already!"

Pompon and Hegoburu would have liked to ask Paulo why four in the morning and not midnight, which would give them six hours' start if the alarm were only raised at the end of the shift, but they were so impressed by their "leader's" self-assurance that they both kept their mouths shut.

Paulo must have read their minds because he came back to the subject of zero hour himself.

"Four o'clock is just before the diesel's last trip. If we left at midnight, it would come to exactly the same thing from the point of view of a head start, because the driver'll have to raise the alarm as soon as he sees our wagons haven't been loaded. So, given the choice, we'd do better to decamp as near dawn as possible. In any case, two hours of night climbing is going to be no joke."

The construction of the false floor was settled, the hour had been chosen. Things were looking good. But the real problem, which would make or break the whole operation, remained. How would they get out of the wagon between the southern entrance and the dump? Who would unhook the heavy door? And come to think of it, who would bolt the door once they were aboard? On this point Paulo had been deliberately vague with Pompon when he'd first suggested the plan. He had winked meaningfully, as if it were all very obvious, as if to say: "So where do you think Yanka fits in?" Pompon hadn't dared to venture any more questions, but by now, when everything else seemed to be settled, he was impatient for Paulo to explain the second half of his plan.

Being tactful went by the board now that they were gambling with their lives.

Alas, Paulo had no more idea than anyone else, except that there were only two possible accomplices who could let the fugitives out of their hiding place when the train, uncoupled from the diesel for the SS inspection, started off again toward the dump, this time pulled by the small *decauville*. The diesel driver was a prisoner and therefore forbidden to go beyond the guard post, so the only men who could unhook the door before the end of the line were the *decauville* driver himself and his assistant, who coupled and uncoupled the wagons, *der Bremser* in German. Obviously they only needed one, but which one—the driver or the *Bremser*?

In order to pick the right man, they had no choice but to rely on Yanko, Dédé's "good civilian." The snag was that he worked on the day shift and so they would have to get the message through via Dédé. It could take several days for the reply to come back, and would it be what they wanted to hear? These unanswered questions forced Paulo to remain vague.

Pompon saw that Paulo was at a loss and, decent fellow that he was, he came to his rescue.

"Getting ourselves bolted in is no problem. We've got plenty of friends on the loading gang. It's no great risk for them—"

"Oh, I'm not worried about that," interrupted Paulo, relieved that he hadn't gone any further. "But we can't just ask anybody. The only discreet and efficient men are the commies. We'll ask them to do it. No more questions, either of you?"

"Yes." The Béarnais spoke up. He wasn't going to be fobbed off. "Where exactly do we get out of the hiding place? As far as I'm concerned they can tip me over the side with the rest of the load, I'm used to slithering down slopes. But you two—"

This time Paulo could hedge no longer.

"It won't come to that, Hego. You've got to trust me, for Christ's sake! I give you my word that there'll be someone to unhook the door before we get to the dump. I know the three civilians at the end of the line, they're real bastards. If something goes wrong and we get to the dump without being let out, there's no way we're going to be tipped over the side,

Hego. We hang on to the wagon for all we're worth, and we beat those bastards' heads in with iron bars, so they don't start yelling *'Zwei Mann weg!'* You haven't forgotten that, have you?"

That was the sort of language Pompon liked to hear, and he backed him up. "Let me handle the weapons too. I promise you, they won't be rubber clubs."

Thanks to this diversion, Paulo was able to adjourn the briefing without letting them see the full extent of his worries. He would settle the question of who would unbolt the door as quickly as possible by using his contact with Dédé and Yanko. The rest was chickenfeed.

Sure enough, before the week was out the three friends found themselves together again, in the loading gang. Two days later, three iron bars a foot and a half long and four pine planks sawed to perfection by Kapo Bayer himself had been quietly hidden away in the ham hole.

When explaining his plan to Dédé Ménard, Paulo hadn't simply asked him to contact Yanko. If Yanko agreed to find them the man to unhook the door, they might as well ask him, while they were at it, if he would help them right to the end. In short, what Paulo was after was for his partisan friends to be lying in wait for them by the dump at the critical moment. An armed escort, once they were out of the camp, would be as good as a life insurance policy.

Dédé caught on quickly. By the end of their conversation, Paulo was certain that his message would be swiftly passed on. It never occurred to him that the Breton must have been thinking of the local maquis to help his own escape too, and that what they were asking of him might very well put his own plan in jeopardy. But Dédé was too generous to let that influence him, and to prove it, he immediately gave Paulo a vital piece of information: they could discount the Italian *decauville* driver. He was a shit of the first order who had been marked out a long time ago by Tito's men, a genuine Fascist who had volunteered to work at Loibl. The Krauts were so sure he was ideologically sound that they had even let him keep his revolver. Not only was he to be regarded with the utmost suspicion, but they shouldn't even think of trying to put him out of action.

As for their last hope, the *Bremser,* Dédé knew only that he was Croatian. Clearly, they were going to be kept in suspense right to the end, for there were good and bad Croats, and some were not only bad, they were bloodthirsty as well.

"Looking at it logically, he ought not to care for the Krauts," Ménard had remarked. "Otherwise he wouldn't be spending all his nights on a menial job like coupling and uncoupling wagons. He'd be in the mountains with a big saber, like his guerrilla brothers, lopping off the heads of the Titoist *Banditen*!"

Everything depended on this man, and Paulo resolved to observe him very closely from now on.

"Believe me, Dédé, he'll be in my sights every time he shows up! I want to hear him tell me himself that he'll slip the hooks! I don't want any misunderstandings at this stage in the game."

While they waited for the reply, it was crucial for them not to give way to their growing excitement. Staying calm and giving nothing away, not even by the expression on their faces, was also part of the plan. And the most natural way of achieving this aim was for them to load the wagons conscientiously so that no stray Kapo, seeing their work fall off, should get the idea of transferring all three to the vault where they would be given pneumatic drills and put to work up on the scaffolding. But they couldn't shovel the loads too efficiently either, for they risked being labeled greasers by the fifty-odd others in the gang, half of whom were Polacks who had the reputation of being stool pigeons. In short they had to work normally, but then it still gave them enough time to talk, particularly when the full hoppers were shunted off to the dump. There were a hundred and one details which they hadn't tackled. The question of food, for example. What provisions should they take? Given the present shortages in the camp, they wouldn't find it easy to build up any reserves. Paulo quickly resolved the point.

"We mustn't weigh ourselves down. If the partisans are at the rendezvous, they'll have food for us; and if they're not there, we'll have to run like hell, in which case we're better off traveling light. Grub would just be extra weight."

"And what about shoes?" Hegoburu suddenly announced.

"What do you mean, shoes?" Paulo sighed.

"I mean we'll be going ass over teakettle every ten yards

with these fucking clogs. I'd rather go barefoot. God, if only I had my espadrilles!"

"You fucking Basque!" Paulo exclaimed. "Why don't you go and steal Bullseye's slippers then!"

When they had all stopped laughing, he went on.

"Seriously, though, Hego's got a good point. We've got to get ourselves into shape for climbing these fucking mountains. And since there's no way we can buy leather boots—which, by the way, would make us stick out a mile—there's only one thing to do: we'll have to go into training. Lungs and legs are the most important, but since the tunnel's no help to our breathing, we'll have to exercise in the camp. There's a good stretch between the *Appelplatz* and the *Waschraum* and it's steep. So starting from tomorrow, we'll all do two or three laps every day."

By now Paulo was quite confident. Every evening the three of them worked together, steadily filling three wagons per trip, looking completely relaxed. The few Kapos who glanced in their directon turned away again without even bawling at them. So during the night, at least, there was no danger of any hitch occurring to foul up the machinery they had so patiently put together.

Down in the camp, however, the atmosphere was more tense. Jealousy and quarreling had again come to the fore since the resumption of the shootings and famine, and the end of the war, which everyone had seemed so sure of in August, faded from their minds a little more each day. Of course, it hadn't taken the bastard block chiefs long to do a complete *volte-face*. It now seemed far less definite to them that their friends the *Haeftlinge* were going to win the war. And the Frenchmen, their ex-associates, had rapidly turned back into *Scheisskubel* whom they could carry on beating with impunity. At any moment something could happen to knock the team's plans for six.

Paulo had no need to warn his two partners in crime to be on their guard and to hold their tongues if any detainee or Kapo started picking on them. Like him, they had instinctively become model prisoners: first up, first to bed, first at muster, anticipating extra duties, and avoiding extra rations at soup time, a likely place for scuffles and, therefore, beatings and getting noticed. Those who already knew Hego found his behavior quite normal. Rarely had a man been so inconspicuous at Loibl. He had no close friends and had never gone looking for a single favor or soft job. Since his arrival, he had spent all his free time gazing at the chain of mountains ringing the valley, even though he considered them far inferior to his beloved Pyrenees.

On the other hand, Pompon's new line of conduct had aroused great curiosity. He was renowned for his joviality at Loibl and he was on good terms with everybody. It wasn't long before his blockmates noticed the change in him.

"It's finally caught up with him too," they grumbled, but they were sympathetic and wisecracks like "Hey, baker, run out of yeast?" stopped almost as soon as they had started. It was the same for Paulo. Apart from the odd man who had come back from the north and who had seen him go downhill there, all the others wondered immediately what he'd been up to for the last fortnight. He'd been skulking in the shadows, bedding down as soon as he emerged from the *Washchraum*, talking in monosyllables to discourage idle chatter and avoiding potentially awkward questions. But all the convicts at Loibl knew what it meant to be under a cloud, and since the latest developments, including those of the war outside Loibl, were not exactly cheering, Paulo's low spirits were understood and excused as readily as Pompon's. If the trio stuck to the prescribed behavior, and kept out of everyone's way, they would have no more reason to fear being shopped during the day than during the night among their anonymous fellow workers.

Unfortunately, for some time now, things had been happening down below which were impossible to ignore. First of all, there had been the Bullseye affair. While he had been away visiting the north with Sladek and Eddy one day, some of the starving men in his block had strangled and carved up his tomcat. When he returned late that evening the chief hadn't smelled the aroma of stew, but as a veteran of the camps, he immediately knew what had befallen his puss. He had seen red, and despite his animal lover's tears, not a single man in his block had escaped the hose of the one-eyed brute. Luckily neither Pompon nor Hego belonged to Bullseye's block, but the thought that either or both of them could get themselves damaged made Paulo tremble with fear.

Another unpleasant episode might have gone badly if he

hadn't mastered his feelings and stayed absolutely cold. He could hardly have been subjected to a more foul test, comparable in its repugnance to the afternoon the previous summer when he had been spat upon by all the *Posten* on the work site.

He had been sound asleep one afternoon, doubtless dreaming of freedom, when the doyen, for no apparent reason, dragged him from his bed for what he termed an urgent chore. He was to empty out and clean the latrines along with three other night workers who had also been collared at random. Not the block latrines, but those of the camp—all eight of them. There was a ton of liquid excrement to be pumped out, then carried sixty-five feet in oil drums to a specially dug ditch. Ferrying this disgusting cargo had taken them five whole hours and when they had finished, Paulo's striped uniform had been dyed all one color, the color of his fellows' shit, at least three months' worth of shit. Ten times he had been on the point of running away to hide under his bed, anywhere—and each time he had managed to control himself. But the time he really did almost commit a fatal blunder was when one of his stupid companions on the shit duty had lobbed a heavy stone into the ditch as a joke, just when Paulo was bending down to fill his bucket. It splashed straight in his face, in his open mouth, in his eyes, everywhere... The farmer had literally plastered him with shit. Luckily, as it turned out, Otto chose just the moment when Paulo was about to christen the cackling peasant with his overflowing bucket to arrive on the scene. If the doyen had seen Paulo retaliate, the consequences might have been severe; he might have found himself strolling across the line. He had stopped just in time and Otto, who was doubled up with laughter, had given him permission to go and rinse himself under the *Waschraum* tap—from head to toe and fully dressed...

That evening, as he loaded his wagon in the tunnel, he was still boiling with anger. There had better not be too many more jokes like that before his departure. And departure seemed more imperative than ever since a young Yugoslav named Josip, who had the same Christian name as his idol Tito, had landed in the *Revier*. Less than ten days had separated his arrest in a Slovenian maquis cell from his arrival at Loibl together with about twenty of his compatriots—further proof that Herr Kommandant was eager to accelerate the work in the galleries. They couldn't have looked at these new boys very carefully at Mauthausen, because when Ramsauer's successor gave Josip his medical he had discovered a machine-gun bullet lodged in his dick!

"It hurts when I piss," the ex-partisan had complained.

"I'm not all that surprised," the doctor had answered, probing the abnormal swelling under his foreskin. But he too found it hard to believe, and it was only after he had made a small incision and seen the bullet that he was convinced.

Before he operated, the good doctor had insisted on showing this unique case to all who doubted its truth. Kapos and block chiefs had immediately appeared on the doorstep of the *Revier.*

"What a thing!" Sailor gaped, and nobody knew whether the old lecher meant the bullet or the tool.

The Yugoslavs didn't need this piece of publicity to boost their standing in the camp, but underlying the affair of the shot-up prick was a note of warning. Loibl was moving into the firing line.

Paulo had also been to the *Revier* to have a look and that evening he felt he had to make this clear to the other two. "After what I heard today, none of us can have any more doubts. I talked to Josip, and he says there's going to be big trouble in this sector, and sooner than any of us thought. If our Croat doesn't show himself before the end of the week, we'll do like Hego said, and jump at the dump itself with our iron bars." His accomplices said nothing. He went on.

"Watch out, you two, we're going soft. With or without the Croat, we'll be free or dead within a week. Perhaps you hadn't thought of that."

As if to justify his words, Dédé Ménard accosted him that very evening before they left for the tunnel.

"Okay, we're all set. The Croat says yes. It was Yanka who set it all up. I've got a lot to tell you, but it would take too long, so I'll see you tomorrow before muster behind the kitchens. I've got to show you something—"

"Show me now then, there's plenty of time."

"I can't, you've got to see it in daylight. But I repeat, it's all on. You're to contact the Croat tonight. He's on nights all this week and he'll arrange to hang around in the tunnel for a minute or two between trips. Incidentally, he's called Stefan and he speaks a bit of French. He's a stocky little fellow of about twenty-five, and he always wears a black oilskin cap. Don't get the wrong man, will you!"

Later, when the three friends were alone by one of the wagons, Paulo called for silence.

"Listen to me, both of you. This is it. The Croat has given his okay. He'll unlock the door, and we won't even need to take our iron bars with us! I'm going to see him a bit later on to hear him confirm it in person, and to fix on a day."

"Who told you? Ménard?"

"If you like. All he did was take the message; Yanka was the one who did everything. She gave him a note which he translated for me. I told you she was more than a pretty face."

A couple of hours later, as the men on the neighboring crews began to arrive with their loaded wagons, Paulo slipped quietly from his post and went down to the end of the line, where he joined the men pushing the last wagon forward. He reckoned it was about nine o'clock, and already the diesel's small yellow headlights were winking in the distance. In a moment, the driver would get down to check that all the wagons were properly hitched, and then he would reverse toward the exit.

Paulo had flattened himself against the side of the tunnel pretending to pee, and he waited for the train to move a few feet before catching up with it. In three strides he found himself hanging from the ledge of the last wagon. He had moved so quickly that nobody, perhaps not even Pompon or Hego, had seen it happen, and in any case the only real danger was the driver. For the SS to have given such an easy job to a *Haeftling*, they must have had a hell of a lot of faith in him.

"That guy could make a real nuisance of himself on the big day," thought Paulo as the train gathered speed. And he shrank down farther so that the squealing sneak wouldn't catch sight of his *Mütze* in the mirror.

It was barely two thousand feet to the southern entrance, and Paulo's second problem was not to jump down too near the SS guard post, nor too far away for Stefan to hear his whisper when he came to check the coupling on the last wagon.

In this kind of undertaking, you had to know how to calculate things down to the last inch, you had to have split-second timing. Paulo loved a challenge like this and if the stakes hadn't been so high, he would certainly have allowed himself a smile of satisfaction as the train came to a halt. He had jumped off thirty feet before it stopped and he had barely had time to flatten himself against the wall again before Stefan's silhouette appeared with a lamp in his hand. He was not flashing it on the wagons but along the sides of the tunnel, looking for Paulo.

"Looks encouraging for later on," Paulo thought, simultaneously registering another interesting item. To give the *decauville* enough room to back up to the wagons, the diesel driver had to take his engine into a small siding, which meant that the Croat was in sole charge of the train. He, and he alone, would roll the wagons forward one by one for the Krauts to begin prodding the loads with their steel lances. That, too, was reassuring. Stefan looked like a cool customer and if the Germans should linger a little too long over the crucial wagon, he might be just the sort to roll the next wagon forward.

Relieved by these observations, Paulo stepped forward into the beam of Stefan's flashlight.

"Stefan, it's me . . ."

"*Du bist Paulo?*"

"*Ja, nicht sprechen französisch?*"

"*Si . . . ein bissel.*"

The Croat's French was rather elementary. Paulo was struggling to find German words to continue the conversation when Stefan went over to a wagon and slipped a hook with a sharp tap on his wheel lever. Paulo didn't need to go on, Stefan had understood everything. But setting the time and the day wouldn't be quite so straightforward, and Paulo had to dredge up his best jailbird German.

"*Wann raus? Welcher Tag?*"

"*Freitag, es ist ein gut Tag.*"

"Friday?"

"*Ja, ja,* Friday."

It was Monday today, four days to go! Paulo wished he could explain that Friday was a long time off, but he'd be there all night if he started going through the days of the week in his halting frog-Kraut.

"Okay for Friday," he replied. "But . . . *wieviel Uhr?*"

"*Vier Uhr, gut Uhr.*"

Four o'clock was perfect. Paulo repeated to make sure that there was no misunderstanding.

"Friday, *Freitag*. Four o'clock, *vier Uhr*, okay?"

The Croat lowered his eyelids to show he had understood and, raising a clenched fist, he spat out, "*Smort fascism, sloboda narodu!*"

Death to the Fascists, liberty for the people!—the password of the Yugoslavs at Loibl and Mauthausen, the rallying cry of the maquis throughout Yugoslavia in revolt. Stefan couldn't have done better if he had given his word of honor. He'd knock the hooks out, even under fire.

As Paulo groped for Stefan's hand in the dark to take his leave, the other grabbed him by the sleeve to indicate that he had something else to say.

"Wagon . . . *welcher Wagen*?" he murmured, pointing to the string of at least fifteen wagons stretching down to the tunnel entrance.

"Hell!" exclaimed Paulo, smacking his forehead. "I forgot the most important thing! How am I going to let him know which one we'll be in? He wouldn't thank me if he had to open all fifteen!" Picking up a soft stone, he drew a swastika on the wooden side of one of the wagons.

"Understand? *Verstehen?*"

"*Nicht gut*," replied Stefan, rubbing out the cross with the back of his sleeve. Taking the chalky stone from Paulo's hand he sketched three letters, S Ü D. South, like the camp . . .

Not a bad idea, it was more discreet and looked less suspicious. Anyway, Stefan seemed so pleased with his ruse that Paulo was only too happy to agree now that everything had been arranged so quickly.

"*Gut*, Stefan, Friday, in the wagon marked *Süd*! *Auf Wiedersehen!*"

And he vanished into the darkness of the tunnel. He was in such a hurry to tell the other two that he automatically broke into a run.

Back at the loading place they were taking a break as they waited for the empty wagons to come back. Pompon and Hego, impatient to know how it had gone, walked forward to meet him.

"Well?" they asked in unison, as soon as they recognized his tall silhouette.

"It's all sewn up! Stefan's good news. He knows exactly

what to do with the hooks. It can't go wrong. When I said 'this is it' just now, it might have been a bit premature, but now it's for real, this really is it."

"When do we go?" asked the practical Béarnais.

"Friday, four days from now. We also fixed the time: *vier Uhr*! It'll seem like a long wait, but I couldn't press him too far. Anyway Stefan chose Friday because he doesn't work on Saturdays. If the Fritzes get a sniff that we had outside help, they'll start poking around the civilian camp and if he's not working, Stefan will see them coming. He'll have plenty of time to pack his bags."

Pompon and Hego had a thousand other questions they wanted to ask, but in the distance, they could already hear the diesel chuffing toward them.

"Let's make ourselves scarce," Paulo said quickly. "Can't let that squealing driver see us hanging around together. We can talk while we walk back. You know it all now anyway."

There was only one more thing for the tall prisoner to deal with, and that was to get Dédé to show him whatever it was he had been talking about, the mysterious thing which could only be seen in broad daylight. What on earth could it be? Surely not a map of the area! Although you could expect anything from an amazing fellow like him. He had a whole pile of maps in his glory hole, and some of them were very hot property indeed, with their little pinholes marking the Germans' line of retreat on all fronts.

The following afternoon, when Paulo appeared at the rendezvous behind the kitchen block, Ménard was already there, gazing at the mountains.

"It's me," said Paulo, breaking the spell.

"Ah, hello there. How did you get along with Stefan?"

"Terrific! We leave on Friday, everything's fixed to the *n*th—thanks to you, Dédé. We all want to thank you."

"Don't thank me, it was Yanka who organized it all."

"Really? Well, what do you know! I thought she'd gone off me. But listen, you said you had something to show me. I'll bet I know what it is—a map of the area?"

"Not quite, but you'll still have to use your eyes. Come and stand behind me and look exactly at where I'm pointing."

"I'm there."

"Good. Can you see that minute light-colored line about a hundred and fifty feet to the left of the outer civilian blocks?

It's a shepherds' trail. Follow it up toward the summit where it starts winding. You still with me?"

"Uh-huh."

"Well, that's the way you've got to go, don't take any other path. On the other side, it goes down to the bed of a stream and cuts through a forest on the lower slopes of the next mountain. As soon as you get to the first trees you'll see a shepherd's hut. That's where the partisans will be. Yanka's passed them the word."

"But she doesn't know which day we're going—"

"She will, don't worry. In any case, you won't reach the forest before daybreak. With the clothes you've got on, it'd be pretty surprising if the partisans mistook you for an SS patrol and started shooting at you!"

"I'm sure they wouldn't, but we haven't gotten to Tito yet. The first thing is, how are we going to find your shepherds' trail in the dark? Looking at it in broad daylight, it looks dead simple, but—"

"Agreed, and if I were you, I wouldn't tackle it down the hillside. I'd head straight down the ravine to the road. The path cuts straight across it. The lights in the civilian camp will give you your bearings. The few yards of road will be nasty, but it's the only way you can be sure of not getting lost. And despite the detour, you'll make up a minute or two that way."

Paulo was taking it all in, the ravine, the stretch of road to be crossed, the civilian camp, and most of all the steep track which he was imprinting on his memory foot by foot as Dédé gave him his instructions.

"Have you taken a good hard look?" Dédé asked.

"A bit too hard; I'm feeling dizzy! I'll get my Pyrenean onto it tomorrow. He's an expert at climbing, night climbing too. He probably doesn't know what dizziness means."

"Good idea. Do you want me to come back and explain it to him?"

"No need. We'll stay in our corner, good as gold, and rehearse it all. In case I don't see you before I go, tell me to piss off now, Dédé!"

"I won't say piss off, but I will say good luck—and see you soon!"

It had completely slipped Paulo's mind that Dédé was also pushing off. The way he had put himself out to help an escape which, if successful, was bound to jeopardize or at the very least complicate his own, was truly noble. If Paulo was a free man again in three days, his first thoughts would have to be for Dédé Ménard, the purest friend he had ever had. How could he say so? Perhaps he could somehow, in a roundabout way.

"Listen, Dédé, don't you think I ought to say goodbye to Joel? If both of us manage to join Tito's men, he'll be furious—being able to fight again is all he ever thinks about! Maybe I didn't twist his arm enough—"

"He must have forgotten, or else he didn't believe you. Either way, don't start on it again. But that doesn't stop you from shaking hands with him on Friday. Just make it a little warmer than usual, that's all."

"Dédé, your advice is solid gold. I'll do what you say. As you're on the day shift, maybe I won't see you again, so . . . *A bientôt!*"

"Goodbye, Paulo, and piss off anyway!"

An hour later, Hego and Pompon had been fully briefed: the dive into the ravine, the run across the road, the track, the hut, meeting with the partisans . . . The jigsaw was complete, they had only left to check that the wooden planks were still in their hole and to carry the four cement blocks to their departure point. The first half of the schedule, inside the tunnel, was settled; after that they were in Hego's hands. Ten minutes behind the kitchens had been enough for him to etch the geography of the track on his mind. He was convinced he would be able to lead them straight to it, even in the pitch dark of Friday night's new moon.

When he returned from the observation post, he had declared happily, "Piece of cake. I could take you there with my eyes shut. All you've got to do is follow the guide."

From the beginning, the idea of going around in circles, once they were out, had been a source of worry to Paulo. But seeing that Hego, who had been smuggling in the mountains ever since he could walk, was so confident, he had absolutely no need to fret. The hardest thing now would be the waiting. Some of the time could be spent rehearsing their plan, but they couldn't do it all night long. Yet none of them dared to talk about what they would do when they were out for fear of bringing bad luck on themselves. In any case, the job they still had to do reminded them constantly of escape. Which one of the wagons rolling backward and forward would be *the* wagon on Friday? They simply couldn't concentrate on anything else.

They kept coming back on the absurd question. Why had they endured almost a year and a half of unparalleled brutality before making up their minds? For Paulo the whole thing had been a gradual process, but what about Hego and Pompon?

"They're only running because I decided to, they're not really prepared," thought Paulo.

It was true they were unlikely companions; there were other, more natural associates at Loibl, like the men who had known each other before being picked up: the Party members obviously, or Gaullists from the same network, crooks arrested together for a job that had gone wrong, the peasants from neighboring villages, and nationals of a small country like the Norwegians or Luxembourgeois, who were lost in the mass of Frenchmen and Poles, and stuck to each other like glue, especially the latter. They numbered about ten and there was not one useless one among them. They were all first-class Resistance members and they taught quite a few men a lesson in unity and patriotism, although they came from a country whose population was smaller than that of a Paris *arrondissement* and which the Reich had simply invaded and annexed. They had proved themselves in their clandestine work, and they all spoke German, sufficient reasons for them to set up a clever escape plan and make it succeed.

And what about the Campana brothers, weren't they a natural team? And there were several other family groups besides. There were no less than three brothers in the north, two of whom, Pierre and Jules, were twins, and had made a fleeting appearance in the ring. They were so alike that the Kapos would beat them both at the same time for fear of making a mistake. Only their friends from Grenoble, their hometown, could tell one from the other, because one joked all day long and the other one never smiled. Prison had done nothing to change them. But the south had a better example: a father and son who were finally reconciled after months of estrangement over some extra soup which hadn't been shared!

Joining forces to put your life on the line was understandable where there were such close ties. But what the hell was Paulo doing with Pompon and Hego? Barely a month before he hadn't known Hego existed. And even with the former, he had never been as attached to him as he had to Dédé, Joel or poor little Belloni. The nearer they got to zero hour, the more this unnatural union between a baker, a shepherd and a crook bothered him. In fact, it was the only thing which was wrong about this undertaking whose every other difficulty he had managed to resolve. Death might be waiting for all three of them at the other end of the venture, so the least each could do was tell the others why he had agreed to share this enormous risk. Paulo had never mentioned the matter to Pompon. Now was the time to do it. Afterward, if they failed, it would be too late, and if they succeeded, they would all invent grandiose reasons, except perhaps for the Béarnais, who wasn't the type to boast.

"Listen, Hego," Paulo tackled him, "when we asked you to come with us, you said yes immediately, and now that we know you better, it's not at all surprising. What you didn't tell us, on the other hand, was what made you do it. You must know you could catch it. You could get gunned down or hanged if you're taken. This isn't a POW camp, you know. You have to have a good reason to accept that kind of risk. Is it because you want to fight, or because you want to get back to France?"

Hego was amazed. "I don't understand you, Paulo. You're not going to go over all that old ground again—"

"No, of course not. It's just for something to talk about. Reciting what each of us has to do on Friday every five minutes is getting on my nerves."

"Oh good, I prefer that," the other replied, trying to find something intelligent to say. "Well, it's quite simple really. An hour after I got here I made up my mind to go. It's so like my Pyrenees that even just looking at it, I know exactly where the escape routes are. Your trail's not the only one, you know—"

"Glad to hear it. But why are you still here then?"

"Because I never had the right chance. I was always in the line of fire. Even I need ten minutes' head start to shake off the Krauts and their dogs. But I can tell you now, Paulo, if you hadn't approached me, I might have been long gone. I had it all worked out. One evening as we were coming up to the tunnel, I'd have jumped and, so long, boys! Why do you think I asked to work nights?"

"Okay, fair enough, I believe you, but you haven't answered my question. Are you going to fight or go back to France?"

"Go home? I'm not that stupid! With my scalp, the only chance of getting through would be to stay up in the mountains. The ridges all join up, you could do it, but you'd need a year. By the time I got back to Pau, the war would have been over for ages."

"So you're going to fight?"

"What else? Don't you think there are a few scores to settle with this crowd? Back in the Pyrenees I was happy to let the Resistance get on with it, I was a pacifist. Now I want a gun in my hand, like everybody else—"

"At least he's said it. Now I've got a better idea where we stand."

"You approve?"

"Of course I do!"

"Me too," added Pompon.

Since Pompon had opened his mouth, Paulo would see to it that he came clean too. "From what I can see, you're beating it to have a bash at the Krauts as well, Pompon. The difference being that Hego's from the resistants, so he's motivated differently."

"And I'm not from the Resistance, I s'pose!" Pompon exploded. "Next thing you'll be saying is I'm from the bloody Gestapo!"

"Don't get so shirty, we know you stayed clean. Some of the men around here used to use your bar. But you've got to admit that you never really went into action in the same way as Joel and his friends."

"So what if I didn't? Doesn't stop me from thinking like Hego. There're a few bills to be paid, and not just our own. What about all the friends we leave behind? When they hear we're with Tito's men, they'll take it for granted we're out there to avenge them. You'll soon see, if we get out of here, that Pompon doesn't forget the debts he's owed, and he doesn't take prisoners!"

"How about that!" Paulo smiled, and the ex-baker thought he detected a hint of incredulity.

"So you don't believe me?" he bristled. "Well, you're in for a few surprises. Besides, between ourselves, didn't you think it was funny I said yes when you offered me a place? I didn't even ask you if your plan meant braining a few Krauts like the Russians did. I don't care if you don't believe me, but I'd have said yes all the same."

It was the truth pure and simple, and Paulo felt uncomfortable. These two fellows he had picked almost at random were turning out to be a lot tougher than he was, and far more aware of the reasons behind their escape. Even before they were out they were plainly showing their hands. They were breaking out so that they could fight! Perhaps it was because neither of them, before they'd been arrested, had really had the opportunity. But that was irrelevant; today it was their strongest desire. Paulo had wanted a straight answer and he had gotten it, even if it hadn't been the one he had expected.

How stupid of him to have wanted to cross-examine his friends on their beliefs so late in the day, when there was no going back. The operation was in motion, and outside all three of them were expected. Pompon and the Béarnais might have been angry, they might have told him to get stuffed, and left him to find his own way to the trail, in the dark. Paulo should have thought before he opened his mouth.

Neither was it any comfort to have discovered that they were so determined, so "motivated," as he had said to Pompon, intending to embarrass him. Indeed, his own desire for revenge lessened as the hour approached. Of course, if Tito's men gave him a gun in a few days, he would use it. He wasn't an old woman, after all. But if they said to him, "Go back home," he wouldn't make a fuss about that either. Revenge wasn't the only exciting prospect about being outside. What about eating his fill, not having to work anymore, staying in bed, sitting by the fire, smoking, boozing, maybe even getting in a bit of bayonet practice? These things were not to be sneezed at; they justified escaping ten times over.

Earlier on he had been evasive, and his friends might have thought he was even more anxious than they were to get his hands on a gun. All the better for the unity of the trio—his childish reason for questioning them—but deep down, he knew that the reasons which had pushed him into this business had not altered. There were four main ones: Yanka to some extent, or rather, his mad desire for a woman, any woman; the rapidly approaching winter, which he might end up spending in the north, like the year before; the renewed shootings which could degenerate into a bloodbath as the front drew nearer; and finally, the risk of being sent back to Mauthausen at a moment's notice, like Belloni. Pompon's reasons paled into insignificance next to his list. In a word, he was getting out first and foremost to save his own skin!

If he succeeded there would be quite a few raised eyebrows in the camp. Those who knew him to be neither hotheaded nor suicidal, but a particularly cautious and shrewd fellow, would soon be wondering whether he hadn't chosen the lesser of two evils. When they found out that the partisans were aiding and abetting them, they would be even more distressed. Some would be tempted to say, "The Yugoslav maquis are going to get a damn funny idea of the Resistance at Loibl when they meet *that* bunch of good-for-nothing jokers!" Or even, "There are better men in the camp. They should have been stopped . . ."

It had been inevitable from the start that if Paulo and his companions succeeded in their escape, they wouldn't make many friends by it. Especially as it was bound to provoke retaliation in the form of a general horsewhipping as the Russians' escape had done. Everyone, without exception, would be in for the dose of *fünf und zwanzig* which so outraged Pompon. The barman-baker couldn't have thought of that . . . Nor that Herr Kommandant might well decide to execute a few innocent prisoners in reprisal, or as a means of discouraging future escapees. Paulo had always known this might happen, but he had never let it deter him, which proved it was only his own skin he wanted to save.

On the morning of the big day, before they left the tunnel, he held a last briefing.

"Listen, you two, we've got to stay in our bunks all day, because there'll be no rest for us tonight. Too bad about saying goodbye to your friends, you can send them a postcard . . ."

Rather hypocritically he himself had gotten up shortly before the day shift returned to the camp to be sure not to miss Joel. He couldn't leave without saying goodbye to this man who had been like a brother to him, even if he had to lie and keep quiet about the escape.

"You looking for me?" asked the Breton, seeing Paulo scanning the column.

"Yes, I was. With this timetable we hardly ever come

across each other. I wanted to know how you were doing. You don't look bad, I'd say. You've still got some of last summer's muscle on you."

"You too, Paulo. I'd even say that you've gotten fatter. You wouldn't by any chance have come up with another of your rackets, would you?"

"Not really. I've got a bread subscription with a civilian, but it doesn't go far."

It was not in his interests to prolong their chat unduly, in case he jogged the gym teacher's memory. Since the day Joel had refused to go along with him, they had hardly spoken to each other. "Morning, Paulo," "Night, Joel," was as far as it went. Any minute Joel might say something like "How's your project, any news?" But he didn't, not a word about it. He had clearly forgotten, or as Dédé thought, he hadn't believed Paulo. What a shock he'd get tomorrow when he heard about the escape! Paulo felt slightly ashamed, but he stuck it out, and the Breton didn't seem to notice that as he left Paulo had clasped his hand longer than usual.

It was time for muster. In five minutes, they would leave for the tunnel, and the long night would begin.

As they drew level with the track they would be following in a few hours, Paulo glanced at Hego two rows behind him. The Béarnais had his eyes glued to their path to freedom, as if about to make a dash for it. No need to worry on that score, he wouldn't miss it when the time came.

A little farther on Paulo turned around again to see the camp disappearing below. But just as he had not allowed himself to think: "Adieu, Loibl, this is the last you'll see of me," as he walked across the *Appelplatz*, past the blocks and the watchtowers, superstition prevented any similar thoughts now. If they failed, the disappointment would be too great. And more importantly, from now on he mustn't let his mind wander for a single second.

"Well, Pompon, what luck did you have with the commies?" he asked as soon as they were out of range of any eavesdroppers.

"It's all fixed, there'll be a man there to shut us in."

"Who?"

"They didn't tell me, but don't worry, our Party member will be there on time and he knews what he's got to do."

"I'd still feel happier if we could have seen him beforehand," Paulo persisted.

"Don't worry, I tell you, there won't be any snags."

The baker seemed so sure of himself that Paulo soon gave up worrying and concentrated all his attention on another task: the removal of the planks and the cement blocks. By the ten o'clock break, everything, including Pompon's three homemade clubs, had been assembled next to the lines and camouflaged by a few shovelfuls of earth.

When this little job was done, Paulo said, "On the next trip I'll go and take a look at the entrance to see what sort of SS are on duty this evening, see if we've got greasers or slackers to deal with. I'd also like to know exactly how many of them stick their steel poles into each wagon. With a bit of luck, if they take it in turns, there'll only be one to poke about in ours."

At midnight, as he had done five days previously to meet the Croat for the first time, Paulo grabbed the last wagon as the train moved off for its third trip. Sixty feet before it stopped, he jumped and, hugging close to the wall of the tunnel, he began his observation.

"Fuck a priest!" he breathed. "The bastards have had fucking antiaircraft lights brought in!"

So brightly lit was the train that from where he was standing he could easily make out the hooks on the wagons. If one of them had been half shut, he would have seen it from a good hundred feet away, and those same hooks were right under the Krauts' noses.

"How could I have missed that the other night!" he groaned. Hardly surprising. The other night he had been so afraid of missing the Croat that he had forgotten everything else. Now that he thought about it, Stefan had saved them from really landing in it by refusing to identify the hopper with a swastika. In this glare, the Fritzes would have pounced on it. They would have smelled an enormous rat when it occurred to them that not a single one of their *Scheisskubel* enemies in the tunnel had thought to rub it out. SÜD was definitely much less suspicious.

The bad news of this brilliant daylight was fortunately not the only item Paulo could report to the others. There was good news too: only one Fritz prodding each wagon. If it were the same weedy fellow later on as the one he was watching now, they ran little risk of getting their asses jabbed.

He had seen enough. He doubled back to the points where he knew the diesel would have to slow down and concealed himself behind an outcrop of rock. No point walking the fifteen hundred feet back, he'd take the train. His legs would be needed for another purpose tonight. Ten minutes later, after the obviously blind driver had dropped him off, he was back at HQ. Pompon greeted him thankfully.

"We were beginning to get worried."

"And so you should, in a sense. It's as bright as day down there. If the hooks aren't on properly, we're screwed. We've absolutely got to talk to this commie of yours, he can't be working very far from here. You really don't know who it is?"

"I swear it! But I promise you, he'll be there. The communists don't mess around—"

"Hang on," Paulo interrupted. "Maybe they're pissed off that we're clearing out without asking them first."

"No way. They know they can't do anything to stop us. They know me and they were impressed with you in the tunnel this summer. So they've given the green light and the rest obey their orders without question. As a Resistance member our man sees it as all in a day's work. In fact, up to muster this evening, he didn't even know what the job was. He was only told what he had to do on the way up to the tunnel and only then was he given my name. These guys aren't half organized!"

"I suppose you're right," said Paulo, privately hoping that the comrade in question would disobey the rules and do a small recon before the appointed time.

At about one o'clock, he thought he saw their man. But he had made a slight mistake. The man he had glimpsed in the distance, pausing at each wagon to chat with the shovelers, was wearing a docker's cap!

"Shit, it's a Kapo!" Paulo almost shouted.

It was indeed a Kapo, and a Kraut to boot.

"Where the hell did he spring from?" he had time to say before the Kapo was upon them.

"No idea, never seen him," Pompon and Hego replied in turn.

It wasn't surprising, the night owl had come from the north in defiance of all the rules. If, in the darkness he caught a fist in the face, he wouldn't even be able to report it.

Paulo was toying with the idea when something about

the man caught his attention: the busybody was not wearing the badge of the common criminal. On the German's jacket was a red triangle, which meant he was a political prisoner, and that was unheard of at Loibl.

Perhaps this Kapo was not a bad type. If they handled him right, they ought to be able to suggest that he go back home. As a complete stranger, he couldn't have been very well versed in tunnel procedure.

"*Gute Nacht, Kapo*," said Pompon, who knew how to deal with the breed.

"*Gute Nacht, Kamerad. Franzosen?*"

"*Ja, chef*," said Paulo, willing himself to smile amiably despite his terrible urge to take a shovel to this bloody nuisance who seemed set on chatting to them, only three hours before they took the greatest risk of their lives.

He really had come just for a chat! The unsuspecting fool didn't know how lucky he was. Three hours later, it wouldn't have been one clout with a shovel that he risked, but three!

"The only way to get rid of him quick," muttered Paulo, "is to pretend we don't understand a word of German. He'll soon get fed up." Just then, the Fritz asked, "*Sprechen Sie Deutsch, Mensch*?"

"*Nein! Nein! Nein!*" the three *Menschen* answered emphatically.

If he had been an ordinary Kapo, that reply would have cost them a certain beating. No danger with this simpleton, he hadn't even brought his hose with him on his visit. He truly seemed to have his head in the clouds.

"If he finds he can't chat to us he might just decide to flop down next to his French *Freunde*," thought Paulo. "That'd be just marvelous!"

The extraordinary Kapo didn't seem to want to sleep, but he certainly intended to stay. He went and sat down—right on top of the small heap of earth covering the planks and cement blocks! Appalled, Paulo could just see the Béarnais, convinced that their game was up and that that was all the Kapo had come for, seizing his shovel.

Such a move would have been hasty, to put it mildly: they still had three hours to go before resorting to that extreme course of action.

Interposing himself between Hego and the Kraut, Paulo

said quickly, "All we've got to do is keep on working and take no notice of him. He'll get tired long before we do." As if to prove him right, the lout belched an "*Arbeit Mensch*" which was supposed to be an order, and every five minutes he repeated it in a voice which progressively thickened. It was looking serious; they would have to do something before he fell asleep.

Again it was Paulo who found the solution. The hopper was almost full and if they were unnecessarily enthusiastic with the last shovelfuls, they could accidentally on purpose shower the dozy Kapo with dirt and pebbles. It did the trick; having twice dusted off his cap the spoilsport got up and with a resentful "*Scheisse Franzosen*," he pushed off back toward Nordfeld.

"Christ!" the fugitives all breathed, and they were still shaking ten minutes later. However, they had to admit that the episode had helped fill the time. It was nearly two o'clock, but then the diesel had barely left on its penultimate trip when Paulo saw a shadow approaching.

"The interfering cunt's coming back!" he exclaimed.

It wasn't the Kapo this time, but like him, this man was stopping at every wagon. He was obviously looking for someone.

"Does Pompon work around here?" he yelled from a good way off, in French.

"That's my contact," said Pompon. "To hell with keeping quiet, I've got to talk to him."

He went up to the man. "Thanks for agreeing to do this, comrade, and it's good of you to come early. We're a bit anxious. How are you going to knock the hooks in? You can't do it by hand, they're all rusty; you'll have to smack them hard, with something solid."

"I'll have a sledgehammer," the man replied, laughing. "Will that do?"

Paulo was amazed at the guy the commies had delegated to this risky job. He was a decent sort whom Paulo knew very well, since they both belonged to Block 3, but never had he heard him talk politics or Resistance. Clearly Paulo must have been going around Loibl with his eyes shut.

It was to be hoped that tomorrow, once he was free and his own problems were over, he would open his eyes. Then he might understand at last that many of the men whose wretched existence he had shared for so long had not been sent here by chance, including those he had thought were nonentities, like this Front National agent.

Before he went back, the envoy (who was called Rouanet) explained how he would operate:

"I'll be nearby from half past three onward, but I won't turn up with my hammer until the hoppers have all been coupled, because of the driver. Don't wait for me before you climb in. It's going to have to be timed to the second."

"By the way," said Paulo, "the right wagon'll have SÜD chalked on it, with an umlaut on the U."

"Okay, fine. See you in a while." And Rouanet disappeared as anonymously as he had come.

Dead on two o'clock, the planks and the cement blocks surfaced, and half an hour later, the false floor was in place. One after the other, the three friends slid in, taking care not to be seen by the neighboring teams. The test proved conclusive: they could carry on and load the wagon.

"But this is stupid, we don't need to shovel at this speed!" said Paulo after a moment. "We've got to take the false floor into account. We've already caught up with the other teams."

It was fair comment, and by slowing down they would save their strength for later.

By a quarter to four, the stones and earth were heaped up as high as in the other wagons, and it would have taken Sherlock Holmes to guess which of them was rigged. They put down their shovels. The time had come for more serious matters.

XXVIII

Suddenly, as if by a prearranged signal, the diesel driver gave a blast on his horn. He wasn't usually the type to play trains, and the three friends exchanged a look.

"It's nothing," said Paulo. "The imbecile's only tooting his last trip of the week. Come on, let's go. Get rid of your coats; we'll fit in more easily and we'll be able to climb better without them later on. We won't feel the cold."

No sooner said than done. He stuffed his coat under the pile of sand which had served to hide the planks and ran back to the wagon. Raising the flap door, he bent right down, stuck his head through and, by wriggling along on his stomach, managed to squeeze his whole body up against the door on the other side. He was quite unable to turn over—the box was less than sixteen inches high—but there was at least some room to move, and they could still talk.

"Hurry it up," he called. "Has Rouanet—"

He hadn't finished his sentence before Hego was inside, saying reassuringly, "He's there, with his sledgehammer. Everything's okay!"

"We forgot the iron bars," said Pompon. And before he slid inside to join them, he passed one to within easy reach of each man.

They were all in, or just about. Despite frantic efforts to cram his bulk into the space, the baker's right thigh and shoulder were sticking out by a good two inches, making it impossible for Rouanet to push the flap home.

"Squeeze up, for God's sake!" Rouanet yelled, giving Pompon's thigh a mighty shove with his foot. One, two inches . . . the flap finally swung to, and with a blow from his sledgehammer, the hooks came flush with their catches. Now he just had to ram them home.

"One!" said Rouanet, bringing his sledgehammer down. He was about to do the same to the second when the train jerked forward. Someone less conscientious than he might have said to himself, "That'll be all right!" or just prayed for the best. But when Rouanet did a job, he did it properly. He started running and without letting go of the flap, he was preparing to jump onto the rear ledge to drive the second hook in, when there was a violent jolt.

One of the front wagons had come off the rails! It was too good an opportunity to miss and Rouanet took it, slamming the second hook into place. Then with his sledgehammer over his shoulder, he calmly went off to see what was going on. Luckily, only two of the wagon's wheels had been derailed and only a little of the load had been shed. If everyone lent a hand, the damage could be repaired within five minutes. A crowd was gathering around.

"Okay, you men, let's get this lot moving again," Rouanet

commanded, dropping his sledgehammer to grab the wagon's chassis with both hands.

He was a damn good guy. And had Paulo and his friends seen his veins standing out from his efforts to get the wagon back on the rails as quickly as possible, they would have thanked him even more. But they would have been even more surprised to learn that the derailment hadn't been an accident. Some bastard had thrown a molding joist onto the track just as the train, which had already traveled a hundred feet, was approaching a slight incline, and this bastard was a Frenchman. He had spotted the fugitives' game and, frightened stiff at the thought of the inevitable reprisals, rather than inform on them he had come up with this feeble idea to foil their escape.

If that coward who worked on the leading wagon had been able to see something of them from where he was, then the entire loading Kommando, all fifty of them, had seen too. The remarkable thing was that not a single man, apart from the Frenchman with the joist, had tried to remonstrate with them or stand in their way, not even the Poles, who were all too often accused of treachery. Everybody knew what to expect if the escape succeeded, and yet, if they were afraid at this moment, it wasn't for themselves but for their fleeing comrades.

It was undoubtedly to tell the trio that they were on their side that suddenly all the men began to whistle a tune which was amplified by the perfect acoustics of the vault:

Si tu vas à Paris
Dis bonjour aux amis

It was an old song which had been all the rage in France when Paulo had been at the height of his career, but tonight it affected him as strongly as if it were a personal message, like those the BBC transmitted to the Resistance to inform them of the arrival or departure of agents: "Okay, runway clear for takeoff, over." Tonight the agents were Paulo and his companions in their cramped wagon (for lack of an airplane) and their protective network the fifty convicts in the loading Kommando.

Paulo's spine was tingling, but it was too late now to thank all these brave men whom he had thought untrustworthy.

And anyway this was no time to let himself be carried away by sentiment, or by fear.

Unfortunately, this was what seemed to have happened to Pompon and Hego, who had stayed mute, as if paralyzed, since the train stopped. They hadn't even reacted when Rouanet drove in the second hook.

Taking a terrible risk, Paulo decided he must rouse them.

"Hey, you two, wake up," he hissed. "We'll be off again soon."

"But why the hell have we stopped?" Pompon muttered.

"Must be some kind of fuck-up ahead by the points. Can't be serious, I can't hear any Kraut voices."

Paulo had no idea whether it was serious or not, but it was his role as leader to reassure them; if he had had to say what he really felt, it would have been more like: "We're fucked, caught like rats in a trap. Our coffin can only be opened on the outside!" But he had dragged them into this ambush and it would have been too cruel to throw that at them. Of course, he had never tried to hide it from them that between the closing and the opening of the flap, there would be some nasty moments, but he hadn't figured on it lasting longer than five minutes at the most.

Breaking down when they had gone only a hundred feet was so stupid; it was screwing up all his calculations and needlessly fueling their fears. The wait seemed endless.

God must have been on their side for the train suddenly moved off as a whistler struck up again "Si tu vas à Paris" . . . It was the green light! The halt had been a false alarm. There were no Krauts in the tunnel. They hadn't been given away. Thanks, friends.

"I was right, we didn't need to panic," Paulo ventured softly. Pompon and Hego didn't have to know what he had just been through.

All his confidence had returned. It was just as well because he was going to need it in the next five minutes to tackle the real moment of truth. In his thoughts and dreams he had lived the moment a hundred times over, holding his breath as he imagined the Krauts trampling on the heap of stones above his head before sinking their steel lances into it. He knew everything depended on this moment and he had experimented several times with a sharpened mining bar similar to those used by the SS at the guard post. He had been pleasantly surprised to find that nine times out of ten, the mining bar struck a stone halfway down. It would take a strong fellow to touch the planks, which were only sixteen inches above the real bottom. Assuming the SS on duty that evening were not javelin champions, there was room for hope.

Provided none of the three moved, got a tickle in his throat, got a cramp or had to piss—and no insomniac hound stuck his inquisitive snout into the wagons. They could only trust to luck. By invoking the goddess of fortune nonstop from inside the wagon taking them to the most important rendezvous of their lives, they had, unconsciously, rid themselves of their fear. By the time the train slowed down and then stopped, Paulo could say, without spreading panic, "Hold on to your iron bar, Pompon, because if Stefan's made a mess of it, it'll be up to you to get out first and take care of the civilian who's supposed to slip the hooks. We won't be able to back you up straight away, so you'll have to move fast."

Paulo must have recovered all his sangfroid to anticipate trouble getting out when the *Kontrolle*, on which everything depended, had not even begun on the first wagon.

The chuffing of the *decauville* brought him back to reality. A moment later, there was a clanking and a jolt which meant that the diesel was in the siding and the leading wagon was being coupled to the good little *decauville* which would steam toward freedom. There was a second jolt almost immediately, followed by the grating sound of the steel lances sinking into the loads at the front end of the train.

"No more talking," ordered Paulo. "And when it's our turn, don't move. Bite your lips, hold your breath, play dead. Got it?"

Pompon and Hego got it so well that they didn't answer, and the silence was only broken by the agonizing scraping of the lances. From time to time, a *Scheisse Arbeit* was heard from an SS furious at having to dirty his beautiful boots in the filthy mess still moist from the humidity in the tunnel.

After three or four *Scheisse Arbeit*, the same Kraut yelled, "*Folgend!*" to the Fascist loco driver. The first wagon had just been cleared and he was to bring the next one forward. Paulo was counting up the *Folgend*—seven, six, five—and the prods which were averaging about half a dozen per wagon. The waiting was becoming unbearable. *Folgend! Folgend!* Three, two to go . . .

"Look out, it's us," Paulo warned them in a whisper. The three stiffened like corpses, heads glued to the floor. Ten seconds later, their wagon was in the glare of the floodlights.

It was damn lucky with these blinding lights that the wooden sides of the hopper which they had picked at random weren't splitting, like many of the others!

Already a grumbling Fritz had hauled himself up onto the wagon and at once the load shifted above their heads. Crunch! Crunch! The shit was tramping about all over the pile heedless of the earth and stones which spilled from the pyramid so carefully heaped up by the fugitives. The SS must have been a hefty fellow because, at one point, the lance touched the false floor. Luckily, he must also have been very arrogant. Convinced he had touched the real bottom, he withdrew his pole sharply to attack elsewhere, over on the left-hand side, just above Pompon. Once again, he hit the bottom, but this time the lance slid between two planks which the weight of the material had parted slightly. An inch farther on, the bar met Pompon's buttocks bang in the middle.

If the trio got out alive, the baker's story of what it felt like to have a steel rod poking him up the backside was bound to give his audience a good laugh! But at this moment, it wasn't funny at all, especially as the rasping had resumed, from the side now. This, however, didn't worry them in the slightest, because even if these thick Krauts spent all night at it, they would never detect the hiding place. Clearly their contempt for the French had not diminished, if they still thought them naive enough to try to escape by hiding under a few shovelfuls of earth! If he had had space to do it, Paulo would have patted himself on the back. It had to be admitted that his false floor was a stroke of genius.

Another few more and more halfhearted jabs, and there was silence. For the wagon marked "SÜD" the search was over.

"*Fertig, folgend!*" shouted one of the Krauts, and the wagons rolled forward to put the next one under the beam of the floodlights. The frontier between death and freedom had been crossed! Paulo groped for Hego's hand and clasped it hard.

A moment later, the fearful rasping which had haunted his dreams for the last two weeks started up in the wagon behind them, but his head and his heart were pounding with such wild hope that he scarcely heard it. It must have been the same for Pompon and the Béarnais. Thump, thump, thump . . . the thudding beat a fantastic tattoo inside their heads, blotting out even the guttural curses which still punctuated the Germans' *Kontrolle*. Had Paulo dared, he would have said, "Calm down, the Krauts will hear us," in order to ease the atmosphere. For even if the greatest danger was past, there was still plenty of opportunity to tremble before they got to the dump: the snuffling of a wakeful dog, for example, or that ass-licking Italian who had climbed down from his engine to give a hand with the inspection.

And even when the train had moved off, it wouldn't be over. The second nasty moment, guaranteed to send their blood pressure sky-high again, was still to come when the flap was opened. If the first face they saw was Stefan's, then, and only then, could they rejoice. Although it was what he longed for with every nerve in his body, Paulo was seized by doubt. The Croat's job was to check the couplings, so why hadn't he given a sign? He could have given the wagon a tap as he went by. He knew which one it was, the chalk marking stood out like a eunuch in a brothel. Had Paulo been misunderstood?

There must have been about ten wagons still to search behind them. To avoid thinking about Stefan, Paulo began counting again each time the train moved, backward this time, one less, two less, three . . . Then a longer silence, and at last *fertig* rang through the night, yelled by the full complement of guards. It was the signal for the wop driver to steam off with his train and all it contained.

Oof! In perfect unison the three fugitives heaved a huge sigh of relief. There had been no dogs around, and the train was rolling again. They could unclench their teeth, let out their breath, move their numbed arms and legs, and above all talk, in spite of the racket made by the *decauville* going full steam ahead.

"We got the greased wheels, guys!" Paulo shouted.

He had always had a liking for the expression, but here it was particularly apt, and if his friends could have read the determination on his face in the dark, they would have understood that Stefan or no Stefan at the rendezvous, nothing would stop him now. But he wasn't on his own; his pals had better not let their euphoria go to their heads. Just to make sure, he said to Pompon, "You've still got hold of your bar, haven't you? We're nearly there. You know what you've got to do—"

"Don't you worry."

His tone of voice made it plain Paulo had no need to worry on his score. No one was going to stop him getting through, either.

As for the Béarnais, he hadn't said a word, but the idea that in a few moments' time he would be racing down the mountainside must have been tormenting him, for they could feel him fidgeting and grumbling like a bear in a cage. He too would not easily be stopped.

As the train reduced speed, none of them could think of anything except overpowering the collaborators manning the dump, but the luck which had followed them from the beginning stepped in once again to help them over the last hurdle.

"The flap's moving! Someone's trying to open it!" Pompon yelled.

The train was still rolling, so it could only be Stefan. "We're saved!" Paulo blurted out. "It's my Croat, we're saved!"

There could be no doubt that it was him, if only because they could hear him swearing in Yugoslav at the imbecile who had driven the hooks home so hard: *"Yeboni! Yeboni!"* Poor Rouanet! If he had known that his bravery was going to get him cursed as a fucker by one of his party comrades, he might have thought twice about hammering so hard. But Stefan was no weakling either, and after seven or eight blows with his wheel lever, the first hook gave, and all at once fresh air rushed into the hiding place through the half-open flap.

The other hook, which the good Rouanet had knocked into the place first, was much looser and it slipped out at the first attempt. The double bottom was a coffin no longer, the way was clear, they had only to jump! Without a second's delay, because the driver was applying the brakes.

"We get out together so we don't lose each other," said Paulo. "Pompon, wait for us."

"Just say the word, I'm ready."

He was bursting with impatience and half his body was already hanging out of the wagon.

Stefan too was anxious for them to hurry things up. "*Schnell, schnell,*" he was shouting. What an excellent fellow! Not only had he kept his word, but instead of going off now that his mission was accomplished, he stayed crouched on top of the wagon to see whether the Frenchmen had any further need of him. If he, too, was getting impatient, it must mean they weren't far from the end of the line.

"What can you see down there?" Paulo cried to Pompon. "Is it steep?"

He couldn't see anything, of course, because there was no moon and it must have been almost dead on four. In a few minutes the pitch darkness would be to their advantage, but for the moment, it was a fucking nuisance. Another consideration which had escaped Paulo's notice! But there was no time for tears, they would just have to jump quick, or they'd find themselves grappling with the Yugos at the dump. Stefan couldn't understand what the matter was. Remembering his French, he called angrily, "Jump, *Franzosen*, jump!"

"Okay, let's go," ordered Paulo, bracing himself against the flap on his side to shove Hego out. Hanging on to Pompon's jacket, Hego tumbled out with him into the void, and Paulo followed them less than a second later.

Their luck was holding. They had jumped blind, and had landed at exactly the right spot! Here, at the end of the bend, the ballast was wider than elsewhere. So instead of rolling straight into the ravine, the three found themselves sprawling six feet from the track, and completely unscathed for the train couldn't have been going at more than ten miles an hour as they jumped. In fact the wheels were screeching continuously on the rails and the train was about to come to a complete stop; the last wagon was less than a hundred feet behind them.

As Paulo jumped, he had distinctly heard the ringing "*Sloboda narodu!*" with which Stefan sent him on his way. *Sloboda*, freedom . . . it was still going around in his head as he started down the slope to the road hard on the heels of Hego and Pompon. The worst was over, but freedom, as the Croat rightly understood it, would only be theirs if Yanka's friends were at the rendezvous at the shepherd's hut . . . on the other side of the mountain.

For the moment the descent to the road was going all right. Hego, who was as much at home in the dark as a wildcat, led the way by slithering down on his backside. He had already found the next way through by the time Paulo and Pompon caught up with him. Unfortunately, the shortest route to the road forced them to cut across the bottom of the dump itself, which meant that as soon as the civilians above began to empty the wagons, the rubbish would land right on top of them. They'd have to slide down fast if they wanted to avoid it. But as they slid, the ground tore at their jackets, their trousers and their skin. The group had barely got halfway down when there was a terrible rumble, and the avalanche began.

"Get down on your stomachs," yelled Hego, knowing better than anyone else the damage that could be done by a stone bouncing down a ravine.

It was lucky he had warned them because even lying facedown, they all got their fair share of earth and stones.

"Come on, up, let's go," he said when the bombardment had stopped, and they slid on down.

The next wagonload might have done even more damage, for among the debris were long planks of wood, which mowed down all the bushes in their way. They were the planks from the false bottom! As their wagon was right in the middle of the train, it could only have been Stefan who had tipped it without asking for the go-ahead of the three Yugos on duty. What style the man had! It made them even more eager to join up with his partisan comrades, and before the third wagon had been tipped they had reached the road.

There was no time to hang around, but they couldn't all three cross the road at once. A car might suddenly come around the bend or, since it was Friday night, a group of civilians who'd been out drinking. There was the work site floodlight to watch out for too, as well as those on the camp watchtowers—which all added up to them taking a well-earned breather after their mad slide down the ravine.

"The heat's off now," said Paulo. "They didn't notice a thing up at the dump. Two minutes break and then we go."

"Right."

Together with the inspection of the wagon, getting past the road was the most dangerous moment of the escape. All three knew it and they were as quiet as they had been in the hiding place earlier. It was a pity. They should have been shouting for joy to be on the loose on this road which had been the scene of so much suffering and bloodshed, this road which each one of them had had to march up and down hundreds of times flanked by killers whose guns were always loaded against them.

Hegoburu had not been boasting, he really knew his way about mountains, with all their perils, including the prime danger for a man in his line of work—echoes. He had immediately pointed out that their worst mistake would be to rush out onto the road as Pompon and Paulo were about to do. Their wooden-soled clogs would sound like tap shoes on the tarmac; they would wake up the valley as surely as the SS in the guard post with their rifle shots when they discovered that three men had escaped.

"Stop!" hissed Hego. "You'll get us spotted!"

Paulo had realized at once what he meant and was already taking off his shoes when the Béarnais stopped him.

"Don't bother. Just follow me."

He dropped down into a sort of natural gutter which ran between the road and the mountainside. It was damp but full of leaves swept into it by the autumn winds, and to the ears of the sentries in the watchtowers the faint rustling made by the fugitives' feet would probably sound like an early-morning breeze.

Hego must have had the eyes of a lynx, the way he was belting along this treacherous ditch. The others were hard put to keep up with him, and every thirty feet he was forced to stop and wait for them. As soon as they caught up, he would set off again looking for the path, and when he discovered it between two trees, he carried on up to make a swift reconnaissance. Running back down again as quickly, he was just in time to catch Paulo and Pompon who had passed the path without seeing it.

"This way, you two," he said. "I've found it. From here on, it'll be a piece of cake."

A piece of cake! For him maybe, but Paulo was already out of breath. Even so, if he had to climb the path on his hands and knees, he was determined to keep going, for this path to freedom—the only one, according to Dédé Ménard—was no longer a distant thread, they were standing on it!

"From now on, no more stopping," Hego had ordered. But despite the seriousness of the moment, he couldn't conceal his joy at the prospect of the climb ahead, which he had done in his dreams so many times over the past year.

For him, it was quite straightforward; he had been released into his own world, the mountains; he was already free. Automatically he took the lead and this time, amazingly, the others kept up.

They reached the first ridge at about five, but beyond it there was another one, as there always is in the mountains, and that one was too much. In the early light of dawn, it looked like a wall.

"Let's take five," said Paulo, disheartened. It was a wise move because to tackle the monster before daylight would have meant broken necks for all of them. The path itself seemed to have given up too. It branched off in all directions into narrow furrows in the rock to where the Béarnais was standing, looking far from happy. Bounding from rock to rock like a mountain goat, he had scouted right and left to see if they could skirt the obstacle. It was impossible. This part of the Karawankens was like the Great Fucking Wall of China!

"It's our only way," he said. "The left leads to the dump and the right leads back down to the camp. We've got to go over the top."

There was no alternative. And all three of them managed it, but at a terrible price! They struggled upward, crawling on all fours and giving each other leg-ups. Then, against all expectations, the Pyrenean cracked. The small man had asked too much of himself, running on ahead as their scout, doubling back to find the others and setting off again, ever since they had left the road. He had traveled twice the distance, as he used to at home in the days when he guided Jews and airmen through the mountains. The poor fellow had thought that just breathing mountain air would suddenly bring back all his strength! But he was forgetting that in the meantime there had been Mauthausen and Loibl, starvation, forced labor twelve hours a day. At his age, it was too much to expect and he had collapsed only sixty or seventy feet from the top of the ridge. Paulo was close behind and almost trod on him.

"Any bones broken?" he asked, thinking he had fallen.

"No, Paulo, I'm all right. I just felt faint, a dose of altitude sickness, that's all. Go on without me, I'll catch up with you as soon as I feel better."

With one accord, Paulo and Pompon each grasped him

by the shoulder and managed to drag him up to the ridge, despite his protests. "Leave me, both of you, go on ahead, I'll manage."

"Shut up," retorted Paulo, indignant that the Béarnais had even suggested it. Even if he'd broken both legs, they wouldn't have left him behind, and he didn't need to ask Pompon to know that he felt the same way. They weren't in much better shape than Hegoburu but they had better reserves of strength. For the last two months, both of them had gotten by pretty well as far as food was concerned, and it was that, those few extra pounds, which kept them going. Still, they too collapsed when they got Hego over the ridge and into shelter.

A pleasant surprise lay before them: the rock had given way to a meadow moist with dew, which sloped gently down to the edge of a forest. Then it climbed again, but under cover of the trees. If Ménard's information was correct, it was under this cover they would find the partisans' hut. They were almost there. Carefully, Paulo turned away and went off to look for some higher ground from where he would be able to see the whole of this plateau and the forest which would finally witness the end of their afflictions. The highest ridge on the peak was what he was looking for, and he began his survey at once, taking good note of any landmarks which would help him, in a little while, to lead his team straight to that gap in the trees which was invisible from lower down. That must be where they would find the path to the hut, it couldn't be anywhere else. It was vital that he make no mistakes, and to be sure of not forgetting a single detail, Paulo would have liked to give the signal to depart there and then, but, fascinated by the beauty of the scenery, he couldn't bring himself to leave his perch. How could he have lived less than half a mile from this haven of peace for a year and a half without suspecting for one minute that it existed? In peacetime, the meadow must be alive with cows and sheep at this time of year; with birds too, of which not a feather had been seen at Loibl, as if the sparrows had spread word to avoid the valley of death. What a contrast between the two sides of the mountain! The one spread out at his feet cried life and liberty, but the other...

The day had dawned clear with no trace of morning mist, and he could see what Loibl looked like from above. In one sweeping glance, he took it all in—the dump, the tunnel mouth, the road, and the camp itself, inoffensive and absurd at this distance. It didn't seem possible that five hundred men who were tough, both physically and morally, could have let themselves be starved, tortured and everything else, for so long, without ever having tried anything. Those shabby blocks and the wooden watchtowers, those frail-looking poles supporting barbed wire which wasn't even electrified: all of it could have been trampled in their path, had all five hundred attempted a mass breakout.

The partisans must frequently have come to stand on this lookout point to watch what was going on below, and like Paulo they must have told themselves that if they sprayed the watchtowers and the SS quarters with machine-gun fire, a rebellion would have every chance of success, and yet they had never lifted a finger. No doubt it was in order not to burden themselves with extra mouths to feed, as Dédé Ménard had claimed. When they saw three of Loibl's five hundred sheep turning up in a short while, maybe they wouldn't be all that pleased, even if Yanka had prepared them for the surprise.

"We'll know where we stand soon enough," Paulo thought to himself.

Their wisest course would have been to run hell for leather across the meadow separating the two worlds, but his fascination was stronger than his desire to flee from hell, and he couldn't tear his eyes from the camp.

Besides, down below he could see signs of life. Like ants, the tiny striped figures were swarming onto the *Appelplatz*, which meant that within a few minutes, the day shift would be on its way. At six o'clock sharp, for things always happened on time at Loibl, and the work force clocked on and off punctually. In other words, up in the tunnel they must also have been assembling and the subaltern in charge of the night crews would shortly be counting his *Stücken*. Once, twice, five times over . . . until he was prepared to admit that he was missing three.

Paulo would have given anything to hear what his friends would say when the shots signaling the escape rang out. In the square formation, which looked more perfect than ever seen from above, the news would flash around like lightning: "It's Paulo! The tall guy!" Only Dédé Ménard would not be surprised, and since he knew the path, he wouldn't be able to help glancing in the right direction. What a joy it would be to give him a wave!

Pompon's anxious voice broke into Paulo's thoughts.

"Hey, Paulo, what the hell are you up to? We thought you'd gone off without us—"

"How's Hego?" asked Paulo, clambering down from his observation post.

"He's all right, he's recovered."

Indeed, the Béarnais was coming toward them, apparently over his momentary exhaustion. Taking great lungfuls of air, he was even doing limbering-up exercises. Nothing was stopping them now from going on.

"Come on, let's make a move," said Paulo. "We've got to be in the forest by six. Follow me, I know the way."

He set out down the meadow on the double. The view of the camp he had savored lent him wings, but it also set him thinking hard. How had he been so ignorant as to let himself stay caught for so long? Now that he was out, he realized that giving these dull-witted SS the slip wasn't so difficult. So why had he repeatedly thrown out poor Angel Belloni's appeals, and refused even to study the matter?

He was angry at himself, too, for not having pressed Dédé or Joel hard enough, since Angel was out of it, to come with him. He was leaving them in the hands of maniacs who would undoubtedly take it out on them first, as his best friends. Sailor, knowing the friendship which bound them together, would make straight for them with his hose.

Poor Joel, poor Dédé! Forcing the pace, Paulo swore he would avenge them and tear them from the clutches of their executioners. His last glimpse of the camp had just supplied him with the true justification for his escape. Up on the ridge, he had felt sick with shame to see the formation of men who would go on being humiliated, beaten, raped and killed. He, who only a few days ago had been willing to mock Pompon when the latter spoke about taking up arms as soon as he was free, now desired more than anything in the world that he be given a gun too. Suddenly winter, going back home, the huge feasts, and the women, meant nothing to him. Even telling the world what was happening at Loibl was less urgent. Bang, bang, from the top of his ridge at all those gray-green assassins—that was why he was pounding toward the wood with such angry urgency. The partisans wouldn't be taking on a bunch of spastics, and just three more mouths to feed!

Bang! Bang! Bang! Three distinct shots shattered the silence. The alarm!

In spite of his optimism, Paulo's heart skipped a beat. Although he had expected them, the detonations echoing interminably in the mountains were dreadfully impressive. If the Russians' escape was anything to go by, an entire army would soon be after them, every available SS and *Feldgendarme* in both south and north . . . Thank God the bastards had no planes left. On the other hand, they were well supplied with dogs and, already, barking could be heard, together with the revving of the flat-loading trucks. In less than a quarter of an hour, the col road above the tunnel would be crawling with manhunters. Knock-Knees had learned his lesson from the Russians' escape; this time he would catch the escapees by cutting them off. Instead of climbing, his lazy underlings would only have to descend. Their two hours' head start was as good as written off. Paulo had not foreseen the use of trucks, and he scowled.

"Let's get moving, you two," he said. "They'll be over there on the left in a few minutes."

Alas, there was another nasty shock in store for them when they found the path through the trees leading to the hut. It was deserted!

"Fucking partisans' day off!" exclaimed Pompon with a look of reproach which Paulo thought was meant for him.

"You're wrong to say that. They wouldn't let us down, something must have happened." As he was trying to think of excuses, it suddenly came to him. The rendezvous was for Friday, by God! And what day was it? Saturday, of course! Everything had happened very fast last night and even if Stefan had realized they were at cross purposes, as was probable, he wouldn't have had time to tip off his maquis contacts.

Besides, it was obvious that the hut had recently been visited. There were traces of a fire and even a meal. But there wasn't a single crust of bread or a bone left for them to gnaw. Tito's troops must also be badly short of food. In any case, it wouldn't have been wise to linger. The barking was getting louder and they could even hear the sound of men's voices in the distance.

They paused just long enough for Hego to get a bearing on the south, and then set off through the forest. Although badly shaken by the failure of the rendezvous, Paulo still didn't despair. Lengthening his stride so as not to be separated from the Béarnais, who had again taken the lead, he tried to reassure Pompon, who was also lagging behind.

"It's not too bad. We'll come across the partisans soon enough, they control the whole area."

"I'd love to believe you, but can you hear those dogs? They're right behind us!"

He was right, they had gained ground during the brief halt at the hut. But the dogs had left their masters standing, for they too were on foot, hampered, what's more, by their cleated boots which weren't particularly suited to this kind of chase, and by their guns and ammunition.

"Don't worry, Pompon," Paulo answered. "They're fat on soup, and they'll get fed up before we do. As long as we're still going in a straight line, and not running around in circles. Thank God for the Pyrenean."

Hego had regained his great mountaineer's form. He was holding his course as if guided by compass, thanks to the sun, which was peeping over the mountains behind Loibl to their right. So it couldn't have been far short of eight o'clock and on the *Appelplatz* the whipping must have begun, particularly for the men on the night shift, all of them guilty.

The three fugitives forced the pace harder still. Not because they were imagining the scene down below in the camp, but because the forest was rising sharply up the mountain, and the yelping of the dogs was suddenly amplified by the echoes bouncing off the slope. From all sides, in front, from right and left, as well as behind, came the baying of hounds on the scent of death, moving in for the kill. Paulo and Pompon were terror-stricken, and stopped, despite Hego's frantic cries of "Follow me! Follow me!"

The furious howling hadn't thrown the ex-smuggler off course for a second. Straight as a die he was heading south, as impervious to the barking as if he had cotton wool stuffed in his ears. His self-possession inspired the others to go on, but he had forged so far ahead that Pompon and Paulo almost had to bust themselves to catch up with him.

"Stop! You'll kill us," Paulo gasped at him as he caught up. And he forced Hego to sit down.

"We've got to take our bearings," he said after he had gotten his breath back. "The trees stop six hundred feet farther on, and we'll be out in the open again. We can't risk just belting on . . ."

But Hego was in full command of the situation.

"Leave it up to me, lads," he said. "In the mountains, there's an absolute rule if you don't want to get caught: take to the ridges and stick to them. And that's what we're going to do."

Paulo nodded, without even daring to point out that it might have been a damn sight easier to have tackled the ridge some way back by zigzagging up to it. Whereas what the Béarnais was proposing now was an ascent only ten degrees off the vertical. Luckily, there were trees to cling on to but every time they hauled themselves up a few more feet, the effort was enough to burst a blood vessel. After the extra strain of dragging the Béarnais to the summit of the first ridge, then the mad dash through the forest slithering and stumbling over the dead leaves, it was inevitable that Paulo, or Pompon, or both, would crack. Pompon was the first to let go.

"I can't go on, boys. Keep going, leave me here," he panted, clutching his chest before collapsing onto the stump of a recently blasted pine.

Jesus, now he was starting to pay the martyred hero! Paulo couldn't decide whether he was moved or furious as he tried to rally him.

"It's not up to you! I give the orders around here, and there's no way we can carry you up this fucking mountain, so we stay with you for as long as it takes—"

"No, don't, I won't be able to go on. Just clear out quick before the Krauts arrive." Pompon was on the verge of tears.

The best thing to do was to wait for for his crisis to pass, and his heart to stop pounding. In any case, a breather was imperative for all of them, after their killing climb. They rested for half an hour, and as they sat, the barking seemed to be getting fainter. The dogs must have lost the scent down by the hut, and this gave Pompon new courage.

"I feel better, let's have another shot at it," he finally said.

Now that the danger from the dogs had receded, they could take things more slowly. Even the gazelle-like Hego had realized this and he didn't rush off ahead this time. In fact, he positioned himself behind Pompon to shove his backside over the difficult bits, and the climb went on, so slowly this time that when they reached the summit of the wooded mountain the sun was hanging directly overhead. It must have been around twelve or half past—eight hours since they had pulled off the escape. There were no Krauts to be seen anywhere, but no partisans either, which posed another problem. Should they wait here, above the forest where they could look down on the enemy, or should they carry on along the ridges in the hope of finding a friendly face? To complicate the issue, there were two ridges which ran parallel for a while, but one or two miles farther on, they resolutely turned their back on each other. The right-hand one, which veered more obviously to the south, unfortunately looked as if it led straight back to Loibl.

"What do we do now? Toss a coin?" said Pompon.

Now that the climbing was over, his good humor had come to the fore again.

"I would take the left-hand one," said Hego. "It's farthest from the road."

Paulo backed him up. "He's right, it's safer. And we've got just as much chance of coming across some partisans. There's no border at this height."

Before setting out, they waited long enough to thoroughly absorb the geography of the area. Mountains, mountains, and more mountains whose knife-edged ridges reflected the brilliant early autumn sun like burnished bronze. Here and there, they could see a farm and a few sheep, but no sign of human life. Choosing between one ridge and another was truly a question of heads or tails, but once they had decided, they had no chance of changing their minds, for between the two ridges there was a bottomless ravine.

"Well, do we toss a coin or not?" Pompon repeated.

"Don't be a prick, Pompon, it's no game!" Paulo said sharply. "We take the one on the left and that's final. I'm only sorry that it rules out taking a look at that farm, down there on the right, halfway up the slope. There's smoke coming from the chimney."

There was indeed a comforting trail of white smoke which was spiraling steadily skyward.

At this time of day, it could only mean that someone was

cooking grub. The last drop of soup the three fugitives had swallowed had been pissed away ages ago—exactly twenty-four hours ago.

"Perhaps I was a bit hasty. We've got to eat too," Paulo thought with some regret. "But fuck it, if we go off to the right, we're likely to end up smack on top of Loibl. No thank you!"

It must have been easily two o'clock by the time they started again toward the left-hand ridge. Now and then they could hear barking, but it was halfhearted and a long way off. Their ramble might have been quite pleasant if they hadn't constantly had to get up to all sorts of acrobatics. One false move would have sent them crashing onto the rock six hundred feet below. Once again, only Hego was really at home on this obstacle course. He showed them all the footholds and, thanks to him, they covered the first half mile in less than an hour. The fact that the ridge line dipped more often than it rose also helped, and the occasional mossy patch allowed them to rest their aching feet. By about five o'clock, as the sun was going down, the trio could no longer be seen from the wooded peak, from where they had set out at the end of the morning. It had disappeared suddenly behind a twist in the ridge, taking with it the SS manhunt. At last, they could breathe freely.

Their one overriding concern now was how to get themselves picked up by the partisans, who were too unobtrusive. Not just in order to be safe from Kraut patrols once and for all, but also to get some food inside them. It was becoming a matter of extreme urgency to satisfy their hunger, aggravated by the keen air and the constant exertion. Paulo halted his men to make a new announcement.

"The first farm or hut we see, we leave the ridge and make straight for it. It'd be a real bastard if there were Krauts inside, but it's pretty unlikely."

It took them another hour's scrambling before they found one, about six hundred feet below the ridge. Three cheers! The partisans could fucking well make it up to them by laying on a real spread. It was the least they could do after abandoning them to fend for themselves. Pompon was quivering with anticipation, but Hego, all of a sudden, looked anxious.

"Are you sure they're going to be Yugos?" he asked. "It's

my opinion that we've gone much too far to the left since midday."

The small Béarnais's words were like a bucket of cold water in their faces. But he'd done his friends a good turn too, seeing that they damn well must be Germans or Austrians living on this farm. He was right: for some time the ridge had been curving to the left and, since there were no boundary marks to show them the way, the three had unwittingly crossed over into Austria!

Thank God Hego had spoken up in time! Paulo instantly ordered asses in reverse, and they pelted back up to a small wooded rise from where they could observe what was going on below without being seen. There was no movement and no sound, but the farm was certainly inhabited because again there was smoke rising from a chimney, and it gave them the same feeling of reassurance.

"Perhaps I got it wrong, and we are still in Yugoslavia," ventured Hego, after fifteen minutes' close watch.

Paulo was also in two minds, and he was about to do a brief recon when the sound of voices and footsteps to the right froze him to the spot. The voices were talking in German and getting closer. Unexpectedly, they were women's voices, and instead of ordering the others to run, Paulo grabbed the first dead branch to hand, and Pompon and Hego did likewise. If the *Hausfrauen*—there seemed to be two of them—came just thirty feet closer, their days of washing dishes would be over . . .

"We can't let them get away," Paulo whispered urgently. But the scene didn't develop as he thought it would. The two biddies were certainly coming toward them, but far too slowly, pausing every couple of steps to pick mushrooms. A surprise attack was no longer possible, and they were still out of range of the sticks when they caught sight of the three convicts.

"*Zu Hilfe!* Help!"

They were Krauts all right. Throwing themselves on top of the pair to stop them shrieking would have been the answer, but they were lively bitches, and on their own ground. A hop, skip and a jump, and they were scurrying down toward the farm, still shrieking.

"Quick, let's beat it, back up to the ridge," shouted Paulo.

And not a moment too soon, for the cows' screeching had brought the farm's occupants running out, three beefy slobs in shirt sleeves, shooters in hand. At their heels, to put the lid on it, two hounds! "*Feldgendarmes!* We're fucked," Pompon gasped.

"Shut up and run," Paulo yelled. "It's getting dark, we've still got a chance."

It was undoubtedly thanks to the bad light that the first salvos whistled way above the heads of the fleeing men. These particular Krauts had obviously not been trained by the SS. The *Feldgendarmes* must have been reservists, or customs men, for the firing quickly ceased. The old farts were even calling their dogs off! Perhaps they thought their old girls had been having hallucinations! It seemed more than likely, because they were now shouting at each other, and so loudly that their racket was drowning the baying of the dogs. Still, it had been a close shave and it left them no choice but to retrace their steps and go all the way back, along the same bloody ridge, back toward Loibl!

"Oh no, I can't," moaned Pompon.

"C'mon, old man," said Hego, dragging him forcibly on. And patiently he started his fantastic work all over again, guiding his comrades step by step, rock by rock. They had to press on; in less than an hour it would be pitch-dark, even darker than the night before, and any further progress along the ridge, their only line of escape, would be suicidal. Paulo sensed this and suggested that as soon as they were out of sight of the farm they should scramble down into the ravine and hide until daybreak. But that still involved another fifteen hundred feet of tightrope walking. Once more, Hego showed them what to do to avoid a premature trip to the bottom. Like a monkey in the zoo he went hand over hand from one rock to the next, only letting go when Paulo, behind him, had gotten his hand to it. Pompon did the same behind Paulo, cursing every foot of the way, "Fucking SS! Fuckers! We'll be dead before they kill us . . . fuckers! Fuckers!"

Paulo would dearly have liked to tell him to wrap it up, but the sentiments of the old master baker were impossible to disagree with. And the bastard *Totenkopf* didn't even need to be around to make them sweat blood. Pompon and Paulo were near to passing out. In the end, the farm disappeared from sight and the fugitives were finally able to give up their hellish crawl. They paused for ten minutes to make sure the big brave men in shirt sleeves hadn't had a last-minute fit of enthusiasm and then, with the Béarnais in the lead, they set about slithering down the side.

Very quickly, Hego found the ideal spot to spend the night in safety, about a hundred and fifty feet down on a bed of dead leaves between four tall larch trees whose exposed roots formed a sort of balcony overhanging the precipice. Behind them was a screen of trees which were smaller, but stepping all the way to the ridge, they concealed the men from above. A whole regiment could march by and even in daylight, they wouldn't see a thing. If the friends could manage to forget what was waiting for them next day, they might spend the most peaceful night of their lives on their leafy mattress. The one slightly disagreeable thing was that now that they weren't on the move, they began to feel the cold. After nearly twelve hours on the run, their shirts were sticking to their skin with sweat, making them shiver. It couldn't have been more than 5 or 6 degrees in the ravine, which was swept by a light northerly breeze; before dawn, the temperature might well drop below zero. Hego, who must have had to deal with this sort of situation more than once when smuggling his charges through the mountain, took things in hand.

"Exposure gets you in the back first and there's only one thing you can do about it: we've got to sleep like spoons, stomachs against backs. Every quarter of an hour, the man at the back goes to the front."

It was the huddle principle, the sardine snooze, just like in the quarantine blocks at Mauthausen. Suffering is also the mother of invention. Feeling the warmth of another human being at your back had been enormously comforting there, but tonight it meant more than that. Perhaps it was friendship, a friendship born of their incredible adventure, of the achievement of getting out of hell together.

Difficult to sleep when you think about that, but their tremendous weariness helped them find rest all the same. Their sleep was broken each time the last man in line moved to the front to warm his back. But it was worth it, for what other joy can a convict wish for than to discover when he wakes that he is out of prison, that he is free? If after more than a year of nightmares, you wake up to this twenty times in the same night, all the other petty discomforts—cold, hunger, exhaustion, and even the fear which the new day brings with it—become almost irrelevant. There was a very good chance that for Paulo and his friends, this night in the open would forever be the most wonderful night of their lives.

When the day began to break, their morale was still set fair. As they stretched on their mattress of dead leaves, their fears of the day before, their bloodied feet, and the climb they faced to get back up to the ridge, were all far from their thoughts. After a moment, Paulo spoke.

"Come on, you guys, we've got to move. We'll have plenty of time to sleep when we're with the partisans."

As Pompon kept his eyes firmly shut, Paulo gave him a shake.

"Get up, you lazy bastard. You seem to have forgotten we're still in Austria!"

Austria! The word was like an electric shock and the baker was on his feet before Paulo. As for Hego he had already gone off to nose about, and what he discovered was not without interest.

"Grub up!" he cried, and to make himself clear, he whistled the mess bugle call, "*C'est pas de la soupe, c'est du rata, c'est pas de la soupe . . .*"* As the Béarnais wasn't renowned for his wit, it couldn't have been soup or ratatouille which he had rooted out. His head was poking out from some bushes and Paulo and Pompon realized at once that he'd discovered some kind of wild fruit. A brief orgy ensued; the three men crammed blackberries and bilberries into their mouths by the handful, groaning ecstatically like goats in a field full of thistles. For once God had done his homework right in these filthy mountains, and Hego got ten out of ten too. The marvelous thing about this manna from heaven was its fruity, sugary taste, such a treat for their palates. Trying to remember when he had last tasted it, Paulo had to think back to his cell in the Cherche-Midi jail, when he had received a parcel of apples and pears by mistake which he had gulped down there and then before it could be taken away from him. That was two years ago.

"Okay, that's enough blackberries, they give you the runs," ordered Paulo, shoveling in one last handful.

---

*"It's not soup, it's ratatouille . . ."

Setting the example, he began clambering up toward the ridge, which they could just make out in the early light. Reluctantly, Pompon and Hego tore themselves away from the blessed bush and ten minutes later they were all up on top. They took advantage of the bird's-eye view to check that there was no sign of life in the vicinity, before starting out again on their hazardous crawl along the ridge toward yesterday's departure point.

Coming, the ridge had dropped down about fifteen hundred feet, so now they had to make up that ground, and it very quickly told on their calf muscles, especially Paulo's. He had noticed that he wasn't at his best as he set out climbing the stretch from the bushes to the ridge. The others had very quickly caught up and then overtaken him, as if their blackberry treatment had had some kind of stimulant in it. And now they had gone on ahead, skipping from rock to rock, and sprinting on the flat stretches. Christ, they were in high gear.

After half an hour of superhuman effort, despite willing himself to go on, he had to stop. His legs just didn't want to know, and Hego and Pompon were already a thousand feet ahead. Ashamed of being so feeble, he nevertheless resigned himself to calling them back.

"Why are you running so fast, you maniacs? You trying to kill me?" he yelled after them, cupping his hands to his mouth.

Pompon came running back. "You all right, pal?" The good fellow was worried to death. If Paulo was all in, things were serious. "We'll give you a lift. It's nothing to worry about. It was Hego's and my turn yesterday. As you saw, it'll pass. Where does it hurt?"

"My legs, both of them, feels as if I've got cramp."

"All right, we'll go slower, take a long breather in the trees . . ."

"That's out of the question, we're not going back into the woods. We do as I say, or from now on we split up."

He said it so tersely that Pompon knew it was not just his legs which were giving his friend trouble. And indeed, the reason Paulo had suddenly felt so drained was that it had just come home to him that to get back to the other ridge, the one which led to Yugoslavia, they'd have to cross the V-shaped ravine a long way from the forested mountain. It was the only way they could stay out of sight of Winkler's patrols, who couldn't have abandoned the chase that easily. The bastards would certainly have their binoculars trained on the edge of the wood, and they might very well have laid a trap for them around the hut. To continue on along the ridge that far would mean certain death. Paulo knew that he wouldn't make that mistake but what he didn't know was whether he would be strong enough to climb down the near-precipice, still less scale the other side.

"Now listen to me, Pompon," he said in a completely different voice. "In case I don't make it, don't be an idiot and try to reach the other ridge through the forest. It'll be crawling with SS, I'm certain of it. They'll be waiting for us, to gun us down. The only way we're going to get out of this is by dropping into the ravine."

The Béarnais, who had also come back, pretended to treat the whole thing as a joke.

"You're right, we'll cut straight across where you say, but let's not make a mountain out of it, to coin a phrase. It's a lot less steep than what we were up against yesterday. Take the expert's word for it, and this time I guarantee I won't need the smelling salts. Neither will you, boy—just leave it up to me."

Their kindly concern was so touching that Paulo found the strength to struggle to his feet.

"Thanks, boys," he said, "I'll give it a try. It'll be all right going down. After that, we'll just have to see."

Pompon heaved a great sigh of relief. Never would he have abandoned the friend to whom he owed his freedom, but having to drag him with them would have complicated things badly. Had he not been afraid of the echo, he would have yodeled for joy.

This time, they all stayed together, and the pace set by Hego was moderate enough for Paulo to forget about his stiff legs. After an hour of this snail's pace, it was actually he who fixed the point where they should leave the ridge.

"We'll do another six hundred feet up to those trees whose tops you can just see, and then we'll have a try at getting down. Okay?" He must have been feeling better.

According to the sun, it couldn't have been much later than eight o'clock when the three friends reached the group of trees, so they had plenty of time to climb down the ravine and then up the other side before nightfall. Unless, as often happens, the ravine was deeper than it looked. Paulo proposed another halt to spy out the land. Below them, there were no nasty surprises, unless they stumbled on a pack of wolves or a bear, neither of which could be ruled out in this savage country. On the heights, for as far as they could see, there was nothing to arouse their suspicion either. Nature stretched away to the horizon—nothing but forests, mountains and ravines bathed by a sun holding out as much promise as the day before. Captivated by the beauty and tranquility of a countryside free from man and hound, Paulo couldn't help thinking that luck was still with them; if, instead of this glorious weather, there had been black clouds and pouring rain—as there could well have been at this time of year—their shortcut into the ravine would be doomed, and everything else with it. So what was the use in getting despondent? He set off confidently down the slope, behind the Béarnais, and Pompon happily brought up the rear.

Barely sixty feet down, they all found themselves on their backsides again, like the day before when they had slithered down from the dump. It was impossible to stay upright with their wooden-soled shoes, which skated on the layers of dead leaves, and even Hego took extreme care. His method of slowing down the helter-skelter was to slalom on his backside, grabbing hold of trees on the way. Not only was the good fellow testing out the way, but at the dangerous points he braced himself against a tree and waited to catch the next man down. The three of them might have been taken for boys out on a giant toboggan party had it not been for their unmistakable stamp of convicts, shaved and uniformed.

They had no choice but to reach the bottom quickly, and they were surprised, even disappointed, to find it took so little time. The slide hadn't lasted ten minutes. Neither had their trousers and underpants, and the sight of their three bare backsides gave them an opportunity, for the first time since they left Loibl, to let themselves go. Their feeling of security was total at the bottom of this thickly wooded and inaccessible trough, and they could well afford their noisy laughter.

When they moved on a little to look for the least difficult way up the other slope, they came to a stream of wonderfully clear water, and with one movement they plunged their heads into it, their mouths open. Their bodies desperately needed water to replace what they had sweated out in the last thirty-six hours.

"That'll wash down the blackberries," said Pompon, having lapped up a good half quart.

He was right. It was better not to tackle the last part of the program with an unsettled stomach. It was disheartening to see how steeply the slope climbed away. It was a mirror image of its partner, the major difference being that this one would force them to use their bare hands rather than their bare bottoms.

Before attacking this new mountain, they could afford to recharge their batteries. Paulo had spotted a slab of stone jutting out into the stream and he stretched out on it full length, as if to sleep, announcing to his astonished friends that he was going to have a snooze.

"Now that we're out of harm's way, there's no great hurry," he said by way of explanation.

They needed to sleep as much as he did, and a quarter of an hour later, soothed by the gurgling of the water, all three fell asleep.

Hego was the first to wake, at about midday, and as he knew exactly how long the climb would take, he shook Paulo.

"Listen, man, we've got to make a start if we want to be at the farm before nightfall."

Paulo was still in dreamland and it took him some time to come to. "What start, where? What farm?" he mumbled, heaving himself up. One look at the immense slope soaring above his head, and he was wide awake—more wide awake than any hose had ever made him.

"Oh no," he groaned, "it can't be true! We can't be going to climb up that, it's not possible!"

But it had to be possible. As long as he followed the instructions Hego was giving Pompon: they weren't to try going straight up, they were to tack up the flank the way skiers did it on snowshoes, leaning carefully, but hard, into each step. It was the long way around, it would more than triple the distance they had to cover, but since they had neither rope nor pitons to climb the rock face, they had no real alternative. And so they started their climb, fervently hoping it would be their last.

Well rested and with the Béarnais keeping a close eye on him, Paulo easily kept up for the first half hour, even daring to glance down from time to time despite his morbid fear of heights. Seen from where he was, three hundred feet up, the stream looked like no more than a trickle and each time he saw it glinting below, he drew a little more courage from it. Taking an interest in how far they had gone naturally stopped him thinking about how far they still had to go—judging by the first half hour's progress, they had four or five times as much ground to cover and it was easily as steep. Pompon was nose to tail with Paulo, and he couldn't help drawing the other's attention to it.

"At this rate, we'll be at it for another two hours," he said morosely.

It was the worst thing he could have said! Another two hours of these bloody antics! Paulo's legs immediately felt shaky, his pulse quickened and within ten minutes he had a bad stitch.

"Hego, stop, my lungs feel blocked," he gasped, collapsing onto a rock.

Once it starts, altitude sickness won't let go, and they had to pause every ten minutes for Paulo to get his breath back. The result was that the two-hour ascent which had so appalled Pompon was turned into a clear four. By the time all three of them were within three hundred feet of the top, from where, in theory, they ought to be able to overlook the farm, there wasn't any sun, even on the tops of the tallest trees.

A dozen times during the climb, Paulo had thought he had had it, a dozen times he had been dangerously close to blacking out. The sweat stung the cuts on his hands, his knees, and one of his feet as well, for he had lost a shoe on the way, and the pine needles buried themselves in the bare sole of his foot like pins in a pincushion. But it wasn't just a question of external aches and pains: his ears were buzzing and it felt as if someone were hammering inside his head. Twice he coughed up a reddish fluid, and this only added to his panic. Pompon, who had been splattered the second time, made the happy observation that it wasn't blood at all, but blackberry juice. He even tried to cheer his friend up with a weak joke. "Wasteful bastard," he said.

Paulo was inching up the last stretch on his stomach, his legs unable to support him anymore. Not once had he complained, but his friends knew what he was going through, and it was they, in turn, who had demanded pauses every ten minutes to make him think they were in as bad a state as he was. They would have done anything to pull him through; despite their own exhaustion they would even have carried him on their backs. For them he was still the boss, the inspiration of this whole adventure which wasn't yet over, and for his strength to fail him when they were so near their goal seemed to them unjust. Illogical too, because he looked the strongest, the least skinny. Why this weakness?

The truth was that Paulo's fatigue was mostly spiritual. He had felt it first at dawn that morning up on the ridge. All at once he'd been sickened by everything, by their present state, the past and the future. The warmth and encouragement of his friends and later on, the slalom down the slope, had temporarily revived him, and, the whole way up the steep ravine, the fear of letting go and the pain in his hands and knees had occupied all his attention. But now they were almost there, and in about fifteen minutes the nightmare climb would be at an end and they would know whether the farm was in friendly hands or not, his depression had returned, worse than ever. He was near to breakdown. He wasn't crying, but the murderous looks he shot at Hego and Pompon, as if they were to blame, were worse. Especially as he let out, at the same time, a stream of abuse: "Fuckers, fuck you, fuckers, you won't get me," abuse which might well have been intended for them.

His delirium was getting progressively worse, and when the floods of insults dried up, it was succeeded by hysterical laughter which worried them even more. His two friends decided to turn a blind eye to his behavior. In spite of their urge to grab him by the shoulders and force him to climb the last three hundred feet, his two friends decided to sit it out with him. It was the best thing to do because the only thing they could think of saying was: "It's almost over, Paulo, just one more effort," and that would only have aggravated his state. The fact that it was almost over was the very cause of his depression. He was almost at the end of an interminable chain whose every link of horror and humiliation he was reliving, like so many daggers thrust into his heart. He must have felt that the small farm on the other side of the ridge, which they could get to in a few minutes if only he would move, was the end of the whole long nightmare. But instead of thinking what that meant, thinking about freedom, returning home, or even revenge, he willfully turned back to the nightmare, floundering in it, incomprehensibly picking out all the bitterest memories—the gobs of spit they had hawked in his face, the *fünf und zwanzig* on his bare ass, the prick parades in front of all the queer block chiefs, the thousands of slaps and blows he had taken without a word, even taking off his cap. Not one of all these could he forget, and each one made him tremble with shame and disgust. He would have thrown up on the spot if he'd had anything left in his stomach.

Was it worthy of a man to have accepted these vile humiliations for all that time? But on the other hand, how do you judge something which has never existed before, where prisoners of war are held in an institution run by guards who are all, from the governor to the lowliest Kapo, raving madmen, licensed to kill, with being called to account? There were never any good reasons, it was enough that your face didn't fit. Quick march, over the line, into the oven with the weak, the ugly, the lame, the hunchbacks, the boys who slopped their soup, the old men who queued up twice for bread and the men whose friends got away—like the whole Russian contingent, a hundred and fifty in one go! Meaningless fucking excuses the whole time, which weren't even worth two days in the cooler in a POW camp. In no other camp in the world, in no other war, in no other prison, had that ever been seen before. "It's beyond human understanding," he heard himself muttering.

The crisis was passing. He no longer felt ashamed, either of himself or of the others. But his anger had not subsided. It didn't matter, he would tell the whole story in all its nobility, all its baseness. Who then would dare see the self-seekers, the cowards, the greasers, and the boys with their ass stove in, as anything other than victims? It was only in the case of informers, the likes of Pozzi, Riton and a few other bastards, that the question might be posed. Even that would have to be weighed carefully, if everything was to be put in the balance. Anyway, he wasn't going to stand in judgment and point the accusing finger now. That's all too easy when you're out of the cage. He would defend all his fellow deportees, all of them, without exception.

But to achieve such a fine aim, he had first of all to get back to France, with perhaps a brief combat stop among Tito's men. All right, on your feet, we're wasting time. He got up, feeling more himself than ever. His depression was gone. Hego and Pompon saw this, and they greeted him with two big smiles.

"Looks as if you're feeling better, boy," ventured the latter.

Paulo didn't reply, as if Pompon had stated the obvious, and without even waiting for the Béarnais to show the way, which had become the established pattern, he began climbing the last crag. This time he did very well at picking out the best paths between the rocks. Never, since the beginning of their escapade, had the trio made such rapid progress, partly because Paulo's crisis had forced everyone to stop and rest but also because the slope was markedly less steep. If they hung on tightly, they could even stand straight. This combination of things meant that fifteen minutes later, they were up and over the ridge.

"Stop and lie flat," Paulo ordered. "The farm's three hundred feet to the left, they might see us."

And there it was, the farmhouse which they had missed through thoughtlessness the previous day. It may only have been an illusion, but it looked reassuring, even though it was inhabited, judging by the thin wisp of smoke escaping from the chimney. It bore no resemblance to the one they had seen the day before in Austria. First of all, it looked very poor; it had no shutters, makeshift planks supported its thatched roof, and it certainly had no electricity or telephone, which was another good sign. Best of all, it could only consist of one room, or at the most two, which ruled out the possibility of a squad of *Feldgendarmes* being billeted there.

"We'll still wait a bit longer before moving in," Paulo ordered in a low voice.

There were the surroundings to be scoured, for women picking mushrooms, for example, like the day before. Five minutes of listening and observing put the men's minds at rest: besides a few scrawny sheep, there wasn't a living soul in the area. Not even a dog . . .

"If there's nothing to eat in the farmhouse, we'll grab a lamb," Pompon said. "At least we won't have come all this way for nothing."

An unsuspecting sheep was just at that moment heading toward them, and Hego instantly began to crawl nearer to it.

"Don't be a fucking idiot," said Paulo, pulling him back. "It'll start yelling its head off and the peasants'll shut themselves in, and then we'll look pretty stupid."

That made sense, and the other two obediently resumed their reconnaissance.

Around the farm there was still nothing suspicious and below it, to the left and the right, there was absolute silence, nothing. The ridge really was very high, easily six thousand feet, and it dominated the whole area, all the cols, woods, clearings, and paths. It was the ideal spot to see the partisans coming from a long way off . . . or the SS.

Still keeping an eye on the farm, Paulo tried to figure out where they were in relation to Loibl and the tunnel. But the view from this lofty perch made everything look different and he was about to give up, when his eye was caught by a long crevice tucked between two mountains to the right.

"Listen, you two," he said, "can you see that landslide of white rocks over there, where it looks if there's been an avalanche? Do you think it's the one we saw from the *Appelplatz*, on the mountain which had the chamois? It looks damn like it . . ."

"You're right, I recognize it now," Pompon and Hego replied, almost simultaneously.

They couldn't have been mistaken. The three of them knew that dreadful gash in the mountain only too well; they must have looked at it a thousand times, ordered to do so at attention, because it was forbidden to turn your head, especially when your neighbors were getting beaten, which was every day, twice a day, at every roll call. There was no mistake, it was indeed the same nightmarish view etched forever in their memories, photographed for life.

"Well! It's nice to be back again!" Pompon remarked sarcastically.

"No, you're wrong, it's a very good thing," answered Hego. "The rock spill is due south, we're on course, we're in Yugoslavia."

Whether or not they were the same rocks wasn't the problem. They had come for the farm. Paulo brought them back to the subject.

"Before we creep up on the house, we've each got to get

ourselves a stick. Not dead wood this time but good solid sticks . . ."

Without knives, it wasn't easy to snap off green branches, but they managed, and a few minutes later, each man had a respectable staff in his hand. They fanned out and began their descent down to the farm.

They were only about sixty feet away when the door swung smartly open, and out stepped a little old lady in mourning, with a black shawl, a black dress and a bowl in her hand. They were too close to run away, but not close enough to knock her out. Fortunately, the poor woman must have thought she was having a hallucination because instead of shrieking like those stupid Austrian bitches, she fell to her knees, put down the bowl and rapidly crossed herself three times. Once for each of the devils she saw before her.

Paulo seized the chance to move several steps closer, poised ready for flight should the old woman, realizing her vision was not the devil, but three very real convicts, start to yell. But this particular old woman's reactions were utterly unexpected. Instead of shrieking with terror, she burst into tears. Nonplussed by this behavior, Paulo quite forgot to grab hold of her.

"Why's she crying? Why isn't she shouting for help or fainting?" he wondered. The answer didn't immediately occur to him, which was why he had stopped. But turning around to see what his followers thought—they, too, had stopped dead in their tracks—he understood. These weren't human beings which the poor widow had seen descending upon her farm, they were ghosts whose skeletons showed through their tattered garments. And with their weird heads and wild staring eyes, they could only be emissaries from hell come to claim her. It wasn't surprising she had lost the power of speech in front of such an apparition, and was weeping, without daring to call for help.

"Hm, maybe there's no one else inside," thought Paulo. In a hurry to find out, he took another step forward, but the old woman, still on her knees and crossing herself more and more frantically to exorcise the demons, was blocking the way.

"Don't cry, old lady, we won't hurt you," he said.

With his free hand, he helped her to her feet, and at the same time, he kicked open the door which had half closed.

They had been right behind him too and the three of them burst into the main room almost simultaneously. What a pleasant surprise! Not the slightest trace of a Kraut or *Feldgendarme*, even in shirt sleeves; just a benign old fellow who looked about the same age as the woman in black, and was probably her husband. With his pipe in his mouth he was quietly warming his toes in front of a cozy log fire. A young girl of about fifteen sat meekly beside him, also in black but as pretty as a picture. The little girl couldn't have known what a convict was, but that didn't stop her from springing from her chair like a scalded cat, and the only reason the old man hadn't done likewise must have been that he had trouble with his legs. Instead, his face assumed the terrified expression of an old man realizing he's about to be murdered.

However intense their emotions were, they were nothing compared to what Paulo, Pompon and Hego felt as they entered the room. For months and months they had lived in a hectic world of brutality, screams, hoses and guns trained on them day and night. Abruptly, they found themselves transplanted into the midst of the gentlest, rustic scene: the family gathered around the wood fire. They felt ridiculous.

To show their hosts that they had no violent intentions, the uninvited guests threw their sticks into the fireplace one after the other. The atmosphere immediately relaxed and the little girl, hearing them talking among themselves, said:

"You, *Franzosen*?"

What incredible luck! She understood French. They would be able to explain themselves and apologize.

Just then the unhappy woman decided to come back in, but she was still sobbing and Paulo went over to take her hand in the hope of calming her down and reassuring her. It was no good, the tears flowed more and more copiously. God, what waterworks! But they weren't tears of fear now. The only reason the old dear was still so upset was because of her shock at seeing the state that these creatures had been reduced to. She had of course heard bad things about the Germans, but the sight of these three poor emaciated boys in rags, shaven-headed and covered in sores, standing in her own house, was too much for her. Perhaps she was also thinking about her sons who would have been in the maquis like the rest of Yugoslavia's youth. They too might be taken prisoner. One thing was for sure, the farmer's wife had a heart of gold, because she rushed to the larder without even pausing to dry her tears. They hadn't even had to ask.

They couldn't be rolling in it at the farmhouse and all they could offer, almost apologetically, was bread, boiled potatoes and milk. Nevertheless the three devils fell upon it like wild animals, teeth bared, peelings and all. But the most fantastic thing for them was the milk. They each downed a quart, straight from the jug, watched by the old man who was staring openmouthed.

He would have been much more in favor of offering them a pick-me-up of slivovitz, and he was already casting sidelong glances at one of the shelves. He couldn't have thought of a better way of laying them out cold if he'd tried. The poor old boy didn't understand that after what his visitors had been through, milk was the life-giving elixir. But their stomachs had shrunk on the Loibl diet and one after the other, they had to admit defeat, just as Serpette eventually had after his seven quarts of soup.

The little girl, who had been watching them in silence as they crammed themselves with food, clapped her hands as enthusiastically as if she had just witnessed the breaking of a record.

"Bravo! A little more eat?" she asked mischievously, grinning and showing her sparkling young teeth.

"No more, thanks, *kein Platz,*" Pompon excused himself. To get the message across, he clasped his stomach with both hands.

"*Danke schön,* thanks," Paulo said in turn. But he felt embarrassed at the idea that these worthy folk might think badly of them, assuming from the way they had thrown themselves on the food that they had only come for grub. So, choosing his words carefully, he added, "Please excuse us, sir, madam, we hadn't eaten anything for forty-eight hours. We have just escaped from the camp at Loibl Pass. Do you know it?"

Of course they knew it! Their farm was the nearest to the camp and they must also have been fully aware of the risks involved in sheltering escaped prisoners. Paulo's question was hardly sincere. Even the little girl had heard about the camp.

"SS Loibl, bad men. You go partisans," she said, anticipating Paulo, who had just been trying to work out how to steer the conversation in that direction. The child's words confirmed that the Krauts must send occasional patrols as far as her grandparents' shack.

"Where are the partisans? Which way?" Paulo interrupted.

"Yesterday come here. They not far, in woods. Come often, you wait here."

What a sweet little thing she seemed as she said it! Her big dark eyes shone with pleasure at the thought that she would be able to keep her new friends in her house. They could teach her some new French words. She must have been on vacation, and it couldn't have been much fun for her on her own. Besides, despite their peculiar outfits and their bald heads, these three rough-looking lads who had appeared out of the blue were young and not bad-looking. Maybe she found them exciting, she was old enough and beginning to blossom . . .

But that was the last thing on Paulo's mind. What excited him at the moment was knowing the partisans were nearby. He questioned her again. "The partisans, how many hours' walk are they? Two? Three?"

The pretty girl burst out laughing again. "No, very close, half a mile. Come here tomorrow."

Half a mile! In less than an hour, it could all be over, the whole affair could be concluded. No longer interested in the little girl, who continued her chattering, the three friends exchanged glances. They were all thinking the same thing. Not for anything would they spend the night here, they would make straight for the partisans, get themselves to safety before nightfall. It was a hundred to one against the Krauts turning up at this late hour, but it would be foolhardy to take that chance. Their little angel didn't realize that for them a barrage of submachine guns was more important than any hospitality. Neither did her grandmother, who had begun taking out blankets and arranging beds for them in a corner of the room.

"No, madame, we can't stay," Paulo stopped her. "If the Germans come back, we're *kaputt*! We're going to leave at once. Thank you again for everything."

Solemnly the young girl translated, but she wanted to keep open a small chance for herself, so she offered to go and fetch the partisans.

Paulo jumped up from his chair, suddenly wanting to hug this miracle of a girl.

"What's your name?" he asked.

"Tina."

"Well, Tina, when we're back in France, we'll write you long letters in French and we'll send you lovely dresses from Paris. Come on, gorgeous, show us the way, we'll follow you."

But Tina wasn't to be gotten around so easily. She had said she would fetch the partisans, not that she would take them to the partisans. There was a subtle difference. Without giving Paulo time to explain why they should go with her—it would be dark soon, at her age she shouldn't be out at night on her own, and so on—she opened the door and disappeared into the twilight.

Her grandparents' attempts at friendly conversation in Yugoslav were in vain, the atmosphere around the table was not the same, and within ten minutes they all felt so uneasy that Pompon couldn't help saying, "What if she's gone to the Krauts?"

"You can drop that for a start, she's not the type," Paulo retorted.

His comment had nonetheless had its effect, and each of the three fugitives began thinking hard. Why hadn't Tina wanted them to go with her to the partisans? Perhaps her pretty little head had been concocting a plan in the hope of keeping her French friends at home. Anything was possible. For example, she might come back alone and tell them that she had found the partisans but they couldn't come to get them until tomorrow morning, so they'd have to sleep here, wouldn't they?

Now that suspicion had got the upper hand, it was impossible for them to wait for the girl's return. Paulo preferred to make a move immediately.

"We'll go and hide ourselves behind a ridge. We'll be safer. If the brat comes back alone, we'll see what we do."

It was too difficult to explain to the old couple. "*Auf Wiedersehen*," said Paulo, motioning the others to come with him. Five minutes later, the three friends were safe behind the first trees on the ridge, taking up their lookout positions even more intently than before. Their morale had taken a turn for the better, not simply because their stomachs were full, but this time there was a strong chance that the whole adventure would be over before tomorrow morning, even if the girl came back emptyhanded. She couldn't have made everything up; there must be a partisan bivouac somewhere in the area. It was the one thing of which Paulo was sure; he had generally played his hunches right in civilian life, and what was he now, if not a civilian? As if to bring it home to himself a little more, and to help fate along, he furiously tore off his registration number, the five cursed digits, two, eight, two, one, four, which they had forced him to sew on his jacket himself.

"Stuff Mauthausen! Stuff Loibl Pass!" he yelled, hurling the faded scraps of cloth as far as he could.

"You ought to keep them as a souvenir. They're a sort of relic," Hego remarked mildly.

Paulo was momentarily taken aback by the Béarnais's strange comment; it sent him off into a tirade again.

"A relic my ass! A fucking whore's number, you mean! Twenty-eight thousand, two hundred and fourteen! Fuckers! Ten thousand times, they made me repeat it, and in fucking Kraut too! I know it by heart: *Acht und zwanzig tausend, zwei hundert vierzehn*. Assholes! Fuckers! Bastards! When we get to Tito's men, tonight or tomorrow, it'll be their whole fucking uniform I'm going to throw into the dustbin. I'm going to burn my relics, as you call them, the first convict's uniform ever to get to the crematorium . . . Yes, until they're a heap of ashes, even if I have to go back to France stark-naked. I'll bet you've never seen striped relics in your priest-ridden part of the world?"

It was good to hear Paulo letting fly at last. Besides, it had all been said half tongue in cheek, and it bore no resemblance to his angry despair of that afternoon. He was finding his feet again, beginning to feel his freedom, and the meal with the Yugoslav peasants had probably had something to do with it. His stomach decided to rumble, reminding him of his feast, and instinctively, he glanced gratefully over to the farm.

The old man had moved his chair to the doorstep and was waving his bony old arms in a kind of would-be semaphore which was obviously for them, whatever it meant.

"He's telling us to come back," said Pompon.

Indeed they could hear him calling, "Back! Back, *Franzosen*!" Like his little girl, he was vexed at the strangers' lack of trust in him.

"You just step this way, granddad, we'll have you as a hostage," Paulo offered flippantly, feeling more relaxed by the minute. Seeing that his friends were enjoying the joke, he added: "Myself, I'd find it rather pleasant to spend another night under the stars. This mossy little bed suits me fine. In any case, I'm not going to kip down with grandpa and grandma."

"Quiet, don't make a sound," said Hego suddenly. "I saw something moving on the path down there to the right."

God, the smuggler had sharp eyes! Nobody else had seen Tina coming.

"Can you see whether she's got anyone with her?" asked Paulo.

"No, she's on her own."

"We still don't move, she might have been followed. Keep looking, Béarnais."

As he watched her skip from rock to rock as if playing hopscotch, Paulo suddenly felt ashamed of his suspicions. How could such a little treasure, with her childish smile, have gone to tip off the Krauts!

She flew into the farmhouse in a whirl, but when she rushed out again almost immediately, her delightful, reassuring smile had given way to tears! Gone! Her French friends were gone!

"We've made a lot of fuss about nothing," said Paulo, feeling awkward. "Let's go down and get the news."

"Yes, it's safe, she wasn't followed," the Béarnais confirmed.

When Tina saw the trio emerging from the trees on the ridge, she gave a joyful shout and came hurtling to meet them. Around the table a few minutes later, they all sat and listened to what she had to say.

"I see partisans. Say to them three French escape Loibl come here."

She could hardly speak, she was so excited, so Paulo gently took her hand. "Calm down, Tina. Did you really see the partisans? Did you talk to them?"

"Yes, really saw, yes talk to them."

"How many are they? Why didn't you bring them back?"

If they didn't believe her soon, she would burst into tears, so Paulo dropped his interrogation. Besides, he was sure she wasn't lying now, his old instincts told him. "We believe you, Tina," he went on, "but you've been there and back in only half an hour, so they must be very near."

"Yes, partisans very near. Not far!" she said, thrilled that they at last believed her. Paulo sensed that this was the right moment to press her.

"Can you lead us to them?"

"Yes, monsieur."

"Tonight? Now?"

"Yes," she said reluctantly, pouting a little. The tall man who was tormenting her was stronger than she was. In any case, she had realized that he and his friends wouldn't be staying, so she might as well do her best to please them. She got up, saying "We go," and Paulo couldn't resist. He seized her around the waist, lifted her up till her face was level with his own and gave her a resounding kiss on each cheek. The color in her cheeks from her mad dash deepened another shade. Trust Paulo! He still had a way with women, whatever age they were!

On the way out he kissed her grandparents too, thanking them much more warmly this time, and following his two accomplices he set off after Tina.

There wasn't a proper path but she seemed to know the way like the back of her hand, and the good thing about it was that it was downhill, unlike all the others the trio had had to negotiate since leaving Route 333. But that wasn't what made them hurry so eagerly. The real reason for their haste was that for the first time they were absolutely unafraid. The more they all thought about it, the more certain they were that the Yugoslav family, right from the start, had only thought to help them, to protect them from the claws of the hated Germans who were bleeding their country dry. They knew the partisans would be there, waiting for them, thanks to brave little Tina. They knew that in a few minutes their long nightmare would be at an end.

Superstition prevented them from picturing the moment when they arrived in the other camp, the camp of freedom, and from wondering whether they would jump for joy or hug their saviors, but the closer they got, the faster their hearts raced. And they would soon be there, very soon, led by the inexhaustible Tina. Even when their delightful little leader veered off to the left and began to scale a fairly steep bluff, no one trailed behind. The team literally flew behind their light-footed guide, but it was not wasted effort because it would be dark within the half hour, and it wouldn't do for the partisans to hear footsteps and start firing at them. The good Tina must have realized this and that was why she was running so fast. Come to think of it, how was she going to get home in the dark?

We'll keep her with us for the night, Paulo decided. He was firmly convinced that the end really was in sight. And with justification, for when they reached the top of the bluff, Tina pointed to a dense clump of trees and announced triumphantly, "There, the partisans!" Then, flinging her arms around Paulo's neck, she kissed him back.

As he had done on another occasion in the tunnel, he held her in his arms longer than was necessary. With this little girl he had no ulterior motives, but he couldn't help himself comparing the two scenes: two girls, both young and pretty too, had helped him out of hell. Why? Because of his good looks? That was difficult to believe, seeing the state he was in after eighteen months of prison, and yet there was no other explanation, because he had scarcely talked to either of them and had offered them nothing in exchange. It was a very gratifying thought.

"Aren't you coming with us, sweetheart?" he asked, seeing her give a goodbye peck to Pompon and Hego who were also very moved.

"No, I go home, night comes. But you not need me. Partisans straight, in the wood, three hundred feet . . . Good luck, *Slobada narodu*."

And she set off back down the bluff with even more grace and speed than before. The three convicts waited until she was no more than a tiny speck in the distance before going on, and long after she had disappeared from view they were still waving their battered *Mützen*. Like the scene at the fireside, this was another extraordinary moment which Paulo would certainly have dwelled upon had he not been so preoccupied with the last act of their escape. What sort of welcome would they receive from the partisans? Had Tina warned them adequately? Yes, they no longer doubted that, but she had forgotten to tell them what the partisans' reply had been, and it was no myth that the Titoists were not kindly disposed toward extra mouths to feed.

"Bound to be able to work it out somehow, they can't send us back to Loibl," Paulo tried to persuade himself, but he knew the suspense would hold right up to the last of the three hundred feet or so which lay between them and the copse.

It was up to him to take control again for this final test, and so, as soon as they had stepped into the open on the other side of the wooded bluff, he took the lead. Never since the start of their adventure, except perhaps during the wagon inspection, had he felt such dread. In an attempt to ignore it, he avoided looking in the direction of the wood, and it was Hego behind him who first noticed a movement.

"Stop!" he called. "There's someone behind the first bush, and he's got a gun on us!"

"Just keep moving, as if there's nothing wrong," replied Paulo, walking on. "If they were Krauts we'd have been cut down long ago."

It was disquieting that ahead of them no one seemed to want to show themselves; all they could see was a Bren gun whose barrel was looking bigger at every step. Behind the gun were two uniformed figures blending with the foliage. Paulo had quickened his pace, and he could just make out their faces, faces which looked so unfriendly that the moment he was able to see the fellows' uniforms properly, he stopped in his tracks. Behind him Pompon had seen them too. "We've been had, let's get the fuck out of here!" he shouted. They were wearing Kraut uniforms.

Fortunately, these were far from being Krauts. The two men standing guard were partisans, in spite of their Wehrmacht tunics which they had doubtless stripped from the enemy. But whether or not they had been informed of the French fugitives' arrival, they probably wouldn't have hesitated to fire at men who took one look at them and then ran. But reassured by the three unarmed men in tatters who stayed rooted to the spot, they eventually decided to emerge from their cover. The Bren gun was still pointing uncomfortably in their direction, however.

"*Kamerad!* Franzoșen*!*" Paulo called to them, holding out his arms in a gesture of friendship. He had just seen the red star of the Yugoslav communists on the two men's caps. There was no possible doubt that they were among Tito's men. They had won! *Fertig Loibl!*

"*Smort fascimus!*" he cried, to break the ice once and for all.

"*Sloboda norodu!*" the two unsociable-looking fellows replied together, and almost simultaneously, their faces split into broad grins.

"Hurray! We've won!" yelled Pompon, throwing his cap in the air. He couldn't contain himself a moment longer. Less than a minute before, he had still had doubts and almost blown everything with his "We've been had, let's get the fuck out of here!" and now he exploded, half laughing, half crying, grabbing Paulo and then Hego and shouting in their ears, "Thank you, thank you. Let me kiss you, brother!"

The kissing and hugging went on for a good five minutes, watched by the two Yugos, who were smiling indulgently. Even the normally reserved Béarnais was leaping in the air, falling on his knees, and kissing the ground. So was Paulo. They looked like football players who had just scored the goal of their lives, and it was indeed their lives which they had played for and won. Their striped uniforms hanging from them in shreds bore witness to the length and bitterness of the game.

It was the older of the Titoist comrades who took it upon himself to interrupt their joyful antics. He too spoke a few words of French. "You come to Kommissar Politik," he ordered.

Paulo and the others had been so carried away by their emotions that they hadn't given a thought to the fact that there had only been two men to receive them. A whole maquis was quite a different matter.

"Perhaps we haven't gotten there yet," Paulo started thinking. But the Yugos reassured them that they had. The maquis was in the wood itself and the Kommissar's HQ was less than three hundred feet away.

Fortunately, it was still light when the three convicts, escorted by their guardian angels, arrived at headquarters. It would have been a pity for them to have missed a single detail of the tableau which was suddenly revealed as they turned the last corner. It was a scene worthy of the great revolutionary epics: a flag bearing the red star fluttered in the wind and around it stood young men and women, submachine guns and cartridge belts slung across their chests, and belts with German hand grenades. There was a whole battalion whose commander, the Kommissar, couldn't have been more than thirty. What a picture of fraternity, faith and quiet strength! It was incredible how pathetic the SS at Loibl looked by comparison! You didn't need a crystal ball to see that these were the true victors here in this maquis and in all the other cells which were dotted the length of Yugoslovia from Macedonia to Croatia, just as Dédé, Joel, and poor old Etcheverry had so often explained to them. What a magnificent chapter the old teacher could have added to his history books, if the murdering Ramsauer hadn't sunk his syringe into his heart. And it was Paulo who was living that true patriot's dream in his place, and in the place of Dédé, Joel and many others too, all of them volunteers for this war.

Well, it didn't matter either way, he would take their place, he would avenge them. How wonderful it would be to fight alongside these amazing men and women. Maybe even Yanka would join them. His happiness would be complete! In any case, she had kept her word. The Political Kommissar confirmed that he had been informed of their escape and that it was indeed because of the confusion over dates, Saturday instead of Friday, that his men had not been at the rendezvous in the hut. They had hung around in vain the whole morning of the previous day. The important thing which emerged from what the kommissar said was that the partisans had accepted them. Yanka must have made it clear that the three Frenchmen she was sending them would not just be extra mouths to feed. At last they had definitely won. Paulo, the ex-crook, had accomplished the impossible: via Loibl, he had escaped from Mauthausen, the camp of a hundred thousand murders.

This time, he was the one who dragged his companions into a new victory dance under the moved gaze of the whole battalion, who, as a mark of respect, had formed a circle around them. Some of them must have known what life was like at Loibl and what it meant to have escaped. Some of the girls were crying and when the three convicts had finished their celebration, everybody came to embrace them.

Paulo, Pompon and Hego had just had their own Liberation, as wonderful in its way as the Liberation of France.

France, incidentally, was still just as far away, and there were many things which remained to be done up here in the mountains.

Liberated? Well, perhaps not quite yet . . .

XXIX

PARIS, MAY 1945

On the boulevard Raspail a few feet from the entrance of the Sèvres-Babylone Métro station, there is a strange gathering in front of the Hotel Lutétia. Nothing but men in pajamas. Despite appearances and the early hour, these are not local residents out to fetch their croissants. They are deportees who have returned home. And Paris is not there to see them, Paris is still asleep. The faces of these Frenchmen bear the marks of the hell from which they have come and their clothes smell of its ashes, but when they emerge again singly, they will be washed, fumigated and properly dressed. Then it will be too late to understand. These ghosts must be seen now, before they go inside.

Even the two policemen (wearing the shoulder braid of the Légion d'Honneur, if you please!) who are channeling the stream of new arrivals look disbelieving. And horribly embarrassed too. With the utmost gentleness they guide the phantoms through the revolving door of the hotel, one by one, trying to find the right words for the occasion.

"Don't push, take your time, you'll hurt yourselves. You've suffered enough already."

They speak so kindly that those deportees who are thinking that the ways of the Parisian cops have dramatically changed for the better keep their thoughts to themselves. Anyway, the line is moving fairly quickly. There is no need to show any papers, a shaven head is enough. In fact, it is the only pass accepted.

So when a new group stepped from one of the buses which was ferrying to and from the Gare de l'Est and a tall fellow with curly hair tried to join the line, one of the policemen barred his way.

"Someone's made a mistake. This is for deportees only."

"I know, I'm one of them," Paulo Chastagnier replied.

"No, young man," the policeman insisted. "The POWs, STOs and voluntary workers register elsewhere. You were misdirected at the Gare de l'Est."

It had to be admitted that this deportee was a very odd man out among the mass of shaven heads, and not just because of his thick hair. Everything about him was different. Unlike the pale men around him, he was tanned and bursting with health, although still quite thin. Above all, his eyes lacked that terrified expression of a beaten dog which was the most striking thing about the others. As for his clothes, although they too looked strange, they were not slave's rags; he was wearing the uniform of a soldier from an unknown army, complete with Sam Browne and boots. It wasn't going to be easy for Paulo to persuade the cop on duty, who had orders to let through only shaven men in pajamas, that the reason he didn't look like them was because seven months earlier he had escaped from one of the notorious camps known as the slow death camps. Keeping his temper in check, Paulo persisted.

"Listen, Officer, I told you I was a deportee. Let me through."

The unhappy policeman hadn't been told that there might be deportees with long hair. He hesitated, trying to find an answer among the other shaven heads who were waiting their turn.

"What camp were you in?" one of them said to Paulo.

"Mauthausen."

"And you escaped? Well done."

"Well done's right. Isn't there anyone here who was at Mauthausen?"

Nobody knew Mauthausen, but one look at Paulo's set face, and the cop decided to open the door. He wasn't unduly worried, because he knew that inside there were other checks to weed out gatecrashers.

They had even gotten it fairly well organized. Written up on placards like the names of military victories were the places where these men had fought their war: Buchenwald, Dora, Dachau, Oranienburg, Auschwitz, Birkenau, Struthof, Flössenburg, Ravensbrück, Neuengamme, Bergen-Belsen... At the end of the hall Paulo saw the name Mauthausen and he made straight for it.

"Can I help you, young man?" a charming woman's voice said from behind him.

It was the hostess who had been assigned to welcome the Mauthausen repartriates. Her bosses had chosen her because she wasn't the pin-up type, and so the men who had lost so much blood there wouldn't burst a blood vessel at this late stage. Seeing Paulo staring at her oddly, she spoke again, still smiling, "Perhpas you're looking for a relation who was at Mauthausen?"

"No, I was the one who was there, and they told me at the Gare de l'Est that I was supposed to come to the Hotel Lutétia."

He was going to have just as much trouble with this patronizing female as he'd had with the cop just now, explaining that a Red Cross convoy wasn't the only way out of Mauthausen. Already, she was smiling her vacant smile again. Paulo anticipated her next question.

"You're looking at my hair, it's like that because I escaped seven months ago."

"I beg your pardon, monsieur, I couldn't have known that," stammered the matron. "Wait for me here. An officer will attend to you."

She left Paulo standing there. Since he had nothing better to do, he walked over to a huge bulletin board on which were pinned dozens and dozens of missing person notices together with identity photographs, like the boards in police stations. The families who had sent these photos, hoping that someone coming back from the camps would recognize their loved one, would have done better to white out the hair and retouch the face. These photos of well-fed civilians meant nothing to a man who came from a world of shaven heads. Paulo scanned them in all turn, without stopping at any particular one. Above each face were the same words: "Does anyone know Jean-Pierre X... transported from Compiègne on July 5, 1944? Jacques X... last seen at Fresnes in February 1943... Paul Z... Does anyone know? Does anyone have any news?" If only they had written up the registration numbers.

As the hostess was still not back, Paulo turned to the board again, this time looking at the names. They were more or less in alphabetical order and when he got to M, he stopped. There was a Ménard, André, born at Rennes in

1922. Dédé! It was him, it was him in the photograph.

A moment ago, Paulo had naturally passed over it. This young man of good family, clean, wearing a tie, and with a schoolboy haircut, bore no resemblance to the convict with the high forehead that he knew. But when he looked closer, there was no doubt that the face in the photograph had the same defiant gleam in the eyes, the same mischievous smile. And the information beneath the photo matched: arrested in Rennes, February 1942, Fresnes, Compiègne, March 1943—and then it stopped. The postcard with the Führer's stamp saying "I'm in good health" had obviously never arrived. The poor Ménard family! Who saw him last? Who has any news of him?

Of course there was only one person, and that was Paulo. But the news was bad, very bad. Dédé had died three months earlier, somewhere in the mountains of Croatia. He had died as a hero, as he had lived since June 1940, and as a free man. For he too had pulled off his escape from Loibl, exactly as he had told Paulo he would. Except that he had not gone alone. There had been four of them, both real and bogus electricians, and their method had been straightforward. Using their irons, they had battered in the skulls of the two SS escorting them to repair a line which had collapsed under the weight of the snow, and it was with the guns and ammunition of their guards that they had presented themselves to the partisans. But from that moment on, as it had for Paulo and his companions, a new kind of hell had replaced the one from which they had come. There was still the cold and the hunger, but no beds now, no *Waschraum*, sleeping out in the open on the frozen peaks in 20 degrees below, and almost daily skirmishes against the SS, the *Feldgendarmes*, the Oustachis and other Tchetniks. Jo from Oran, the ex-convict, had become famous at Loibl for coining the phrase, "Give me life in Cayenne rather than a year here." In Tito's army, Paulo had borrowed it and adapted it to "Give me life at Loibl, rather than a year with Tito." He was exaggerating, of course, but Loibl had had its moments during the summer of 1944: there had been boxing, his sunbathing, and there had even been food. Whereas in that maquis of savages . . .

Yet after him, there had been a fair number who had run from the camp. Exactly twenty had turned up to join Tito's troops, counting the three Soviet officers, Paulo's team, and the electricians.

The first had been a White Russian who had vanished from the south camp, carrying a tree trunk on his shoulder, without saying a word to anyone. He couldn't have found life as hard as his fellows, firstly because he was a strict vegetarian, but mainly because before the outbreak of war he had spent a few years in a Soviet labor camp. He had become a fireman there and, during an alarm call, seized his chance and just kept going, on his own, as he had done at Loibl. He had crossed through Turkey and Italy, and ended up in France, where the Krauts, utterly unimpressed by his adventures, had thrown him in the first train for Mauthausen. When he got there, the commies had pointed out to him that this was neither the time nor the place to go around telling everyone that extermination camps existed in comrade Stalin's country, too, but he didn't give a damn. For all that, he didn't feel at all like a traitor and he had demonstrated as much by taking up arms again as soon as he was out of Loibl. He had displayed such zeal that very soon the Titoists had entrusted him with the command of one of the famous Russian battalions, the terror of the SS.

Three other solo escapes had followed. There was a young Frenchman from the north camp, a racing cyclist and Resistance worker, who had run for it without any warning either, leaving his colleague holding the coffee urn which they were both bringing back from the SS field kitchen. Shortly after that, an Italian, who had just arrived after only a flying visit to Mauthausen, had made enquiries about Loibl's position in relation to the Italian border.

"Fiume, Trieste, *dove*?"

They showed him, and he left the same day. His luck had been astonishing: the SS sentry was sleeping, and it wasn't until evening muster that his absence was noticed.

Lepreux's escape had been much more of a drama. Like Dédé Ménard, he had stuck to his original plan. Climbing up to the tunnel one evening in the column of miners, he had purposely dropped his hurricane lamp. Bending down as if to pick it up, he had dived into the ravine. It was such a swift tumble that the SS in the rear was not altogether sure that anything had happened. He had taken a couple of pot shots, but before they could give chase, the *Stücken* had to be counted, and the time it took them to establish that there was one man missing gave Lepreux a clear fifteen minutes, which was more than enough for a mountaineer of his kind. When the hounds found his jacket a little while later, he was already over the ridge. Instead of going away from Loibl, he had come back toward the camp, foiling all the patrols Winkler had sent into the Yugoslav side of the mountain. When he turned up at the partisans' camp after countless feats of endurance, he looked so small and frail that Tito's men never suspected they had acquired a champion marksman. They ended up entrusting him with the only machine gun in the battalion, to which he had been assigned. For him to merit such an honor in Tito's army, without being a Yugoslav, he must have been an absolute crack shot.

The last group which succeeded in taking to the hills must have been the final straw for Knock-Knees. There were no fewer than six of them, a whole Kommando led by the brave Rouanet. After all he had done to help the others, he deserved to succeed even more, and although the escape took place under heavy machine-gun fire, they all got through. The escape had been copied from Paulo's plan. It was to take place at night, from the tunnel, the main difference being that instead of making a false floor (impossible with six), Rouanet's team had taken off in an iron hopper. One of them had taken over the controls of the diesel, and with the throttle wide open, the train had smashed through the guard-post barrier. This time the Krauts didn't stop to wonder, as they had when the three Russians had gone, they immediately opened fire. But their bullets bounced off the metal, and a little farther on, the six men were able to jump down and run for the mountains, zigzagging to avoid the continuing fire. After that, it was the same story as Paulo's: mountain scaling, successive bouts of exhaustion, an involuntary detour into Austria, doubling back, a farm inhabited by people as sympathetic as Tina and her family, and finally finding the partisans.

Paulo tore himself away from his memories to read the notice about Ménard properly. The last line gave the address of the person to contact: Mme. Ménard, rue Alfred-de-Musset, Rennes. No need to take the notice down, he would remember. But how could he tell a man's mother what had happened in a letter? Especially the end. He'd have to lie, make something up. He couldn't possibly tell her that her son had died barefoot and exhausted, still wearing his convict's uniform, four months after his escape. Still less that the partisans, forced to retreat, had had to abandon Dédé because he was so weak.

Paulo, who had been the last Frenchman to see him alive, didn't even know whether he had been killed in the course of a rearguard action or shot by the SS because he was wearing Mauthausen's striped pajamas. The only thing he did know for certain was that in the Delnice region of Croatia there was a common grave beneath a monument to the glory of the unknown maquisards.

But did he have to pass on news like that? It must have been the same story for all the faces in the photographs pinned to every wall of the hall. Nine out of ten would be dead, anyone who knew how efficiently the ovens worked would know that. It wasn't even worth his looking to see if he recognized any other faces. Moreover, he had no idea how Loibl had finished. Perhaps his fellows were all dead, gunned down in the camp, walled up in the tunnel, or sent back to Mauthausen to roast. The only story he had to tell the officer whom the hostess had gone to fetch had little to do with deportation. It concerned a savage, pitiless war, a war with no prisoners taken, with the wounded either abandoned or finished off. One Yugoslav in eight had died since 1941, shot, hanged or exterminated in the camps, and yet they had needed no one to liberate them, in spite of an army of 450,000 Germans, Italians and Oustachis out for their blood—more than all the Axis troops deployed to hold back the Allied advance into Italy! Should the officer want to hear about a real war, he'd have his money's worth. On that subject, Paulo was inexhaustible. His own campaign alone would be enough to make the ex-FFI jealous. He had had another long march, seven months on the mountain peaks, running, attacking, killing... He had done it all, the Russian battalion... the Political Kommissar of a company of SS who had deserted from Alsace-Lorraine with all their weapons and baggage. It was a miracle that he had come home with his arms and legs intact.

Not all the escapees from Loibl had had the same luck. Among those he had met up with in Tito's army, as his unit moved around, there were three, apart from Dédé, who would never come back. Two were the Russian officers from the first escape and the other was brave Hegoburu, who fell only a few feet from him during the last great offensive launched by an SS division, which had wiped out everything in its path in order to get back into Austria. The only consolation for Hego, the Pyrenean smuggler, was that he died and was buried where he felt at home, in the mountains.

At the Hotel Lutétia, the deportees seemed to be regarded as heroes, both those who had come back and the others. So how would the likes of Hegoburu and Ménard have been received! And what about Paulo, didn't he have some small claim to glory? It wasn't his fault that he was still alive, or that no one had sent his photograph to the Lutétia! Granted, he had come back with a full head of hair, which posed something of a problem, and he would have to explain himself... But that hostess must think him a complete good-for-nothing to keep him hanging around for so long.

She must have guessed his impatience, for just as he was about to go and look for her, she turned up with a young captain in combat uniform.

"This young man," she said, indicating Paulo, "claims to have escaped from a Mauthausen Kommando."

"What do you mean, 'claims'?"

"Calm yourself, young man," the captain intervened. "Take a seat, and give me your full name, address and date and place of birth. Afterward, you can tell me your story."

He had no choice but do as he was told, and the officer made notes, but only about Paulo's personal details, not about his story, to which he seemed supremely indifferent. For form's sake, he did at least ask Paulo the date of his arrest and his departure from Compiègne. Then he left with his notes, saying: "Madame de Dunant will deal with the rest of the formalities for you."

You didn't have to be a genius to work out that he was going to hotfoot it down to the copshop for a spot of research before he carried on with the interview.

"I should have had a haircut before I came here," thought Paulo. "Or not come at all."

He was just looking around to see how he might slip out unnoticed when the Dunant woman, who had her official smile back on, caught him by the arm.

"I'm going to take you for some light refreshments," she said. "Afterward, I'll show you to the bathrooms."

Refreshments! She couldn't even call it a bite to eat, or

just breakfast, the toffee-nosed old bat! But she had unwittingly found the right formula to stop her client from leaving. Paulo was famished, he had been for two and a half years and his hunger took precedence over all other considerations. The old trout's refreshments weren't bad at all, and Paulo soon felt less morose.

There was a good atmosphere in the showers as well. Out on the pavement earlier, the shaven heads had turned away from Paulo because of his hair, but now they all vied with each other to talk to him.

"Hey, civilian, at least you can have a shampoo, you lucky bastard!"

General laughter.

It was time to set things straight:

"I was probably shaved a long time before you lot were, see. For eighteen months I was shaved with a big fucking part in the middle. Didn't any of you get the *Autobahn*?"

Now that they did find interesting. As Paulo was drying himself they listened to him sketching his story, and none of them felt like ribbing him anymore. His explanation was too detailed for it to be completely unfounded. But it was only a little later, as they were being disinfected, that the still skeptical recognized him as one of them. As they came out of the shower room, a cardboard hand pointed them toward a room where two medical orderlies in white jackets and trousers, each armed with a spray, squirted DDT at any visible hairs.

"Raise your arms, turn around, part your buttocks"—the same bloody rigmarole as Mauthausen! Paris was obsessed by crabs too.

It was too much for Paulo.

"Listen, soldier boys, we haven't got the plague! I suppose you learned all this rubbish from the SS, did you?"

His protest made its mark. The others in the room began to mutter: "He's right, what kind of a welcome is this? We're old enough to take care of our own crabs!"

The poor orderlies were paying dearly for their senior doctor's lack of tact. But this time, Paulo had definitely convinced the others; he was a deportee, no doubt about it.

"I wasn't at Mauthausen myself," a tall, bony Parisian said to him. "But I traveled back from Switzerland with a couple of guys who were. They spent the whole day telling me about the camp you escaped from. What can I tell you?"

"The whole story."

Paulo thought he had heard it all as far as extraordinary adventures were concerned, but he had to admit the story the other man was relating about how Mauthausen had finished went way beyond anything he could have imagined. A secret committee had been formed, just like at Loibl: there were eight hundred prisoners organized into military units and nationalities under its orders. The Russians were the most numerous, then there were French, Belgians, Spaniards, Poles, Yugoslavs, Czechs and even a group of Germans and Austrians. The commanders of this cosmopolitan army were a Spanish major, a Russian lieutenant colonel, an Austrian captain and about fifty other officers from twenty different countries. The alliance was sacred.

The insurrection had been worked out by these professionals in the minutest detail, and when the chosen eight hundred stepped out of the shadows, at least a quarter of them had revolvers, grenades and even a submachine gun. How had they gotten hold of them, and how had they been able to hide them in a place where no one had ever possessed anything, not even his own soup bowl? It was a mystery. But these weapons, together with a few Molotov cocktails, wire cutters to cut the electrified fence, rope, ladders and all the fire extinguishers in the camp, had enabled them to attack first the watchtowers and then the SS armory. When the first Americans entered the fortress the following day, the thirty-five hundred convicts who could still stand had welcomed them with weapons in their hands, singing the "Marseillaise" in every tongue. Of course, before that there had been a massacre, informers, Kapos, block chiefs, and any SS who had not managed to get away, had all been dealt with, beaten, strangled and even kicked to death. The murderers' commanding officer, Ziereis, had escaped the lynching. An American sergeant had taken it upon himself to execute him without trial, by a bullet in the back of the neck.

In spite of his eagerness to hear the rest of the story, Paulo couldn't help interrupting "The fucker! He should have torn his eyes out!"

"That's what the two fellows on the train with me thought, too," the Parisian went on. "They told me that only a week before, this Ziereis character had had all the women in one convoy decapitated with axes, and burned all the prisoners who'd been working in the crematorium, guys who'd been working there for years, so that they wouldn't talk. Apparently, they'd gotten up to the two-hundred-thousand mark."

"Listen, comrade," Paulo interrupted again, "did your two guys mention a Kommando at Loibl Pass? D'you know whether the SS shipped them back to Mauthausen?"

"That name doesn't mean anything to me, I'm afraid, but they didn't really go into details. Mostly they talked about the liberation of the camp—"

"Yes, sure! I'm sorry, go on. How did it all end?"

"Very well. When there wasn't a single live Kraut left in the camp, the able-bodied men formed into a division, armed almost by the book with the weapons they captured—fifteen heavy machine guns, twelve Bren guns, thirty bazookas, three thousand rifles and as many grenades. Instead of waiting patiently in the camp for the Swiss Red Cross trucks to arrive, they went out to meet up with the Allied troops, wiping out anything that looked like an SS on the way."

Unbelievable! Paulo felt a shiver of emotion and pride, tinged with regret. How he would have loved to be part of that beggars' army who had had the profound satisfaction of being able to settle their accounts on the spot! Only a man who had been through it could fully understand the meaning of this impossible insurrection, this rebellion of mere skeletons. The army of revenge Paulo had dreamed about when he arrived at Loibl had become a reality at Mauthausen, inside the gates of hell itself. To have missed that! He almost regretted having left . . .

Paulo was going too far. He was forgetting that he hadn't done badly in the way of great moments and heroism himself. His escape and his seven months in Tito's army were no mean achievement. In the Mauthausen epic, too, he had had a part, if only by bearing the number 28,214, one of the early registrations. Come on, Paulo, even if you weren't there for the rebellion, you still have a right to respect, you can hold your head up proudly—even if it is curly!

"Chastagnier!"

The person who had just called out his name obviously didn't go in for hero worship. There was a touch of the martinet about the man's voice, not to say ill temper. And yet this lout was only a private. Not one stripe, not a single gong. He had certainly bitten off more than he could chew with Paulo, whose morale was sky-high after what he had just heard.

Luck was with the little upstart because Madame de Dunant was close by. She had her orders, and there was no question of anyone else kidnapping her curly-haired deportee. She was to take him for a medical after he had showered. The suspicious captain had insisted on it, hoping no doubt that the doctor would be able to prove whether this suspect character had been in a camp or not.

The consulting room was a classic hotel bedroom, fitted out like a proper surgery with all the necessary bits and pieces: pulmometer, scales, height measure, piss-specimen bottles, Red Cross cabinet crammed with medicines, an X-ray machine and a stretcher on wheels. Enough equipment to screen beings from another planet.

"Take your clothes off, young man. Everything," said the doctor.

While his guardian angel's back was turned—she was busy whispering something in the doctor's ear—Paulo was able to begin undressing. Anyway, the Dunant woman wouldn't be shocked at seeing his cock if she was no more prudish than the other women medics he had met since crossing the border. Indeed, the emancipation was the first change that had struck him. When he got to Constance, in the French zone, he had found himself naked and alone in front of a superb blonde with three stripes and a stethoscope balanced on her pear-shaped tits. She was a captain in the Medical Corps, and did her job like a proper M.O.: she squeezed his prick to see if she couldn't coax a little drop . . . militarily speaking. Paulo was aghast at this reception; even when he'd joined Tito's army, he had kept his fly firmly buttoned up. And although he had never ceased, for all that time, dreaming of girls and imagining how he was going to sow his more than two years' stock of seed in them the minute he got back, this doctor's audacity had made him blush like a schoolboy. The minister in charge of repatriation couldn't have had a very subtle mind not to foresee that making prisoners and deportees, deprived of love for years, parade naked in front of women might damage them psychologically, or even finish them off entirely. Constance was no exception; it had been the same everywhere else, from what Paulo had gathered in the showers.

Granny Dunant, on the other hand, could stay for the strip-tease. She was easily on the wrong side of fifty, and in no danger of Paulo pouncing on her. Yet she must have felt apprehensive for, modestly, she withdrew.

The Lutétia's doctor was of the old school. He preferred asking questions to touching his patients.

"How much did you weight before? How old are you? Any previous illnesses? Why were you arrested?"

He too was interested in that. Surprisingly, he didn't make Paulo raise his arm to see if he had the tattoo mark of an enlisted SS as the orderlies had done earlier on the way into the showers. Naturally, the young fanatics who had followed Doriot and his associates were not all dead, and some of them must have had the idea of shaving their heads in orders to slip out of the former Great Reich incognito. But for genuine deportees, this kind of inspection was hard to stomach, just as hard as having their balls sprinkled with crab powder.

But the doctor was only after general information before going on to the full medical: blood pressure, weight, lung capacity, the state of his mouth, and so on.

"It doesn't look as if you've eaten very well since leaving the camp."

"Hardly more than I did when I was there," Paulo agreed.

"I can see that. Now go in there," the doctor continued, pointing to the X-ray booth. "I'm going to take a few photos."

Back, front, profile. By the tenth X ray, Paulo was becoming uneasy. Perhaps the tunnel had left some scars on his lungs? Or maybe it was the thousands of times he'd been caught out in the rain at Loibl and in the maquis, never able to take shelter or dry himself off.

"If there something wrong, doctor?" he asked.

"Your lungs are in splendid condition. I can tell you've been in the mountains, and you can't have smoked very much. On the other hand, your heart isn't so good. It's abnormally large like your ankles, and the two go together. You're going to have to take things easy. What line of work are you in?"

"Work can wait. I did enough in Yugoslovia to last me a lifetime. But look, doctor, I'm not dying, am I?"

"No, my boy, of course not. The main thing is to avoid any strain. You've overdone it, and there are various deficiencies. Cheer up, it's not too serious. You can get dressed. There are a few other formalities, but in the meantime we'll give you a room so you don't have to wait in the hall."

Old Madame Dunant must have been peering through the keyhole. Paulo had scarcely slipped on his demob partisan's uniform before she poked her refined features around the door. Even more obliging than before, she ushered her favorite repatriate upstairs.

"Here we are," she said, showing him in to one of the bedrooms. "I shall be back to fetch you in about an hour. If I were you, I would lie down and have a little snooze." And before he could reply, she had turned the key twice, from the outside. Paulo was just too slow in working out what she had done and his good hostess had gone by the time he realized he had been locked in.

"The bitch! The double-crossing bitch!" he yelled, pounding his fists against the door. There was no latch on the inside of the window either, the two-faced cow had gone and locked him in a cell, not a bedroom at all. But since there was a bed, he stretched out on it. If the doctor had been right about his heart, he'd better avoid sending his blood pressure up.

"I'm getting worked up for nothing," he decided when he was calm again. "They'll soon find out I'm not on their list of collaborators. So I was picked up? So what? It was a Nazi dealer I knocked over, he won't have boasted about it, and he definitely won't have filed a report—anyway, after what I've done, they can all go and get stuffed. They ought to be congratulating me, giving me the Légion d'Honneur, or at least the Croix de Guerre. Still, they're being damned unfriendly just because I've come back with some hair on my head. There'll be plenty of other hairy escapees turning up, and if they're Resistance they'll be really impressed with the trusting atmosphere in this coop."

They would already be surprised enough to find out that the whole of France was behind de Gaulle, so if they were going to be grilled about their deportation as well, there was bound to be trouble. Quite apart from the fact that some of them might well have been tortured right here at the Hotel Lutétia, maybe in this very room. Jesus, how ironic! Paulo didn't even feel angry anymore, he just felt sickened by it all.

"Oh well, what the hell do I care anyway," he shrugged, and he fell asleep.

The hour Madame de Dunant had mentioned turned into four; by the time she reappeared, it was past midday. So the captain had taken four hours to get his research done! Which proved he hadn't been very convinced by Paulo's story of escape, and that he'd be starting up his catch questions again.

"You just try me, we'll have some fun," muttered Paulo, jumping out of bed.

His four hours' sleep had done him the world of good. He was chuckling to himself as he thought about what he would say to the officer cop if he persisted with his suspicions. Look at all the witnesses there would be, for in the hotel dining room his hostess had led him to, there were a dozen shaven heads and the same number of soldiers interrogating them. Above each table placards were pinned up on the wall indicating, as in the entrance hall, the names of the camps; and on each table there were printed cards and blank sheets of paper laid out for the men being questioned to fill in, if they wouldn't mind.

"Trusting atmosphere, isn't it?" said Paulo, loud enough for the soldier sitting beneath the Mauthausen sign to hear. He had just motioned him to sit down at the table.

It wasn't the captain he had given his details to a few hours before, but some vague kind of officer with just one pip who looked even more unfriendly. You could tell he was the law a mile off. Hs had a snout like a weasel, and gimlet eyes.

Paulo's remark had made him frown, but like a typical movie cop, instead of getting annoyed, he put on his most professional voice.

"You must understand, Monsieur Chastagnier, that traitors might infiltrate."

At least he didn't beat around the bush, he didn't give a damn about upsetting anybody. Paulo saw he'd have to tackle him head on.

"Look here, Inspector—"

"There's no inspector. It's the army here."

In spite of his training, he had reacted. Paulo felt he

had just scored the first point and he gave a faint smile.

"Sorry, Lieutenant, a slip of the tongue, but your reception room looks a bit like the Quai des Orfèvres* with all these tables and typewriters."

"Ah, so you know the Quai des Orfèvres?" he asked, walking into the trap.

"Yeah, seen it loads of times in films. But it looks even more realistic here with all these convicts—"

"All right, let's leave that, shall we?" replied the lieutenant with a nasty look in his eye. "I want to know your story from the beginning, your arrest, why you were arrested, what happened in Germany, and how you got back. And I want the exact dates."

So it was a full-scale interrogation! Monsieur the officer wasn't being at all friendly. His native meanness had come to the surface, and he was calling him *tu*. It was a fucking liberty.

"Since we're on friendly terms," Paulo snapped, "you listen to me. Do you really think I'd have come here on my own if I'd been shacking up with the Krauts? And if I'd wanted to make out I was a deportee, what was stopping me from shaving my head? I suppose that didn't occur to you, did it? You're not going to catch me out, so don't waste your time trying. If there's a single guy in this room who's clean, it's me—"

"B-but . . ." the lieutenant stammered, suddenly softening and addressing him formally again, "I'm not trying to catch you out, Chastagnier. On the contrary, I'm here to help you. Repatriates are entitled to a number of benefits: discharge gratuities, special ration cards, clothes coupons . . . I just need certain information to put on file."

What he said made sense. Paulo relaxed. Besides, he'd need the cash, and the grub tickets, since they still seemed to be around.

"Okay, I'll give you my story," he said. "Arrested by the Gestapo in January nineteen forty-three. Cherche-Midi jail boulevard Raspail, right opposite. Three months. Left for Mauthausen in April, via Compiègne. In June, sent to Loibl Pass, Kommando on the Austro-Yugoslav frontier. Escaped in October nineteen forty-four, seven months in the maquis with

---

*Headquarters of the Paris police.

Tito's men. Is that enough for you? I'm sorry, but no one gave me a residence permit anywhere along the line."

This flood of information was to the cop's liking. Now he could ask him some nasty questions.

"Arrested in January nineteen forty-three? Which day?"

"The third, at dawn."

"Did you have a registration number at Mauthausen?"

"Two eight two one four, but I threw it away with my uniform."

The number was all the cop wanted. He glanced at his notebook to check that it corresponded to the date of his arrival, then he went on, "April, yes, that fits, but which block were you assigned to?"

"Block Seventeen, one of the four quarantine blocks."

"Very good. Can you draw me a sketch of the camp? Use this piece of paper, I want the position of your block in relation to the others, to the kitchens, to the infirmary—"

"I suppose you want to know where the crematorium was, too, do you?" Paulo burst out. This flyfucker was beginning to get on his nerves. But as he glanced around the room, he saw that the shaven heads at the other tables were sketching away with good grace, like schoolboys on exam day. The sight calmed him, and he too set about his little sketch: Mauthausen, the *Revier*, the *Appelplatz*, the quarry, the electrified barbed wire, the *Krematorium*—he wasn't likely to forget them! Every night for two years he had dreamed of them. His plan of the camp turned out rather well.

"That's a pretty good likeness," the lieutenant nodded, as if he'd been there, the insolent bastard!

"Let's go back to your arrest," he went on. "What did the German police accuse you of?"

He consulted his notebook again, but Paulo, who knew how to use his eyes, like all deportees, could read upside down. There was nothing on the page about him, except for a few peccadillos before 1940. The Krauts must have burned the Chastagnier file before they left, or maybe they had never even made one. The accusation, as the cop had called it, was the black market, and practically the whole population had had a finger in the pie at some time or other. Oh, no, they weren't going to get him on that.

"Why was I arrested?" he repeated. "I'm still asking

myself the same question, but maybe you can help me. Isn't there anything in your notebook?"

"You must know whether you were involved in the Resistance—"

"And how! I did two and a half years of it, more than anyone else here. If you want me to tell you about it, I could go on all night."

The officer didn't want to be told. What he was interested in, now that he was more or less certain his client had been at Mauthausen, was the reason for his arrest. The sketch, the registration number, and the dates could not have been made up. But Paulo's self-assurance irritated him. If this tough thought he could start playing the hero, he had another think coming.

"Since you were at Mauthausen, you must have noticed that there were other men there besides Resistance. Criminals, collaborators and men who were just rounded up were sent there too. Which of these three categories would you put yourself in?"

By ruling out the Resistance so blatantly, the weasel had overstepped the mark. Sabotage, escape, the maquis, didn't that qualify as Resistance? Paulo felt like grabbing him by the lapels and hauling him across the table.

"Why don't you fuck off?" he shouted instead. The heads of the other twelve convicts jerked around simultaneously.

His outburst was partly because of them, and all they represented. How could such humiliation be inflicted on them the very day they got back? To suspect Paulo because of his hair and his relatively healthy appearance was just understandable, but forcing survivors of the death houses to sketch plans of their camps, to answer hypocritical questions designed solely to trip them up, was shameful, disgusting—there was no word for it. Even if there were a few collaborators mixed up in the crowd, what the hell did it matter? Couldn't they have waited until the prisoners had seen their families, and kissed their wives, their kids and their mothers, before starting their snide little investigations?

It made him furious to think that a true hero like Joel, if he made it back, would also have to lift his arm to show he didn't bear the SS brand, have his balls dabbed with crab powder, and draw all the camps and prisons he'd been through. Dédé Ménard, Etcheverry, and many more would have had to endure the same outrage if they hadn't died. It was intolerable and Paulo's "Fuck off!" was the only proper reply to make.

What it all boiled down to was that doddering old Pétain had been right when he said the French had short memories. Less than nine months after the liberation of their country, they had already forgotten that these ghosts who were trickling back were the ones who had paved the way for the new France, which they, at no danger to themselves, had brought to power in 1944, when the Krauts were packing their bags. These pioneer Resistance members should have been asked to parade beneath the Arc de Triomphe instead of being received on the quiet, as if they were tainted with some dirty disease, and interrogated like criminals. They were the ones who should have been asking the questions of all the profiteers who had snatched control of the ministries, the army, the brothels, and everywhere else. They had already sliced up the French cake between themselves, a full year ago, and these poor wretches who were now stumbling back, worn out and half dead, were hardly in a state to challenge their spoils. So why were they treating them like this?

Perhaps it was all intentional, organized even. Thinking about it, the returning ghosts were a source of embarrassment: they had been presumed dead two, three and even four years ago for some. Most of them had been denounced to the Krauts and in many cases they knew who had done it, and they might have recognized a few of the men who had turned them in among the officers in the Lutétia. Naturally, there were fewer of them now—only one in ten had survived—but before their friends had died back in the camps, they could have passed on the names of a few traitors as a legacy.

If they were too well treated, they would get ideas above their station, they would want to reopen the books and settle the accounts they found. Think of the god-awful mess there would be if the Resistance were allowed to blab, if the men weren't brow-beaten as soon as they got back. With what France was beginning to find out about the camps, it was easy. The prisoners were all coming back half mad and riddled with complexes. You men with the shaven heads, to heel! Look at me! Draw! Raise you arms! And it was precisely because it was working that Paulo's "Fuck off!" had had such an impact.

He wasn't likely to denounce a fake Resistance member and neither did he have any illusions about picking up a few crumbs of the cake, but as so often at Loibl, now he felt compelled to tell the bastards what he thought of them. And this jerk who had dared ask him whether he'd been a crook, a collaborator or rounded up was one of the worst of his kind. He would coldly have asked the same question of Joel, and Paulo could imagine the Breton paling at the insult. The thought made him even angrier, but against all his expectation, the lieutenant seemed to want to let it go.

"Look, Chastagnier, there's no need to be rude. I know you're tired, but there are limits," was all he said.

"In the camps, that's how we talked, friend. You'd better get used to it if you want to deal with us."

The lieutenant from Military Security was no fool. He could see he wasn't going to get anything more out of his "suspect" except a public scandal, for Paulo's outburst had woken up the other deportees, who were beginning to protest loudly: "How much longer are you going to keep us? . . . We're not strays off the street . . . ," and so on.

"All right, that'll do," said the lieutenant. "I'll make out an attestation for you to get your repatriate's card and food coupons."

Paulo watched him write with ill-concealed satisfaction. It was written all over the officer-cop's face that he was annoyed at not being able to send yet another man to Fresnes . . .

"Do you still live in the Eighteenth Arrondissement?" he asked suddenly.

"In theory, if my landlord hasn't locked me out."

As he replied, Paulo guessed what the muckraking cop was up to. Before you could say knife, he'd be on the blower to his colleagues in the Eighteenth so that they could follow it up. Maybe over in Montmartre they'd know why this Chastagnier had been picked up.

The ploy was so unsubtle that Paulo almost yelled at him again, "Fuck you, you and your copper friends." The only reason he restrained himself was that everything he had seen since that morning, since the moment he had set foot in

France in fact, made him feel more sick than angry. Nothing had changed in the dungheap of a society. Everyone was pigeonholed as he had been before 1943. Cops were still cops, the rich were still rich, the old cunts were older cunts and were more stupid, and the deportees coming home so late were more of a pain in the ass than anything else. France had managed very well without them for the last nine months.

He had been bitterly disappointed to see the deportees so docile in front of the so-called soldiers, who should have stood at attention before talking to them. Now his one desire was to get out of this depressing company as quickly as possible. During his seven months with Tito, he had managed to forget the camp and now, just because he had wanted to get properly demobed he'd gone straight back into it, up to his neck. And to top it all, he was being insulted.

"Paulo, you were a deportee, weren't you?"

"Me? You must be fucking mad."

That was the reply he vowed he would make to any ghoulish voyeur who tried to get him to talk about the camps. At a pinch, he might consent to talk about the war he had fought with Tito, although he had always thought old soldiers were suckers who were only good at getting shot up so that the top brass could go on lining their pockets. He had been just as big a sucker as they had in the end; his heroic adventure hadn't earned him so much as a thank-you. He had come home sick, without a penny to his name, without a clean shirt or suit, with no means of existence, and maybe without a roof over his head—unless someone had been kind enough to pay his rent these last three years. Obviously, the government would end up doing something for the recognized Resistance men, once they had been vetted. They'd be decorated, given pensions and back pay, and they'd be provided with apartments. But for him—nothing, he wouldn't get anything, he had no right to anything. Yet, in the bitterest of trials, in the camp, not all had conducted themselves as well as he had. Far from it. He could not be reproached with a single dirty trick or base action, and moreover nothing had forced him to risk his neck by escaping, nor to fight once he was free. Out of all the men who were coming home, he was certainly one of the best, one of the most deserving. Alas, apparently good conduct in prison didn't rank as serving your country, and neither did fighting in a people's war.

"Well, they can all go and get stuffed, fuck them all, deportees included," he thought to himself, pocketing his attestation.

But his rage had subsided. It was even beginning to amuse him to find himself back to square one again.

Paulo had always enjoyed gambling, with his life as well. At Mauthausen, at Loibl and with the partisans, he had continued to play high stakes, it was right up his alley, and all things considered, he had won, because each time he had got out of trouble, and now he had come back alive.

Of course, it had been ten to one against, but for a man who likes betting and the smell of danger, ten to one is good odds. Winning under such conditions gives you an incomparable thrill.

Thrills and good times to the end of his days was how he saw his future, now that he'd realized there was no place for him in the France of the Resistance. Yet he had come to the Lutétia with good intentions—and a few illusions, too; he thought he had redeemed himself after all he had endured in the camps and with Tito. He had had some vague hopes that he would be congratulated and fêted as a brave fighter. Balls! At the Lutétia, fighting in any army other than the French Army didn't count, and he could consider himself lucky not to be slung back into jail.

Crossing the hall, he couldn't help saying out loud, "Deportation, Resistance, the army, I've seen enough of you. I'm finished with you. Forever!"

If he had said everything he thought, he would have added, "I've seen enough of all you men, too." He'd had more than his fill of the male sex over the last three years, thousands and thousands of men, physically and morally stripped naked, and none of it was very attractive. What he needed now was to be with girls, so that he could talk about something else! Love suited him so much better than war! And, from what he had seen since crossing the frontier, it suited the liberated Frenchwomen too. He had picked up any girl he had wanted, and he'd only had to snap his fingers for them to come running. All these girls were far prettier than what he had left—better fed, better togged up, better in bed.

What a fool he had been to come and get demobed! Demobed from what, anyway, since he had never enlisted?

"What a waste of a day," he said, and he meant it. At this point, he would have shot out through the revolving door but for Granny Dunant collaring him and dragging him into what was supposedly a records office. This was where you were issued with all the paraphernalia which allowed you to become a civilian again: temporary identity card, ration card, and there was a dressing room full of suits and shoes to choose from.

"Might as well," he shrugged, and he fell into line. But when he saw how ridiculous the men coming out of the dressing room looked, he almost turned tail and ran. Where on earth had the military authorities requisitioned these peasants' outfits? Skimpily cut and in impossible colors, the material was hardly any better than the Mauthausen pajamas.

"Got anything in stripes?" he joked to an AFAT who had gone to fetch him a jacket in his size.

The shaven heads who were waiting their turn roared with laughter, and Paulo took advantage of it to skip a few places in the line. The important thing was to get hold of an identity card quickly so that no one could give him any bother when he found himself out on the Paris streets in a little while. This business was the last straw, he was completely pissed off with the whole damn circus. Shit, he was a free man, wasn't he? He'd even freed himself, seven months ago. So what the hell was his comedy all about?

"You are entitled to the rations of a forced laborer," said the records office chief, a staff sergeant of the female variety, handing him his ration card.

"What a coincidence, I was one!" retorted Paulo. Suddenly he saw himself back in the tunnel holding his pneumatic drill. Work was another thing they'd better not talk to him about once he was out of the Lutétia.

"What do I put down as your profession?" the staff sergeant asked him.

"None, or . . . retired."

Pleased with his own wit, he went and sat down, hoping that the piece of card which would make him a legitimate citizen again would soon be back signed and rubber-stamped. Ten minutes later, he had his precious document, smudged with his fingerprints for lack of a photo. About fucking time too! Life could finally start again, he could turn his back on the lot of them.

"Goodbye, one and all," he said, and brushing aside the AFAT who had just been to dig him out a pair of wooden-soled clodhoppers which were even more unwearable than the suit, he headed toward the hall.

A day train must have just unloaded a new shipment, for there were as many shaven heads outside the revolving door as there had been that morning. Added to those who were getting ready to leave after passing all their tests brilliantly, they made quite a crowd. Laughter, backslapping and general babble—it wasn't going to be easy to get through this forest of heads without joining in the hugging and kissing. But Paulo wasn't having any of that now; he was saving himself for the girls.

"Christ, I'm not going to wade into that sea," he said to himself. But all the same, he had absolutely no desire to spend even five minutes longer in this five-turd hotel.

He skirted around to the left where the crowd was slightly thinner; using his elbows, and looking as nonchalant as he knew how, he managed to push his way into the crowd. There wouldn't have been any problem if he had been shaved like the others—pushing and shoving had become second nature to the deportees. But his hair provoked them.

"Hey, you, civilian! Don't mind us, just walk all over us," growled a terribly emaciated man still wearing his striped jacket.

"Excuse me, boys, someone's waiting for me outside."

"Oh, feel free, make yourself at home, walk all over us," the man went on. By now he was shouting, and all the shaven heads paused in their exuberance to get a look at this heathen who dared to lack respect for deportees. A torrent of insults started up: "Fucking bum . . . you civilian bastard . . . no more Kapos now, you know . . ." But in the confusion Paulo had managed to get nearer the door. One, harder, shove and he found himself ejected onto the pavement, rather faster than he had expected.

Unfortunately, the new arrivals outside were more than ready to take over the argument. Instead of going on his way, Paulo tried to calm them down.

"Give me a break, fellows. I was deported too, you know."

"Deported—like fuck you were!" shouted one tall skeleton.

Obviously it was Paulo's hair that was upsetting them, but he had had enough of trying to explain. He had already turned his back on them when someone right in the middle of the group hurled the final insult.

"Poofs' Paradise is where you were deported to!"

That was too much. Clenching his fists, the ex-prisoner 28,214 retraced his steps, determined to flatten whoever had dared insult him.

"Who said that? Let him repeat it, and he'll see whether I'm queer," he said, putting up his fists.

The deportees couldn't have noticed the murderous glint in his eyes, because the jeering got louder and louder: "Poofs' Paradise . . . Who's a queer? . . ." He'd have to beat them all up, like a Kapo.

The thought stopped Paulo cold, and suddenly he saw the jeering men in their true light: they were just poor bastards who, a week earlier, still didn't know whether they would get out of the camp through the gates or via the chimneys. His rage subsided, and instead of hitting out, he turned around and walked away forcing himself to ignore the laughter which accompanied his retreat.

He had lived through some terrible days, at Mauthausen and at Loibl, but this day had beaten all the others for sheer humiliation. Sickened forever by this universe of which he had never really been a part, he crossed the boulevard and made for the Métro station, eager to be among civilized people again.

Still he was deluding himself, believing that all he needed was willpower to forget the hell he had been through. Sèvres-Babylone—the name of the Métro station—was enough to bring it flooding back: it was Joel and Dédé who suddenly came to life again at Sèvres-Babylone. "The two of us have got a secret, we'll tell you about it one day," they had said to him during the first days at Loibl.

Little by little, their story had come out. It was in front of the Sèvres-Babylone Métro station on the boulevard Raspail, one evening in May 1942, that Joel, with his hands tied, had jumped from the Mercedes which was bringing them back to Fresnes, after a day's interrogation. Because it was late, the car was going faster than he'd anticipated. He fell badly, and was hurt. The Krauts had piled out and caught him, and while they whipped him with their gun butts, Dédé had stayed sitting quietly in the back of the car for three minutes.

It had happened exactly three years ago. Poor Dédé! How many times must he have regretted his slow reflexes! But perhaps the only reason he hadn't seized the unexpected opportunity to escape was so that he could stop the Germans from murdering his friend there and then. They were like wild animals. One of them had even thrust the barrel of his Lüger into Joel's mouth, and perhaps he would have pressed the trigger if Dédé hadn't spoken to him in German and made him realize that his superiors would not forgive the execution of a terrorist who could still talk. It was thanks to his initiative that Joel had arrived at Fresnes alive, but Dédé's reasoning turned out to be false: in spite of everything, torture included, Joel still didn't talk.

That was the two boys' secret, and in the end, given what both of them had done later, it was probably better for France's sake that their attempted escape on the boulevard Raspail had failed.

Paulo was unable to tear his eyes away from the pavement which Joel had stained with his blood. He pictured the scene exactly as his two friends had described it: the two Krauts battering Joel with the butts of their guns, stopping only to point them at a French cop on duty at the Lutétia-*Kommandantur* who had come over, eager to give them a hand.

"*Raus*, we don't need you," they had screamed at him.

"Wouldn't it be funny," thought Paulo, "if that cop were one of the ones assigned to process the deportees."

Why not? After all, the local police station must still be supplying men for the Lutétia. Duty and service! Nevertheless, if that same policeman saw Joel turn up one of these mornings among a group of shaven heads, he might just feel ashamed of himself. He might even blush redder than his heroic shoulder braid.

"There's still a whole world between men like Joel and Dédé Ménard, and the pen-pushing soldiers in the Lutétia and the cops who were cops under the Germans too," Paulo reflected, watching the traffic stream by.

He didn't even count himself part of it anymore. He had drawn a thick black line through his war. But for the two Bretons, for their memory, he felt sick at heart. Who would listen to him telling their story, when no one even wanted to hear his own?

"Joel will come home, he'll talk," he tried to persuade himself, as he went back to the Métro entrance.

It had to be hoped, otherwise France would never know that one of its first, one of its greatest, Resistance fighters was a student from Rennes called André Ménard, who had been arrested because he had wanted to complete a radio message announcing the destruction of his network, and had died in combat three years later, still wearing the red triangle of Mauthausen over his heart.

"Come on, I've got to forget all that. Time to start thinking about number one," said Paulo, tearing himself away from his memories.

Nothing brings you down to earth more quickly than realizing you haven't got any cash on you. The good souls at the Lutétia hadn't even given him a Métro ticket! He was broke, stone fucking broke.

"The repatriate's card, will that do?" he asked the ticket man on the off chance.

"Yes, where are you going?"

"Montmartre."

"Take the corridor for the porte de la Chapelle, and get off at Pigalle. It's direct."

Pigalle? Wasn't that Poofs' Paradise, too?

Perhaps Sailor had already started work.

Epilogue

Paulo's story ends at the Sèvres-Babylone Métro station in May 1945. If the author, himself a veteran of Loibl Pass, had to give one reason for recounting it thirty-three years later, it would be that despite the passing of time and the perspective it has made possible, nothing has ever been said about one particular form of deportation—the "active" deportation practiced by some of the camps which were annexed to the great death factories like Mauthausen and Auschwitz.

In general, the citations of captured Resistance members

end at the gates of the camps; nine times out of ten, the words "deported to X" serve as their epitaph, testimony to an honorable death in action. Even for the handful of survivors, there is nothing to add to their service records after the word "deportee," nothing except the darkness and shrouds of mist which Himmler, the inventor of the system, intended there should be. And the survivors' stories are all alike, set against a backcloth of starvation, the *Revier*—death's threshold, the gas chamber and the crematorium.

For the men of Loibl Pass, as we know, activity did not come to an end with their registration in the camp, but the measure of their achievement is better assessed when one remembers that at Mauthausen, from where they were snatched in June 1943, the average life expectancy was four and a half months, and that 225,000 of their comrades, out of a total of 250,000, were to end up in the crematorium. The fact that Kommando X did not go back to Mauthausen, although the SS who went with them did everything to bring it about, is perhaps their greatest achievement of all, and in itself justifies the writing of *The Tunnel at Loibl Pass*, even thirty-three years later.

Every event, every scene, is rigorously authentic. Only the names of the heroes have been changed, out of respect for the families of those who were lost. With one exception: that of André Ménard, to whose memory this book is dedicated.

The other actors may want to recognize themselves, they may not, but one point on which they will all agree is that none of the savagery, none of the degradation, none of the heroism has been exaggerated—nor even the language, closer to prison slang than that common among POWs. Nonetheless, in order to be completely true to history, it is essential to tell how Loibl Pass ended, and that is why this epilogue has been written. What has already been said makes that end easy to guess: Loibl liberated itself. There was an insurrection, though not the bloodbath Joel had hoped for and Paulo had feared. It was a victory of intelligence, of well-chosen words, much the same as all the previous victories over their SS overseers.

In the early afternoon of May 5, 1945, Knock-Knees almost had a fit when he saw a delegation of *Haeftlinge* come to ask for a meeting. He immediately summoned the doyen, the block chiefs and the Kapos to restore order, but it had been obvious, ever since the German stampede had begun on Route 333, that these gentlemen had been asking themselves some serious questions. Faced with their reluctance to quell the revolt, he wisely dispatched them to the other side of the barbed-wire fence.

An hour after their dismissal, the French flag was flying over the five blocks, the kitchens had been taken over, and the Front National, faceless no longer, was taking control of camp administration. There was no reaction from the SS, who were already packing their bags. The next day, the most fantastic "Marseillaise" ever sung shook the walls of the tunnel, and it was thus, amid tears of joy and pride, that Loibl Pass ended. There was only one regret, and that was that Paulo, Pompon, Hegoburu, Lepreux, Dédé Ménard and all those who had set such an example of courage were not there to participate in the triumphal parade, as the convicts marched arm in arm from one end of the tunnel to the other—the tunnel which was to have been their common grace.

And it very nearly had been. Winkler had planned to round up all the prisoners and civilians involved in the construction of the tunnel, herd them into it and dynamite the exits. Any survivors were to be finished off with flamethrowers. The operation was called off at the eleventh hour by an order from the *Gauleiter* in Klagenfurt, who was afraid of reprisals against the local population.

So death had hung over the heads of Kommando X right up to the last second. One might have thought that the moment they found themselves free again, their one desire would have been to get back home, to France, as quickly as possible. Absolutely not! Hardly had the partisans rushed to greet the column coming out of the tunnel before at least half of them had decided to join up with Tito's troops and carry on the fight.

Naturally Joel was among them, with all the French and Polish communists, but there were also many young men like François of Burgundy and Jeanblanc, the abscess king, who were impatient to get their hands on their first gun. The rest, crooks included, had taken the wider course and, led by the banker-interpreter, went to join up with the Red Cross. The division between generations and social classes took place barely a few hundred yards from the tunnel.

The tunnel itself was finished; it was high enough and wide enough to allow through both the tanks of the British Eighth Army and the partisan trucks. Mission accomplished. Kommando X had outlived its usefulness. The men could go their separate ways.

It would have been interesting to know which way Paulo would have gone, if he had been there. It was by no means certain that he would have followed Joel; the column of new partisans was singularly lacking in *joie de vivre*. Right from the start, they took themselves very seriously, automatically forming up by fives, snapping to attention for their comrade commander, one of the two commie leaders, saluting the colors with raised fists, singing the "Internationale," the "Jeune Garde," the "Chant des Partisans," and forward march, left, right, off to the nearest garrison at Klagenfurt to arm and equip themselves. Men were badly needed to clear the area of the last SS. Making absolutely no concessions to their lamentable physical state, worse than ever during Loibl's last months, Joel and his comrades had thrown themselves into the breach for the last time, risking at every minute the lives which had cost them so much to preserve.

Even so, there was one thing which had given them great satisfaction: Winkler, the murderers' Kommandant, and a few other SS who had the most blood on their hands—Perrier, Medal-Man and Mère Michele—had fallen into their hands.

It was only after this campaign that the soldier-convicts had consented to take some time off, but by then the Freedom Brigade, the name they had given to their force, was already a legend in Yugoslavia. Belgrade had asked them to join the victory parade, carrying their guns and wearing their pajamas whose Mauthausen triangles had been replaced by the red star. It was a great day for Joel, the greatest in all his young life. Staying at Loibl hadn't been the wrong decision, he hadn't lost his war as Paulo had told him he would, when trying to get him to join his escape party.

Thirty-three years have passed, and yet every year on the first Sunday of October, Loibl comes to life again at a banquet held at the Mutualité Hall in Paris by the veterans of Kommando X. Curiously, although one or two more names, with their registration numbers, appear each month in the "In Memoriam" column of the association's newsletter, just as many attend now as did at the first reunion celebration in 1946.

During the early years, the parents came to fill the empty seats and to meet the friends of their sons who had not come home. Then, as the years went by, they were replaced by the children of the survivors, now old enough to understand. Even when their fathers were too old to make the journey or had died, the children continued to come to hear the story of Loibl again and again. The best-loved parts of that story, more popular than any of the tales of heroism and escape, were the witty Gallic anecdotes and comic episodes, the adventures of Serpette, or Professor Reboux or Fatalitas. Every year without fail, the memorial banquet ended in laughter and singing.

Neither young nor old ever tired of it, even those who had come to mourn, like the sister of a plucky redheaded boy, son of a town mayor in the Midi, who had been shipped back to Mauthausen when he became too weak to work in the tunnel. There was little the veterans could tell the poor woman about her brother's last moments, for he had been in the convoy of the hundred and fifty exhausted men along with Angel Belloni, almost all of whom had died or disappeared in the smoke screen of Auschwitz, but that hadn't stopped her from making the journey for twenty years afterward. Sitting at the bottom of the table, she would listen in silence, asking no questions, and in the later years, carried away by the atmosphere, the tears she shed were tears of laughter.

This annual dinner was a service to history too. The veterans pieced together the log of Kommando X with the exact date of every execution, of every transport to and from Mauthausen, of the escapes, and of the freedom fighting. It was important and worthwhile work, and it obliged French and Yugoslavian chroniclers of the Second World War to add a few more lines to their accounts, especially since Loibl had had its own mini-Nuremberg. Two men were hanged as a result of the trial: Knock-Knees, the chief executioner and Perrier (*Oberscharführer* Briezke in the SS), one of the few of Winkler's staff careless enough to get caught. For Mère

Michele (*Oberscharführer* Gruswitz), twenty years, but for a man of his age, it came to the same thing. For Tits, twenty years too. Medal-Man, judged less bloodthirsty, got off with ten years and Uncle Franz, an old SS from Nordfeld, had even been acquitted, thanks to the testimony of François of Burgundy, whose life he had saved one day.

As for the syringe-happy Ramsauer, who had also been caught, he was so obviously mad that the bewigged English colonel presiding over the tribunal ordered him to be imprisoned for life. As Tito's men had already shot Fossil-Face in the heat of action, Loibl's SS had come out of it well with only two death sentences. So had the Kapos, who the day after their incorporation into the *Volkssturm* threw away their uniforms so as to conceal themselves in the mass of refugees.

Kapos Bayer and Bullseye were the only ones to be caught up with. Bayer's mother had come to France to ask Pompon for a certificate of good conduct for her son, but he had paid for his absent colleagues: five years and no parole. The accusations against Bullseye were so numerous that the court had requested the search for him to be extended all over Europe. His judges were overestimating him. With his distinguishing features he hadn't been able to get very far, and he was picked up in an Austrian prison less than thirty miles from Loibl. Bullseye felt completely lost as a free man, so he stole to get himself taken again. He was so lost, in fact, that when the car taking him to court overturned in a ditch, leaving him the only one without a scratch, he waited two hours for the military police to arrive. His bovine stupidity had earned him the tribunal's indulgence: ten years' hard labor. Not a high price to pay for all the wretched men he had beaten toward the crematorium.

At first, the veterans of the Mutualité banquets were somewhat embarrassed to admit to all the relatives that they had let Sailor, Fritz, Otto, and some of the SS like Green Bean and Helmut the *Rapportführer*, slip through their fingers, when all of them were guilty of several assassinations in broad daylight. But there was more than enough to satisfy the guests. There was the end of the southern camp, for example, which had been bombed and set on fire in the course of a bloody battle between White Guards, SS and partisans for possession of the tunnel and Route 333. Nothing was left of the camp, and it was a miracle that only one of the twenty men who couldn't be moved and had been left in the care of one of the two doctor-deportees had been killed. Another story which caught their imaginations was the arrest of the lovely Yanka and her liberation by a squad of partisans commanded by Zimmerman, the Slovenian SS, who had become a captain in Tito's army. But the warmest toasts were reserved for Yanko, when one year he made the trip to Paris. Not only had he played a major role in the French escapes, but he had also achieved a brilliant tactical coup at the end of the winter of 1944. Soon after Paulo's departure, he had joined up with the partisans and paralyzed the tunnel for a whole week by intercepting two truckloads of civilian workers—a hundred and three of them—and unceremoniously packing them off to the maquis.

Inevitably, out of all this reliving of memories came a desire on the part of everyone—veterans, parents and children—to see for themselves or see again the extraordinary tunnel. And every year, when the weather is warmer, the great Loibl family sets out in trains, coaches and cars for the Karawankens.

The survivors hadn't misled their families. The countryside was even more beautiful than they had said, and their tunnel was indeed a real tunnel, with a border post at each end. What an extraordinary experience it was for them to travel over the mile which they had dug with their hands and with their blood! The Austrians and Yugoslavs had finally agreed to restore it jointly, and had laid a tarmac road and installed lighting. It was the kind of perfect surface which makes travelers want to put their foot down and hoot their horns gaily, and yet none of them dared. The former slaves all drove through at a walking pace, stopping frequently to reflect, to pray, and to thank God that they had gotten out alive.

But the biggest shock is waiting for them at the southern entrance. They know that all the camp buildings have been destroyed, but where the refectory once stood, where Serpette had won his sordid soup wager, stands a three-star hotel, the Loibl Hotel!

Route 333 has been the subject of some improvement too. Out of necessity it has been widened to accommodate the enormous numbers of tourists who for five months of the year drive up to Zelenica, the ski resort built on the same mountain through which the tunnel runs. Zelenica is ultramodern, with chair lifts and competition slopes, and 80 per cent of the visitors' cars are Mercedes, BMWs and Opels filled with Germans and Austrians who are bursting with health and happy to be alive. At any rate, they are untroubled by complexes, even when they happen to read the inscription on the two marble plaques at either end of the tunnel as they wait to go through customs: "*Here, from 1943 to 1945, stood the annex of the Nazi death camp of Mauthausen-Loibl. Working on the construction of the Loibl tunnel, here suffered and here died political deportees from France, Poland, the Soviet Union, Czechoslovakia, Belgium, Luxembourg, Italy and Yugoslavia.*"

The tunnel, for which the earliest plans go back to 1691, and which Hitler in his turn adopted to facilitate the movement of his troops into Yugoslavia, continues to fulfill its purpose. As the Führer had intended, it still serves the Germans, even if they have become skiers or holiday makers in a hurry to take a dip in the Atlantic.

Obviously, the motorized procession of tourists in Tyrolean hats is not a particularly welcome sight for the pilgrims from France. Their children ask questions, they don't understand.

"No, son, they aren't the same ones, the bad men are all dead or in prison."

But as they say it, the ex-convicts still can't help scrutinizing the faces of the beer drinkers lounging around the Loibl Hotel bar. After all, it is not beyond the bounds of possibility that some of the assassins too might want to revisit the tunnel of their youth.

Not Sailor or Willy from the Saar—their features would be too easily recognized—but there are so many other less conspicuous sadists who must be itching to come back: a tormentor and his victim coming face to face in this holiday atmosphere would not, one must admit, lack piquancy.

In the meantime, there is a group of Krauts who remain utterly unmoved by the rancor of the former *Haeftlinge:* the bosses of Universale. They are not ashamed of the tunnel, nor of the way it was built. Far from it. They use it for their advertising. On every road in the area, as far as Vienna, there are billboards rattling in the wind, and that too is hard for the survivors to swallow. But as soon as they cross the border, the welcome they receive from the Yugoslavs is so overwhelming that they soon forget, along with everything else, the slave-trading company from whom they had naïvely hoped to recover back pay for two years' work, twelve hours a day. Not one penny has Universale ever paid them. Of course, it would have been too much to pay—but the company could at least refrain from taunting them.

As for the Yugos, their hearts have never forgotten. The French have remained their friends and brothers, especially the escapees and the veterans of the Freedom Brigade, all decorated with the partisan medal, at Tito's personal request. And so, when they come back in the summer bringing with them their flags and Mauthausen pajamas, it is a special occasion at Loibl. Stands are set up on the ruins of the camp, speeches are made, a band plays, there is a procession to the crematorium religiously maintained and decorated with flowers, and a minute of silence before the monument to the dead erected on the side of the road where both the camp and the tunnel mouth are visible. It is a very fine piece of work, a skeleton sculpted in bronze whose immense arms seem to call the heavens to witness, symbolizing the appeals of all the martyrs shot down on the line. Engraved on the pedestal in French are the words "*J'accuse!*"

After the solemnity comes the celebration. They go down to Trzic, the little town at the end of the railway line where one night in June 1943 three hundred Frenchmen were unloaded, never suspecting that they were going to dig a tunnel which their ancestors had dreamed about for twenty generations.

At Trzic, there is no question of the ex-convicts staying in the hotel. Every household claims the honor, and throughout their stay there is feasting and dancing with as much slivovitz as they can drink. But the hero of the festivities is invariably François of Burgundy, whose reputation for indomitability and record-breaking endurance of beatings had already impressed Trzic well before the camp was liberated. Everyone there still remembers that when the SS had made him sew onto his jacket the red circle of men condemned to cross the line, the partisans had warned Winkler that he would pay for François's life with his own. Since by then it was all over for Germany, Knock-Knees had spared François, but this most unusual intervention on the part of the Titoists gives some idea of the esteem in which the Yugoslavs held François even before he joined their ranks.

Nothing is too good for him, no act too generous to make him understand that he is the darling of the district. The town has offered him a piece of land on which to build a house and a permanent hunting and fishing license valid in all seasons, and the day after he arrives a photograph of him in partisan uniform appears on the front page of the local paper. In it, he looks very dashing, with his submachine gun and his cap bearing the red star, but that isn't why a local girl called Boja ("caress" in Slovene), the doctor's sister-in-law, became his wife. She had fallen for him, she claims, a long time before, having picked out his shaven and bloody head from among a thousand others when, like her friend Yanka, she was employed in the civilian camp and working as a partisan liaison agent.

That Loibl should culminate in a wedding should not come as a surprise. The men of Kommando X were no ordinary men. But the sad thing is that their extraordinary adventure is only of interest to Yugoslavia. In France no one has ever heard of Loibl Pass, which is a pity, because there could be a few lessons learned from this unprecedented human experience: men of all ages and from all walks of life, from the tramp to the managing director via the criminal, uniting like brothers, pooling their respective talents and their national gifts, to overcome several hundred SS whose mission was to wipe them out.

It is likely that even now, thirty-three years later, if some of the surviving guards were questioned, they would say, as the Yugoslavs do, "The *Franzosen* of Loibl Pass, ah yes, what men they were!" At his trial, even Knock-Knees had not hidden the fact that he had had to give way on more than one occasion to men he had thought to be only *Scheisskubel* at the beginning. And yet as kommandant of the camp and a long-serving officer in the SS, he should have been the last to be surprised. Hadn't he and his Nazi associates carefully selected these tough men themselves, several times over? The first time in France, since the Gestapo generally picked up only men who had committed some crime, which in '42 and '43 was not so commonplace. Then, there was the slave market on the *Appelplatz*. Three hundred men chosen from 2500 candidates—a hell of a selection when you know that 8205 Frenchmen never came back from Mauthausen. Finally, at Loibl itself you had to have real balls to last out for two years, and avoid the return to sender. Any man who had managed to survive this selection process could not be a man like other men.

For some, this was soon to be proved conclusively. Barely out of their hell, they had gambled with their lives again, double or nothing. In Indochina Jeanblanc, the abscess king, was one of the first paratroopers killed by the Vietminh, and the tall lanky fellow whose gold tooth Paulo had yanked out, a genuine French baron, was killed in Korea.

Without traveling quite so far from home, one of the two Bretons who had arrived with Dédé Ménard met his death the year he got back in a knife fight in Brest, where he had taken up his old job as a docker. A few months later, the racing cyclist, the only escapee from Nordfeld, was run over by an escort car during a race. Finally Perrimond, the old glory of the rings, who had wanted to make a comeback although he was almost blind, had chosen to kill himself rather than end his days as a tramp.

There were other reckless men who came to a fitting end, like the elder Campana brother, the champion of reduced sentences and murder acquittal for insufficient evidence. Not in the least bit sobered by his experience, he had tried to relieve some thugs of their spoils from the gold theft at Orly but, indifferent to his status as a former deportee, they turned him into a sieve. But it was the old boy who had been the first to taste Sailor's ladle on his mouth who had had the nastiest surprise. Hardly had he set foot on French soil before he was notified of his death sentence *in absentia* for alleged collaboration! He would have smiled, had it not been for the enormous circumflex-shaped scar which distorted his mouth. It took him several months to extract himself from this unfortunate misunderstanding.

The worst fate, however, was reserved for Pozzi, the ex-caretaker from the rue Lauriston. He had come back in the Red Cross convoy with the others, and overnight he had forgotten everything, his disgusting betrayals as well as his Kapo's stripe. Apart from the odd fist in his face during the journey home, everyone had left him alone, and even the security officers at the Lutétia Hotel had leveled no accusations against him. For the next three years, he was to be seen loafing about the *grands boulevards*, his new beat, proud to have passersby stare at his buttonhole to which he had pinned the deportee's insignia, the small red triangle inverted against the striped background of blue and gray.

The ex-Kapo would have been better advised to lie low, for the commies were patiently building up a damning file of accusations: collaboration with the enemy, informing and accessory to the deaths through exhaustion of several young prisoners, together with his spell as concierge at Bonny-Laffont. One fine morning they had run him in, put him on trial, and despite the impassioned defense of his fellow sufferer, the lawyer from Limoges, he was condemned to death and shot in the fort at Montrouge.

The terrible thing was that right up until the last minute he thought they only wanted to frighten him as a punishment for his zeal at work. It was only when his lawyer came to tell him his appeal had been refused that he realized the judges' severity was no sham. Anyone else in his position would have begged for mercy and cried out against the miscarriage of justice. But he was of another school, he was from Loibl. Refusing the blindfold which was offered him, he died as they had learned to die at Loibl, without a word.

Thankfully, the survivors of Loibl Pass have not all met such tragic and premature ends. Although over the last thirty-three years, many have died naturally, somewhat earlier than the national average, as might be expected, there are still well over a hundred of them to bring to the Mutualité or to the tunnel pilgrimages the rebellious spirit of Kommando X.

But when the laughter is over and the story of what happened to So-and-so has been told for the hundredth time, the conversation turns to the present, to how each man is getting on and how business is going. Painful to relate behind all the warm camaraderie, behind their unusual fidelity to their memories, the social barriers are still in place. None of them have ever gone into business together. Ths farmers have stayed on their farms, the shopkeepers in their shops, no boss has ever taken on a comrade in difficulty, and only those who were militant communists at the beginning have remained true to their beliefs. After the banquet or the trip to Yugoslavia, each man goes back to his own patch. It is perhaps a shame, but on the other hand, it's hard to imagine what the common interests in civilian life would be between a senator (the lawyer from Limoges), a managing director (the banker-interpreter), a professor of literature (old Reboux), a ready-to-wear tycoon (Eli Katz, the little Jew with the charmed life), a bailiff from Bayeaux, a vet from Nogent-le-Rotrou, the director of a flying school, a market-stall holder (the ex-champion boxer Pommier), a customs officer from Frontignan (the heavyweight Templier), a sailor (Leblond, the man with the cast-iron head), the director of a ski resort (Lepreux, the escapee from Chamonix), a bartender (Paulo's companion Pompon), a chatelain (the former scrounger Pierrot Martin converted to the hotel trade), a carpenter, an offal butcher, a hotelier from Sète (the brain behind the generator escape), a dishwasher in a restaurant (the Franco-Polish miner with a thing about dirt) and a journalist, the former gym teacher, Joel Le Goff, who today regards physical effort with abhorrence. Even so, all these men do have two things in common: a taste for work and, each in his own sphere, a desire to succeed. But to try and include certain others in one big family, the down-and-outs, the scroungers and the crooks, was not reasonable to expect, and they cannot be blamed for going their separate ways after the liqueurs.

In any case, the crooks have always stayed well clear of the Mutualité banquets, two in particular: Maumau, Bullseye's hustler, and Riton of the *Zwei Mann weg*. They too came back alive, but after Pozzi's execution they were extremely reluctant to come and hear about Loibl. Far more effective than any sentence had been the grapevine set in motion by the Campana brothers, as soon as they got back. They were forever barred from the milieu, and had both become tramps. On the pavements they had boasted would make them the richest pimps in Paris, they are now the streetwalkers.

Speaking of tramps, there is one, on the other hand, who would be welcomed as a guest of honor if he could bring himself to turn up for the veterans' banquet—Serpette, the legendary soup drinker. Perhaps everyone would lend a hand to get him out of his present mess, because his last job is almost an affront to the memory of Loibl. The trouble is, he hasn't been able to find anything better than to be taken on at a fairground sideshow, where he sticks his head through a hole and tries, when he can, to pull it out again before the rotten tomatoes thrown by the merrymakers land on it. To have been through Mauthausen and Loibl only to be reduced to that is indeed pitiful, but again it is proof of Kommando X's lack of pretension. None of them has ever made a song and dance about his war.

Of course, the best example is Paulo. "I'm finished with you forever," he had said as he left the Lutétia Hotel, and he has stuck to it. Like Serpette he has never come to collect his metal, and not once in thirty-three years has he been seen at the Mutualité. But not a single banquet or pilgrimage has gone by without them talking about him and his mad escapades, his love affair with Yanka and his legendary escape. Even in his absence, he remains the star, and the youngsters, whose heads are full of his adventures and his wit, cannot understand why they have never seen him.

"Why doesn't Paulo ever come, Papa? Isn't he invited?"

"No point trying to understand some things, my boy."

As for Loibl, has it served no purpose at all?

The Germans think it has. They find the border tunnel, with its easy access to Yugoslavia for weekend skiing trips, very convenient.

ABOUT THE AUTHOR

ANDRÉ LACAZE is decorated with the Croix de Guerre, Medal of Resistance, and the Legion of Honor. After the war he went into journalism and became editor of *Paris-Match*. Then he worked for RTL, one of the main French broadcasting networks, until recently, when he retired.